The Gates of Carthage

The Last of the Romans: III

The Gates of Carthage

A NOVEL OF BELISARIUS

WILLIAM HAVELOCK

First print edition October 2022

Book cover design by Dusan Markovic
Maps by Cyowari

ISBN 978-1-7379808-3-4 (hardcover)
ISBN 978-1-7379808-2-7 (paperback)
ASIN: B097ZK2X8SB (ebook)

www.havelockbooks.com

For Jacob & Joshua

For him, with sails of red,
And torches at mast-head,
Piloting the great fleet,
I swept the Afric coasts
And scattered the Vandal hosts,
Like dust in a windy street.

~Henry Wadsworth Longfellow (1807 – 1882 C.E.)

CHARACTERS

Aetius	Long-dead general of the Western Roman Empire, Attila's nemesis
Agathias	A slave to the Imperial Palace in Constantinople
Aigan	An officer of the Hun foederati, succeeds Simmas
Alaric	A junior officer amongst the Herulian foederati, slain at Dara
al-Harith	Ghassanid King, brother of Mariya
Aliya	Handmaiden to Mariya
Al-Mundhir III ibn al-Nu'man	Lakhmid Arab King, sworn enemy to the Ghassanids
Altan	A young Herulian horseman
Amalasuntha	Queen Regent of the Ostrogoths in Italy
Amalric	Grandson of Theodoric, King of the Visigoths
Ammatas	Brother of Gelimer, and Lord of Carthage
Anastasius	Deceased Roman Emperor of Varus' Youth
Antonina	Young Roman aristocrat, daughter of Basilius, wife of Belisarius
Archelaus	A former excubitor and leader of the Thracian Army, killed in a trial by combat
Ascum	Alani ballista commander, serves the Cappadocian Army
Athalaric	Boy-King of the Ostrogoths, grandson of Theodoric
Attila	Long-dead Khagan of the Hunnic Empire
Auria	A princess among the Mauri
Aya	An Egyptian slave to the Imperial Palace in Constantinople
Azarethes	Commander of all Persian armies
Baduarius	Ostrogoth, tribune of Belisarius' spearmen
Basilius	Former East Roman consul, chief advisor to Justinian
Belisarius	Former Magister Militum of Rome's eastern forces

Bessas	Armenian, leads Belisarius' cataphracts
Cassiodorus	Justinian's priest and religious official
Cephalas	Greek, former spearman of the Thracian Army, aide to Varus
Chanaranges	Personal excubitor to Justinian
Dagisthaeus	Ostrogoth, brother of Baduarius, a deceased tribune under Belisarius
Domnicus	An elderly general in Egypt
Fastida	A deceased chief amongst the Gepids
Fulcaris	Centurion within the Herulian foederati
Gelimer	Usurper of the Vandal Throne
Germanus	Justinian's cousin, general of the Thracian Army
Gibamund	Nephew of Gelimer
Godilas	Deceased general of the East Roman armies, and a close friend to Justin
Gratian	One of Solomon's centurions
Gunderic	A respected warlord of the Vandal armies
Hakhamanish	The magus, a priest of the Zoroastrian religion
Hermogenes	Imperial minister and legate in the Persian War
Hilda	Illegitimate member of the Vandal royal family
Hilderic	Former king of the Vandals
Hormisdas	The Catholic Pope in Rome
Hypatius	The eldest nephew of Emperor Anastasius
Ildico	Attila's final bride
Indulf	Ostrogothic chieftain
Irilar	A Herulian recruit, cousin to Fulcaris
Isaacius	A Jewish soldier in the Thracian Army, killed in battle against the Avars
Jabalah	King of the Ghassanids, killed at Thannuris
Jamila	Handmaiden to Mariya
Joannina	Daughter of Belisarius and Antonina
John	Belisarius' second-in-command
Justin	Deceased Roman emperor, former master of Varus and Samur

Justinian	Roman emperor, husband to Theodora
Kavadh	Shahanshah of the Persian Empire
Kazrig	Khan of the Avars
Khingila	Warlord of the Hephthalites, slain at Dara
Khosrow	Heir to the Persian Throne
Leo	Long-dead Pope, met with Attila
Liberius	A senior advisor to the Emperor
Magnetius	A chariot racing champion
Marcellus	Lord of the excubitores
Marcian	Latin centurion, second-in-command to Solomon
Mariya	Princess of the Ghassanids, wife of Varus
Mundus	Tribune of the Thracian Army, Germanus' second-in-command
Narses	Theodora's chief spy and advisor
Nepotian	A wealthy Roman senator, and Solomon's father
Nzamba	An Aksumite spearman
Odoacer	Ostrogoth who overthrew the last Western Roman Emperor
Opilio	Centurion of the Herulian foederati, slain at Dara
Patroklus	Trainer of Green Chariot Racers
Paulus	The Roman emperor's minister of the treasury
Perenus	An exiled Lazic prince, and Varus' second-in-command
Perozes	Persian noble and general
Petrus	An aged Roman priest
Phocas	Personal guard to Hermogenes
Pompeius	A nephew of Emperor Anastasius
Probus	A nephew of Emperor Anastasius
Procopius	Imperial scribe and historian
Rosamund	A captured Gepid pagan and healer
Samur	Formerly a Herulian slave to Justin, Varus' only sibling
Sembrouthes	Commander of Aksumites guarding Princess Mariya

Sergius	Latin centurion under Belisarius
Shaush	Prince of the Avars, eldest son of Kazrig, slain in battle against Belisarius
Simmas	A commander of the Hun foederati, slain at Callinicum
Sindual	New centurion of the Herulian foederati
Sinnion	An officer in the Hun foederati, succeeds Sunicas
Sittas	A Roman general in Armenia
Solomon	A young Roman aristocrat and komes, son of Nepotian
Sunicas	A leader of the Hun foederati, slain at Callinicum
Symeon	A spearman of the Thracian Army
Theodora	Roman Empress, wife of Justinian
Theodoric	Late hero-king of all the Goths
Theudis	Regent for the Visigoths in Hispania
Thurimuth	An Alemanni, first-spear centurion in the Thracian Army
Tiberius	Hypatius' young son
Tribonian	The Roman emperor's minister of laws
Troglita	A centurion in the Thracian Army
Tzazon	Brother of Gelimer, and general of the Vandal armies
Uliaris	A Frank, leader of Belisarius' bodyguards
Valerian	A centurion in the Roman Empire's eastern provinces
Varus	The narrator, a Herulian, and leader of the joint foederati under Belisarius
Vitalius	A youth of the Imperial household
Wazeba	An Aksumite spearman
Wisimar	A young warrior among the Vandals
Xerxes	Persian prince and commander of the Immortals
Zenobia	Varus' daughter

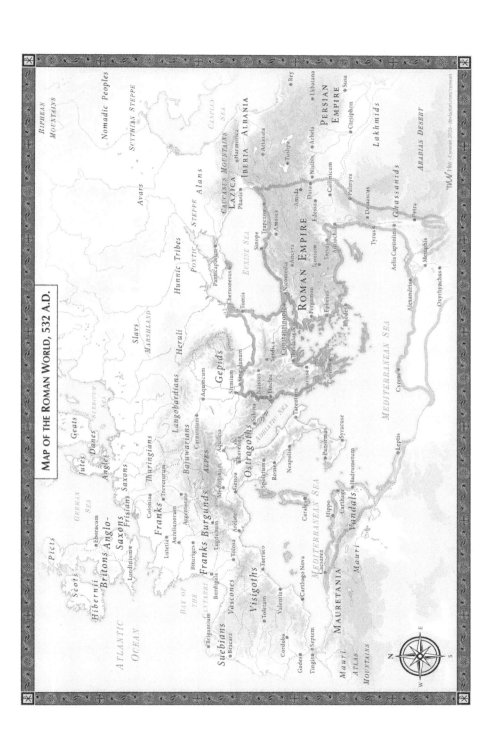

MAP OF THE ROMAN WORLD, 532 A.D.

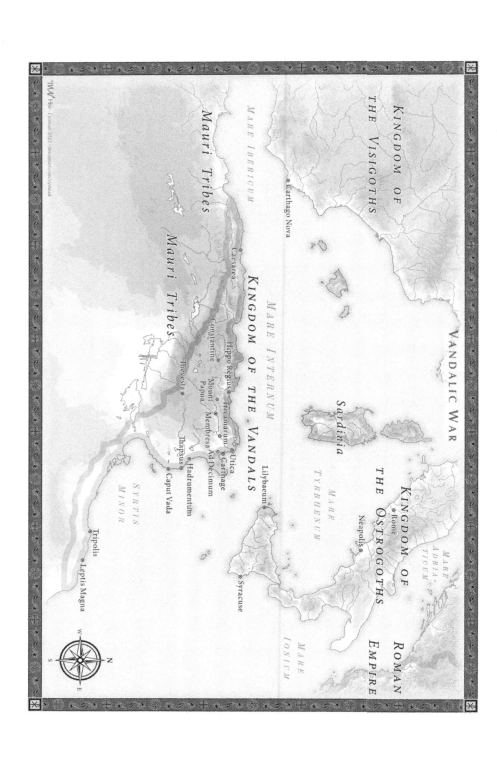

VANDALIC WAR

KINGDOM OF
THE VISIGOTHS

KINGDOM OF
THE OSTROGOTHS

KINGDOM OF
THE ROMAN
EMPIRE

Mauri Tribes

Mauri Tribes

KINGDOM OF THE VANDALS

MARE IBERICUM

MARE INTERNUM

MARE ADRIATICUM

MARE TYRRHENUM

MARE IONIUM

SYRTIS MINOR

Sardinia

Rome

Neapolis

Carthago Nova

Caesarea

Constantine

Theuesta

Hippo Regius

Mount
Papua

Tucamatrum

Membresa Ad Decimum

Utica

Carthage

Thapsus

Hadrumentum

Caput Vada

Lilybaeum

Syracuse

Tripolis

Leptis Magna

10% off* when ordering direct from our Websites

www.healthyfeetonline.co.uk
www.freshbreathonline.co.uk

using promotion code TK007,
free UK shipping as well !

*Min £10 Order for Discount

TK Logistics
Unit 2 Innovation Centre
Festival Drive
Ebbw Vale
Gwent, NP23 8XA
Phone: 01495 356732
E-mail: sales@tk-logistics.co.uk

£ 1-25

2003 DO3

Dear Valued Customer,

Many thanks for your recent purchase !
TK Logistics huge product range include :

- Foot Health Care Products
- Dental Products
- OTC Pharmaceuticals
- Computer Sales & Repairs

We sell direct through our main websites and on Amazon and eBay under the user IDs :
TK Logistics, Inter-Dentals & Healthy-feet-online

Feedback is so important for us as a small Family run Business, and we welcome all positives on our seller accounts, if however you have an issue with an order please could we kindly request you contact us for a rapid resolution prior to leaving any Negative comments.

Kind Regards,
TK Logistics

Book 4
The Pillars of
Hercules

Book 5
The eternal city

Constantinople, 6th Century AD

Bosporus

Golden Horn

Palace of Blachernae

Neorion Harbor

Prosphorion Harbor

Harbor

Strategion

Acropolis

Basilica Cistern

Hagia Sophia

Great Palace

Cistern of Aetius

Cistern of Aspar

Forum of Theodosius

Forum of Constantine

Hippodrome

Church of the Holy Apostles

Valens Aqueduct

Forum of the Ox

Harbor of Julian

Melantias Gate

Wall of Theodosius

Wall of Constantine

Forum of Arcadius

Harbor of Theodosius

Sea of Marmara

Gate of Romanus

Cistern of Mocius

Gate of Rhesios

Xylokerkos Gate

Golden Gate

Lycus River

Via Egnatia

PROLOGUE: THE WASTREL

Warriors mocked him in their cups. Many called him brutish within his hearing, thinking it a slur, not knowing it bothered the wastrel little. Others called him a fool, a lunatic, and a drunk, and those were the words that tugged at his patience. His father had amassed great wealth that, while not initially entrusted to the wastrel, had been in his possession for several years now. That inheritance made things worse, for the wastrel's people disdained those who lived on the backs of their father's successes. Now not only a fool; he was thought a weakling, a child, a drunk.

His father had been a careful man and made it difficult for any warrior not of his bloodline to raise a challenge for the throne. Ruling with an iron fist, the wastrel's father ground down resistance like blades of autumn grass, cracked at the root and blown away into the chilling wind. The wastrel followed his father's example in this, even going so far as to use some of his father's most trusted servants and advisors to administer torture or execution of supposed malcontents. The man relished those moments, when voices full of secretive scorn were shattered by swords and hooves alike, now forever silent and unable to mock any further.

Despite his best efforts, however, the wastrel had failed where his father had succeeded. This confused the unlucky son greatly—his father's cruelty had been met with swift obedience, yet the wastrel's own malice only stirred further resentment and resistance amongst the common soldiers. Chieftains and threadbare spearman alike rose in resistance to his orders and destroyed his army, though it had been superior in numbers and in blood rights. The wastrel escaped capture, barely, with a half dozen loyal followers who were either too stupid to realize their leader's time as autocrat had ended or too fearful to strike out and forge their own paths.

The traitorous bastards could rot in whatever underworld would take them, for he would not give them the satisfaction of lashing iron chains about his neck and wrists. For his faults, the wastrel was no coward.

Light rain had fallen three days after the battle, washing away crusted remnants of a shallow wound. With his followers warm and dry in their tents, the man ventured outside to a low knoll and surveyed the vast grasslands that had once been his own.

They had laughed at him, but they would not take him alive. Of this, he was certain.

He drew his blade, its wicked edge whetted sharp for its purpose, and turned its point toward his own exposed stomach. Many would have struggled at the task, yet he did not flinch. He seated the sword in his large middle and offered a final prayer to the gods.

Satisfied, the man sheathed the blade into his guts. Blood spilled onto the grass, mingling with the rain in its quickening staccato. The man winced as his strength evaporated, and he fell forward, driving the blade's pommel ever further into his body.

As he rolled onto the grass, he cursed those who had brought him to this wretched place, and all who would hope to succeed him. He would have gone on cursing had his spirit not departed. Exsanguinated, lolling, lifeless, his sword-impaled body would not be discovered until the darkest hours of evening.

FROM THE ASHES OF
DARKNESS

There is little justice in life. Wicked men grow fat upon pilfered goods, living to a ripe age in their hedonism while their providers sweat and toil for the most meagre keep. It is the nature of people blessed with wealth to desire comfort at any cost, even if it means the suffering of countless unmet strangers in foreign lands, or even one's own countrymen. That imperative is why thousands of young men venture off to war, shield and spear in hand as they batter at the warriors of other peoples. It is avarice that fuels war, grinding the souls of the young beneath the grindstone of power and want. Those who resist the temptation of grandeur are fleetingly rare, as if they were saints living amongst the fallen.

What prevents some women and men from succumbing to that dark path is a sense of duty. For some, it is their love and fear of their god or gods, the divine forces who permit us mere mortals to exist in their chaotic world. For others, it is an innate drive to protect one's immediate family, or at least bide time until starvation or violence claim them for the afterlife.

The rarest few take their honor from the bond of camaraderie and an oath to something greater than their own selves, agreeing to sacrifice personal comforts so that others may live in relative prosperity. From my experience, all but the final sort are malleable, and easily forgotten when hardship becomes too great to bear.

In the smoky dawn after the Battle of Callinicum, all that bound Belisarius' army together was a love for one another and the firm belief in the cause of Rome. Most of us were not even Italian or Greek, though we fought and died all the same under the Imperial Eagle and obeyed commands from a Greek or Latin tongue. It was that sacred sense of duty, battered and exhausted though it was, that I counted on to bring Rome's survivors through the smoking ruins of defeat.

Stinging from exposure to smoke and exhaustion, my eyes ached for cool water and rest. Torn between sitting beside the prone figure of Samur on one hand and setting the remnants of Rome's army to rights on the other, I knew rest was unlikely to arrive for another day.

In a makeshift tent that had been prepared for Belisarius, I pored over a map of the region. Stacks of scraped animal skins had been dotted with my Greek handwriting, containing orders to assess the state of the army as well as to inform local forts and cities of our plight. Through it all, I felt a strong urge to gather a hundred of my foederati and storm into Hermogenes' tent, demanding Belisarius' immediate release from captivity. Few beyond the legate's personal guard would protest at the maneuver, and even those unlucky soldiers would be tempted to abandon Justinian's representative to our beleaguered Mesopotamian army.

Belisarius would have been mortified by these actions, which would also condemn me to the status of an insurrectionist and place my wife and unborn child in mortal danger. Ergo, I permitted that unholy temptation no more than a few minutes of my time before fixing upon the task of securing the general's rightful freedom. Only a handful of hours had passed since our organized retreat from the battle, with the first rays of sunlight caressing the Syrian plains and the hundreds of slain warriors that dotted the opposite bank of the river.

Uliaris poked his head into my tent, announcing the arrival of the several senior officers who remained of Belisarius' retinue. Uliaris the Frank had been chief among Belisarius' bodyguards and swore to protect me in my temporary command, assuring me that the legate would be discreetly monitored by one of his men, and that all visitors to my command tent were to be identified and searched before being granted entry.

My first visitor from the officers was Baduarius, who had to duck to avoid banging his skull against the wooden doorframe. The huge Gothic man had dark circles rimming his eyes and the detritus of the previous day's battle still caked on his foul-smelling body, yet I did not flinch as he offered a squeezing hug in greeting.

"Commander Varus, then!" he joked. "I should be calling you sir and sweeping your shits into gilded buckets!"

"It is only temporary," I replied. "Until Belisarius returns, which should be soon."

It was a lie—one that Baduarius understood as the words departed my lips. I had no notion of whether, or how, Belisarius would be freed of Hermogenes' clutches, even with the might of our battered army under my command. Unspoken altogether was the doubt that I felt— leading a foederati of my kinsmen was nothing compared to leading thousands of scared, hungry, exhausted, and wounded men far from safety or comfort. Belisarius was younger than I was at that time when Justin first appointed him as head of the Cappadocian army, though I possessed none of the calm surety that he had come to be known for. There was simply too much to do, and too many looking to me for guidance, and I lacked adequate answers for all of them.

If Baduarius nursed similar doubts in my abilities as Belisarius' temporary successor, he gave them no voice. "Don't worry, my friend. Belisarius chose wisely. My talents are best used to crack a man's skull, not sign papers or listen to hours of reports."

"I doubt I am very different from you," I confessed. "I'm a battle commander, not a prefect."

"Nonsense!" Baduarius bellowed. "For starters, you can read. That's rare enough. In all seriousness, though, there are only two men besides the general that I wouldn't hesitate to take orders from: you and John. There's no explaining why—it's just some innate energy that separates leaders from other men. You may be young, but you are cursed with that rare trait."

"Cursed?" I held back a smile.

"Aye," Baduarius responded. "As I said, I wouldn't want your present job. Look at the situation we find ourselves in!"

I nodded sadly. "I've already dispatched orders requesting the tally of the dead and wounded," I said. "Any update on Ascum?"

"Up with him all night, I was." Baduarius nodded, uncorking a wineskin and taking a thunderous gulp. "Never seen a man in such continuous pain without dying or losing consciousness. Half of his body is charred, but the doctors insist that he stands a good chance at surviving if illness does not cut his recovery short."

Sighing, I closed my eyes at the bittersweet news. "I will ask Father Petrus to pray for him," I said, "and please bring me regular updates of his progress."

"Ascum's no Christian," Baduarius replied, "but I don't think that he'd resist a good word to any god in his present condition."

We were interrupted by another shout from Uliaris, declaring the arrival of additional officers. With my permission, Marcellus and Valerian filed into the tent, looking little better than Baduarius.

"Lord Varus," Valerian said, grinning as he saluted.

"Commander Varus," Marcellus offered next, correcting Valerian's improper name for my temporary title. The commander of the excubitores winced as he placed a hand over thickly layered bandages at his side that, while worrisome, showed no signs of damp blood from an open wound.

"Valerian, Marcellus," I replied, nodding to each man and turning my attention to the excubitor's damp binding. "How's your wound?"

"Like a bee sting, nothing more," Marcellus replied gruffly. "I've had Greek women hit me harder than that lucky Persian bastard who stuck me with a spear."

"I think you're doing it wrong with the women, Marcellus," Baduarius said. "Unless that's your idea of foreplay?"

"Any sign of the others?" Valerian asked, breaking up the conversation between the two more senior commanders.

"Not yet, although I've sent couriers to assemble them at daybreak."

Valerian nodded. "Any worry that Germanus would insist upon command of the army? He is the ranking general with Belisarius out of office."

Marcellus flared his nostrils before I could respond. "Germanus doesn't think like that—he's got his own men to take care of, which is responsibility enough. He'll respect Belisarius' wishes."

Our conversation continued as we waited for the Thracian officers to arrive, with our chief concern those close friends who still fought against death in the nearby tents. Several questions as to Samur's well-being arose, while Baduarius cuffed away a tear in remembrance of Sunicas and Simmas.

"I should have stayed with them," he said, his voice cracked with a light sniffle. "Gods help me, but they deserved better than to be butchered like cattle."

"I'll send men to reclaim their bodies as soon as it is safe," I promised, a pitiful consolation. "Their sacrifice worked—we are testament to that. We need to make sure that their actions were not in vain."

Marcellus and Valerian both nodded at that statement, and each drank from Baduarius' wineskin as they toasted to the memories of the fallen Huns. Our melancholy continued for several moments more until a final contingent of officers arrived at our first formal meeting.

Sembrouthes entered first, his yellow robes shredded and stained; he had lacked the time to bathe and dress. Along with the doctors and supplies, Belisarius had planned for our wagon train to be sent to the other side of the Euphrates before the onset of battle with Azarethes, yet most lacked the time or energy to take advantage of that small boon.

"Rosamund said to tell you that Samur is stable and is finally resting," Sembrouthes said in his accented Latin.

I nodded, clasping his arm as he entered the room.

Behind Sembrouthes entered King al-Harith, the Ghassanid monarch whose forces had splintered under the strain of Azarethes' armored Persian and Lakhmid cavalry. The king was flanked by two guards whose duty seemed more to prop their king up as he walked more than to protect his life from unseen threats. A chair was drawn, and al-Harith sank into it, letting out a mixed gasp of pain and relief as he lifted bandaged legs onto a footstool.

Last to arrive were the Thracians, each of whom had been covered in healing cuts and bruises from their extended time in Belisarius' infantry. Troglita entered first, and like al-Harith, he was carried into the tent, a deep gash at his hip. Shaking my head, I protested that Troglita should leave for the doctor's tents at once, yet he merely shrugged. He was helped into an open chair by Mundus, whose scarred face bore a deep gash where the nosepiece of his helm had cut into his flesh. Behind the two strode Germanus, his eyes rimmed red from a perilous lack of sleep.

"Christ almighty, what a mess," Germanus grunted as he entered the tent. Finding my gaze, he nodded in approval and offered his greetings.

"Damned fine work you did shoring up the Thracian lines, Varus. I mean it," Germanus said, deflating any conflict that may have existed between us. He offered an outstretched arm that I grasped tightly as a sign of friendship and respect. The other men seemed to relax, as though finally ready to consider the limitless needs that our army would require.

"As you already know," I began, "Belisarius has been removed from command and jailed by Hermogenes for not defeating Azarethes at Callinicum. Before he was taken away, Belisarius appointed me his interim replacement until he is able to rejoin the army."

Germanus spat at Hermogenes' name, while Mundus suggested that we assemble enough men to bop Hermogenes over his balding skull and take Belisarius back. Smiling, I shook my head and insisted that we would respect Roman law in this matter and work according to Belisarius' wishes that we exonerate him legally and with no bloodshed.

"We need to put the army to rights," I said. "What is the status of those who joined us on this side of the Euphrates?"

"The Thracians have several hundred dead, and likely twice that wounded. Another hundred of those will likely die of infection or some other cause," Mundus recounted, his eyes falling to the ground as he spoke.

"Same as the Cappadocians," Baduarius followed, "and even though we fought nearly the entire time, archers and ballista bolts kept the Persian attacks lighter than those against our right flanks."

Having fought within Baduarius' lines of spearmen, Marcellus and Valerian concurred, although Marcellus warned that the excubitores had already taken considerable losses at Dara prior to this most recent campaign.

King al-Harith winced, though whether this was from pain or from mention of his men's failure, I could not know. "There's no way to know my exact number of casualties," al-Harith began, "for only a small number joined Belisarius' men across the river. Several thousand mounted Ghassanids retreated toward Callinicum with John, but many of those were grievously wounded."

I nodded, taking pains to show respect to the Empire's defeated ally. Turning to Sembrouthes, I asked for an update of the Hunnic and Herulian foederati, who had been battered by extensive use throughout Belisarius' Persian campaign.

"Only a half dozen losses from the Herulians and Aksumites," Sembrouthes reported, "but at least two-thirds of the Huns were killed with Sunicas and Simmas. A bit over one hundred remain, but like your brother, they are generally wounded to the point of limited use in a fight."

Baduarius groaned, which I quickly hushed to prevent the spread of demoralization amongst the officers. "Who remains of the Hunnic leadership?"

"Other than your brother?" Sembrouthes replied. "Simmas'

centurion Aigan, and a dekarchos from Sunicas named Sinnion, but no others with considerable leadership experience."

I sucked between my teeth as I absorbed the gravity of our losses. The Hunnic foederati had been the most dependable core of Belisarius' army, yet they possessed few leaders whose talent and loyalty could be assured.

"Inform Aigan that he will be the interim commander of the Huns," I replied. "And bring me a list of junior officers with leadership potential."

"And what of Samur?" Mundus asked. "Would he be able to lead?"

Bile churned in my gut at the question. Samur's grievous wounds from Callinicum, while stabilized, had left my brother perilously close to death. "Sunicas always said that only a Hun can lead other Huns," I responded, "and while they respect Samur, he is too young, too foreign, and presently too injured to ensure their discipline and loyalty."

We continued with status reports of the other sections of the army, allowing me time to craft our next move. Complicating matters were the army's conflicting needs, chiefly the competing desires for rest and for progress toward a more secure location. Though Belisarius had provisioned our escape with several days' worth of full rations, we needed to move toward a city before the supplies ran out. Furthermore, our forces remained utterly exposed on the Syrian flatlands, our lone stroke of luck being Azarethes' lack of boats to pursue our battle further. After the completion of the final status report, I issued my first orders to Belisarius' diminished staff.

"Valerian, take a dozen men across the river and recover the bodies of Sunicas, Simmas, and the other Hun officers. Bring more bodies if you are able, but do not engage in battle, and return by sundown."

Baduarius gave the table an affirmative thump, while others noted their agreement. Most armies—especially those in defeat—abandoned their dead and dying where they fell, though Belisarius would never support that sort of indifferent cruelty. Azarethes had departed the battle site before the break of dawn, leaving little time for the Persians to have completely mutilated the corpses of our fallen brothers.

"Sembrouthes, order Fulcaris and six others to take whatever horses remain available to us," I said. "They will find a shallower river crossing, find John and Bessas, and order them to meet us in Barbalissus."

"So that's where we're headed?" Baduarius asked with a grunt.

"For now," I replied. "It is the closest settlement that can support an army of our size and will allow us to keep watch of Azarethes without risking another fight."

"Or allowing Hermogenes to force us into another engagement." Germanus gave a throaty spit as he mentioned the legate's name.

"Yes," I allowed, "although we need to send scouts to shadow Azarethes' movements."

"My men can do it," Germanus said. "With the butchery we inflicted on the Persians, they can't be moving too quickly. If there are no more horses, runners could spy on the Persians from a safe distance."

I nodded. "Do what you can to find horses—maybe some will have been left behind from the battle. Send relays, and let your men know that we need daily reports until reaching Barbalissus."

"And when will we reach the city?" Marcellus asked.

"We leave tomorrow," I said, ignoring the groans of exhaustion that escaped several officers at the news. "Those unable to move will be tended by doctors and guarded by a full century. They shouldn't be at any risk, but I won't take any chances."

Most nodded, and all ignored the fact that any man unable to walk with support by morning was unlikely to return to full health in the coming days. Hundreds of wounded lay along the riverbank, their moans filling the midmorning air as their blood mingled with the slow current of the Euphrates.

"Go now," I commanded. "We leave after midday tomorrow and will be in Barbalissus within four days."

The men grunted their assent, although Baduarius raised a question that had been on the minds of all.

"What can we do for Belisarius in the meantime? Any plan to free him?"

Again, Baduarius touched on fears that capped my newfound command. Hermogenes was intractable, and he had little love for me. I could simper or bargain or threaten him, but no matter my approach, Hermogenes was unlikely to view any attempt to secure Belisarius' freedom as anything other than a challenge to his authority—a grave transgression. After all, Callinicum was the cursed fruit harvested from Hermogenes' insistence upon engaging Azarethes' better-trained host, and none of us possessed the authority to counter Hermogenes' will. Not Belisarius, nor me, nor even sage Liberius. Short of driving a dagger between the man's ribs, I had no notion of how to turn Hermogenes' intended course. And therefore, I feared him.

But the others could not know of my doubts—of this, I was resolute. "I will meet with the legate privately, although I doubt he will listen to those pleas," I admitted. "I will insist on making his conditions more comfortable. Hermogenes would not be so obstinate as to refuse that."

Yet, indeed, Hermogenes proved he was. Hermogenes scowled after I was permitted entry into his tent and seemed further irritated at not being consulted regarding the army's next movements toward Barbalissus.

"By the blood of Christ, we are still at war! You would allow a Persian army to traipse around Roman territory unhindered?"

He did not brook any argument, even when I pointed out that an exhausted and depleted army could hardly resist Azarethes further, though neither did he force me to obey. Grumbling, Hermogenes merely nodded as I promised regular updates regarding Azarethes' movements and waved a hand in dismissal, his mind presumably already trained upon another letter bound for Constantinople.

At last, I dared to ask whether I could visit Belisarius. Hermogenes shook his head without even turning his eyes from his quill and scroll.

"Another time, perhaps," he said.

Back in Belisarius' tent, a dozen officers from various contingents of the army waited, nursing bruises and using an awning as shade from the sun. My thoughts blurring, I forced myself to meet with each man and listen to his needs and complaints, and to promise what help I could manage to dispatch in Belisarius' stead. The audiences would have continued well past sundown had Uliaris not ordered the tent closed after a half day's exertions.

"Varus needs his rest, the same as you! His brother is with the healers, and you're keeping them apart. Leave petitions with me, and I'll see that they're addressed in due time." With that, Uliaris shut the tent's heavy cloth flaps, blocking out the light of the midday sun, and I fell back into a small cot into a sleep known only to those pushed well beyond the limits of their endurance.

Aromas of rich meat and roasted vegetables drew me awake near sundown. I found Cephalas carrying heavy trays of food and drink, resting the simple clay cups and wooden bowls next to a low table filled with maps and scrolls. Rising, I nodded to my friend and gave instructions to commence our camp's departure for Barbalissus.

Despite the depleted strength of the army, our departure was uneventful. Centurions and *dekarchoi* of various units barked orders for the men to gather their packs into larger carts and form into wide columns, with most of our supplies borne by the few oxen that had been herded toward our makeshift camp. Sweltering in the Syrian heat, most men opted to pile their armor into our wagons and walk in boots and a light tunic.

Each of the officers transferred reports of his wounded—those who were too frail to travel. All told, I was required to leave three hundred Romans along the Euphrates riverbank and an equal number of men to serve as their guards and caretakers until additional carts could be commandeered to carry all to Barbalissus. Two spaces were reserved for wounded men to be carried with the remnants of the army—one for Ascum and the other for Samur.

Pus oozed from Ascum's scorched flesh. While gruesome to behold, his wounds were far more contained than might have been expected. His left arm was a mess of burns and scabs that tendrilled their way across the chest and left leg, although his face was largely spared from injury. Though the ballista fires had claimed an ear and some of Ascum's left cheek, he still retained capability of movement. Largely unconscious for the previous two days, Ascum moaned as he rolled in his sleep, with a doctor fighting against the searing inflammation that still threatened the officer's life.

Far more stable than Ascum, my brother, Samur, bore a sallow face that left Rosamund wary of leaving him unattended. While successful in dislodging the Persian arrowheads from Samur's body, she'd insisted on accompanying him west to Barbalissus.

"There are enough doctors here," Rosamund said, "and I serve *you*, Varus, not the army."

I did not press her further. I ordered one of my Herulians to keep watch over Rosamund and deliver me any changes in Samur's condition. With both wounded men lodged safely on wooden carts, the army progressed away from the Euphrates River, and I prayed that the pitifully small detachment I left to guard those too injured to travel would not be caught and murdered by Persian raiders. Tongues must have wagged that I granted a prone Samur special privileges against the common spearmen of Belisarius' army, yet I was deaf to any complaints. He was my brother, and I would not leave him behind again.

With much grumbling of the men, most of whom were bruised and torn from Callinicum, we arrived in Barbalissus five days later. At the onset of our march, I had hoped to meet with Belisarius, making one last attempt before departing, but Hermogenes, it seemed, had dispatched the imprisoned general well before the army was ready to leave our campsites. Uliaris, Sembrouthes, and I confronted the legate angrily at the news, yet Hermogenes merely shrugged off our concerns and insisted that I had no right to consort with Belisarius until further guidance from the Emperor was made available regarding his punishment.

Barbalissus was a relatively minor city in Roman Syria, serving as a staging point to support Roman military operations along the Euphrates River. Its stone walls had recently been repaired under orders from the late Emperor Justin, however city leadership had taken few measures to sufficiently staff the fortifications with trained spearmen. The neatly uniformed limitanei of Barbalissus' walls hardly deigned to formally identify our army's officers, which was a serious breach of protocol of any Roman city during wartime. Moving toward the front of my column, I began to shout angrily at the gate guards to grant us passage, only to draw back in shock and surprise.

For the limitanei of Barbalissus were cheering wildly, shouting the Emperor's name and hugging one another along the walls. That sight was a portent that God had smiled once more on the Roman cause, giving us hope for another day. Ignoring decorum, a gate captain called down to me, sharing the news with all present.

"Commander, have you not heard?" he exclaimed. "Kavadh is dead!"

Soon enough, I found his tidings to be true. And the logic was sound, for the tidings explained Azarethes' desperate movements to escape east for the safety of Nisibis.

The wily Persian Shahanshah, who had ruled for decades and had destroyed dozens of Roman armies, had perished, struck down by old age. And with that, we were saved.

ETERNAL PEACE

Shahanshah Kavadh's death was verified from two sources. First was a dispatch from Narses who, still ignorant of the events of Callinicum at the time the missive had been written, had sent riders to inform Belisarius of our fortune.

Wait for further instructions, and take no measures to engage Azarethes or any other Persian force unless attacked, Narses wrote, words that would have saved thousands of lives and would have given Belisarius the means to resist the legate's Imperial decrees. *The Emperor has convinced the Hephthalites to break their alliance with the Persians and paid the Göktürks to invade Persian Sogdia. With luck, the war will conclude soon.*

Scanning the fine ink of the scroll, the familiar thin characters of Narses' script, my gaze settled upon Theodora's seal, stamped at the bottom of the document. This alone convinced me of the truth of Kavadh's death, though it did little to instruct me on the best course of action.

That second piece of information came a week later—yet not from Antioch nor Constantinople, though I wrote several missives to the Emperor and Empress, as well as Mariya and Antonina in Antioch. Instead, a message arrived from a darkly cloaked figure atop a Nisean stallion that reminded me of Ignis, bearing a banner of truce to the gates of Barbalissus.

I was summoned to the city's eastern gates by Fulcaris, who had assigned sentries from our army to accompany Barbalissus' limitanei. The city governor complained at first, yet desisted when even Hermogenes growled at the incompetence of the city's levies and guardsmen.

Signaling for the gates to open, I moved out of Barbalissus' walls, Uliaris and Sembrouthes following closely behind. Both men were heavily armed for the occasion, with Sembrouthes favoring a lengthy pike while Uliaris held multiple franciscas at his waist.

"No violence," I ordered. "We don't need to start a fight over a messenger."

"I'll be cordial if he is," Uliaris muttered.

I shook my head and walked to greet the Persian messenger, signaling for my two guards to remain behind. The Persian dismounted, his cloth trousers billowing, and saluted in my direction with a respectful greeting in the Persian tongue.

"Well met," he said. "Do I have the pleasure of addressing General Flavius Belisarius?"

"No," I responded, my Persian sloppy from misuse. "Komes Varus, interim commander. Roman Mesopotamian Army."

The Persian nodded. "Well met then, Komes Varus. I bring greetings from Astabadh Azarethes, lord of all warriors of great Persia. The Astabadh would entreat with Rome's leadership in these parts." He spoke smoothly, flourishing Azarethes' flowery title at each mention.

My limited Persian was considerably more curt. "When?" I asked. "And where?"

"Within eyeshot of this city, if you like," the Persian said. "The Astabadh fears no man but trusts in Lord Belisarius' honor... wherever he may be."

I nearly blurted out that Belisarius no longer commanded the army but mercifully did not. In hindsight, Azarethes likely needed to strike a peace with us Romans regardless of our ability to withstand further attack. The death of Kavadh would have placed the Persian Empire, and all of its military leaders, in a tumult of tension and dangled it on the precipice of civil war. Absent Belisarius, the Empire's eastern frontier was more of a sieve than a fortified border, incapable of preventing Azarethes from rampaging through Syria and even Cappadocia or Cilicia. Therefore, I opted instead for a casual tone, even as my words came slowly and clumsily. "Very well," I said. "Five days?"

"Three would be better," the messenger said. "We are under considerable urgency to conclude these matters and return to Ctesiphon."

I nodded. "Very well," I said again. "My man here, he shall provision you, give you a fresh horse. Travel well, stranger."

"And may Sarosh Yazad protect you at night, good commander. The world could use a bit more civility, don't you think?"

I nodded and turned back to the city. "See the man has supplies and a fresh mount," I said to Uliaris. "We meet with Azarethes in three days."

"So soon?" Uliaris responded. "Where?"

"Here," I grunted. "They're coming here."

Sembrouthes spat. "That means one of two things. Either Azarethes took horrendous losses at Callinicum, or we're about to be besieged and slaughtered."

Unintentionally laughing, I said, "Either way, we lack the strength to do much else but wait and make the Persians think us well armed and supplied. Double our sentries, and keep fires burning every ten paces of wall."

And so we waited. Whether for a declaration of peace or for another conflict, I am still not sure to this day. I spent my days dictating letters to nearby towns and cities, demanding support from some while begging from others. I wrote to Mariya, assuring her that all was well and that we would be reunited before meeting our child. And I wrote to Liberius and Father Petrus, asking for their advice on how to wield the biting weight of command, how to uphold Justinian's will while preventing further needless death. I even tried to force my way into Belisarius' personal prison, yet I was continually turned back by men who knew their deaths were at hand if I was not refused. Seeing a half dozen men reluctantly bound by duty rather than by any love to Hermogenes, I relented, if only to spare their lives for another day.

Where my days were an agony of bureaucratic monotony, it was the nights that I feared. With my tapers down to the wick, guttering from lack of fuel, I stared blankly into the dark expanse of my rooms, twitching at random creaks and groans from the old stones and boards of Barbalissus. I held no esteem for the Persian gods, yet in my solitude, I was taken back into my cell at Nisibis, alone once more with the magus and his curse, his gods as real as my savior.

Sleep offered little succor. Long deprived of inebriation, I began to drink greedily from a wineskin in an attempt to induce a dreamless sleep, but it was in vain. The first night I awoke slathered in sweat, screaming defiance as I rose from my bed. The next, I dreamt of the men I had killed, from the Gepid chieftain to the molded features of an Avar warrior to Khingila and even Archelaus—though it was not until the face of Hakhamanish that I drew back in horror, forced to behold that mocking laughter once again.

Heed my words, Roman, and be wary. The Great Lie is already upon you, the scion of sin!

I awoke screaming, reaching for the runed sword that was never more than a few paces from my bedside. My room door creaked open, and a head poked inside, to which I roared a challenge and lowered my blade. The door closed, only to be swung open several moments later by a more familiar figure. Her white hair tangled and gaze slackened with recent sleep, Rosamund approached slowly, calling out my name as a sign of friendship. She slowly offered an upturned hand, raising it in my direction.

"Varus, it's all right! It's me... It's Rosamund. Put down your sword."

My grip loosened from the pommel, and I let the blade fall

dully against the woolen rug. Rosamund eased me back to bed, still cautious, and I remember little other than what others have told me. I do know that Rosamund sat outside for the remainder of the evening, instructing the guards to find her for any future disturbances.

The day before Azarethes' arrival, messengers arrived from the surrounding region. Most promising among these was a note from John, who had rallied Belisarius' mounted survivors near the walled enclosure of Callinicum.

Most of the cataphracts survive, as well as a few thousand Ghassanids, John wrote. *I'm leaving for Barbalissus as soon as I can requisition enough boats to ferry us across the Euphrates. Reinforcements from Dara have arrived as well.*

A mixture of writing dotted the scroll, telling of the relative strength of each banda that had joined John in his retreat. Bessas went into considerable detail regarding the condition of the armored horses and offered a happy note in the margins that the Herulian mounts, including Ignis, were safe and well. However, near the bottom of the scroll, a more ominous warning awaited me.

Do not allow Hermogenes to move Belisarius away from the army, John said. *The legate cannot be allowed to make unilateral decisions. I'm bringing Liberius from Dara to help. Keep yourself safe, Varus.*

The note was signed John of Armenia, Tribune, in flowing letters that stood in contrast to the rushed blocks of the longer letter. I called Perenus and Sembrouthes to discuss the letter's contents, desirous of keeping their warning a secret.

"I think Hermogenes is going to force Belisarius into a trial," Perenus said. "Blame the general for our troubles at Thannuris and Callinicum."

"Yes, and take all the credit for Dara." Sembrouthes scowled. "I wouldn't put it past an old politician."

Nodding my agreement, I ordered Perenus to keep a constant shadow over Hermogenes. "Send a report each time Belisarius is moved," I said. "Even if it is just to walk in a courtyard, I want to know the moment Belisarius is taken from his quarters."

They obeyed, taking trouble to keep out of Hermogenes' way. When I wasn't addressing the growing mound of messages and orders demanding the attention of the army's commander, I spent my hours visiting detachments of wounded men who had been slowly carried from the banks of the Euphrates and visiting my maimed brother, who moaned as he turned in discomfort.

I woke well before dawn the next day, pleased to find the walls of Barbalissus teeming with braziers and torches. Narrow stone parapets were choked with soldiers, yet the ruse was well worth the curses and blundering of half-blinded sentries if it made Azarethes waver even slightly in his desire to pursue his luck against Rome any further. Scouts had placed heavy braziers at regular intervals as far as five hundred paces from Barbalissus' gates, which allowed us to spy the first Persians who advanced against our position.

To our surprise and relief, the Persian Astabadh arrived with an honor guard that we estimated at a mere five hundred men and servants. The late Shahanshah's banners flapped against the light western breeze as a few dozen Persians erected embroidered tents along the horizon, taking few measures other than a lightly guarded perimeter to defend against their Roman enemies in Barbalissus.

A short time after dawn, the tent village was completed, and cookfires blew thin trails of smoke across the clear skies. Astride a pony, a Persian messenger galloped the remaining distance to the city and beckoned for the army's leaders to follow. When none answered his call, the messenger tried again in rough Greek words that further confused the men.

"You may bring your weapons if you prefer," the messenger yelled over the walls. "Astabadh Azarethes will wait unarmed and hopes that you will sup with him at his table."

As the rider departed, I ordered Fulcaris to inform Hermogenes of the invitation and send couriers to gather Belisarius' senior officers for a meeting with the Persian commander.

Not long after, Hermogenes rustled to the gates of Barbalissus, leading a contingent of Roman officers toward Azarethes' encampment. Other than myself, attendees included Germanus, the Ghassanid King al-Harith, and Marcellus, with Sembrouthes and Uliaris as our heavily armed guardsmen. Lastly, Hermogenes invited a recently arrived Procopius to accompany our party, so that the scribe might note any agreements made and dispatch them quickly to the Emperor in Constantinople.

My hopes were Janus-faced — simple in their desires and endlessly complex in their execution. Simple in that I yearned for a definitive agreement to end our war, concluding the threat of hostilities that would otherwise result in our destruction if carried out. Complex, however, in that our Empire must not be seen to lose standing in the process of negotiations, lest Hermogenes provoke further enmity with our Persian counterparts. Tributes and prisoners must be exchanged, of this there was little doubt, but otherwise I lacked the skills to win a war of words with our Persian adversaries. I could only hope that God saw the righteousness in my longing for peace, and that Hermogenes would not waylay our negotiations in favor of something wholly disagreeable to Azarethes and his men.

A hundred paces from the tent village, a white-robed Persian approached, the yellow sash at his waist swaying as he raised his arm in greeting. His thick beard, neatly combed and curled, parted as he smiled, formally welcoming us into their encampment.

"May the Ahura Mazda light your path, friends," the man said in smooth Persian. "Surely it is time to exchange our weapons for plows and sickles, so that the common people can once again live in peace?"

Hermogenes looked at me impatiently for a translation, which I gave as best I could. "He's a Zoroastrian priest of the Persian religion," I added, not concealing my shudder.

Before Hermogenes could answer, the priest coughed lightly into his sleeve and offered another thin smile. "Indeed I am, Varus the Herulian. I pray that your own nights are kept in safety and comfort," the priest said in flawless Greek.

"How do you know my name?" I asked incredulously in Persian.

"The Magus Hakhamanish said much of your conversations," he

replied. "He mourns the foul treatment that you and your comrade were subjected to at Nisibis but prays that you keep his words close to your heart."

Hermogenes grunted. "We have no time for this," he complained. "See us to your master."

The priest smiled. "I shall accompany you to meet the Astabadh, do not worry," he replied in Greek. "But Azarethes is not my master, nor is any man of flesh and bone."

Hermogenes waved at these remarks, leaving further arguments unsaid. Politely, the Zoroastrian priest guided us past Azarethes' sentry lines and into one of the larger jade tents, its edges bedecked with golden embroidery. Inside, we found a number of cushioned benches, a low table filled with cooked foods and exotic fruits, and Azarethes.

The Astabadh was a surprisingly common-looking man. Nearly bald, Azarethes kept what little hair remained to him cut close to his russet scalp, taking no measures to hide the cuts and scars that leather caps and metal armor had dug into the thin layer of skin above the skull. His eyes were round and his mouth overlarge, making this feared Persian commander appear something of a human-sized frog rather than the leader of the largest army currently in arms.

"Welcome, welcome," Azarethes purred in accented Greek, gesturing to the couches around the table.

A half dozen servants rushed to our side, making Uliaris and Sembrouthes jump in alarm and place hands upon the pommels of their swords. Hermogenes looked on, uncertain of the situation, though Azarethes merely laughed.

"Friends, it is against Persian honor to violate the peace of a meal," the Astabadh said. To further alleviate our concerns, he tore at a loaf of bread and filled it with a section of meat, taking time to savor each small bite. Once finished, he raised a large pitcher of wine and filled a green-hued glass, which he drained within moments. "Now, please, sit and enjoy."

I was the first to copy Azarethes' example. Only then did

Hermogenes and the others follow as well. Thus satisfied of our safety and the Persian general's lack of complaint at our blades despite his own men being unarmed, we sank into our cushioned chairs. I nodded at Azarethes' servants, who returned to continue serving our food and beverage, yet noticed a constant wariness amongst Uliaris and Sembrouthes throughout this ritual. The two men did not relax in the slightest until the servants retreated behind Azarethes, and even then, they remained on alert for any sign of treachery.

"Now that we are more comfortable, let us turn our minds to see what can be done to end this war," Azarethes said. "Are you prepared to negotiate on behalf of your emperor?"

"We are," Hermogenes replied stiffly, "if the terms are genial."

Azarethes smiled. "I would expect nothing less. But tell me, who among you is General Belisarius? I must compliment him, for even as adversaries, I recognize talent when I see it."

As Hermogenes grumbled a reply, I shot into the conversation. "General Belisarius is not with us," I said, drawing a heated look from the legate. "The Emperor's representatives do not approve of lost battles."

"Lost?" Azarethes asked, his eyebrows raised. "You mean Thannuris? Or Callinicum? You can hardly call those engagements outright losses, not when you have deprived your enemy of any strategic advantage or victory."

I smiled weakly. "Yet here we are."

Hermogenes cleared his throat as though to change the subject, but it was fruitless.

"Sadly, I do understand your point." Azarethes sighed. "I have no doubt that I will face my own inquiries from the Shahanshah into the loss of Persian men at Callinicum, but such is the life of a commander."

"Our condolences at the passage of Shahanshah Kavadh," I replied. Hermogenes and Germanus echoed similar sentiments. "He was a fearsome and wise leader."

"Indeed he was!" Azarethes replied, his face brightening. "And we fully believe Shahanshah Khosrow will be the same. I thank you for your kind words, but I do not know your name, soldier."

"Komes Varus, Commander of the Herulian foederati," I said, adding, "… and interim commander of Rome's Mesopotamian Army."

Azarethes smiled and raised his eyebrows at the mention of my men. Whether this was from true respect or a polite gesture, I do not know, for Azarethes' honeyed words flew freely that morning on subjects near and far. Regardless, I took his compliments as he laid them out, deflating the tension in the room.

"Perhaps we may move on to resolve our present situation," Hermogenes said, once again cutting into talk between military officers.

Rather than take offense, Azarethes merely nodded. He clapped his hands, summoning two burly Zhayedan into the tent, their status denoted by the fine scale armor that covered their bodies. Between them was a collection of heavy calfskin scrolls that, once laid across an adjoining table, revealed a painstakingly detailed map of the border between Justinian and Khosrow. As long and wide as a man, the display showed even small villages within each of the major provinces, and client kingdoms from Lazica to distant Himyar, where Rome's Aksumite allies had dislodged the Persians months ago.

Azarethes snapped his fingers, signaling another batch of servants into the room. These carried thick linen bundles that, it seemed, held dozens of wooden figures, each representing a key Roman or Persian armed band. Under the Astabadh's instruction, the pieces were arranged at various points, identifying present locations of large army groups by both forces. Such an exercise gave away little that Narses' extensive web of spies had not informed upon, but nevertheless, the Persians' confidence drew me to pause. Azarethes spoke first.

"As you can see, the forces of Shahanshah Khosrow now occupy several regions of Roman Mesopotamia and Syria," Azarethes lectured, using a finger to sweep across the map.

"But no major cities," I pointed out.

"Nor any Ghassanid territory, despite Lakhmid brutality against my people," King al-Harith said acidly—speaking for the first time in our meeting.

Azarethes frowned, his attentions trained upon me. "True, but how long will such isolated cities hold? Only time will tell, and the sands run low for many a Roman garrison."

"Your army has sustained significant casualties, though," Germanus grunted, his eyes following the locations of each Persian army.

Azarethes made a sucking sound, a stream of air whistling between the gaps of his frontmost teeth. "Apologies, but I do not know you either, good commander."

"Lord Germanus, general of the Thracian Army," Germanus replied formally, "and cousin to Emperor Justinian."

"Ah, very good," Azarethes said. "Yes, we have taken casualties. But Persia is vast, and her sons are many and near. Tell me, can Rome say the same?"

Veiled bickering continued for some time as Azarethes and the Roman delegation traded barbs. While the Persians were clearly endeavoring to give away little that we Romans could not deduce on our own, it was surprising to see how few figures represented Azarethes' massed men. In the chaos of our retreat across the Euphrates, it was impossible to get a close estimate of the forces remaining to Persia and the Lakhmids, although Germanus and others had testified to the horrendous level of dead and wounded that our spearmen had wrought.

Hermogenes grew more active in the debate, frequently referring to Roman prowess on the fields of Dara. He was not incorrect, though the boasts made me cringe, for the author of that impossible victory currently resided in Hermogenes' confinement. However, Hermogenes continued, referencing other Persian advances farther north that had been muted, with General Sittas and the Persian Iberian princes prowling along the pre-war borders. Our allies in Lazica had retained their freedom, ejecting a larger Persian warband from their borders and preventing easy Persian access to the Euxine Sea. Even in Mesopotamia, Hermogenes argued that Persian blood had accomplished no major goals, to which Azarethes' subordinates furiously retorted the damage wrought against Rome's frontier provinces.

Sunlight grew and waned as discussions continued well into the afternoon, with Procopius furiously scribbling notes of the negotiations on a number of flax scrolls. Despite mistrust and considerable differences in opinion, Hermogenes and Azarethes reached an agreement amenable to the monarchs of both nations. Persia would withdraw all of her armies from pre-war Roman territory, and in return Justinian would pay 110 centenaria of gold, a bloodcurdling sum that could have paid the costs of the Roman army several times over.

When I asked why the Persians were so eager to end the fight, Germanus framed the issue bluntly. "They've accomplished little, and Khosrow lacks the love of the Persian nobility that Kavadh commanded with a breath. Worse, they're facing another sizeable war in the east against the Göktürks and Hephthalites, so tying up their Roman war with a handsome payment is an easy decision to make."

"And our willingness to pay so much for that peace?" I asked, thinking of what damage Hermogenes might bring into the negotiations.

"Would you really want to fight the Persians again?" Germanus asked. "Even if this so-called 'Eternal Peace' fails in five or ten years, the cost is more than worth the pain and blood that continued war would wreck upon us."

As the conclusions waned and oaths were sealed, Azarethes added one additional requirement to the terms of the truce—something confusing to us Romans, and that no Roman would have ever offered voluntarily.

"As a token of good faith, we ask that you host our beloved Prince Xerxes for the foreseeable future," Azarethes said.

"As a hostage, you mean," replied Hermogenes.

Azarethes smiled in a manner that sought to convey his innocence. "A gesture of friendship, surely. I'm certain that you will learn much from Prince Xerxes, which would very much please the Shahanshah."

A tense hush swept through the Roman party. Hermogenes whispered into Procopius' ear. The scribe nodded and replied in an excited murmur. That seemed to bring the matter to a definitive close.

"The Emperor Justinian would be delighted to host Prince Xerxes," Hermogenes declared. "Procopius here will take the details of his household and requirements as requested."

Azarethes clapped his hands. "Excellent! Although you will find that Prince Xerxes wants but little in this life, I will make his conditions known to you privately."

The Astabadh snapped his fingers, and a man was ushered forward under the pressures of the two Zhayedan. His hands shackled with heavy gold, Prince Xerxes was a handsome man, perhaps only a few years older than myself, with a neatly cropped beard and dark eyes. He raised one of his bushy eyebrows as he caught sight of his new Roman hosts, yet said nothing at his change in fortune.

"It is done!" Azarethes exclaimed in delight. "By the truth that is the Ahura Mazda, let our Eternal Peace see our children grow fat and carefree in their idyll."

Such a future was not meant to be. For a brief time, Rome found itself at peace with its eastern enemy. It would only be with time that truce's effects would be revealed: it did nothing to allay the foes within Justinian's government, nor even within my own army.

Through all my years, I have discovered that the deepest wounds are not struck by foreigners or barbarians, but instead by those who bear the standard of ally.

UNHEEDED WORDS OF
WARNING

Jubilant bonfires roared outside of the walls of Barbalissus. Wineskins made their way through the ranks as men danced around the flames, hollering in joy at the honorable end to the Persian war. I spied Fulcaris nearly stumbling into his certain death as he pissed onto the stacked logs, drunkenly boasting to his cousin Irilar that he alone could stamp out the Persian god's fire. Nearby, Perenus gorged himself on an entire sheep's leg, the rich juices flooding down from the corners of his mouth and staining his beard.

Most of my foederati joined in the revelry, accompanied by a fair number of the surviving Huns and Ascum's Alani archers. Baduarius led many of them in a bawdy song, quickly establishing impromptu wrestling matches against the more intoxicated of the men. He even managed to entice al-Harith and several Ghassanids to sing and dance, goading the Greek-speaking Arab officers to teach him lewd insults from their native tongue.

Even Solomon, flanked by a small cadre of junior officers, had joined in the festivities. Withdrawn from other groups of the Roman and Ghassanid contingents, camp servants carried food and wine toward the few dozen spearmen that formed a ragged circle around Solomon's fires. Catching my gaze, a noticeably drunk Marcian smirked, spitting throatily into the fire as he leaned to whisper in Solomon's ear. The komes drew back in confusion and seemed to ponder Marcian's words until finally nodding in agreement.

"He has no right to celebrate," Sembrouthes said. "His men, maybe. It's not their fault that he is a coward. But Germanus should have whipped Solomon and Marcian raw."

"Nepotian would never allow it," I said, groaning. "Any injury or insult would be paid back a thousandfold."

"There will come a time that this pain will be worth it," Sembrouthes muttered.

Amidst the reverie, Germanus and I handpicked a hundred of our more disciplined men to keep watch over the city walls. Largely consisting of members of Germanus' spearmen, the unit's command was given to a young Alamanni man named Thurimuth on the basis of his courage at Callinicum; Mundus had attested to Thurimuth's strength as pivotal in staving off a complete collapse when Marcian and Solomon retreated from the right flank.

"Keep the men from doing anything too destructive," Germanus ordered Thurimuth. "And stay sober. I'll be sure to compensate each of your men handsomely for their discipline and discretion."

Thurimuth nodded excitedly at the charge, eyeing the opportunity as a rare chance to rise above his station as an enlisted spearman of one of the more battle-worn armies of the Roman Empire.

Another fifty were requisitioned to scout the countryside to anticipate any ambush. Our horses were poor, with most as older swayback mares that would have struggled to pull a plow, yet they were still better than blundering in the dark on foot.

Gathering together what few sober Herulians and Huns I could find, I ordered them to keep a loose perimeter a few miles from Barbalissus, remaining a careful distance from Azarethes' camp. With my surviving officers drunk or useless by dusk, I gave the honor of command to a half-Herulian, half-Greek rider named Sindual. Dark and clean-shaven, Sindual had been Alaric's second before Dara, and he'd promised to serve me as faithfully as his predecessor had against the Hephthalites.

With our defenses set, most of the senior officers joined the celebrations in a rare show of social fraternity with the common soldiers. "After all that we've been through, I think I will make myself drunk. You should join me, Varus." Germanus chuckled, beckoning me onward.

I smiled but declined. "Someone needs to keep a clear head," I said, "and I'd like to try to meet with Belisarius to tell him of our good news."

Germanus relented. "Very well. As good a reason as any, but don't be surprised if I'm useless in a few hours. I'll have to order Mundus and Troglita to join me, but they will obey like good subordinates."

As we parted, Uliaris and Sembrouthes soon approached. "So we're meeting with Belisarius, then?" Uliaris asked.

"A good bodyguard doesn't let on that he's eavesdropping," Sembrouthes said with a groan.

I laughed. "Yes, we are. With Hermogenes and Procopius busy sending notes of the peace terms to the Emperor and the provincial governors, this is our best chance to force an audience."

And so we stayed alert and sober while our friends descended into a depravity known only to soldiers and those who have seen the carnage of battle. Waiting for the festivities to continue, we received a gift of honeyed wine and seasoned meats from Azarethes' camp as a gesture of further goodwill. Cursing myself and Hermogenes for not preparing for the ritual, I yelled at Baduarius to requisition several heavy skins of Greek wine and Thracian cheese to return to the Persian host. He grumbled at the loss, but he complied so as to respect decorum in the face of our former enemies. I entrusted the skins to Valerian who, despite hiccupping and giggling like a child, was the steadiest on his feet of the officers available to me.

As the sun surrendered into the darkness along the Syrian flatlands, we made our move to Belisarius' buildings. Fearful of being accused of insubordination or treason, I commanded Sembrouthes to hoist torches in the air in the event that Hermogenes spotted our arrival. Yet the legate was nowhere to be found, leaving us direct access to Belisarius' modest quarters at the center of Barbalissus.

A single spearman stood watch at the doorstep. A young man, he bore ceremonial armor that denoted his status as an Imperial guardsman entrusted to care for Legate Hermogenes in Justinian's absence. Hermogenes commanded at least twenty such creatures who, while handsomely equipped, lacked the skill of even the most junior excubitor. Many amongst those guards owed their position to parents wealthy enough to purchase a commission from one of Justinian's ministers, or at least bribe a leader of Constantinople's city watch for a safe position and a dependable salary. That lone spearman, the only man who separated me from Belisarius, looked as disinterested and unfit as I had eventually become as a servant in the Imperial Palace.

"The windows are boarded up, and that building has a single door," Uliaris whispered. "I could drive a francisca into his gullet and hide the body before morning."

"Hush!" I hissed. "No bloodshed, especially against Hermogenes' men. Can't we just bribe him?"

Uliaris grinned. "Anyone can be bribed, given enough coin. But what we need is a distraction as well. Do you have coins in that belt?"

I nodded, unfastening my pouch and producing a golden solidus. Uliaris' eyes widened—this was the sort of wealth that few warriors in the Empire would hold at any given moment. I placed the solidus into Uliaris' gloved hand. "Do you have a distraction?"

"The best!" Uliaris nodded, patting the wineskin at his belt. "If our friend is stuck with sentry duty on the evening of a celebration, it's not by choice. Wait for my signal."

"This cannot end well," Sembrouthes muttered.

Immediately thereafter, Uliaris rushed into the street and toward Belisarius' confinement. The guard did not react at first, but he lowered his spear as Uliaris drew within ten paces of the entrance.

"Friend!" Uliaris shouted, raising his empty hands into the air. "Thought you might appreciate some of our swill!"

The guard relaxed, raising his spear again as he gestured to the door. "Would that I could..."

"Nonsense!" Uliaris insisted, unstopping his wineskin and gulping a draft. "Whatever you're guarding isn't likely to run away from a mouthful of wine."

The spearman's soft cheeks creased in a smile, and he nodded, propped his spear against the door's entrance, and thrust a hand out for Uliaris' bounty. Uliaris complied, although he mocked the guard for taking an unsatisfactory sip. "It's a celebration, man! Perhaps I should take my bounty elsewhere..."

The guard laughed and upended the skin in several swallows. As he drank, Uliaris stepped closer to the spearman, tensing with each step, until he suddenly turned in my direction. "What was that?"

"Wha—" the spearman half choked in reply.

"Over there!" Uliaris said, pointing in my direction.

Wiping his mouth against his tunic, the spearman moved toward Sembrouthes and me. I froze, silently cursing Uliaris for including me in his foolishness. "You, eavesdroppers!"

In a swift motion, Uliaris glanced up and down the street. Then he snatched up the propped spear. Its wooden shaft cracked into the back of the spearman's helmeted head, producing a sickly thud. He crumpled to the ground, moaning.

Uliaris sighed. "I swear, the world is becoming stupider. I would say you have ten minutes, Varus."

"You didn't have to hit him so hard!" I growled, emerging from the alley. Inspecting the fallen soldier, I found no blood and heard no approaching footsteps of any who might have spotted Uliaris' attack in the darkness. "What was the solidus for, if not a bribe?"

"I didn't promise that I'd bribe the man, and the solidus is for the wine!" Uliaris winked, tossing me the skin to offer to Belisarius.

Sembrouthes frowned. "Ten minutes at most, Varus. You and Uliaris can go speak with Belisarius while I stand watch."

I did not waste the opportunity, and I gestured for Uliaris to follow. I wrapped my knuckles against the heavy wooden door and unlatched the handle. With flickering candlelight emanating from the room into the street, I led my two companions into Belisarius' quarters, meeting with him for the first time since Callinicum. I expected to find a bedraggled man, unwashed and unkempt in his deprivation of anything more than basic staples.

What I encountered, however, was the same well-dressed and clean Roman commander I had known throughout our time in Tauris and Mesopotamia, albeit absent the lines of exhaustion about his eyes and minutely plumper about his waistline. In this, at least, Hermogenes had displayed a measure of respect.

Belisarius had not expected me, nor likely any friendly face. Abandoning his usual calm, measured demeanor, Belisarius jumped from his chair as he recognized me. His mouth curled into an overlarge smile, teeth flashing behind lips lightly stained by wine as he beckoned me to enter, pointing excitedly toward a bench adjacent to his own.

"Varus! Uliaris!" Belisarius exclaimed happily. "So good to see you. But how are you here?"

"No time, Lord," I said, eager to convey as much information as possible until our audience would be cut off by the fearful guard or the inopportune return of Hermogenes. "Kavadh has died, and his heir Khosrow made peace with us. The terms were agreed with Azarethes earlier today."

"My God, incredible," Belisarius replied. "But how?"

We shared cups of Uliaris' wine as I regaled Belisarius of the army's challenges and progress since the retreat from the banks of the Euphrates. Belisarius grimaced as I described Ascum's injuries, nodding in cold approval as I told of our recovery and burning of the Roman dead.

"Azarethes left the battle early the following morning, leaving little enough time to defile our men's bodies. We had scouts track their progress east, but he didn't make it far until hearing of Kavadh's death," I said. "And Azarethes specifically asked to compliment your generalship, Lord. All the men agree with him."

Belisarius smiled weakly. "That is nice to hear," he said, cordially dismissing the subject of battle skill. "But what of Hermogenes? Any word from the Emperor?"

We discussed further, hurrying through the details, as rustling could be heard coming from the street. "I'll fillet the old weasel myself, if you would allow it," Uliaris said tersely. "I don't think the man's own bodyguards would deign to stop me."

"No." Belisarius glowered, shaking his head. "Despite his faults, Hermogenes is the Emperor's representative and speaks with his voice... until we return to the capital. We place our trust in Justinian and Theodora to see the truth in our situation."

We spoke for a moment longer before being interrupted by banging at the entrance. "Time's up!" a muffled voice called from behind the heavy wooden door.

"Thank you for visiting me, both of you," Belisarius said, touching me on the shoulder. "But don't take these needless risks again... I need you to see to the men."

We stood and saluted him, pausing as Belisarius rose from his chair. "An incredible turn of events, though. Getting back all of our lost territory... Even John did not dare to dream of so remarkable an outcome."

Uliaris departed first, yet Belisarius held me back before I followed into the streets of Barbalissus. With his smile erased, Belisarius held a stern gaze as he lowered his voice to a whisper.

"Varus, you need to be more careful," he said, voice low and urgent. "Hermogenes is far from your only concern until we reach Constantinople... and you will be vulnerable to criticism as the army's commander."

My eyebrows perked up in suspicion. "But the war is over."

"No," Belisarius said. "Justinian's wars are just beginning. Keep your guards close, and don't allow disrespect or defiance to stand. Once John arrives, you will have more friends to help share the burden, but for now, you are in considerable peril."

"Is that what you would do?"

Belisarius chuckled. "No, but look at where I have ended up. A prisoner eligible for hanging or public disgrace."

"I won't allow that to happen, Lord," I said. "And the Emperor will set things to rights."

"I hope so, for my sake," Belisarius said. "For now, just promise me to keep on your guard. Lead by example, but do not hesitate to delegate tasks to those you trust. No more foolish risks... including coming to see me."

Belisarius placed his arms on my shoulders, halting further discussion and my burgeoning protestations. "You can do this," he said firmly. "You're a good man, Varus, and you'll make the right decisions."

Belisarius could not have known how wrong he was. For I would violate my promise to the general mere moments after parting from his company.

UNSPEAKABLE

Leaving Belisarius' quarters, I chuckled as I spotted Belisarius' lone guardsman, soft groans suggesting that he would soon wake. Plucking two silver coins from my belt, I placed them upon the guardsman's chest, whispering to ears that could not hear me.

"For your candor," I muttered, pacing away from Belisarius' temporary prison.

Moving away from Barbalissus' governmental center, we passed a number of taverns and brothels that had been stuffed to capacity. One Greek spearman leaned against an alley wall and vomited a torrent of undigested wine and meat scraps, moaning and laughing as he rubbed at his forehead. Another alley held a man and a woman who had taken the barest of moments to hide their nudity as they grunted in pleasure. Seeing his fellow soldiers pass by, the man drunkenly waved to me, wishing me favor with whatever god I chose as my own.

Upon reaching the east gate facing Azarethes' distant encampment, I was greeted by Sindual, caked in sweat and dirt as he gulped down cups of water.

"No sign of Persians, Lakhmids, or any enemy, Lord," Sindual rasped, panting. "And no movement or signals from Azarethes' camp."

"Good," I said. "Keep watch nonetheless. I wouldn't want the legate to use lax sentry duty as a reason to punish our foederati any further."

Sindual saluted and snuck underneath the gate, which was closed firmly behind the man as he remounted his horse and galloped to the east. Soon thereafter, Thurimuth walked forward, offering a crisp salute as he reintroduced himself.

"Apologies, Lord Varus," Thurimuth said, his Greek stilted and awkward as he addressed me. "I had thought to meet with General Germanus, but the commander has taken to drinking with Komes Troglita and Tribune Mundus and seemed unable to issue viable orders."

"He's piss drunk, you mean," Uliaris translated.

"In a manner of speaking," Thurimuth said. "At any rate, the city is rife with drunkenness, fornication, and petty vandalism. I even caught one dekarchos greasing up a hog and organizing bets as to who would catch it first. The hog broke several windows and destroyed several carts as it dashed to the forum."

"Aye, but who caught it?" Uliaris asked, smiling.

Thurimuth narrowed his eyes. "Lord Varus, I am unsure of how to handle this situation with only a banda. The local limitanei are useless, mere boys or crookbacked old men, and Barbalissus is not as small as it seems."

I shook my head, clapping Thurimuth on the shoulder. "It's an impossible task, Thurimuth," I said. "Any violent offenses or significant destruction beyond the pig?"

"None, Lord," Thurimuth answered. "My men are escorting women in the streets and protecting religious houses, but overall there's been no word or sign of anything worse than debauchery."

Laughing, I waved Thurimuth's fears away. "Keep vigilant, but don't look so dour. Believe me, you will know when a city is being savaged by an army. Belisarius' men wouldn't do such a thing."

"God willing, Lord," Thurimuth said, his hand rising to a wooden cross that hung at his neck. "I hope it continues."

Offering him another encouraging slap on the shoulder, I sent Thurimuth back toward his work. The young officer barked orders at his men to form up, leading them on a trot back to the center of the city.

"Strange people, the Alemanni," Uliaris observed. "Joyless, but dutiful."

"I like a man who takes his job seriously," I said.

"Or a woman," Uliaris agreed. "The first woman I ever took to bed was an Alemanni when I lived in Lugdunum. An awful place, filled with joyless, pious people."

Aside from Thurimuth's report, nearly all men and women that we passed in the streets were enraptured in celebration. Some within my camp had become so inebriated that they had turned to lamentations for the fallen, signing pagan tales of grief and loss that had long been outlawed in Constantinople. The Huns took to this behavior with renewed energy, singing the glories of Sunicas and Simmas as men who could have ridden alongside Attila. A half dozen languages filled the expanse around Barbalissus, and none seemed to mind the confusion or the basest lack of harmony in the tune. We three joined several fires, admiring the men for their happiness, but abstaining from any strong drink.

It was as I finally began to relax that horror curled its gnarled hands around my fate once more. As we moved from the eastern gate back to the commander's residence, a cloaked figure barreled against my position. Sembrouthes and Uliaris both raised their weapons at the faceless interloper, with Uliaris stepping two paces ahead.

"Identify yourself immediately!" Uliaris shouted.

"Cephalas, assistant to Lord Varus," the voice called back. As he drew nearer to a lit torch, I saw my friend and servant's distinctive harelipped face and nodded reassuringly to my guards. Cephalas waved a hand in thanks, closing the final few paces that separated us.

Panting, Cephalas rubbed at a sore spot on his mangled arm, proof of his stand against the Avars far to the north. His chest rose and fell as he gasped for air, mumbling apologies for raising our alarm.

"Never mind that," I said. "What brings you running frantically into the night?"

"Samur, Lord," Cephalas said. "You must come quick."

At the sound of my brother's name, ice streamed through my veins despite the warm Syrian air. Samur had shown signs of recovery over the week, and had even begun to sit up and perform basic tasks. His mobility remained diminished, and the muscles in his legs were exhausted from even a short time of supporting his weight.

"Speak your meaning," I barked. "What happened?"

Cephalas lowered his gaze at my impatience. "Lord, I went to visit him and…"

"What happened?"

"He's been attacked, Lord. A guard is still with him, but he won't speak to any of us." Cephalas was practically stammering, the words pouring out of him with frantic energy.

Without even responding, I left, darting in the direction of Samur's semi-private quarters, which I had provisioned for his treatment and recovery. Closer to the interior of the city, I cursed my ill luck at not visiting Samur on my way to Belisarius.

"We could not have known," Sembrouthes said as we ran along Barbalissus' cobbled streets. "Besides, he may not be seriously hurt. Cephalas could be wrong."

I doubted this, doubted it deeply, but said nothing. As we arrived at the threshold of Samur's building, I threw the door open and swept into the dimly lit room, barely minding the guard within, and found the truth of my brother's condition.

Samur lay crumpled against the ground, an arm bent in an obscene angle. Thick welts covered the exposed flesh of his body, which had been hastily covered by the black cloak common within my foederati. Beside the crumpled flesh was a cracked spear and a dented candlestick, both of which were laced with blood. Thick gore pooled near Samur's mouth, while cuts near his bum hemorrhaged copiously.

I crouched beside him, and Samur moaned piteously as I cradled his head with my gloved hands.

"Out, now!" I roared to the guard.

"Lord, is that wise? Surely I can be of some assistance in catching the—"

"If you do not leave this building this instant," I snarled, "I will have you lashed to a wagon wheel and rolled back to Antioch. Get out, immediately!"

His hesitancy evaporated at my fury, and the guard saluted and hustled outside. Uliaris and Sembrouthes followed suit, despite no such order being delivered to them, and I did not care to stop them.

The corners of my vision faded into a bleached haze as I struggled to keep my attentions on Samur. With one eye swollen shut, he cracked the other open, meeting my gaze with his own.

"Varus..." Samur croaked, reaching a hand to my face.

Slick with blood, his fingers weakly clenched my own, and I lowered Samur's head into my lap. A tear streamed down his face as he coughed up another gob of dark crimson, threatening to choke on the viscous fluid.

"Who did this to you, Samur?" I said, pleading. "Who did this?!"

Samur's chest strained to rise and fall as he gathered the strength for a single word. Barely audible, it was a word that would burn in my memory forever. Not only for the pain it had wrought against Samur on that evening, but for all the chaos and destruction it would cause for years to come. It was a word that I hoped Samur would not say, but in my heart, I already knew the answer. And in a moment, the world trembled.

"Marcian," Solomon whispered, his voice but a rasp against the stone floor.

My grip tightened as the name flowed into my consciousness, infecting my every muscle. Marcian, lapdog of Solomon, a man who I had pitied and hated. A man whose onetime betrothed was now my wife. A man who had now seen my brother brutalized in return.

"Sembrouthes!" I screamed, my voice cracking against the walls.

The Aksumite leader stormed into the room, his bare sword twinkling against the naked flames along the walls. Energetically scanning the room for threats, Sembrouthes soon trotted to my side, kneeling next to Samur.

"Lord?" Sembrouthes asked, his voice stilted and formal.

I took several deep breaths before turning to him. "Tell Uliaris to fetch a doctor. Then sit with my brother. Let no one else intrude on his peace until I return."

Samur clenched my fist, offering one final request before I moved to depart. Unable to make out his first words, I leaned closer, my ear a mere finger length from his cracked lips.

"No Romans," Samur sputtered weakly. "Bring Rosamund."

Patting Samur on the head, I nodded. "Tell Uliaris to bring my Gepid household servant Rosamund," I amended. "None other."

"But what of you, Lord? I should be at your side," Sembrouthes asked.

"Do as I command!" I yelled. "Stay with Samur, and see my will done."

Sembrouthes bowed his head in submission. As I released Samur into Sembrouthes' care, the Aksumite called for Uliaris, who glanced curiously at my figure as I moved back into the streets of Barbalissus. Standing watch over the door was the lone guard, his chest racing as his eyes remained fixed into the darkness.

"What is your name, soldier?" I asked, my voice low and full of danger.

"Symeon, Lord Varus," the man replied. "Of the Thracian Army."

I nodded. "I am only going to ask this once, Symeon. Did Marcian come here this evening? Did he attack my brother?"

Symeon hesitated, biting a quivering lip as he refused to meet my eyes. Furious at the delay, I drove a gloved fist into his unarmored gut. Symeon crumpled in painful groans.

"Yes, Lord," he finally replied, spitting the words between clenched teeth.

"And was he alone?"

This time, Symeon did not pause to reply. "No, Lord. There were others."

"Who?"

"I know not, Lord. I do not know their names," Symeon said piteously.

I kicked at an exposed thigh with my boot, and Symeon yelped as he tried to shield himself from my blows. "I swear, Lord, I do not know them. Marcian ordered me to depart and used his rank to enforce the command."

Ignoring the man's pleas, I clenched a handful of tunic with an outstretched fist. Drawing Symeon to his feet, I straightened the spearman and looked him in the eye. "Was Solomon with them?"

"Komes Solomon?"

"The fucking banda commander," I yelled, losing my patience. "Was Solomon party to the attack?"

"No, Lord," Symeon said, crying out as I raised a fist at the answer and desperately attempting to shield his body. "I swear on the living Christ! I swear to you, Solomon was not present. I'll regret leaving your brother until my dying breath, but the command was Marcian's alone."

I released the tunic, and Symeon fell into a squat, weeping into his hands. My heartbeat racing in my neck and my head pounding with violence, it was all I could do to turn into the street, to the quarters which housed Marcian's banda, ignoring the stupefying concoction of drunkenness, pleasure, and rank suffering that filled Barbalissus or any Roman town or city. Losing track of time, I snapped to attention as I came within twenty paces of the barracks door, my mind haunted by images of Samur's broken body once again.

A single guard leaned the bulk of his weight against the stone wall of the barracks. Using his spear to keep balance, the man took regular swigs from a wineskin, swaying lightly as he did so. The guard seemed to have been at this activity for some time, as he did not register my presence until I was nearly at his doorstep.

Spitting wine onto his beard in surprise, the man gripped his spear shaft and barked an uneven warning.

"Who... who goes there?" the guard said.

"Your army commander," I said. "Stand aside at once."

His eyes widening, the man seemed to consider his options. Absent my bodyguards, I may have seemed a liar in the glazed eyes of the inebriated, for few army commanders would travel the slightest distance without a retinue. A hint of recognition spread across the man's face. He straightened his stance.

"Aye, I know you. You saved my arse at Dara," the guard said. "You and your black-shielded Herulians."

"You're very welcome," I replied discourteously. "Now, please stand aside and grant me entry."

"I should inform the officers of your arrival, Lord," the man said, hiccupping at the end of his words that were half statement, half question.

"No, you shouldn't."

Meeting little resistance from the befuddled guard, I unlatched the barracks door and kicked hard at its lower boards. Crashing through the door, I was greeted with a foul scent of mold, sour wine, and unwashed bodies. Sounds of laughter were curtailed by the surprise as a half dozen faces swung around to meet mine. Most were crimson and slackened by rich wine and looked on with faint confusion.

Including Marcian.

"Varus," Solomon hissed. "You are not welcome here."

I ignored my old rival, who alone appeared relatively sober on a bench in a far corner of the room. Instead, walking into the enclosure, I scanned the other unknown members of Solomon's banda and issued them a single command.

"Leave. Now," I said, a warning as much as a command.

The four enlisted spearmen looked to Solomon in bewilderment, unsure of how to accommodate this conflicting request by a superior officer. As my breathing heightened and muscles tensed, I refused to cater to their more delicate sensibilities.

Covered in thick leather, I slammed my fist into a nearby wooden beam. Two men jumped to their feet as the beam moved with a lurch, the rumble from the impact echoing across the far stone walls.

"Leave!" I screamed.

This time, the four men obeyed, averting eye contact as they slipped by me and escaped into the streets. A light breeze wisped through the open barracks door, though the men did not even grumble as they left their commanding officers to face the wrath of a stranger.

"What's the matter, Varus?" Marcian said, his words slurred from heavy drink. "Angry about something else?"

I moved a pace closer, eyes narrowing on Marcian's frame. He remained armored despite the truce, his cloak soiled by spilt wine and whatever other foul humors he'd found that evening. A sly grin carved itself into his spittle-laden lips, baring teeth and crinkling his eyelids. His mirth stood in contrast to Solomon's stony silence, who sat apart from his centurion, a hand resting intently over his pommel.

"Did you visit my brother earlier tonight?" I asked, my voice low enough to force Marcian to hear each word.

Marcian laughed. "The slave? Ah, yes. With his Hun cock lovers gone, Samur had mentioned that he was lonely. I just wanted to make him feel at home, so I did."

Amidst his laughter, I smiled as my eyes narrowed. I approached quickly, my footsteps rattling. The wooden floorboards of this barracks—distinct from others dressed in stone—were so loose I nearly lost my footing against one, yet I did not stop.

"No further, Varus," Solomon bellowed, though he took no initiative to intervene.

Ignoring him, I closed the distance between me and Marcian. Alarmed, Marcian hopped to his feet, lowering a hand to a weathered sword that hung from his belt. He shot a glance to Solomon but soon snapped his eyes back on me. At three paces distant, Marcian drew his blade, shouting defiance and cursing my name, and all but licked his lips in anticipation as its pommel reached my eye level.

He moved to strike, and I grabbed it, catching his sword hand by the wrist, grinding sinew and bone, and Marcian winced in pain and struck at me with his free hand. Standing a full head shorter, he lacked my advantage of sheer size and could gain no leverage in his blows. I closed my other fist and smashed it into Marcian's left cheek, snapping his head backward. Marcian's eyes slackened as he struggled to free his trapped wrist as it crackled under my grip.

"Get the fuck off of me!" he shouted.

Marcian launched his forehead at my jaw, yet I smacked him again just below his eye. Retreating a half pace, Marcian attempted another headbutt, hissing as he failed to escape. He moved in reverse, step by step, until his back connected with the far stone wall. He seemed prepared to strike again, until I lashed with my other hand, gripped his throat, and squeezed.

Eyes bulging in surprise, Marcian let his mouth fall agape as he struggled for air. Feebly, he struck me with his free hand, each blow bringing slightly less force than the last. In response, I dug my fingers further into his muscled neck, feeling his blood pulse hard in protest.

I watched as veins burst in his yellowed eyes, as his tongue lolled from cracked lips, as thick bubbles of saliva lathered at the corners of his mouth and slid onto his beard. At last, his jerking began to still, and his blows ceased. He was growing weak. The sour odor of fresh piss steamed from his trousers, forming a wet pool along his left boot. His wild eyes met my own, pleading for release, though I merely smiled as I tightened my grip further, feeling the centurion's life ebbing from my hand.

In moments, it was over.

I released Marcian's limp body, watched it slide across the barracks wall and crumple onto the floor. Rough hands grabbed at my shoulders as his slumping form let his skull crack against a floorboard. As my unnamed assailants disarmed me and carried me away, my eyes fixed upon the lifeless stare of my enemy, and I knew the fear in Marcian's gaze would be burned into my memory forever.

FALL FROM GRACE

My memories of the hours that followed are shrouded in an uncomfortable haze. I remember vague orders from Thurimuth, though his voice seems drowned in water when I try to recall his words. Likewise, I remember the dungeon door slamming home against its lock, yet I cannot recall the men who led me to that dank enclosure, or even how much time had elapsed since my encounter with Marcian. All that can be concluded is that I had been placed under guard as a prisoner, with the men in Hermogenes' employ as my jailors.

As with many such memories clouded by time, the first one that stands clear is the smell of that place. Dungeons are never known for their opulence, and I had spent a fair bit of captivity in Persian Nisibis to understand the deprivations that imprisonment inflicts upon one's mind and body alike. Nor was I unaccustomed to unpleasant scents — life in the army makes one immune to all but the most pungent odors. Neither in my slavery nor the rancid filth that was part of my soldierly life had I encountered the pungent odors of that cell.

Slime-covered stones held a sickening wetness that was only surpassed in fetid stink by a cracked wooden bucket in the corner. There, flies feasted upon its foul contents, their buzzing and whirring somehow making the cell all the more unwelcoming. Disarmed and still bedecked in the robes and clothing of a senior army officer, my uniform hem soon grew dark and stained from the room's filth despite my initial pains to stay clean.

Hours passed. As I coughed against the sweltering heat from a room with few avenues to filter fresh breeze, a voice—a foreign voice—made me start.

"So, what fortune has brought you to this lovely place?"

Masculine and somewhat nasal, its Greek words were stilted and unconfident, yet bemused all the same. As my eyes adjusted to the room's near-total darkness, I followed its lone source of light from a distant candle to the opposite end of the cell. An outline of a figure sat against a wall, moving but slightly as its head faced me.

"Do you not understand my words?" the voice asked, sounding irritated to have to slow its procession of accented language.

"Yes, I do," I responded weakly. "Who is that?"

"None you would know," the figure said, rising to its feet. "But I recognize you, Komes Varus."

Squinting, I watched the figure—the man—approach, more of a shadow than the flesh and bone of any man. His outline grew clearer as he closed within five paces of my position, though his head was partially covered by a hood. Instinctively, I took a step back, silently chiding myself for demonstrating fear. The figure halted at my movement and introduced himself.

"I am Prince Xerxes, Marzbān of the Persian Immortals, youngest son of Shahanshah Kavadh." His chest puffed as he recited the titles.

"Or I was," he added. "Now, I am not so sure."

"Xerxes? From Thannuris?" I was dumbfounded. Why was he locked away in this prison, rather than in more opulent quarters befitting his position as a great lord?

"My only battle," Xerxes confirmed. "A victory that nearly saw me executed."

Lowering his hood, the Persian prince drew closer. Half a head shorter than me, Xerxes nevertheless stood proud as he measured himself against me, our revolting conditions notwithstanding. Beads of sweat glistened against his forehead, faintly outlining the bushy eyebrows and thin beard that had denoted his regal stature during our negotiations with Azarethes, and his dark eyes appeared sunken—though he had been in captivity for less than a day.

"But Hermogenes received you as an honored guest on behalf of the Emperor," I wondered aloud. "How did you end up here?"

Xerxes laughed sharply. "You know, I thought for sure *you* were to blame. Now I'm having second thoughts." He composed himself. "Still, no Persian would allow an enemy to languish in these foul conditions if it was in our power to do better."

"The garrison of Nisibis held me in a cell not dissimilar to this one for a month," I could not help but retort. "It was Persians who beat my friend senseless each day, all the while asking if we were agents of Perozes sent to harm Prince Xerxes."

At my words, Xerxes took several steps away, his back coming to the wall of his original resting space. He considered this, lowering his head to run a hand through his cropped hair.

"I heard of that while I was still in command of the front," he admitted, "although I never knew the identities of the spies who snuck through the fortress gates. Once the priests took control of you, I assumed you had been released or killed."

"Then Persians are guilty of equal cruelty, for you didn't care too much for our fate then," I said. "But what should I expect from a man who employs Hephthalites to burn churches and rape women?"

Xerxes shuddered violently, though he did not move from his seated position. Instead, he sat like a statue, with no noise and little motion, barely needing to breathe the fetid air. Rather than draw another fight, I allowed myself to surrender to my depleted muscles and my sleep-deprived eyes and curled against a far corner. So spent I was that I nearly did not mind the thin layer of damp slime that became caught in my hair as I closed my eyes. My spirits were crushed at a sudden realization: I had damned myself, but I no longer had Theodora, or any powerful sponsor, to rescue me.

With no window, it was difficult to comprehend the passage of time. I may have slept an hour or a day or a year, I do not know. All I remember of that first night was the bulging face of Marcian, his bloodshot eyes impossibly wide as his tongue wagged, the rattle of death resonating in his broken throat. I awoke in a thick sweat, tense and alert for any nearby movement, yet found none.

Except Xerxes. The Persian warrior made no utterance as I adjusted to my surroundings, seeming to study my movements and consider his own.

"You have seen violence and battle," Xerxes said. "Much, by the looks of it."

"What business is it of yours?" I replied, squinting at the dark figure that blended against the shadows of the wall.

"I've seen many Zhayedan awaken in panic and violence. Stern and fearless in all their waking hours, yet crying like babes in their sleep. There is no shame in it," Xerxes said, ignoring my terse manner.

"I have no need for advice from child killers," I answered angrily, eager to return to the dull silence of the cell.

Xerxes sighed. "So much rage. Such flames burn hot but quickly expire. I wonder if that's why they've sent you to this happy place."

I grunted. "You claim to be a son of Kavadh, but our spies say that you are a distant relative, nothing more. How is a son of the Persian Shah voluntarily handed over to his enemies? The most logical answer is that you are a liar."

Xerxes shook his head. "Your spies lacked the finesse to see behind my father's ruse… but such is its purpose," he said, his words hinting at a riddle. "Tell me, Komes, what happens in Greek society when the Emperor has more than one heir?"

I let the cell fall silent for a time, not wishing to entertain Xerxes or give satisfaction of any sort to an enemy who ravaged Roman Armenia and Mesopotamia. Eventually, flattened by boredom and spurred by a desire to speed along the passage of time, I relented.

"They're sent to a monastery or awarded an ambassadorship to some faraway land in India or Francia," I answered.

"They're exiled, blinded, or killed before they can become a nuisance," Xerxes corrected, sounding pleased that our limited conversation was regaining momentum. "Such were the options available to my father, who had many sons from many wives. We all knew Khosrow as his favorite, though my father was a pious man and was incapable of the barbarity required to kill or exile his progeny. So my father's advisors invented a tale of my status as a far-flung nephew rather than a son."

"Forcing children into the Persian military is a perfectly acceptable solution? Or imprisoning them in the midst of war for no reason?" I snapped, still skeptical.

Xerxes snorted. "Perhaps your spies were not worthless after all. Yes, my father committed me to the Zhayedan as a child—a great honor, at least in Persia. I am... or was... the youngest Persian general since Cyrus," he said, a note of awe in his voice as he mentioned his Achaemenid forebear.

"Then why did they imprison you after winning a battle?"

This time, it was Xerxes who allowed the conversation to fall silent. After several heartbeats, he sighed and offered a more conciliatory tone. "That is a much longer conversation for a different day."

Slowly absorbing the noxious smells of the dungeon, we continued our conversation in that manner for a considerable time denoted by guards depositing grubby meals at the edge of our cages. Our nourishment was a far cry from the starvation rations at Nisibis, consisting of twice-baked bread and overripe fruit that would otherwise have gone to the army's camp dogs. Fearing future deprivations, I forced down all that was deposited before me, noting Xerxes' revulsion at following my example.

Though I remained hostile through much of our conversation, we still traded stories of our childhood and time in the army, noting odd similarities. Xerxes was particularly amused by our mutual proximity to the emperors of our nations, who offered military service as the only means of gaining honor and serving our peoples. Whenever I pressed Xerxes regarding the reason for his disgrace, he merely shrugged and changed the subject.

Besides irregular mealtimes, our on-again, off-again discussions were only broken by the arrival of two of the legate's spearmen. Unlocking the cage, one lowered a spearhead against Xerxes while the other hoisted me to my feet, controlling my movements with a mailed hand clenched against my armpit. After shackling my hands and feet, the guards ferried me into another room with high windows and fresher air that initially stung as I breathed it in. They bade me to sit at a small wooden table, sunlight sending sparks into eyes that had grown unaccustomed to any sort of luxuries.

My two captors stationed themselves behind me, their spear butts thudding against the floor's stone tiles. Not that diligence was required, for with a locked door and little else in the room but other chairs, there was little else to do but to sit and wait for fate to throw another curve in my destiny.

That, and wonder at how those who depended upon me fared upon my downfall. Mariya, carrying my child. Samur, who lay broken by wounds from more than combat with an easily discernible Persian foe. Rosamund, Cephalas, and many more who comprised my household—all of whom counted their survival in the Empire based upon my favor in the army. Though I fought to keep my mind clear, the monotony of imprisonment left me with few distractions from considering their predicament and the shame that my disgrace would have. At moments, the guilt was overpowering, and the urge to bash my skull against the nearest wall grew more tantalizing as time slithered on.

Eventually, the outer door was once again unsealed. Rather than face the legate, however, my interrogator was Marcellus, who was oathbound to serve the legate in his duty as an excubitor. The pockmarked and scarred veteran looked at the two neatly attired guardsmen and scowled.

"Leave us," Marcellus barked, his voice full of an authority more suited to Constantinople's Imperial Palace.

"But Lord Marcellus, Legate Hermogenes commanded that we

not leave the prisoner unattended," the shorter of the two guards said. As Marcellus raised an eyebrow, the guard added, "He's dangerous, you know."

"I am fully aware of Lord Varus' talents," Marcellus said in a disinterested tone. "And as the komes excubitorum, I'm telling you to leave my sight. Tell Lord Hermogenes of my decision, if you require."

Hesitating for only a moment, the two guards looked at one another and summarily darted through the door. Marcellus checked to ensure the door had closed and withdrew a keyring from his belt, locking the room from the inside. The excubitor ran a hand through his thinning hair and took a seat opposite me. He let his elbows rest on the table so his hands could support a weary head.

At last, he cleared his throat and raised his gaze to meet my own, heavy bags weighing upon his eyes. "Varus, this isn't good. Hermogenes wants you hanged for assaulting and killing a Roman officer during wartime. I argued that our peace with Azarethes renders the laws of an army at war moot, and the other officers supported my efforts. But Hermogenes is still demanding a trial and insists that he sit as your judge."

It was all I could do to absorb these grim tidings. "Soon?" I asked.

He shook his head. "In Antioch," he said. "The army leaves Barbalissus in two days."

Closing my eyes, I stifled a groan. I pictured a pregnant Mariya welcoming the return of her husband, chained like a dog and damned in the eyes of the Roman people. Bile rose into my throat as a heavy weight fell into my stomach, and my skin began to itch in discomfort. Even as I fought for composure, I wanted nothing more than to break open the door and ride far from Hermogenes and his hangman. Death was a constant companion that I had little fear of, as a soldier familiar with its many forms.

However, my heart raced at the thought of impoverished loved ones and a disgraced child forced to bear the lineage of one who was cast out from Roman society. Such a fate was sadly not uncommon and was typically reserved for the family of rapists, murderers, and traitors to the Emperor.

"Any chance Hermogenes will listen to the cause of the violence? Of Samur's attack?" I asked, unsure of how much information Marcellus had been given of the night's events.

"None," Marcellus answered. "Hermogenes wants to claim credit for the peace with Persia while laying blame for losses at the feet of others. With your execution, none would remain to challenge his version of events."

Seeing my despair, he added, "I've staffed two excubitores to stand vigil over Samur at all times. What Marcian did is unforgiveable."

I nodded in thanks. "And if I refuse Hermogenes' gambit? If I demand a trial by single combat?"

His unreadable visage broke into a feeble smile. "That is your right, and Hermogenes could not deny you any privileges. But he has already selected a champion, should you elect that choice."

"Who?" I asked, already certain of the answer.

"Me," Marcellus said. "And if I fall, Hermogenes would call other excubitores to fill my void until you are dead or surrender."

I shook my head. "I couldn't fight you," I admitted to the excubitor. "I wouldn't."

"That's what Hermogenes anticipated. And there is no other choice."

"There is," I said firmly, drawing Marcellus' interest. "Give me a dagger, and leave me to my prayers."

Marcellus grimaced. "Don't even think about it. I'll station my men to never leave your side, even to shit or piss."

I laughed darkly, spawning a single tear from the corner of my eye. "So there's nothing to be done?"

Marcellus shook his head. "I will do all I can to find a better solution," he said, "but I'm afraid that Hermogenes has total control of the situation, unless your friends in Constantinople can pressure him to act differently. I can sneak a message out to someone if you believe it could help."

Grateful for the opportunity, I nodded. "Send a note to Narses explaining my situation. If Theodora still has any affection for me, perhaps she will intervene."

"I will. It may take weeks to hear a response, though," Marcellus said. "Well after Hermogenes' trial."

"Such is life," I sighed, quoting a favorite lamentation from the taciturn Simmas. "I thank you for your help nonetheless."

Before concluding, Marcellus also informed me of the repercussions of my arrest. After fetching Rosamund to care for Samur, Uliaris gathered several of Belisarius' bucellarii and scoured the streets for signs of where I had departed for. Soon arriving at Solomon's barracks, the Frankish bucellarii learned of my detention for Marcian's murder and were prevented from seeking an audience with Legate Hermogenes by a half dozen armed spearmen outside of Barbalissus' dungeon. Rather than seek out Germanus for instruction, Uliaris warned Perenus of my capture, unleashing hell on Hermogenes' tenuous grip over the celebrating Roman ranks.

"Even pissing himself drunk, Perenus rallied the foederati and closed himself inside their barracks. They aren't taking up arms against the legate, but nor will they obey commands to allow themselves to be disarmed," Marcellus informed me.

Picturing Perenus stumbling in drunken fury, I chuckled heartily. "But how are they supplying themselves? Even with our numbers diminished, that's near two hundred mouths to feed... and worse."

"Hermogenes posted several of his household guard to block the entrance, but other segments of the army have been ferrying supplies," Marcellus said. "Hermogenes initially commanded me to support his blockade of the Herulians, but he soon found that I was all the more ineffective."

At that, I grinned. "My men are few in number, but they have heart. But how does the standoff end?"

Marcellus sighed. "Hermogenes will allow them to end their resistance with full forgiveness for their insolence, but only if they do so immediately after my consultation with you. If I give my solemn oath that you are unharmed, and that it is your desire that Perenus accede to the legate's wishes, the foederati will obey."

Considering his words, I relished the thought of Hermogenes struggling for command, my men inspiring disobedience that would free not only myself, but Belisarius most of all. These thoughts were fleeting, for they went against my oath to the Roman Emperor and people and would place my men in grievous danger.

"Give Perenus and Fulcaris my command to obey," I said.

Marcellus nodded, visibly relieved at being able to deliver a rare spot of welcome news in an otherwise fragile situation. Our meeting drew to a close as he rose from his chair, straightening his excubitor's armor, which had folded into uncomfortable bunches. Offering an embrace, he promised to improve my conditions, to which I simply waved, as though my surroundings were a trifle of no concern.

"If I'm to be moved in two days, perhaps conditions in Antioch will be better," I said dryly.

"I doubt it," Marcellus replied.

However, the excubitor did promise to dispatch a note to the Empress with all haste, hoping that a favorable reply would reach Antioch before my sentence was executed. Unlocking the door, Marcellus barked away the legate's two idling guards, offering instead to personally lead me back to my prison. Raising an outstretched palm for the keys to the dungeon lock, Marcellus did not even glance at the guardsmen as he led me back to captivity, with few words passing between us on that somber march.

"Stay brave, and trust in God," he offered as my cage door slammed shut. "Know that we are doing everything we can to get you out of here."

"Who?" I asked. "How might they free me?"

Marcellus, normally a dour man, yielded a sliver of a smile. "You have powerful friends, Varus. As an excubitor, I have found that counts more than any law."

THE ROAD TO ANTIOCH

Well, *that's* certainly interesting," Xerxes said. "Interim commander and friends with the leader of Rome's excubitores. You weren't telling tales when you said that you were close to the late Emperor."

I rolled my eyes but humored Xerxes' goading and answered what questions I could. His curious manner left me on edge in a mixture of annoyance and curiosity speckled with a healthy layer of disdain. To his credit, he never once made a threatening gesture or otherwise used his skill as an elite Zhayedan to pilfer scraps of my food or to establish dominance in the cell. Instead, Xerxes merely asked an incessant battery of questions, soaking up information about Roman life.

Xerxes took particular interest in my proximity to women. Voicing skepticism at my description of Rosamund as head of my household servants, he flat-out refused to believe in my marriage to the late King Jabalah's daughter.

"Jabalah seemed a decent enough monarch, but a terrible commander," Xerxes said offhandedly. "I regretted his death, even if it contributed to my victory at Thannuris. But what Greek marries an Arab? Did the Emperor command you?"

"Quite the opposite." I laughed, explaining my tryst and eventual marriage to Mariya. "And I'm not Greek. I'm Herulian."

"A Herulian fighting in a Greek army that calls itself Roman. Destined to marry an Arab princess and fight in a Persian war," Xerxes mused. "It seems too ridiculous for even the most outlandish of campfire tales."

I ignored his comments and all his further attempts to goad me into conversation. Xerxes babbled on to himself, his accented Greek flavored with a confusing mixture of sarcasm and curiosity. After a time, however, his tales of training and battle faded, and he questioned my silence once again.

"I don't understand your hostility to me," Xerxes said, feigning offense. "We are essentially the same person under separate banners... two unappreciated commanders, unloved by their people, caged for doing their duty as best they know how."

"We are nothing alike!" I yelled, although I feared the falseness in my words. "You led savages into Roman territory, unprovoked, and raped and massacred thousands of innocents. I know, for I found and buried many of their bodies."

Xerxes paused at my rebuke, offering a light grunt as he considered the condemnation. Raising a hand before his face, he analyzed each digit in turn. After several moments, he broke from his trance and offered a response.

"Do you remember the first man you killed?" Xerxes asked, his voice deeper and darker than usual.

"Yes," I replied hesitantly. My mind drifted to that long-ago Hippodrome riot when Theodora and I had fought of a mob of rapists and looters in the burning Hagia Sophia.

"Mine was a farmer in some nameless village near the Tigris," Xerxes said. "Some shaggy-haired Armenian who seemed weathered beyond his years. When other villagers complained about rough treatment from my army, the man snuck into his hut."

He paused, breathing slowly as he recounted the memory. Rubbing his thin fingers together, he continued his tale, taking a slower pace as he described every detail of the village.

"The man returned with a sickle, its iron so poor that a well-made bronze blade might have sheared its metal in half. Even so, he raised its curved edge to the air, roaring for his god to send blazing fire onto we heathens. He had even begun to yell for others to eject my men from their dung heap of a village, and the younger men of the area even began to join in."

"All men and women have a right to defend themselves," I said.

"Yes. And I, too, am a man among those men." Xerxes frowned. "I gave him a chance to stand down, and he spat in my face. Before the man had a chance to wipe his mouth, I disemboweled him with the cleanest sword stroke that an arms instructor could ever ask for. I cut his throat with my backstroke, and the man fell dead in moments."

"So you attacked an untrained villager that hadn't struck first," I said. "Forgive me if I fail to see the honor in your actions."

"Not at all," Xerxes replied. "I join you in that failure. Yet I did learn a valuable lesson that day—honor is secondary to survival. If I had showed mercy to that farmer, a hundred of his friends would have risen up to harass and kill my men. If I returned to that moment in time, I would make the same choice."

"Monstrous," I muttered, albeit with less venom than before. My thoughts flooded back to Rosamund's village in the Gepid Kingdom, when my friends and I burned huts and slaughtered dozens of Gepids guilty of nothing else than having some distant relation to raiders who had recently plundered Moesia.

I had been sleeping poorly ever since my encounter with Marcellus, my mind racing with concerns for Perenus and the foederati as well as Samur and Mariya. Was Samur safe from reprisals? Perenus? Mariya? All fell into a more precarious situation due to my captivity and would likely not be safe until completing the long journey back to Constantinople.

When sleep did come, the only face I saw was Marcian's, his features filling a thousand bodies of men who had departed violently from my life. He faced me on the dueling grounds of Scythian Neapolis and stood against me in the shield wall in that nameless Gepid village. He was an Avar, a Persian, and a Hephthalite… and also none of these things. In his many forms he held the same pitiless laughter, tinged with the death rattle that rang in the back of his throat. Last of all he was the black-cloaked rider of my potion-induced sleep, his red eyes and burning hands yearning for company in that dark hell from whence he came.

Xerxes remained silent throughout the morning of our departure. A half dozen of the legate's guardsmen flooded into that dank cellar, hands covering their noses in disgust as they positioned themselves for a prisoner transfer. Two men lowered spears as the other four hauled us to our feet, half dragging us up the stairs and eventually out into Barbalissus' open streets. A wagon met us near the building's entrance, and Xerxes and I were herded inside. Pulled by two oxen, the wagon was covered on all sides with thick wooden boards, with a single barred window serving as our only portal into the world beyond.

Blessedly, beyond the faint odor of ox dung and the unwashed bodies of two warriors, the interior of the cart did not stink. Its air soon grew thick and close, since there was little means to whisk away the stale humors, yet still it was a marked improvement from Barbalissus' constricted prison quarters.

We did not find out until later that much of the army had already departed Barbalissus in the predawn hours. Among them were my own foederati who, led by Perenus, had relented in their resistance to Hermogenes at Marcellus' word. The army had been in the titular control of Germanus, though the Imperial legate had sent the watchful Procopius to document all our lone remaining general's actions.

Though loaded into our mobile prison around breakfast time, the cart's driver did not lash his oxen into a forward movement until midday. Our expedition to Antioch began smoothly enough, with dressed stone lining the cart's path as it departed through Barbalissus' western gates. The cart's spoked wheels rumbled over the stone, sending vibrations into our cabin that contrasted against the dull silence of our former quarters.

"Well, at least we aren't being forced to march," Xerxes said. "I was beginning to worry about the blisters these Romans were going to force onto me."

While I replied in a rare moment of agreement with the Persian, I soon came to rue those words. Riven by centuries of conflict and strife, the old Roman roads in the nearby countryside of Barbalissus had become rough and uneven. Our cart rocked and tumbled about, frequently sending one or both of us sprawling from one narrow bench to the other. On one occasion, one of the cart's wheels plunged into a hole masked by the grasses sprouting between the once-orderly stones. Xerxes slammed a shoulder into the cart's wall, and we were forced to make camp at that spot while several men hauled the cart upright, straining against the wagon's weight.

Xerxes and I were only allowed to exit the cart to relieve ourselves in a nearby ditch. Abandoning all pretenses of modesty, we both hustled to the welcome opportunity, drawing noises of disgust from our neatly attired guards.

"After shitting into a bucket for a few days, you really begin to appreciate the luxuries in life," Xerxes said dryly.

"A few days means little," I said. "Antioch may be far worse."

"One dung heap is the same as any other," Xerxes said with less bravado this time.

Even in the fading light as we were ushered quickly back into the cart, Xerxes' features became clearer. Similar to Samur, the Immortal possessed a wiry physique. Where my brother always appeared sickly, Xerxes showed all the vitality of a man who, until recently, had been well nourished and well kept. He bounded lightly on his feet, as though hinting how easily he could outrun his captors, and more than once stole a glance at an unprotected blade that hung from a guard's hip. Xerxes made no attempt to break free, and besides his blunt sarcasm and muted disdain for Roman customs, he behaved like the ideal prisoner.

Before lowering my head and joining Xerxes in the cart once more,

I caught a glimpse of something familiar: the outline of Belisarius near the front of our formation. Flanked by two of Hermogenes' guardsmen as well as the legate himself, Belisarius sat tall in Xanthos' saddle, his silhouette framed by the fading sun. Though I cannot be sure, I thought I saw him turn his head toward me, bobbing with a nearly imperceptible nod of recognition. Pleased at even so insignificant a sign, I jumped into the wagon and did not begrudge the guard for turning its lock for an uncomfortable evening.

And so began one of the worst journeys I had experienced in my entire life. The cart's narrow benches were just long enough to support the torso and thighs of a man of normal height, forcing me to bend and twist to find a position that would reasonably take me into another night of fitful slumber. Xerxes, on the other hand, leveraged his smaller frame to position himself into a near immediate rest, and his light snores were an infuriating percussion at the corner of my mind. I was tempted to slam a fist into that sharp Persian jaw and its unkempt, unaristocratic beard. I relented in my desire, settling for an occasional violent kick against the cart's walls when Xerxes' snoring reached a cacophony resembling a dying animal.

Our journey continued for three more nights, including a brief lull where a small fleet of riverboats ferried our retinue across the Chalos River. Though we skirted the outer perimeter of a prospering city named Berrhoea, Hermogenes ordered the caravan to proceed to Antioch. We stopped for another evening of contorted sleep, with Xerxes and me waking well before dawn to find our wagon proceeding ever westward. He made few japes as our journey lengthened, merely staring out of our barred window as the dry Syrian flatlands gave way to the lusher hills of Phoenicia.

"Cyrus once led an army here," he said in a rare moment of reverence. "So, too, did Ramesses, and Alexander, and Pompey."

"Would that they could save us now." My complaint did little to faze Xerxes' fixation with the region.

Indeed, my patience wore thin as we reached the final day of our travels. Though Hermogenes had ordered his guards to keep silent around our mobile prison, the men inevitably broke the legate's rules, sharing with us updates of our progress on the road to Antioch. Rather than put our souls at ease, the news only made us more impatient for release. Worse, my hands began to tremble as we grew nearer to that ancient Seleucid city, which I attempted in vain to hide from Xerxes.

"Worried?" he asked, an eyebrow raised. "I would be, meeting a pregnant wife I hadn't seen in half of a year. Practically strangers!"

"Leave it," I gritted out.

Xerxes only smiled broadly.

Antioch's walls were blocked by our wooden enclosure, yet several signs indicated our approach to the city. Our path grew smoother as we neared the city, the loose and broken stones lining the Syrian countryside giving way to recently repaired and uniformly aligned stones that left our wagon less likely to pitch and rumble unexpectedly. Even more telling was the gradual increase in ambient noise, which shifted from wind-swept silence to the clattering sounds of commerce and civilization, getting louder and clearer with each passing turn of our cart's wheels until it was possible to discern individual voices of Romans who lined the entryway into Antioch's eastern gate.

There, our procession slowed to a crawl, the cart's wheels no longer vibrating through the wooden benches that had been our seats. We ventured forward, passing small groups of onlookers whose gazes paused upon our locked and barred cart. Initially no more than a half dozen, the press of humanity grew into a dense throng that crowded around Hermogenes' column. Soon after, we made out a muffled roar falling over Antioch's walls and under its open gate, a sound that eventually swelled into a sweet tune shared on battlefields across the length of the Empire.

"Belisarius! Belisarius! Belisarius!" the masses called out, with more voices joining in the cheer with each passing chant.

"At least the Roman people have some sense," Xerxes said. "Persia has long profited from the thickheaded nature of your rulers."

Even as men and women rushed to greet our formation, our slow march continued on. I could hear the angry shouts of Hermogenes ordering the men to double their pace in vain, and loudly complaining at their failure. One daring youth even rushed at our cart and slammed uncalloused fingers into its door, only to draw back in tears after one of Hermogenes' guards cracked an elbow with a cudgel.

"Get back, all of you!" the guard yelled, forcing the crowd to form a rough ring to allow our cart to continue unmolested.

Unhindered, our pace quickened, although not enough for the liking of Hermogenes. We soon cleared the city's massive stone gates and crossed the final threshold into the city. Xerxes and I scuffled for a viewing position out of our narrow window as we moved along, seeking interesting sights or a sign of a friendly face.

Instead, we were met with two events that shall be burned into my memory forever. The first begin in dead silence, the noise of the crowd's adulation fading into a hushed curiosity of the two men kept under strict guard. About twenty paces into the city, I met the eyes of Fulcaris, who immediately called out a near-wordless order.

"Foederati!" he barked, slamming his spear into the ground and clattering it against the stone.

On either side of the wagon, total cacophony followed Fulcaris' lead. At each turn of the cart's wheels, the sounds grew louder, and I recognized another of my men, their expression angry and spiteful as they beat their spears into the ground. Irilar and Sindual stood out among those men, their blows surely grinding the stone underneath into useless rubble as evidence of their fury. Trailing along the end of the formation, I found Perenus, his centurion's plume dancing as he led the men in their percussion.

"Roma Victrix! Roma Victrix!" Perenus called out.

The foederati's thumping grew ever louder—if such a thing were possible—interwoven with chants from the crowd as they joined the tempest forming against Hermogenes' caravan. The legate yelled for silence, threatening discipline against the unruly Herulians, but none even so much as hesitated in their chants of defiance.

I sat grinning only briefly, for soon a pang of guilt brought me to sink back into my seat.

At the end of the Herulian foederati stood a neat row of Aksumites, their elongated pikes joining my men in their show of camaraderie. In their midst stood Sembrouthes, leading his men while retaining an unmoving expression as he met my eyes. A hand tugged on his robes and signaled for Sembrouthes to step aside, and he followed with lockstep obedience.

Mariya bounded to the cart, her favored crimson robes sweeping against the stones as she fought to keep pace with the moving of the wheels. Though she had disguised her pregnancy and lacked the heavy weight that I had seen many women carry in my time as a slave to Justin, Mariya's face showed clear signs of discomfort as she made her way to my door, pressing a hand against the exposed window. Xerxes backed away as I reached out for her fingers. Straining against the rusted metal, I was unable to meet her grasp.

Behind Mariya ran Sembrouthes, who had deposited his spear with one of the other Aksumite men. Sweeping Mariya into his arms with a gentleness that belied his scarred warrior's physique, Sembrouthes raised his longtime charge closer to the window, trotting to keep pace with the cart's ceaseless motion. Only then, as Mariya glided in Sembrouthes' arms, could I reach out to touch her.

"Varus!" Mariya cried out, thick tears smearing the kohl that lined her eyes. The scent of her perfume wafted into the carriage, and for a moment I imagined that I had returned to the Imperial Palace, that I was whisking Mariya away from an unwanted marriage and into the freedom of the Thracian countryside.

Mariya's fingers curled around mine, digging hard into the flesh of my palm. "I will get you out of this, no matter what I have to do," Mariya promised, her chest fluttering from heavy sobs.

"No," I responded. "Rest, and stay under the care of Sembrouthes."

Mariya's honed fingernails dug harder into my skin, threatening to draw blood. "Too late," she replied. "I will not let them take you from me again."

Bending her head over, Mariya planted a kiss on the back of my hand, showing no revulsion at my unwashed body. Her signature imparted, Mariya's amber eyes burned into my own as she fought back further tears.

"I love you," Mariya said.

And with that, Mariya's hand slipped from my grasp, and the beautiful Ghassanid princess who was my wife quickly fell from my sight.

I drew my exposed arm back into the cart with a cry of anger and frustration, with tears matching Mariya's own. My screams must have filled the skies above Antioch, a dull rage smoldering as I beat at the walls of my cage with fists and boots alike.

PURGATORY

Broken skin and flecks of blood covered my knuckles, evidence of my foolhardy attempt to break free of my containment. I did not hear the guard yell for me to keep calm or even remark his presence at all until he jabbed his cudgel into the window, where it collided against my jaw with a concussive thud. Dazed, I sat in a heap in the cart, my hands swelling and vision blurred from tears and injury. All I had to remain sane was the outline of Mariya's lips, the only gift she had been able to impart.

After a time, I glanced over at Xerxes, my eyes narrowed in annoyance. He merely raised his hands in mock surrender, all signs of bemusement replaced by a countenance of inquisitiveness. Indeed, he said nothing for a time until he finally broke our silence with a low remark.

"I'd butcher a man who did that to me," he muttered. "That's what I don't understand about you Romans, so willing to sow horror into each other's lives. And for what? A few coins? Power? Why do you bother to fight for a government that despises and mistreats you?"

"I doubt it is much different in Persia," I said in return.

"Oh, but it is," Xerxes replied. "In Persia, we geld anyone who seeks too much power from the Shah or send them to join the army.

None are allowed to outshine our monarch."

"That explains your predicament, then," I shot back, seeking an end to idle talk.

Xerxes seemed to acquiesce to my wish, leaning against the farther end of the cart. We eventually came to a halt outside of a massive stone complex, its design flavored with a similar style as the great fortress of Nisibis. Guards unlocked our door and barked for us to jump out, leaving us no option but to obey.

Herded inside the building, we were guided up along several flights of stairs, their polished stone offering little traction against the thin leather boots that had been offered to us. Despite his rigorous training as an Immortal, Xerxes grew winded at the exertion, his body wracked by a week of poor nutrition and little sleep. I fared somewhat better, having prepared myself for the deprivations that most prisons afforded their residents.

To my surprise, however, our holding cells were almost pleasant, with wide barred windows that allowed breezes from the Mediterranean Sea to whisk away the otherwise fetid humors in the air. The room was well lit, and its walls lacked that crusted layer of filth and grime that had characterized our quarters in Barbalissus. Folded clean clothing waited for our use, while white rags and buckets of water were available for cleaning at designated times when we were allowed outside of our cells.

Even with these amenities, that prison in Antioch was the most hopeless I had faced. A dull ache burned in my chest as Mariya's devastated face mixed with the cringing features of Marcian plagued my thoughts. The twitching in my hand grew more pronounced, and it took considerable effort to conceal my unsettled behavior from Xerxes.

"Not so bad, then," Xerxes muttered cheerily. "No need to worry about cockroaches slinking into my mouth as I sleep."

"Don't test your luck."

"You know," Xerxes began, "I'm beginning to think that you're a rather dour fellow. And I heard so much about the rowdy cheer of

Rome's barbarian allies… the Herulians in particular."

"I've lived amongst the Romans for as long as I remember," I replied listlessly. "The majority of my interaction with other Herulians, outside of my brother, have been over the past year with the foederati."

"It shows," Xerxes said. "Although I wouldn't have taken you for a Herulian anyway. You could even pass for a Hephthalite, miserable creatures that they are."

I grunted. "I killed the Hephthalite leader at Dara," I said angrily. "Drove my sword into his chest at the end of the battle."

"And the world thanks you for your efforts," Xerxes said. "Khingila was a rife bastard."

"And your ally," I added.

Xerxes sighed. "Yes, he was," he said. "In conflict, sometimes the greatest allies are those we despise."

"No," I countered, thinking of Belisarius' maxims. "The greatest ally is one you can trust."

"As you say, then."

Xerxes gathered a thin blanket and lay upon a small wooden cot that had been propped in a corner against the cell wall, his head turned toward the cool stones, leaving me to my thoughts. With that, I had nothing else to pass the time other than reliving my shame a thousand times over.

Our first day passed with a tedium that bordered upon madness. A hooded servant deposited our meals at appointed hours but offered nothing to betray their identity. In the times between, one of the legate's guardsmen inspected the room for any signs of escape—or suicide—but did not dawdle long after. My only company was Xerxes who, given better food and the opportunity for rest, slept nearly the entire day and throughout the night. His only contribution to my troubled state was a constant wheezing and snorting as he fought for air in his sleep, leaving me to wonder whether the prince might choke to death in his slumber.

Though my eyes ached with weariness, I could not easily share in

Xerxes' peace. When sleep did come, it was followed by fevered dreams, my mind racing as dozens of thoughts pervaded my consciousness simultaneously. I could hear the magus' curse, feel burns from the dark rider's unholy grasp, and feel the dozens of wounds I had taken since pledging my service to the glory of the Emperor. Underneath all, I could hear the bloodcurdling screams from long ago, a wordless sobbing for mercy as a blade hacked against a woman's exposed neck.

I have rarely been a good Christian, but I have always feared God's wrath and the punishment my actions have earned me. Such fears may be easily smothered by the comforts of an army campfire, or even in the urgency of the shield wall. Stripped of protection, I never feared God more than in that moment, recounting the torments awaiting those possessing murderous wrath.

Haggard from little rest, I felt every movement as an agony the following morning. I even shunned my normal morning bathing, drawing scoffs from Xerxes, who remarked at my ripening stench. I did not care; the ritual seemed futile, and what little vigor it required was beyond my now meagre reserves.

Then, after a morning meal, the outer door to our rooms opened. At first I assumed it was another circuit from the duty jailor, and I paid little heed to the heavy footsteps that slapped against our stone floor. However, as the man's steps drew closer to our cell door, I raised my head, eyes meeting a beardless youth whose body seemed ill-suited for the armor and uniform required of the legate's men.

"Lord Varus," the voice called respectfully, "you have a visitor. Take a moment to prepare yourself, and I will escort you there."

"Who?" I asked, wondering at the type of man who had the political power to thwart the legate's order that Xerxes and I receive no guests.

The youth shrugged. "No man I have met, although he seems eager." His tone lilted in the manner of Italian aristocracy.

Rushing to straighten my disheveled and spotted clothing and splash lukewarm water over my face, I followed the boy out of the room and up a flight of stairs. Revealing his inexperience, the young man walked a pace in front of me, looking over his shoulder only to check if I followed his lead every dozen paces or so. Pale skinned and thin limbed, he held his short spear loosely from his body, making it perilously easy for someone to steal the weapon and jam it into his guts before mounting a defense. The darkness in the pit of my stomach urged me on, but I meekly followed the boy to his intended room until we reached our destination and my escort beckoned me inside. And then—

"Father!" I exclaimed, falling to my knees in subservience.

"Thank you, Vitalius," said Father Petrus. "If you will permit me some privacy, I will be quite safe with Lord Varus." A warm smile broke the deep crags that lined his face as he spoke.

Bobbing his head, the youth stepped from the room and closed the door. A lack of footsteps suggested that he remained on just the other side, whether to forestall any potential escape or merely to eavesdrop, I could not be sure.

"Lucius Vitalius is a distant relative of mine, of the old Vitalii family," Father Petrus explained. "A good boy, or so I'm told. Wants to be a soldier, but his mother paid enough bribes to see her son in a less dangerous role."

"I've missed you, Father." I was blubbering, my eyes still facing his black slippers.

"Lucius does not know me, but unfortunately for his mother, he will," Father Petrus said, ignoring my welcome.

After a moment of awkward silence, save my sniveling, the priest cast his gaze to the floor, and sighed. "My son, if you would be so kind, a chair would be lovely. The good Lord has seen fit to worsen my arthritis, and my knees trouble me considerably."

At his command, I snapped to my feet, fetching a cushioned bench that had been stationed near a high narrow window. Far more ornate than my modest rooms, the chamber was handsomely outfitted. Violet drapes hung near each window, with decorated columns lining the room's expanse, giving the space a cozier feel while allowing natural light to spill across the floor, with no need for tapers.

Taking my arm for support, the old priest groaned as he sat, his knees popping from the exertion. Father Petrus fixed his black robes and rubbed wrinkled fingers together, teasing at one particularly crooked finger that seemed far too pale to be healthy.

"By the looks of you, Varus, you have not been taking care of yourself," Father Petrus observed. "I am quite disappointed."

"Father…" I struggled for words that could unravel the knot in my chest.

The priest silenced me, gesturing for me to sit at his feet. "When telling a story, it is best to start from the beginning," Father Petrus said. "So that is what I suggest we do."

Nodding, I did so. I returned to the blood-soaked riverfront near Callinicum, telling of our desperate yet unwanted stand against Azarethes for a day and a night. With no filter upon my thoughts, I told of Hermogenes' insistence upon the fight, of Solomon's retreat, and of Samur's near fatal injury that still had not fully healed. Father Petrus listened intently as I recounted our retreat across the Euphrates River, Hermogenes' arrest of Belisarius, and of our peace accord with Azarethes that spawned riotous celebrations across Barbalissus.

Lastly, as Father Petrus sat back upon the seat's cushion, I told without interruption an account of Samur's assault, and of my final encounter with Marcian. My words came with difficulty in detailing the evidence of Samur's wounds and the burning hatred I held for the world in that moment—a fury and resentment that drove me to choke the life from a Roman man with nothing more than my two hands.

Eyeing me carefully as I rocked slowly at the end of my tale, the old priest sighed again.

"These are terrible times we live in," Father Petrus began. "Rome has seen dark days, of course, but rarely has there been so little hope for a better future."

"But, Father, we have held off the Avars, the Persians, and the Vandals… How could these days compare with those of Attila or Odoacer?"

Father Petrus smiled, undoubtedly thinking me naïve. "Enemies at the gates make for a considerable trial, but they are only successful if our society is internally fragmented. That is where I fear we are now."

Such dark words of warning were common with Liberius and the late Emperor Justin, who worried over the future of the Eastern Empire. Even Belisarius had echoed the sentiment, optimistically arguing that Rome's clear solution was for a small number of good men to sacrifice all. I had sworn an oath to fight for the future despite whatever hardship may come, yet now I wondered whether my actions condemned me as unworthy of this company.

"Father, how can I serve God, honor the Emperor, and care for my loved ones, especially when those goals come into conflict with one another?" I asked, allowing a note of frustration to rise in my voice. "If I keep the Emperor's peace, my brother or my household will be brutalized by the privileged. If I defend my men, I dishonor God with grave sin. But if I do nothing, I will be deemed weak and unworthy in the eyes of all three."

His chest rising and falling, Father Petrus considered my words. With cracked nails, he scratched at the stubble on his otherwise bare chin, a rare clean-shaven man who harkened back to the Roman emperors of old. A lank strand of white hair fell onto his forehead, though Petrus ignored the nuisance, his attention locked upon one of his flock.

"Any man who would have you betray the Lord is no friend to you, for even with their gratitude, these offenses against one who sacrificed all for your immortal soul will cost you eternity," he said. "We knew you would walk a difficult path, Varus, but we were also fully confident that you had the heart to overcome your trials."

"Who?"

"Justin, Liberius, Godilas, and myself," he responded. "And even Basilius, although he dislikes putting too much faith in the goodness of any man. In a twisted way, he may be the purest minded of all of us, even if it is for the pursuit of worldly glory."

Petrus' calm did little to assuage my anxieties, or my conscience. "Father, I killed a man against the orders of my commander or the Emperor. I see his face each waking moment—and when I fall to sleep. God condemns me for such a heinous sin."

His face grim, Father Petrus nodded. "Perhaps, perhaps not. The commandment against murder has been sacred since the age of Moses, even if it is in defense of a victim of a terrible crime. But the Lord has the power to forgive all things, and while I cannot know His will, I do not believe that He is finished with you."

"But how?" I begged. "What can I do to bring myself back into His favor?"

Closing his eyes, Father Petrus shook his head in disappointment. "Sometimes I wonder if I have failed to teach you anything, just as Liberius japes so often. That is not for you to decide, but for the Lord to make the opportunity available for you. But be prepared, because the cost of atonement will be considerable, and more than you would wish to give."

"And Samur?" I asked. "What do I do to help him?"

Father Petrus' expression grew dark. "Do what you can," he said, "but your brother must walk his own path. What happened to him was monstrous, and those responsible will be punished for their crimes."

I hoped his words were true, but I found myself deeply skeptical. "But will the Emperor give me the chance to redeem myself? Will Hermogenes? How can I atone if the Empire will send me to death?"

"That I cannot say, but you will have your chance... of that I have no doubt," Father Petrus said. "And even after all the horror and grief you have suffered, we still believe in you."

I sought to pry further on his relationship with Justin but lacked the opportunity. The priest beckoned me to my feet, drawing me into a tight embrace against his rough blackened wool, and promised that he would do all that he could on my behalf.

"Now, my son, I should hear your confession before you leave, else I will be accused a liar in the eyes of our dear legate."

After the confession, Father Petrus resummoned the young Vitalius. He offered one final blessing as I followed the youth into the hallway and back to my cell. Feeling a mixture of relief and nagging worry, I offered no insolence as I walked calmly into the cell, where I took a seat on my cot as and watched Vitalius fumble the keys to the door's lock.

"Anything good?" Xerxes asked as the cell door closed. "Maybe a roast chicken?"

After my visit with Father Petrus, nightmarish faces still plagued my dreams, but they began to appear more sparingly. I put my efforts into maintaining a more familiar, ordinary routine—bathing, sleeping, and whatever degree of physical movement remained possible while imprisoned—in order to be in the best position possible when my opportunity for atonement arose.

Xerxes grinned at my newfound vigor, and even joined me in a few wrestling scrimmages, just enough to keep both of our instincts sharp. Hearing the crashing noises of our tussle, a guard burst into our rooms with his spear leveled, only to find the two prisoners panting but unharmed from our mock combat. After that, in a rare show of mercy, several rugs were laid out in a neat square to cushion our falls. I can only assume the guards reasoned that the exertions would leave us too fatigued to mount any resistance or escape and therefore encouraged it.

For Xerxes, the most irksome worry came from the complete uncertainty of his fate. Since his imprisonment after being handed over by Azarethes, few Romans even spoke to him, refusing to answer any questions regardless of the language he used.

"All I know is that the Greeks are not doing this without the approval of Perozes and Azarethes," he grumbled that evening. "When I am freed from this hell, I will find a way to repay their kindnesses."

"You're sure you will leave?"

"It is not my fate to die in this dark place," he said confidently. "All I require is an opportunity."

"An opportunity," I replied bitterly. "If only Hermogenes were that charitable."

Xerxes laughed. "Have patience, but be vigilant. When your chance at freedom comes, I doubt it will be pleasant. But you do have one advantage that Hermogenes does not."

I frowned. "I fail to understand."

"You're far more desperate than he is," Xerxes answered. "Even more than me. Just don't bungle your opportunity when it comes."

THE INQUISITION

The next day began uneventfully, with no sign to mark the occasion. A thin breakfast of fruit and day-old bread, served with a rare skin of wine that our guard handed over with a grin, one that faded when I handed the skin to Xerxes, favoring a pitcher of water for myself. Xerxes took the skin back to his cell but did not drink either, arguing that wine so early in the morning would only beget problems later in the day.

Shortly after finishing our meal and changing into fresh garb, the relative peace within our cell was rocked by a half dozen of the legate's men. Morning sunlight glinted from their polished lamellar armor as they formed a protective half ring around the door to my cage, with several lowering their spears in a protective stance.

"Lord Varus, you are to come with us," the nameless leader said, his face masked by the decorative iron of his helmet.

"Where?"

"To your trial, of course," called a lighter voice that, despite the helmet and heavy armor making him appear larger, clearly belonged to the young Vitalius.

It did not make sense. "I was not informed that a trial would be soon, let alone today!"

"Such affairs are conducted as Legate Hermogenes commands and are not at your leisure," the leader replied with the formal tone of one who has rehearsed a line several times over.

After withdrawing a key from his belt, the leader unlocked my gate and let two guardsmen rush into the room. One pinned me against the wall while the other clapped heavy manacles around my arms, leaving no potential for resistance or escape.

"He's a military commander of your countrymen," Xerxes bellowed in Greek. "Show him some respect!"

"Quiet, Persian," the leader of the guards returned.

"Insanity." Xerxes sat on his cot, observing with a sharp, wary eye.

Satisfied with their preparations, the two guards fastened leather-gloved hands tight under each of my armpits and hoisted me to standing. Marching from the cell, I took one last look at Xerxes before departing, and the prince offered me a final nod. We descended several flights of stairs before arriving once more on the ground level, my retinue wary of my every twitch. Seeing it to be futile, however, I allowed myself to be guided along, offering no resistance other than an occasional hesitancy as my feet slid across the smooth stones at each stairwell.

At the base of the stairs, the guards repositioned me along a row of ornately decorated rooms built to house various representatives of the Emperor. I assumed that, per Roman law, we were intended for the Great Hall, with plenty of room for public observation. That notion was soon wiped away, for we arrived at a more secluded, and far smaller, room at the end of the hallway, its heavy wooden doors propped open in anticipation.

After whisking me inside, the guards shoved me onto a worn bench a few paces from the doorway and took their position along the walls of the room, leaving the outer door propped open. Following the benches and tables that filled the space, I found Procopius leading several ink-stained clerks scratching hurriedly onto scrolls, with the chief scribe angrily pointing out mistakes that had to be corrected.

In another circumstance, it would have been a comic scene, but here, any mirth was soon blotted out by the looming figure of Hermogenes.

Clad in verdant robes with intricate gold embroidery, Hermogenes projected a measure of wealth that few in the Empire could match. True, Justin had promoted me to the same rare company upon his death, that fourth gift of seven that remained shrouded in mystery, yet these privileges did little to elevate my position to anything like that of Justinian's Imperial legate. Sitting atop an elevated throne with a high desk screening his legs and body, Hermogenes looked down upon all others, his scowl infecting all present with a feeling of unease.

"Now that the prisoner has arrived, we may begin," Hermogenes cried, signaling for any loiterers in the room to either take a seat or depart.

A dozen sets of eyes fell upon me as I resisted the urge to squirm. I had faced numerous shield walls and gazed angrily upon certain death, though those situations did not cause half of the fear and discomfort that Hermogenes' trial instilled within me. Despite my familiarity with Imperial decorum as a former slave to the late Emperor, little could have prepared me for the intensity and resentment held by the Imperial legate and the formal power he wielded to strike against his enemies. Hermogenes allowed the room to settle, waiting for a signal from Procopius that the trial may proceed as intended, which soon arrived.

"Komes Varus, of Herulian descent, commander of the Herulian foederati and former slave to Emperor Justin, may God protect his immortal soul," Hermogenes began formally, reading from a thin scroll at his desk. "You stand accused of the heinous crimes of wrath, assault upon a Roman officer, a breach of the Emperor's peace, and the murder of a Roman citizen with significant military rank. Such villainous crimes carry with them the gravest of penalties."

Hermogenes' words spilled across the room, painting an image of the hangman's noose. Unfurling another scroll, Hermogenes' eyes shot an angry glance in my direction before continuing.

"Komes Varus, in the name of the Emperor Justinian, first of that name, may God bless him with abundant and prosperous life, I, Hermogenes, Imperial Legate and Magister Officiorum of that same Emperor, implore you to acknowledge your guilt in the abovementioned manner," he pronounced, his voice resonating across the stone walls for deliberate effect. "We will easily demonstrate your guilt. If you save the Emperor's time and resources on this trifling manner, we will take those measures into consideration for your sentencing."

Dumbstruck, I stared up at Hermogenes. Irritated by my silence, he rolled his eyes and pounded his right fist onto his desk.

"Well, Komes Varus? You can end this amicably now or subject yourself to considerable hardship. Your guilt is already well known to the Emperor's Court." Hermogenes smirked, his face lit with triumph. "All we desire is that you acknowledge your crimes and be done with formalities. What say you, the accused?"

Defeated, I opened my mouth, prepared to surrender to the legate's will. Raw frustration boiled within me at the injustice of the proceedings, and for the fruitlessness of mounting a defense that my judge had little interest in considering. Thus, my head bowed, I leaned onto the table and began my confession. I cannot now recall my precise words; all I know is that I started by acknowledging Hermogenes. And it was as I continued, with platitudes to the Emperor's justice and honor, that the door behind me burst open with a crack.

"Lord Varus wishes to say that he is thankful our Empire has not descended into a state of tyranny, lawlessness, and a shocking lack of decorum," a voice boomed behind me.

"Liberius!" I whispered. My eyes filled with tears, as I wished for nothing more than to rise from my shackles and hug the man.

"Additionally, Lord Varus compliments Legate Hermogenes on his fine clothing and desires to know the tailor," Liberius continued, his sarcasm balanced with the precise sort of evenness to make a casual listener wonder if he was serious.

"Lord Liberius, it is a pleasure to see you've arrived safely in

Antioch," Hermogenes hissed, "yet you disrupt a formal legal proceeding, which I cannot tolerate."

Liberius nodded, hacking violently into a sleeve. My old teacher remained standing as he moved next to me, motioning for a cup of water from a nearby servant. Gulping greedily, Liberius licked his lips and grinned, his wild beard and gray hair fully grown out from his former disguise in Nisibis.

"A formal legal proceeding indeed, to which I took considerable pains to attend all the way from Dara," Liberius responded. "But the announcement of these matters was delayed—a wayward courier, I trust? Regardless, had I not received a message from the dear Princess Mariya of the Ghassanids, I would be blissfully ignorant of this unhappy affair."

Hermogenes cleared his throat, his brow furrowing. "Lord Liberius, as I said, this is a formal proceeding. While your status entitles you to attend, I would ask that you seat yourself silently within one of the benches."

"Ah, yes, I understand your concern," Liberius offered apologetically. "However, along with my status as an Imperial Councilor, I am also Lord Varus' lawyer in this case."

Procopius fumbled his quill at the pronouncement, with others rustling in excited activity. Hermogenes' eyes widened, banging a fist to instill order into the room. My mouth agape, the legate's gaze turned to me, his teeth grinding.

"My lawyer?"

"Indeed, Lord Varus. Please do keep up," Liberius said. He turned back to Hermogenes. "They say the youth are our future, but so often I cringe at that thought."

With significant reluctance, Hermogenes admitted Liberius to the floor, granting him the right to speak on my behalf. When Liberius asked the legate to recount the charges against me, the wily old counselor merely smiled and brushed a thin layer of dust from his robes.

"Pardon me for my unthinkable rudeness, Legate Hermogenes.

I fear the Syrian roads have done little to quicken my addled brain," Liberius said sharply. "But is it not proper for this case to be open to the noble classes of Antioch, to ensure that no motion is made improperly?"

Hermogenes grunted again. "Such a measure is more efficient, less costly," he said, "and spares the public the macabre details of Lord Varus' crimes.

"Truly? Then I must inform the Emperor immediately. He will be *quite* pleased to discover additional cost savings in tedious legal matters," Liberius said. "And we shall not object to those methods, provided that our conditions are met."

"Conditions?" Hermogenes asked. "It is not your place to make demands of the Emperor's tribunal."

"Of course. Forgive me," Liberius said smoothly, emphasizing each word. "We merely ask the right to present witnesses, test the statements of those previously committed to the record, and of course, demonstrate Lord Varus' innocence in this matter."

"Innocence?" Hermogenes bellowed. "He was seen by a half dozen men killing Centurion Marcian with his bare hands!"

"And I thank you for recounting the charges against Lord Varus, to which I have no doubt of your impartiality," Liberius continued. "Such measures will not require much of the legate's precious time, and may even commence after a brief interlude for me to confer with my charge."

Hermogenes considered Liberius' words, possessing little recourse than to agree to Liberius' request if he intended to keep the proceedings a closed and tightly controlled affair. Though he may have been sorely tempted to shut down the longtime Imperial advisor, to do so would invalidate even the barest assumption of legitimacy in the proceedings, making Hermogenes appear to act against the Emperor's customs and wishes even if he condemned a known murderer. Similarly, Hermogenes had likely gambled upon a quick resolution of the case by bullying me into submission before outsiders could interfere with his work.

Outmaneuvered, Hermogenes acceded to Liberius' proposal but ordered a brief interlude before witnesses could be called.

No sooner was his minor victory granted than Liberius dragged me from the courtroom, assuring my captors that he would take full responsibility for my safety. Grabbing the collar of my robes, Liberius forced me into an adjoining room, slamming and locking its door firmly behind.

"We have little time," Liberius muttered, transforming in an instant from the mischievous rogue into a visibly weary statesman. "I need you to tell me everything that happened. Spare no details, however gruesome."

As with Father Petrus, I recounted my tale from the cataclysm of Callinicum through my capture and arrest. Unlike the priest, however, Liberius' face held the same stern intensity as he absorbed each detail, from the battle through my discovery of Samur. As I concluded, Liberius frowned and coughed into his sleeve.

"Water..." Liberius croaked between coughs.

Jumping to my feet and cracking open the door, I beckoned for a palace slave to fulfill Liberius' wishes. Within moments, the slave returned with an overfull pitcher, water sloshing on either side of its mouth. My old teacher drained the cup and held it out for more. After another cupful, he pawed at his mouth, wiping away excess droplets that threatened to stain the collar of his robes.

"Apologies," Liberius began. "Travel at a gallop does not ease with age, even when the region isn't at war."

"But how did you know about the trial?"

"Your wife sent Perenus and Fulcaris to find me, and they nearly killed their horses doing so," Liberius said, catching his breath. "John and I were stalled crossing the river, with Hermogenes conveniently having forgotten to inform us of your movement."

A prayer of thanks darted through my mind. "How did Mariya know to find you, Lord?"

"Women can do more than bear children, especially that wife of yours," Liberius teased. "Truly, if it weren't for her and Theodora, I'm not sure where you would be. I really do wonder if you've listened to anything that I've taught you over the years."

It was true, of course. I owed much to both women, though I worried whether I would live long enough to repay their kindness. "Lord, is Hermogenes going to hang me?"

Liberius shook his head, his seriousness returned. "Not today. Your wife found one piece of evidence that the legate is not counting on."

I could not think what such evidence could be. At that point, I did not care. "But will it be enough?"

"I doubt any sane man would have acted differently than you did after discovering Samur," Liberius said. "I've sent John to check on him to verify our account, but even Hermogenes will have difficulty condemning you outright for defending your brother."

"But he could still imprison me? Sever me from the army?"

"You and Belisarius both," Liberius replied. "But tell me, would you be unhappy with that outcome? Do you wish to continue to serve if the people you're protecting are willing to do such evil things?"

Pondering the question, I drew back. The voices of Rosamund, Samur, and even nagging Xerxes filled my head with their doubts, their opinions, their desire to leave behind the treachery and danger of the Empire in favor of a free life along the plains, caring for nothing other than family and friends. For the briefest of moments, I was tempted to join them.

My doubts were swept aside by the other voices in my mind—the lectures of Justin, Belisarius, and Liberius himself. "Yes, I wish to serve, if the army will still have me."

"As I suspected," Liberius said, nodding. "While I cannot promise anything, I will do everything I can to free you from this place. If we can get to Constantinople, Theodora will solve everything."

"What about Justinian?" I asked. "Wouldn't he support Hermogenes?"

Liberius shook his head. "Hermogenes can mask his crass

decisions and military mistakes if you are dead and Belisarius is disgraced, but he'll have no chance if you make it to Constantinople. Justinian supports Hermogenes but does not love him. That privilege is held only by Theodora, and we can exploit that weakness to rid ourselves of that loathsome creature as soon as possible."

Impatient knocking rattled our door. My session with Liberius appeared to be over. Brushing off remaining dust that covered his robes, Liberius composed himself for another duel with Hermogenes, a sarcastic grin returning to his face.

"Don't let them see your fear," Liberius warned me. "Right now, Hermogenes is confused. We need to keep him off balance until he is ready to end this charade."

Throwing the door open, Liberius arched his shoulders back and glided into the hallway into Hermogenes' makeshift trial room. Several onlookers had converged near the door, including a few whose features were concealed with thick leather hoods. I had little time to discern their identity as a guardsman grabbed my arm and shackled me once again to my chair.

"Well, Liberius," the legate said, "are you satisfied with the proceedings?"

"Ah, Lord Hermogenes, but *my* satisfaction is irrelevant," Liberius said, gesturing to me. "Instead, I must transfer your polite question to Lord Varus. Are you satisfied, Lord Varus?"

My eyes fell to my shackles, and I shrugged. "I can't say that this is the most pleasant room I've been in. But neither is it the worst."

"No indeed!" Liberius said merrily. "But the shackles are hardly necessary for one so valorous and loyal as Lord Varus. Perhaps they may be done away with, just for now?"

Hermogenes rolled his eyes at Liberius' theatrics. "Very *well!*" he bellowed. "But perhaps we may begin with our business at hand."

After Vitalius released my wrists, Liberius nodded gratefully. "Of course," he offered. "After all, we are nothing but the Emperor's servants."

His face shifting into a smug grin, Hermogenes beckoned to the door. "Bring the Emperor's witness," the legate's voice boomed over the walls.

As the door opened, one of the hooded men entered and revealed himself.

"Identify yourself for the record," Hermogenes ordered, gesturing to Procopius.

"Thurimuth of the Alemanni people, first centurion of the Thracian Army," the speaker said.

Thurimuth's tall and lanky body had difficulty fitting in the squat, short bench made available for him, and a loud thud sounded as his knees struck its heavy paneling. He winced, rubbing the thin trousers that covered his kneecap. Thurimuth was nondescript beyond his height; he could have passed for a lowborn Roman villager had it not been for the pale features and sinewy form that gave the Alemanni considerable strength. He met my gaze with heavy eyes, unyielding in his duty, yet uncomfortable in the role he was required to play.

"Centurion Thurimuth, you were the first to apprehend Lord Varus after the murder," Hermogenes stated, hardly a question by his tone of voice.

Thurimuth raised an eyebrow. "I isolated Lord Varus in a holding cell after finding Marcian dead," he said simply.

"Yet Lord Varus was standing just over the body, still warm in its repose," Hermogenes stated again.

"Yes, Legate."

"Ahh," Hermogenes said. "And was it well known that Lord Varus held little affection for Centurion Marcian within the Thracian Army?"

"I'm not sure who initiated the feud, but the grudge was certainly known," Thurimuth confirmed again.

"Thank you, Centurion," Hermogenes concluded.

As Thurimuth sought an exit from the proceedings, Liberius hacked violently into his sleeve, clearing his throat of some unknown obstruction. "Apologies, Legate," he said, once finished. "When you are as old as I am, even soft cheese becomes a choking hazard."

Hermogenes rapped his table lightly. "Is there something you wish to say, Liberius?"

Liberius nodded. "Legate, if I may ask the centurion a question or three?"

Hermogenes sighed. "Yes, of course."

"Centurion Thurimuth," Liberius began, straightening his robes as if to venture into a gaudy speech, "who gave you command of the city watch that evening?"

Thurimuth straightened. "Lord Varus did."

"And why Lord Varus? Why not the city governor or another senior officer?"

Thurimuth's brow furrowed. "Lord Varus was one of the few officers still sober after the truce with Azarethes. He alone was clearheaded enough to receive and deliver orders, especially as the head of the army in place of General Belisarius."

"Indeed." Liberius smiled. "And finally, did you see the events that led to the death of Centurion Marcian? What was your understanding of Marcian's behavior that evening?"

"No, Lord," Thurimuth responded. "I saw Marcian drinking with Komes Solomon's men. The next I saw the centurion, he was dead on the floor of Solomon's barracks."

A further rustling rose from the scribes, with glances flitting to Thurimuth's gangly figure. I struggled to understand Liberius' strategy at all, but it plainly struck a nerve with Procopius, who furiously scribbled onto a lengthy scroll.

As though sensing the momentum sliding from his grasp, Hermogenes interjected one final time.

"Centurion, based upon your soldier's knowledge of death, and of your observations of Marcian's corpse, would you say that Lord Varus is the most likely person to have killed Marcian?" he ventured, his voice now oddly sweet.

"Yes," Thurimuth said reluctantly. "Most likely."

"Gratitude for your testimony." Hermogenes bowed, signaling for him to depart.

The air was all but sucked from the room. Thurimuth's assessment seemed to have speared my chances of walking free. Strangely, however, a small part of me rejoiced, for it seemed absurd for me to refuse to acknowledge my role in Marcian's death, justified or not. I had committed that sin, and masking that fact behind the benign persona of mistruth would only compound my guilt.

"Well, Lord Varus, it seems that you have been condemned by the very soldier you had entrusted to keep Barbalissus' peace," Hermogenes declared. "This is enough evidence for judgment, don't you agree?"

"Not quite," interjected Liberius, smiling. "After all, even if Lord Varus slew Marcian, an important question remains."

Hermogenes leaned forward. "What's that?"

"Why, I'd think it obvious," Liberius said. "Why would Lord Varus seek out Marcian, in the centurion's own barracks, in the midst of a celebration? After all, as Thurimuth informed us, Lord Varus was one of the most in-demand individuals in the entire city at the time."

"Your point?" Hermogenes said. "Such a reason changes nothing."

"On the contrary, it changes everything." Liberius narrowed his eyes as they locked upon the legate's. "I'd like to call a witness of my own."

Not waiting for the permission, Liberius yelled for the door to open. Within moments, a second hooded figure emerged, taking Thurimuth's place near the center of the room. Withdrawing his hood, a buzz of questions arose amongst Procopius' scribes, the stranger's identity unknown to those in the room.

"And you are?" Hermogenes demanded.

"S-Symeon, Legate Hermogenes," the figure said cautiously. "A spearman of the Thracian Army, and a duty sentry on the evening of Centurion Marcian's death."

My jaw dropped. "How?" I whispered to Liberius.

"Again, you underestimate your wife," Liberius hissed back. "Pay attention. I might be able to improve that straw-filled head of yours."

Hermogenes shot a murderous look at Liberius, who raised an

open hand in apology for the disruption. "And what relevance have you to Marcian's murder, Symeon? Did you observe the death?" Hermogenes barked.

"No, Legate," Symeon responded, his voice wavering further.

"Perhaps you heard Lord Varus speak of the murder? Or a desire to kill?"

"No, Legate," Symeon bleated, sweat forming on his brow.

Hermogenes growled. "Then why are you here? The Emperor's time is ill used by these interjections."

Liberius raised a hand deferentially to the legate. "Perhaps you should allow the lad to speak," Liberius lectured. "Symeon, you mentioned sentry duty. Where were you stationed?"

"At a doctor's private quarters," Symeon said. "For the entire evening."

Liberius nodded reassuringly. "And you were stationed there to protect property? The building?"

"An injured man, Lord Liberius. Recovering from wounds taken at Callinicum."

Liberius paced near Symeon, affording the scribes a rare moment to catch up with the conversation. His face drained of color, Symeon peered at Liberius, visibly unsure of his intentions.

"Do you know the identity of the man you were tasked to guard?"

Symeon nodded. "Samur, brother to Lord Varus."

"And was your duty that evening uneventful? Boring, even?"

"No, Lord." Symeon shook his head. "Samur was attacked by others. Nearly beaten to death."

Liberius drew a bony hand to his mouth. "Nearly beaten to death," he echoed. "Did you know the men who committed this act?"

Symeon nodded but said nothing. He shuffled in his seat, likely unused to courtly decorum after a crude life of sleeping in barracks and relieving himself in trenches.

Liberius remained unsatisfied. "Why would you allow anyone into Samur's presence without strict orders to do so? What would cause you to abandon your sole duty that evening?"

Symeon's eyes flitted toward me, and then back to the ground. "Because Centurion Marcian ordered me to," Symeon said. "He said that his rank gave him the rights."

Liberius drew back in theatrical horror. "So it was Marcian who attacked Samur! But do you know exactly what Marcian did?"

Hermogenes muttered an angry retort, though he was unable to halt Symeon's testimony. His words slow and deliberate, Symeon recounted the muffled screams that he had initially shrugged off as noise from nearby celebrations. Until the screams grew louder, more desperate, and then suddenly silent. As he turned to investigate, Marcian burst through the door, not even looking over his shoulder at the hurt he had caused. Symeon even told of the bloodied and broken spear shaft, evidence of the horror that the injured Samur had borne.

By the end of Symeon's tale, nothing and no one moved. Even Procopius' quill halted its motion. Color departed Hermogenes' face as he watched the testimony conclude, dumbstruck. Liberius craned his neck to the quivering Greek man until his face a handsbreadth away from Symeon's, where he held it motionless for several heartbeats.

"Now tell me, based upon your soldier's knowledge of death," Liberius said slowly, his words taking the lilt of his aristocratic status, "and of your observations of Samur's injuries, would you say that Centurion Marcian was the cause of Samur's considerable pain?"

"Yes." Symeon nodded, his voice hardly more than a whisper.

His gambit concluded, Liberius turned to Hermogenes. Though stock-still, my old teacher's thin figure rose ever higher, his eyes locked onto the legate's fearful ones. At least ten heartbeats passed, the tension of the room bringing me to involuntarily grasp at rough wool of my trousers.

"These proceedings will cease for today," Hermogenes finally ordered. "And Symeon, you are dismissed from the Emperor's service." He descended from his perch and snaked out of the room, ignoring Liberius, Symeon, and even Procopius as he sought solace from another disappointment. Many gaped. Symeon merely hung his head low, hiding a blushing face and a thin wet streak that fell to a scraggly beard.

"Time to leave," Vitalius said, moving to my side.

"Indeed," Liberius confirmed. "Allow me time to absorb our trials together, and I shall have further instructions prepared for your later."

With neither need nor desire to remain there, I rose and allowed Vitalius and the other guards to lead me back into my cell without protest. Though I should have felt a measure of gratitude to Symeon for speaking his truth, it was resentment gripping my heart as I left the trembling guardsman behind. If it were not for him, I reasoned — reasoned at the time — my brother would be much further to full health. He would have been spared another of Solomon's tortures.

Back in my cell, I found Xerxes sitting lazily on his cot, gnawing at the pit of a plum that had been hidden since our breakfast meal. He smiled as I returned, as though noting the kinder manner of the guards around me.

"So, still alive?" he asked.

"For now," I returned, my mind awash in a toxic mixture of hope and despair.

"Well, then," Xerxes deadpanned. "Any chance they'll let us go?"

HARBINGER

Another two nights passed before the aftermath of Liberius' intervention had churned to its intended end. Two days of idle discussion with Xerxes, who jabbered incessantly about whether my freedom would bode well for his own chances at the same.

"There's no telling what Hermogenes will do," I told him. "All that Liberius proved is that Marcian provoked a response, not that I am, in fact, innocent."

"In Persia, we would not stand for such injustice," Xerxes said confidently. "But then again, I've heard tales of Greek habits, so I'm not surprised."

Though irritated, I did not respond, too lost in thought. Could Liberius free me? Would Hermogenes insist upon my execution despite Symeon's revelations? Time passed slowly in that cell, with only meals and the occasional sparring session with Xerxes to interrupt our doldrums. Even those exertions soon lost their appeal, my mind too full and too occupied well beyond the walls of our enclosure.

When the time finally came for Hermogenes' decision, I quickly regretted my impatience. For rather than the relief of a satisfying conclusion, all that remained was the worst possible outcome that anyone could have imagined.

The proceedings began innocuously. After an evening meal that, while far from delicious, was at least fresh and nourishing, a light knock thumped against our outer door. A moment later, young Vitalius slipped into the room and beckoned for my attention.

"Your presence is requested," he declared, arching his back and puffing his chest.

I nodded and rose. Vitalius unlocked our cage and led me into the hallway, moving two paces ahead as he directed me to my intended destination. Similar to my last venture with Vitalius, I had assumed my meeting would be with Father Petrus, who had not offered his tutelage for my prayers since our last assembly. While Vitalius led me to the same room, however, Father Petrus was not the one within.

Instead, I found Liberius, sitting motionless as he peered out a window into the streets of Antioch. He did not react as the door creaked and slammed shut, nor did he turn in greeting as I gathered a bench. I anticipated an extensive discussion, yet none came. At last, I kicked a heel against one of the thick wooden legs of my bench, coughing loudly to get Liberius' attention.

"Lord?" I asked apprehensively. "Did you call for me?"

Liberius bobbed his head, saying nothing. With bony fingers, he smoothed the thick moustaches and wild beard that engulfed much of his face, then traced the length of the gray beard down to his chest, where he rested upon the onyx robes of the council.

"Is something wrong?" I asked bluntly, beads of sweat forming along my neck and brow.

"No victory is complete without the vanquished," Liberius responded. "A better question is whether the knowledge I hold will lead you to freedom or prison."

I had no patience for riddles. "Will I be freed, then?"

"If you desire as much, it can be so."

My spirits lifted at his answer, and I even chuckled. "Of course I do! How soon?"

Put off by the mirth, Liberius turned from his window, his face gaunt and stern. With grace unusual for a man his age, Liberius glided onto a vacant couch near me, positioning himself close enough to whisper.

"Never ask a favor until its costs are made manifest," Liberius said, quoting some long-dead philosopher from a long-ago age of the Empire's glory.

My loyalty to Liberius knew no limits, but I had grown impatient at these indirect answers. I felt my nostrils flare, and I ran a hand through my hair, returning Liberius' stern gaze with equal measure. It took a considerable measure of disciple to not lash out and demand clarity, demand what it would take to free me from bondage and return to my wife and unborn child.

Sensing my frustration, Liberius offered a halfhearted smile. "How do you imagine that we convinced Hermogenes to reconsider his desire to see you swing from the nearest gallows?"

I shook my head. "I don't know, Lord. I assumed that, seeing my motive, Hermogenes would have no choice but to let me go."

Liberius guffawed. "I'm truly disappointed, Varus. Years of education, all for nothing."

This puzzled me. "Lord, I don't underst—"

"That much is obvious," Liberius interrupted, "and I will stop, just this once, to instruct you once more. Now, what would make Hermogenes change his mind?"

Meeting his gaze, I scratched at my beard, which was still disheveled by a lack of grooming. "My reasons for attacking Marcian?"

Liberius groaned. "Of course not. The legate would not care if you were the resurrected Messiah come in white robes and a flaming sword. No, no, men like Hermogenes care for only one thing. What is that?"

"Power?" I guessed.

A look of delight brightened Liberius' face. "Indeed," he responded. "And how was his power been jeopardized by our questions for Thurimuth and Symeon?"

I opened my mouth to speak but found no words. Rather than

hazard a guess, I raised my hands in surrender.

Another look of displeasure. "You gave me hope for a moment, but alas, it is gone," Liberius said. "Varus, who was Marcian's puppet master?"

"Solomon, of course," I responded immediately.

"Ah, good, still somewhat alive," Liberius said. "And who is Solomon's father?"

My eyes grew wide in realization. "Senator Nepotian... We just accused Senator Nepotian's son of rape and assault of a wounded veteran of Rome's army!"

Liberius nodded. "Sadly, yes. And the senator will not appreciate the news reaching his comrades across the Empire. Ruinous, if his son is shown to be the petty thug we have always known him to be. If he were from a poorer family, Solomon might be burned alive for the crime."

Accounts of Solomon's misdeeds had nearly spread throughout Constantinople before, from our childhood scuffles to his near-arrest in a drunken brawl in the Hippodrome. Senator Nepotian had always found methods to silence his son's detractors, either with gold or with intimidation. By Liberius' telling, Hermogenes was clearly a target of the latter, for the legate and the wealthy senator had long been confidantes.

"So Hermogenes will allow me to go free if I keep silent?"

Liberius sighed, the mischief fleeing his eyes. "That is certainly a requirement, though not the most difficult one."

"Then what?" I asked. "What could Hermogenes possibly want that could protect Solomon?"

"Your brother," Liberius said solemnly. "He wants your brother to testify that Marcian acted alone. That neither Solomon, nor anyone else of his banda, attacked Samur on the night of the Eternal Peace."

Eyes wide, I sat back in shock. "Samur? But why should he defend Solomon? Even if he did not commit the attack, Marcian would not have acted alone."

Rising from my chair, I balled my fists, feeling thick veins rise to the surface of my skin. Liberius raised a hand, seeking silence and peace that I was little prepared to offer. The old man gave me a moment to pace and rage, sitting motionless until I returned to my bench.

"Samur would never forgive me," I muttered. "To force him to ignore Solomon's role in this… it's monstrous."

"I know," Liberius said. "Truly, I do. But it is this or the hangman. Hermogenes needs to squash any rumors of what Nepotian's son has done with his time in the army, and for that, he's willing to free you of all charges."

Guilt flooded into the pit of my stomach. "How long do I have to decide?"

Liberius shook his head. "Until tomorrow." He handed me a scroll for Samur's signature. "I know what is being asked of you is an awful thing… but it is the only way. I wish to God it was not, Varus. I did everything that I could to give you justice, but the world rarely rewards us with our desires."

We sat in mutual silence for a time, the Phoenician sunlight beaming through the glass windows and warming our room even further. Liberius sat back as I hung my head at my knees with embarrassment, imagining what words I could muster to ask Samur for such a repugnant favor. I could find none.

Soon thereafter, I asked for time to consider my path, which Liberius granted happily. The old man even shrugged off Vitalius' insistence that he escort me back to my cell alone, matching my thundering steps with a swift gait and swishing robes. Liberius winked at Xerxes as the cage was locked behind me, then offered his final words of guidance.

"All great men are called to do terrible things," Liberius said in Latin, "and that does not stain their memories. All that matters is how we strive to do better, and to be better. This decision has been taken from your hands… and all you can do is identify the proper path to rise from its ashes."

Before parting, Liberius held out a closed fist through my bars.

Reaching out with my own, I felt a thin metal pressed into my grip. My old teacher beamed.

"Father Petrus and Mariya felt that you would like these back," he said. "See that you do not lose them again."

As the door closed, I unfurled the cross and pendant that I had always worn close to my heart. Their weight around my neck felt strange after so long an absence, yet oddly reassuring all the same.

"Jewelry?" Xerxes asked, an eyebrow raised.

I shook my head and explained the seven gifts that had been promised to me by Justin and the others. Xerxes seemed amused by the puzzle but viewed the cross with an awe that seemed strange on the face of a Zoroastrian.

"If that was truly borne by Pope Leo against Attila, treat it carefully," he said. "As for these other gifts... Well, I doubt those will lead to anything good."

"A cross, a dagger, my sword, and tremendous wealth," I replied. "I would argue that I've done well so far, whatever they mean."

"Trust me," Xerxes said, "no man or woman receives a bounty like that without a terrible cost. Perhaps not now, or for a while, but there is a reason you have been given these items. And I would gamble that your seventh gift will cost you far more than all of the gold and glory these four have brought you."

Unable to process further grim tidings that day, I shrugged Xerxes' premonition away, thinking instead of Samur. Liberius had given me that solitary evening to reflect upon what to say or do. Adding to my troubles was that I had not seen Samur in the days since Barbalissus, having been secluded from all except Father Petrus or Liberius. While I trusted that others would inform me of any negative turn that Samur took from his injuries, I could not even be sure that my brother was in any state to listen to my request or was even conscious at all.

Against my better judgment, I explained my situation to Xerxes, who grew cold as I recounted it to him. He agreed with Liberius' position, arguing that my hands were tied — though not so much as to prohibit me from taking revenge in the future.

"As I said before," he mumbled, "I'd kill the man who put me through that sort of shame."

"Agreed," I answered. "And Samur... he'd never agree to forget this crime."

All mirth disappeared from Xerxes' face. "You must convince him. Whatever it takes."

"Oh?" His directness caught me off guard.

"As I said before, honor is secondary to survival," Xerxes explained. "Do what you must to survive. Not merely for yourself, but for those who need you in this life, if only for a moment longer. That includes your brother, from what you've told me."

Xerxes may have been a smug, cocky bastard, but he spoke truth. Above all else, I valued truth, the plain facts washed of misdirection or equivocation. I had only one choice.

Like every other night in Antioch, I found sleep came only with significant difficulty. Unlike other nights, however, I struggled not with dreams of the men I had killed, but instead with a wish for time to slow and separate me from the meeting that was destined to ensue. After tossing in my cot, I rose several times through the night and lifted myself to peer through our barred window, the fresh air temporarily stalling my racing thoughts.

As dawn broke, I dressed in fresh clothing and took a meal when it came. Xerxes said little to me as I stared, entranced, at the stone floor, my ears trained for any footsteps in the halls outside of our prison. My attendants did not arrive after breakfast, nor even after a light midday meal of hard bread and goat's cheese. As the sun reached its peak and began to fall, it seemed as if my punishment might be canceled for good, awash in the golden glow of dusk that heralded the end of Antioch's day.

Such a reprieve was not to be, however. With the first hints of darkness snaking through our chambers, four of the legate's burlier guards stomped into our rooms. Their leader unlocked the door and ordered me out, while a second threw an opaque cloth hood over my eyes, making it uncomfortable to breathe.

"Just as a precaution," the guard said. "We'll take it off soon."

Rather than take me to an adjoining room in that same building, the guards led me down the several flights of stairs to the ground level and out to the cobbled streets. Grubby hands lifted me onto another cart, guiding me through its narrow entrance to keep from slamming into a wooden panel. Seemingly in haste, the cart darted away with my captors gripping my arms tightly.

Our journey did not take long, nor did it take long for sweat to pour from my face beneath the thick covering. Our cart bounced from each pace of uneven stone that, while better than the winding roads from Barbalissus, brought me to the precipice of retching. I resisted just long enough for us to arrive at our destination. My guards jumped into the open air and hustled me into another high stone building. Creaking hinges noted the movement of a heavy door, and the guards withdrew the sweltering hood just time for me to watch it slam shut behind me.

"Phocas here will take you to the appropriate room," the leader of the guards said, pointing to an older guardsman with a heavy scar lashing the right side of his face.

Before I could ask any questions, Phocas seized my shoulder and pushed me two paces in front of him, guiding me up another flight of stone-dressed steps. Far less ornate than the governor's palace where Xerxes and I had been imprisoned, this building was nevertheless clean and well lit, its halls lined with thick rugs and tapers flickering every four paces. Moving quickly, Phocas led me to a locked doorway that he unfastened with a key from his belt.

"The legate told me to give you whatever time you need," Phocas said roughly, "but to stay close by. When you are finished with your business, knock on the door."

A knot in my throat, I nodded, and Phocas swung the door open and beckoned me inside. I slid past my captor, my sword hand shaking as he slammed the door behind me.

Judging by its high ceiling and wide dimensions, the room must have been built to house many of Antioch's sick and dying.

Such vaulted stone ceilings had been engineered in the lost styles of Agrippa and Augustus to promote good health. A light breeze flowed inside, and ambient light from the glowing moon inundated the high windows, amplified further by dozens of torches and low braziers that gave a healer vision even in the darkest watch of night.

But there was no multitude of ailing soldiers here. Instead, just two occupants resided in the room's center, engulfed by its cavernous expanse.

"Varus!" Rosamund jumped from her chair, half skipping toward me and tumbling into an embrace. She buried her face in my chest as I returned the hug but only briefly. Less-pleasant thoughts occupied my mind.

"How is my brother?" I whispered.

Rosamund grimaced, glancing over her shoulder. "Much better over the past few days. He should even be able to walk soon, with the help of the gods."

"Rosamund," rasped a voice from the bed next to her now-vacant chair. "My brother has come to me at last. Let me speak to him in private."

Rosamund turned to me, concerned, her wide lips pursed, but I nodded in agreement with Samur. Complying, however reluctantly, Rosamund grazed her fingertips across the back of my shield arm as she moved to the room's exit, signaling for the guard to unlock the door.

Alone with Samur, I went to take Rosamund's empty chair. The bed was facing away from the door, allowing its occupant to absorb the light breeze fluttering in from the windows. Outlines of thin limbs rose from a woolen blanket, which shifted in sync with pained grunts from a voice hidden from view.

Moving alongside the cot and looking down, I could see only a small portion of Samur's injuries. While his legs and torso remained covered by blankets, one of his arms was heavily wrapped and its motions restrained, hinting at the broken bones underneath. Yellowed bruises cloaked his other exposed arm and neck, eliciting shocks of pain at each movement he took. These injuries paled at the heavy gash along the left side of his face, with a deep red-and-black line bisecting his eyebrow and continuing across the length of his jaw. Several neat stitches bound the flesh together, their knots sealed with a stinking paste that I had only seen in Rosamund's box of supplies.

"Even with these injuries, I'm still the more handsome brother," Samur croaked. His face strained with the effort of the conversation.

"That's right." I laughed politely. "Even Mariya would say so."

Samur's mouth contorted into a grotesque smile, the left edge of his gashed lip frozen and unmoving. "So." He coughed, spittle forming along his wounded lip. "Have these fucking Romans come to their senses and freed you?"

Though intended as a joke, Samur's barb made me almost regret the task I had agreed to. If I had been the one so brutally assaulted, would I have signed a document that absolved my attackers? I wanted to believe I would, yet the thought was unpalatable. And Samur was less likely than I. My brother had many honorable traits, but a tendency to forgive was not among them—especially not for Solomon, who had haunted every step of Samur's life.

"Not quite," I said, my gaze dropping to the floor. "Hermogenes wanted to hang me in secret, but Liberius intervened."

Heavy lines formed along Samur's brow, a vein pulsing in his neck. "You have my thanks for killing that motherless bastard," he said haltingly, "but nobody told me how he died. Tell me, did he feel fear?"

"Yes," I murmured, envisioning Marcian's final moments, bile surging in my throat. "I strangled him. His eyes bulged as he tried to break free, but I broke his wrist to end his resistance."

Coarse laughter rumbled from Samur's chest. I placed a hand behind my back to disguise its trembling, taking no pleasure in recounting Marcian's murder. Yet vengeance lit a fire in Samur's undamaged eye. He bared his teeth in macabre celebration.

"Good," Samur rumbled. "Very good."

Straining against the cot and his broken arm, Samur rolled his body in my direction, his face coming level with my own. His joy was replaced with skepticism as he scanned my body, taking in my simple yet clean robes and an otherwise healthy body.

"At least they've gone easy on you this time," Samur said.

"In Antioch, yes," I replied, thinking of the slime-caked walls of my Syrian dungeon. "Barbalissus was another tale altogether."

Samur's head bobbed in acknowledgment. "But tell me, why would the Romans allow you to visit me if you have not been freed?"

The temptation to abandon Hermogenes' gambit was unbearably alluring. The letter I held was nothing less than poison to Samur, shattering whatever faith he had placed within me through our years of struggle together. I wanted to hurl the wretched thing aside, to find another path to freedom. But Xerxes' words echoed in my mind, urging me onward.

Do what you must to survive. Not merely for yourself, but for those who need you. "Like I said," I began hesitantly, "Liberius intervened before Hermogenes could pass a sentence of murder against a Roman officer, but the reasons for the delay have less to do with my motives and more to protect Hermogenes' own interests."

"And these are?" Samur asked impatiently.

"Solomon," I responded, the name flowing from my mouth like bile.

Samur's face contorted for a few heartbeats, the pace of his labored breathing quickening at that cursed name. His eyes then narrowed, and a snarl took his features, spittle dribbling onto his injured lip.

"Nepotian," Samur spat, echoing Liberius' words. "That bastard Hermogenes is worried about saving Nepotian's reputation, and therefore his own."

"Yes," I replied, "and a condition of my freedom is that I argue that my attack was solely directed at Marcian, with no one else at fault."

Samur laughed again, a certain cruelty behind his incredulity. "But of course, you wouldn't agree to that," he said. "And besides, they could just kill you later in some back alley or poison your food to close any loose ends."

My eyes burned as I looked on at Samur's confusing laughter, allowing him his final moment of trust in his only living family. As another bout of coughing spasms wracked his body, I shook my head and continued to explain the conditions of my freedom. Whatever rage Samur might inflict upon me, I had earned it.

"You're right," I began. "If it were only me, Hermogenes would cut my throat and be done with all of this. Yet my silence isn't enough."

My words trailed off. Still, Samur seemed to grasp the hidden meaning of my indirect explanation, his eye again narrowing at my suggestion.

"You mean he demands my own," he whispered, words clipped and slow.

His face pinched, half from agony, and the other a look of menace. A grunt of pain rumbled from his throat as he adjusted his body, with his lone hale arm tensing as if prepared for a fight. I had no choice but to continue, whatever the cost.

"Your death would be far too suspicious," I said miserably, "and what Hermogenes needs is for rumors regarding Solomon's involvement to die. If you sign a statement that it was Marcian alone who attacked you, the legate will let me go free."

Samur recoiled, saliva dribbling down his chin as his face contorted in a mixture of pain and fury. I offered no interruption as he turned to me, gathering the strength for further discussion.

"But there were five of them." Samur moaned. "All laughing like a pack of monkeys as they urged Marcian on. It wasn't even Marcian who suggested they use the spear!"

There was no hatred in his reply. That, at least, I could have understood, and acted upon. But as color faded from Samur's face, his bruised face fixed upon mine, he quivered. For a moment, he shook his head and drew a hand over the blankets covering his body.

"See what they did to me?" Samur cried, dragging the blanket from his body.

Absent the blanket, his body was completely bare. Same as his arms and neck, the haggard flesh along his torso was rippled with angry bruises, evidence of the continued blows that Marcian and the others rained down upon their prey. The twin puckered wounds where Samur had been struck by arrows at Callinicum had begun to heal, although they remained heavily scabbed and swollen. His legs were little better, unresponsive to his desire to stand from his sickbed and leave this accursed place.

It was too familiar. All the cruelties that Solomon and his ilk had inflicted upon my brother, who, as a slave, lacked the status to protect himself. Images from my last days as a slave, when I discovered Samur in a broken heap as a result of Solomon's torment, reignited the urge to lash out against someone. To do something, anything! Or, barring vengeance, to at least allow Samur to expend his fury upon *me*, his failure of a brother, who once again could not protect him.

Neither fate was in store for me. My freedom, and the safety of my wife and unborn child, depended upon me extracting Samur's signature. And oddly, Samur had no fight to offer against me. And in that moment, I knew that Samur felt betrayal. It was not my intention—God knows, I only wished to help him. But knowledge of self-serving virtue did nothing to alleviate my guilt. My brother's wounds were wrought not through honorable combat, but by our supposed allies, and I lacked the skill—no, the courage—to correct that wrong.

"Roman men came in the darkness and attacked one of their own soldiers injured in battle," Samur cried. "And I'm supposed to give them a reprieve because their leader's father is an important man? What justice is that? They suffer nothing while I cannot even take a piss without help…"

Samur collapsed, his remaining vitality spent in thick tears of frustration. I started to place a hand upon his shoulder, then decided against it. Instead, my brother buried his face in the sweat-strewn cot that had been his sickbed throughout his days in Antioch, his chest heaving as he struggled for breath.

"Samur…" I began, delicately touching his uninjured arm. "I killed Marcian for you. I walked into his barracks and squeezed his neck until I could feel the veins popping underneath. If you do not sign this paper, Hermogenes will execute me for murder, and will likely come for you soon thereafter."

A great deal of time passed as Samur collected himself. I rose and gathered the blanket over his body, temporarily disguising that thick layer of bruises. As his breathing became more regular and his coughing fits less violent, Samur raised his head once more, his eyes swollen and red as spit flooded down his chin.

"We could start a rumor in the streets," he muttered. "You know well how tongues wag over gossip. Rather than let Solomon win, we could win the support of the people."

"Samur, please!" I cried, surprised at my own vehemence. "I want to live long enough to see my child, your niece, born. This is the only option we have that doesn't end in blood."

Again, Samur fell silent but for his painful wheezes, so strong he flinched with each. A single tear streaked down his cheeks and onto his chin. There was nothing else I could say—in truth, I struggled to understand Samur's thoughts. In our years together, we rarely fought, and never for long or over something of monumental importance. After a minute, however, Samur's eyes fell to the floor.

"Where is the letter?" he asked, his voice barely audible.

I withdrew Liberius' scroll, detailing Samur's acknowledgment of Marcian's sole responsibility for the attack. A quill and ink pot had been left upon a nearby desk, which I retrieved for Samur's use. He took the quill in his sole working hand and dipped it in the pot, scratching his name in chunky block letters near the bottom.

"Done," he grunted, thrusting the scroll into my hands.

Though I felt relief, I knew that a grievous blow had been struck. "Thank you, Samur. You're giving me a second chance with my wife and child…"

Samur grunted again, seeking silence. It was not anger that filled his face, but a certain coldness that I had only known him to show in the darkest parts of our childhood slavery. However, this time it seemed different, as if a light that could never be reignited had gone out.

"Varus, you're my brother, and I love you," Samur said. "But I wish you had let me die at Callinicum."

He rolled over and faced the wall, cutting himself off from the world.

"I'll do everything I can to help you," I said.

No response came.

Pausing a few more moments, I finally grazed Samur's shoulder with my fingertips. Samur blanched, and I drew away to permit him the peace he longed for. I walked for the door and knocked for the guard, allowing Rosamund reentry to the room.

"You've been fidgeting, Samur," Rosamund complained. "You will hurt yourself if you don't lie still."

Samur grunted, his slackened gaze glancing to the ceiling. Rosamund inspected Samur's body, finding one of his many layers of stitches severed and bleeding. "See! I'll need to fix this again. Varus, hold Samur's arm still."

I obeyed, with Samur's skin burning beneath my touch. Samur initially lay still as Rosamund tore away the broken stitches, moaning and jerking as she poured hot wine on the gash. "That was the easy part..."

I was no stranger to death or dismemberment. Even so, I lacked the stomach to move torn flesh about as Rosamund did, finding myself squeezing Samur's arm far too tight as I stared at the open and bleeding wound. Rosamund's hand brushed against mine. "This is nothing, Varus. All will be well."

Rosamund's voice was reassuring at first. Soon, however, she began to chant in her Gepid tongue, the words washing into one another with a singsong quality. Though I kept distant from Rosamund's pagan faith, I understood this immediately as a ritual beseeching her ancient gods for some healing power. She seized a nearby candle, dipping the wick close to the wound and allowing it to graze Samur's flesh for a heartbeat, causing Samur to moan again.

"You're hurting him!" I protested.

"Silence!" Rosamund hissed, her eyes wide. "Push the split ends of skin together!"

For those few moments, Rosamund's demeanor changed—far more forceful and possessed by rage. Her yellow irises latched onto mine as I struggled to comply, my hands trembling as Rosamund continued the prayer.

"Keep still, Varus!" Rosamund cried.

As the prayer concluded, Rosamund lowered a needle and thread, reinforcing Samur's broken stitches. The new set stretched taut, but it held, and within moments, Rosamund's features settled back into friendliness and composure, as if whatever had possessed her had been my imagination.

"Stop squirming, and this will close with just a tiny scar," Rosamund scolded Samur.

Her eyes again returned to my face, finding my mouth agape as I tried to make sense of what I had observed. "Something bothering you, Varus?"

"I-I suppose I have never watched your healing process before," I stammered. "Did you do the same to me?"

"The prayers, you mean? Yes, although every setting is different. Some gods prefer the day, others night. There are spirits of water and earth and flame, although fire is the best purifier. This place is not ideal to channel the gods, though this injury was minor enough."

Phocas, my guard, left me little time to reminisce with Rosamund, instead ordering my return to the prison for further instructions. I made no complaint. Though I treasured Rosamund's friendship and was grateful for her care of Samur, witnessing the pagan rite left me feeling unclean. As if I was a willing adherent, absconding from Christ the Savior for these elements of darkness. And if Petrus was correct, spirits of evil. Rosamund offered one final hug as I meekly joined Phocas and the others, surrendering to the dark hood that saw me back to my joint cell with Xerxes.

I was freed the following morning. A guard had ferried the signed scroll to Hermogenes, and a notice of my release followed soon thereafter. The sole point of confusion was a note scratched along the bottom of my release orders, adding a condition for my newfound freedom from the legate.

"Lord Varus is to take Prince Xerxes into his custody until further notice," the note read. "Given their familiarity with one another, and Lord Varus' proficiency with the Persian tongue, Lord Varus is the best equipped officer currently disposable for this task."

Though little could disrupt the joy of my release from prison, I grew wary of Hermogenes' intentions. True, Xerxes and I had bonded during our time together, yet he was still the man responsible for the sacking and burning of dozens of towns in Roman Armenia and Mesopotamia. Worse still, he would be easily spotted in camp, making him a tantalizing target for a vengeful spearman or an Armenian refugee whose family had been butchered or village put to the torch. Even in our shared misery spanning two different Roman dungeons, that fact had never been far from my mind.

As an escort, Fulcaris and Perenus led half the foederati to accompany me from the building that served as my prison.

"Can't take a chance that Hermogenes might change his mind," Perenus said, "and besides, it's good to see a spot of fear on the faces of these painted boy-lovers. If Belisarius would have allowed it, we could have annihilated the legate's entire guard without so much as a stubbed toe."

Laughing, I clapped my old friend on his back. "It's good to see you, too."

Fulcaris, however, was instantly suspicious of my newfound companion. "A new recruit?" he asked rhetorically. "Looks Persian. They can't join up."

"No," I said. "This is Prince Xerxes, and he will be staying with us, per the legate's orders."

Fulcaris snarled at that comment but did not disobey. With all the pomp that our battle-hardened group could muster, the foederati traipsed through the streets of Antioch to my established quarters, the men singing a victory march that had so recently filled the skies around Dara.

Honor dictated that I return to the assigned barracks of my men and learn of all that had transpired in my absence. Many still recovered from wounds taken at Callinicum, while everything from armor repair to purchasing fletched arrows, and a hundred other errands needed tending. A foederati of a few hundred warriors, let alone an army of several thousand, consumed greedily, requiring a considerable levy from Justin's bequeathment to me to feed, house, heal, and equip those under my care. All would be addressed in time, yet not even the apocalypse could have kept me from an alternative course.

"Perenus, lead the foederati back to the barracks, and tally every item that requires fixing or replacement," I commanded. "I will meet with you shortly about this."

Perenus raised an eyebrow. "You're not coming?"

"Soon," I promised. "There's something I must do first."

Xerxes grinned. "She's pretty, that wife of yours."

Fulcaris punched Xerxes on the shoulder, and the Persian raised his hands in surrender. "No offense intended, my young mustachioed friend."

Fulcaris huffed and turned to me. "Varus, I swear to God," he said in Herulian, "if he keeps this up, I'll kill him."

"Keep him safe," I ordered. "I made a promise to watch over him."

I parted from the others, allowing Sindual to lead me to the building assigned to my household, a modest brick structure on the eastern bank of the Orontes River, separated from the city's agora by a double-wide roadway. Dozens of merchants and farmers hawked their wares to the many thousands who walked by. I ignored them all. As I approached my destination's doorway, I was greeted by Sembrouthes.

He nodded, offering a smile. "They're inside."

Restraining the urge to burst through the door, I unlatched the handle as calmly as I could and stepped inside.

It was home. Aromas of fragrant soups and roasted meat emanated from a distant kitchen, a tantalizing distraction from so many weeks of poor fare. The house rumbled with activity, although passing servants paused as they recognized me. Chief among them was Rosamund, who discarded a pail of water as she sprinted to greet me.

"I prayed hourly that they would release you!" she exclaimed. "I knew they would, but still…"

I could not refuse her embrace, and though it was welcome, I had one destination before any further conversation would be entertained. "Thank you for your prayers, and for tending to my brother once again. Can you lead me to Mariya?"

Rosamund sobered. "Follow me."

Through one meandering hallway after another, Rosamund guided me to a staircase. "The top level. Mariya's near the end of her pregnancy, and the past weeks have exhausted her."

I thanked her and ascended the smooth stones that had likely carried the feet of so many others for half a millennia or more. Occasional windows bled sunlight onto each level, cooling the building with gusts from the nearby sea. Quickly, I arrived at Mariya's rooms and rapped my knuckles against her door.

"Enter!" Mariya called from inside the room.

I obeyed. Peering inside, I discovered Mariya, adorned in a silk shift that kept her skin cool, lying upon a feather mattress. Her pregnancy—our child—was clearly in its last months, forming a pronounced bump along her once-slender torso.

"Thank God!" she sighed, beaming. Raising a hand to her mouth, she gave a half laugh, half whimper. "Varus, I didn't know if the legate's men would let you leave…"

"Only because of you, they did," I said. Striding to her bedside, I tossed aside my cloak, and sat on the bed beside her. "Liberius told me everything. I owe you my life, Mariya."

Struggling to pry herself from the soft mattress, Mariya sat. She placed one hand upon my cheek, and then another. Then her arms slipped about my neck and shoulders, and she squeezed with a surprising grip. I returned her embrace, with one hand resting upon our unborn child. After a few seconds, I felt a vibration where my hand grazed her skin, and I jerked in surprise.

"It's constant, the kicking." Mariya laughed, snatching my hand and pressing it once more against her stomach. "I wager we'll have a fighter in this little one, given all this punching and kicking."

I was at a loss. The sudden sensation of freedom, mixed with the realization that my child would soon greet the world, left me giddy, weightless, yet strangely queasy. In my lightheaded state, Mariya kissed me, resting her body against my own. We lay there for several minutes, cradled together.

"I'm sorry about your brother," Mariya whispered. "Poor Samur."

I flinched. Even then, I still could picture Marcian's face, tiny veins bursting in his eyes as his mouth tried and failed to suck air. Though I trusted Mariya, there were parts of me that I knew I could not share this with her. I dared not. That hesitancy was the only stain on our reunion, and I prayed that our future life together would not possess further horrors that must be kept unspoken.

"Samur is resilient, above all things," I said at last. "I will continue to care for him."

Mariya's head raised to my shoulder. "So will I, whatever comes."

REPRIEVE

Following my release were three months of relative bliss. Hermogenes kept his visits to a minimum, preferring to seek out Liberius anytime further instructions had to be delivered to the remnants of Belisarius' army. The return of John and Bessas further eased my burden of serving as Belisarius' proxy. In truth, I was relieved to have John take leadership over the army. Given Belisarius' orders outside of Callinicum, I still retained some rights as overall commander, yet did not balk at yielding duties to John and his considerable skills of strategy and organization.

Perhaps the most significant change, however, was the chance for unprecedented, unrestricted time with Mariya. Liberius had sequestered a series of apartments for the more senior officers of the Herulian foederati near Mariya's apartments, making it easy for me to steal additional time with my family between bouts of training and planning. The building had likely been built from the old Seleucids, judging by the frescoes on the walls detailing their long-dead ancestor's triumphs alongside the undefeated Alexander.

One in particular, a retelling of the Battle of Issus, which had raged not far from where a Seleucid king had built the city of Antioch, held Mariya awestruck, her long fingernails grazing the painted tiles.

Though I led the foederati in drill each morning and met with the army's officers each afternoon, our responsibilities ebbed due to our cessation of hostilities with the newly crowned Khosrow. This afforded more precious moments of laziness for Mariya and me to lie in bed, sharing stories of our time apart, as Cephalas and other servants brought news, food, and anything else we could need. In those moments, Mariya would place my hand over her swollen belly, holding it close until a kick bumped against my outstretched palm. Initially, I drew back in concern, fearing that I would somehow hurt mother or child, yet Mariya laughed heartily at my ignorance, and she nuzzled close against my chest.

My uselessness in aiding Mariya with the household was apparent from my first day of freedom. I assumed the work would be predictable and simple—years of survival in the viper's nest of the Imperial Palace could not be any easier than lording over a few dozen servants, or so I thought. Where the Palace demanded its own hierarchy and handlers to manage chaos, I discovered that a smaller household needed just one careful eye, someone unflinching and precise in their direction. In that regard, despite my experience as a minor warlord, I simply could not equal my wife.

A childhood as a Ghassanid princess made Mariya easy and decisive in doling out responsibilities and tasks. At Mariya's instruction, servants swept floors of crumbs that attracted vermin and used tiny silver coins to purify water for safer drinking. Copper and silver coins were allotted for daily purchases of food and wine, providing a diversity of meals prepared in a manner that mixed Grecian love of fruit, eggs, and grains with the fragrant sauces, curds, and roasted and boiled meats and nuts of Ghassanid tradition.

Moreover, Mariya seemed attuned to every flaw of our abode, accounting for wooden boards that needed mending or a rusted nail that required replacing, or squeaking hinges in dire need of greasing. Every afternoon, Mariya would dispatch gifts of food to select friends and local figures of authority, from a soft goat's cheese for Liberius or a jealousy-inducing Falernian wine in green glass to Troglita, to a sticky-sweet tray of *lauzinaj*—an Arab delicacy composed of thin wafers of bread, ground almonds, and rosewater—to the city governor. I could not stomach the stuff, yet I was alone in my tastes. Others who sampled Mariya's favorite childhood sweet soon lined our doors for more.

"The cost of these gifts is nothing in comparison to the influence they bring," Mariya explained. "You never know when you you'll need their gratitude."

And then, of course, there were the squabbles. A kitchen scullion stealing a freshly trimmed goat's leg, exchanging it in Antioch's forum for a few silver coins. A handmaiden sneaking out for a midnight rendezvous with one of Germanus' slaves. An occasional eavesdropper, vaguely resembling a retainer of Solomon's, stalking our household a ways off, remaining just distant enough to avoid intervention.

All these were but a tiny portion of Mariya's duties, though she made them appear trifling and required none of whatever poor aid I could offer.

Mariya also insisted that we regularly visit Antonina, a chore I was considerably less fond of. I sympathized that she remained separated from her beloved Belisarius due to his continued imprisonment in Antioch, yet I knew Antonina had a small army of servants to cater to her every whim, many of whom were holdovers from Belisarius' own household attendants, and I could not see what she might gain from our social calls. Protection, perhaps—arguably my only domestic skill—except that Belisarius' estate paid the salaries of Sergius and his hundred spearmen to serve as Antonina's personal guard.

Still, I acquiesced to Mariya's judgment. On our first such visit within a week of my freedom, Mariya bounced an infant Joannina on her knee as Antonina pried me for information and made a request.

"If Hermogenes was willing to release you, maybe he'll do so for my husband?" Antonina's suggestion was more a desperate plea than a well-reasoned supposition.

"I fear that is doubtful," I said, gently as I could. "Although once we arrive in Constantinople, Hermogenes' authority evaporates, and I will be able to petition the Empress."

Antonina scowled for a heartbeat but soon resumed her placid indifference. Though she had kindled a friendship with my wife, it was apparent that Antonina had little desire to do the same with me. Not that her unkindness yielded any special hurt—on the contrary, I had never known Antonina to be anything more than a privileged, spoiled child, even once we were no longer actual children. Why Belisarius doted upon her was beyond my understanding.

"Belisarius will be freed and honored soon, I'm certain," Antonina continued. "And when that day comes, all the wives and courtiers that mocked us will simper and plead for favor."

In my peripheral vision, I saw Mariya grimace, but she voiced no retort.

"You have had many disrespect you?" I asked. "Any threats?"

"Vandals and hecklers mostly. Nothing too worrisome." Antonina shrugged. "And if there were anything serious, I have Sergius and his men. I cannot tell you"—she pressed a hand to her chest—"how fortunate I feel to have him."

This was a sort of admiration I had not realized Antonina was capable of expressing—not for another person besides herself, anyway. I had spotted Sergius on the street with four other Roman spearman, and while I knew him as a fit and capable centurion, I could not recall any particularly unique strengths or abilities not possessed by any of the other hundreds of officers in Belisarius' army.

"I'm sure Varus would be *pleased* to lend some of his men to guard your household," Mariya interjected.

My wife's eyes sparkled with near mischief as they caught my gaze. Certainly, I would happily grant such a favor for Belisarius' sake. Yet for his wife, a woman I held no particular love for… "Yes, of course," I said, too late and too clumsy. "Rotate Sergius' men back to the barracks for a time."

"Oh, no, that would not do." Antonina's mouth was firm. "Sergius knows my servants, my preferences, the daily requirements of my household…" She waved a hand. "All I ask of you, Varus, is to free my husband from that dotard Hermogenes."

"Then our wishes are the same," I agreed, for freeing Belisarius was nothing less than a core objective of my present business in life.

I thought nothing more of Antonina's particularity as to Sergius and his men until Mariya raised the subject in private later that evening.

"Do you remember when Sergius refused to return to Dara?" she asked me, taking care to keep her voice muted even though we were alone in our chamber.

"Of course," I replied. "The roads were unsafe, yes. But a hundred men would have hardly made a difference against that horde of Immortals and Hephthalites."

Mariya sighed, twisting her head to free her hair from its bindings, sending a breath of perfume my way. "Safety may have been an issue, but that's not what Sergius was concerned about." She ran her fingers through her loosened strands, thinking. "Nor was Antonina."

"I don't follow your meaning," I said. "Did Sergius tell you this? Did he have some other business in Antioch?"

"He was…" Mariya paused, a light frown on her features. "Disloyal."

I grimaced, but my senses still were intoxicated from the mixed scents of Mariya's perfume. For a moment, I was transported back to our first meeting even before the Avars, when Mariya was presented before the Imperial Court as Solomon's betrothed. Her scent had snared me even then, infecting me with a wild and untamable hope that she would be mine.

I brought myself back to present. "A spy, you mean?" The very thought made me angry.

"Not that kind of disloyalty." Mariya stood, lightly slapping my chest with her open palm. "The kind between him and Antonina…"

My eyes widened as Mariya's voice trailed off. "I see," I muttered. Then I shook my head. "Such a thing is not possible."

"Why not?" Mariya asked, almost amused. "Antonina may be

THE GATES OF CARTHAGE

haughty, but she is a beautiful woman who is unused to being left alone. And Sergius is hardly a saint."

"That is hardly proof."

"Yes, but hardly an alibi, either."

"Did you see them together?" I asked, keeping my tone level.

"Not as such, no," Mariya admitted. "But I've seen them walk together through the markets alone and enter private rooms together. And I have spent enough time with Antonina to know something was wrong."

"Then we cannot be sure," I said firmly, although I was unsettled by the notion that Sergius and Antonina had been allowed to enter private quarters while absent attendants. "We should not assume anything, Mariya. Even a rumor of this nature would destroy Belisarius and lead to both Antonina's and Sergius' deaths."

Mariya rolled her eyes but did not argue the severity of the situation. "Trust me, Varus. They have crossed a border that is beyond retreat, and not for the last time either. Antonina is far too clever to be left bored and aimless while you men go off on campaign. She will find something to amuse herself. The impropriety only adds a flavor of excitement."

There was no point in pursuing the issue. "And what about you?" I joked. "Surely you are every bit as witty as Antonina? Perhaps I'm the one that should be worried."

Feigning anger, Mariya jabbed me gently in the chest before drawing closer for a deep kiss. Sliding her body level to my own, Mariya leaned closer to my ear, offering words of reassurance.

"You are mine, and I am yours," she purred. "There will be no others for the rest of time."

Even with my waking hours filled with Liberius' scolding, Petrus' sermons, and the endless needs of the army, I doubt we were ever happier than those days in Antioch. Whether invigorated by the relief of my exoneration or by that odd feeling of fulfillment when a journey is finished, I cannot say, but Mariya and I ended each day in each other's arms with a feeling of contentment that is the true embodiment of love. Yes, there were times of unhappiness—my brother's frail health and broken spirits chief among them—though even these moments were tinged with optimism, as Samur's strength soon allowed him to walk again and beg to train with my men soon thereafter, though Rosamund insisted on rest for more several months.

Two months after my release, our joy was magnified: Mariya gave birth to our daughter. The babe did not come easy, nor quickly, and when I overheard the physician murmuring fears that Mariya's narrow hips and thin frame would not survive the stress of childbirth, I threw the quack into the streets and summoned Rosamund. She came galloping up, clutching her medicine chest atop a borrowed horse, and did not even pause to ask me for details as she sprinted up the stairs to our bedroom.

"Send up four female attendants," Rosamund called behind her. "And hot water. And do *not* come up here yourself, Varus!"

Thus banned from the birthing room, I left to pace the barracks in search of any omen that might dispel my uncertainty. Father Petrus sat with me throughout my ordeal, and even Liberius paid a call for a meal and some advice.

"Trust me, your wife is in good hands," Liberius said. "That Gepid of yours might be half a savage, but she is the best healer I have ever met."

Father Petrus said nothing, clearly uneasy with Rosamund's power in this situation, but kept any concerns muted as always. He and I prayed frequently, with my words a mix of begging and threats as I asked God, Jesus, and all of the saints to see my Mariya through her ordeal. Even in one of the largest cities of the Empire, childbirth remained a dangerous affair that claimed women from all stations of life, and my mind frequently imagined terrible outcomes that drove me to shaking fits.

As Mariya's labor carried into another day, I sought out my men, seeking sparring and drilling as a weak measure of distraction. Hearing of my situation, Troglita joined in our camaraderie, even extending a welcome to an aloof Prince Xerxes. While Perenus had given strict orders that Xerxes was not to be harmed, few of the foederati had any desire to associate freely with a man they blamed for much of the carnage of the Iberian War, and so the Persian prince was left alone within a group of soldiers who spoke neither Greek or Latin. Troglita's arrival eased those tensions somewhat.

He invited Xerxes to join the sparring and show what an Immortal was capable of, which he did gladly. Trading blunted swords against Troglita, Perenus, and myself, Xerxes easily took command of any fight, his lithe body far faster than anything the Romans could pit against him.

Removed from my private rooms, I spent that first night with my men, harkening to days before my rise in the army, sharing tales and singing old battle songs with even the humblest soldiers of the Herulian foederati. I even ventured out to our stables for a private moment with Ignis, who had been safely returned by John on their long journey back from Callinicum. Any trivial matters or requests for orders did not reach me for those long days of waiting; I can only assume that any issues were intercepted by John, Liberius, or others less distracted than myself.

On the second night of my vigil, I was lost in my prayers with Father Petrus when someone burst into the barracks: Rosamund, silent, her tunic soiled with blood. Many in the barracks rose to their feet. For a moment, my heart sank, until Rosamund's smile broke all the evil omens that clouded my mind.

"A girl, Lord Varus," Rosamund declared. "Hale and whole."

The men broke into cheers, and my legs went weak with relief. I launched forward, my hands wrapping about Rosamund's shoulders. "Thank you, Rosamund," I blubbered, joy flooding my entire being. "Truly, I am in your debt."

Rosamund smiled and pushed me away, gripping my wrists. "You're a father now, Varus! Everything is going to be better. You'll see."

She guided me into the birthing chamber, where I found Mariya cradling a tiny bundle.

Exhausted yet beaming, Mariya handed our daughter over, cautioning me to hold her head safely as I took her tiny form into my arms. Though much wailing would come later, she shed no tears as I brought her close, placing a finger into her small, clumsy fist. For a rare time in my life, I wept tears of joy, sitting at the foot of Mariya's bed and staring at this fragile creature that bore my blood.

"What shall we call her?" I asked at last. "I did not know my family and have no names to share, so the choice is better left with you."

Mariya grinned, thinking. "I've always been partial to Zenobia," she said. "I grew up on her stories, and she's a hero to my people. And if this little one is anything like her father, then I expect she will be far tougher than most."

"Zenobia it is, then."

After a brief time together, Mariya and I were joined by Rosamund, who asked that I give Mariya more privacy to recover from her ordeal. Reluctantly, I handed Zenobia over to one of Mariya's attendant ladies and returned to the barracks. No sooner had I opened the door than over a hundred voices cheered my name, and someone thrust a cup of wine into my hand.

"To Varus! The crazy bastard who fought the Avars and the Hephthalites and lived to sire a child. Roma Victrix!" Perenus yelled.

"Aye, to Lord Varus!" Fulcaris replied.

I saw the faces of so many I had fought and bled with over the previous years that I was nearly overwhelmed at their number. Cephalas and Troglita, Father Petrus and Sembrouthes—even a number of Belisarius' bodyguards and Uliaris. The Frankish officer had split his men between myself and John after my release, yet always kept a watchful eye over Belisarius' more luxurious prison than my own. They all cheered with me as I gulped down the wine, as sweet as ever despite its rank sour quality.

The following day I received another surprise: a message from Belisarius, all congratulations and words of good health for Mariya and the babe. Though I cannot be sure how Belisarius heard the news, or that the child was a girl, I was touched to read Belisarius' words, assuring me that Zenobia would receive the finest of what the Empire had to offer, and that she and his little Joannina would become the best of friends.

Several other visitors offered similar sentiments, with Baduarius inflicting a famous, though still potentially deadly, bear hug upon me when we met again. Mundus procured another barrel of wine for my men, yet he did not share in their mirth upon his visit later that evening.

"If I had not been drunk on the night of the peace, you wouldn't have been imprisoned," he said, voice full of regret. "I'll never drink another drop again."

We had two remaining visitors of note. The first was Mariya's brother, King al-Harith, who bestowed a necklace of heavy white pearls upon the wailing infant before kissing his sister twice on her cheeks and declaring that her family would always be his own as well. Two days after Zenobia's presentation to her uncle, al-Harith led his remaining Ghassanid forces back to their home territory in Arabia, seeking to rebuild from the merciless raids that the Lakhmids still inflicted despite our hard-won peace with the Persians. The Lakhmid king, Mundhir, would certainly never admit that the attacks were sanctioned or organized beyond a disgruntled chief or foolish youths, though we all knew that the Lakhmids were probing for any signs of weaknesses for the future wars to come. Eternal Peace be damned.

After al-Harith, the second visitor was Samur. Arriving by cart, Samur embraced me and offered a kiss to Mariya, who did not blanch at the angry red scar that lined Samur's face. All his anger temporarily evaporated as he held Zenobia, at first smiling and then laughing suddenly as urine spouted from her cloth wrappings. So much heavy laughter made the babe start her cries once again, yet Samur good-naturedly rocked her into a calmer state before returning her to her caretaker.

Yes, even with the lingering horror we had experienced, and the unknown hardships the Emperor had prepared, we were happy.

Despite all that came later, I thank God for those days, their tranquility proof that He does provide a measure of peace to the weary.

Such idyll was soon broken, however. Ships intended to carry us back to Constantinople had arrived in Antioch's port and were quickly provisioned. Despite my attempts at political maneuvering, Hermogenes kept Belisarius well away from the other soldiers, yet relented to Liberius' demand to spend the voyage with the jailed general.

And so, three months after Zenobia's birth, as autumn gave out its final days for winter, we set sail from Antioch, enmeshed in a tempest that would consume the Empire's future.

STEALING WAR FROM PEACE

Despite the lateness of the season, our sea passage from Antioch to Constantinople was largely uneventful. The seas grew choppy as we entered the Aegean, skirting the dozens of Ancient Greek cities that were capped by the ruins of Troy. Mariya went green-faced as our ship rocked in rhythm with the waves, requiring servants to care for a swaddled Zenobia for that section of our voyage. Even that minor disturbance abated as we entered the Straits and steered to the capital's massive fortifications, which extended well into Constantinople's extensive harbor system.

Despite the hive of activity in Constantinople's harbor, our disembarkation was relatively simple. Horses and armor were unloaded by teams of dock workers, while spearmen and cavalry riders alike exited their transports and formed columns. Perhaps the only unusual instructions passed to the army's officers was that no steps should be taken to repatriate the Cappadocian or Thracian soldiers to their provinces, which had been assumed given the Empire's return to peace.

Most of our army units were dispatched to nearby Thrace or Bithynia, although accommodations for select detachments were allocated in the Imperial Barracks. My foederati were among those assigned to remain in the city, joining several detachments from

Mundus and Troglita as well as smaller personal commands for other notable officers.

With all the pomp he could muster, Hermogenes led the army through the brocaded streets of Constantinople. Though the legate had taken care to move Belisarius separately, onlookers cheered the victorious general with shouts of *"DARA!"* that brought further spirit to the column of marching men.

Despite the excited welcome from the city's masses, more ominous signs were etched along the city's streets and buildings, hints and remnants of less happy behavior from the Emperor's citizens. Though I was no stranger to the charred walls and rotting vegetables that presaged riotous behavior, here it seemed that few buildings had been spared destruction. As we paraded to the Imperial Barracks, such omens were echoed in the hollow cheeks and gaunt eyes of a people that, despite their cheering for their army's victories, had been visibly sapped by malnourishment.

Upon reaching the barracks, the legate gave a ceremonial order to disband the columns, allowing the centurions and tribunes to lead their men to their assigned quarters in the city or nearby. After instructing Sembrouthes and a half dozen Aksumites to escort Mariya, Rosamund, and our household servants to a private building that Narses had procured for my use, I initially joined my men in settling into their familiar quarters in the vast barracks.

"Go easy on the wine and the women, men," I ordered half-heartedly as I distributed an additional bonus of a half year's pay to each of my foederati. "You'd be amazed how quickly this coin will evaporate amongst strangers and strong drink."

"What he means to say," Perenus interjected, winking at Sindual, "is to pick your women before burying yourself in a wineskin."

"Aye, and don't start what you can't finish," Fulcaris added. "For example, I intend to consume enough wine to make some tavern owner wealthy enough to close for the rest of the week."

"No women for you, then!" Perenus called out, drawing a playful fight between the two men.

My moment of camaraderie with the men was interrupted by a palace slave, sweat dripping from his brow. After passing through the barracks sentry, the slave sought me out and delivered a message for me to return to the Imperial Palace at once. Apprehensive, I asked by whose authority this order was given and got no direct answer.

"It is not an order, Lord Varus. Merely an urgent request from one who is your friend," the slave said, bowing deeply before disappearing back into Constantinople's narrow alleys.

With neither Sembrouthes nor Belisarius' personal guard, I asked Cephalas to help prepare my armor and ventured into the building of my childhood. Though the armor's scales glinted and its ornamentation identified me as a wealthy lord, the dents and rends in its helmet and body bore witness to the extensive combat my men experienced in Mesopotamia, and it would require considerable repairs before long. Even so, I wore that battered scale coat proudly as I made my way to the Palace, already finding a detachment of excubitores manning the palace gates alongside the more ornamental guardsman.

Unlike my previous engagements in that massive stone complex, the excubitores welcomed me by sight, opening the doorway without requiring written orders for access. Crossing the palace threshold, another slave flagged me down, apologizing for the break in decorum as he guided me to the bearer of my summons. After ascending multiple flights of stairs, the slave directed me to the offices reserved for the Emperor's more senior ministers and advisors and knocked on the door of one of the more ornately decorated doorways. Hearing a muffled response from inside, the slave held open the door as I entered and darted back down the hallway.

To my surprise, the sole occupant of the room was Basilius. Eschewing wine for honeyed water, the skeletal councilor had aged since my departure for the war against Persia, his hair now completely white and thin. Hollow cheeks and sunken eyes made Basilius appear a walking corpse, an effect he had long used to intimidate his rivals in Constantinople's government.

"Thank you for coming, Varus," Basilius offered formally. "I know your journey has been a lengthy one, and that you have a child to attend to now. But as you know, so do I, thus the purpose of our meeting."

"Lord Basilius, I'm afraid I do not follow your meaning," I said quizzically, wondering at the intent of a man who had rarely treated me as anything more than an up-jumped foundling of Justin's.

"We are safe to speak in this room," Basilius replied. "Candidly, I need to know… Did Belisarius purposely or negligently lead the army to multiple defeats? Did Hermogenes save the army? As Belisarius' interim successor, I can trust your judgment over the pack of rumors floating through Justinian's Court."

Drawing back in surprise, I replied to each question in turn. "If it wasn't for Belisarius, every man and woman of the expedition would be rotting in the Mesopotamian desert," I said, "and I can safely say that the legate's rashness and inflexibility was the primary cause of our defeat at Thannuris, and the sole cause of the unnecessary carnage at Callinicum."

Basilius nodded. "As I thought."

Taking a seat at desk richly carved with scenes of the Argonauts, Basilius offered a cup of his honeyed water, which I accepted with gratitude. Wincing, Basilius rubbed his chest and sipped at his own cup.

"Heartburn," he explained. "Liberius prattles on and on about aging, and I fear he is correct. Experience is no worthy replacement for a healthy body."

Another knock rapped at the door.

"And here he is now," Basilius noted. "Enter, please."

Sure enough, Liberius strode forward, his weathered travel garb replaced by the black silken robes of a man of rare talent and privilege. Liberius disdained unnecessary shows of grandeur but allowed that some displays of power were warranted in moments of need. Despite his clean and austere appearance, however, Liberius was clearly tired from the voyage, having disembarked his ship less than a half day prior.

"While I always relish each of your company, I do wonder what is so urgent that it could not wait for another day," Liberius said politely.

"Quit your jabbering," Basilius sputtered. "You've been away from the capital for too long, and if what Varus says is true, we will need to act quickly before Hermogenes destroys everything we've worked for."

Liberius looked at me kindly. "If Varus has given you some information, it is indelibly valid. But perhaps you would do me the favor of elaborating?"

At that, Basilius rose from his chair, his arms leaning heavily upon the desk for support. He locked the doors, then turned to Liberius with a wolfish grin of triumph.

"With the peace with Khosrow paid and sealed, Justinian is planning a new war... the first effort at expansion in generations," he said, his voice hushed despite his excitement.

To my surprise, Liberius returned the glee. "At long last, my friend," he said warmly. "But what is the intended target?"

"Africa," Basilius declared. "Carthage, Septum, Utica... all are in our sights."

Basilius' words evoked the years-old declaration of then-Emperor Justin, who had declared that the surviving Empire of the East would no longer cower, but would retake its heritage in Carthage, Ravenna, and in Rome itself. Though the gathered lords and generals cheered wildly at these pronouncements, they were little more than unrealizable dreams for those of a more practical mind. And, as Justin was dead, and wars in Tauris, Moesia, Egypt, and Mesopotamia all threatened to crack Roman provincial control, most assumed that those dreams had been put to rest. Yet the invading Avars were slaughtered, the alliance of Gepids, Lombards, and Sclaveni put to heel, and the Persians and Lakhmids had fought to a bloody stalemate and truce, giving Justinian the previously impossible opportunity to seize upon his predecessor's dream.

As intoxicating as these sentiments may have been, Africa remained removed from Constantinople's battered armies. Taxes would have to be raised upon an already beleaguered public, and supplies hoarded for an expedition to a land as dissimilar to Greece or Asia Minor as one could imagine. Even accounting for these considerable logistical hardships, however, an even greater obstacle had prevented previous emperors from even considering the liberation of Roman Africa after generations of its subjugation.

It was this issue that Liberius, still sharing Basilius' enthusiasm, latched onto immediately.

"The Vandals will have something to say about that," he answered soberly.

Basilius nodded. "Yes, but their attacks on Cyrenaica give the Emperor a legal justification for a military response. That, and the Arian heresies that the usurper Gelimer has allowed to spread while butchering other Christians—a scandal against the Pope and the Patriarch alike. I can't remember another instance when the two offices agreed with one another."

"Nor can I," Liberius replied. "Varus, what do you think of Justinian's little proposal?"

Taken aback, I quickly gathered my thoughts and rendered an answer, albeit one that likely disappointed Basilius. "Even though it was nearly a century ago, the army remembers Basiliscus and Cape Bon," I demurred. "True, we fought off the Persians, but the cost was significant. It is said that every Vandal is a warrior, and their children are taught that death in battle is a thing to be desired."

Basilius snorted. "Mere tales to scare Roman children before bed. We'll be able to pry away the Mauri from their grasp with a few choice weddings, like your colleague Troglita's."

Despite Basilius' confidence, I had my objections. No Roman army or navy had won a victory in Africa in well over a century, including the infamous attack on Cape Bon. Led by Basiliscus, a hundred thousand hardened Roman spearmen from both halves of the Empire launched an invasion against the fledgling Vandal Kingdom.

However, the Vandals under Gaiseric repulsed the invasion with fireships, slaughtering no fewer than ten thousand experienced Roman soldiers and enslaving thousands more who swam to the African shore. The loss was so pronounced that many still blamed Basiliscus for the Western Empire's fall, arguing that the total loss of thousands of pounds of gold and thousands of casualties had been altogether insurmountable.

The Vandals had not become gentler over the years, either. Now under the warlord Gelimer, they used their reputation as unassailable on African soil to frighten invaders from various sides. They had even reduced the Mauri to utter vassalage, and I doubted that offers of betrothals to men such as Troglita would inspire Mauri leaders to toss aside the Vandal yoke until it was certain that Roman soldiers could secure a victory.

Whether Basilius feared those obstacles too, I cannot be certain. What I did see was that this generally suspicious and cynical man showed an ardor for the liberation of Roman Africa that I had only felt in the presence of Justin. Liberius, too, had been swept up by this dream, quickly arriving at the reason for our clandestine meeting.

"To execute such a complex invasion, you need a seasoned and energetic general to lead the expedition," Liberius said.

"Precisely." Basilius grinned.

"Based upon my extensive discussions with Belisarius on our return voyage from Antioch, I would recommend your son-in-law for the task," Liberius concluded. "Assuming, of course, that he can be cleared of the charges against him."

"Can you outfox Hermogenes?" Basilius asked directly, eschewing Liberius' flowery language.

Liberius chuckled. "A halfwit could. Even Varus here did as much. The greater challenge, I'd say, is to convince Justinian that Hermogenes' slanders against the general are unfounded, and that he is the ideal candidate."

Basilius snorted. "Few have the power to convince Justinian of anything these days, only to simper and aggrandize. That power remains in the sole custody of the Empress."

Liberius nodded expectantly, his gaze turning upon me. Basilius chortled, his laughter almost sinister in its realization that victory was nearly in our grasp.

"Liberius, you really are a clever bastard." Basilius laughed. "Now, Lord Varus, can you convince Empress Theodora to set our plan in motion?"

"Assuming, of course, that Varus agrees that Belisarius is worthy of so difficult a challenge," Liberius interjected.

Though I was hesitant for a new war on the heels of one so recent, I was eager to keep my promise to see Belisarius released and returned to power, so I bobbed my head in agreement. "There is none better for the task," I said, "and I would be happy to try."

"Do better than that," Basilius ordered. "Make Theodora understand our future is intertwined with this single decision. She is intelligent enough to see beyond the machinations of Hermogenes, Paulus, or the other courtiers."

Basilius' need for my aid was off-putting, for throughout my childhood, the man had been an emblem of authority and confidence. "Theodora has her own mind and has no personal patronage over Belisarius. What if she refuses?"

"Then we're all going to die," Basilius replied. "Whether from the Vandals, or the Goths, or corrupt sycophants from our own government."

"Lord..."

"Understand this, Varus," Basilius continued, brooking no dissent. "You are no longer a child. Like my son-in-law, you wield power amongst the army, and any fool knows that the army sways the Empire. You still believe in Justin's dream, yes?"

"Always."

Basilius drew close, his voice hushed. "Then act like it. There's little honor in this world—only power. And if you aren't willing to do anything to save your friend and oathkeeper, the consequences will be severe for all of us. My family... and yours as well."

OMINOUS

An advantage I possessed in my newfound task was Theodora's urgent desire for a report on the army's performance against Persia. After taking an evening meal with Mariya and Rosamund, Nzamba, the Aksumite spearman on duty, notified me of another summons to the Palace.

"A courier from Lord Narses," Nzamba said, handing me the letter.

Recognizing Narses' spidery script, I acknowledged the order to return to the Palace for a private audience with the Empress. Mariya made a tutting noise at the lateness of the meeting, but she did not protest as I donned a heavy cloak and boots.

"Theodora is our household's sworn patron," I explained. "If she wanted me to run naked through snow to make a meeting, I would have to comply."

"And if she did, I would not be unhappy to bear witness," Mariya replied mischievously, drawing a bark of laughter from Rosamund.

Refusing any attendants, I returned to the Palace unarmed and unaccompanied but for the courier. I found Marcellus keeping duty at the main palace gate, chastising a guardsman for dozing while on duty. The chief excubitor hailed my arrival as he concluded his scolding, ordering my passage through the lines.

"There's no discipline in these guards, Varus. If it comes to a real fight, I don't have enough excubitores left to guarantee the Emperor's safety," he said.

"Fight?" I said, alarmed. "With whom?"

His head sank at the question. "You wouldn't believe the assaults and protests I've had to deal with in the two days since we returned from Antioch."

"More violence?" I thought of the riots that had plagued Constantinople just before my campaign against the Avars.

"The worst is arson, for now," Marcellus said. "But it won't take much to spark a real riot... and I'm not sure we have enough trained guardsmen to keep the peace this time around."

"What seems to be the cause this time?" I wondered aloud. "Is there something that the Emperor could do to make the mob happy?"

Marcellus shrugged. "Perhaps, but perhaps not. Costs for basic necessities are skyrocketing, and city dwellers are struggling to feed their families. Just this morning, we had cartloads of grain carried by ox to the main gateway, which I stopped and ordered its driver back to the marketplace. The man laughed and said that none in the market had the gold to take his wares, and only the Emperor could afford more than gristled flour for a half day's rations."

"Jesus Christ," I said, dutifully crossing myself at the oath. "How did it get so bad so quickly?"

"War is expensive," Marcellus said simply. "Building and road repair, ship construction, payments for our peace with Persia... all gold that we didn't have. Paulus has raised taxes to ruinous levels, but the real brunt is carried by the average citizen."

"I'll speak to the Empress," I said.

"I hope you do," he said. "For all our sakes. Until then, I'm left with a city guard of crookbacked old men and boys too young to shave to keep the Palace secure and the city reasonably guarded. A thousand angry peasants could swarm our gates if they were determined enough."

Shivering, I entered the main palace hall. Hundreds of torches cast light along the enclosed space, illuminating walkways for the few servants, ministers, and visitors who remained that late in the evening. One young palace slave, no older than ten, flagged me down, his eyes bright with happiness as he approached.

"Lord Varus? Of the Herulians?" the boy asked.

I nodded. "The very same. Are you to escort me to the Empress?"

"Yes, Lord. Lord Narses sent me."

As we ascended the stairs to the massive building's highest levels, the lad ventured a question that most other slaves would not have dared to ask. Grinning foolishly, he could not help himself.

"Lord Varus, is it true that you were once a palace slave like me?"

The lad relaxed as I smiled. "For many years, yes. I served Emperor Anastasius and was tied to the household of Emperor Justin," I recounted. "But how did you know?"

"All of us know, the palace slaves," the lad said. "You and your brother both, getting your freedom and rising in the army. Some of us wish to follow your path, Lord, but many refuse to believe these tales are true."

"Well, allow me to confirm that they are," I replied, taking in this diminutive and undernourished youth. "What is your name?"

"Agathias. My parents were of Epirus, but they sold me into slavery to pay off a debt to moneylenders two years ago."

"Well, Agathias, it was not much earlier than your arrival that I performed the duties you are tasked with now."

My hand dropped to my belt as I tore at the leather thongs that protected a coin-filled purse. Handing it to the lad, I ordered the slave to keep its contents confidential for his own safety. "Use this to pay Narses for your education," I explained, "and seek me out if you need more. When you have learned all there is to know from the Imperial schoolmasters, we will find a way to set you on your own path from this place."

Agathias stole a glance into the purse, and his eyes bulged at the golden coins within. True, I likely could have freed him within the week, but I could provide only a few opportunities for him to advance his mind. Besides, judging by his size, Agathias would likely never qualify as a soldier for Justinian's army. But even young, he possessed a courage that would make him a fine minister someday.

"Thank you, Lord!" Agathias exclaimed. "I promise I will do as you ask."

He chattered excitedly as we reached the Empress' private offices, their doorways flanked by two excubitores I had met on campaign in Mesopotamia. Patting Agathias on the head before he departed for other chores, I waited for one of the guards to inform Theodora of my arrival and was whisked inside soon thereafter.

Where the Emperor's offices and apartments were spacious and grand, Theodora had always preferred more intimate and spartan surroundings. I found the Empress sitting at a table with Narses, an emerald dress and intricate pearls outlining her slim frame. Spotting my entry, Theodora smiled as she rose from her seat, approaching with a hurried shuffle.

I dropped to my knees, my gaze intent upon the Empress' thin sandals. My deference made her laugh, and she raised me from subservience with the touch of a manicured hand to my shoulder. Infamous for breaking decorum, Theodora kissed me on both cheeks, her hands grasping my elbows with a surprising measure of force.

"Varus, how I've prayed for you," Theodora whispered, drawing a poorly disguised look of irritation on Narses' face.

Relieved at the warmth of her tone, I bobbed my head in deference. "Your prayers have been answered then, Empress. On more than one occasion, I should have been killed, but God has seen fit to deliver me back to Constantinople."

After stealing another hug, Theodora led me back to her table, pointing to a cushioned couch at her side. Her curiosity was insatiable as she asked for tales of my time in the east. Sparing no details, I regaled her with stories of Armenia and Mesopotamia and early skirmishes against Persian outriders. She held a hand over her mouth as I told of our reckless entry into Nisibis in search of Liberius, who truthfully needed little help of our own, and leaned in hungrily for details of Dara and Callinicum. She grimaced at mentions of Khingila and the Hephthalites and inadvertently gripped my outstretched hand as I told of our fight in the shield wall against masses of Zhayedan Immortals.

Indeed, Theodora absorbed each drop of information as if she were a woman dying of thirst, reserving any interpretation or opinions so I might continue uninterrupted. Her only interjection was upon hearing the plight of Ascum and hundreds of other injured Roman soldiers, when she ordered Narses to provision each veteran with medical care and coin that the Treasury could provide.

Though it pained me to recount my brother's assault and my imprisonment in two different cities, I dutifully informed the Empress of my actions there as well. I laid my position at her mercy. Though she would have long known of those events, Theodora closed her eyes as she considered my account, her deep-set eyes dark and sad as she reopened them.

"I need to know—is what Narses tells me true? Did that centurion assault your wounded brother and violate him with a spear butt?" Theodora asked, choosing her words carefully.

I nodded. "Yes, Empress, in a manner of speaking."

"And Solomon was behind this? Nepotian's son?"

I looked around, concerned, but concluded that I had no choice but to tell the truth to Theodora, legal documents be damned. "Without question, Empress. Marcian was Solomon's puppet."

Theodora shivered, balling a bony hand into a fist. "A horrendous crime inflicted upon men and women both. Deserving of painful death," she said, her voice low and dangerous.

"Though it is not Roman law, Empress, I would agree," I said.

"Laws can change," Theodora said simply. "But you again put me in an awkward position, Varus."

My head dropped. "I know it, Empress, and for that I am truly sorry to have violated your trust," I said, my fingers twirling the signet ring that bore Theodora's seal.

"As before, even with your acquittal, if I ignore your crime, men will think me weak. Yet if I punish you, I lose the only true friend I have in the army," Theodora said.

"Not true, Empress," I protested. "You will always have my loyalty."

Theodora smiled weakly and continued with her analysis of her situation. Though the Empress held little love for Nepotian, she knew him well. She seemed concerned of the senator's influence over her husband and knew of Nepotian's distaste for Roman women holding positions of high authority in Constantinople's government besides.

"So, Varus, I have no choice but to reward you," she said, a wicked grin on her face.

"Empress?"

Theodora raised a hand for my silence. "Varus, you have served loyally and ably as a commander of the Herulian foederati. You've placed yourself in considerable danger in service of the Emperor and defeated a Hephthalite commander in one of the most pivotal battles since the fall of Romulus Augustus."

With a rush of heat flooding to my face, I hurried to explain. "Empress, my killing of Khingila was pure dumb luck more than skill. The Hephthalite outfought me and would have killed me easily."

Theodora laughed at my bashfulness. "Ah, Varus, but he did not. One lesson you must learn is that in life, it is far better to have luck than skill. Graves are full to bursting with skilled men and women, yet it is the lucky who survive long enough to enjoy their successes. Be it through God's grace or a happy chance of fate, you live, and Khingila does not."

I started to reply, but Theodora stopped me.

"Besides, it is considered both unskillful *and* unlucky to contradict one's monarch to her face, is it not?"

I could not deny the truth of that statement. Surrendering to Theodora, I answered her remaining questions about Dara, Callinicum, and the general challenge of facing down an enemy with superior numbers, closer supply lines, and generally better training than our own. Her questions regarding Hermogenes' contributions to the war effort required all the tact I could summon, though my diplomatic answers on military authority against the Persians left her unsatisfied.

"Who deserves credit for Dara?" Theodora asked bluntly.

Scratching my chin, I pondered the best answer, and ultimately opted for the truth. "The men, for having the courage to stand against a far superior foe, and to Belisarius for creating the opportunity for victory where there should have only been a massacre."

"But why then was Callinicum less successful?"

I shrugged. "We inflicted horrible casualties against Azarethes' men, so I wouldn't call it a defeat. Besides, it wasn't a fight that Belisarius or any other senior officer wanted."

"Neither was Dara," Theodora shot back, a note of superiority in her voice. She was savvy enough to remind me of the intimate details of our camp discussions prior to that pivotal fight against Perozes and Khingila.

"True, Empress," I allowed. "Except that is because Belisarius dislikes risking the lives of his men for causes that are unlikely to improve our strategic situation. Thannuris, Dara, Callinicum... all rolls of the dice that even a more seasoned gambler would hesitate to pursue. Make no mistake, Belisarius' skill saved thousands of Roman lives in each of those battles, victory or otherwise."

Theodora nodded, taking my meaning. Gathering a green-hued glass with decorative whorls carved into its stem, she sipped at a rich crimson wine as she considered my words, her head slowly bobbing left and right. Then, as though suddenly needing a happier subject, Theodora beamed.

"Lord Varus, for your abilities and successes for the Emperor and Rome, I nominate you an excubitor, a sleepless sentinel to protect against our enemies wherever they may lie in wait."

Thus, with a look of triumph etched across her face, the Empress offered a gift I could not have anticipated.

"An excubitor?" I said, my voice hushed with awe.

Theodora chuckled. "Indeed, and well deserved, my husband and I both agree."

My heart fluttered. This status was what I had longed for since the earliest days of my youth, but my euphoria was swiftly tainted with a hint of doubt.

"But Empress," I asked, "what of my position in the army?"

"I still require your services in leading the Herulian foederati," Theodora explained, "and there are no other senior officers that hold my trust. However, your new position will entitle you to certain benefits, including the ability to carry a weapon in the Emperor's presence. The expectation is that excubitores pledge unyielding loyalty to the Imperial family, well beyond the simple oath taken as a Roman soldier."

"Yes, Empress, I understand," I said, hiding my relief.

Theodora was not finished. "I think you understand our friendship, Varus. I count myself fortunate that God placed us next to one another on that fateful day at the Hippodrome. If you were to accept this honor, you would be pledging your life into my service, even if the service requires your ultimate sacrifice."

This blood oath pounded a dull warning in my gut, but I nodded. "I understand, Highness."

Theodora's face brightened, the pearls at her ears waving about as she turned her head excitedly. She noted that my promotion had come on the nomination of several other sources, including Lords Marcellus and Germanus, and would easily be accepted by Justinian. Given Marcellus' considerable shortage of men, my induction would occur within a matter of days and would require another new suit of armor made for the occasion.

"You can wear whatever you like on campaign—I would hate for your beautiful suit to go to waste," Theodora said, complimenting my customized scales. "Yet in the Palace, all excubitores bear the same equipment, and the Emperor's sigil."

After a time, the subject of our conversation turned to more personal matters. Theodora beamed as she inquired about my daughter, approving of Mariya's choice of name.

"Oh, but you must move your household into the Palace," Theodora said. "It would give Zenobia far more opportunities and future playmates than any little apartment." Hesitant at eliminating any opportunities for privacy, I attempted to raise several excuses, from Mariya's preference for more isolation to the villa in Pella that I had not visited since being named the heir to Justin's fortune, but Theodora waved any concerns away.

"Small matters," she said. "Easily sorted."

Poor Theodora. Even with Justinian as a doting partner, she must have felt isolated and friendless in the Imperial seat. Liberius had lectured previously that if Theodora had been born a man, she would likely be sole Emperor, and a ruthlessly powerful one at that. Instead, she was condemned to navigate the machinations of the Court as was required of a simple minister. True, her status afforded her legal privileges and access to immense wealth, but her power was predicated upon her continued control over the Emperor. In other meetings, I had heard other ministers question when Theodora would have children to carry on Justinian's lineage, at which my sworn oathkeeper would blush and seek another conversation to pursue.

I rarely raised inopportune questions in Theodora's presence, though I pressed my luck before my dismissal in this intimate meeting. "Empress, there's talk of unrest in the streets and of another war on the horizon. I have been away for too long to understand any of this, but if I am to protect you, I should know."

Theodora frowned but did not deflect the question. "Famine has hit our northern provinces hard, and Egypt cannot send enough grain to meet the needs of the capital. Armed gangs have formed illegal markets for grain and other food at ruinous prices, yet there are days where that is all that is available."

"And a new war?"

Theodora nodded. "Justinian wishes to exact revenge on the Vandals for their assault on our towns in Cyrenaica. The usurper Gelimer is sending a delegation to discuss terms for peace, but I fear that few in Constantinople wish to prevent further war."

"But Highness, an invasion at that distance could be recklessly expensive and would require an immense force to take and hold Vandal territory," I said.

"I know," Theodora replied curtly, letting slip just a hint of frustration. "Minister Paulus has already crafted plans for new taxes to cover the cost of the conflict, but whether the people will accept such impositions, I cannot be sure. Unfortunately, this is a rare topic that my husband does not seek my counsel for, nor is willing to listen without invitation to speak."

"And I'm assuming Domnicus and our Egyptian army will lead the effort into Africa?" I feigned ignorance of Basilius' previous information.

Theodora shook her head vigorously. "Domnicus will support but will not serve as the expedition commander. That duty will be asked of our veterans from Iberia and Persia."

"That will be difficult to ask for men just returned home, who haven't seen their families in a year," I said. "And we'll need time to replenish losses taken in Mesopotamia and Syria."

Theodora nodded. "And a commander to lead them in what most will consider a suicide venture, of course." She added, "Perhaps even you?"

I drew back on my couch, a weight settling my gut that threatened to make me retch. Theodora's words seemed serious enough, and it was well within her influence to seek my nomination as commander of the joint expedition into Vandal Africa. For several moments, I imagined myself joining Scipio or even Caesar himself as a victorious general in that storied territory, etching my name alongside theirs for the countless generations to come, and the vision was enticing.

That image was interrupted by thoughts of Belisarius, still lingering in confinement even as he returned to Constantinople. "You flatter me, Highness, but I can think of only one man capable of leading any such army."

Theodora grinned. "Your honesty suits you, Varus, but it makes you hopelessly transparent. I know you favor General Belisarius."

"Indeed, Empress," I said. "If the Empire wishes to conquer an enemy it has never won a battle against, who better than a general who performed similar feats in Mesopotamia?"

"Who indeed?" she replied, her eyes twinkling in the candlelight. "Assuming, of course, that Belisarius is cleared of Legate Hermogenes' charges."

"Which doesn't seem likely, given the circumstances."

Theodora seemed to drift somewhere distant in her mind, her eyes following tapers along the walls. "Poor Antonina," she said after a moment. "Leave the legate to me. Your information about his conduct leaves me quite concerned with his judgment."

"Yes, Empress."

She dismissed me with an embrace and a light smile. "Do consider my request to move your family into the Palace, Varus," she added. "I have need for more trustworthy friends in this hive of serpents and jackals."

With a bow, I bade her farewell and exited the office and was soon joined by Narses closely behind. With heavy yellow robes masking a bulging gut, Narses appeared unthreatening—a cultivated impression on his part, presumably, the harmless eunuch. As we exited the Palace, Narses murmured to me in hushed tones, seeking information that I had not expected to part with.

"Your new charge, Prince Xerxes," Narses began, "do you trust him? Is he useful?"

"It's difficult to trust a man who massacred thousands of your countrymen," I answered, "but he is a skilled warrior and useful for training the men."

Narses narrowed his eyes. "What I mean is, would you protest if the prince were to not survive a tainted meal or an unfortunate accident in training?"

The insinuation angered me. "Explain your meaning," I said shortly.

"Khosrow needs no rival claimants to the Persian throne, however removed and dishonored Xerxes is in the eyes of Persia's families," Narses explained coolly. "He pledged to return a third of the gold our Emperor paid for the Eternal Peace if a rival were smothered while under our care."

Teeth bared, I snarled at Narses. "I am many things," I spat, "but not an assassin. Make sure that nothing happens to Xerxes as long as he remains a guest of the Empire."

Hands raised in surrender, Narses agreed. "As you wish... Unless the Emperor commands differently."

"He won't," I said, though in truth, I was not sure.

Narses offered a shallow bow and whisked himself back toward the Palace, his steps hardly making a sound as he blended into the darkness. Eager to celebrate my promotion with Mariya and the others, I tried to put Narses' troubling comments out of mind. As I eventually ventured off to sleep, a sinking sensation settled over my body, and I realized it was the skepticism of the Imperial Court that I had long disdained in Rosamund, Samur, and several others.

What if my newfound status was only intended to exert control? What unconscionable tasks would be asked of me?

And in that moment of darkness, I considered the cost of my loyalty to the vision of Belisarius, Liberius, and of my old master, the Emperor Justin.

THE MACHINATIONS OF CONSTANTINOPLE

Within days of our return to Constantinople, the Emperor's ministers spurred a rush of activity in reequipping the Empire's armies. Critical among their objectives was the need to replenish our ranks due to losses taken against the Persians, or the retirement of a rare lucky few who amassed enough gold and slaves to enjoy their remaining days in luxury. As a representative of the Imperial Court, I offered the same path to Ascum, though the Alani merely spat defiance.

"I'm not going to let those simpering eunuchs toss me aside to choke to death on my own vomit, drunk and fat," Ascum slurred, his charred flesh stretching angrily as he spoke. "Free Belisarius, and give me something worthwhile to do."

And so Rome's forces were rebuilt with all that could be mustered. While Ascum's ballistae were rebuilt and additional engineers were recruited to replace those who perished in the conflagration at the end of Callinicum, most of our senior officers were dispatched to various corners of the Empire to fill other needs. Leaving Mundus behind with veterans garrisoned in Constantinople's outlying forts, Germanus ventured out into Dacia and Moesia, luring farmers and young boys with the promise of gold and a far more interesting life than driving a plow.

Likewise, Bessas was dispatched to Asia Minor, recruiting cataphract riders from the old provinces of Cappadocia and Roman Armenia. Even Baduarius was dispatched to his tribunal territories of Scythia and Tauris, the surly Goth seeking out men to bear the heavy armor and elongated spears of Rome's shock infantry.

However, by far the most troubling losses were amongst the foederati. While my Herulians emerged generally intact, roughly half of my men had been wounded or killed at Dara, reducing our effectiveness either as horse archers or as reserve spearmen. The Huns, however, had been nearly destroyed after Sunicas and Simmas' final stand against Azarethes, with only a few dozen of the younger and more impetuous riders remaining in our service. While Narses had dispatched his own couriers to recruit additional Herulians for my own banda, John and the remaining Hunnic officers, Aigan and Sinnion, departed for the distant northern plains where the nomadic Hunnic tribes had taken up residence.

Precious few commanding officers remained in proximity to Constantinople in those spring months, and those who were required to stay worked tirelessly to refit the forces for the ill-defined campaigns of the following year. Even with our diminished leadership, we still found causes for celebration.

First among these events was Troglita's long-awaited marriage to Auria, a princess of the Mauri people who inhabited the outskirts of the Vandal Kingdom. Though they had been wed by proxy during our campaign in Mesopotamia, Troglita insisted upon a more formal exchange of oaths upon Auria's arrival to Constantinople. The usually taciturn Troglita gushed over his bride, showering her with elaborate compliments that Perenus mocked with gagging noises behind Troglita's back.

With most of Troglita's friends on dispatch throughout the Empire, and so few Mauri making the perilous journey to Constantinople, their wedding was a small affair. Auria seemed relieved at being spared a public ceremony and confessed as much to Mariya in the days following their union. Where the Mauri nobles had descended from a union of nomadic tribesmen and wealthier Roman governors and merchants, Auria appeared a darker-skinned version of Troglita, with long hair curled and piled atop her head with thin golden chains bedecked in pearls. Though bearing a relatively conservative dress of her people, Auria's athletic figure and aquiline features belied a shy creature underneath—a feature that contrasted against the more cunning and self-sure behaviors of women like Antonina or Theodora.

The second included the announcement of a massive circuit of chariot racing in the Hippodrome to commemorate the Emperor's successes against Persia. Though the Imperial coffers could hardly afford the extravagance of hosting the event and paying lavish rewards for the race's victors, Paulus reasoned that the gold would purchase the amusement and distraction of an otherwise dissatisfied populace.

Liberius spoke angrily against the proceedings but was overruled, and the tournament was scheduled for the Spring Equinox. Undeterred, Liberius requested that the city guard be tripled during the tournament, arguing the need to dissuade the budding street gangs from seeing these events as invitations to cause chaos throughout the city, and Paulus and Tribonian acceded.

Though I shared Liberius' concerns, I did not dampen the men's excitement. Most had not experienced the massive and lengthy production of the Hippodrome, yearning for tales of prowess at the games by the number of factions who dominated its circuit at various points in time. Several favored the Reds or the Whites, but most held loyalty for the Greens, which represented the common men of the Roman Empire. To the derision of many, I was honor bound to support the Blues, who represented the aristocracy and normally possessed the fastest horses and richest carts available in Constantinople.

Of all those who relished the incoming games, Perenus remained aloof from the others. Even when goaded by Fulcaris and Cephalas for stories of past victories for their beloved Greens, Perenus simply shrugged and offered a dispassionate account of his victories. Perturbed by his uncharacteristic malaise, I sat down to an evening meal with him.

"Not excited for the races?" I asked, gnawing on the bone of a sinewy and off-putting chicken.

"Too much else to do," Perenus said, "and it doesn't seem wise, given what happened last time."

I grinned. Perenus frowned—perhaps in offense—and wiped greasy hands on his trousers.

"I suppose I'm confused, is all," I explained. "I thought you would be happier after the Emperor granted you permission to return to the games."

Perenus' mouth gaped at my words. "What did you say?"

"Well, not Justinian, per se, but his ministers agreed to anonymous requests that Perenus, the onetime champion of the Greens, be reinstated to the Hippodrome," I explained, feigning surprise. "You didn't know?"

"Truly?" he shouted, jumping to his feet.

"Indeed," I said, smiling as Perenus pumped his fists with unmitigated joy.

He laughed. "Are you sure they are referring to the same Perenus? I was a champion more than once…"

Punching his arm playfully, I whispered to him of my agreement to fund his equipment and training, noting that not much time remained to assemble a winning team. Perenus initially refused my gold, but eventually he offered a vigorous embrace as I insisted.

"Just keep my role a secret," I told him. "Theodora would flay me if she found out I was financing a member of the Greens."

Perenus roared with laughter.

Unfortunately, these causes for celebration were not devoid of equally taxing stresses. Indeed, on the day of my induction into the hallowed ranks of the excubitores, emissaries from the Vandal Kingdom docked in Constantinople's port.

With Cephalas' help, I donned the bright lamellar coat that all excubitores were required to wear in the Palace. Though made of quality steel and reinforced with woven layers of thin chains and boiled leather, the armor lacked the custom fit of my campaign chest plate and fit snugly around my chest and shoulders. Its accompanying helmet bore a gaudy white plume, with cheekpieces and a nose plate that exposed little of my face—perhaps an intentional design, as excubitores possessed no identity but the Empire's and no loyalty but to the Imperial household.

"You look like a giant bucket," Mariya teased, using one hand to straighten my cloak as she balanced Zenobia on the other.

"Better a living ugly bucket than a pretty corpse," I replied darkly. Mariya shuddered.

Reaching for my belt, I inspected each loop and pouch, my fingers running across each leather knot. When I went for my scabbard and drew a hand length of Justin's sword out of practice, Zenobia began to cry. Children cry, I knew well enough, yet the sound was both unfamiliar and off-putting.

A servant fluttered into the room, but Mariya waved her off.

"Zenobia does not recognize me," I mumbled, my throat surprisingly thick with emotion as I looked to the welling eyes of my baby daughter.

"She rarely cries," Mariya replied. "And now that the war is over, Zenobia will have time to learn more about her father. I promise."

Though I nodded, uneasiness lingered. Belisarius' warning of continuing war rendered doubt in Mariya's hope for blessed idyll. And worse, there was little I could do to avoid further deployment, maintaining my status as a stranger to my child.

As we had not acted upon Theodora's request to move into the Palace, I left my quarters with Sembrouthes but was forced to continue alone after reaching the Palace gates. Sembrouthes bristled, but he accepted the guard's explanation that only the Emperor may intrude upon a gathering of the excubitores.

Guided by palace servants, my induction was to occur in a

large, secluded hall that went unused outside of gatherings held by Marcellus. Initially instructed to wait outside, Marcellus eventually permitted me entry into the darkened room, its heavy curtains blocking all sunlight in favor of several braziers that lined the center of the room. Two of Marcellus' excubitores grabbed me by either shoulder and directed me to the center of that room, flanked on either side by rows of grizzled veterans lucky enough to survive the maw of Thannuris, Dara, and Callinicum.

"Kneel," one of the excubitores commanded, helping me fall to my knees before he, too, joined the ranks of his comrades. After all had taken their places, a heavy spear butt rapped against the stone floor, silencing what little rustling had been permitted.

That hush prefaced the arrival of Emperor Justinian, followed close behind by two senior excubitores who carried a long iron rod between them. His gait slow and deliberate, Justinian paused two paces before my kneeling figure, signaling for me to bow deeply in submission. The spear butt clapped once more on the ground, instructing Justinian's followers to hand over their iron rod and fall into place behind me.

Justinian soon broke our silence with a prayer. "Divine Father, your children ask for blessings to guide their hand," he began. "I, Imperator Caesar Flavius Petrus Sabbatius Justinianus Augustus, seek your guidance to shepherd the Roman people."

Their faces blurred by the thick gloom of our surroundings, dozens of excubitores stomped their boots. The floors rumbled under their weight. Justinian turned his gaze upon me, his features cold and impassive as I remained in submission to his will.

"Holy Father, a warrior of the Roman people comes before you. He claims to be Varus of the Herulian tribesmen," Justinian cried out. "Who among the ranks of the worthy speak to this man's identity, his courage, and his loyalty to Rome?"

"I do!" a voice rumbled behind me in the gravelly tones of Marcellus.

Justinian nodded in acknowledgment. "Varus the Herulian,

komes of the Empire, your name has been proposed to join the ranks of the excubitores," he said, his voice carrying high to the rafters. "Is it your will, free of any encumbrance or pressure, to bind yourself to its ranks?"

"Yes, Highness," I replied, keeping my head lowered as I sought to make my voice carry from the walls.

Justinian's chin rose at the response. "Komes Varus, do you understand that the excubitores serve until death, bound and sworn to the Emperor, to whom there is no higher loyalty?" he asked. "That you shall keep the Emperor's confidence and sacrifice your life, should that be the Emperor's desire for you to do so?"

"Yes, Highness," I replied again, more intense.

Justinian took a pace closer, his Imperial purple sliding across the floor and brushing against my hand. "You may leave now, Komes Varus, and none will think less of you. For if you take the excubitor's oath, there is no going back. What is your intention?"

"I shall remain, Highness," I answered.

He nodded, summoning one of the other excubitores. Handing the iron rod to the man, its ornamented end was plunged into a white-hot brazier, turned every few heartbeats to evenly spread the heat of the flames.

"So be it," Justinian yelled. "May God burn your soul to ash now if your heart is false."

On that note, the excubitor handed the rod back to the Emperor, its tip burning an angry orange hue. While still on my knees, the two excubitores behind me propped me into a more upright position. One man held fast onto my shoulders, while another unfastened the bracer that protected my forearm. My flesh exposed, the second excubitor grabbed my wrist and stretched the arm away from my body, baring the inner forearm to Justinian.

With no warning, Justinian plunged the rod onto my exposed forearm. Searing pain rocked through my body as sizzling fat and burning flesh crackled through the room, making me skip a breath in shock. As he held the rod to my arm, Justinian stared into my eyes for a sign of weakness or surrender, and eventually, finally, seemed satisfied at my response.

"Lord God, a simple man came before you today," Justinian's voice rang out with a singsong quality. "Yet no man departs from this gathering. He is now an excubitor, forged in a crucible of pain and duty. May nothing prevent him from fulfilling his oaths."

A hundred voices roared in approval, then fell instantly silent. Mercifully, Justinian removed the branding iron, placing it alongside the brazier before returning to face me.

"Lord God, we beseech you. May your servant know no fear save disloyalty and seek no calling but service. May his enemies tremble at his coming, their spirits shattered and bodies broken from his skill," he called out. "For he is no ordinary man, but a sworn sentinel of the Empire, and of Your will."

After the Emperor's pronouncement, a deafening cheer arose from the ranks that was not soon quenched. Such noises washing over him, Justinian nodded again, finally deigning to smile in triumph.

"Rise, Komes Varus, excubitor. Welcome to the brotherhood," he declared.

My knees stiff, I was helped to my feet, and a thick woolen bandage was applied to the throbbing flesh along my arm. As Justinian slinked out of the room, a dozen men circled around in congratulations, bearing their own brand that bore the Emperor's sigil of the Chi-Rho. A channel through their massed bodies formed as Marcellus made his way to the fore, a cumbersome bundle in his hands.

"Welcome, brother," Marcellus roared, launching another round of raucous cheering.

My arm held at an awkward angle, I bowed to the lord of the excubitores, who clapped me lightly on the neck. Returning upright, I accepted Marcellus' bundle, finding my dragon-hilted blade hidden underneath.

"You've earned the right to carry weapons in the Emperor's presence," Marcellus said. "While you will be exempted from many duties due to your command role in the army and service to the

Empress, you are expected to respond when called upon to defend the Palace and its inhabitants."

His words rang through the hall as I considered my new sworn brothers, finding them to either be relatively young and vigorous or gruff and thin-haired from extended years of service. While Marcellus was closer to that older cohort, they were few enough in number that they were easy to miss at first glance.

"Few excubitores live more than ten years after accepting the Emperor's service," Godilas had once lectured in his training yard, "for they're called upon in the direst of circumstances. They serve for life and almost always meet a bloody end."

Those teachings from my mentor now seemed impossibly distant as I reveled in my boyhood dream. Though my shield lacked my personal sigil, and my cloak was fashioned in an identical white with the others, the excubitor's costume had seemed closer to my true self than any other I had borne in peace or in war.

Our celebrations were kept brief, however, due to the arrival of the Vandal mission to Justinian's Court. Though my presence was not required on the first day of my induction, I followed the others to the Palace's Great Hall, covering my woolen bandage with a thick steel vambrace favored by most of the others. Led by Marcellus, three dozen excubitores filed through a hidden doorway into the hall, finding most of the Imperial Court already assembled.

Making an uncommon appearance at a public gathering, Liberius was the first to spot my entry, signaling his approval at my newfound status. Speaking in hushed tones, he turned back to Basilius and Father Petrus, paying little heed to the actions of Justinian's sprawling Court. Among the scurrying ministers, clerks, and ladies was Hermogenes, dressed in expensive silks and heavy golden chains, his face powdered to appear far younger than his fifty years. Scuttling close behind the legate were a number of wealthier senators, Senator Nepotian among them. Though I had not so much as glanced at Solomon since Barbalissus, relief washed over me as the senator made no sign of recognition of my helmet-clad face as he walked by.

My disguise did little to fool Theodora, who waved excitedly and gestured for me to stand at her side. Leaving our formation, I complied, and I positioned myself on Theodora's right, adjacent to the perfumed figure of Narses. While Procopius had been tasked with keeping an official historical record of Justinian's decrees and Court gatherings, Narses' extensive ring of invisible spies kept more sinister dossiers, any signs of disloyalty or disrespect soon reaching the Empress' eyes and ears.

From the high dais of Justinian's and Theodora's thrones, I held an ideal vantage point to survey the burgeoning crowd. Cassiodorus jostled his way to take his place behind Justinian, who was already deep in conversation with Paulus and Tribonian, a wolfish grin lining his face. Along the rear of the hall I even spotted Mariya, accompanied by Antonina and the recently married Auria. Bedecked in the dark crimson robes she so often favored, Mariya stole a glance at Theodora, then offered a wink as she momentarily made eye contact with me.

Normally, supplicants would have gradually approached the Emperor with some proposal or petition, preassigned an order of audience by Procopius, Narses, or another of the Imperial ministers. On that morning, none were allowed to present business before Justinian, although several senators sought the Emperor's notice with honeyed flattery.

Instead, a buzz filled the hall as the Emperor's visitors arrived and were checked for weapons that might be disguised in the loose folds of their rough flaxen robes. Finding none, the guards permitted the group of five to approach the Emperor's throne, albeit at a slow and respectful pace.

"The Vandal delegation, Highness," Narses said, whispering into Theodora's ear.

The five Vandal men were all thickly bearded, with moustaches curled below their lips and blending in with their coarse chins. With few Vandals living within the Empire's borders, the men struck a curious figure amongst Justinian's Court, their muscular bodies bulging underneath their robes and trousers. Some were dark haired, while others bore manes the color of ripe straw, their heads a mess of tangles and knots as they walked into Justinian's presence. Though each of the five men were well above average height, their leader was an especial giant of a man; his blonde head would have rose well above my own if we had stood upon level ground.

Ten paces from Justinian, the Vandals halted their advance. Several looked around uncertainly as their leader scowled in defiance as he waited for further instructions. As he grew closer, the leader's age appeared far younger than his matted beard and heavy physique would suggest, with his skin unmarked by disease and otherwise showing the resiliency of youth despite thin scars that lined his jaw and cheekbones.

"You stand before Justinian, Emperor of the Romans," Paulus called out in Latin, smirking. "Identify yourselves and be welcome in his Court."

Where most men would have bowed, the Vandal leader remained stock-still. Nodding at Paulus' words, the Vandal raised his chin to Justinian and roared his response.

"My name is Gunderic, son of Hunneric, who speaks for King Gelimer on this day," the Vandal leader said, his Latin accented and confident. "But tell me, why does your Emperor require a toad to speak for him?"

Paulus recoiled, gritting his teeth at the insult. "Careful, Gunderic. It is unwise to insult your host."

"Yet the question remains," Gunderic replied. "If you were to come to Carthage, Gelimer would not allow an inferior man to speak in his presence."

A light chuckle murmured near the front of the audience as Paulus seethed. Glancing toward the disruption, I found Liberius stifling further laughter as Basilius scowled and elbowed him, seeming to shrink back as more eyes turned to face him.

Paulus moved to interject again, interrupted by Justinian's raised hand. "Tell me, Gunderic, is your master prepared to repay damages caused against Roman territory in the previous war?" he asked, a hint of cold anger in his otherwise measured voice.

Gunderic raised an eyebrow. "The strong never pay debts to the weak. That is the Vandal way. They take what they can until another comes who is harder and more powerful."

Piqued by another insult, red-faced Tribonian fidgeted with affront, eager to chastise Gunderic, as though he'd not seen Paulus' failures just moments before.

"Watch your cheek, Vandal, or you will not find your way back to Carthage again," Tribonian threatened, his heavy jowls quivering in frustration.

Gunderic merely laughed. "Aye, and who among your perfumed eunuchs and bent-backed priests is going to whip me? My men would laugh for months to come."

Tribonian's features flooded crimson, but he was disallowed from offering further retort. Instead, atop his throne, a visibly annoyed Justinian offered his ultimatum.

"Gunderic, I will speak plainly so that you do not misunderstand," he intoned. "If the Vandals do not pay the weight of a hundred men in gold by the Summer Solstice, I will seek repayment of those debts by invading your lands and enslaving your peoples."

Cassiodorus shuffled closer to Justinian, whispering in the Emperor's ear. With a nod, Justinian affirmed the priest's words, adding, "Further, we also demand the immediate freedom of bishops imprisoned at the will of your Arian heretics, and their guaranteed freedom of proselytization to the peoples residing within the Vandal Kingdom."

Gunderic translated Justinian's words to the other four Vandals, and within moments, they burst into laughter. One of the older Vandals, his heavy beard thinning and streaked with silver, offered what was presumably a retort in the Vandal tongue, drawing further bouts of chortling from the gathered Vandal envoy.

"What did he say?" Justinian demanded. "I find little humor in our current situation."

Catching his breath, Gunderic grinned at the Emperor. "He notes that some men possess greater girth than others and wonders whether that weight will be measured against Roman men or Vandals. As for the priests, you leave us to our religion, and we won't begrudge the Greeks their own."

Gasps and whispers from the audience grew into a din that threatened to reduce the gathering to an unruly mob. The Vandals spoke again amongst themselves until several excubitores thundered their spears onto the stone floors, instilling order to the Emperor's proceedings. Curious, Gunderic returned his gaze to the Emperor and his ministers, seeking further banter and opportunities for insult.

Instead, however, it was Theodora who spoke next. Her hands clasped tightly together, the Empress sat comfortably back onto her chair, her voice rising well above the ambient noise of the room.

"Gunderic, you stand before men who stood against the unlimited might of Persia and slaughtered thousands," she began. "Slayers of Hephthalites, of Gepids, and of the Avar hordes. Think carefully, because our Emperor would love nothing more than to turn such men upon your people and erase their stain from a once-proud province of our Empire."

Gunderic paused as he considered this young empress, whose emerald eyes bore into his own with no sign of apprehension. After a moment, he nodded with a smirk and offered a shallow bow to Theodora. The Empress looked only bemused, her thin fingers clasped together.

"Your success in our previous war—and it was extremely limited," Theodora continued, "was due only to other more important distractions our army faced in other corners of the Empire. Those distractions are now dead or pacified, yet the Emperor's hatred of your kingdom and your king remain."

"Aye, my lady, your men have had some recent success in the field, and you may even outnumber us," Gunderic conceded, his eyes locked upon her. "But most Greek soldiers long for little more than to return to the farms of their childhood. Few Greeks have a thirst for battle, while every Vandal man, woman, and child is bred for nothing but war."

Theodora considered his words and leaned onto her throne. "Fanciful stories for children!" she declared. "Let's be serious. Are you willing to gamble the future of your people, especially for a usurper like Gelimer? Or will your leader make amends for his atrocities in Roman Cyrenaica?"

Gunderic chuckled. "Gelimer is a cunt, that much is true." The coarse language drew several gasps, but he continued unfazed. "But Vandals respect strength, and he stood against your painted and costumed soldiers and sent them pissing in their breeches. And will do it again against you, as Vandals have done to Romans and Greeks for a hundred years."

At the suggestion of this ultimatum, Justinian rose. All but the Vandals and excubitores knelt in supplication. The older of the Vandals looked around in confusion, shrugging at his comrades. Even Liberius paid tribute, although where others like Paulus and Tribonian kept their eyes glued to the floor, Liberius fixed upon the test of wills between Gunderic and the Emperor.

"Then let it be known that Rome comes to make war on you barbarians," Justinian declared. "We shall take our armies to Africa, burn your villages, and enslave your women and children. Tell Gelimer that the Mauri and the enslaved Romans will cheer as we liberate them, parading the Vandal lords back to the streets of Constantinople like the dogs they are."

Gunderic grinned. "And this time, we'll give you a proper whipping. I hope to see you there, Your Highness, although I doubt you will find the time to experience real Vandal hospitality."

In truth, I doubt that Justinian ever intended to resolve our dispute with the Vandals peaceably. Nor could Gelimer acquiesce to any demands by paying such unreasonable tribute—to do so would be an unforgivable weakness in the eyes of his warriors. While I trained my attentions on the Vandals for any potential sign of attack against the Empress, I did steal a brief glance at Basilius, who beamed.

Raucous applause erupted from Justinian's pronouncement, with Roman nobles jeering at Gunderic and the Vandals. They were quickly escorted from the Court and to a nondescript building near the city wharf, then were given instructions to depart on the morning tides. Along with a half dozen other excubitores, I followed Marcellus as he guided Gunderic's men to their designated residence, saying little as Gunderic asked about the availability of rich wine and soft women.

"After spending a month getting here, surrounded by nothing but these stinking shits, I'd love to show a nice Greek girl a happy time," he belted out, instigating further laughter amongst his men upon translation of his words. Seeing me, Gunderic winked. "Now this big fucker, he must know what I'm talking about. Some wine, good conversation, and the chance to carry a half-barbarian babe!"

Stifling a chuckle, I scowled at Gunderic. "Roman law strictly forbids violence against women or forcing them into coitus," I said.

"Violence? Force? I think you're doing it wrong, lad," Gunderic said, his accent emphasizing syllables in an unusual rhythm. "When you're in Africa, I'll show you how to really woo a woman."

Marcellus grunted. "If I see any of you in Constantinople by tomorrow at sundown, I'll hang you by a gibbet and let the gulls pick at the jelly in your eyes."

As with all other threats levied against him, Gunderic merely laughed. "I'll see you soon, I'm sure," he replied. "We'll show you what a real war looks like."

Upon reaching their lodgings, Marcellus and the other excubitores promptly returned to the palace, leaving me a moment to gain better measure of our soon-to-be enemy. Gunderic raised an eyebrow.

"I was only half joking, you know," he said. "I could use a local guide to show me where the least pox-ridden women and more honest tavern keepers reside in this stink hole of a city."

Laughing, I shook my head. "I have a wife and a newborn babe. Perhaps another time."

A moment later, I hailed a slave boy running through the streets with a few quick notes in Greek. Plucking a dozen silver coins from a pouch at my belt, I offered one to the lad in return for his delivery of enough food and wine for our Vandal guests. Gunderic, evidently having no command of the Greek tongue, looked on in curious confusion as the slave grinned and skipped off to his task.

"Even if we're at war, it is poor manners to not offer guests food and drink," I explained. "The lad will deliver them to you by sundown."

Gunderic nodded in gratitude, extending an arm. "What is your name, stranger?"

"Varus, komes of the Herulian foederati," I replied.

To my surprise, Gunderic's smile widened. "Ah, but you're the man who slew the Hephthalite king at Dara!" he cried. "You don't look like a typical Herulian—but who knows nowadays, with all these tribes intermarrying."

"Yes, I slew Khingila," I said. "Although it was pure luck more than anything else."

Gunderic clapped me on the shoulder with a hoot of mirth. "Don't ever disparage luck, Varus," he instructed me. "My first battle, I'd been shitting my pants from diarrhea all morning. We tangled lines against some Visigothic war band, and their leader had me pegged as another green boy in his father's armor. When the Goth's axe swung against my head, my boot slipped on a recent batch of wet shit, and I tripped along the lines. Buried my dagger in the man's calf, and the men behind me did the rest."

I wrinkled my nose, but I believed it at once. Though singers and poets spoke in flowered terms of the glorious meeting of shield walls, of men fighting valiantly and praising their commanders, in truth, battle was a vile affair. Shit, blood, and piss were an expectations for men on the wall, that mixture the perfume of human suffering. I politely laughed at Gunderic's tale, acknowledging his own good fortune in surviving so long.

"Well, Varus, I thank you for your hospitality," Gunderic declared. "If you want to leave these treacherous people and be honored and appreciated for your sacrifice, come to Carthage."

Offering a thin smile in return, I shook my head. "My place is here," I affirmed, "although I thank you."

Gunderic nodded. "Well, it seems we are destined to meet in Africa," he said. "Keep well, and stay alive. As for the others, I'm coming to slice their balls and split their entrails with my blade."

God help me, but despite his coarse manner—and loyalty to a mortal enemy of the Empire—I liked Gunderic. And while I wouldn't hesitate to cut his throat on the battlefield, I hoped that such an unhappy event would not come to pass.

Alone, I marched from the city wharf back to Mariya, retracing steps taken twice before as part of an army departing for campaign. As I was welcomed home and held Zenobia in my arms, a grave sense of foreboding flooded my veins, chill as the ice chips cut and carried from high mountains for the Emperor. Zenobia shot me a wide soundless smile, her pink gums making her mouth seem all the larger—a sight of playfulness and joy, yet my senses were filled with the offal of death.

"I wish I could halt time," I cooed to her in Herulian. "Even for just a few weeks. You would like that too, wouldn't you?"

Zenobia gurgled her reply. In that moment, thoughts of war felt repulsive, tainted by the thought that war could rob Zenobia of a father in the earliest days of her childhood. That was the fate that had befallen me and Samur—the fate that transformed us from boys, from sons, into property. That Zenobia could ever suffer even a tiny measure of my childhood pain was unthinkable.

"You'll never see the world with the eyes of a slave," I promised her. "I would give all the gold I possess to guarantee you a different fate."

Spittle pooled on her chin. More the better, for I would not want my daughter worrying about her father pondering a violent death along the shores of Africa.

"God," I begged, "if you can't sway Justinian toward peace, just let me make it back home safely. Not for my sake, but for hers."

PREPARATIONS FOR WAR

By winter solstice, my household was relocated to the Imperial Palace. Theodora was overjoyed by such news, providing Mariya with spacious accommodations overlooking the Golden Horn and just below those of the Emperor and Empress. I found out later that these quarters also had a private staircase in the Empress' foyer, which Narses said would make it easier for me to reach Theodora in an emergency.

News of Justinian's declaration of war burned through the provinces with incredible speed. Within a month, we had even received missives from Cherson, Singidunum, and Antioch, all noting the relative peace we enjoyed along those often wild borders. More nearby provinces had also pledged grain and other supplies as requested by the Emperor's ministers, although several provincial governors pled for a reduction in the quota they were expected to provide.

Though several provinces had begun to recover from famine that struck much of the Empire's wealthy growing provinces in Egypt and along Moesia, it would be several more months until a new harvest could alleviate the pangs of hunger afflicting the Empire's plebeian classes. Inspired by advice from Liberius, Justinian agreed to reduce production quotas for scarce foodstuffs in return for the province offering up new recruits for our army. Combined with the dozens of recruiters previously dispatched throughout the Empire, replacements for our losses against Persia began to fill into several units of spearmen, archers, and much-needed cavalry. Among those included several hundred Huns and Herulians, who were quickly assigned to their respective foederati in Justinian's service.

However, while the more rural provinces of the Empire rose in patriotic energy at news of the Vandalic war, public reaction in larger cities was far more muted. Such urban centers faced greater deprivations from drought and hunger, while new taxes had been raised by Paulus atop the impoverishing collections that were already required of the common Roman citizenry. Constantinople was perhaps chief victim of this resentment, with crude paintings of Justinian engaging in sodomy with Paulus and Tribonian appearing on several building walls throughout the city. Even before Gunderic and his men departed for Carthage and Utica, angry outbursts had been noted in the marketplace and at several of the city's gates, although these frustrations had yet to boil over into something far more sinister.

Our attentions in the army were placed elsewhere, for a thousand tasks had to be completed before our intended voyage to the African coast late in the following spring. Absent the support of other senior officers than Troglita and Valerian, I did what I could to prepare the logistical necessities for thousands of men on the march, all the while seeking new avenues for Belisarius' release and reinstatement to command. Antonina grew increasingly impatient with my lack of success, visiting my office and even seeking guidance from Mariya and the Empress regarding how to petition for Belisarius' freedom.

"Belisarius trusts you!" Antonina chastised me in my office, joined only by Sembrouthes. "And you sit here, bargaining with clerks and ministers. I thought you were supposed to be a fearless warrior?"

If I did not love Belisarius, I would have dismissed Antonina outright. After all, in all our years together, she had never demonstrated the slightest kindness to me or to Samur. "If Belisarius were held captive in an enemy shield wall, I would happily charge in headlong to rescue him. But I can't wave my sword about in Justinian's Court and expect anything good to happen."

Antonina groaned. "Then do better, Varus. If your positions were exchanged, Belisarius would sacrifice anything to have you freed."

"I know it," I replied. "And that's why I will continue working to free Belisarius, even when those far more powerful would happily imprison me alongside him. But I won't be a fool, Antonina."

"I should hope not," Antonina countered. "All I ask is that you do something. Even John sits idle, despite everything Belisarius has done for that man."

Her nose crinkled at the mention of John, Belisarius' dearest childhood friend. Some enmity, I wondered? If so, I doubted John deserved it, for his position in Justinian's Court was no better than mine. All we could do was find allies, wait for opportunities, and keep Belisarius' army well-maintained until he returned to favor.

Outside of such command duties, I led daily drills with the Herulians in Constantinople's nearly vacant training yard. After morning prayers with Father Petrus, I ordered Fulcaris and Perenus to rouse the men, who grumbled. For the veterans, it took little time to sweat off the soft layer of fat that had grown on their bodies, evidence of easier living since the affirmation of the Eternal Peace with Persia.

Unfortunately, the newer Herulian recruits who trickled in from our recruitment efforts required considerable effort to form into a single coherent mass of mounted death. Their first few weeks of training primarily concerned sword, shield, and spear, leading many of the younger and more cocksure in their ranks to boast that this education was unnecessary. Fulcaris spat furiously at one man, scarcely older than sixteen, who argued that the Herulian people had little to learn from Romans who had not won an offensive war in generations.

"Please, idiot, enlighten me on your superior fighting skill," Fulcaris yelled.

The youth refused to answer until Fulcaris gave him a shove. "A generation ago, these Romans cowered before our people. We were never conquered, but still we serve them. Why should Herulians fight and die for a weaker people?"

Before Fulcaris could beat the man senseless, I intervened with a sinister smile on my face.

"Perhaps you are correct, Altan," I said, addressing the youth. "And I would not deprive you of a more appropriate education, which is why you will duel a man of considerable skill."

On that note, I summoned Xerxes, who trotted forward with an indignant scowl on his face. Shunned by most other men, despite their developing familiarity with the Persian, Xerxes had trained assiduously alone, ending each day caked in dried salt and layers of sweat that warranted a visit to the city's many baths. I had provided Xerxes with private barracks quarters befitting a tribune and saw little enough of my former prison comrade until the foederati's training regimen resumed with vim.

Xerxes looked over his opponent for a heartbeat and shrugged. "This peacock has no claws. Send me a real man."

"Lord, I meant no disrespect..." Altan began in Greek, yet was quickly silenced by Sindual, his new centurion.

"Altan, Prince Xerxes is a former commander of the Persian Zhayedan. He has killed men for no other reason than it was expedient for him to do so," I bellowed. "If you can defeat Prince Xerxes in single combat, I will provide you with half of your weight in gold and permission to leave the Emperor's army."

Altan blanched upon hearing of Xerxes' status as an Immortal, but was tugged convincingly by the pull of greed. Agreeing to the terms, Altan took up a blunted sword and turned to Xerxes, expecting him to follow suit.

Xerxes refused to draw any weapon. "A sword isn't necessary here," he explained mischievously. "Nor a shield."

"Insane!" Altan yelled out. Inspired by the considerable advantage he enjoyed over his unarmed foe, Altan charged Xerxes, swinging his sword astride the Persian's neatly coiffed beard. Xerxes stood motionless at the onslaught, feigning terror and bounding from one heavily booted foot to the other. Altan raised his blade for a stroke that, though it could not cut flesh, may well have bashed Xerxes' skull in, as though seeking the handsome reward that would leave his grandchildren wealthy within.

Xerxes merely sidestepped—little more than a hop, really. Altan followed his attack with two more swings, both easily dodged as Xerxes barely paid his enemy mind. Then, when Altan sought to charge once more, Xerxes darted forth and smashed a fist into his chin.

To this day, I am not convinced Altan ever saw the blow coming. Few in that training yard could track Xerxes' raw speed, his limbs a blur as he rushed ahead and connected his fist with a sickening crack. Altan dropped to the ground, knocked unconscious even before his body fell to the earth.

A mixture of anger and fascination rose from the Herulian recruits, their grumbling full of slurs in a language that Xerxes did not speak. Before the resentment grew further, I addressed the two hundred Herulian trainees.

"As I said, Prince Xerxes is one of the most skilled warriors currently living," I yelled in Greek, "and as the Emperor's guest, he will accompany us to Africa. Learn from Xerxes, and I promise you that no slobbering Vandal will outfight you in the shield wall."

Though few counted Xerxes as a friend, even the veterans of my foederati began to avidly pursue his instruction. After those initial days of training, I gave Xerxes and the other foederati officers greater independence in their tutelage, occasionally visiting to inspect their progress. With several weeks of gradually improving weapons education complete, Perenus and Fulcaris led the men on mounted archery exercises outside the walls of Constantinople, returning well after sundown. Where the swordsmanship of the younger recruits was generally lacking upon their arrival to my foederati, their horsemanship and skill with a bow belied their heritage as a people who had previously rode and conquered with Attila.

Our murderous pace continued as more frigid weather blustered into Constantinople, blanketing its streets with a thin layer of snow. Aside from martial planning, I spent my time visiting Samur as much as possible, finding him doted on by Rosamund throughout the day. Soon enough, Samur regained enough strength to walk unassisted, and within a week, he begged to be included in the foederati's drills.

"More war," Rosamund scolded. "It's disgusting. You both nearly die in battle, and now the Emperor wants to do more of the same. Why don't you take their offer to retire in peace?"

"I'm still young," I pointed out, "and I've made an oath."

Rosamund shook her head. "Oaths are wind," she spat. "Words to keep men bound to acts of stupidity! But you could end this, Varus. We could leave this cesspit of a city and live wealthy and free for the rest of your days."

"You know that won't happen," I said, rolling my eyes. "This is our chance to bring peace back to the world... to bring back order where there was only chaos."

Wringing her hands, Rosamund walked to me, her fury abandoned for her usual wispy voice. "The people in your lost provinces aren't asking to be liberated," she said, "and all your efforts will bring are death and suffering. Even the people of Constantinople don't want this war."

"Rosamund, if you do not wish to go, you are welcome to remain in Constantinople with Mariya. Although I would prefer to have you with us again."

Rosamund laughed in a resigned tone. "I'll never leave you," she said, "but I wish you would listen to me, even occasionally." She offered a light embrace. "Your brother also shouldn't train, but he is more stubborn than even you," she mumbled. "Keep vigilant around him... I worry that he will do something reckless."

"I promise," I said. "For now, take whatever coins you need to purchase your healing supplies and any other equipment you require.

Even with all our planning, we have no idea what we'll face in Africa."

And so, as Rosamund monitored with a disapproving gaze, Samur rejoined his training, preferring more private lessons with select members of my foederati. When asked if he wished to rejoin the Huns, Samur shrugged.

"The new recruits are in training near Scythia," he said, "and I only know a few of the survivors from Callinicum. Sunicas was always convinced I'd return to fight with you... and perhaps he was right."

Nodding, I gave him gold to equip and arm himself, and instructed trusted friends to spar with Samur for the time being. His body drained of its strength from months of bed rest, Samur became easily exhausted from simple efforts, although all his skill remained intact. Troglita offered to train with Samur while the foederati departed for mounted exercises, while Xerxes and Fulcaris remolded Samur's body into a lean physique. Such efforts were an agonizingly slow process, while Samur insisted upon his readiness prior to our voyage to Africa.

As the foederati's training progressed, so, too, did the capital's measures for the multi-day racing tourney set for just after the start of the new year. Justinian spared little expense in anticipation of the event, which would gather hundreds of charioteers from across the Empire, with purses of gold and silver disbursed to the final twelve who reached the championship circuit. Though Constantinople's residents brightened at the week-long games designed to showcase the Empire's successes against Persia, many grumbled at the coin required from an already depleted Imperial Treasury to finance such a complex operation. Angrier residents vandalized one of the Hippodrome's gates, calling for the overthrow of "Justinian the tyrant."

Any bitterness had little effect on Perenus, who jabbered excitedly at his progress. Though my coin had provided Perenus with a significant advantage over other would-be racers, the sheer expense of the endeavor required a measure of frugality in balancing the need for well-bred horseflesh against elite craftsmanship of the chariot itself. Understanding these limitations, Perenus invested his funding into finding the two fittest and best-natured horses available to the city's markets, spending the remainder upon a worn, serviceable frame for Perenus to stand upon. Concerned, I offered Perenus further coin to fund his venture, but he declined with a boyish grin.

"No need for baubles," Perenus said, "besides, it makes the other teams more likely to ignore me at first."

In those early months of winter, Perenus insisted upon meeting all training obligations with the foederati as its second-in-command. After returning from afternoon drill, he raced to the Hippodrome track, working with trainers who had been rented from the Greens to supervise Perenus' return to form. Other than two craftsmen to repair any damage to the chariot body, Perenus hired a weathered old Green named Patroklus whose every utterance was laced with profanity and scorn. In my few visits to Perenus' training bouts, I frowned most of the time I watched, worried that my friend would grow disheartened from the considerable time he had spent away from the all-important Roman sport.

On one particular instance, one of Perenus' wheels collided against a stone disguised in the Hippodrome's sands, sending its rider careening into the dust close by. Such falls had snapped the necks or twisted the limbs of many chariot racers, and I rushed onto the track in fear that a similar fate had befallen Perenus. Weak-kneed and frail, Patroklus sprinted all the faster, lambasting Perenus for his poor showing.

"You shame me, boy!" Patroklus yelled. "If I'd wanted some cunny-brained braggart to train, I'd snatch one of the wharf urchins. Now get up and do it right this time!"

To my relief, Perenus laughed in between coarse coughs, wiping the dust from his face. Later, I asked whether such abuse dampened his spirits, worried that Patroklus would shatter Perenus' return to the circuit.

"This is nothing compared to Archelaus," Perenus chided me.

"I hardly notice it anymore. If anything, I probably frustrate him by laughing at everything he says."

The first month of Perenus' training followed a similar course, with frequent falls and angry bruises as evidence of Perenus' extended time away from his former period as a champion racer. Even after particularly gruesome falls, however, Perenus never seemed to lose confidence, ending each day with a broad grin at the prospect of being allowed to return to his beloved Hippodrome. By the second month of training, he handled the chariot reins as deftly as ever, and by the third he was able to execute breakneck maneuvers around sudden obstacles common to the races, such as a broken-down chariot blocking a swathe of track.

Through it all, the initially small gathering of Greens grew into a veritable cult around Perenus' practice sessions. The Hippodrome was closed to spectators, yet the circus' guards were easily bribed, and few were willing to chase away interlopers who would surely return moments later. All the better, for Perenus seemed to relish the crowd's adoration, with several speaking in hushed voices of his final victory in the years prior.

In the final month before the games, I disallowed Perenus from participating in the more physically taxing training with the foederati. While he initially resisted, Perenus relented once several other officers added their voices to my own.

"The army will be waiting for you when you're finished, don't worry," Mundus muttered to Perenus during a visit to Constantinople. "In the meantime, give us something to feel happy about."

Finally, as winter's chill bit deep into Constantinople's flesh, the great tourney arrived. Hundreds of teams from every Imperial province flooded the Hippodrome, paying handsomely for the scarce rooms available even along the city's outskirts. Poorer drivers even begged for space on the floor of the Imperial Barracks, something that was adamantly disallowed by Marcellus as an unnecessary risk to an already overtaxed Imperial Guard. As Constantinople's population swelled, its already expensive foodstuffs grew exorbitant in cost, forcing Paulus to release a small portion of the grain reserves set aside in the Imperial granaries.

Driven by the prospect of gold and timeless glory, racing teams arrived from distant lands well beyond the Empire's borders. A number of Ostrogoths journeyed to Constantinople, invited by a show of goodwill between Justinian and the Ostrogothic Queen Amalasuntha. Their racing teams appeared of poor quality against those of the squat and thickly bearded Franks, whose carriages were studded with precious amber and thin sheets of gold that glinted in the sun.

"Damned peacocks," Sembrouthes whispered upon seeing the display. "Flashy, but far too heavy to win in a distance race."

"Then why bother decorating their chariots with jewels?" Fulcaris asked.

Rosamund laughed, rolling her eyes. "Why do men do anything? To show that their spear is mightier than all others."

Though the Hippodrome remained one of the largest buildings known to the civilized world, its capacity was fully reserved the week prior to the initial race. Wealthier patrons had ordered slaves to cordon off seats in the more desirable sections, while less scrupulous members of Constantinople's underbelly auctioned off higher vantage points for heavily inflated prices. Though this fervor stirred the city's masses into greater excitement at the first races, it also drew resentment as another reminder of the Emperor's unwillingness to intercede on a desperate and unaffordable life in the capital.

Protected by the high walls of the Imperial Barracks, my men thought little of the rising protests, their bellies full from grain and wine from the Emperor's granaries and cuts of meat paid for from my own purse. God knows that several of those meals were traded for prostitutes or strong drink, nevertheless I preferred to believe that the men's ventures into Constantinople's evening chill were full of altruism and charity.

Perenus never joined those ventures, despite a clear desire to do so, preferring instead to take on additional practice circuits along the

Hippodrome until his legs bowed from exhaustion. He even eschewed the company of women at that time, save Rosamund, and only to see to the blisters that formed on his chafing hands and aching feet. The evening before the race, Perenus even abstained from rich meats, preferring lighter fare as he chatted idly at an empty barracks bench.

"Dreading this?" I asked, eyeing Perenus' peckish behavior.

"No," Perenus said unconvincingly. "It's just another shield wall. Besides, I used to be good at this sort of thing."

"Aye," I answered, "until you burned down half the city after winning."

"True, true!" Perenus laughed. "This time, if I win, I won't take it for granted. If this is to be my last race, I want to remember it forever and tell my children one day that I was a victor in the Hippodrome."

It was odd to hear Perenus, ever one prone to jokes, express sentimentality. "That's if you can find someone willing to bear your children!"

Perenus slapped the back of my head playfully, and we sat together for a time resharing the same stories that had been told countless times on the march. Cephalas joined in our melancholy vigil, his crippled arm shrouded in a sling underneath his cloak. As the sentry duty switched for the evening watch, Perenus insisted upon sleep and disappeared into the centurions' quarters that had been his makeshift home in Constantinople.

Absent the thousands of bodies it once held prior to our departure for Trapezous, the barracks echoed with an emptiness that somehow seemed unnerving, a reminder that the capital's defense rested entirely upon an overdressed city watch and a few hundred trained soldiers. All for a population of over one million souls who teemed with the dichotomy of excitement and hopelessness on the eve of the largest games since Constantine himself founded our capital, the cost of which was still untallied.

It was a price that Justinian, and all who followed him, would pay in blood.

THE DIVIDED PATH

The following morning, I awoke well after Mariya, who had already been attended to by a half dozen servants in a vain attempt to prepare for a public audience with the Empress. One burly woman wove strands of golden thread into Mariya's raven hair, which hung in thick curls between her shoulder blades. Another drew layers of kohl around Mariya's eyes and applied a thin powder to her face that gave her something of an aloof expression. Two others prepared the layers of thin silken robes that flowed in azure and gold, decorated with the sigil of the ouroboros that decorated our household banners.

She pursed her lips in a smile as I approached, gifting me a red kiss that smudged the red ochre along her mouth. The burly woman grimaced in frustration and reapplied the cosmetic, crowning her work with a rich golden clasp in Mariya's hair, shaped like a dragon similar to the one that decorated my neck and sat at the hilt of my sword.

After washing, I joined Mariya in preparing for our audience with Theodora. Cephalas helped tie together the overlapping plates of my excubitor's armor and offered a selection of weapons I had accumulated in my personal armory. Other than the sword of the late Emperor, I tied Aetius' dagger along my opposite hip, concealing its hilt and sheath inside the white cloak that all excubitores wore inside the Imperial capital.

Entrusting Zenobia with the nursemaids who also watched over Joannina for much of the day, Mariya and I slipped out of our palace rooms and navigated the labyrinth of halls that led to the Emperor's private box in the Hippodrome. As the dawn sun flooded its feeble winter warmth through the palace windows, we were quickly joined by Sembrouthes and a half dozen Aksumites, unarmed yet armored to discourage any hint of violence against their mistress. Rosamund, with a bemused Xerxes in tow, also joined as the host of my household. Samur and the rest of my foederati preferred the solace that came with an anonymous and nameless existence within the rows of stone benches that lined the Hippodrome stands in the thousands.

We were preceded only by Marcellus, his polished armor glittering against the dawning sun as he stood against the railing nearest the Hippodrome track. Removing his plumed helmet, Marcellus greeted Mariya and nodded to Sembrouthes before extending a hand to me in embrace, clutching tightly as I offered my own. A slave boy scurried from behind Marcellus to finalize duties of arranging furniture for the Emperor's box, and I caught a chipper wink from Agathias as he completed his task and snaked out of the room.

Though many years have passed since Justinian's games, I can still remember the roar of the Hippodrome's crowd. A sea of noise, percussive and rhythmic, as if the building were some mythic beast that hungered for countless teams of the Empire's most beloved chariot racers. With the first races nearing their start, camps of hundreds of Whites and Reds held crude banners supporting charioteers of their camps that sported names from one of the dozens of provinces that comprised Justinian's Empire. Smaller circles were bedecked with feathers and exotic animal skins and even a cavernous elephant skull, seemingly serving as the rare centers of support for racers from Persia, Frankia, and other provinces who held chariot racing as an ancient and beloved tradition as did the populace of Rome.

The overwhelming majority was swathed in various shades of

green and blue, their chants rising and falling like waves upon the shores of the Euxine Sea. Their colored banners bore the names of dozens of riding teams, and more than one bore the likeness of a favored horse.

As had been the case throughout my childhood, the Blues were dressed in finer silks and appeared plumper than their pockmarked and frail rivals in the Greens. Holding the more spacious seats and better viewing angles, the Blues congregated close to the track, sending servants and slaves to fetch refreshments or place bets. One larger mob of Blues congregated immediately opposite the Emperor's box, with no fewer than a hundred of the wealthier merchants and senators coalescing in a flowing mass of sapphire.

Marcellus pointed out that the mass was largely the responsibility of Hypatius, the eldest of old Anastasius' nephews and a onetime possible heir to the Imperial throne. Still wealthy despite the loss of Imperial patronage, Hypatius appeared to command a sizeable following, including Senator Nepotian and his sniveling son Solomon.

Despite their threadbare appearance, the Greens held dominance over all other parties, though few managed to secure the more ideal seats close to the sands or near the Emperor's box. Thousands of curious eyes fell upon our luxurious quarters, which included a violet canopy to shield the Emperor from excess sun or inclement weather.

"Do you not favor the games, Lord Marcellus?" Mariya inquired.

Marcellus shook his head. "They're an excubitor's nightmare. I'd rather charge at a wall of a thousand Immortals than deal with public games."

"Take care of your words, excubitor," Xerxes retorted, a smile creasing his manicured face.

Ignoring him, Marcellus turned back to Mariya. "But I see that you favor the Blues, my lady."

Mariya nodded, patting my chest with her lacquered nails. "My husband," she explained. "It would be quite a scandal if I sided against the Emperor, no?"

An aroma of freshly baked bread wafted through the morning chill, melding with the stench of stale sweat and animal dung. Agathias flitted along the edges of the Emperor's box bearing heavy lamps whose oil burned with scents of citrus and lavender, yet even this expensive measure did little more than mask the odor that the men pretended to ignore and the women blocked with silken rags. Instead, we chatted about the races, new laws drafted by Tribonian, or additional taxes levied by Paulus, all in an attempt to ignore the logistical nightmare of our looming war with the Vandals.

As the sun's orb rose fully above the horizon, a knock rang through the palace doorway, preceding the entry of a dozen other richly attired Romans and their retinue of servants. Other than a half dozen palace guards, the Empress Theodora held the arm of Liberius, both of whom held a knowing smirk on their faces as they crossed over their private entrance into the Hippodrome. Behind Theodora walked Antonina and Auria, who both assumed responsibility of handling the train of the Empress' ocean-blue dress as it glided over polished stone. The last two figures were more somberly dressed, including Narses in a muted gray cloak and Father Petrus in the raiment of a Catholic priest.

"Lord Varus!" Theodora called. "It's hard to think of you enjoying life's leisures."

Liberius snorted. "Varus? When he was ten, he'd pretend to have the pox so he could skip my lessons and play with toy soldiers."

Theodora beamed at my embarrassment.

"He'd even have rotten cherries ready to rub on his face if we were able to find him. Clever trick, that."

"I know nothing of the sort," I said, heat rushing to my cheeks.

Theodora offered a playful pat on my shoulder, her fingernails rapping against the strips of metal that all excubitores wore. Pearls danced along Theodora's headdress as she found the gold-encrusted seat that would serve as her throne, offering a wave to the crowd with that curious mixture of glee and reserve I had seen in other monarchs. Several near the Emperor's box applauded in a polite, muted tenor, only temporarily dulling the crowd's roar in anticipation of the first races.

"Shall we begin?" Theodora inquired, unfazed by her lukewarm welcome.

On Theodora's left, Liberius chuckled. "It is customary to name an editor, Empress," he said. "But I fear the crowd may not have ears for such proclamations."

"My thoughts exactly," she agreed. "Narses, perhaps you might give the signal for the initial races to commence? My husband is quite preoccupied and will make an appearance in the later championship bouts."

Jumping to his feet, Narses scuttled to the edge of the Emperor's box. Rolling a silken sleeve past a pudgy elbow, Narses raised a flag bearing the Emperor's eagle and waved it against the winter breeze that circled the Hippodrome's expanse. Horns blared at this sign. The crowd's thunder rose to a boil as a banda of city guards fanned out along the Hippodrome's walls. Dressed in white surcoats over polished ringmail, several had belts that strained under the weight of bulging guts, while others were likely far too old or inexperienced even to fill a position with the limitanei. Still, they provided a modicum of protection, as their honed spearpoints warned against unauthorized entry to the racing sands, which had always been a nuisance in major Hippodrome events.

No sooner had the last guard taken place along the Hippodrome's circuit than the first chariots burst into the circus, their riders assisted by attendants nudging the harnessed horses forward. Twelve teams rumbled onto the racing circuit and along the starting line, including a Persian, a Goth, two Reds and Whites apiece, and an equal number of Blues and Greens in the remainder.

Eager to demonstrate grandeur in the opening race, the Emperor's ministers had scheduled several recent champions in the early circuit, with their drivers decked in torques of gold, silver, and precious gems. One rider amongst the Blues even bore a burly fur coat that had been dyed a deep cobalt that was held together by sapphires the size of an eagle's egg. Easily mistaken for an emperor in his own right, the man raised a hand in salute as the crowd chanted his name, beaming a broad smile from a hairless head that had been tanned from the winter sun.

"That's Magnetius," Marcellus murmured into my ear. "He's dominated the major races for the past year and was granted an Imperial patronage after the Emperor received word of Dara."

"Patronage?" I asked. "He's that good?"

Marcellus bobbed his head side to side, indifferent. "I've only watched him once, before the Persian campaign. But I've seen few more skilled."

"Magnetius! Magnetius! Magnetius!" the crowd roared, the Greco-Latin name shortened to a single syllable in the throats of well over a hundred thousand. Others shouted "Nika! Nika! Nika!" the famed Roman victory cry.

On cue, Magnetius spurred his chariot before his peers, guiding the cart in a tight circle before returning to the race's starting position. Within moments, an attendant of the races signaled readiness back to the Imperial box. Narses raised the Imperial banner again, the hem of his sleeve flapping against the wind as the twelve teams gazed intently to Theodora's advisor and spymaster. Pausing for several heartbeats, Narses then brought the flag down with surprising force, leaving it hanging along the lower levels of the Hippodrome. Amidst a burgeoning flow of cheers as the teams surged along, Narses returned the flag to its rightful holster and scurried back behind the Empress, whispering into her ear.

Though the energy of the Hippodrome reverberated throughout the crowd unabated, that initial race left much to be desired. After shedding his accoutrement to a nearby slave, Magnetius kicked his chariot forward, driving his twin horses beyond those of the competition. Bedecked in a deep onyx without any sock or blemish, Magnetius' horses surged ahead a full cart length by their initial circuit around the Hippodrome, and five by the following. By the end of the race, Magnetius had even begun to ease off from his riding crop, trotting peacefully across the finish line a half circuit ahead of the nearest rider. Despite the lack of drama, the Blues rose in celebration at the success of their champion, roaring his name as he saluted in a lazy victory lap.

The pattern continued for the rest of the races. Despite the crowd's clamoring, that first day held little of note. Though each team required previous victories to gain entry to the racing lists, several had done so in the minor games of Epirus or Alexandria, where the quality of competition flowed like cheap wine. Several bouts contained serious collisions, with one unfortunate Red driver losing his balance as his chariot thundered over a dust-veiled stone at full gallop. The man's spine snapped like kindling, leaving him lifeless before the attendants could hear his final words.

Justinian did not appear that first day, nor the second or third. Led by Paulus, the Emperor's ministers had scheduled twelve days of games, honoring the apostles who had served our Savior five centuries prior. With quality of those first days so low, we often escaped back to the Palace, enjoying a respite from marathon planning sessions for the upcoming invasion of Africa or angling to free Belisarius from his lengthening house imprisonment.

Among the few events of interest was the murder of a wealthy businessman at the hands of two ardent, drunken members of the Hippodrome audience, cause unclear. Consisting of one Blue and one Green, both were quickly condemned to death by Tribonian's city guards, with angry protests falling upon deaf ears as the men were imprisoned until their visit to the city gallows could be noted in Procopius' ledger.

We paid little heed to such trivial matters, for our thoughts were captured by Perenus' anticipated return to the Hippodrome's track. Clad in coarse green wool, Perenus rested stiffly at the helm of his chariot, ignoring applause and recognition from those in the audience who remembered their onetime champion. Pitted against erstwhile contenders and those who held greater love amongst the crowds, Perenus offered a salute to the vacant Emperor's chair and surged to cross the initial flag.

"He looks strong but unconfident," Sembrouthes muttered. "Like a young champion's first time with a woman."

Mariya pretended to not hear the remark but stifled a smirk at the edges of her mouth. "He's been preparing day and night, and I have full confidence in him," she declared. "Even if he is a Green!"

Despite the insistent urging of the Greens in the Hippodrome's vast audience, however, Perenus lost. Of a dozen in his heat, Perenus finished third behind two jeweled veterans of the Blues, drawing the red-faced ire of Patroklus as he screamed his displeasure. Perenus' head bobbed as his chariot slowed, his hands clenched over the reins as his face etched into a scowl. The placement advanced Perenus into the championship bouts later that week, though that success did little to ease Perenus' fears regarding his return to the racing sands.

The races grew more competitive as the week progressed, with few upsets as favored champions edged their way to the top of the lists. Perenus performed far better in his next two bouts, including a victory over a previously retired Blues rider and a second-place finish in a particularly close heat, pushing Perenus' bid to meet those of the top twenty-four riders for the Emperor's tournament. Slated for the sixth and penultimate day of the games, Perenus was positioned against a Red, two Persians, and a half dozen Blues, and just two other Greens in their goal to achieve a slot in the championship race. Perenus merely nodded as the names were announced, showing no emotion as Magnetius was named the marquee rider on behalf of the Blues.

On the morning of the penultimate races, I left Mariya to fulfill my daily audience with Theodora, who had taken considerable interest in the army's training and refitting after its heavy losses in the east. Bedecked in my excubitor's armor, I was greeted by Theodora's guards, who waved me close.

"The Empress is attending Court with Justinian," one of the guardsmen said. "No explanation."

Thanking the guardsman, I headed to the Palace's lower levels, my nailed boots thudding against the marble floors. Their echo rang against the marble visages of long-dead emperors, their glories detailed on thin tablets at the base of their busts. Having dusted and polished their features on dozens of occasions throughout my youth, the features of each had become etched in my memory, with every fold of skin or twist of hair hiding stubborn veins of dirt that justified a caning for an unlucky palace slave.

On the final steps before the main palace floor, I jumped in surprise at one bust that stood apart from the rest. Recently rubbed to a smooth finish, the bust's features bore a man with thinning hair and piercing eyes, a look of distant melancholy lining a thin mouth and hollow cheeks.

"Justin would be upset that the sculptor captured his likeness as an old man," the frail voice of Father Petrus called from twenty paces away. "But it's a fair memory of the man, even if they didn't quite capture the eyes."

"He would have loathed this statue," I replied, recalling my former master's aloofness.

"Justin often warned that history only remembers the great emperors," Petrus continued. "Conquerors, tyrants, visionaries, and fools. He often told me that it is better to not be remembered at all, or for more deserving subordinates to claim victories under his rule. How will history remember Justin, I wonder?"

"As a good man," I concluded, "and the spark that reignited Roman valor."

Father Petrus shook his head. "Perhaps, but perhaps not. The answer depends upon Justinian, who has all the makings of a great man in his own way."

Shrugging, I turned to him. "What brings you to the Palace this morning?"

"Other than to see an excubitor inconstant with his prayers?" Father Petrus asked rhetorically. "I need to see Liberius and Basilius about a private matter. Perhaps you will allow me to accompany you into the Emperor's Court?"

His paper-thin skin flexed over an outstretched hand, which I took, and guided the priest toward the looming doorway to the Great Hall, guarded by two other excubitores. My brethren permitted my entry, triggering the thick bronze lock, and the door cracked open to unveil a veneer of incense and flickering light. I helped the priest over a low wooden step as we entered the Emperor's presence. As predicted, we were far from alone.

"My lord, I recommend the races be postponed until further notice," Marcellus said, his armor catching the light of a hundred tapers as he held his plumed helmet at his side.

Justinian scowled. "Marcellus, I understand and respect your fears, but to take such drastic action would be seen as unacceptable weakness. Surely doubling the city guard would cease any rumblings from the plebs."

Marcellus bobbed his head deferentially but returned his gaze to the Emperor's. "Highness, the recent arrests and threats of hanging have brought Constantinople to a boil. It may not seem so dire, but all that prevents another riot is its lack of a leader. Stop these races now, before this anger ignites into something we are incapable of stamping out."

Justinian sighed, running a hand through his bushy hair and along the golden circlet of his diadem. He shot a look to Theodora, pausing a moment as she narrowed her features in consternation. At last, motioning in disagreement, Justinian rose from his throne. Marcellus fell to his knees.

"An emperor cannot appear fearful of stories and shadows," Justinian declared. "How can I take Africa from the Vandals if I'm afraid to walk my own city streets? Marcellus, do what you must to keep the peace, but these games of celebration shall continue."

Awkward in his armor, Marcellus rose to his feet and bowed low. A flock of ministers scuttled behind Justinian, with Paulus swishing his silken robes as he emerged at the Emperor's ear. Justinian nodded in recognition and waved Paulus aside as he returned his attentions to the petitioner.

"You may leave, Marcellus," the Emperor declared. "You have your orders. See to it that my grateful people remain tranquil in their celebrations of our Empire's recent successes."

Marcellus bowed once again, his movements crisp and halting. Retreating several steps, the excubitor eventually turned his feet and filed through the door, either not recognizing me or ignoring my presence as he moved out into the hallway. Justinian returned to his throne and waved a courtier into his presence, who heralded the next petitioner as Lord Basilius Venantius. Theodora pursed her lips in a friendly smile as the name was announced, leaving Justinian to permit the entry of a further supplicant.

Basilius limped forward, his skeletal frame somewhat bereft of the superior airs that the old minister and consul was famous for in his service to Anastasius and Justin. Basilius grimaced at every other pace but refused the assistance of any palace slave. Despite his stiff joints, he reached the feet of the monarchs and offered a crooked bow, a strand of his nearly absent hair sweeping across his face as his spotted pate came level with the richly carpeted floor.

"Rise, good Basilius," Theodora boomed. "What have you come to present before the Emperor?"

"Opportunity, dear Empress," Basilius replied. "An opportunity many thought we would never see again in the Eastern Empire."

Justinian's eyebrow rose in muted interest. "I've never known you to mince words, Lord Basilius. Speak your meaning."

"All in this Court remember the death of the accursed Theodoric, who united the hundreds of Gothic tribes from Hispania to Illyria," Basilius said, his words slow and deliberate as he boomed each syllable. "His passing has driven a rift between the Visigoths in Hispania and the Ostrogoths in Italy once more."

Frowning at Basilius, Tribonian whispered into the Emperor's ear. "I'm well aware of the discord amongst the Goths," Justinian declared, "but perhaps you have some news to share?"

"Indeed, Highness." Basilius bowed. "My spies inform me that Amalric, Theodoric's grandson in Hispania, sees few supplicants or even his teachers. Amalric's reagent, a onetime sword bearer for Theodoric named Theudis, speaks for the Visigothic throne."

Paulus snorted, his features curled in disdain until the Empress shot him an angry glance. "We can assume that Theudis will use the lad as his puppet," Theodora concluded. "A tragedy for one so young, but a gain for Rome if the Visigoths are no longer collaborating with their cousins in Italy."

"Indeed, Empress," Basilius agreed. "What's more, the Ostrogothic nobles have rejected the regency of Amalasuntha, mother another of Theodoric's grandsons named Athalaric. That boy-king was taken by a council of Gothic nobles, leaving Amalasuntha powerless."

"But not without friends," Justinian interjected. "Amalasuntha has given her word to root out the Arian heresy in Italy, and to protect Roman citizens under Athalaric's control."

Basilius flashed a rare smile. "Yes, Emperor. But whether the Gothic queen is able to keep her word, who can say? Tragedies befall powerless queens with alarming regularity in the barbarian world."

Not offering a retort, Justinian considered Basilius' information. In truth, I doubt that much of his words were news to the Emperor, who was a voracious reader and pored over the thousands of reports from spies and provincial governors alike. Leaning forward, the Emperor raised an elbow to the arm of his throne, using his thumb and forefinger to scratch at the hollow, hairless chin that rolled into a light cleft.

"I thank you for your information, Lord Basilius, but I already have one war to win in Africa against an enemy that the Empire has never defeated," he declared. "Why should I commit scarce gold and men to plan for another in a distant Hispania or an Italy teeming with millions of Ostrogoths, all who despise the Empire and its traditions?"

Basilius lowered his head, keeping his features impassive. "Because, my emperor, this is the opportunity that many emperors before you have longed to seize." His voice was hardly more than a murmur, yet conversations around the hall faded in rapt attention.

"It was a great dream of my youth, and that of your predecessor, the Emperor Justin, that Rome's east and west should once again be reunited. One land, one religion, one emperor."

Basilius' final words stirred the few in attendance. The excubitores on duty beat their spear butts against the marble tile to call for silence. Amidst the din, Justinian leaned toward Theodora, her features framed by a bemused look as her eyes narrowed with a thin smile. She whispered into her husband's ear, and Justinian nodded and returned to a stiff, dignified seating position.

"As you say, Lord Basilius, the opportunity is a tempting one. Yet the Ostrogoths are presently my friends, and the Vandals are more than enough of a challenge for the time being than to assemble an expedition to Hispania against Theudis," Justinian declared, pausing as he glanced through the hall. "However, your counsel is always welcome. If the situation were to change, how might the Empire best seize my beloved uncle's dream of a united empire?"

Basilius bobbed his head again at the compliment, straightening his thick robes. He seemed to shiver against a light draft that flooded into the hall, and Narses signaled for a half dozen slaves to light braziers along the hall's columns. Basilius remained unperturbed by the interruption, his brow furrowed as he answered the Emperor.

"Free General Belisarius and give him command of all Imperial armies. Any other will repeat the failures of Basiliscus... or worse," Basilius declared, sending up another round of excited chatter amongst the few in attendance.

Justinian absorbed Basilius' request with reserved silence, leaning back into his throne as Tribonian and Paulus alike rushed to the Emperor's ear. Furious, Hermogenes addressed the charge, a vein pulsing from his temple.

"Belisarius was relieved of command for multiple failures in the east, and you would have the Emperor give him even more authority?" Hermogenes balked. "In the days of the Republic, that kind of man would be asked to fall upon his sword, not enjoy further glories."

Basilius did not wait for the Emperor's permission to speak, his mouth breaking into a grin. "We are no longer in the days of the Republic, Hermogenes."

Hermogenes scowled. "Without my leadership, our eastern armies would be buried in the Mesopotamian sand instead of enjoying the fruits of hard-won peace. I tell you now, it is unwise to tempt fate once more."

"And we thank you for your service, even though it ended the moment you stepped foot in Constantinople," Basilius answered, "and I have consistently denounced those who whispered of your role in destabilizing our army and forcing losses in Thannuris and Callinicum. We owe you much for your heroics at our outpost in Dara."

Hermogenes' face purpled in rage. "Your son-in-law will not return to command, Basilius! The Empire is not a plaything for you and your cabal to manipulate to your whims!"

"Enough," Justinian commanded, raising a hand for silence. "I have heard councilor Basilius' words and will consider their import. For now, preparations for Africa remain the priority of this government."

Basilius bowed low, a hand clutching his thigh for support. Hermogenes did the same, returning to the shadows behind the Emperor's throne and grumbling to Paulus and Tribonian. Dismissed, Basilius departed from the Emperor's presence, taking Father Petrus' arm before leaving the hall. Before the next petition was announced, Marcellus waved for my attention and gestured for me to follow Basilius' exit.

Leaving through the heavy oaken door, I trailed Marcellus to a distant corner from the hall doorway. The excubitor commander's face was pale, and his lip trembling, but he shrugged off any concern.

"Just a winter sickness, as any other," he said.

I nodded, changing the subject. "You have particular reasons to fear unrest?"

"I always do," he answered. "It's always there, just behind every hooded face that walks the cluttered streets of Constantinople. Only this time, there are far too many to keep the troublemakers separated from the less reckless."

"I remember the riots before leaving for Cherson, and in Justin's games before that," I replied. "They were terrible, but not a major threat to the Emperor. Moreso to the moneylenders and food mongers."

"For now," Marcellus said, "just keep your mind sober and sword sharp in case you are wrong."

And I was. God in heaven, was I wrong.

FOOD FOR THE GODS

As the Emperor's Court ceased for the day's business, Theodora emerged with her retinue of guards and ladies. Notable among them was Antonina, her face flushed from the excitement of her father's request to Justinian, gripping Auria's veiled forearm for support. Theodora beckoned as she met my gaze, smiling as she slipped her hand around my arm.

"The Emperor will join us shortly," she explained cheerily, "but that should not stop us from enjoying the day's games! Right, ladies?"

Auria fluttered in agreement as the others offered their praise for the Empress. Unfazed, Theodora strode up the marble steps to the Emperor's private box in the Hippodrome, her delicate fingers grazing the marble busts of a half dozen emperors from the distant past.

Even before unbuckling the door into the Hippodrome, a crush of noise battered against the door's rust-speckled hinges. An attendant unlocked and opened that portal, showering Theodora and me with an overwhelming sensation of humanity that thronged the Hippodrome's sands.

Several others had already assembled in wait of the Emperor and Empress, including Mariya, Liberius, Rosamund, Troglita, and a number of unarmed Aksumite guardsmen. As with prior racing days, Agathias skipped along the outskirts of the box, lighting incense and fragrant herbs to ward off the rising stench of shit and cooking meat. Though many others clenched perfumed silks over their faces, Theodora remained open to the people, radiant in triumph as she waved to the ravenous hunger of the masses.

"It's about time," Mariya whispered into my ear as she tugged me away from the Empress' grasp.

I grinned. "Miss me?"

"Always," Mariya replied, planting a kiss on my cheek, "but don't press your luck any further!"

Antonina rolled her eyes at our affection but remained silent as Theodora nodded in welcome to my wife. "Shall we begin?" the Empress said, a command more than a request.

On Theodora's signal, fifty trumpets thundered angrily against the crowd's energy, their sharp notes carrying above the din and throughout the circus. Though many hissed against the Imperial sigil, most cheered wildly as the charioteers of the semifinal circuit took to the sands, each trailed by a number of servants and slaves that hoisted colorful banners. Magnetius' retinue outstripped the others by a significant margin, and even included a number of slave women who threw loaves of bread into the grasping fingers of the audience.

Perenus followed soon thereafter, his ear cocked toward Patroklus' grizzled form. The riding instructor screamed to be heard over the swirling noise, yet Perenus nodded in comprehension as he took Patroklus' forearm into his own as a sign of acknowledgment. Each of the dozen riders performed a slow circuit around the Hippodrome, waving to the crowds and flexing stiff limbs as their horses plodded along. Magnetius' name echoed within tens of thousands of throats, and the champion returned their love with a toothy grin and a broad salute to the heavens.

"The Blues seem favored this day," Theodora remarked, bringing a half dozen attendants bobbing like string puppets.

"A positive omen for the Emperor," I replied, keeping to myself that positive omens for the Emperor were to the detriment of Perenus and his lonely Green companions.

One after another, the twelve charioteers formed a line and faced the Imperial box. Several threw flowers onto the Hippodrome track, which in the dull gray of winter were little more than withered poppies. Their faded pink and reddish hues mixed with the soiled sands and were quickly scooped up by attendant slaves, fearful that the horses might swallow the flower and succumb to its tranquilizing medicinal properties.

As the crowd's fervor for Magnetius grew to another deafening crescendo, the army of trumpets croaked again in a march that signaled the arrival of the Emperor. Within moments, the door to the Imperial box swung open, permitting Justinian and a number of ministers and excubitores to file into the confined space. The Emperor shaded his eyes from the treacherous winter sun as young slaves drew up cushioned benches for the ministers, with most eschewing the frocked Cassiodorus as the expensively draped priest carried his girth onto the balcony.

While the chanting for Magnetius continued unabated above the brass, a number of disgruntled voices speared through the din. "Justice!" one cried, and "Mercy!" came from several others, producing a befuddled look on Justinian's face.

"What do they want?" he asked Tribonian.

"To free the imprisoned arsonists and looters from both factions," Tribonian declared, secretly signaling to several palace guards to silence the interlopers. "A minor thing, Highness, and one soon forgotten."

"Hmph," Justinian responded, his eyes narrowing. He straightened the diadem perched atop his hair.

Tribonian's guardsmen slipped into the crowd and conducted their brutish business, though such measures did little to cease the discontent amongst those nearest the Emperor's box. Several picked up the cry for the Emperor's mercy, their causes diverging into topics of crippling taxes or increasing lawlessness and gang violence in Constantinople's streets. Outstretched hands reached toward Justinian as if he were a god onto himself, supplicating for relief that only Justinian had the power to provide.

However, Justinian ignored their pleas. "Commence the games," he ordered Paulus, who bowed and moved to the frontmost edge of the enclosed balcony.

"Citizens of the Empire!" Paulus began in Latin, screaming to be heard. "In his gracious generosity, the Emperor Justinian has—"

Yet Paulus could continue no further, as a chorus of boos pelted him. His shoulders drooped, his words inaudible as Romans screamed indignities at the jeweled figure.

Theodora summoned me again to her side. "Tell Paulus to speak Greek; the people can't understand him," she ordered, her face stern and eyes darting in multiple directions.

Throwing a diminutive salute, I shifted toward Paulus and offered the instruction. He ignored my words at first, his nose curling in a barely perceptible scowl as I interrupted his hallowed status as editor of the Emperor's Games. When he did acknowledge my presence, he turned completely from the dais, shaking his head in disgust.

"Send Cassiodorus," he muttered, waving for the gold-layered priest to take his place.

The crowd muted itself as the bearded priest held a cross into the sky, his combed beard brushing against golden silks that glittered in the sunlight. Cassiodorus attempted a prayer, calling upon God's blessings to Justinian and the Empire as they paid glory to the Father and Son through these games. Many in the audience dutifully turned their heads to the floor as Cassiodorus invoked the Savior of the world, yet many still shouted for Justinian's assistance for their plights. More than a few even began slur the Emperor's name, although these voices were soon silenced as Tribonian's handpicked men of the city watch sought out any sign of dissent.

Cassiodorus continued undeterred, his crackling tenor easily swept aside by a frustrated audience. The silken priest raised another arm to the heavens as he began another prayer, only to be smacked in the nose by a maggot-riddled tomato.

Off balance, Cassiodorus slipped backward, his hands grasping at air as he fell to the ground. His protruding gut connected with the carpet first, which softened the descent, though Cassiodorus wailed in pain as two slaves rushed to his side. A single maggot wriggled from the depths of the blackened tomato, burying itself in Cassiodorus' beard and leaving the red juices to stain an ornately decorated woolen rug.

Other than dispatching additional guardsmen to take the offenders into custody, Justinian took no revenge against the slight. "Tell them to begin," the Emperor said in a stern voice, although his left eye twitched slightly, and he ground a fist into a wooden armrest on his throne.

Mouth agape, Paulus made motions to argue, but demurred to Justinian's wishes and signaled for the trumpets to sound again. In a moment, much of the crowd's anger was diverted back to the racing sands as each of the twelve charioteers saluted the Emperor, who returned their gesture in kind. The formalities observed, the teams were dismissed to return to the starting line as teams of slaves brushed the disturbed track and removed debris that could easily crack a wheel or split a hoof.

Veins pulsing from his neck, Patroklus' pockmarked face turned an unhealthy shade of garnet, and the diminutive trainer came to resemble an unappetizing cherry. His words were inaudible in the hundred paces or so that separated the Emperor's box from the line of chariots, although Perenus seemed to appreciate the encouragement, as he released one hand from the reins and gripped tightly onto Patroklus' gnarled fist. Within heartbeats, Patroklus darted back to the distant Hippodrome walls with the other trainers and servants, leaving the dozen racing champions standing alone in the baskets of their chariots.

Not to be denied some note of glory in the proceedings, Paulus took the Imperial banner into his arm. Its golden eagle crumpled in the minister's grasp, the violet hues turning a shade of blue-black in the sunlight. Each of the twelve riders strained to follow Paulus' movements as he raised the banner high into the air, dangling it in the sweeping breeze and threatening to billow onto the heads of those below. His back arched and chin protruding, Paulus basked in the moment with a grin, then finally let the flag fall.

"Go!" shouted Rosamund excitedly, her voice melding with thousands of others as the charioteers lurched forward.

Startled by the noise, Narses shot my Gepid servant a sour look. "Surely your favorite cannot hear you from here."

"Oh, hush, Narses," Theodora said. "If the races aren't meant for fun, why do we take on such an expense at all?"

"Too true," Justinian murmured, although his face remained melancholy. The Empress patted her husband's jeweled hand.

Swirling dust clouds curled into the air as the horses fought against their harnesses. Though the ordered position of each charioteer had been randomly assigned prior to the race's beginning, within a half circuit, each of the respective cliques had separated into more cohesive units, with smaller clumps of Persians and Greens riding further back as well as a larger mass of Blues in the center. The lone Red rider whipped his crop forward, pelting his nearest horse as his chariot shot far into the lead ahead of the larger pack.

"He's pushing too hard, too fast," Sembrouthes said. "Foolish or worried."

"Or both," Mariya replied tactfully. "And why not, to be out there alone?"

"At least Perenus has two friends out there," Rosamund added in a low voice.

True to Sembrouthes' words, the Red rider held a lead only until the close of the initial circuit, which was the first of ten. Slick spittle caking his horses' mouths, the Red cracked hard at the whip, yet could only look on in futility as the half dozen Blues surrounded his chariot on all sides. Alone, the Red tried to veer to one side and break out of their grip but found himself further enclosed in a tightening noose.

Dust veiled the chaos that ensued, but within moments, the Red rider was seen vaulting from his chariot, which skipped harmlessly away as its horses continued to pull astride the Hippodrome walls at a more leisurely pace. A slave rushed to the prostrate body of the Red rider, who was nearly trampled by Perenus' horses, and the man stirred weakly as he was lifted by the shoulders and dragged to safety. The few Reds in attendance groaned and complained, while cheers for Magnetius grew all the more fevered.

A half circuit later, one of the Blues raised a hand and tore away from his pack. The Blue gestured angrily at one of his chariot wheels, which I could see had splintered even from a great distance.

"Do you think he's responsible for downing that Red?" Antonina asked with a frown.

"Likely," Theodora responded, "and it cost him the race. He's disqualified for exiting the track."

Disappearing into a long tunnel, the rider yelled angrily as his chariot was guided to an exit. Perenus' head turned momentarily to follow the departure of two of his competitors, then quickly snapped back at attention as the three Greens bore down on the leading Blues. Cheering them on from the more distant seats, a cacophony of noise rained down from the Greens in the audience, with Perenus' name rising just above the fray.

With the chants as a warning, Magnetius raised a hand into the air and turned his gloved hand in a tight circle. On cue, the four other Blues pulled back on their reins, slowing the gallop of their horses and allowing their chariots to slink back near those of the Greens. Anticipating the maneuver, many in the audience booed their disapproval, their Green cloaks and scarves flailing into the air with indignity.

Magnetius closed his hand into a fist, signaling at two of the Blues charioteers, who began their next movement. One bearded Greek steered his chariot left, its wheel spokes slamming into those of a Green rider with a sickening thud that nearly threw its rider to the ground. Likewise, a Sicilian Blue jerked his horses violently right, connecting squarely with another Green rider's mounts in a spray of sweat and pain. Near the center of the Green formation, Perenus narrowly avoided the collision by urging his horses forward, his rear wheel grazing the leg of a gelding that screamed as he toppled over.

Even amongst the deafening noise, we could hear the snap of the horse's foreleg. Bone pierced horseflesh as its leg bent at an impossible angle, the beast screaming as the pressure of the invading chariot pressed against its body. The wounded gelding fought to stay upright but soon succumbed to the inevitable, rolling onto its haunches and lifting the chariot basket into the air. Its rider did not even have a moment to scream as he was catapulted into the air, momentum pulverizing his face against a stone wall at a narrow portion of the track. Blood misted into the air as the half-crushed body twitched heedlessly, its features distorted into a macabre nightmare.

"Dirty," Xerxes muttered.

"Tactical," Narses corrected. "The best way to use one's numerical advantage is to take even losses."

"Cowardly, then," Xerxes countered, and scowled when Narses kept his silence.

Though not falling to the same fate as his victim, the offending Sicilian did suffer a wheel that splintered and cracked from the assault. Cursing the inevitable, the Blue jumped free of the chariot and sprinted to the safety of a nearby wall, watching as his cart bounced and skidded, inadvertently causing further damage as an unsuspecting Persian driver collided with the riderless cart, slamming his face violently into the rear of his right horse.

Perenus turned his head back to find one comrade missing and another flailing for control of the reins. His chariot slowed to a crawl as the Green tore away from his Greek attacker. An irate Green in the audience hurled a stone toward the bearded Blue, cracking the man's exposed forehead as his chariot slowed from untangling with its victim and sending him crumpling to the sands in a lifeless heap.

Paulus snarled with rage. Wasting no time, Tribonian dispatched a full ten to arrest the offender and his accomplices, ordering the dekarchos to use force if necessary.

"Is it always this violent in these games?" Mariya asked, her face drained of color.

"Not this bad," I admitted. "This is far worse than any I've seen."

The furious ride continued as the six remaining charioteers struggled to free themselves from the dust and debris of the various collisions. Green supporters continued to jeer at the display of the Blues, with one raving peasant jumping onto the track and sprinting by the inattentive guard of the city watch. Sopping wine dripped down the man's once-white tunic as he charged at another of the Blues, reaching out a hand to grab the halter of a speeding Blue's right-side horse. The Blue rider snapped a whip at the man's arm, its leather thong trapping itself under the drunkard's armpit and driving the rider from his chariot. The drunkard wailed in pain as his arm popped out of its socket and did not resist as the city watch hauled him from the sands and into a hidden tunnel along the stadium's side. The Greens in the crowd cheered as the drunkard fell from view, with many laughing as the dismounted Blue rider sprinted, failing to catch his rumbling chariot.

"You see that, Justinian?" a nasally Greek voice called from a nearby seat. "We won't stand for the antics of you or your fucking men!"

The Emperor snapped his head to the origin of the insult, his eyes wide and wild. "Who said that?"

"He will regret such affrontery, Highness," Tribonian swore, sending off a just-returned detachment of guards to arrest the offender. It should have been a simple and expeditious assignment, yet as the charioteers rounded the halfway marker of the race, the guards had not returned.

Thus, Tribonian dispatched another detachment of five to assist with the arrest, charging an Armenian excubitor named Chanaranges with responsibility of leadership. The Armenian nodded to Marcellus and me and saluted before raising his shield and leading the guardsmen of the city watch out of the Emperor's box and through a hidden entrance into the Hippodrome's marble benches. Justinian visibly relaxed as Chanaranges left for his duty, ignoring a swelling anger from the populace as Perenus rolled ever closer to Magnetius and the Blue compatriots flanking him.

Shortly after the completion of the seventh circuit, Magnetius again stole a glance behind, finding Perenus trailing by a mere chariot length and the remaining Persian rider flagging far behind. As before, the Blue champion raised a hand into the air and gave his gloved fingers a broad swirl, signaling immediate action from the other two Blue riders. Drawing back on the reins, the twin chariots moved to flank Perenus, their platforms coming parallel to his. Patroklus roared a warning at the assault as a hundred thousand Romans gaped.

But Perenus had anticipated the threat well in advance. He yanked at the reins, slowing his horses to a trot. Before the Blues galloped beyond their prey, Perenus unfurled his whip and lashed at the left attacker, its studded tip twisting around the Blue rider's arm. With a twitch of the whip, Perenus sent the would-be attacker spiraling to the dust, leaving his chariot to career into his would-be ally. The riderless chariot pushed its partner against the stone walls of the Hippodrome, grinding its spokes to a useless pulp and sending its horses crashing into a centuries-old statue of Mars the War-giver. Perenus urged his mounts back into a sprint, desperate to regain ground that Magnetius had taken to move further into the lead.

As Greens cheered wildly and the Blues chanted Magnetius' praises at the start of the eighth circuit, Chanaranges burst into the Emperor's box. Marcellus and I drew our swords in surprise, initially not recognizing the panting and blood-soaked figure, then soon rushed to the Armenian's side as he collapsed into an empty bench.

"What happened?" Marcellus growled, shaking the man.

"The crowd..." Chanaranges rasped. "Knives, cudgels, all dead."

Just two paces from my position, the Emperor drew back in horror, his eyes glued to the blood pooling ever closer to his slippered feet. He leaned forward on his throne, as though to escape back into the Palace, until Theodora broke his trance with a light graze of her fingertips over his hand. His brow furrowed, Liberius shuffled close to the Empress and murmured into her ear, earning a nod of approval.

"Dearest, it's just blood," Theodora whispered to Justinian. "Stay with me, and let your people see how strong a Caesar you are."

Reluctantly Justinian nodded and raised a foot away from the congealing mass. Chanaranges insisted that his wounds were relatively minor, gesturing to small rents in his excubitor's armor that blunted the force of a half dozen weapons. I patted Mariya's arm as I rose to meet Marcellus inside the palace entrance, finding the scarred commander's face riddled with worry.

"We need to get the Emperor out of there," Marcellus urged. "While we still can."

I shook my head. "Theodora won't allow it."

"Damn Theodora!" Marcellus cursed in a hushed voice. "This is no game. Constantinople is ready to explode, and it won't stop until Justinian's blood quenches the flames."

Sighing, I considered Marcellus' words. "Two more circuits," I reasoned. "Then we can put the Emperor on a ship and sail for Thessaloniki—or Corinth, even. Justinian saves face and leaves the city for a much-needed respite while tensions ease in Constantinople."

Marcellus scowled but relented. "Fine. But the moment this race is over, the Emperor is leaving—with or without Theodora."

I nodded, taking what victory I could. Marcellus and I returned to the Emperor's box as Chanaranges was carried off by two city guardsmen, a thin trail of blood squelching in his cowhide boots. Most of the Emperor's retinue pretended not to notice; only Antonina slid heavily into her chair, nearly fainting away. Agathias fetched a pitcher of cool water and shavings of precious ice that Auria placed gently near Antonina's mouth, cooing as Basilius' daughter sipped at the cool liquid.

Down in the thick of it all, Perenus bellowed for his horses to push harder in the final stretch. Magnetius did the same, but he lacked the men to block Perenus' approach. He was further impeded by the growing frequency of rotten vegetables and moldy crusts of bread that rained onto the Hippodrome track, including a soiled batch of lettuce that exploded into gray-black mush all over his shoulder.

Members of the Blues and Greens broke into a hundred minor brawls along the Hippodrome track, with one rising conflagration near Hypatius gathering as two armored city guardsmen jabbed knives into the ribs of an offending Blue spectator. Members of the Blues and Greens alike swarmed the guards, their bodies disappearing in the swarming mass. Justinian's wide eyes followed each bout of violence as the riders entered their final circuit, with sounds of hatred matching cheers for Magnetius and Perenus in intensity.

Perenus drew within a quarter length of Magnetius as the champion of the Blues slashed his whip at the exposed noses and gaping mouths of Perenus' horses. Though quickly covered by white foam, the whip left angry welts on their horseflesh. One of Perenus' mounts veered away from the offending sting. Perenus banked hard into Magnetius' basket in defiance of the horse's pain, raising a sheathed forearm as Magnetius turned his weapon onto Perenus himself. As the two chariots began their turn of the first quarter circuit, they stood in a dead heat with one another, although Magnetius jealously guarded the shorter interior of the track.

Both men tugged hard at their reigns, ignoring the horses' pants of exhaustion as a final sprint loomed ahead. Magnetius turned against Perenus once more, raising his whip against Perenus' leather-capped head. Patroklus screamed in rage at the display, his words fanning the flames of the crowd as the two champions vied to complete the Hippodrome's gauntlet.

As Magnetius' elbow raised in attack, Perenus jabbed with his own riding crop, driving the leather into the Blue's throat. Magnetius sagged but kept his balance atop the chariot as he fought for air, eventually rising to his feet as the half-circuit marker flitted by. Now standing and enraged, Magnetius banked his chariot hard into Perenus', bouncing off the spokes with a dangerous crack.

Despite the warning of their impending mutual disaster, Magnetius screamed defiance as he banked again into Perenus, who had no time to maneuver away from the assault. More detritus flew from the stands as the champions grappled in their dance, hurtling at full gallop to the final turn on the Hippodrome track. One of Perenus' wheels buckled and bent from the attack, while Magnetius' chariot began to list wildly from side to side. The two chariots remained tangled as Perenus fought desperately to free himself from Magnetius' grasp, one eye placed firmly on the nearing finish line before the Emperor's box.

As the damaged chariots slowed from an all-out gallop to a fast trot, Magnetius' axle burst at last from the abuse, dropping its basket into the sands and sending its champion tumbling to the ground. Perenus' own cart tore free and careened sideways, leaving the Green champion screaming in victory for a glorious moment.

Until Perenus raised his head and saw doom approaching him.

For the Persian cart continued unabated and bore down on the turn.

His view blocked by dust from Magnetius' attack, the Persian came within finger lengths of colliding into Magnetius' wreck, whooping as he cleared the debris. The Persian had no time to see Perenus' cart fighting to right itself, sending the Persian's horses into Perenus' team.

A spray of blood and splinters painted the Hippodrome track just twenty paces from the Emperor's throne. The Hippodrome's sands swirled into a hundred minor cyclones, then a vast plume arose, shielding the crowd from the worst of the wreck, its mangled bodies and pulverized wood. For a heartbeat, the world drew eerily silent as my heart pounded against the walls of my chest. All the Hippodrome fixed upon the plume of dust, a sensation of utter wrongness rippling through the benches.

Rosamund screamed in horror, breaking the trance. "No!" she yelled, brushing past our silk-and-jewel-clad retinue to lean over the frontmost railing of the box. Without thinking, I followed her example, grinding my fists into the gold-lacquered wood as I sought any sign of movement in the wreckage.

"Where is he?" I screamed. "Find Perenus!"

But I knew the answer. As the Hippodrome dust thinned, the crumpled heap of the chariots formed a grisly sight of splintered wood and gore, with limbs of horses and men strewn about. "God!" I screamed. "Perenus..."

A projectile blurred into the Emperor's box, revealed as a stone as it clattered against the nearby wall.

"No time!" Marcellus yelled. "At attention, Varus! We need to evacuate!"

Incensed by blood, what restraint had limited the crowd's resentment evaporated in an instant. Younger partisans of the Greens and Blues alike rushed onto the Hippodrome track, overwhelming the guardsmen of the city watch as they crowded around the three-chariot wreckage. Several guardsmen attempted to restore order by driving more hesitant Blues supporters back to their seats, yet the efforts were short-lived as the press of humanity drove the thinly armored and poorly trained security forces ever backward. Their discipline vanished in moments as several guardsmen backed away and ran for any openings available, with several throwing down the spears and shields that encumbered their escape.

"Go! Now!" Troglita yelled, his call echoed by Marcellus and Sembrouthes alike. For his part, Troglita snatched Auria by the elbow and directed her back into the Palace, and the Mauri princess skipped to safety without further complaint. Guarded by the Aksumites, Antonina and Mariya led the other ladies inside. Mariya stole a glance back to me, her kohl-lined eyes wide with fear.

"Get Zenobia, and stay with Sembrouthes and Wazeba!" I yelled to her. "I'll be right behind you!"

"Varus..." Mariya replied hesitantly, pausing before entering the Palace.

"I'll take her," Rosamund said, breaking through any standstill. In one swift movement, she grabbed the priceless dagger that had been gifted to me by the late General Godilas and slid the sheathed blade into her own blackened leather belt, securing it with a loop of cloth.

"Just in case," she explained. Then she grabbed Mariya by the hand and pulled hard toward the Palace. Mariya followed, reluctant, as Wazeba and a half dozen Aksumites formed a barrier around Theodora's ladies, leaving Sembrouthes and another detachment of the elite spearmen to retrieve Zenobia from the apartments above. Temporarily satisfied of their safety, I turned my attention back to the Hippodrome, a painful knot forming in my throat as I squinted for any sign of Perenus in the swirling maw of the mob. There was no sign of Perenus, Magnetius, or any other charioteer as more reckless members of the riled mass toppled statues and attacked the few remaining guardsmen, using those newfound weapons to attack vendors of precious fruits and bread.

"Marcellus, get me out of here!" Justinian yelled.

Liberius rose in anger, towering over the seated Emperor.

"Justinian, if you do not restore order now, it will mean the end of everything we've worked for!"

Justinian glanced at the masses, which began to turn its attentions to the Emperor's box as a dozen Green youths scaled the Hippodrome stands. Paulus and Tribonian stared at Justinian with pleading eyes, while Xerxes smirked in curious interest. Shaking his head, Justinian surrendered to the disorder.

"Retreat to the Palace and barricade the doors," he ordered. "That is a command, Marcellus!"

Ignoring Liberius' frustration, Marcellus summoned a dozen excubitores and led Justinian and his ministers into the safety of the Palace. As with Magnetius, a barrage of rotten vegetables flew into the Emperor's box, striking several ministers and staining multiple cloaks and gowns. Cassiodorus was again hit by a blackened apple, while Hermogenes was splashed with a pungent vinegar that made the other ministers gag.

Theodora alone remained seated. "Can we not restore order?"

I shook my head, struggling to imitate her calm as my friend's sudden and violent death replayed in my mind. "No, Highness," I answered, eyeing the palace door as Tribonian slipped inside, the last of the Emperor's retinue to seek safety. "It's time to leave the Hippodrome."

A heavy stone crashed onto the floor, shattering into multiple shards as it slammed against the polished surface. Theodora jumped in surprise and searched furiously for her attacker, accidentally elbowing Xerxes as she twisted left and right. Unable to identify the culprit from a dozen Blues and Greens climbing slowly to the box, she nodded.

Drawing his shield, Troglita joined me as I used what bulwark I could to protect Theodora's body from a rising hail of missiles and filth. The Empress initially sought to brush her gown but quickly changed her mind as I gently shoved her through the door. Liberius and Xerxes followed closely behind, allowing Troglita and me to guard their escape until we, too, followed the others into the relative safety of the Palace.

Though a dull rocking echoed through those hallowed rooms, lacquered frescoes and ornate decorations lining the palace walls muffled the din. For a moment, a feeling of eerie quiet flooded my mind as I considered what had just transpired, the knot in my throat returning in realization of the sheer horror.

"Perenus…" I moaned.

"I know," Troglita cut in, "but we can't grieve now. Get what boards you can and jam this door closed."

Two other excubitores joined our efforts, with Marcellus commanding others throughout the Palace to follow suit. A wounded Chanaranges guided Justinian and his ministers back into the Great Hall, further locking and barring its doorway as more excubitores and loyal guardsmen lined the entrance. The Empress followed soon thereafter, turning to me for one final command.

"Varus, summon the foederati," the Empress ordered. "I will not lose this Palace."

On instinct, I saluted. "Yes, Highness," I shouted, followed close behind by Troglita.

Liberius remained in the palace hallways to organize the defense of its various doorways with Marcellus, his wild mane frayed and eyes wild.

"You're going out there?" Liberius asked, straightening his back and seeming taller than normal.

I nodded. "To the barracks," I said. "Less than an hour?"

"Don't take any foolish risks," Liberius barked, "but bring Father Petrus back to the Palace if you are able. He declined to attend the Games, saying his sore back was not up for the task."

"I will," I said.

"Your brother too, Varus," he commanded. "You know the way?"

I bobbed my head a final time. "As if my life depended on it," I answered—then regretted the poor choice of words.

Liberius glanced down at the dragon-hilted sword at my waist and nodded. "Go," he grunted. "Do your duty."

And so I did. Into the maw of the greatest and most terrible riot that Constantinople has ever seen.

CONFLAGRATION

There are wise men who argue that there is nothing more abhorrent than war. The wanton loss of life, often for little more than a few miles of rock-strewn land, all against the most sacred commandments of God. War is the aberration brought to us as the burning mark of Cain, who slew his brother Abel for little more than petty jealousy and brotherhood rivalry.

Those men are wrong. It is not war, but civil strife that is the ultimate evil that plagues the sanctity of the Lord's vast creation. For it is rioting and civil war that locks once-peaceful kinsmen into a bloodlust that is never sated, fed only with paranoia and depravity.

Multiple palace entrances rumbled under the strain of the ravenous mob outside, their iron hinges creaking in protest of the mistreatment. Justinian's elite excubitores sprinted to each doorway and reinforced as many as possible with heavy oaken beams that stood twice the length of a man and half as wide—a momentary bar to the unorganized mass of rioters on the other side. Sweat poured from a hundred faces as many of the elite bodyguards panted under the exertion, calling upon palace servants to join in the defense of their Emperor.

"Why are they doing this? The riots? All it does is make their plight worse," Troglita wondered aloud, his voice more frustrated than inquisitive.

Despite the risk of violence to my friends and family, I found myself sympathizing with the rioters—even if only in some small way. Would I behave any different, were I them? As slaves, Samur and I might not have lived in opulence or gluttony, but we never feared starvation or homelessness. Our scholars claimed that such penury would have been far less common in the great cities of Rome or Carthage in centuries prior—or at least blunted by generous donations from the pagan temples, early Christian churches, and Imperial government alike. At the onset of the Nika Riots, many such programs had been curtailed due to lack of funds. Paulus and many other Imperial treasurers before him had transitioned coin from servicing the public baths or providing donations of bread or constructing new housing for Constantinople's burgeoning population, while constant warfare drained many provinces of further wealth.

And, God forgive us all, but in the many years that followed, things have not improved since, despite all our sacrifice.

Not that I would hesitate to slay any who raised arms against my emperor, my men, or my family. A web of oaths demanded it. Nevertheless, rather than a howling mass of mindless enemies, I saw the mob for what it was—people, desperate and angry. Even protected within Justin's household during my bondage, I understood those emotions well.

"They're starving, overtaxed, and otherwise ignored," I said, "even many of the patricians."

Troglita frowned, unconvinced. "But how does a revolt improve that?"

"Does it matter?" I snapped. Troglita shrugged in submission. "I'm headed to the barracks."

"I'm coming with you," Troglita replied, summoning a palace guardsman to commandeer their sword and shield. "I want to rescue Father Petrus too, and Samur."

"Fine," I said, "but follow my lead, and keep silent."

Catching the attention of a nearby servant, I asked for strips of woolen cloth and two cloaks, then stripped out of my excubitor's armor before sending another servant for my previous chestpiece and helm. Troglita looked at me quizzically, his hand patting at the thick cowhide belt with frenetic energy.

"To keep the swords from making too much noise," I explained, wrapping the cloth over strips of iron that reinforced my scabbard. "Armor won't draw too much attention with as many guards as there are out on the street, but an excubitor would be suspicious. We're just two veterans from Dara caught in the middle of the riot."

"And the cloaks?" Troglita asked.

"To dissuade curious eyes," I said. "It's fine if they see our armor, but I'd rather be invisible in the crowd."

Troglita nodded, checking his own armor for signs of Imperial loyalties and selecting shields bare of any painted Imperial device. He then quickly helped me don and secure my chestpiece, unknotting its polished scales and shoulder guards. Grasping my helmet, I removed its plume and threw the helm and faceplate over my head, tying its leather straps firmly under my chin. Troglita followed suit, removing his own plume, which denoted his status as a senior commander within the Thracian Army. After a brief inspection, I signaled for Troglita to follow me down a hall and into a servants' entrance, memories of my childhood guiding my steps in the darkness of that place.

Barely adequate for children to sneak by unencumbered, Troglita and I cursed and fought our way in pitch blackness, our armor clanging against exposed wooden beams and loose stones along the walls. At one point, Troglita stumbled when an iron strip in his shoulder guard snagged a beam, sending him hard to the ground, and he used my body to pull himself upright, keeping as silent as possible as he did so.

After what felt like an hour of bumbling in the dark, my hand instinctively caught a rail that signaled a change in direction.

"Headed down," I whispered to Troglita, gingerly using my

right foot to search for a descending step.

My boot pressed lightly upon a creaking wooden board. As I stepped down, the board sagged, yet held true under my weight as I shifted from one step to the other. Eight steps guided us through more flat hallways that we followed for another twenty paces. Eventually, however, the walls at our sides evaporated, giving way to a junction where multiple hallways intersected.

"Where now?" Troglita asked, a twinge of fear in his voice as his hands reached for stone walls and wooden pillars.

"Wait," I replied. "Be still."

Grasping Troglita's shoulder, I stilled him with an outstretched palm. Together, we sat in silence for several heartbeats, the only noise reaching our labyrinth of underground hallways the distant thunder from the streets. Holding onto that sound, I placed my other hand against the wall, its vibrations coursing into my arm and nearly causing me to drop my shield.

"To the right," I said. "That will lead us to the street."

Fixing my shield, I traced the wall along a right turn, leading Troglita close behind with my other arm. The noise of the mob grew sharper as we closed in upon the hallway's end, with the blended roar transforming into a number of discernable voices of Roman men and women. We stumbled another fifty paces in that blackness until reaching a wide doorway that curiously consisted entirely of metal rather than wood. Tracing its edges, my gloves eventually wrapped around a ponderous knob that creaked as it moved. I tugged hard, straining my elbow as I wrestled against the door.

It did not budge. I tried again—still no success.

"Do we need a key?" Troglita offered.

"No," I said, my voice strained as I tugged for a third time. "These are servants' doors, and most don't even have a lock. The entrances are hidden and usually guarded by agents of the Imperial spymaster."

"Narses," Troglita concluded, and I nodded before realizing my movements were invisible to the other man.

Breathing in the damp, fetid air, I withdrew my helmet and

placed an ear to the door. While thick crowd noise rumbled overhead, the other side of the iron door was soundless. My knuckles rapped against the center of the metal, answered by a hollow ringing that betrayed little.

"Any idea where we are?" Troglita asked.

"Outside of the Hippodrome, but close by," I said. "There are dozens of entrances, and this is one I'm unfamiliar with. But it's our best chance to get to the streets for now."

Removing a glove, my bare fingers traced the iron once more. Callused skin grazed against rough patches that interrupted the smooth metal, and I drew back my hand in fear.

"Rust," I declared. "The door's hinges and knob are rusted through."

"So it just needs a bit more muscle," Troglita said.

He gently nudged his way to my side and placed his sword hand around the dangling knob. After replacing my glove, I followed his example, flexing my arm before placing my fingers adjacent to Troglita's.

"Pull!" I hissed, jerking my arm and leaning backward with all my weight.

The door groaned under the strain of our labors and initially resisted in a similar manner as before. After several more moments of cursing and spitting, a scraping sound echoed through the hall as the door began to move and its hinges buckled under the pressure. I exhaled as I tugged all the harder. The door creaked open and unveiled its hidden rooms. Our whoops of triumph quickly transformed into panic as the door slammed against the wall, pushed forward by an unseen force and nearly crushing our hands in the process.

Freezing water rushed into the hallway. Troglita and I grunted in shock.

"We're in the Basilica Cistern!" I whispered urgently as water continued to rise in the hallway, its current attempting to drive us back. "Justinian must have built a direct entrance from the Palace."

"The Cistern? Won't we drown?" Troglita said, panic in his voice.

"Not here. It's probably a shallower reserve," I grunted, shivering as flecks of water sprayed my face. "There's a door to the street nearby."

Wading into the frigid water, I prayed that my words were true. The Basilica Cistern was one of many underground storage yards for Constantinople's water reserves, ensuring that the Palace and the barracks would have ample supplies of the precious liquid in the event of a siege. The cistern rose three times the height of a man and was fully flooded during times of rain, although its engineers warned against overuse of the stone walls.

"Inside, and close the door behind us," I decided.

Troglita, however, was more apprehensive. "I can't swim," he confessed.

"It won't be too deep. Come on!" Holding on to Troglita's outstretched hand, I guided him as we waded through the door into waist-deep water. Other than the rush of swirling waters, a clacking noise filled my skull, and it was not for several more heartbeats that I realized it was the clattering of my own teeth. Fighting against my body's convulsions, I latched onto the door alongside Troglita, and we tugged again, struggling against the pressure from the cistern's waters. Panting, we eventually succeeded. The cistern's waters rose to our waists, slowing further movement, and the current pushed hard against my shield. I growled, but I drew my sword and cut at the straps that lashed the shield to my forearm.

"Cut your shield!" I yelled desperately to Troglita. "It will only hold us back!"

Troglita acknowledged the order and struggled to seal the palace door. After the outer door screeched shut, my eyes adjusted to the room that contained a faintly visible light on its far corners. Against the damp stones, the light danced as it rose and fell, revealing the vaguest outline of an outer door.

"There!" I pointed. "The torch!"

Driven by the signal, we rushed forward. I prayed at each step, fearful of dropping into the cistern's abyss from some hidden drop-off. What I did not explain to Troglita was that the cistern regularly fell to well over the height of a man, and our dim light gave us no way to see where those traps may lie. Scooting into the blackness, I eventually brushed my foot against a step and rose against the sucking waters, reaching for the sole burning torch.

Shivering uncontrollably, I dragged Troglita up behind me and tore the damp gloves from my hands. Raising my fingers to the dancing flames, my skin held a bluish tinge as all my instincts centered on the need for warmth. I would have paused far longer than needed had Troglita not disturbed my trance.

"Let's go!" he said, teeth snapping violently.

Forcing numb fingers back into their leather gloves, I moved to the cistern door. Unlike the entrance from the Palace, this door cracked open readily, allowing Troglita and me to file into the stone-lined streets of Constantinople.

Though we poured into one of the city's innumerable alleys, the riot's din instantly returned to our ears. Where the Hippodrome's rancor was a cacophony of thousands of voices, a single curious word rang from nearly all throats in unison.

"Nika! Nika! Nika!" The noise echoed from the cistern's outer walls, making the ground rumble as though a minor earthquake.

"Victory?" Troglita asked as he tugged off his boots and dumped water onto the street.

"No idea," I responded. "I've only ever heard that call after a Hippodrome race. Must be some dark attempt at symbolism."

"Ah. Doesn't matter, I guess."

After taking a moment to collect ourselves, we threw cloaks over our damp armor and moved into the street. The cistern alley connected to a nearby road to the Palace, and I stole a glance upon one of the many palace doors that served as Justinian's refuge, and Mariya's and Zenobia's as well.

Hundreds of bodies gathered near the vaulted doorway, their fists pounding fruitlessly against the thick iron and wood boards. Others threw stones that generally clattered in a similarly useless fashion, although one of the larger stones gored an ugly groove into an exposed wooden plank. Other than that one spot of danger, however, the stones did greater damage to the unsuspecting heads of those closest to the door, with several rocks falling short of their mark and connecting with exposed hands and skulls. Despite cries of pain, the crowd kept roaring their mocking chant of victory, leaving Justinian's diminutive force cowering behind the palace walls.

"We need to move before they set fire to the door," I told Troglita. "Marcellus doesn't have enough men to mount a sally."

With the crowd's attention on Justinian's looming Palace, we blended into the throng, tugging our cloaks tight and throwing loose wool hoods over our helmets. Damp boots and trousers made for an excruciating march as our feet grew sore and numb, made all the worse by the chill winter air and a light blanket of flurries that spat onto Constantinople's streets. Adjacent to the Palace was the still-full Hippodrome, now marked by several pillars of smoke that rose well above the highest floors of the Palace as chants of "Nika! Nika! Nika!" jeered them on.

We avoided the main thoroughfares, out of practicality as much as stealth, for the main streets that linked the city's port, markets, and Palace were choked by the press of thousands of unwashed bodies and rotting food, all accented by a hint of smoke and flame that never seemed far off. Constantinople's lesser streets wound circuitously around the less pleasant of professions—butchers, tanners, and other handlers of dung, blood, and various byproducts of death—yet these roads made for easier travel to the Imperial Barracks. Not to mention that the otherwise putrid miasma that permanently wafted outside of those shops was little worse than the odor around the Hippodrome.

Navigating the coarser cobbled streets of the dimly lit alleyways, we slinked along a rear entrance of the barracks.

The foederati's temporary home was far less encumbered by a riled mob than the Palace had been, with a dozen Greens and Blues loitering outside each door. Many swayed on their feet, roaring challenges to whoever resisted behind the locked doors, while most searched opportunistically for alternative entrances to the building that housed a broad assortment of the army's weapons and armor.

"Draw your sword and follow my lead," I whispered to Troglita, who raised an eyebrow.

Throwing back the cloak and unsheathing my blade, I rushed toward the barracks door. Heads turned in bewilderment as I approached, with most backing away at the hulking armored figure charging in their direction. One of the Blues stood defiant, staggering as he copied my movements and ran for me, ignoring pleas from his comrades to turn in the opposite direction.

"Lapdog!" the man slurred. "Bastard!"

I would have pissed myself laughing had the situation around the barracks not been so hostile and urgent. Then, as I thought of how Perenus would react to such a confrontation, my mood soured irretrievably. My oldest friend in the Roman army would not share in laughter ever again.

Rather than stabbing with my blade, I tossed the hilt to my opposite hand and slowed my advance to the would-be attacker. Reeking of sour wine, the man attempted a lunge and slipped upon wet stones and landed hard at my boots. The man drew support from my greaves and waist as he pulled himself upright, drawing a knife as he stabbed clumsily down at my neck.

I balled my hand into a fist and smacked the drunken attacker hard enough for his head to snap back with a violent jerk. He stumbled and was caught by one of the Greens, allowing the man time to bring a free hand to his face. The Blue winced as his hand recoiled from an open wound, blood pouring from swollen nostrils and into his mouth.

"You broke my nose!" he cried. "Fucking bastard!"

I feinted, scattering the half dozen or so men who loitered near the barracks door. Troglita walked calmly to my side, chuckling as he nodded for us to continue to our destination.

"A brave enemy!" Troglita joked.

"A drunken fool," I said bitterly, "filled with more wine than sense. I fear the city will be overrun with that sort of men and women soon enough."

"Surely that works to our advantage?" Troglita replied, a wide grin still spanning his cleanshaven jaw.

"It only takes one drunken fool to set the city alight," I answered seriously, "or to stick a knife between your ribs when you aren't looking."

Troglita grimaced and let the subject dissipate. Together, we reached the splintered and gashed doorway, its panels covered in a malodorous stench that reeked of fresh urine. Troglita hammered against the door and demanded entry and was answered by an aggressive baritone whose Greek was accented with telltale signs of the Heruli tongue.

"It's Varus, your commander!" I bellowed, adding my commands to Troglita's. "Open the door while the passage is clear!"

Bustling with confusion, the door eventually unlocked and propped itself open. Two spearheads glistened as they shot into the daylight a handsbreadth from our throats, close enough to shave away several loose hairs of my beard. The Herulian faces on the other side glared at us with a fury that melted into relief, the spears lowered to a resting position.

"Komes!" Sindual replied, bowing his head. "I thought you were just another drunkard, or one of the wild ruffians that's been slamming clay jars into the barracks walls."

Sindual pushed two of the Herulian guardsmen aside and allowed Troglita and me to slide through. Against my desire to appear calm and dignified, I followed Troglita to a nearby fire, tugging free my sodden boots and placing wrinkled flesh near the dry flames.

"What happened to you two?" Sindual asked.

"It was hell getting here," I explained. "The Palace wants the foederati back as soon as possible."

Sindual's eyes widened as his mouth drooped ajar. "The Emperor? He's still alive?"

"Of course," I cried. "Why wouldn't he be?"

"The crowd is calling for Justinian to hang," Samur answered, announcing his presence. "A long time coming. The race was just an excuse to burn the city."

Dropping formalities, I drew Samur into a tight embrace, ignoring the instinctual twitch in Samur's torso before he returned the gesture in kind. "How do you know this?" I asked.

"We managed to sneak into the Hippodrome, Fulcaris and I," Samur explained. "I saw what happened to Perenus but couldn't get close to the crash. We were barely able to push our way out of the mob and back to the barracks."

I nodded, dropping my head in melancholy. "Where is Fulcaris?"

"Holding the main doorway," Samur said. "A mob tried to rush the barracks with clubs and torches, and Fulcaris had to lead an attack to ward them off."

Troglita shook his head, veins protruding from his neck and forehead. "Absolute madness," he yelled, fists clenching.

"For you," Samur replied cautiously. "But for most? Roman livelihood means less than Roman justice. The poor are treated like horse droppings and are swept away all the same."

Troglita eyed Samur warily but did not pursue an argument. "Did all the Herulians make it back?"

Sindual nodded. "Most weren't able to get seats in the Hippodrome, and many were sleeping after training when the riot broke out. We've been waiting for someone to come and give orders. Varus or Mundus, or Belisarius even."

Belisarius. The name seized my throat in a moment of horror. For in our rush to take action, we had forgotten the man who remained in comfortable but unyielding confinement.

"Did anyone go to free Belisarius or Ascum?" I asked. "Any others that need to be brought to safety?"

Samur shook his head. "Since Fulcaris and I returned, the barracks has been locked tight. There hasn't been time to do much more than douse fires and threaten drunken Greens."

I nodded. "Spread the word. The foederati are commanded back to the Palace. We need to bring Petrus, Ascum, and Belisarius with us."

Troglita turned to me, an urgent look on his worried face. "Belisarius is on the other side of the city, and not in our orders."

As dozens of eyes took in my movements, I sighed, considering what few terrible choices remained available. The rising din of the street riots denoted an equally grave risk facing the Palace, which had fewer than five hundred excubitores and city guardsmen to cover its dozens of possible entrances. My instincts told me to run back to Mariya, Zenobia, and Theodora, and I quickly saw the reason behind Troglita's worry.

But given my promises to free Belisarius, I could not abandon him. "Any chance we can reach the horses?" I asked.

Sindual shook his head. "They're heavily guarded and difficult to access. While this makes it easy to resist an attack, it also makes it nearly impossible for us to reach the stables without fighting our way through resistance. Even then, the horses will scatter from so much chaos."

"I see," I replied, cursing inwardly. "If no other options remain, we will split the foederati in two. A smaller portion will reach Ascum and our other wounded and carry them to the Palace through back alleys. You'll be attacked, but the crowds will be smaller and unlikely to test a few dozen armored veterans."

"With your permission, I'll lead them," Samur insisted. "I'm not leaving Ascum to be butchered by these animals."

I nodded. "Take Sindual's men. Forty should suffice, but go with a full kit. Leave nothing valuable behind."

My next order was interrupted by Cephalas, who came running with eyes wide. "Lord!" he exclaimed, spittle dribbling onto his beard. "Is it true about Perenus?"

As Cephalas drew close, I nodded. The crippled Greek wailed, fat tears trailing down his cheeks. No longer able to check my own urge, I shared in his misery, and I draped an arm over his shoulder. We three had shared Archelaus' torturous training and had stood together in the shield wall. Though I had witnessed Perenus wounded before, the thought of him dead seemed incompatible with the world, no different than if God plucked the sun from the sky. He was like my brother, and his passing felt somehow more piercing than that of Godilas, or even Justin.

"We will mourn him soon," I said at last, "but we have a job to do now. Prepare to leave with Samur, and take anything valuable with you."

Cephalas turned back to me, his eyes blotched with misery. "But, Lord, I can help you if you'll allow me to go with you."

"I know," I answered. "That's why I need you to get back to the Palace. Zenobia, Mariya, Rosamund... They need your protection as quickly as possible."

Biting his slackened lip, Cephalas nodded. "Where will you go?"

I sighed, resigning myself to a far more difficult fate than Theodora had intended. "I'm taking the rest of the foederati and rescuing Belisarius. We'll grab Father Petrus along the way and fight our way back to the Palace."

Troglita cleared his throat and sought a moment to speak privately with me, which I declined. "It won't take long," I explained. "Go inform the men. Have them form up and prepare to depart."

And so they did. As stones clattered against the barracks walls and Roman men and women screamed for Justinian's blood, the Herulian foederati donned armor and prepared for war.

THE NIKA RIOTS

It did not take long for the men to squeeze into their mail and assemble their weapons, their leather kits sagging from the abnormal weight of each man's earthly possessions piled together. Several of my veterans tied thick pouches of gold and silver coins to their belts, while others strapped torques and bracelets to their leather and armor-protected skin. Even the newer recruits with little wealth and no plunder gathered artifacts from their homeland, their eyes closely surveilling the more experienced men for any sign of distress.

Troglita and I each replaced our thick cloaks that had been weighed down from our sojourn to the Cistern and grabbed a replacement shield from a stack in the barracks central corridor. Tightening its leather straps to my arm, I smiled as I saw its ouroboros sigil, a reminder that my men and I had fought through far worse circumstances and emerged alive to tell the tale.

"If you're not back at the Palace by sundown, I'm coming to look for you," Samur said, securing an iron helm and cheekpieces over his head.

Frowning, I stole a glance from a high arched window, its wooden frame crusted with frost and wet snowflakes. Though the day was still early, the winter sun had already reached its peak, its descent casting shadows into the barracks hallway.

"That doesn't give me much time," I said.

"I know," Samur said. "So don't waste your time, and get the task finished."

We clasped each other at the forearm before Samur and Sindual gave the order for their group to file out a rear doorway. An equally armored Cephalas stood at their center, his sword arm hanging limply at his side as he clutched at a heavy pack. Cephalas nodded heavily in my direction as he shot past, his lids rimmed with heavy shadows and swollen from his tears. Samur paused for nothing as the barracks door swung open and his men filed into the streets, quickly forming a shield wall and threatening those who loitered about for any food or goods that might be pilfered from the Roman army.

Enraged by Perenus' death, a bloodied Fulcaris barked demands for the remaining foederati to fill the barracks hall and prepare for departure. Amid the rustling armor and equipment, I pulled Fulcaris aside.

"It's not my blood," he insisted, seeing my concerned eyes on his armor.

I offered a weak smile. "We have a long road to trudge through, and we need to avoid bloodshed if at all possible. Are you ready for this?"

"Perfectly," Fulcaris replied with a snarl. "Some of the men are untested, but they won't disappoint you."

Though many appeared worried, I agreed with Fulcaris. As the column formed into a tight mass that filled each crevice and empty space in the barracks hall, I walked to the front of the formation and hoisted my body atop a wooden bench.

"Foederati!" I yelled out. Over three hundred men snapped to attention. "You are being called to protect the Emperor and his interests. The crowd outside these doors is rabid and will not hesitate to assault any of you if given the chance. So no matter what happens, keep tight behind the shield wall, don't engage in violence unless attacked first, and never stop moving!"

Fulcaris slammed his spear butt into the ground, echoed by the roar of the column. The younger and unbloodied members of the foederati yelled loudest, clanging spears against their blackened shields with a frenetic energy. I raised a hand for silence that brought the foederati to a sudden stillness, their hush made more pronounced by the cacophony beyond the barracks walls.

"We have two stops to make. One is for the old priest, Father Petrus, who is close," I explained, watching the men's unflinching reaction. "The other is for General Belisarius, who is currently being kept under house arrest near the docks."

My veterans broke out once more into raucous cheers at Belisarius' name. For a moment, I was transported back to Tauris, my battered body struggling to remain mounted as the survivors of our fight against Kazrig yelled in rapturous thanksgiving for their general. I subconsciously rubbed at my shoulder that, even two years after that battle, still throbbed in soreness during colder days.

"Leave nothing behind!" I yelled.

Turning to Fulcaris, I threw a slight gesture that ordered him to begin the advance, and he snapped to the order with relish. The column positioned itself just before the wide barracks doors, their holds barred with heavy wooden beams. At Fulcaris' order, the beams were removed and the doors kicked ajar, allowing a rush of smoke and afternoon light to pour into the enclosed space.

"Advance!" Fulcaris yelled, an order immediately obeyed.

Standing eight abreast with shields locked and spears pointed high into the air, the column's vanguard rushed into the streets. Dozens of Greens and Blues thronged the door's entrance and struggled to move away from the armored foederati, causing several fights to erupt as men and women sought to avoid the sudden shock. Nevertheless, several younger men skipped close to the shield wall, spitting insults and calling for Justinian's destruction. Our column edged forward as the crowd grew denser, our final ranks coiling a thick iron chain around the barracks door in a vain attempt to frustrate would-be intruders.

Standing in the second row of the walled column, I assessed the crowd's willingness to attack and grew unsettled at the conclusion. "Foederati, advance!" I growled, echoed by Fulcaris and the other centurions. At the pace of a slow walk, the column marched away from the barracks doorway and toward the nearby building housing Father Petrus. Thankfully, its modest trappings and lack of affiliation with the Imperial Palace made it an unlikely target for early mob violence—at least I hoped.

Within three paces of the foederati's departure from the barracks, members of the crowd swarmed into the gap near the barracks doorway, leaving our formation surrounded on all sides. Though my eyes remained trained on our intended destination, I could hear several in the crowd taking clubs and axes to the barracks doorway as many jeered at their failure to break the barracks' iron lock.

"That won't hold long," Troglita said, referring to the door.

"I know," I grumbled. "Anything that's left, they're welcome to."

Out of the corner of my eye, I saw a small stone zip through the air, connecting against the iron helmet of the spearman diagonal to my position. Dazed but otherwise unharmed, I slapped the man on the back, finding Altan shooting a toothy grin in my direction.

"All right, Lord!" he cried.

"High and tight, Altan! We need your shield steady today!" I replied cheerily.

He straightened with intensity.

A few other projectiles rang out against our formation, yet the crowd kept a fearful distance as we neared Father Petrus' quarters. An older girl ran close to tap one of the ouroboros on our shields and was promptly sent sprinting away by a furious Fulcaris, who snarled obscenities in two different languages and cursed the poor child's soul to the deepest of the Herulian hells, waving his spear about for effect.

Another man drew too close as he threw rotten vegetables at one side of our column and tripped after one of my men smacked his forehead with the shaft of a spear. Other than these minor engagements, we drew no blood as we formed a protective ring around the doorway to Father Petrus' building, the men's spears now facing outward in warning.

Inside the ring, I gestured to Troglita and moved to the building's doorway. Finding it locked, Troglita tugged against its bronze bolt, sweat pouring from his brow despite the afternoon chill and sporadic flurries falling amidst a backdrop of smoke, excrement, and terror. Shaking my head, I turned to Fulcaris and gave my instructions.

"Wait here, and draw no blood if it can be helped."

Sliding beside Troglita, I rested my spear against the building's front wall and drew my sword. Gripping hard, I bashed the bronze with the sword's pommel, secretly checking that the dragon decorating the sword's crosspiece was undented. After two blows, the lock bent at a crude angle, sending sparks onto the cobbled stones at our feet. The door's loose hinge allowed Troglita to kick the door open and rush inside.

Father Petrus' quarters were on the third level of the brick-and-stone building, whose lowest level had been one of the hundreds of fletchers in Justinian's Empire who were responsible for carving, straightening, and decorating the Army's arrows. That first floor was vacant and dark upon our arrival, yet sheaves of arrows had been stacked against a far wall, while mounds of loose feathers and iron-tipped arrowheads lined a nearby workbench that encompassed much of the room's floor.

"Empty," Troglita said nonchalantly, scanning the room. "Might be in the mob."

"Or he might be dead or out of the city," I answered. "It makes no difference. Let's check upstairs."

Mindful of each footstep, Troglita lowered his spear and slid up the stairs. I followed closely behind with my sword drawn, flinching as an angry boom resonated from the street. We continued undisturbed to the building's third level, the interior rooms dark and silent as we passed by. Finding the doorway to Father Petrus' quarters propped open, Troglita lowered his spear and edged forward, using its honed point to break through the faded wood.

Into nothing. As with other rooms, Father Petrus' sleeping room was as plain and empty as ever, holding barely more than a single thick scroll of the Gospels, a worn onyx robe, and the oiled leather sash bearing the Imperial Chi-Rho that I had first laid eyes upon as a raw recruit to the Thracian Army. Conspicuously missing was the priest's cross, which usually rested upon a flaxen cord bolted to a wall when the priest rested. The floor was free of shoes or trousers, and the straw mat of his bed was unkempt.

"Search the side rooms; he was recently here," I said to Troglita. "Someone may have tried to loot the place and surprised the old man."

Just as Troglita moved to obey, a rustling clattered against a far wall. Twitching toward the noise, I raised my sword to my chest, prepared to brawl against any man or woman who had assaulted Father Petrus.

"Varus?" a weathered voice croaked in a frail and uneven manner.

"Father?" I replied, lowering the blade.

Father Petrus poked his head from behind a tiny storage closet whose door was little more than a loose wooden plank held with a creaking bronze hinge. His wrinkled hand shaking, he gripped the wall as he withdrew from the crawlspace, his eyes blotchy and irritated.

I sheathed the blade and hustled to help. "Father, are you all right?"

"Don't put away your sword, Varus," Father Petrus begged, his face pale and jaw quivering. "I fear it will be needed before this day is completed."

I hugged him, feeling his thin body shiver. "Father, no harm will come to you, I promise. There is no need to fear."

Father Petrus shook his head in uncharacteristic pessimism. "You don't know what the death of a city is like, Varus, but I do," he said mournfully. "What the sound of blood clogging the city gutters makes as men and women commit all measure of depravity."

"It won't come to that," I said. "We'll bring things back to order soon enough. And help solve the people's grievances."

"It is too late for that." Father Petrus sobbed. "Any chance for peace slipped from the Emperor's fingers when he spent his coin on games instead of bread and medicine. There's an evil in each of God's children, Varus, and once awakened, only divine retribution will send it back to whatever hell it spawned from."

Troglita cleared his throat. "We need to leave, Father."

Father Petrus shrugged. "Just leave me here. I've seen too much death and survived it all. I pray the Lord will take me before I have to do that all over again."

Growing frustrated, I cuffed my gloved hands together with a muted slap. "I won't leave you, Father, but the Emperor has ordered us to defend the Palace. I'll leave that order to you."

"How cruel!" the priest responded with fresh tears. "Just leave me to whatever fate claims me."

I did not reply to the self-pity and leaned lightly against the grease-stained wall. Its boards had recently been scrubbed, yet buildings this old had been caked in generations of filth that predated every person currently living and would likely remain well after each of us had gone to the ground. Provided, of course, that the building was not destroyed.

After several heartbeats, Father Petrus raised his hands in surrender. "Very well, Varus. Liberius was right—you are too stubborn for your own good."

"Count yourself lucky, then." I grinned at him. "Forgive me for this indignity."

Before Father Petrus could reply, I grabbed him in my arms and lifted him high into the air. Weighing little more than a child, Father Petrus huffed in surprise, patting my shoulder insistently.

"My bag!" he cried out, his voice cracking once more. "I can't leave without it!"

Without another word, Troglita grabbed the rich dark leather satchel, carrying it gingerly under his arm. The three of us descended the creaking stairs and reached the lower door. I grabbed my spear before we ventured back to the foederati.

"Lord!" Irilar called out to me. "We need to get moving again!"

"Trouble?"

"Mainly stones and rotten food, but some are lighting torches and throwing them into nearby buildings," he explained. "Most are Imperial property, but fires are breaking out in at least a dozen sites on the road ahead."

Nodding, I released Father Petrus onto his feet, and ordered Irilar and a half dozen Herulians to shield the priest above all other orders. "Not a single hair on the old man's head is to be disturbed," I ordered in Greek.

"That's easy. He doesn't have many!" Irilar said back to me Herulian, spurring laughter despite the apocalypse that billowed within a spear's length of our formation.

Father Petrus scowled. "Just because I can't understand your language doesn't mean I don't follow your meaning," he hollered at Irilar. "Such horrible respect for your elders!"

"Don't worry, old father, we will see you to safety," Irilar responded, and at his words, a vault of shields formed over the priest's head, held by a half dozen black-shielded spearmen.

Satisfied, I gave the instruction to reform into columns and brought the ponderous foederati back to marching order. As before, the crowd at the front of our formation parted to allow us passage, with most struggling to escape the thundering mass of armored Herulians that bore down relentlessly on one of Constantinople's busiest streets.

True to Irilar's warning, many of the buildings we passed showed signs of a blaze recently doused with water, while others freely burned into the afternoon sky. Black smoke wafted into the air, choking the men whose position in the column sent them perilously close to the charred and smoldering wood and plaster.

"Keep your shields tight!" Fulcaris barked. "A little fire never killed anyone."

"Clearly you don't remember Callinicum," one of my veterans

laughed as he bashed his shield at a drunken Blue who wandered impermissibly close to the shield wall.

"Point taken," Fulcaris muttered. "But keep the wall tight all the same."

Our boots slapped against slurry-crusted stones as we continued down the path. Block by block, we ventured to Belisarius' house of imprisonment. We were aided by the still-plentiful daylight and the generally wary crowd that seemed content to be little more than a nuisance, albeit one that made progress painfully slow. The exertion was minimal as we trampled steadily downhill, the weight of our armor carrying us through the Forum of Arcadius along the capital's southern coastline. The sun continued its descent as we snaked adjacent to the Imperial docks and found ourselves approaching Belisarius' quarters. Despite scorch marks and piles of waste lining the walls, the place appeared otherwise intact.

"About time!" an armored soldier growled at my column. "I wasn't sure you were coming!"

"Uliaris? What are you doing here?" I asked the man as our column approached twenty of Belisarius' armored bucellarii, his household guards.

"Just because they locked Belisarius away doesn't mean we don't keep an eye on things," the Frank answered as he extended a hand in greeting. "Are you here to take him away?"

I nodded. "Back to the Palace. It's not safe in this part of the city."

"Aye, true," Uliaris said. "The mob broke into an armory and have been passing out daggers and axes. A few even charged at us but did little enough damage."

"We've had few disruptions, although the foederati is too large to be hit directly by untrained city dwellers."

"I wouldn't gamble on that," he said, "but at any rate, let's get Belisarius out of this shithole."

Though crude, Uliaris' estimation of the place was accurate. The buildings leading to the Great Harbor of Theodosius housed Constantinople's poorest residents, with drafts that billowed the stench of fish guts and seaweed into every nook and cranny. Belisarius' building was a tall and unpainted structure that bore signs of several years of neglect, including multiple scorch marks that had been doused with water.

"Halt in the name of the Emperor!" yelled a petulant voice that I quickly recognized as one of my captors from Barbalissus. "No man is permitted entry to this building. Turn and depart this place at once, and commit no more crimes."

A dozen Imperial guards flowed out of the doorway and into the street to face the halted foederati. Though better trained and armored than the feckless city watch, the guardsmen looked warily onward as their limited numbers stacked suicidally against our own. Young Vitalius formed up at the center of their small band yet shrunk slightly behind as his lowered spear wavered.

"I am on the Emperor's business and mean you no harm."

"Which Emperor, though?" the guardsman said in a challenge.

"Justinian, the only Emperor," I answered in frustration. "If you don't leave here now, the mob will tear you to pieces when the sun falls."

The guardsman looked back to his supporters, hanging his head in surrender. "I remember you," he replied. "You're taking Belisarius to the Palace?"

"And you and your men as well," I said. "That's the best we can do for now."

As the crowd inched closer at the display, the guardsman nodded. "Gather your things. We're leaving!" he said, allowing the Imperial guards to sweep into the squat doorway and retrieve their packs and other gear. Vitalius' shoulders rose and fell in a deep sigh as he ran inside to collect his belongings with the other veterans.

Following the guardsmen inside, I left Troglita and the foederati to secure the building's entrance. Belisarius' assigned rooms were kept in a windowless section of the second level, its floorboards weak and creaking from the slightest movement. Though Hermogenes had initially promised to leave him in more luxurious surroundings, gaps in the walls and piles of rat dung made it clear that the legate had failed to keep his word.

Ignoring questions from the excited guardsmen, I climbed the uneven staircase, hoping to God it would not collapse under my weight. The shouting and banging outside the building grew worse as I reached the second level, and I nearly tripped when my foot caught a loose beam on the landing.

"A sturdy building to be sure, but in desperate need of the loving attention of a craftsman," Belisarius remarked matter-of-factly as I came into view. "It's wonderful to see you again, Varus."

"Lord!" I exclaimed, dropping my head in supplication. "I would have come sooner, but—"

"You did your duty, nothing less." Belisarius offered an embrace.

Though he had spent several months in captivity, Belisarius remained as spotless as if an audience with the Emperor was imminent. Left with no weapons or armor, he seemed somehow denuded, somehow smaller as he stood in that dank and mold-infested hallway. Belisarius remained healthy, so at the least, he had not been deprived of meals by the Emperor, a courtesy that my experiences in Nisibis and Barbalissus convinced me was a rare one.

"Lord, we need to leave immediately."

"I've heard commotion all afternoon, but the guards tell me little," Belisarius replied. "What has happened? Is the Emperor still hale?"

"For now," I explained curtly. "The Hippodrome games broke out into rioting, with the Blues and Greens overrunning the city guard."

"The Blues and the Greens together?" he asked. "I wouldn't have thought that at all likely."

"I don't pretend to understand it either, Lord, but we do need to leave immediately. Please gather any belongings and join me outside."

Belisarius offered a warm smile. "My family is at the Palace. Let's leave this wretched place."

Grabbing little more than a handful of text-covered scrolls in a courier's bag, Belisarius marched down the stairs and shadowed me into the courtyard beyond. Though his jailors were the first to greet Belisarius as he entered the open air, veterans of the foederati began to call out his name, almost matching the riotous mob in vigor. Though Belisarius presented a terse greeting of thanks, I thought I caught a momentary twitch of his lips, and I can only imagine that he, too, was transported back to times of glory for an all-too-brief heartbeat.

"Form up!" I commanded, instructing the jailors and Belisarius to blend into the center of the column. "Back to the Palace!"

As the sun bled its dying light onto Constantinople's slush-stained roads, the foederati returned to formation, chants of Belisarius still heavy on their lips. Uliaris and the other two dozen bucellarii that comprised Belisarius' household guard formed a protective ring around him, scorning the feeble attempts of the jailors to retain custody of their ward.

"Belisarius stays with us," the lead guardsman grumbled, stepping two paces in front of Belisarius' other guardsmen.

Uliaris, however, had no patience for the whims of Hermogenes' men. "And you're going to fight for him here, are you?"

With his hand dropping to his belt, Uliaris slid his sword from its scabbard. The guard wavered as he glanced back to his followers, finding little support to keep Belisarius from my custody. Uliaris glanced to me, seeming to seek permission to cut their throats.

"There's no time for this!" I roared. "Join us, or don't. God help me, Belisarius is coming with me if I have to burn half of this city down to keep him safe."

That was all Belisarius' jailors required to surrender their charge. "No offense intended, Lord. Lead us out of here."

As a measure of goodwill, the jailor fell back into the safety of the foederati's center, joined by his comrades. Uliaris grinned and nodded, though I felt only irritation at the delay.

"We're headed to the Palace," I roared to my column. "Obey my commands. Do not let the column break, and we will all live. If anyone runs away, we're all dead. Understand me?"

Dozens of hoarse throats boomed a reply. "Yes, Lord!"

Our path back to the Palace was guaranteed to be far more treacherous than our initial journey to Belisarius. Slick sleet that carpeted Constantinople's smooth stones made for hazardous marching, with several of the foederati cursing as they stumbled and briefly left a gap in the tight cluster of shields that protected each of us from the swirling mob just paces away.

I should have given closer attention to elderly Father Petrus. Pacing over a particularly slick section of road, Petrus fell so hard to the pavement that I feared that he had shattered a knee, but he merely waved away my concerns and promised to be more careful. After his initial anguish, the priest mentioned nothing of his fears of Constantinople's conflagration, although Father Petrus flinched when a stone connected with our shields, one hand clutching a cross while the other trembled at the fraying rope that served as his belt.

With darkness beginning to fall, a graying sky illuminated the many fires that had sparked throughout Constantinople's Second and Third Hills. As we ascended toward the Forum of Constantine, we were able to glimpse the military's quarters and the Hippodrome beyond. The Imperial Barracks was engulfed in white flames, with angry black clouds swarming overhead. The plume was further lit up by a dozen smaller fires rising from the Hippodrome, which remained a center of hellish roaring as thousands chanted prayers to the Goddess of Victory.

"I never did like that barracks," Fulcaris shouted. "Maybe they'll make a better one."

"If we survive, that is," his cousin Irilar replied. "The whole city is going up in smoke."

"Quiet in the ranks!" I barked. The men slammed their shields back to attention. "Keep pushing to the Palace!"

As we approached the Hippodrome's northernmost entrance, the crowd grew thick, not just in numbers but in sharpened steel as well. Well-muscled, these men were clearly no strangers to physical toil, brandishing stolen torches, swords, and shields, all bearing the Emperor's sigil. Most unsettling of all was a heavy ox cart at the center of the mass, its carriage stacked with thin logs that dripped an ominous liquid onto the road.

"Brothers!" one bearded Greek called out to the foederati. "We are not your enemy, but your friends! Join us in overthrowing that usurper Justinian and restoring Hypatius to his rightful throne! Hypatius will put an end to Justinian's illegal wars and bring bread and work to the people!"

"Hypatius?" Troglita muttered in my ear. "Anastasius' nephew?"

"Must be," I answered. "He was a prat when his uncle was emperor, and I doubt he has the guile to stage a coup on his own."

The Greek frowned and repeated his greeting. "Brothers, we have suffered under the tyranny of Justinian for long enough! Free yourselves of an illegitimate emperor!"

Walking two paces before the shield wall, I faced the mob and their sea of smoldering torches and blades. "My name is Komes Varus, Commander of the Herulian foederati," I said, leaving a slight pause between each word for effect. "In the name of the Emperor, I demand that you allow us passage and offer no further hindrance. This will be your only warning!"

Laughing, the Greek hefted a torch with a thickly muscled arm. Curling his arm back, the man hurled the torch directly at my chest. As the torch sailed through the air, I squared my shield atop my body, allowing the flaming wood to clatter harmlessly against my shield and onto the ground. It was a feeble attack, yet my tormenter was not finished with me.

"You are what, three hundred? We are thousands, and you will not leave here this day."

The man's laughter was cut short as a spear pierced through his chest. Eyes wide in surprise, the man choked as he attempted to speak, but no words gurgled from behind a froth of blood. His strength sapped, the man collapsed into a twitching heap, the crowd roaring in anger.

"Go fuck yourselves!" Fulcaris screamed in accented Greek, drawing a sword to replace his absent spear.

"Idiot!" I yelled at Fulcaris in Heruli. "Form up!"

"It couldn't be helped, Lord," Fulcaris insisted with a wicked grin. "They attacked you first."

Dozens of armored Greens and Blues descended upon our formation, all screaming in rage and vengeance. Many seemed intoxicated as they stumbled fearlessly to our lines, cursing the Emperor's barbarians as a blight upon Constantine's city. Incensed by blood, they rushed at our column, the weight of hundreds pressing each side of our crude rectangle in on itself.

"First rank, kneel!" I commanded. "Second rank, spears up!"

The foederati obeyed flawlessly. The formation was one disdained by most Roman infantry as no more than a delay to an inevitable defeat, as it allowed an enemy to maneuver, yet in the tight corners of Constantinople's streets I found it the ideal approach to ward off a horde of angry plebeians. While some of the mob may have been military veterans themselves, most had little to no training in combat. They rushed us headlong, with no sense of order in the sort of charge that would terrify a levy or another undisciplined rabble. But my men were trained killers and saw the unorganized mass as easy prey.

Those first waves fell upon an even wall of Herulian spears as many of the mob were unable to maneuver away from the sharpened spearpoints. Pressed forward by hundreds of those who followed behind, men screamed as their momentum impaled them on the iron and ash weapons, forming a macabre fence of dead and twitching corpses. I gave an order for the men to only defend themselves against attack and to mount no offensive assaults of their own, which they generally followed.

As the pressure of the mob dissipated, a voice at my back warned of new threats ahead. Turning, I found Belisarius, eyes fixed on the road ahead.

"Varus, the cart!" he yelled. "Get the men to move!"

His words immediately preceded the torches that brought the oiled cart alight, its flames dancing well above the towering buildings on either side of us. One woman screamed in agony as her thick woolen gown caught fire from the pooling flames, crying for help as the fire snaked up her body and consumed her veil and hair. Dissuaded by such an example, others of the mob grunted as they pushed against the cart, its wheels gathering speed as it rolled downhill.

Straight for the foederati.

"Split!" I yelled, wide eyed.

Though the cart was slow in rolling in our direction, many of the Herulians shouted as they pushed to either side of the flaming ram and leaned against the relative safety of a nearby building. Belisarius was quickly surrounded and carried off by several of the bucellarii, while Father Petrus clung perilously to my cloak as I half carried him to the opposite side. Flames licked at exposed flesh as the cart jolted past, popping and rumbling as its wheels hit uneven stone.

I discovered later that other than minor burns and abrasions my men emerged unscathed from the cart's passage. As my men called to one another, the more courageous of the mob surged into the gap left in the cart's wake, splitting the foederati into two incomplete halves.

"What do we do, Lord?" a voice called from my left. I saw Altan, his face caked in fear and his shield wavering as a gang of club-wielders charged in our direction.

"Keep your shield high, Altan!" I screamed. "And butcher the bastards!"

Rather than waiting for the men's reaction, I jammed my spear into a Latin man who laughed carelessly as he charged into the fray. My spear caught the man in his unprotected midriff, and he arched back as its point split his spine and drove cleanly through his body. Unable to wrench the spear free, I discarded the weapon and drew my sword once again.

"Recover! Re-form!" I yelled, my words echoed by a dozen other voices down the line. Fulcaris and Irilar screamed and snarled for the wall to reassemble, and slowly the centermost lines in the column reknit themselves into a coherent mass. As the last of the interlopers fell to blades or fled, the shaky column shaped itself into marching order and again continued to the Imperial Palace.

"Wounded?" I called to the back.

Each centurion replied in turn.

"A broken wrist, but all alive!" called one.

"No casualties!" replied another.

"Knife cut in the arm, but nothing major," noted Irilar with some irritation.

"General Belisarius is safe, as is Father Petrus," Uliaris shouted behind me.

Though dozens of onlookers continued to throw stones and flaming projectiles into our formation, few others volunteered to throw their bodies into a Roman banda hardened by war against thousands of Hephthalites and Persian Immortals. We were the victors of Dara and had survived the maw of Callinicum, giving Rome a rare taste of victory against a vast Persian Empire that had been the bane of many an emperor in generations past.

We squeezed through alleys and avoided the Hippodrome's ominous entrance, finally snaking our way to the palace doors. Immediately adjacent to the Palace was the Hagia Sophia, still only half rebuilt, its scaffold fully alight like a cruel candle to Constantinople's destruction.

"Awful," Belisarius said.

"Better the church than the Palace," I replied, earning a sigh of disgust from Father Petrus.

As the palace doors came into view, my heart sank as my words took on new meaning. For the mob had stormed the palace entrance, with dozens snaking into the once-austere gates to the Emperor's residence.

"Foederati, follow me!" I cried out, my mind swimming with fear as I begged God to spare my wife and child.

Like any well-trained Roman infantry, the foederati kept pace with their commander, their shields locked as we swept aside stragglers eager for loot and spoils from the Palace's many rooms. Resistance grew stiffer as we ascended the marble stairs to the doorway, the passage littered by dozens of corpses that included several members of the city watch in their number.

Storming through the palace doorway I stumbled into an angry mob of Greens, many of whom were heavily laden with all forms of silver and gold instruments. The only lights of that hallowed place were fostered by a handful of dancing torches that rose and fell amongst the masses, leaving most helpless as they grasped at shadows to determine friend or foe. Seeing the foederati, dozens slinked away with their plunder and out into the streets, while others dropped the heavy candlesticks and medallions in fear for their lives. However, the bulk of the mass turned in resistance, slamming hard into our shields and nearly pushing the foederati out of the Palace and back into the blood-soaked stairway.

Leaning hard into my shield as I stabbed forward, even that resistance ebbed and allowed the ranks behind me to press our way into the palace entrance. A thousand voices screamed and roared in a mixture of agony and ecstasy, the noises accented by the smell of coppery blood and the fearful musk of fresh piss. Ignoring it all, I charged forward, occasionally risking my eyes as I glimpsed my next victim as my armored body propelled me through the malnourished and uncoordinated rabble that had filtered through the Palace's main level. The foederati surged ceaselessly, chopping at the limbs and heads of any who resisted or failed to move from the carnage.

Until, in the darkness, my shield slammed hard into another. The foederati's advance came to a sudden halt.

"Cease! Withdraw!" Samur yelled in Heruli. "Friends!"

My back popped as I stood straight and sheathed my sword, and I sprinted to Samur. Though the sight of my brother, blood-soaked but otherwise healthy, kindled a hope that we could still secure the Palace and all inside, bile rose in my throat at the realization that many hundreds of the mob had swarmed past the palace guards. I wanted to vomit, jam my blade into an enemy torso, and to know that Zenobia, Mariya, and my circle of beloved remained safe.

I suppressed panic, taking three deep breaths before answering Samur. "Where's Zenobia? Mariya? The Empress?"

"Upstairs with the excubitores!" Samur replied hurriedly. "I took your men and held off as many as I could, but the bastards just keep coming."

"They're upstairs?" I asked, referring to the mob.

"Some," Samur said, panting. "We couldn't cover every entrance. They came shouting how Hypatius is the new emperor."

"Same with us," I said, my eyes on the stairs. "Can you clear out the main level with the whole foederati?"

"Already done," Samur replied darkly. "Take whoever you need and go relieve Marcellus."

Signaling Belisarius and Troglita, I explained our situation. Belisarius bit his lip, understanding the jeopardy Antonina and Joannina were in, and nodded at my plan to take a small force to the upper levels of the Palace.

"You know the Palace better than any here," he said. "You have command."

I nodded, turning to the bucellarii and Belisarius' former jailors. "Men, the Imperial Court is under siege. We're going upstairs, but don't attack unless struck first, and keep your eyes sharp in the darkness."

"No brutality," Belisarius added. "We don't know who stormed the Palace, or why."

Impatient, I ascended the stairs as Samur organized the foederati for their intended tasks. Already slick with blood, my boots had little grip on the marble steps, and what little light was available hardly illuminated the treacherous outline of that winding staircase. Multiple bodies had been pushed to either side, littering all manner of guts and excrement on the landings, yet I forced my attention ever forward, my sword drawn and heart begging to find my family healthy and safe.

Though the din grew softer as we reached the second level, sounds of struggle still rang down the various corridors leading to the Emperor's guestrooms. Having grabbed an abandoned shield and blade, Belisarius stood at my left, his eyes scanning the near-pitch-black hallways for signs of enemies or friends.

"Keep going," I said in a muted voice. "Listen for the excubitores."

Our pitifully thin shield wall crept down the hallway, our boots occasionally connecting with severed limbs or a body drained of its vital humors. After twenty paces, we found our first evidence of battle as an armored body sent Uliaris tumbling to the ground. He scrambled back to his feet in expectation of an attack.

"Excubitor's armor," I concluded, feeling its grooved steel layers. "They're close."

Despite the danger of tripping and falling, we accelerated our pace down the hallway. Boards creaked in the near-total darkness as our boots navigated to whoever still lived among the Emperor's retinue, guided by a steady trail of bodies that grew denser with each step.

Until, in the distance, a single flame erupted in the darkness. A woman's scream followed, echoed by a bloodcurdling moan as a deeper Greek voice pleaded for his life. Such pleas went unheeded just moments later.

"That was Auria!" Troglita yelled.

"Don't break ranks!" I called fruitlessly, though Troglita did not even pause as he ambled towards the flames, sword drawn.

"To Troglita!" Belisarius yelled, a command that I echoed.

Without a second thought, our shield wall disintegrated. Any half-decent master-at-arms would have wept, yet we had little choice as Troglita followed the shrieks of a woman pushed far beyond the limits of fear any person should experience. Moving just a handful of paces behind Troglita, I held my eyes on the torch, its embers tracing the silhouette of a half dozen cloaked men.

"Auria!" Troglita screamed.

The men raised their heads in warning of his advance, while Belisarius and I dashed close behind, blades drawn.

Troglita gutted the first man, his sword digging into his stomach with a sickening lurch. I followed by stabbing at the eyes of another, feeling a slight tugging as my enemy wailed in the darkness. Belisarius and Uliaris dispatched three others. The last man raised his sword high above Belisarius' head and swung down with a crude scythe, leaving him no time to react.

The man's sword arm swung limply to his side, its strength evaporating as a spear pierced his chest and punctured the heart protected within. The man was dead before he hit the ground, killed by young Vitalius.

Grabbing the torch, Belisarius nodded his thanks to the lad, whose jaw trembled at what had been done.

"Was that your first?" I asked.

Vitalius nodded. "I did the right thing?" he asked, white-faced, his shaking hands dropping the spear to the ground.

"You protected your commander, and there is no higher honor than that," I said. "And we will discuss it later when there is more time."

Troglita had already bounded down the hallway, using the light of Belisarius' torch to find the prone figure of a Mauri woman behind an open doorway. For a moment, my chest seized as I thought Auria dead, until she blinked.

"Oh, thank God!" Auria cried in her Mauri-accented Latin, draping her arms over Troglita's armor.

"Are you hurt?" Troglita asked, his eyes sweeping the hall for any further sign of intruders.

"I don't think so," Auria replied. "I got separated from the rest of the group, and my guards were overwhelmed by the mob…"

She sobbed as her gaze fell upon the slain guardsmen, their eyes staring blankly upward as their bodies cooled. Both bore the sigil of a city watchman rather than the heavier steel of an excubitor, who were trained to never leave the Emperor's side unless commanded.

"Where did the others go?" I asked urgently. "Mariya, Antonina, the Emperor and Empress?"

Sniffling, Auria wiped her face, her slim fingers clutching at Troglita's collar. The Mauri princess jumped as a great crash sounded from the floor below, evidence of the desperate fight facing Samur and the foederati. I guiltily thought about siphoning a few dozen

Herulians to aid in rescuing Mariya, then shrugged away the idea, as it would only delay my search.

"Marcellus tried to hold the mob back in the Empress' private hall," Auria recounted, indicating the series of rooms dedicated to Theodora's private audiences on the second level. "It seemed to work for a time, yet more started pouring in from the Hippodrome door and overrunning several of the guardsmen."

"But where are they now?" Belisarius said, his urgency adding to my own.

Auria stuttered. "T-top level, at the Emperor's private hall."

In that moment, her words brought me back to my final visit with Justin, his frail body able to do little more than rise for a few moments of minimal exertion. Back to the oath that he administered to me in hopes that I would become a good man and an honorable servant of Rome. When Justin gave me his runed sword, its blue-green blade rumored to have been forged from the fires of the gods themselves.

"Let's go!" I cried. "Auria, there isn't anywhere safe to go right now, so you'll need to stay close to our formation."

Auria nodded, her hand outstretched as she pointed to a far staircase where Marcellus had led what remained of the Imperial party to safety. The press of bodies grew denser as we approached those stairs, a sickly humidity filling the air from their heat. Where our initial sojourn had encountered only members of the dead, here, the prostrate bodies moaned, calling out for water, or God, or merely for an end to suffering as their flesh leaked blood and bile. I hardened my heart as we passed those poor fools, for I could not jeopardize my family even to offer them a mercy stroke.

Ascending the stairs to the highest levels of the Palace, the sound of battle on the main floor diminished, only to be replaced by more desperate fighting on the floor above. True to Auria's words, hundreds of the mob pressed against Justinian's enclosed quarters, their voices chanting a mixture of familiar cadences, with dozens roaring the chant of "Nika!" Yet, as with the foederati's struggles through the streets of Constantinople, others called for Hypatius, while others called for the deaths of Justinian, Paulus, and Tribonian.

We encountered stragglers of the mob as we scaled the final steps, their arms heavy with weapons and torches that contrasted angrily against the pitch black of the floors below. A woman yelled furiously as she saw our shields. Dozens turned and threw loose wooden boards and flaming torches at us. Instinctively, I squared my shield against the fray, its rim locking against Belisarius' and Troglita's as we carved through flying missiles and a thickening mass of fighters. Auria prayed fearfully as we marched a half step at a time, using our weapons to fend off those who ventured too close to our formation.

However, there was little we could do against that press of humanity. Our diminutive shield wall curled as the mob threatened to quickly outflank our ranks, forcing Uliaris and the other bucellarii to push hard against this fate that would force our lines to fight back to back. We called out to one another for encouragement as, heads guarded by our shields, we pressed on toward the Emperor's private hall.

Even upon reaching that goal, however, we were met only by fearful omens. Rather than being shut and barred, the hall door had been battered to splinters, its handles caved in, allowing dozens to pour into the gap. Using the crowd's momentum, I directed our wall through that gap, fighting off a number of Greens as we stumbled over a carpet of the dead and the dying. As we pushed into the room, I caught a glimpse of the far dais where, guarded by several dozen excubitores, the Emperor had made a final stand.

"To the Emperor!" I cried, pleading with God to find Mariya and Zenobia within that protective ring.

Atop the raised dais, Marcellus shouted ragged commands through the crowd's chanting, despite his hoarseness. Using his voice as a guide, I bashed forward with my shield, cutting a path to Justinian's position. However, the claustrophobic press of bodies forced our shield wall to curl once more, yielding fatal gaps in the overlapping shields. The commander of Belisarius' jailors took an axe to his exposed throat as he struggled to parry blows from three different attackers, red mist spraying high into the air.

Unable to carve through the dense center of the mob, our shield ring succumbed to the crowd's pressure and waded to the right side of the raised platform. Few attempted further violence against us in the press, although whether that was from an inability to move their arms or greater attention placed against the thin ring of excubitores in the other direction, I cannot be sure. All I know is that we fought desperately to reach our comrades, and that Mariya and Zenobia were amongst them.

Even with salty sweat blurring my vision, I could make out Mariya's raven-black hair, shimmering in the torchlight even absent the usual gems and combs. In her arms was Zenobia, red-faced and screaming, both beside a weeping Antonina and her own squirming child. Sembrouthes and Xerxes stood guard over that small cadre, as most of the other Aksumites were positioned along the Emperor's defenses. Shielded by an additional ring of defenders, Justinian and Theodora were surrounded by an inner circle comprised of Marcellus, Chanaranges, and a dozen of the more senior excubitor commanders. While Justinian's ministers huddled close to that inner mass, Liberius snarled as he directed the last bastion of the palace's defenses, cracking his gnarled cane over the heads of those who threatened to swarm past overwhelmed guardsmen.

Even in the presence of babes, the crowd bayed for the blood of the nobles. With cries of "Nika!" and "Hypatius!" on their lips, Blues, Greens, and various other factions swarmed against Justinian's frozen form, undaunted by the screams of the wounded and the rising mound of the dying. Nearly all excubitores were caked in gore, panting in exhaustion and struggling to retain their defenses from a flurry of wounds.

Despite a valiant effort, even these Herculean excubitores had slowly cracked from the pressure of hundreds of attackers, leaking several invaders into the inner circle of the Emperor's Court. Helpless, I screamed as I watched two Greens haul themselves onto the dais and brandish their weapons, advancing to beat down an excubitor a mere ten paces from my position. Xerxes took down the first attacker with a rapid slash to the throat, the choking body falling to the floor. Sembrouthes speared the second attacker, then was tackled by another as their followers joined the melee, with one raising her club toward Mariya's uncovered head.

With a nimble, catlike grace, Rosamund lunged for Mariya's attacker and drove the woman to the ground with a sickening thud. Aetius' dagger in her hand, Rosamund keened an eerie cry as she jabbed at the woman's exposed neck, a fountain of blood staining her normally bone-white hair. She hopped to her feet as she spat a red mist that blinded her second would-be attacker, ignoring the man's pleas as she drove the knife into the man's eye, then turned to fend off a third Green, who clubbed her hard in the face, sending her crumpling into a heap.

I screamed in rage, an otherworldly fury fueling strength that was beyond that of even my overlarge form. Slicing through the crowd, I led our shield ring to the dais and severed the ankles of those who sought to overrun the remaining excubitores, leaving four squealing in pain as they rolled helplessly on the sodden floor. Eyes rising in recognition, Xerxes hauled himself to his feet and cut down the wounded attackers, opening a space for me to join the desperate defense.

Taking advantage of the momentary gap in the crowd, I hauled myself up, raising Belisarius and Auria as soon as I was able. Our shield ring slid into the gaps of the Roman formation and drove the attackers back from the dais, offering momentary respite from the constant press of unwashed bodies. Leaving Belisarius in command of our motley unit, I stole a glance at Mariya and Zenobia, then quickly turned to an unconscious Rosamund. I lifted her from a suffocating mass of slain bodies and placed her gently on safer ground.

"Varus!" Sembrouthes yelled, wincing as he clutched at his side. "Thank God for your timing."

"Are you wounded?"

"A broken rib or two, nothing more."

Xerxes snorted. "And I'm just fine, thanks for your concern."

"Enough jabbering!" Liberius bellowed. "Are the foederati coming?"

I nodded. "Samur's leading them. They're clearing out the lower levels and following close behind."

Liberius beamed. "All the more reason to chase these dogs off," he replied. "Lord Belisarius, perhaps you would be so kind as to clear the room?"

Belisarius nodded, visible relief framing his features as he stole a kiss from a howling Antonina. He signaled to Marcellus the need for a charge, and the excubitor commander offered a rare smile as he nodded at Belisarius' return.

"Men, for Rome and the Emperor!" he cried, lowering his sword and bashing with his shield.

Joined by the forces remaining to Justinian, the reserve excubitores and guardsmen pressed hard against the crowd, slamming iron shield rims against exposed hands and skulls from those who pushed to the edge of the platform. The mob's pressure began to wane at this sudden offensive. Those closest to the Emperor's forces backed away fearfully into a more constricting mass. I followed Belisarius as he jumped down and formed a wall on the lower level, with Uliaris and the bucellarii following closely behind. We gained ground as many of the mob ran for the exits, leaving only a few hundred behind who still strove to drive a blade into Justinian's heart.

Not long after, screams rang out from the back of the hall as dozens of black-shielded infantry stormed into the room. Many vainly attempted to throw down their weapons in surrender, but whether from the darkness or a fury against this insurrection, they were butchered by Herulian and excubitor alike. Most of the remaining mob went down fighting, even ones surrounded by the Emperor's most hardened killers.

Within moments, the affair was over, leaving behind a few hundred panting warriors, a shaken Imperial Court, and a Palace that more resembled the lair of Satan than the residence of God's chosen ruler in Christendom.

The stench was horrid, made all the more unbearable by the oppressive heat of the room. Men and women alike cried from fear and relief of certain death, with several of the more senior ministers joining in praises for their salvation. Paulus raised an abandoned blade and hacked angrily at wounded attackers that had been unable to flee from the Herulians' final attack, while Justinian clutched at Theodora's gown as she lowered his head to her chest.

Checking for potential ambushes, I soon sheathed my sword and ran back to the dais, crashing to the arms of Mariya. Zenobia screamed louder as she gazed at the crimson-soaked stranger who wore her father's skin, yet I could not resist planting a kiss on her smooth forehead. With her free hand, Mariya dug her fingers painfully into my face as her amber eyes locked onto mine, a heavy tear causing the kohl along her eye to run darkly down her almond cheek.

Our trance was soon snapped as my mind turned to Rosamund, who still lay in a heap along the back of the platform. As I lifted her into my arms, I felt her stir, her hollow voice barely more than a whisper.

"Varus," she said weakly, a question as much as a statement.

"I am here," I replied foolishly, unsure of what to say.

"Next time, I'm taking your sword instead of your dagger."

Despite myself, I laughed. "Not for a good while, with this wound."

"I'll be fine. No paralysis." She wiggled her hands and feet. "I just might not be able to work for a few days."

I shook my head. "After saving Mariya, I owe you my life."

Rosamund smiled as she nestled her head against my armor, her eyes closing as she winced. Careful not to disturb her head, I handed Rosamund to the Aksumite officer Wazeba, telling him to take a retinue of a dozen Herulians and find secure quarters for his charge to rest. Rosamund protested lightly at being taken from the battle's aftermath, but soon fell into a deep sleep as Wazeba set off to his task.

Other detachments of Herulians and excubitores were sent to clear the Palace of its remaining interlopers, leaving the Court behind to process the evening's horror. At Theodora's command, I formed teams of men to haul bodies down to the Palace's main level, a task that Belisarius and the bucellarii joined in with no complaint. Excused from those detachments was Vitalius, who I ordered to depart with Liberius to the Palace's lower levels. Liberius placed a hand on Vitalius' back as the youth strode away from the carnage, silent and unblinking, and murmured soft words of reassurance.

As Troglita and I detached our shields and joined in the grisly work, Samur and Fulcaris shook their heads in refusal of our help.

"I'll make sure the Empress' orders are fulfilled," Samur said. "Take your family and get some rest."

Soon thereafter, a decision was reached to allow the Court to rest for the evening, for no reasonable strategy could be formed from the exhaustion of the Palace's defense. Those with weapons not given the task of corpse removal were assigned to protect the Palace's various entrances and were provided with the right to form any type of barricade necessary to ease the burden.

Theodora also sent the few remaining city watchmen to seek out the palace slaves and servants who'd scattered to the dozens of hidden hallways and tunnels that lined the Palace's more ornate rooms. After ordering those secret passages further manned with armed soldiers, the Court retired to the rooms on the Palace's mid-levels that had not been ruined by fire, blood, and plunder, with the Emperor and Empress followed closely by Marcellus.

Surrendering to weakness, I took Mariya into my arms and led her to our apartments. Sembrouthes moved to follow, but I commanded him to rest.

"You think I will sleep after this?" Sembrouthes gestured around us. "Give me something to do."

I began to speak, but Mariya interrupted me. "Bring a half dozen of your men and guard the entrances to our doorway."

"Of course, Princess," Sembrouthes replied. Snapping his fingers, he issued orders in the Aksumite tongue, dismissing half of his men to rest while the remainder scurried to obey Sembrouthes' call for assembly. Navigating pools of slick blood, we departed the massacre. Mariya held a hand over Zenobia's eyes as we stepped carefully along less dangerous footing and filed downstairs, and as soon as we escaped the view of my men, both of us wept.

AS THE WORLD BURNS

Located at the far end of a second-floor hallway, our rooms bore no bloody signs of violence, yet they had not escaped unscathed. Our apartments had been ransacked by plunderers, its featherbed overturned, furniture gashed and broken along the walls. I let out a guilty sigh. While I was infinitely grateful for the deliverance of my wife and child, I hated to think that our prized possessions would be hacked and bartered by those of Constantinople's streets. Mariya grinned weakly at my display, offering a lone sliver of positive information on a ruinous day.

"That servant boy, Agathias, gathered several men and carried our things to the tunnels below," she explained.

"A good lad," I said.

Mercifully, a thorough examination of Zenobia's rocking cradle found the wooden frame undamaged and its cloth only lightly torn. Overtaxed by an exceedingly long day, Zenobia had already begun to snore lightly in Mariya's arms, tiny tears drying upon plump cheeks. Slowly, we placed Zenobia in the cradle, covering her exposed arms with a clean swaddling cloth. Zenobia twitched in her sleep from our interruptions, and I jerked back in alarm, which brought another smile to Mariya's kohl-smeared face. We set the cradle in a secure adjoining room, its windows barred shut to block out the winter cold and the constant hum of the ongoing riot.

Mariya sped into the hallway as I used our single lit candle to readjust the broken furniture and mattress within our room. My mind in a fog, I did not even think to question the wisdom of her venturing out into the possibly dangerous and dimly lit Palace until she returned with two of her Ghassanid servants, freshly returned from the relative safety of the palace tunnels. The young women sobbed loudly as they each hugged Mariya, sharing a moment of relief as they praised God for their safe return. Mariya then whispered into the servants' ears, and they nodded in unison.

"Yes, we will wait for you, Princess," one of the women, Alia, replied, gracefully slipping into Zenobia's room. "Guards have secured the building and are stationed at the junctures of each hallway."

"And Sembrouthes' men guard your household rooms," Jamila, the second household servant, added. "We are all safe, at least for the evening."

I frowned. "What's this?"

"Just follow me," Mariya replied, gathering a heavy bundle with the help of Jamila.

"Mariya, I'm exhausted, and the Palace might still be crawling with rioters."

But Mariya shook her head, allowing Jamila to speak. "No, Lord Varus, the guards have checked each room. We should be safe now," Jamila offered. "They will be cleaning for some time, however."

Undaunted, Mariya grabbed my hand and dragged both of us into the hallway. Even with her statement of confidence, Jamila locked the door behind us as we exited, its wooden latch slamming home upon an iron holster on the other side. Navigating by the few torches that had been raised to illuminate each hallway, Mariya led me down a side passage and further into darkness.

"Where are we going?" I asked insistently, making no effort to hide my annoyance.

"Where I decide we go," Mariya responded. "Be patient."

A reassuring grumble of patrolling Herulians echoed in the distance as Mariya moved farther from the central corridor toward the rooms least affected by the crowd's intrusion. Chilling drafts swept at our feet as we neared a high window at the end of the hallway, allowing light from the smoldering Hagia Sophia and a hundred fires beyond to filter into the shadowy Imperial halls. Dropping her bundle at a heavy door adjacent to that window, Mariya turned its brass handle and pushed, forcing me quickly inside.

Into the Emperor's private baths.

"We aren't supposed to be here," I whispered.

Mariya's hand tightened around mine. "I don't care."

I dug in my feet, listening carefully for any sounds of approaching footsteps. "If the Emperor finds us…"

"Then the Emperor is an idiot."

Baths had long been a Roman tradition, and the emperors in Constantinople had attempted to mimic their Latin forebears by constructing a number of public bathing facilities, yet their maintenance and use had declined during my lifetime. Petitions to thoroughly clean operational baths and to reconstruct those allowed to succumb to decrepitude had frequently been raised in Justinian's Court, but those expenses had been largely ignored by Paulus as he hoarded taxes for Justinian's other projects. The Emperor had never balked at the maintenance of his own private thermae and frigidarium, the bathing rooms reserved for heating and cooling the body as it was wet and scrubbed clean.

The greatest luxury of that bathing complex was its ready access to clean, fresh water. Piped from an aqueduct system that carried water from the hills of Thrace, the baths funneled fresh water into the room as quickly as it was expended, allowing the Emperor as much time in relaxation as was desired. The water could even be heated by a great furnace that quickly burned white hot from a discreetly disguised bellows. Dropping her bag to the floor, Mariya ducked back into the hallway and returned with a stolen torch, which she threw into a furnace that had been heavily laden with stripped logs and branches. The flame ignited the stack as Mariya closed the furnace door, inflating the bellows and bringing the room temperature to a summer heat levels within moments.

"Mariya…" I began.

"Until a few hours ago, I thought my husband and daughter were going to be torn apart," Mariya muttered, her amber eyes narrowing on mine as she spoke. "Let me have this one happy memory."

Mariya drew close, hints of her rosewater perfume still present despite the day's carnage. Raising her slender fingers to my shoulder guards, Mariya unclasped the spare cloak I had taken from the barracks. As the thick wool dropped to the floor, Mariya slammed me hard against the thermae wall, using her spare hand to secure the bolt to prevent intruders from disturbing her peace. She struggled to unknot sections of my chest armor, chuckling at her failure as she wondered aloud how Cephalas could perform the task one-handed. Eventually she succeeded in her task and helped me pull the overlapping metal scales over my head and atop the cloak on the floor.

"Varus," she cooed, her voice a mixture of concern and awe as she traced her manicured nails against the sheet of fresh bruises that covered my body. Mariya drew back hesitantly as I winced in pain but returned to her ritual as she found a dozen scars from Dara, Tauris, and the Gepids.

Steam billowed in thick clouds as the furnace brought its steady stream of water to a boil. Satisfied, Mariya traced her hands up my jawline and along my exposed neck, tugging hard as she beckoned me lower. Her lips met mine with a ravenous anger that made me draw back in surprise, but she continued nonetheless.

As I enveloped her in my embrace, she leaned hard into my exposed torso, and I winced again as her forearm pressed against an already blackening bruise. I raised my sword hand to Mariya's throat, plucking at a golden ouroboros clasp that held her stola in place. Slowly dropping each arm in turn, Mariya gracefully slipped off the sleeves and allowed the silken stola to join my cloak on the floor, its rich azure spotted with blood and torn in a half dozen cuts at the hem.

Mariya's soft, unmarked skin betrayed her status as a Roman aristocrat, her hands and body spared the grueling labor from tilling a field or bending ceaselessly over a loom to fashion coarse clothing for her family. Nevertheless, her body had changed from pregnancy, the skin about her hips and stomach softer to the touch, her stomach and chest fuller. And unlike upon our wedding night, I feared I might hurt her, taking my touch cautious and slow. As my hand grazed her navel, she inhaled, seizing my fingers.

"I still feel different, from Zenobia," Mariya explained, placing my hand upon her bare hip. "I know it's normal, and I regret nothing, but still…" Her voice trailed for several moments. "I miss how I used to look."

Since she first arrived in Constantinople, I had never known Mariya to lack confidence. Nor had I been aware of this new discomfort, the doddering oaf that I am. "Every night in Mesopotamia, I begged God to grant me one last moment with you. But even that pales in comparison to now. You are more radiant now than ever."

"Varus the flatterer!" she teased, her broad smile illuminated by blushing, dimpled cheeks. "Not a skill I suspect is popular in the army."

As the thickening steam further blotched the remaining kohl around her eyes, I tugged her hips closer, making her shiver and laugh at the grazing touch. With her lips still locked upon mine, Mariya unfastened the leather belt at my waist and slowly sank to the floor to unbuckle my iron greaves. She did not slink away from the muck caked onto my boots as she guided my feet free, using my body to climb back to her feet as my trousers sank to the thermae floor.

Leading me to a shallow pool of water, Mariya guided me to sit on a heated stone that had grown slick with precipitation. Stealing a brief moment away, Mariya disappeared into the thickening steam, only to return after the sound of fresh logs being thrown into the furnace and a swift crank of its bellows. With a self-sure smile, she dipped her entire body into the pool, emerging just heartbeats later at my feet. Pushing me back against the stones with unabashed forcefulness, Mariya drew her hips atop my own, her nails digging hard into my chest.

We made love in the Emperor's thermae, our only lights the bath's furnace and the fires that lined Constantinople's expanse just outside our window. The flame from the Hagia Sophia's scaffolding had transformed into reddish embers, and other Imperial buildings had been put to the torch by one gang of rioters or the other. But in that moment, I did not care, for I felt and thought of nothing else beyond the wild energy that Mariya wielded.

Later, as the heat drew down and the furnace's flames lowered to a more muted level, Mariya and I lay against the pool in each other's arms. She smiled as her finger traced the outline of my beard, occasionally clutching at my side as she drew me into another tight embrace. Our skin matted together from the steam as we lay there watching Constantinople burn for a rare private moment in the Imperial Palace.

Even that peace felt hollow as my thoughts drifted to Perenus. Fleeting images whirled about, first of a cocky recruit in a poorly fitting bronze cap, his feet bleeding and swollen from our hellish march to the Euxine Sea. Then, of a burlier man on horseback, patient and lighthearted as he instructed me in the art of horse archery alongside the Herulian foederati. He was like a brother, exultant in my victories and consoling in my hurts, and incorrigibly optimistic.

It seemed strange that such overwhelming sadness would arrive at that moment, yet as I lay next to Mariya, tears flooded onto my cheeks, blurring my vision as I attempted to disguise my weakness. The efforts were futile, however, as Mariya's forceful hands brought my nose to graze hers, her soft thumb brushing just below my eye. Brows knitted with concern, she demanded an explanation for the sudden shift, and I confessed my grief—for Perenus, for my friend.

Mariya pulled my head to her chest, her fingers running through my hair.

"Perenus loved the races," she murmured. "He was so excited to return to the Greens."

I nodded, my head swimming from the overwhelming mixture of grief and intimacy. "It's all he talked about in the last month," I agreed. "Even if he knew how it would have ended, I doubt I could have convinced him to do anything differently."

Helpless, my body softened as Mariya bestowed all the strength and comfort she could muster. We lay again in silence as the fires smoldered unabated, the thermae's steam beginning to clear over our drenched bodies.

After a time, Mariya cocked her head at me and wrinkled her nose. "You stink!" she cried in mock horror.

I raised my arms in defense, pleading forgiveness. "I didn't really have a chance to bathe," I explained, splashing water onto her exposed back, where its cool temperature raised a layer of bumps. She shivered, stretching her legs, then rose and skipped to the furnace to additional fuel to its dying flames. Her wiry arms tensed as she operated the bellows, her energy heating the water once more.

Satisfied, Mariya jumped into a deeper section of the pool, where she dunked her head underwater for several heartbeats, only a swirling mass of hair visible that rippled on top of the waves. When she resurfaced, she tied her sopping mane into a thick bun before beckoning for me to join her.

Relaxed, my eyes grew heavy as I lowered my body into the heated water, my legs and torso aching. Mariya would not allow any surrender to sleep as she pried brushes and scented soaps from her bag, ordering me to follow her example and immerse myself in the water. I obeyed and was immediately subjected to one of the more invasive Roman baths of my life.

While many wealthy or senior members of Roman society utilized the services of slaves or servants to assist with the complex bathing ritual, my own years as a slave and general awkwardness with nudity left me to generally bathe alone. Outside of my early experiences with Rosamund, I had only allowed servants to clean my body in the aftermath of considerable injury from battle, and even then reluctantly so. Mariya showed no aversion to the normally degrading task, scrubbing my body as she clicked her teeth at the state of my injuries. With the brushing completed, Mariya finished her work with a bronze strigil, scraping away any grime or gore that inevitably found its way into the crevices of soldier's bodies. She mocked my sheepishness, dunking my head once more into the water before nodding in acceptance.

I paid her the same respects, patiently scrubbing her body as she closed her eyes and leaned back onto the warm stones. Her stomach hinted at the recent pregnancy that had ended less than a half year prior, yet even then Mariya remained a delicate and slender figure, seemingly too thin by Roman standards. Her breathing slowed as I drew the soaps over her body, and she yelped in surprise when I dragged the strigil along her flank to scrape away remaining impurities. She splashed at my face and leaned over for a lingering kiss before instructing me to complete my task.

Finally succumbing to fatigue as the furnace burned low, we raised ourselves from the pool. Mariya retrieved several washcloths as we did what we could to dry away the excess water and don fresh clothes. As I gathered my cloak and armor, Mariya placed her soiled stola and bathing instruments into the bag, grabbing my hand as we unlatched the thermae door.

Sneaking back through the dark hallway, we turned a corner and were stopped by a detachment of Herulian sentries. One lowered his spear and ordered us to stop in a halting Greek accent, then begged forgiveness when his partner's torchlight revealed my identity.

"Everything all right, Lord?" the sentry asked.

"Perfect, given the circumstances," I replied.

Mariya stifled a giggle.

Sporting confused looks, the guards allowed us to pass with no further questions, and we soon returned to our rooms. Mariya's servants bowed and exited without comment, and we collapsed onto the remnants of our feather bed. Then, two heartbeats later, the bed's frame collapsed under our weight, weakened by some unseen damage from the earlier Palace attacks. Cursing under my breath, I sat up to inspect the damage, only to find my wife hooting with laughter.

"Leave it be," Mariya gasped, her fingers interlocking with my own.

Lulled into a stupor by the dull roar of the crowd outside, my body sank into the cushions as my senses faded, allowing only the trailing scent of her soap to cloud my sluggish mind.

AN IMPERIAL SHROUD

The next morning came painfully soon. After a polite knock, Cephalas cracked open the door, gently sliding his feet along the floorboards to limit unnecessary noise. Mariya groaned as she slung an arm over my chest, offering a feeble defense to protect her husband from further unpleasant duty.

"How early is it?" I asked groggily, my eyes fixing on Cephalas' outline as I realized the babe still slept in the next room.

"Before dawn," Cephalas responded, "although the Court is assembling, and the Empress asked me to retrieve you, with her apologies."

Grumbling, I pried myself away from Mariya's warmth and drew upright, the muscles in my flanks protesting from lack of rest. Cephalas helped me dress before disappearing out into the hallway, summoning an unseen servant.

Agathias returned with my excubitor's armor, beaming with delight as he entered the room. Spotting a sleeping Mariya, he blushed, handing each piece of armor to Cephalas as he strapped the leather and metal to my body. With that step complete, Cephalas placed my sheathed sword on my belt, adding to it the dagger that had been a gift from Godilas.

"Rosamund said to return this to you," Cephalas whispered. "Although both dagger and sword will need to be cleaned and sharpened before further use."

"How is Rosamund?" I asked.

"Pained," Cephalas answered truthfully. "Although she says she will recover soon enough. Agathias returned her powders and elixirs this morning, and Rosamund insists that she is well enough to treat herself."

"Keep an eye on her," I said. "She's independent but too proud to know when to ask for help."

Cephalas nodded, then hesitated. "Do you think…"

"Yes?"

"Should we say words for Perenus?" Cephalas asked. "Christian or pagan, I'm not sure if he really cared for either. But something so that he may know peace?"

Perenus. Images of the man's death again flooded my thoughts, mixed with the crushing horror of so many fights from the prior evening. "Of course. But perhaps after we find and cleanse his body."

That satisfied Cephalas. "Of course. I just wish I could go and retrieve him… It's hard to sit here knowing that the mob might desecrate his body."

A knot formed in my throat. "I doubt they would. Perenus is… *was* a Green. That should spare him most indignity."

Following Cephalas into the hall, I found Agathias next to two yellow-robed Aksumites standing silently outside the door. I offered a word of thanks to the men and patted Agathias on the head, offering my thanks for preserving so much of my estate.

"Think nothing of it, Lord," Agathias replied cheerily. "A small repayment for the gold for my lessons."

"As you wish," I said, placing a hand on the boy's shoulder. "When you're ready to leave the Palace, I would be happy to welcome you into my household."

Agathias flashed his teeth again. "Yes, Lord! That would be wonderful."

I nodded. "Let's make sure we survive the riots first, and that your lessons are not interrupted. But see Cephalas if you need anything while I am away."

Agathias bowed deeply as he bobbed with excitement and disappeared back into the servants' hallways. Cephalas directed me to a secondary room on the same floor that, while not nearly as large or grand as the Great Hall, still left ample space for Justinian's ministers to discuss matters of state. Standing guard outside the doorway, Sindual saluted as I passed, remarking on the continued high spirits of the foederati despite the prior day's street violence.

Inside, the room was occupied by two rectangular wooden tables, and I quickly spotted Theodora at the far end. Though deep in conversation with Liberius and Basilius, she raised a hand as she caught my gaze, summoning me into the private meeting as other ministers and guardsmen entered.

"Enjoy a restful evening after your dismissal, Varus?" Theodora asked mischievously.

I fought to remain emotionless as she inspected my reaction. Despite my efforts, a slow heat trickled up my neck. Mirth shone from her weary face, but she kindly did not press further, allowing her councilors to speak their business.

Liberius' eyes twinkled as he offered his greetings. "Father Petrus told me that you treated him quite ignobly the day before," he teased. "In my years with you, Varus, I know I lectured on the importance of showing respect to your elders."

"Not now, Liberius," Basilius mumbled, rolling his eyes.

"We are in your debt again, Varus," Theodora added, "but we are at a crossroads regarding what to do next."

"What the Empress means to say," Basilius cut in, "is that it is unclear how we can remove ourselves of our current predicament, and whether the foederati will be enough to defend the Palace."

I frowned. "My men will hold this building until the apocalypse. But what do you mean by *our current predicament*?"

It was at that moment that the Empress unveiled the extent of the danger facing Justinian. Shortly after the attack on the Palace had been quelled, a message was nailed to the outer palace door, proclaiming that Constantinople's Senate had voted to install Hypatius as the new and rightful emperor of the Romans. With the backing of nearly all senators, most remaining pockets of resistance against the mob had crumbled, leaving Justinian with the Imperial Stables, a select number of guard posts along the city's famous double walls, and a few other locations of little importance. In the span of a day, Justinian had been reduced to the tiniest fraction of his power, with the mob howling for his death as the fool Hypatius promised milk and honey for all.

And worst of all, only a few hundred men remained to hold hundreds of thousands at bay. For the mob had continued to arm itself, surrounding the Imperial Palace with a cautious ring of clubs and spears as chants to the old Goddess of Victory sporadically filled Constantinople's shoreline.

"But how could the Senate do this?"

"Weakness." Basilius snorted. "Most are old greedy men looking to see which way the wind blows. Everyone knows Hypatius is a glutton and an idiot, yet a sizeable amount of silver has been spread amongst the people to buy their love."

"By whom?"

"I have my suspicions," Basilius said, "and my doubts. A few names are curiously absent from Hypatius' confirmation, yet they haven't sought Justinian's protection either."

My eyebrow raised. "Any of note?"

"A few senators who never agreed with Justin's initial ascension to the Purple," Liberius chimed in, "and Nepotian, curious as it is."

"Solomon's father?"

"Indeed," Liberius replied. "Clever enough to not pick sides while the dice are still rolling, although his choice may be forced soon enough."

Amidst the conversation, I noticed Theodora's head had dropped to her hands, stiff fingers rubbing her eyes. Her nails were chipped and torn, while dark circles shadowed her emerald eyes, giving her a rare look of utter exhaustion. Untouched by the powders that colored her face and lips for Court, her face looked haunted yet strangely more alluring.

Theodora grabbed at my gloved right fist, tugging the soft leather free and exposing my hand underneath. Theodora turned my hand over to expose my callused palm, the flesh nicked with a half dozen abrasions and cuts.

"If I released you from your oath, would you leave me?" Theodora asked, her voice slow and viscous with intent.

I frowned again. "Never, Highness."

"Even if it meant saving your wife and child?" she asked innocently.

I sighed. I was caught again in Theodora's tangled web. She judged my reaction carefully, her fatigue forgotten.

"I have promised God to defend you, Highness, and that oath cannot ever be revoked," I concluded, bringing a sad smile to her face.

Returning my glove, Theodora rose to her feet and pulled me into a tight embrace. The pearls of her headdress brushed uncomfortably against my beard as she rested her head on my chest, her breathing slow.

"If I could trust all of my servants as I trust you, the world would be reshaped entirely," Theodora whispered, just loud enough for me to hear.

Liberius cleared his throat aggressively, and Theodora snapped back to attention. She returned to her chair as other ministers filed into the room, consuming the limited available space. Cassiodorus complained at the cramped quarters as his beefy shoulders rubbed easily against Paulus, as though he'd forgotten the fact that all present had nearly been butchered not a half day prior and were lucky to be alive at all.

"How many men were stationed in the outlying forts?" Theodora asked in another whisper.

"Two thousand? Perhaps three? Mundus leads them."

Theodora nodded. "Do you trust them?"

"Mundus is a born soldier and would never forsake a vow," I reasoned. "His men followed him to Dara and Callinicum—they would not abandon him now."

Several excubitores beat their spear shafts into the pavement, signaling the entrance of the Emperor. Justinian rushed into the room, followed closely by Narses and Procopius, yet absent any other pomp, his appearance more haggard than his wife's. Paulus attempted to get his attention, but either from lack of awareness or deliberate avoidance, Justinian remained silent as he moved to his improvised throne. Pecking Theodora on the cheek, he ordered all present to sit, an order obeyed in rapt silence. He surveyed the room and set his agenda.

"The people of Constantinople have risen against our throne and have crowned the patrician Hypatius as Caesar," he said, oddly nonchalant. "Our palace retains less than a thousand that may be called to arms, while reliable estimates place the forces available to Hypatius and his conspirators at a hundred times that number."

"Outrageous!" Tribonian wailed. "Hypatius must be skewered like the dog he is!"

"As should all senators who supported him, hanged for their treason," Paulus added.

Justinian glared at the interrupters, rendering them silent once more as he addressed the Court. Paulus nodded to several of his sycophants, who murmured agreement.

"I have been assured by Marcellus that with reinforcements by the Herulian foederati, the Palace can withstand a frontal assault for at least another day or two," Justinian recounted. "We have enough food stored to last for several weeks, and water remains in ready supply from the outer aqueducts. This is so, Lord Liberius?"

"Indeed, Highness," Liberius responded. "Preparations carefully made by your predecessor as a measure of last resort."

Justinian bobbed his head once in acknowledgment. "Yet it is inevitable that the forces arrayed against us will strike, and they will eventually overrun the Palace's defenses. So I ask you gathered here: What shall be our course of action?"

None spoke at first. Even Liberius sat motionless in his chair, his eyes glazed over as if in a distant trance. Others muttered in side conversations, their thoughts guarded and formal. Paulus stood just moments later, seizing his opportunity to take charge.

"Highness, you mentioned that we have one thousand of the Empire's most deftly trained warriors within these walls," Paulus began. "Even against considerable numbers, the rabble cannot withstand such discipline."

Basilius shuddered as Paulus finished his pronouncement, his chest rising and falling with violent motion. Standing along the wall behind Theodora, I began to rush toward the old consul, believing him struck by some illness, yet stopped when his convulsions turned into unfiltered laughter.

"Paulus, of all of the moronic ideas you've had over the years, this is by far the most selfish." He chortled. "Perhaps you'd like to join our intrepid warriors as they face down the enemy?"

Paulus rose to his feet, scowling at Basilius. "See here, you old codger," he said, "your entire generation has left the Empire in nothing but ruin, and you blame me for these riots? What of your guilt, Basilius?"

Before Justinian could intervene, Basilius cocked his head toward the finance minister, a self-sure smirk on his face. "Oh, I have many failures, Paulus," Basilius lectured, "but it isn't my head that the crowd called for last night. They want you... and Tribonian too."

A half dozen men vaulted to their feet, pointing and shouting. Some added their voices to Basilius while others rose to the defense of Paulus. Enjoying the spectacle, Liberius merely sat back and absorbed the moment, offering a sly wink as I caught his fleeting look. The room's chaos grew serious enough that Herulian guards in the outer hallway entered with spears drawn, ready to end any potential violence.

Justinian slammed his palms against the table, silencing the chatter. "The next man who disrupts the conversation will be thrown outside to the crowd," he warned. "I swear it."

The meeting grew more somber after that. Reports were given about Justinian's remaining strength, including flags bearing the Imperial sigil flying over the Golden Gate and the Melantias Gate to the south of the Theodosian Walls. Narses noted a remaining garrison at the Imperials Stables that, while promising, would likely be unable to assist with any military action, consisting of fewer than a hundred lesser wounded from the Battle of Callinicum. Other buildings remained unmolested by looting or fire, yet those tended to be churches, whose occupants could do little to enforce order at the point of a spear.

"Other pockets of loyalists are likely," Narses explained, "yet it isn't possible to tell from our current vantage point atop the Palace. The only sizeable force within a reasonable distance is the Thracian detachment under Tribune Mundus."

"And is Mundus loyal to Justinian or the rioters?" Cassiodorus asked. "The Thracians have long been questionable in their allegiance."

"Unquestionably loyal," Theodora replied icily.

"That is well and good, but there's no telling how long it would take Mundus to reach the city gates, let alone the Palace," Paulus said. "If our current forces are insufficient, we must make preparations to abandon the city."

Despite Justinian's previous warnings, the room erupted in chaos. Paulus and Tribonian squawked at ministers responsible for the city watch, while red-faced Hermogenes bellowed his anger at the crowd for forcing this fate. Even Liberius offered a comment, leaning toward Theodora with a predetermined vote of confidence.

As Justinian stood once again, the assembly silenced. "Marcellus, can you guarantee that your men could restore order to the city?"

Withdrawing his helmet, Marcellus paced to the tables, his face dripping with sweat as he took a deep sigh. "Including the Herulians, the men are willing to fight until the end, Highness," he began. "Yet they are tired, and many are wounded. If all were fresh, we would have a chance, but even then, it would be a slim one."

Justinian closed his eyes, his brow furrowed. "And do you believe that the Palace can hold out against another assault like last night?"

Marcellus paused, weighing his words carefully. "That sort of assault would lack the same measure of surprise. But if dedicated enough, the Palace is at risk of falling. There are simply too many entrances to guard effectively at the same time."

At Marcellus' words of doom, none replied. Eyes turned first to Paulus, and then Tribonian, and then back to the Emperor, yet none wanted to give voice to the hopeless situation that Justinian found himself in. It was Hermogenes who finally spoke up, his voice hoarse and somber.

"Highness, I am no coward," he began, "but if what Marcellus says is true, we have no choice but to abandon Constantinople."

Justinian's eyes glued themselves to the table, unable to meet Hermogenes' face. "Leaving Constantinople in such circumstances is tantamount to abdication," Justinian replied.

Hermogenes nodded. "Yes, Highness. But you would live, and in splendor. Enough gold and other riches can be assembled for a lifetime of leisure in a distant territory."

Justinian's head rose as he turned to his other councilors. "What say you, Paulus?"

"If Marcellus is unconfident of our safety and chances of success, then I agree with Lord Hermogenes," Paulus declared. "Bugger the people. Take the gold and sail away."

"I concur with the other lords," Tribonian said. "We cannot force the Roman people to aspire for grander dreams of the future. Khosrow would likely give us lavish accommodations in Ctesiphon, or at least allow safe passage to the rich cities of India."

Cassiodorus opted to speak next, yet Justinian turned back to Basilius. "And you, Lord Basilius?"

Basilius shook his head. "If you leave, Rome dies," he said with finality. "I won't ask you to sacrifice yourself in defense of an idea if you are unwilling to take risks."

"What Basilius means, Highness," Liberius butted in, "is that Hypatius lacks the strength to rule, and the remnants of the Empire cannot afford another weak man at the helm. Within a generation, the provinces will fall into chaos or foreign rule, and the last light of civilization will die with them."

"God will provide for his servants!" Cassiodorus cried. "To risk our lives for the vanity of kingship is a fool's errand."

Justinian raised a hand. The excubitores present beat their spears into the floor, and the Emperor sat heavily back into his seat, his face sinking slowly into his outstretched palms. Likely by accident, the Imperial diadem fell from his head and rolled onto the floor. Even those servants who carried food and drink halted in horror of the omen. Justinian looked down at his mark of overlordship and shook his head.

"I thank you, ministers, for your honesty and service," Justinian began. "Given the enormity of the threat that we face, and the few unlikely options to overcome that challenge, it is my decision that the Court vacate Constantinople. I leave it to your collective wisdom to determine where our initial destination might be."

While the other ministers bobbed and voiced their agreement, Liberius closed his eyes, a look of pain lining his features. Basilius likewise clenched his jaw with a grinding force, yet he did not speak against Justinian's pronouncement. Justinian bent down to retrieve his lost diadem, placing it not on his head, but on the table.

"Make preparations to leave as soon as possible," he ordered. "Ships for the army's voyage to Africa have already been provisioned and can serve as our vessels into the Mediterranean Sea."

Leaving his diadem, Justinian gathered the other ministers, dismissing the Court with unceremonious brusqueness. Many snuck out into the hallway, while others gathered around the former Emperor for more detailed instructions. In that hive of activity and defeat, few heard a calm voice at the head of the table, speaking as if the Court were still in session. Eyes looked up as the voice called out once more, side conversations in the room slowly muting.

"I respectfully disagree." Theodora sat straight on the throne, still bedecked in her emerald-and-pearl headdress.

"Disagree?" Paulus frowned at her. "Disagree with what?"

"I will not abandon Constantinople."

Justinian shook his head. "Theodora…" he began, yet this was promptly curtailed as Theodora smiled politely at her husband.

"My dearest, I would not dream of countermanding your orders. You must think of the safety and welfare of your people."

"But—"

"But as for me, I will remain in this palace," Theodora interrupted, her jeweled fist curling into a ball. "I will not demand that any woman or man, be they a patrician or a slave, remain with me. But I would treasure the company of friends all the same."

Dumbstruck, men stared at the Empress sitting alone at the head of the table. That silence was only broken by Liberius, beaming as he clapped his hands.

"I'm far too old to start anew," Liberius said, "and I never did like Persian food. Can't stand the stuff, despite what my learned colleagues might say. An old man's bowels, I presume. At any rate, I shall remain here with the Empress."

"As will I," Basilius continued. "I did not dedicate my life to the Empire to see it burn in a fortnight."

"And I," I cried, walking from the shadows. I stood behind Theodora, drawing an irritated glare from Marcellus for speaking out of turn. "I release my men from their oaths of service to me but welcome any who would remain at Theodora's defense."

"Thank you, Lord Varus. Your companionship is most welcome."

Justinian's eyes sank to the floor as he considered Theodora's words. Others muttered angrily to one another at her pronouncement, with several glowering at what they perceived a suicidal errand.

"I will not be cowed into remaining in this city to be butchered!" Cassiodorus boomed. "The Empress would make us appear cowards for departing the city while she remains behind."

Theodora's somber face broke into a wide grin, her rare set of straight teeth beaming at the elder priest. "Dear Cassiodorus, I have never used the words 'you are cowards' before. What a discourteous accusation!"

Her words caused Liberius to choke with laughter as Cassiodorus huffed, his face adopting a shade of unhealthy scarlet. Others interjected to argue against Theodora's intentions, with Justinian doing little to control the fray. It was only a disgruntled Hermogenes who at last rose to challenge the Empress, leaning over the table as his thinning gray hair reflected flickering light from the tapers above.

"Empress, we appreciate your sincerity and loyalty to the Empire, but what you propose is nothing short of suicide," he said, his voice flavored with thick condescension.

"*Prideful* arrogance!" Cassiodorus added.

Hermogenes nodded but gestured for calm from the other minister. "The Emperor could not be seen leaving his wife behind in a falling city. Such a thing is without precedent or excuse, going back to the earliest days of the Republic."

Paulus nodded his assent. He, too, insisted that Theodora drop such pretenses so that preparations could be made for the Court's departure. Her chin held high, Theodora ignored his thinly veiled insults, and she sat unmoved, as if carved from stone. Visibly frustrated, Paulus repeated his assertion with added protestations from Hermogenes.

"Empress, you have no choice," Hermogenes concluded. "You must leave the city with the rest of us."

Thin lipped, Theodora smiled once more and raised an eyebrow as she considered. She paused for several heartbeats, drawing the attention of even those who had previously moved to exit the hall, no better than rats on a sinking ship. She ignored them all.

"Every man or woman has a choice in all things," the Empress declared, "and mine is to stay in Constantinople, whatever the outcome."

"But... but you'll be *killed*!" Hermogenes yelled, his face bright with frustration.

Theodora viewed him impassively, offering little more than a light shrug. "I have come to believe that purple is a fine shroud," she said, sweeping her gaze over the onetime legate before closing her eyes, as though absorbing all that the Fates would soon place on her path.

Justinian's head sagged at the pronouncement, his tired body sinking into an empty chair. Others gasped as they looked to Justinian, Paulus, and Hermogenes with frenetic energy. Through it all, Basilius and Liberius shared a private look of vindication, their wishes obeyed by the only woman allowed to sit in the Emperor's Court.

"Absolute madness!" Hermogenes barked. "They will tear you apart in the street, pleasure for dogs!"

Against my better judgment, I laughed at his warning. Theodora turned slightly in my direction, curious, yet showing no anger as I spoke in her defense. Hermogenes grew crimson as I again approached the table, my gaze fixed squarely on the man who'd terrorized Rome's eastern armies.

"Where was this caution at Callinicum, Hermogenes?" I roared. "Perhaps it's different this time, when it's your own life hanging in the balance?"

Hermogenes spat with unfiltered rage. "Be silent, murderer."

The charge brought fears of damnation rising like bile into my throat, and I instinctively reached for the bronze cross that adorned my neck, temporarily bewildered. For the briefest of heartbeats, Hermogenes' face took on the cragged wrinkles of Hakhamanish, his deep cackle labeling me as nothing more than an agent of death, a peddler of murder. Fighting against an urge to retch, I swallowed hard and trained my attention on the rising and falling of my chest.

"Murderer? What does he mean?" Justinian asked, his first words since Theodora's declaration.

"Yes, Hermogenes, I have killed many men," I replied at last, "but not nearly as many as you. I pray for each one of my victims. I wonder if you do the same?"

Justinian stood, demanding answers, yet the other ministers ignored him as several rose against me. Hermogenes threw his chair back and rushed at me, his pulsing eyes fearless of my heavy armor and looming frame. I have no doubt that Hermogenes would have struck me for insolence had I said a single further word—and had Theodora not interrupted with her own declaration.

"I do apologize, Lord Hermogenes," she said, "but I have decided to reject your sage advice and place my prayers onto God… and on the arrival of Tribune Mundus."

Undeterred, Paulus defied Theodora's station, wrinkling his nose in utter hatred of the Empress, and took one last crack at routing her suicidal defiance.

"Empress, your pet Varus is respected amongst the barbarian Herulians," he said, sneering, "but neither he nor Tribune Mundus have the experience to lead such an operation. Are you willing to put your life, and our lives, in their hands?"

Patiently considering Paulus' words, Theodora offered a warm smile to the minister. Basilius sat up in his chair as the Empress leaned forward intently, her eyes flickering with wicked mischief.

"I would trust Varus with my life," Theodora declared as she waved to me, words that had echoed from Justin's lips so many years ago. "But I would not put this burden on his shoulders alone—that would be grossly unjust. However, it just so happens that one such champion is available to assist Lord Varus with this gravest of duties."

"No!" Hermogenes blurted out. "I will not allow this!"

But Theodora would hear him no longer. Rising from her chair, she gathered her gown and glided to my side, ignoring the curious looks, and spoke the words that freed me of a separate oath sworn a season ago, when the banks of the Euphrates River flowed crimson for a day and a night.

"Komes Varus, perhaps you would inform Lord Belisarius he is to prepare the defenses of our Palace?" the Empress asked.

"It would be my pleasure, Highness."

"Absolutely not, Komes!" Hermogenes exclaimed. "Belisarius is a criminal, and an incompetent. He is unfit to lead the Empire's soldiers."

Theodora glowered, but not at Hermogenes. Instead, she fixed her gaze upon her husband—disheveled, pale, and visibly exhausted as he hunched in his chair. Hermogenes approached Justinian, seeking to whisper malice into the Emperor's ear.

"Enough, Hermogenes!" Theodora shouted.

Justinian flinched. So did Hermogenes, although the older man's face blossomed to crimson as he gritted his teeth, swallowing venom. Again, Theodora glared at her husband. After another minute, Justinian closed his eyes, nodding at Theodora.

Few still live who remember our terrible stand in the Imperial Palace, when Justinian's realm had shrunk to a single complex of buildings engulfed by a sea of his own furious citizens. As for me, I shall never forget the look upon Theodora's face as she took command of the throne of Caesar—standing straight, her expression calm and stern as if mimicking the statues of Augustus that adorned the palace hallways.

"Varus, inform Belisarius of my charge to him," the Empress commanded. "And find me reinforcements. We're taking this city back."

ULTIMATUM

With Theodora and Justinian affirming their joint desire to remain in the Palace, the foederati and other able-bodied men and women toiled at bolstering its defenses. Ancient oak tables were piled against palace doors and windows, thick iron spikes driven through their polished boards and facing any would-be invader. Likewise, smaller entrances were walled shut with stone and mortar available in the palace cellars, with egg yolks mixed in to strengthen the grip of the newly constructed walls at a far faster pace than most engineers would prefer. Weapons were stacked in critical hallways, and thick casks of water and sand were placed at each entrance, ready in the event that Hypatius' men would storm the Palace with all-consuming fire.

Despite the oppressive demands on their limited manpower, the foederati and excubitores offered no complaints as Belisarius transformed the Palace into a fortress as formidable as any the Empire still held. Wafting smoke from the besieging crowd's cookfires, the lingering stench of blood and death that permeated the lower level, the dozens of corpses tossed onto the palace steps as another macabre wall—all only added to the military ambiance.

Of all the endless tasks facing us, none were as desperate as the need to gain contact with Mundus. Less than a half day's ride away, Mundus' encampments would have likely seen the black plumes flying over the Bosporus Strait, but I doubted that the tribune would do more than scout the walls until clearer orders manifested. Not a quarter day after his return to power, Belisarius convened his diminutive officer corps in the ruins of the Great Hall, embracing old friends as Agathias retrieved a detailed map of the local region. Belisarius' lingering embrace was reserved for Ascum, clad in black furs as he disguised his withered hand and stiff limp.

"If Narses' information is correct, we hold two gates near the Via Egnatia," he began, "yet between the Palace and the Golden Gate is more than a mile of armed gangs, burning buildings, and a sea of Romans who have no reason to trust an agent of Justinian."

"Correct," Troglita replied. "It's a miracle Varus was able to reach your position near the harbor, and that was only halfway."

"I disagree," Samur said matter-of-factly. "Once past the Forum of Arcadius, there are far fewer buildings where the mob would gather. Much easier to sneak past undetected."

Troglita nodded and allowed Fulcaris to add additional concerns. "Assuming, of course, that one could leave the Palace under the nose of a thousand Greens and Blues, pass the Hippodrome, and not draw the wary eye of any sentries."

Samur immediately responded, relishing the chance to use his intimate knowledge of the city for his own purposes. "The Hippodrome is a concern, but once past that monument, few will be looking for any Imperial loyalists," he explained. "I doubt Hypatius even enlisted patrols for the streets, thinking that Justinian's men are all trapped like mice in the Palace."

"But how could we get past the Hippodrome safely?" Belisarius asked him.

"How could *you*? Impossible," Samur said. "Your face is too recognizable. But a single man dressed as a common peasant… that person would find the tunnels under the Palace to their favor."

Troglita shook his head vigorously at that statement. "Varus and I nearly drowned last time, bumbling in the dark. There must be a better way."

"Varus' knowledge of the passages is pathetic," Samur said, grinning, "but mine is far more recent. I will guide Mundus' messenger to safety on the streets."

"And where will you go?" Ascum rasped, his gestures awkward as his undamaged hand traced the Via Egnatia's route through the Golden Gate.

"To scout the city," Samur offered. "We aren't sure of Hypatius' numbers, their readiness, or whether the mob is even a single, uniform party."

Belisarius considered the strategy, working out its flaws and risks. Of the men present, Samur held the most intimate knowledge of Constantinople's streets and alleys, while Justinian himself mourned over the lack of information regarding the Palace's enemies. Thus Belisarius authorized Samur to venture out of the Palace, provided he return after no more than the turn of a day.

"I'll travel to Mundus, then, if Samur will guide me past the Hippodrome," Troglita offered. "After all, he's my commanding officer."

After additional discussion of lesser details, Belisarius charged each man with their respective tasks, ordering the mission to commence with all haste. Likewise, he gave me the responsibility of securing the Palace against further attack, with Marcellus taking personal command of the Imperial family's safety. Even in that chaos, however, Belisarius never seemed more content, for as his meetings concluded, he would sneak upstairs to surprise his daughter Joannina, making her giggle as she grabbed at his cropped beard.

Where Belisarius wore a visage of calm, Troglita fought to retain a mask of confidence as he pulled me aside. Leaning close, he whispered to me.

"Auria is pregnant," he murmured. "If anything happens to me when I leave the Palace…"

"Then why take the risk? Send another in your place! Fulcaris or any of my men would take this order gladly."

"Would you allow someone else to shoulder that burden?" he asked. "This is my task, and I pray it is a simple one. But my mind would be at ease if I knew my wife and child would not suffer in poverty if God no longer favors my cause."

Placing a hand around his shoulder, I swore another oath. "They will want for nothing, I swear it by God," I declared. He wrapped his arms around my back and squeezed tightly, offering profuse gratitude before setting off to prepare for his journey.

Samur was far less sentimental than Troglita, his face lit with an older sense of mischief that had been missing since the death of Sunicas along the Euphrates. Initially dressed in a clean, plain woolen tunic favored by palace servants, Samur muttered discontentedly to himself. Grabbing soot from a nearby brazier, Samur rubbed the cool ashes against the cloth, transforming the garment into one more fitting on the back of a beggar.

"Take a look outside," Samur said in response to curious looks. "Do you see any of the crowd dressed in clean laundry?"

Troglita followed Samur's example, using a thin dagger to cut ragged holes along his knees and elbows, and smirked despite himself.

"Reminds me of the march back from our battle against the Avars," he exclaimed. "My clothing was so worn, I might as well have been naked!"

"Oh, I remember," Cephalas added. "I didn't even have use of my arm to hide my eyes!"

Properly adorned and equipped with a plain dagger each, Samur and Troglita readied to depart for the underground labyrinth disguised within the Palace. Troglita clutched at Auria with perhaps too much of his soldier's strength, but she did not complain or perhaps even notice as she whispered into her husband's ear. After handing Samur a rare key to the hidden doors below, Mariya embraced my brother, then he gripped my forearm, holding my gaze as he promised to return soon.

"Give my best to Rosamund," Samur said. "You know how she worries."

Soon thereafter, the two departed, with Samur bearing a torch to light their path ahead. Belisarius offered his own well-wishes, urging Troglita to reach a swift conclusion to his journey. With a brief prayer, the two vanished behind a near-hidden servants' entrance, the creaking of their footsteps growing ever more muffled as they delved further into the Palace and descended into its lowest depths.

Normally my thoughts would have been infected with worry for Samur's well-being, especially as this was his first foray into potentially fatal danger since his attack at Barbalissus. Belisarius' demands filled my time as we continued to bolster the Palace's defenses, stretching our labor to its limits before having to rotate teams of exhausted foederati and guardsmen to rooms for fleeting rest and sleep.

Though the fear of imminent attack was never fully extinguished during those days of waiting for salvation, there was a measure of tranquility in the work that lulled many into a sense of security. The palace grounds were extensive, yet not so large that work to survey potential zones of attack or clean dark stains that emitted an evil humor was insurmountable. Every healthy man and woman volunteered to assist in the efforts, with even Antonina patching holes in soldiers' clothing and Paulus honing spear points to a wicked point. Cephalas helped me keep track of each of the hundreds of duties that needed to be performed, often reminding me of neglected rooms of the Palace whose walls required strengthening or a servant in need of a mace or dagger for possible defense.

In my limited free time, I visited Rosamund, whose face was smothered with bruises, her gaze slack as she struggled to sit upright in her private rooms. Tears trickled down her cheeks, and she winced, swearing that all would be well in due time.

"Sometimes I wonder why you don't listen to me," she said bitterly, and rolled her eyes at my confusion. "We could be far away from this evil place, with only the sun and stars to determine our daily routine."

"Evil?" I sputtered. "How? There's nothing evil here."

Rosamund shook her head sadly. "I'm not angry with the people outside of this stone monstrosity," she whispered. "Not most of them, anyways. It isn't their fault that their children cry from empty bellies, or that they live in gutters after injuries keep them from being able to earn coin from their labor."

"I understand your point," I offered. "But I'm not willing to let that mob in here to butcher you or anyone else."

She sighed. "Then why stay here? This is all Romans are... death and misery, while a corrupt few hoard what wealth they can for as long as they are able."

For all her stinging words, Rosamund brightened when I brought Zenobia into the sickroom. She used what strength had been accumulated from a half day of bedrest to lift Zenobia high into the air, smiling as the babe giggled merrily and laughing as chubby hands grasped at her long white hair, its silky white strands flitting between tiny fingers like the ethereal pelt of a creature of myth.

Our work was occasionally interrupted by a barrage of rocks colliding against the palace doors, sending contingents of armed spearmen to their assigned stations. Ordered explicitly to not return violence unless the crowd scaled the cluttered palace steps, our spearmen looked stonily upon the howling masses, many of whom still shouted for Justinian's blood. Another notice of Hypatius' election to the Imperial seat was tossed onto a palace balcony, arguing that the man known as Justinian may leave peacefully if he surrendered all claims to the legacy of Caesar.

Other than these temporary bursts of frenzy, the Palace remained quiet and apprehensive as the sun faded into night. Justinian made few appearances as men and women continued to resist the mob in his name, though Theodora often walked beside me as I inspected each station. Where possible, Theodora would take time to speak with each servant or soldier who toiled at the Palace's defenses, hearing stories of their children and sitting in rapt attention as she sympathized with their experience during the Palace's initial assault. We fell into an unsettled confidence as many in the outer crowd disbursed for the evening, leaving only a smaller force to keep the siege lines clearly demarcated.

The Palace was not attacked that evening. Nor were any major assaults mounted as the pitch black of night bled into a blue of the deepest seas, hinting at the frigid morning to come. This relative tranquility convinced Belisarius to allow much of the Palace's forces to rest until called to action, with few complaining. With a note of insistence, Belisarius extended that command to me, brushing away protests that my duty remained to Theodora as the primary officer at the palace gates.

"You'll be no use to anyone if you're falling asleep standing up," Belisarius said. "Rest, and spend time with your family. I need you fresh for the morning."

Though I wished to wait for Samur, a heavy sluggishness of body and mind convinced me to acquiesce. Mariya welcomed me back to our rooms with a flurry of requests to her servants, sent off to fetch food, drink, and other comforts to ease my burdens. I warmed to the gesture, yet after sliding off the hot leather and pinching metal that encased my body, I collapsed onto the still-broken mattress and drifted off to deep slumber before I could eat or drink a thing.

Unlike the previous day, neither Cephalas nor any other servant nudged me awake in the earliest hours of morning. By the time I shook myself awake, the sun melded into a deep orange, hinting at midday in the darkest part of winter. Mariya and Zenobia had long ago vacated the quarters, the bed cool to the touch. A sickening pop clicked in my knee as I rose to my feet, my joints and muscles tense and sore from overexertion and an unfamiliar excess of sleep.

Cephalas entered as I groaned from stretching—presumably he'd been sitting quietly in the halls outside—and eagerly fetched clean clothes and nourishment that had been left over from the morning meal. As Cephalas helped me dress for another day of service, Father Petrus shuffled into my room, carrying the container of food and water requested by Cephalas. My face flushed with embarrassment as I rushed to assist him, only for the old priest to tut at my lack of respect for the physical abilities of the elderly.

Properly attired and armored, Father Petrus led me in our ritual morning prayer, adding a desire that the disharmony amongst the Emperor's people would soon be lifted. These sessions normally helped calm my mind prior to struggling against the day's labors, yet on that day, Father Petrus concluded our meeting with a note of unease.

"Samur hasn't returned yet," he mentioned. "I wanted to be the first to tell you, before you meet with others."

"No other information?" Impatient, I felt a pain rising in my chest, my neck throbbing.

"None," the priest confirmed, "although that is to be expected, given that we are cut off from the world."

Samur did not return later that afternoon, nor in the twilight of evening as the crowd outside the Palace ebbed once more. I filled my time working with Belisarius and Liberius on the endless preparations and repairs needed along the palace walls and interior, throwing myself into each task in a desperate attempt to clear my head. These efforts were occasionally successful, but little prompting was required to bring my worries to Samur and the nagging worry that he would share the brutal fate of Perenus.

The evening's dark hours were more eventful than the previous night's: a halfhearted assault, a heavily armored detachment of a few hundred Greens hauling a brass-capped battering ram to the looming palace doors. Despite their rich attire, the troops had little skill and no discipline as a fighting unit. Without the unstoppable mass of the thousands who stormed the Palace on the first day of the riot, many of the armored Greens panicked and ran as the foederati rained stones onto their exposed heads, while the remainder dropped the great log and sprinted away as I led a sally onto their exposed ranks. Shouting glory to Emperor Justinian, we set the log alight and rolled it down the palace steps, watching enemies scatter fearfully as the projectile threatened to snap legs and crush those too slow to escape.

As the first ray of orange sunlight pierced the elevated palace windows, fate threw another maelstrom into my path, one that rendered me paralyzed with indecision. Having slept well beyond my normal routine, I volunteered to remain on watch through the heart of the evening's darkness. With Belisarius sneaking in a few hours of sleep after the destruction of the battering ram, I was relieved later by Liberius, who alone seemed to enjoy the Palace's chaos.

"Still alive, then, Varus?" Liberius asked.

"God hasn't seen fit to take me yet."

The two of us sat for a brief time, exchanging few words as we watched the ram smolder and turn to ash along the cobbled streets. My foederati exchanged their duties with several of Marcellus' excubitores, their voices bright with appreciation for the day's rest as my Herulians and Belisarius' bucellarii shouldered the greater portion of the Palace's defensive duties. As leader of that pack, Chanaranges acknowledged Liberius' status as duty commander before setting off to assign sentries to the Palace's defensive posts.

"In some way, this entire experience reminds me of your last days as a slave to Justin," Liberius remarked as the excubitores disappeared into other rooms.

"When I fought Solomon?" I asked with a mixture of resentment and embarrassment.

"I could tell you feared the worst," Liberius confessed. "And truthfully, so did I. But even then, Justin and Godilas knew that you had the potential to be something special in this world. If there's one thing I have learned in my all my years is that the laws of common men are easily skirted by those with talent and promise."

I blushed, unsure of how to take Liberius' rare turn for the serious. "I miss them," I replied weakly. "And I wonder if things would be different if they were still here."

"Me too," Liberius said, placing a hand on my shoulder. "We mocked the old men in our youth, thinking that we would never join their ranks. Yet here I sit as they remain lost to this world, leaving their dreams for the youth of those who follow to suffer through."

"It is a dream worth dying for," I said. However, some part of me knew that the hope of the Empire's reunification might be extinguished at any moment by the forces gathered just beyond the palace walls.

"And many will," Liberius replied darkly. "I foolishly believed that I could absorb the losses myself and spare the likes of you and Belisarius, yet I fear that more sacrifices will be demanded of you before our struggles are over."

I stiffened at Liberius' worries, my thoughts trailing off once more to a previous conversation in the aftermath of Dara. "I am ready, Lord. Just name the challenge."

Liberius' dark demeanor melted to a smile. "Not yet," he said. "But you have my word: you will know everything at the appropriate time."

"Through the remaining three gifts?" I asked, more bluntly that I might have otherwise, assuming Liberius would obfuscate the answer. But though his face registered surprise, he was forthright.

"Yes," Liberius said, chuckling. "A childish way of sharing secrets, but a symbolic one nonetheless. A cross, a dagger, a sword, and more gold than Croesus... There is a riddle that even the Oracles at Delphi would blanch at."

Liberius' mirth only stirred my irritation. "But when will I receive the next?"

"In due time, and not a moment sooner," he said. "In the meantime, perhaps you would benefit from rest as I haunt Justinian's battlements for the evening. I cannot imagine that Hypatius' armed thugs will leave us in peace for too much longer, and your sword will be needed on that day."

Tacitly dismissed, I accepted Liberius' embrace and returned to my sleeping quarters. Shedding my armor and slipping next to the warmth of Mariya, my thoughts raced. I wondered at Liberius' riddle, even as my mind numbed from my wife's lingering perfume and Zenobia's carefree snores as she dozed just paces away from her mother and father. Sleep came slowly, but when it did, it yielded dreams of Justin's oath, Hakhamanish's curse, and Rosamund's dark rider, whose red eyes and dark laughter pervaded my nightmares.

I awoke near dawn the following morning, my body drenched in sweat and muscles tense. I sprang to my feet, ready to brawl against my unseen attacker. Startled, Mariya sat up and grazed my skin, cooing in a singsong voice to calm me. Realization dawned, and I dropped to sitting, weeping. I buried my face against Mariya's thighs, and she drew me into her arms, rocking my head and shoulders and stroking my matted hair.

Another day passed with little to distinguish it. Reinforced in the late morning, a mixture of Greens and Blues raised another force to test the Palace's defenses, yet the attempt was even more halfhearted than the prior evening. A half dozen dead and an equal number of wounded convinced the rioters to remain entrenched in their siege lines, occasionally throwing stones or flaming torches at a palace window.

"It's a miracle they don't have any ballistae," Belisarius remarked that afternoon.

"Yes, a miracle given to us by Azarethes," I muttered darkly, stealing a glance toward a resting Ascum. Dark leather and furs hid the twisted flesh that covered much of his body.

With the Palace's defenses largely complete, our routine became more tedious as one shift bled into the next. I began to form a plan to go search for Samur, but was promptly dissuaded by an insistent Theodora. My job was to protect the Palace, and by the Empress' logic, there was no possible way to determine where Samur may have gone at any rate. The day ended with a whimper, concluded by a light exchange of violence with the rioters as the Emperor's forces waited for the crossroads of rescue or annihilation.

The tedium was broken just before dawn the following morning. Cephalas barged into my sleeping quarters carrying a silver candlestick. Panting forgiveness to Mariya, he trained on me.

"Come quickly, Lord," Cephalas whispered in excitement.

"Samur?" I asked groggily.

"Yes, he's returned," he said. "But that's not all."

Pausing only to don a shirt and trousers, I stumbled across the darkened room, carelessly bumping my shoulder into the wooden doorframe and staggering into the hallway. Following Cephalas' beacon, I rushed down the hallway and through the stairs, where I grinned at a familiar face. Leaning heavily against a far wall, huddled closely with Belisarius in an energetic meeting, was my brother.

Samur gasped for air as he peeled away sweat-stained clothes splattered with dark splotches of human blood. A servant handed him a bucket of water that he greedily tipped over his head, washing away a layer of filth that ran black to the palace floor. Most disconcerting were his hands, caked in a deep red that appeared fresh before it was washed away by another heavy water pail.

Belisarius leaned close to Samur as my brother responded with insight regarding Hypatius' numbers and the general state of the city, Procopius and Narses taking down every word. Samur stopped as he caught my gaze, raising a weary arm in welcome.

"You're late!" I bellowed, squeezing him with affection despite the unsavory aroma that clung to his skin.

"Trouble returning to the Palace. Couldn't be helped."

I nodded. "And Troglita?"

"Completely fine, and safely reached the Golden Gate," he wheezed. "But Varus, that's not what I need to tell you."

Time seemed to freeze as I waited upon Samur's every word. A painful knot formed in my throat as I feared the worst, some friend killed or other fatal delays that disrupted Mundus' march to Constantinople. A thousand futures flooded into my mind, with nearly all of them ending in a grim fate.

"Perenus is alive," Samur panted, gulping at a waterskin.

My chest seized. *"What?"*

"In the Hippodrome, I saw Perenus," Samur repeated. "Walking with a limp, and bloodied. But he lives."

LAST STAND OF THE
IMPERIAL PALACE

Belisarius flatly prohibited any journey to rescue Perenus from the Hippodrome. Even though Perenus was held less than a few hundred paces from our position at the palace gates, Belisarius reasoned that no fewer than ten thousand armed rioters would make a secretive extraction impossible. When I requested to take a detachment of foederati to retrieve Perenus by force, Belisarius disagreed all the more, arguing that those maneuvers would leave the Palace too weakly defended.

"If Perenus is still alive, it's because Hypatius' men have no intention of harming him," Belisarius explained. "Once Mundus arrives, we will have more options to end these riots and save Perenus."

After nourishment and rest, Samur agreed with Belisarius. He'd had a difficult time infiltrating the Hippodrome, as Hypatius' guardsmen had remained vigilant for any Herulians skulking through the streets, yet thankfully my brother had entered the racing stadium undetected.

"It's pure madness in the Hippodrome," Samur remarked. "Thousands of people milling about, gorging themselves on food from the Imperial granaries. Hypatius' senators try to keep some semblance of order, but the only thing that works are hangings."

"Hangings?" Belisarius echoed.

"Enemies of Hypatius' revolution," Samur explained. "There's at least a hundred bodies rotting along the Hippodrome's entrances, yet what these people did to deserve execution, I cannot say. The city is rife with rape and murder, and only roving street gangs resolve grudges."

"Jesus Christ," Belisarius muttered under his breath, the oath unusual for a man so devout. "And Troglita? The Golden Gate?"

"Still guarded, as are the stables," Samur said. "I saw Troglita rush to the gate's guardsmen, and I know he made it at least that far. But if there are any other outposts of loyalists, I didn't see any."

Though Belisarius requested that Samur's insight be kept private, word of Troglita's escape and the Hippodrome's horrors infected the Palace at a frenetic pace. The rumors reached Theodora, who demurely insisted that this anarchy would soon be put right and the Emperor's justice reinstalled, yet many in the Court wondered whether their properties would remain standing after the conflagration, and whether Constantinople would still be habitable amidst despoiled water pipes, thousands of bloated corpses, and a hundred ceaseless fires that fueled the populace's rage against their government.

Concern only grew as Justinian and his closest advisors kept themselves locked away in separate rooms, emerging only occasionally. Theodora alone served as our conduit to the Emperor, my soldiers brightening as the Empress inquired after their labors. Theodora was frequently seen joking with Herulians, excubitores, Aksumites, and bucellarii alike, granting compliments for faithful service and occasional coins to many. Bearing Theodora's likeness, these silver coins where not meant for use in markets, for Tribonian's laws allowed only Roman emperors to adorn precious metals within the Empire. Wazeba viewed the coin as an item of boundless value and sewed a pocket within the leather lining of his armor, where it remained close to his body for the rest of his days.

Both Sindual and Fulcaris independently volunteered to lead an expedition to rescue Perenus from that evil abode, but I reluctantly commanded the men to obey Belisarius' orders. They grudgingly accepted, agreeing that Mundus provided the best opportunity to pluck Perenus up alive and whole. Even with this restraint, however, men of the foederati became more aggressive as morning gave way to a frigid afternoon, inflicting vicious wounds against another sally that saw another dozen Green attackers slain. Leading the sally, Irilar smiled as two Green wounded pled for mercy from the Roman soldiers and slid his spearpoint deep into the man's throat with a snakelike twist of his arm.

"Mercy?" Sindual said mockingly.

"I killed him quickly," Irilar said. "For that, he should thank his god. In the Heruli tribe, traitors are flayed alive. We dismember the bodies after death to keep their souls from reaching the otherworld."

I shuddered. The Palace had barely enough men and women to stand guard at its walls; none could be spared to house and feed those who had taken up arms against Justinian and his Court.

Where the previous days had seen only targeted attacks that probed for any weaknesses in the palace defenses, a great horde of Hypatius' men swelled before the Palace at sundown. Their chants mixed with an aberrant fear as rams and torches were carried to the front, all at the direction of several Greek officers, urging speed as their assault mounted.

Our sentries had enough warning to spread an alarm throughout the Palace, however, and called all sleeping or resting soldiers to their stations. Armored and organized, the men looked to their officers as the crowd bellowed a thunderous cheer, their sandals and boots rumbling the palace floors as they began their approach. Noting his exhaustion, I ordered Samur to stay with Mariya and Antonina, ensuring their safety if our wall was unable to hold. For once in his life Samur obeyed, disappearing down the Palace's dim corridors and into the upper levels that housed the Roman Court.

"Allow none to step one foot into the Palace!" Belisarius roared, unsheathing his sword. "For God and the Emperor!"

A half dozen languages yelled their affirmation, generating sporadic chants of "Belisarius!" that were quickly suppressed as officers demanded silence and concentration. A four-rank shield wall formed against the palace doors, while a number of guardsmen under Liberius' command ascended to the second level, joined by men and women of the Emperor's servants who had gathered stones and boards near overhanging balconies. A single detachment of archers would have cut the massed enemy to ribbons, yet there were none to be found, save my own bow taken from the spoils of Khingila. Liberius made do with the missiles available, using the height of the balconies to his advantage.

I took my place in the second line of the shield wall, directly centered between the twin doorways. Sembrouthes attempted to shove his way to my right flank, but I chastised him.

"Don't fight with healing ribs!" I yelled over the rising din. "Go voluntarily, or I'll fetch Mariya."

"Fine," he said. "But Wazeba and the others stay with you."

I nodded, and Sembrouthes relayed his commands to the other Aksumites. Wazeba took Sembrouthes' place as he locked his shield against mine and leaned in.

"It is an honor, Lord," he said.

I smiled weakly. "Just keep your shield high and tight, and we'll get through this."

Wazeba responded with a hearty grin.

Though still undisciplined, the mob attacked with a determination that mirrored the initial assault that came within an hour of overwhelming the Emperor's excubitores. Bronze-capped rams were protected by a thick layer of stolen shields, many of which bore the ouroboros symbol of my own Heruli. Stones and other projectiles flew overhead as men from higher levels struck down at the attackers, and while several unlucky Greens and Blues fell screaming with crushed skulls and bleeding eyes, the crowd surged forward as it approached the palace doorway.

Many of the shield wall jumped as the first ram slapped forcefully against the doorway, the wood groaning with a sickening crack. Marcellus barked orders for discipline, reassuring the men of their strength against the rabble.

"Hold this wall, and they stand no chance!" Marcellus said. "Remember, you men held the Immortals and Hephthalites at Dara!"

"Perozes was a fool," a Persian voice muttered immediately behind me.

I turned to find Xerxes. He bore the full regalia of a Zhayedan officer, bedecked with a number of curved blades at his belt but bearing a Roman spear. He glared at the doorway ahead, not even flinching as the ram struck again at the wooden panels.

"What are you doing here?" I replied in Persian clumsy from lack of practice.

"I was bored," he answered. "Now I'm not."

I grunted. "This isn't your fight."

"It is if your men let the mob run amok through the Palace again. Besides, someone needs to make sure you return to your pretty wife in one piece."

I rolled my eyes but conceded. "Just stay behind me."

"Of course, my lord!" Xerxes declared, sweeping a mocking bow. "I remain helpless without your protection."

Additional rams began slamming against the wooden door, their labors beginning to bear results as sections of wooden beams splintered to the floor. The shield wall waited patiently at each stroke, wondering whether the next heartbeat would see an influx of thousands of Greens and Blues rushing headlong into our line of spears.

Our discipline was momentarily broken by the voice of Vitalius, calling excitedly for me or Belisarius. The youth was soon joined by Father Petrus, his rasping tenor mixing with calls for our immediate attention.

"Lords!" Vitalius yelled as loud as his body would allow. "Banners waving at the Golden Gate! Mundus is entering the city!"

A booming roar echoed through the Palace as all present hailed their own god of fortune. Even I joined in the rapture for a single cheer, but was soon called back for attention amongst the ranks.

"Mundus won't get here quickly," I warned, "so do your jobs, and butcher anyone who would attack the Palace."

While the soldiers returned to formation, the first ram broke through the reinforced wood, its bronze cap ripping at once-bolted planks as it was withdrawn to the mob. Other logs soon followed, puncturing holes and sending oaken shards over the heads of the shield wall. One man cried out angrily from a cut, but he brushed off any assistance as he wiped blood from his brow.

After another battery from the rams, the doors burst open. A wave of noise collided with our front ranks like a drum. Many shuddered from the angry percussion. Each of the rams were dropped or hauled free of the doorway, opening lanes for the mob to initiate their assault.

Belisarius refused to wait to be struck. "Soldiers of Rome, advance!"

Our ranks closed the gap to the shattered door, kicking stray boards aside. Though the mob had begun to form their own shield wall, men edged backward from our advance, leaving gaps for our frontmost ranks to exploit. Belisarius' forces pounded into their enemies with devastating force, sending a dozen to the ground and leaving their bodies to be trampled like an old carpet. We lunged with our spears leveled against our enemies' chests, finding frequent success as Greens and Blues yelped in pain as they were gored by Justinian's remaining protectors.

The mob's casualties must have been terrible, but even our disciplined beating was soon blunted under the sheer weight of the thousands of men who, ignorant of the slaughter at the front, eagerly sought to enter the fray. Our forces were slowly pushed back by the press, with Belisarius and Ascum yelling for the wall to remain tight despite the rising onslaught of enemy swords.

Sensing my front rank begin to flag, I whistled for the second line to switch into that role. The first rank let out a coordinated bash of their shields before slipping between our ranks, sliding back to the rear to take on a moment of rest before returning to the fight. I saw little of that as I slashed with my spear, driving its point through the exposed leg of a rare Red rioter, who toppled to the ground.

As I attacked, an Aksumite to my left took a blow to his exposed shoulder. Cursing in his native tongue, he raised his shield to protect against a storm of blows, but he was struck again in the shoulder, and this time the bone was dislocated from its socket. Desperate to buy him time, I drove my spear through the hip of the attacker and drew my sword to attack others.

That decision was a poor one. For a moment after I engaged in my counterattack, the force of the mob drove my shield further back, leaving me stranded amongst a sea of enemies despite Wazeba's best attempts to cut a path to my side. I slashed wildly with my sword, cleanly severing a man's wrist with its wickedly honed edge, staggering as a gush of blood sprayed into my exposed eyes from the stump. I jabbed forward still, my shield taking a half dozen blows in kind as I fought to keep from being surrounded.

Out of the corner of my blurred vision, I saw a larger Green raise an axe high in the air, aiming its curved edge at the armored hinges at my neck. I swung my shield to protect against the killing blow — too slow. As I girded myself for its biting iron, the axe dropped harmlessly to the floor. The man's head hung half severed, his dying eyes flaring impossibly wide from shock.

"Ha!" Xerxes slammed his shield next to mine as he cut at another of my attackers. "How did Perozes or Azarethes lose to you Romans? Come, let's back away to the lines."

At that, hands grabbed at our belts, yanking us to the safety of the shield wall. Wazeba apologized profusely as he lashed with his spear, slicing clean through a weakened shield of a nearby Green and biting deep into the man's knuckles.

"Don't worry," I replied. "Sembrouthes could never stop me from making terrible decisions either."

Additional waves of rioters crashed against our wall like a tempest against stones on a beach. Many of my men absorbed minor cuts and bruises, yet none died as the wild frenzy of the mob broke against our steady layer of shields and spears. As the enemy's casualties mounted and their footing became treacherous with blood, bodies, and shrapnel, the charge was sapped of its intensity. The last ardent attackers were quickly dispatched by our third line. The Herulians burst into songs of long-ago battles in the northern plains.

Though the enemy's lines fell back, thousands remained in the square before the Palace. A handful of leaders urged another assault while a number of fresh attackers flung heavy rocks at our ranks, yet the stalemate continued as we traded insults for another hour. Until another cry rose from the crowd, and we lowered our shields for the resumption of carnage.

Initial confusion rose through the lines as the enemy began to mill about mindlessly, their leaders unable to regain control of the masses and foster another assault up the palace steps. The confusion soon gave way to shouts of triumph as another mass of Roman shields pushed hard at the remaining forces gathered before us. Led by Troglita at the center of their shield wall, the Thracian forces butchered any who did not flee in terror from their march, spearing and cutting without ever stopping the motion of their boots.

Mundus had arrived, and the battle for the Imperial Palace had finally turned in Justinian's favor.

RECLAMATION

As Mundus' soldiers cleared the siege lines facing the Palace, Belisarius and I sent our wounded for treatment and dispatched others to craft a replacement door. Screams from the mob grew more distant as the Thracians marched along the Golden Horn, creating a winding barrier of leather and iron that fostered sorely missed protection for Justinian's Palace. As the Thracian centurions bolstered their defensive perimeter, Mundus and Troglita ascended the palace steps to a raucous welcome.

"We are grateful again for your service, Tribune," Belisarius said, lifting an outstretched arm that Mundus gripped just below the elbow.

"I'm just happy to see you returned to service."

Belisarius nodded with appreciation. "How many have you brought to Constantinople?"

"Three thousand, although many are newer recruits just arrived from Germanus' travels," Mundus replied. "I cleared out all of the forts within a half day's ride from the city."

"Three?" Ascum rasped. "I thought you had less than a thousand?"

"Baduarius returned with another detachment of spears," Mundus replied gleefully. "I've sent him with a thousand men to retake the city gates."

"God be thanked for that," Belisarius said.

"Give thanks when Constantinople is back in our hands," Liberius put in impatiently. "Lord Mundus, are your men prepared to fight against the mob?"

Wiping stray drops of blood and dirt from his face, Mundus shrugged. "I didn't join the army to kill other Romans, but I don't see any other choice at this time."

"Nor do I," Belisarius agreed. "But if we begin to restore order to most sections of the city, the populace may return peacefully to their lives."

Even with Mundus' forces, we were hideously outnumbered. We had incalculably superior leadership, and the men burned to reenter the city to strike against the forces of Hypatius. I found it hard to disagree, for our enemy appeared deflated and ready to flee, and I desired nothing more than an end to the nightmare that consumed Constantinople into a furnace of destruction.

Hurried into a private room, Belisarius' officers assembled as servants unfurled a sweeping map of the city and its districts. Basilius and Liberius carefully placed markers detailing critical control points at various sections, while Narses and Samur informed us on areas with an established armed presence of Hypatius' men. Several dark markers were placed along the Hippodrome, testaments to the tens of thousands who still milled about the racing track, using it as their hoped-for emperor's command center. As the Emperor's representative, Theodora frowned as she delved into the map's details, questioning Belisarius' ability to retake specific buildings and streets with minimal bloodshed.

"Our goal is to cut Hypatius away from his possible supporters, Highness," Belisarius explained. "If the common citizens of the capital feel that Hypatius is losing the fight, they will abandon his cause."

"Agreed," Samur added. "I doubt that Hypatius has more than ten or twenty thousand determined followers—the rest are opportunistic looters or brutes enjoying the city's chaos. It was clear that many are growing tired of the violence, and their food stores are running low."

Despite her remaining concerns, Theodora consented to Belisarius' overall strategy, ensuring Justinian's blessing over the enterprise. While Baduarius continued his mission recapturing towers along the city's walls, Mundus would lead the Thracians along the northern coastline, retaking much of Constantinople's trading quarters and driving away armed resistance along the city's outermost hills.

At the same time, Belisarius would lead near a thousand men along the southerly route, retracing Mundus' entrance and recapturing the Forums of Constantine and Arcadius. Leaving the Hippodrome and its immediate surroundings untouched for the time being, the twin armies would encircle the heart of the city, choking the remaining resistance of further supplies and eliminating any possibility of victory against Justinian's armies.

As commander of the Palace's defenses, I was prohibited from joining Belisarius' attack. I argued against such restrictions, but the Empress insisted upon my duty to defend the Palace.

"If I were Hypatius, I'd attack the Palace as soon as the armies moved away," she reasoned. "We can't risk losing this building so soon after our fortunes turned for the better."

So I watched the armies form up and shuffle in opposite directions, with Mundus' better rested and more numerous Thracians taking on the more daunting task. As the Thracian lines moved north, I caught a glimpse of men from Solomon's banda, their commander's plume bouncing as he marched at the rear of Mundus' column. Likewise, Belisarius absorbed the bulk of my Herulians for his own march, leaving behind a skeleton force to maintain the Palace's more important defenses. Both armies were illuminated by hundreds of torches that were borne by each dekarchos, their fires snaking through Constantinople's streets like some fire demon of the ancient gods.

However, my duties were far from dull, for as the last of Belisarius' column departed the Palace's square, a palace slave approached with fear lining her features. Her bronzed skin hinted at an Egyptian lineage, and despite her attempts to appear a fully mature woman, I doubt she had seen more than fifteen summers.

Timidly seeking my attention, the woman patted the back of my arm, her shoulders turned inward and eyes cast aside as she begged for my attention.

"Apologies, Lord, but Agathias mentioned that I could seek you out if I ran into a problem." Her voice was uneven and low, the accented Greek falling from her lips in a torrent.

"Of course, always," I replied genially. "But what is your name?"

"My name is Aya, if it please you."

"Well met, Aya," I greeted. "Tell me, what is your concern?"

Aya shook her head, tears welling in her eyes. Her lip quivered as she struggled for words. Drawing closer, I pledged for her safety.

"Whatever you tell me, I will keep in confidence," I told her.

"Thank you, Lord," Aya replied. "But it may be easier if I show you."

Though I endeavored to treat her far more politely than the palace nobles she was used to, I balked at the request. "Perhaps later? This is a very stressful time, with the armies moving through the city."

Aya's head shook once more. "Please, Lord Varus, this is extremely urgent."

Her frightened features gave me pause, and I could not refuse. "Very well," I answered. "Show me."

Seizing her opportunity, Aya bounded up the palace stairs, waving for me to follow. Sembrouthes gestured with confusion at my departure, and I promised to return quickly and ordered the Aksumites to remain on the palace floor. There was little need for a bodyguard—most likely, Aya was escorting me into some private squabble amongst the servants or a noble far too comfortable with the whip than honor would allow. With soft footsteps against the hall-length silken carpet, Aya stepped between still-unwashed bloodstains every few paces. Reaching our destination, Aya pointed to a door at the end of the hall, her eyes wide.

"In there, Lord," she whispered.

"What is it?" I asked, beginning to fear some unseen attacker or poison that had claimed many a Roman aristocrat.

"Please, Lord!" Aya begged.

Sighing, I nodded. Disengaging the latch, I listened intently for any sign of someone lying in wait, yet only silence came. I pushed the door open, allowing a sliver of light to enter the room that, other than its eerie silence, had little to indicate anything noteworthy. Then I threw open the door and peered within, and my mouth dropped from shock.

There I saw Hermogenes, his legs dangling above the bedroom's floor, his neck horribly bent.

For a horrifying moment, I thought Hermogenes had taken the form of a phantom, his tongue lolling from a corner of his mouth as froth formed along his chin, yet the body remained motionless as I regained my courage. Grabbing a torch from the hallway, I shone it onto Hermogenes' form, tracing the thick rope that had been knotted to the ceiling and hung rigid with the legate's weight. A foul stench pooled at the man's feet, dripping from his slippers to the silken carpet.

"The legate usually summons me in the evenings, and when I came to check on him, I found him like this," Aya said between sobs. "I did not do this, Lord, I swear to God and his Son."

"Summons you?" I asked, already knowing the answer.

"Yes, Lord..." Aya replied, her sobs louder still. "But I swear, it was not me! I could not do such a thing!"

Stepping gingerly near the body, I hefted the torch near the man's face. His skin had purpled along his collar, matching blood vessels already burst along his eyes and nose. A dull heat still emanated from the limbs. A recent death—within the past hour or two.

"We need to fetch the Empress," I said sternly.

Aya choked. "Lord, the Empress will see me burned! That is the penalty for a slave killing her master!"

"No, she won't," I said. "As you say, there is no way you could have committed this act, even if you wanted to. Hermogenes died by his own hand, or by that of one who could easily overpower the man."

After a time of convincing Aya of her safety, I was soon able to pry Theodora away from her war council and back to Hermogenes' death chamber. Walking alone with the Empress, I prepared her for the grisly sight. I cautiously watched her expression as the door creaked open, but her face remained emotionless. Then, in a flicker of torchlight, I had the briefest impression of triumph on her unnaturally cold features.

"Suicide?" she asked. "Or murder."

"Impossible to tell," I admitted. "If there was a killer, they disguised their movements well. No sign of a struggle, and any bruises on the legate could easily have been wrought by his own hand."

Theodora closed her eyes for several moments, mouthing a silent prayer. "Hermogenes desperately wanted to escape Constantinople. Perhaps he feared the Palace would be overrun during the latest attack and took his own life to spare himself further torture."

"It is possible." I sighed. "But of all the things that Hermogenes was, I never saw him as a coward."

Theodora glided into the room, careful that the hem of her dress did not brush too close to the muck at the corpse's feet. Asking for more light, she examined Hermogenes' body, slowly arriving at my previous conclusion.

"The official word is that this is a suicide," she concluded. "Inform Liberius and the other lords, and I will do the same for the Emperor."

"Highness—"

"Varus, so many have died here, and we lack the time or resources to conduct a thorough investigation," Theodora said sharply. "If there is a killer—and that is a significant if—they specifically targeted Hermogenes and are not likely to pursue further violence."

"How can you be so confident of that?"

"You know better than most that Hermogenes had many enemies, especially in the army," she offered. "Some may even suspect you of the deed, or even me! And even though such accusations would be ludicrous, the rumor of a senior minister's death would lead to disaster. So spread the word of the legate's suicide, and instruct men to burn his corpse as soon as possible."

Though it felt vile to slander a man—even a bitter and bloodthirsty man such as Hermogenes—with suicide, I followed the Empress' order. Many expressed shock at the announcement, and though both Procopius and Narses pried for additional details of the corpse and its immediate surroundings, the questions were uncaring and businesslike. Few seemed bothered by the news, and fewer still attended the legate's cremation a few hours later, although I stared unblinking as the flames consumed the erstwhile enemy of Belisarius, Samur, and countless others who sacrificed their lives for Hermogenes' vanity. Samur stood beside me as the corpse blackened and twisted in the rising blaze, his gaze stern to the point of disgust as Hermogenes' bones were extracted from the fire and pounded into dust, condemning his suicide in the eyes of God and the people of the Empire.

At Theodora's urging, both Mundus and Belisarius ferried updates of their progress through a series of relays that had been successful during the campaign against the Avars. Capitalizing on Mundus' previous success, Belisarius' forces quickly swept along the southern coast, ejecting rioters from the Forum of Constantine and occupying the massive southern harbors along the Sea of Marmara. Even Justinian emerged from his private quarters as Belisarius' messengers described the increasing control the army exerted over the capital, nodding at tales of armed Greens or Blues dropping their weapons and running to the hills on the city's western extremes.

Mundus' Thracians saw considerably more difficulty in recapturing the northernmost road along the Golden Horn, although even these hardened defenses soon capitulated against the furious assault of the Thracian bandae. A messenger even regaled the Emperor with a vivid description of Solomon's banda being the first to reach the Charisius Gate at the city's northwestern extreme, complementing Baduarius' spearmen as they tightened their grip around the city's remaining holdouts.

"He's trying to bring the Emperor to overlook Nepotian's role in backing Hypatius," Cephalas said, reflecting upon Solomon's newfound valor.

"It's likely," I responded, "but Nepotian wasn't on the letter of Hypatius' backers at the beginning of the riot."

"That's because Nepotian's too cunning to leave any evidence of his crimes." Samur scowled. "I've seen his behavior enough to know that he was playing both sides to emerge a victor upon any result."

The progress of both armies slowed as dawn broke over the smoking ruins of Constantinople, with both forming separate camps. Ten thousand Greens flooded out of the Hippodrome in an attempt to take Belisarius' force unawares, yet his scouts informed us of the attack well in advance of the enemy's arrival. The ensuing street battle was over within moments, sending men streaming back to the Hippodrome as they abandoned their crude standards and stolen weapons.

By midday, the armies met along the Valens Aqueduct in the oldest portion of the city, clearing out the few remaining nests of resistance before raising the Imperial Chi-Rho. The gathering was soon joined by Baduarius, raising Belisarius' strength into a veritable field army that was outnumbered by a mere fifty to one by Narses' reckoning.

A select group of senators began to defect from the Hippodrome, pleading ignorance or torture as reasons for their names being included on Hypatius' proclamation. A taciturn Justinian listened to each senator in turn, judging their haggard appearance as much as their honeyed words as they pled for mercy and understanding. Though some were spared at Paulus' insistence—after considerable donations of gold and land to the Imperial Treasury—others were summarily dismissed, taken to the nearby Bosporus Strait, where they were wrapped in chains and tossed from a hill into the sea. I was spared that shameful duty, but I could not avoid hearing the pleas of elderly men and women as their bodies were stripped and coiled in the coarse iron, skin tearing and weeping blood as they were carried to their place of execution.

While many of his colleagues met their inglorious ends, Nepotian returned to the Palace under the escort of Solomon and a full Thracian banda. His fine silks torn and covered with ash, Nepotian rushed to the Emperor, flopping onto the grimy marble floor and kissing Justinian's slippered feet. For the first time in days, I saw Justinian smile, insisting that he rise to his feet.

"I've never doubted your loyalty, Senator Nepotian," Justinian declared, "although it is my wife that you should thank. Without her courage, there may not be a Justinian for you to confess fealty to."

Nepotian stole a brief look of disgust as his attentions shifted to Theodora, quickly replaced by an emotional protestation of loyalty and gratitude. Theodora sat lazily as he planted kisses on each of her shoes, seeming to forget to order the man to rise and rejoin the ranks of the trustworthy. Solomon shifted, visibly angry, as his father remained prostrate along the freezing floor, resembling something of one of the great fishes from the Mediterranean breathing its last on the deck of a Roman sailing vessel. I struggled to stifle laughter as Theodora eventually remembered to honor the senator and relieve him of his supplication, for which she earned a look of pure hatred from Solomon as the family was dismissed.

By the evening, Belisarius declared the city, excepting the Hippodrome and its outlying buildings on the capital's southeastern tip, to be liberated in the name of Justinian. Proof of the newfound peace included the arrival of Epiphanius, the elderly Patriarch who administered the spiritual lives of the Eastern Church and its many adherents in the Empire. Walking arduously with a wooden cane, the Patriarch bowed humbly to the Emperor and Empress, sharing kisses as he praised God for their continued good health. The favors were returned to the city's priests who, despite their general safety during the progression of the riots, maintained their faith in the legitimate Emperor of the Romans.

Leaving detachments of hundreds of soldiers to occupy the city's streets and forums, Belisarius led his officers back to the Palace. Gaunt-faced and downcast, the plumed soldiers followed the general in near silence before the Empress, who called out formal gratitude to each man. Contrasting the somber mood was Baduarius, who sauntered into the shattered palace gateway as though basking in the victory of any other battle. After making polite gestures to the Empress, he approached me with his usual joviality.

"Jupiter's cock, Varus! I leave you for a few months and you let the city burn?"

"The beginning was awful," I said. "At least in a battle, your enemy flies different banners."

"Aye." Baduarius nodded, cuffing me in the shoulder. "But Belisarius set everything to rights. Even with huge numbers, Hypatius doesn't stand a chance."

And that was exactly the point that had begun to nag my mind. While I saw no sin in fulfilling my oath to defend the Emperor, or to slay his enemies on the field of battle, massacring men and women who had a month prior been lawful and taxpaying citizens filled me with apprehension. Like Mundus, I felt resentful at having to kill other Romans—this was not why I had taken Justin's oath, nor why I continued to serve Justinian and Theodora when a wealthy retirement had been mine for the taking.

It was this subject that Belisarius had assembled the various leaders of his fledgling army to discuss. Joined with a surprise appearance of Justinian and his high ministers, the Emperor's general was granted the floor and asked to explain how the crisis may be favorably concluded.

Looming over Liberius and Basilius' map, Belisarius positioned each of his forces to surround the massed mob inside the Hippodrome. "With most of Constantinople pacified, Hypatius only has about a hundred thousand under his command, with supplies dwindling fast."

"Including his most fanatical and loyal forces," Ascum added. "Men and women who have seen plenty of death and are unafraid of more."

Paulus grunted. "So march the armies into the Hippodrome and be done with it!" the minister cried. "If they are determined to be loyal to the usurper, then they cannot be trusted to live."

Justinian's fists battered the table, making Paulus jump. "Sit down and be silent," he ordered. "Lord Belisarius, please continue."

Nodding, Belisarius responded to Paulus warily. "My men are loyal to death, yet asking them to tear apart civilians and peasants is something else entirely. It is a gruesome duty," he explained. "Significant casualties are likely, and those who survive will resent Imperial rule in the coming years."

"Making another riot inevitable," Basilius interjected. "Such things have become too common and keep the Empire from prospering. They must be curtailed here."

"But how?" Mundus asked. "I do not wish to bloody my sword against any more Romans, but the racing gangs are determined to resist. Even if we could evacuate those forced to side with Hypatius or who felt no other option in the early days, our task would be far less burdensome."

Belisarius considered Mundus' charge but seemed to have no ready solution. His eyes searched the room for assistance and eventually rested upon me. Any hope that a miracle solution would manifest itself in *my* mind was fruitless, and I shrugged helplessly. I saw no other solution than conquest, regardless of the growing tug of my conscience.

Of all the warriors and seasoned politicians in the room, it was Narses who broke the deadlock. Approaching the table from the shadows of a rear wall, he giggled as he leaned over the Hippodrome, plucking away blue-painted figurines.

"Gold," he said proudly. "We pry them away with gold."

"I doubt simple bribery would work—" Tribonian was quickly silenced with a glare from the Emperor.

"The entire riot has been about high taxes and little food," Narses said. "Even under such conditions, if we kept the loyalty of the Blues, the riot wouldn't have been more than common thuggery, easily quashed."

"The Blues have always favored the Emperor," Theodora

observed. "Yet Anastasius' nephews were always popular with that crowd. How can we win their favor?"

"By giving them a way out of certain death," Narses concluded. "The Greens are largely lost to us, but spread enough coin and the guarantee of safe passage, and the common Blues will abandon Hypatius in droves. At least, all but the senators who publicly allied with Hypatius."

Chairs creaked as the array of councilors shifted uneasily. "You would have me distribute money to those who are comparatively wealthy, and abandon the poor to slaughter?" Justinian asked icily.

"Yes," Narses said simply. "Spread promises of eased taxes and redistributed grain, and the common plebeians will come around. But for now, give your traditional supporters in the Blues a chance for forgiveness, and your enemy will crumble from within."

"It is highly dishonorable," Belisarius added cautiously.

"Cowardly," Baduarius agreed.

Narses merely grinned. "Which is why it will work. Hypatius' senators are preparing for an all-out battle, but they are lax on security and discipline. I also doubt that all of Hypatius' followers are willing to stand against a charge by hundreds of disciplined veterans. Give me a few bags of coins, and I'll see the task completed before the night is finished."

Many petitioned the Emperor to speak, yet Justinian cared to hear only one opinion: the Empress'. Theodora's head hung low as she considered each outcome, but she soon surrendered to Narses' strategy. Nodding, the Emperor offered Narses his approval, with one caveat.

"No senators or senior officials are allowed to escape," he decreed. "Their fates are in my hands alone."

"Of course, Highness." Narses bowed. "I will see it done."

Another voice rang out. All in attendance turned their heads at the unfamiliar tongue. "With permission, Highness, I will accompany Lord Narses," Samur said.

"Quiet!" I hissed.

Samur shook his head in anger.

"It is a task for two who have knowledge of the Hippodrome," he said. "I will operate with Lord Narses and see this riot to an end."

"As you say. See it done," Justinian declared. "Paulus will see both of you properly equipped to spread coin and goodwill amongst my once-loyal supporters."

And so it was. Despite my pleas for Samur to remain in the Palace, my brother assured me of his safety and disappeared out of the palace gates and into the streets, moving stealthily with Narses against Hypatius' bastion of power.

THE GREAT LORD OF
COMMON MEN

By the orange glow of dawn, a small trickle of stained blue tunics could be seen sneaking from the Hippodrome, many with sagging leather pouches at their waists. That trickle swelled into a veritable stream by midmorning, with dozens walking warily through the Forum of Constantine and a safe distance away from Justinian's soldiers. Thankfully, no violence was reported as Narses' wiles bore fruit, and even small detachments of Greens were seen mixed in with the refugees—largely the elderly, those with children, or those suffering from painful ailments, with few healthy men in their number.

One senator, named Avienus, was caught attempting to escape with a larger contingent of Blues, his hood stretched and robes arranged to disguise him as an old woman suffering from leprosy. The costume allowed the senator to walk past a disgusted and fearful checkpoint of Thracians, yet he was soon recognized by an excubitor who happened to be returning from the Imperial Stables.

Once unmasked, the excubitor smashed an iron fist into the senator's face and carried him to Justinian for judgment. Justinian barely set eyes on the pleading man as he condemned the disgraced senator to the fate of other riotous traitors, albeit with the added punishment of blinding beforehand. Bleeding, Avienus was wrapped in sackcloth and bound in chains, and the wriggling body to be thrown into the sea. I was told that Avienus pissed through the sackcloth as he begged for his life, his cries echoing down the hill until his body connected with the rough waters of the Marmara. I prayed the fall offered some degree of mercy, killing the man upon impact, but I doubted it.

Narses was the first to return, a thick layer of sweat beading against his face. His belt empty of the Emperor's gold, Narses beamed with success as he noted Hypatius' fury at the torrential departure of his followers, leaving the Hippodrome with a mere thirty to forty thousand to carry arms against Belisarius' forces. Though many scoffed at Narses as the eunuch passed, I noted Justinian's approval, for the man had seemingly sealed his victory and ability to continue as Caesar. Narses shrugged off my concerns for Samur, assured that my brother was well and that the two were separated as a precaution to limit their chances of discovery.

Thankfully, Samur arrived at the palace gates as the first stars formed in the sky. Like Narses, Samur was visibly exhausted, his clothes stained from sweat and mouth agape as he sucked air. As he neared the row of torches at the Palace's entrance, I saw his arms and shirt were painted with dark blood. However, he waved off my concerns and cleaned himself at an outdoor basin of cool cistern water.

"Ran into trouble with a couple of Hippodrome guards," he explained. "Now, they won't trouble anyone."

Though Samur's safety was a relief, his reports of violence did little to quell my anxieties for my captive friend. "Were you able to get close to Perenus?"

"I didn't see him. And Narses didn't give me a chance to look. But I doubt I could have plucked Perenus from the mob unawares."

With Narses' plan complete, Belisarius was provided with the Emperor's approval to begin the final storming of the Hippodrome's residents. Justinian had been insistent upon killing any who bore arms against Imperial soldiers, as well as those with clear evidence of theft from an Imperial granary or storage yard, which by this day included most Greens who struggled to feed themselves in the Hippodrome's enclosure. Belisarius protested vigorously but was harangued by the Emperor for timidity, a charge that had cost him his freedom in the aftermath of Callinicum.

As Belisarius began his planning session for the attack, I begged for a temporary delay in the Hippodrome's recapture. Theodora seemed skeptical, but she allowed me to speak.

"Perenus is alive in the Hippodrome," I explained. "As my second-in-command, honor compels me to bring him out of that place."

"How do you know for certain that he lives?" she asked coolly.

"My brother was absolutely sure of it," I told her. "I do not need much time... perhaps a few hours? I'd return well before the moon's zenith."

Belisarius weighed the appeal, seemingly uncertain of how to proceed, raising concerns of my safety. Liberius interjected on my behalf, silencing debate.

"Perenus is a senior Roman officer," Liberius said, "and deserves a chance at rescue. The Emperor needs to show mercy and kindness in the same way that he must demonstrate cold determination to quell the riots."

"But why Varus?" Belisarius asked, his voice laced with caution. "Many of my men would be happy to take on such a duty."

Liberius grinned. "Have you seen the size of him? If Perenus is injured, we'll need someone of Varus' strength to carry the man to safety. Besides, I doubt that Varus would agree to others taking such a risk in his stead."

"Indeed, Lord Liberius." I bowed. "An hour, maybe two... That's all I ask."

The Empress considered our words and quickly agreed. "Accept no unnecessary hazards," Theodora said, "and you are oathbound to retreat if danger rises, whether you have located Perenus or not."

I bowed again and excused myself. Donning a deep-green robe

that bore only a few splotches of blood from its previous owner, I dressed myself as a poor commoner, drawing upon my days as a palace slave for inspiration. Unconvinced of my appearance, Cephalas rubbed dirt and ashes in my hair and skin to complete my disguise, adding additional layers until he was convinced of my safety.

"None in the Hippodrome would have bathed in weeks," Cephalas reasoned, "so any sweet-smelling body would warrant alarm."

Adequately costumed, I headed to the smaller quarters where Rosamund still recuperated from her throbbing head wound. Still looking frail, Rosamund's high spirits shifted as I explained my mission.

"This is not a game, Varus," she said. "Don't take any chances with these people."

I swore upon my preparations and safety and handed her my dragon-hilted sword. "I thought I would trade you until I return," I said, holding a hand out for her to return Aetius' dagger.

Sliding the sword from its leather sheath, Rosamund traced a bony finger along its runes, marveling at its bluish hue and the ornately decorated pommel, then slammed the blade back into its covering and safely tucked it behind her resting head.

"Come back to me safely," she ordered as she handed over the dagger. "I can hardly stand this accursed city as it is. I don't know what I'd do alone."

Lifting herself into a seated position, Rosamund offered a lingering embrace before I left. A crash of melancholy dampened my spirits as I departed, a daydream taking me far away from the crush of Constantine's city and onto the open plains and forests beyond the Empire's borders—Rosamund's recurring dream that, in spite of myself, held great allure in times like these, when my many oaths weighed heavily.

That dream was broken by Samur, who approached with an irritated expression that belied disapproval at my intended actions.

"If you're going back to the Hippodrome, I'm coming with you."

"No," I told him. "Your body is already overtaxed from your excursion with Narses, and I need you here in case I'm unable to return to the Palace."

Samur sighed. "They're killers in that stadium, Varus. I love Perenus too, but he wouldn't want you recklessly risking your life on some wild hunt."

"That's exactly what Perenus would want me to do." I laughed. "At any rate, it is decided. Don't worry, Samur. I will not be gone long."

Samur hung his head in surrender. "As you wish," he replied meekly. "I'll make sure the army doesn't launch their attack until you return."

Before departing, I paced back to my assigned rooms, finding Mariya dozing inside. Waking from the noise at her door, she smiled and placed a finger to her lips.

"Zenobia is sleeping," she whispered, pointing into the adjoining room. "I sent the servants away."

I could not tell Mariya my intention to sneak into the Hippodrome. Even if she permitted me to go, the danger would only cause her to worry, and she had suffered enough over the past week. However, I was not blind to the risk of being discovered and taken captive— if this was the last moment of peace I would share with my family, however fleeting, I intended to make the most of it.

Taking a step toward Zenobia's room, my boot smacked against the floor, drawing Mariya's ire. "Can I see her?"

"Let Zenobia sleep. There is plenty of time later," Mariya whispered. "She hasn't slept too soundly in the Palace."

"Of course."

Mariya rose to sitting. "Can you stay? You have time away from the Empress?"

I bent down to steal a kiss. "Not now, unfortunately."

"They ask too much of you." Mariya sighed. She tugged at my arm, pulling me to fall in a heap atop the bed. "Are you sure you can't stay with me?"

God, but I wanted to. "If only I could, my love. But I won't be long."

Squeezing her hand one last time, I rose from the bed and stepped into the hallway. I had not lied to her—not truly. But that did not make the burden of our parting any easier on me. Instead, I pivoted to how I would find and free Perenus, suppressing the gnawing fear that I might be about to leave my wife a widow and my child absent her father.

I ventured down the palace steps and through its main entrance. Where the Palace's primary doorway had just recently been thronged with Greens and Blues eager to finish the overthrow of Justinian's government, all that remained on those streets were stray dogs who skulked in gutters, feasting on mounds of decaying filth. As I moved away from the palace doors and stepped onto the cracked stones of the street, I was interrupted by an urgent voice behind me.

"Wait!" Xerxes called out in Persian, rushing down the palace stairs. "I'm coming with you."

"Not a chance," I answered in Greek, "and why would you even want to?"

Xerxes shrugged. "As before, someone needs to keep you from killing yourself. I think you might be my only friend in this place."

Visions of charred villages and the desiccated corpses of Armenian children flashed in my mind. "*Friend* might be stretching it."

Xerxes' face twitched for a brief moment, but he showed no anger at the veiled insult. "You Romans hate me for what was done in the war," Xerxes said, "yet here we are in your capital, pondering the massacre of tens of thousands. How is this any different?"

"Because it is in self-defense," I said, pulling away as I continued on my path. "I don't butcher unarmed women and children for sport."

I expected some witty banter in retort, but Xerxes kept any frustrations to himself. "Very well, be angry," he muttered, "but I'm still coming."

"If you jeopardize my chance of rescuing Perenus, I'll think skewer you myself," I replied, seeing no easy path to jettison him.

"At least you're dressed appropriately."

Garbed in a similar torn green robe, Xerxes also sported a boiled leather skullcap and a thin black cloth that covered his nose and chin—likely uncomfortable, but it was thin enough that it did not muffle his voice and served to further disguise his Persian heritage, which would invite unwanted questions. Along a thin jade sash rested a simple steel dagger, its handle worn from excessive use over the years.

"So, how do we get in?" Xerxes whispered again in Persian.

"The long way," I answered in the same tongue. "We can't risk getting caught by sneaking through the servants' tunnels, but Hypatius will have few spies that can track our movements through the streets. We'll follow the northern road until well out of eyeshot of the Hippodrome and then cut through the center of the city to reach its rear entrance."

"And how do you know they will let us in?"

"An opportunity will arise," I lied, entirely unsure of my strategy, "and if any question our intentions, there's always gold to discourage unnecessary questions."

Xerxes chuckled but did not reply. As we moved farther along the coast of the Golden Horn, we encountered greater numbers of bystanders, most of whom bore symbols favoring the Blues. Enough Greens milled through the city's alleys that roving bands of Mundus' men paid us little heed, keeping the pretense of my anonymity intact.

Sensing the fair distance remaining to our destination, Xerxes chatted idly, speaking of his experiences as a child in the Persian Court of Ctesiphon. I allowed the Immortal to continue his conversation without reply for a time, yet eventually succumbed to nagging thoughts and offered polite retorts to Xerxes' observations. The prince listened intently as I offered stories of my childhood under Justin, balking at descriptions of the once-peaceful Imperial capital. He further questioned the logic of allowing chariot racing to continue, given their propensity to stir a thirst for violence amongst the sultrier elements of the city's populace.

Even encumbered by multiple distractions, I could sense Xerxes delaying the true topic of his interest, his words rambling and imprecise. As we turned away from the Golden Horn and toward the Forum of Constantine I shot looks in my companion's direction, curious of his true interests on our journey together. When he finally did ask his question, it hit me with the force of a spear thrust, throwing me off guard as if I were in battle.

"Do you trust the Empress?" Xerxes asked.

"With my life, and my family's lives," I answered. "Why do you ask?"

He shrugged. "Theodora's actions are rarely in line with her private thoughts," he said. "It's difficult to tell most times, but her emotions betray themselves through her eyes, even if just for a heartbeat."

"Explain your meaning," I snapped. "Theodora has given no reason for any mistrust by me and has offered more support and love than I have rightfully earned in her service."

Xerxes shook his head, taking care to keep his voice muted. "I mean no offense," he explained. "I just do not believe that Hermogenes killed himself."

My eyes widened. "And you think Theodora did the deed?"

"I doubt it." He chuckled. "She's far too clever. Some catspaw. Or a hired assassin? Hermogenes did not seem the type for suicide, and the legate was a known opponent of the Empress, even to a foreigner such as myself."

Anger rising in my throat, I clenched my fists as I fought to remain calm. "Impossible, and too difficult to execute," I reasoned. "Those conspiracies may be rife in Ctesiphon, but not in Justinian's household."

"Such things unfortunately do happen in Persia," Xerxes confessed, "yet those men are not worshipped or revered, but reviled by the priests and common men alike, marked as servants for the Dark God."

"The Great Lie?"

Xerxes looked at me curiously. "Indeed," the Immortal replied. "But how does a Herulian soldier know of the teachings of Zoroaster?"

"My instruction in the Palace," I began, "although that name I learned from a priest named Hakhamanish."

"The magus!" Xerxes smiled. "A good man, and a force for truth. Haunted, but good."

"As you say," I answered, "but we should attend to the task at hand."

Xerxes obeyed and let the matter drop. We veered back in the direction of the Hippodrome. Filtering onto the coastal street along the Sea of Marmara, the Hippodrome's vaulted structure rose in the sky, its sections still intact despite their considerable misuse by Hypatius' men. As we approached that ominous place, my thoughts strayed back to Theodora, her emerald eyes caught within a noxious web.

Could she have killed Hermogenes? No, of course not. That would be wildly against her character. The Empress was one of the most closely watched and carefully guarded people in the Empire, and therefore the world, and the assassination of a senior minister was a crime so horrific in Roman eyes that she could be burned alive if proven guilty. Hermogenes may have been a stubborn enemy, but his death would have been too risky to engineer, even if it was desired.

But then I recalled words from the Empress' own mouth. I returned to the day we first met, when the Hippodrome first rose in chaos and the Hagia Sophia burned to its foundations.

Is this your first time taking a life?

There, in the deepest recesses of my memory, nagging doubt wormed its way in. Who else could have killed Hermogenes if not Theodora? Who had the motive, the potential for gain? I found I could not answer those questions, nor could Xerxes' words find a counterpoint to demonstrate the answer's falseness.

After walking in relative silence for a time, we intersected with the continuing stream of Hypatius' refugees. Reduced to a comparative trickle, it still flooded the streets, showing the willingness of hundreds to turn away from Hypatius' cause, or at least save their own lives from the hopeless fight to come. Xerxes and I blended in easily with that crowd, avoiding the armed thugs preying upon those whose infirmity or lack of protection left them open to theft and brutality. Xerxes frowned, and I whispered that there was nothing we could do—any armed defense would almost surely condemn us to attacks from all directions.

Though we approached with little difficulty, the thick forest of fearful refugees made for slow progress. A thick odor seeped from hundreds of bodies, its stench made all the more rancid by a general aura of terror. Xerxes gripped my robe tight as I navigated each layer of the crowd, and gradually, the Hippodrome's walls slowly rose to dominate my view.

Then, as if by an act of divine providence, the mob cleared. A handful of stragglers remained, yet otherwise the Hippodrome's rear entrance was blocked by rows of unmanned barricades, their wooden posts spiked and intersecting like quills on a hedgehog. That would have been curious enough, were it not for the bodies.

There were so many that in the darkness, I took them for a larger group of sentries posted to keep order along Hypatius' stronghold. But any illusions were dispelled as a breeze filtered through the burned-out buildings and piles of rubbish. The bodies swung as if in a macabre dance from hell.

"Evil," Xerxes muttered, a rare note of fear in his voice. "Pure evil."

Hesitating for a moment, I moved one booted foot toward the grisly display. Many of the bodies appeared fresh, their torsos covered in stained Blue robes that leaked the humors of the dead. Others had already begun to stiffen and rot, layers of flesh fusing to the ropes that blackened as they held their burdens. A smaller selection of nooses were altogether vacant, accompanied by piles of half-burnt flesh along the ground as testament to their former occupiers.

Walking through that forest of rot and decay, I mumbled a prayer to God to deliver me from this place. A sudden gust of wind blew one corpse to the side, spraying me with flecks of congealed blood that collected in cold dots along my face. Jerking back, I blushed at my own disgust, at my timidity at the dead when I had seen far worse on the battlefield. I could not calm myself until we passed under the Hippodrome's gates. Its solitary guardsman hardly deigned to inspect his latest two visitors, seemingly amused at young men eager to enter the racing arena as opposed to slinking cautiously away.

The Hippodrome itself seemed something out of a dream—or a nightmare. A dozen bonfires roared into the sky, clouding the stars above with a crimson glow as ash rained lazily onto the heads of Hypatius' citizens. While thankfully absent a sea of corpses that decorated the stadium's exterior, piles of food and weapons cluttered various sections of the seats and racing sands, while makeshift forts and barriers housed hundreds of armored men and women bearing grim and dirty guises.

By their appearance, many had eaten far better than the near-starvation rations that had become all too common in Justinian's Empire, although soiled clothing and rancid piles of waste hung thickly in the air. Clutching his scarf closer to his nose and mouth, Xerxes stifled a gag as he adjusted to what had become of the Hippodrome, once a jewel of the Eastern Empire. All that remained of its memory was a tainted hulk of a building and an ominous stain along the finish line where the final race had met its end in a massive crash of blood and splintered bone.

"Keep sharp," I whispered in Persian. "The sooner we find Perenus, the sooner we can leave."

"Find him? But how?"

Xerxes had a point. Even with most of the Blues and many of the Greens having abandoned the place, thousands remained to gorge on their remaining supplies. Most were younger and fitter, clearly defiant of Justinian's threats as they carved obscenities into the Hippodrome's walls. One rather gifted artist used a dark-blue paint that outlined a fair likeness of the Emperor, his body bent over as another figured labeled Paulus grabbed hold of the monarch's haunches.

I refused to surrender to the rising sensation of hopelessness. I walked between the rows of the Hippodrome's stands, cautious to not appear in a hurry. I regulated my pace to a brisk walk, checking every thirty or so steps to be sure that Xerxes followed closely behind. To his credit, the Immortal looked intently upon hundreds of faces as we passed, scrutinizing those with bloodied wounds or resting filthy heaps on more choice benches that had not been spoiled by dung or rubbish. After making a quarter circuit, however, I shook my head in futility.

"We don't have long," I murmured. "We need to split up. Meet at our original entrance after clearing a half circuit."

"And if you don't arrive soon thereafter?"

"Then you can leave," I said. "Head east to Persia, or wherever you'd like. I won't stop you."

Though his face was heavily shrouded, Xerxes' eyes narrowed as he smirked. "A half circuit," he said, "nothing more."

We separated. I continued down my path while Xerxes paced up to the more elevated benches, many of which contained circles of armored men crouching around cookfires. After nearly tripping over loose boards that littered the ground, I stole one of the hundreds of crude torches that lined the Hippodrome's lower levels, consisting of little more than a thick branch wrapped with layers of cloth that had been dipped in naphtha. Its heavy smoke irritated my eyes, yet the light from its flames eased my task as I searched through dozens of faces, desperate for any sign of Perenus.

As hints of despair began to coil in my gut, I passed by a contingent of richly attired Blues, their faces serious and gaunt as they plotted how to regain dominance over Constantinople. I recognized many as senators who once enjoyed the Emperor's favor, though apparently they resented their declining fortunes as Paulus' taxes eroded even those privileges of the patricians. Many had even longtime colleagues of Justin, my former master. I steered away from those men in particular as I continued my search, but only in vain; my presence was soon noted, and by someone I could not have expected.

Of all the grubby Blues who remained in that section of the Hippodrome, one figure stood out from the rest. His robes dyed in a crude violet paste, the portly figure sat atop a soiled bench, its cushions frayed and its legs cluttered with all manner of chicken bones, rotting apple cores, and a foul brown sludge that warned of a putrid stench. It would have not surprised me to find a gluttonous aristocrat on that chair, fueled by an innate belief of superiority over the masses. What I found was a man weathered beyond his limits, his mind and body neither fit nor capable of bearing the burden as the riot's leader. I lowered my head and raised a hand to disguise my features as I passed close to Hypatius, hoping to pass for another grimy supplicant—this hope was in vain.

"You!" Hypatius yelled, his voice trembling as he spoke. "I remember you!"

"That is not possible," I answered curtly, seeking to pull away from the would-be emperor.

"You were Justin's slave," Hypatius concluded. "The big one! Oh—"

"Varus," I grunted. He rushed to greet me, the thick flesh of his limbs jiggling as he clutched hard at my forearm.

"Of course. I apologize. My mind wanders these days," he confessed. "I've heard that Justin's successor won honors in the east. If only I'd listened more carefully to your words that day in the Palace—"

Shrugging, I tried to pull away from the stained figure, his tattered purple robes swirling in a rising wind. "Then you know that I wish nothing more than to leave this place," I replied, careful to avoid revealing my loyalties to the would-be emperor.

"I didn't want this. Justinian must know that!" Hypatius blubbered. "I told them no, it would never work, but they insisted I go along with their scheme."

"Who is 'they'?" I dropped my guard, observing this weeping wreck that was Anastasius' nephew.

"Nicephorus, Avienus, Suda, even Nepotian," Hypatius whispered with desperation. "They all said it would be over quickly, and that few would need to be hurt!"

My nose flared as I scowled. "They were wrong, as were you to join them."

Hypatius nodded. "I know…" he said, fat tears flowing down his cheeks, "but maybe Justinian will show mercy? He will! He must! I am Anastasius' nephew, after all!"

I shrugged, tried to step away, yet the fleshy hand stopped me once more.

"At least he would spare my son!" Hypatius said, his features lined with greater desperation this time.

"Son?" I had thought Hypatius preferred the company of men.

"Constantine," Hypatius affirmed. "Although in the privacy of our house, we use his cognomen, Tiberius. He's just a little boy, only two summers. Perhaps you could take him from this place?"

Just a boy. Most children had long evacuated those areas most exposed to fighting, but a few stragglers remained, clutching at their parents amidst pyres of smoke and stacked barricades.

I should have refused Hypatius' request outright, for the boy would only jeopardize my safe return to the palace. My own family depended upon my safe return for their safety and comfort—and yet, as much as I loathed Hypatius and sought only to retrieve Perenus and remove myself from this monument of death, I felt my resolve wavering. For would an enemy of mine show mercy to my Zenobia? I would hope so. But how could I expect such grace from another if I could not extend it in my own right?

"I'm on the Emperor's orders," I said, equivocating. "The boy would be no safer with me than with your men."

"Please…" Hypatius begged, his other hand clasping my arm. "I will give you anything that is in my power, if you swear by your god to take my boy out of the Hippodrome. That's all!"

What little defense I had against Hypatius' request evaporated. Even if Perenus' whereabouts were not dependent upon my answer, I doubt I would have decided differently. Others, like Justinian, may have chastised me as a foolish and sentimental man—as Justin knew well, I was not like those men. I could forge my own path.

"Very well," I answered. A wave of joy flashed on Hypatius' face. "With two conditions," I hurried to add. "First, the boy will respond to his cognomen rather than Constantine. If his true identity were to be discovered, both he and my own family would be executed."

Hypatius nodded, although he had little choice. "Cautious, of course. And the second?"

"You must tell me where Perenus is—the Lazic charioteer for the Greens. I'm taking him back to the Palace."

Hypatius' eyes scanned the Hippodrome's track. "My men pulled the Green champion from the wreckage with Magnetius. That Perenus was a lucky one. Both Magnetius and the Persian rider were mangled beyond recognition, yet Perenus was blown clear of the destruction."

"Where is he now?"

Hypatius' face calmed itself as his soft eyes rested upon mine. He began to draw a golden signet ring from his left hand, then paused. "I have your word that you will come back for Tiberius?"

I sighed. "On my honor as a soldier of the Empire, and as a father to my own child, I swear it."

Satisfied, he offered the bauble to me. "This was Anastasius' ring. I rarely got along with the old man, but I did love him," he said, another bout of tears welling in his eyes. "Make sure Tiberius receives this when he is ready?"

"I promise," I replied again. "But I need to leave as soon as possible."

"Thank you, Varus," Hypatius said, swallowing hard.. "Descend to the racing track. Perenus has been kept on a cot between the Obelisk of Theodosius and the Triumphal Quadriga and is likely still there with his injuries. I will have Tiberius ready to leave when you return."

Instinctively, I saluted, which brought a sad smile to Hypatius' face. Turning away, I trotted down to the track. I avoided the bands of Greens that huddled at various points of the Hippodrome's stands, yet few acknowledged my presence, and none questioned my intentions. I dropped onto the sands, avoiding piles of litter and supplies that had been stacked in the earliest hours of the riot, and surveyed my territory.

While I initially assumed that Perenus would be easy to locate, the rows of hundreds of crude cots and tents showed that to have been a vain hope. The Great Obelisk was easy enough to identify, its outer façade covered with inscriptions of the Ancient Egyptian pharaohs whose bones had turned to dust long before Rome was carved out of its Seven Hills. So, too, was the Quadriga, the four bronze horses that personified the beloved races that filled circuses and arenas throughout the Empire. Between them were hundreds of sleeping, farting, and dying Greens, with no semblance of order or organization to simplify my task.

Even with the cool breeze blowing through the Hippodrome's lowest level, open wounds, burnt flesh, and the ever-present threat of dysentery was nearly as bad as the forest of corpses that guarded the Hippodrome's rear entrance. Walking briskly with a hand over my mouth and nose, I perused dozens of faces. Several grunted in anger at being disturbed from their relative solitude. Others moaned incoherently, their skin peeling and green as disease wormed through open wounds and oozing sores.

And then, half hidden in the sickly sweet odor of rancid death, I found him. There was Perenus, his eyes sealed shut, still clad in his racing attire of a stained green cloak, his limbs unmoving where he lay on a crude wooden cot. In the darkness of the Hippodrome's sands, Perenus was still as death.

I could have struck Hypatius in frustration—Perenus' body was as wounded and unmoving as any of the hundreds of others. I placed a hand along the hem of Perenus' wool cloak, feeling only despair. I was too late to help my friend.

"I'll cut that hand off, thief!"

Callused fingers clamped around my wrist. Perenus jerked awake, coughing.

"You're alive, you bastard!" I yelled, then lowered my voice as others nearby gazed warily in our direction. "Perenus, I saw you die!"

For a heartbeat, I did not know what to do. In fact, I giggled and placed a hand on Perenus' chest just to be sure that I spoke with a living, breathing man and not some malicious spirit.

Perenus coughed again, his breathing haggard. "Varus? What are you doing here?"

"Saving your life, or attempting to," I said hurriedly. "If that's acceptable."

He chuckled, giving in to another coughing spasm. "Wouldn't be the first time. But I think you've really stepped in shit, coming to the Hippodrome."

Perenus struggled to sit upright, his usually pronounced physique pale and lacking vigor. I helped him stretch one leg after the other. "Can you walk?" I asked in Heruli. "We need to leave this place immediately."

"Think so," Perenus responded, his own Heruli rough and uncertain. "But why?"

Heart racing, I explained our predicament and the limited time remaining before Belisarius expected my return. Upon hearing Hypatius' request Perenus scoffed, insisting that we leave the traitor to rot. I refused, insisting upon fulfilling another troublesome oath, arguing that despite the sins of his father, a boy that young was innocent of any crime and deserving of a chance to escape certain massacre.

Surrendering to my wishes, Perenus wrapped his arms around my neck as I lifted the man to his feet. He groaned in discomfort, bruised muscles and cracked ribs shifting as I steadied him on his feet. Though he initially threatened to topple over, he remained standing, albeit with significant assistance as he leaned heavily on my shoulder.

We made slow progress back to Hypatius. As we neared the Emperor of the Greens, another figure approached, his breathing rushed and eyes flicking in all directions.

"We need to get out of here now," Xerxes warned in Persian. "The

Greens are getting violent and threatening to hang the remaining Blues. If Hypatius can't control the mob, there will be slaughter even before Justinian's forces arrive."

"Hypatius controls little and shouldn't be counted on to stop anything at this point," I replied. I relayed my plans for escape, and Xerxes nodded in understanding, then grabbed Perenus' other arm. Together, we painfully hauled him toward the plump form of Hypatius, the would-be emperor's guards eyeing us lazily as we approached.

Sitting at Hypatius' feet was a young boy, too old to be a babe but far too young to speak more than a select few words. Still shaped by the layers of fat that followed infancy, Tiberius seemed oblivious to his surroundings, playing with a crude wooden figure that resembled a gray wolf. Tiberius giggled as he tossed the figure into the air, watching it clatter to the ground and kick up a tiny pillar of dust. As we approached, Tiberius handed the figure to his father, who patted the boy on the head and rose to his feet.

"Thank you, Varus," Hypatius said. "You are saving my son's life."

"The boy has done no wrong," I said shortly. "He deserves a chance to live a full life. But I do need to leave soon."

"I understand," Hypatius replied, his eyes beginning to tear up. "If I am unable to reclaim him…"

"Then Tiberius will be cared for."

At my words, Xerxes sputtered with shock. But Hypatius nodded, and thick tears ran down his wriggling cheeks. "Make sure to give him my uncle's ring, yes? And let him know that his father loves him."

I nodded wordlessly. Hypatius struggled to kneel, ignoring the filth that puddled along his throne, and stroked the thin mop of auburn hair on Tiberius' head with a pudgy hand. The boy smiled, offering the toy to his father once more, as though now was finally the moment to play.

"Constantine, you are going to leave with this nice man," Hypatius croaked, his tears rising to a torrent. "His name is Varus, and he will take you to the Palace where you will be safe. You will respond to the name Tiberius from now on."

Tiberius lacked the years or words to question any commands from his father. His age, at least, would make his name simple enough to change, allowing me to avoid the scrutiny of Narses' spies. The boy wriggled as Hypatius drew him into his arms, planting a kiss on Tiberius' forehead as his fingers clutched at the boy's thick woolen shirt.

"You father loves you very much." Hypatius wept, rocking Tiberius as the child slapped playfully at his cheeks.

Father and son remained in the embrace for a time, and I lacked the heart to separate them. My thoughts trailed to Zenobia as I avoided staring at the unfolding scene, wondering how I would behave in this same predicament. At the time, I did not know the answer, and only thanked God that I had been spared such impossible decisions.

Hypatius eventually rose, still holding Tiberius as his knees slowly absorbed his body's weight. As he handed Tiberius into my outstretched arms, the wooden toy clattered to the floor, brushing against a thin trail of blood. Hypatius rushed back to the floor, using the hem of his sleeves to wipe away the stain before handing it back to me. I placed the wolf into a pouch at my belt, feeling it clatter against Anastasius' ring as I resealed its leather straps.

"God protect you, filius," Hypatius said. Nodding to me, Hypatius gave permission to depart before collapsing into his chair, his face buried in a nest of grubby fingers.

Moving away, I clutched Tiberius close to my chest as Perenus leaned upon my opposite shoulder. Where before our pace had been slowed by Perenus' limp, we were now reduced to a crawl. Xerxes and I panted and grunted from the burden of the added weight. Surprisingly friendly with a stranger such as myself, Tiberius eyed me curiously, tiny fingers pulling at my beard as a thin layer of mucus trailed from his nostrils.

"It will take forever to return the same way we came from," Xerxes said, sweat beading on his forehead.

Reluctantly, I agreed. "We shouldn't risk it, but there's no time. Let's head for the main entrance, the gates leading to the road to the Palace."

As we trudged back to the safety of the Palace, however, Xerxes' warning began to yield wicked fruit. Angry shouts rumbled along the edges of the Hippodrome's structure. Hastily armored guards sprinted toward the origin of such cacophony.

Urging our party forward, I heard signs of struggle rising as a small faction of Greens broke away from the rest of the group. Others pointed and called out as they watched us pass by, complaining to the gate pickets of our intent to escape. The half dozen guardsmen ignored such grumbling, with one barking in anger that the Emperor had decreed that our party should be allowed to depart.

"Not good," Xerxes muttered.

"Just keep going," I said, closing the distance to the ornate iron gates that opened to the main city thoroughfare."

Angered by the guards' indifference as the gates creaked open for our passage, one man rushed at a sentry, screaming in the man's face.

"What's the point of a revolution when Hypatius lets some be saved while others are forced to fight?" the man screamed in rage. "At least we were permitted to move where we wanted under Justinian."

The guards lowered their spears and backed away hesitantly as others rushed behind the protesting figure. I stole one final glance as we marched past the gate, met with eyes that burned from anger and hopelessness. And, for an instant, recognition.

"That's Hypatius' son!" the man screeched. "That bastard would save his son but let mine be cut to pieces!"

That familiar wave of anger and violence became muffled as we moved through the open street and the gates closed behind us. Tiberius jerked in my arms as two men shook the iron bars of the Hippodrome entrance, spitting curses at Hypatius' hypocrisy and our purported cowardice. I thought that the threats were the worst of our concerns, until I turned my gaze to the view just beyond the Hippodrome's arch.

Swinging bodies. As with the rear entrance, rows of rotting corpses defended the stadium's gates, their limp forms dangling from nooses. Choking on the wafting stench of death, I threw a hand over Tiberius' eyes. He fidgeted, whimpering.

"Jesus…" Perenus said, limping closer to the display. "How could this happen?"

Tiberius struggled in my grip as another breeze blew a nest of swinging legs in various directions. One grimy foot even brushed the boy's hair. He laughed as he kicked and squirmed in my arms. The task of shielding Tiberius consumed so much of my attention that I did not notice another swinging leg that connected with my face. I jumped in disgust as blood and other death fluids sprayed on my forehead.

Then, from the corner of my eye, a flicker of recognition forced me to glance back at one of the hanging bodies. Far fresher than the others, its blood had not thickened into a congealed mass, its skin resembling living flesh instead of the gray pallor that consumed all men and women as they left their bodies. The corpse differed from the others, its stomach ripped open and intestines serving as its hangman's noose. The face's features were fixed in horror at the man's last moments of suffering, and I soon recognized the figure as one who had drawn my ire in the streets of Barbalissus.

"Symeon?" I muttered aloud.

His tattered green cloak sticking to his torso and legs, Symeon eyed me with a death stare still burned into my mind.

The iron gates behind us groaned open, the sounds of the mob rising for one final bout of depravity. I could not linger.

"Run, Varus!" Perenus shouted, leaning on Xerxes for support.

We dashed ahead, our sandals finding little purchase against the slick stones of Constantinople's streets. Gripping Tiberius tightly, I called out for help from the still-distant Palace, but my voice was drowned out by the approaching anger of the mob. We sprinted another fifty paces, our progress made painfully slow by Perenus' weakened condition. Nearing the halfway point to the palace gates, a small stone struck my calf. I cursed in pain as I struggled to keep my balance.

From the direction of the Palace, a Thracian horn blared four clipped beats, a note of recognition and emergency by the officers on duty. In the distance, a thin wall of armored spearmen formed along the palace steps, their features blurred against a backdrop of darkness and torchlight, still several hundred paces away.

Despite our rising hopes, however, another stone clattered at our feet, with a band of a few dozen closing the distance to our party. Perenus winced in pain as he forced his legs to walk. Xerxes shook his head in futility.

"Not enough time!" Xerxes said.

Xerxes unslung Perenus' arm from around his shoulder, causing Perenus to stumble. Reaching for my arm, Perenus leaned against my body, which was already encumbered by a hysterical child, kicking at my hips and legs in a desperate attempt to free himself. Livid, I snarled at Xerxes' betrayal, turning to curse the man.

Rather than sprinting to the Palace, Xerxes unsheathed his thin dagger. Though small, it had been honed with deadly purpose, moving swiftly in the hand of an Immortal.

"Give me your blade, Varus!" Xerxes yelled.

I protested, but he interrupted. "Take the others and go!"

Propping Perenus momentarily on his feet, I withdrew my dagger and handed it to Xerxes. He nodded, then turned to the oncoming rush, backing away in step with our own retreat. After another twenty paces, Xerxes fell from view, but his warning roar carried far.

We soon approached a detachment of twenty Thracian spearmen. Their leader did not halt the detachment's advance as they passed by, instead ordering that we move to the palace door immediately. Recognizing the voice, I turned and found Solomon, his face dark and hollow from lack of sleep.

"Go, Varus!" Solomon yelled to me.

Before I obeyed the order, I glanced at the fray behind us, a blur of green robes, clubs, and a spray of blood. Xerxes slashed with both knives at a number of hesitant attackers, yet slowly the sheer press of men and women surrounding him were gaining. I strained to make out his figure, finding nothing. Our group had reached the palace doorway. The last I saw of the attack was the arrival of Solomon's men, their wall closing in on the diminutive mob that soon ran from the orderly array of Roman soldiers.

Inside the Palace, servants rushed to produce benches, and Perenus plopped gracelessly onto the first available wooden seat. He moaned as he rubbed at sore legs, the muscles undoubtedly weakened from a lack of use since the onset of the riot. Samur arrived soon thereafter, inspecting Perenus' wounds and summoning a still-hobbled Rosamund to treat the more serious injuries as best as she could. Before departing with Samur on a litter, Perenus thanked me for our rescue, grasping at my forearm before seeking treatment.

As soon as Perenus departed, I was approached by Aya, who spoke with eyes fixed on the palace floor.

"Lord Varus, the Empress wished a notice as soon as you returned," she mumbled, raising a curious eye upon Tiberius. "Shall I inform her of anything of note?"

"Tell the Empress of our success," I said. "Nothing more."

Aya nodded uncertainly, disappearing amidst the servants' hallways and into Theodora's private chambers. Other soldiers on evening guard duty followed close behind with a barrage of questions, including an idle question from Sindual on Xerxes' whereabouts.

Before I could answer, the improvised palace doors swung open once more, allowing Solomon's detachment to march inside before the doors were returned to their barred and locked position. Though uninjured, Solomon's men bore evidence of the violence they had incurred, their cloaks further stained by the crumpled figure that several carried between them.

Handing Tiberius to a nearby servant woman, I knelt beside Xerxes' prone form. Moaning piteously, he spat blood onto the tiled floor, the coarse liquid mixing with his saliva and threatening to block his nose and mouth.

"The Persian took at least a half dozen down before we pulled him from the scrum," Solomon said. "I think he'll live."

"Thank you," I replied, clenching a hidden fist so my voice would not waver.

Solomon grunted acknowledgment, then instructed his men to return to their posts outside of the Palace. Though there was no sign of any further disturbance by the mob, an additional detachment of Thracians filtered through the palace doorways, ordered to call for support the instant any trouble smoldered.

I had no mind for these concerns. In between speaking soft thanks to Xerxes, I called for doctors to be fetched at once. Another servant departed, informing Rosamund to tend to Xerxes after addressing Perenus' aches, for Xerxes placed little trust in any other learned Roman doctor with his care.

"Why would you do that?" I asked, inspecting the dark welts forming on Xerxes' face and body.

Xerxes' clenched his teeth, tears of pain running down his cheeks as he gritted out a response. "Because it was the right thing to do."

Within moments, a bearded Greek doctor emerged at the palace entrance, irritable and disheveled at being disturbed so late at night. But a single glance at Xerxes convinced him to cease his grousing, and he ordered several palace slaves to carry the wounded Persian to more private rooms. With Xerxes' bloodied head in my hands, I followed along, helping him onto a cot, where the physician cut away sodden clothes to inspect the extent of the damage.

Though Xerxes had no open gashes that would have certainly meant a slow and agonizing death, the doctor clicked his teeth at an angry contusion along his patient's ribs. The doctor ordered slaves to retrieve his cups and blades, explaining in disinterested Greek the course of action that would be taken to relieve him of his evil humors.

Thankfully, before the man could administer further pain, the door burst open, and another slave led Rosamund into the healing room. Though her head was still tightly bandaged from her own wound, her eyes burned with disgust at the man for his intended practice.

"Bloodletting? For a battle wound?" she cried, incredulous, and rushed toward Xerxes' pained form.

"Who is this woman to raise such questions?" the physician said to me, ruffled in his response.

"A better healer than you," Rosamund answered for herself.

"All Roman doctors have learned of the value of bloodletting for years from the teachings of Galen," he said stiffly.

"Then all Roman doctors are insipid fools. Leave, before I turn your decorated knives upon your own flesh."

The doctor looked to me in protest, yet I only shrugged and gave authority to one whose opinion I could trust absolutely. Storming out of the room, the doctor cursed "that Gepid witch" but let us be.

"Good. You probably won't want to see this, Varus," Rosamund told me.

I grunted. "I've seen far worse on the battlefield. Tell me how to be helpful."

"By getting out of my way," she said, nudging me. "Perenus is resting nearby, and this one will survive if I can set his rib cage to rights. Go and be useful somewhere else."

Though I desired to help Xerxes in any way that I could, Rosamund had already begun arraying her potions and medicines and again bade me to leave. I obeyed only after instructing a palace slave to find me with any concerns. Sliding into the hallway, I ventured back to the main palace floor, my limbs heavy from another day of overexertion. Thoughts of sinking into a featherbed were pushed away by Tiberius' cries, the boy desperate for long-denied sleep and a respite from unfamiliar people. I instructed the servant to take Tiberius to Mariya, issuing strict orders that no one else was to speak of Tiberius' arrival.

With the boy safely headed to my private rooms, I sought out the Empress to report my safe return from the Hippodrome. Night still firmly gripped the Palace's hastily repaired marble floors and wooden doorways, the rows of torches and braziers casting shadows of the excubitores who guarded the Imperial family as well as the duty guardsmen who remained on high alert for any sign of further uprising.

Following a trail of activity to the Great Hall's sweeping oak doors, the other guardsmen did not stop me as I cracked its panel open to peer inside. Rather than Theodora, I discovered the conclusion of a far more sinister conversation between two men, with one pleading to God to be relieved of the burden ahead of him.

"Please, Highness, I beg you to reconsider," Belisarius was saying. "Do not ask this of me."

"I understand your concerns, Belisarius," Justinian replied. "But you know that I cannot let this mob go free! I have already given ample opportunity for surrender, and the thousands remaining in that Hippodrome would still see me dead!"

"Perhaps if I go to Hypatius myself, unarmed..." Belisarius began.

"No!" the Emperor boomed. "Or perhaps you would betray me as well, General? Others have warned me of placing too much trust in you."

"No, Highness, never," Belisarius responded, sounding desperate. "Never."

Justinian grunted in approval. "Very well, then. Prove your loyalty... or don't."

The room drew muffled for a moment, the only sounds a restless shuffling of men's feet and the burning of a dozen iron braziers. Justinian cleared his throat impatiently, and Belisarius beckoned to respond.

"You have my oath, Highness, always," Belisarius said. "God forgive me, I will do what you ask. But what of Hypatius and the senators?"

The question echoed in the chamber and through the creaked doorway. The Emperor paused to consider this question, as though haste could only bring an undesirable solution. As he reached his answer, however, he gave a cruel laugh clipped short in the audience chamber.

"Hang them all," Justinian declared, his solitary voice echoing across the marble columns. "Leave none alive."

Though his wrath was justified by ancient Roman law, I shuddered and clutched at my cross. May God be more forgiving of us all than Justinian was on that day.

Belisarius clicked his boots together in a formal Roman salute and swiftly departed from the chamber. Throwing open the door, he paused only as his eyes fell upon me, his features darkened by the plumed helmet secured to his head.

"I heard Perenus lives thanks to you," Belisarius said curtly.

"Yes, General."

"You are recovering from injury from the evening's previous ordeals," he said, "and are dismissed from further service until the following morning. Go and rest."

"Injury? No, not I," I replied. "A sore leg, perhaps, but—"

"No, Varus," Belisarius said firmly. "You are to stay here with Perenus and the other wounded."

I balked. Would he cast me aside from the duty to clear out the Hippodrome? "Lord, I can fight and serve. All I want to do is help."

It was one of the few times in my life that I saw Belisarius rise to anger. "Then obey my orders!" he yelled. Seeing my stunned silence, his tone softened. "Please, Varus. Let me spare you this."

My chest tightened in a confusing mess of emotion, but I bowed my head to Belisarius' will. He nodded, then left me, roaring for the Thracian officers to form into battle array in the palace courtyard. Their numbers would be bolstered by Marcellus' excubitores and others from Belisarius' growing bucellarii. Uliaris and Baduarius formed their men into a protective ring around the thickly armored general while Marcellus' excubitores followed, and their orderly discipline caused the less-experienced ranks behind them to do the same.

The Herulian foederati were commanded to remain to guard the Emperor, while Sembrouthes and the Aksumites remained quartered for the evening, their respite shared by young Vitalius and the few

Imperial guardsman who had not been killed or deserted by this point in the riot. Many looked to be questioning why we were not asked to follow, to which I could only shrug and obey Belisarius' orders.

Having returned from sitting with Perenus, Samur looked to me with curious interest, his eyes a mask of foreboding of the cruelty to come.

"It will be terrible," Samur said, his eyes fixed on a nearby brazier. "The Greens, they're all going to die."

I nodded and remained silent as the last of Belisarius' men filed into marching columns. His orders were repeated by Mundus, and the grizzled veteran showed none of the reluctance he had privately voiced upon arriving in Constantinople. Marching along Mundus' side, Troglita glanced at the foederati as he moved through the palace doorway, a look of confusion as our men did not follow in their lead. Other familiar faces followed close behind, like the taciturn Thurimuth or the twisted figure of Ascum, who alone seemed to relish the chaos that had befallen Constantinople, winking in our direction as he reached Belisarius' position.

"Do you think Justin would have given such an order?" Samur whispered, awestruck as the final Thracian spearmen exited the Palace.

"No," I answered firmly. "I know he wouldn't."

Those not on duty snuck to the higher landings to watch the procession to the Hippodrome, and I did nothing to stop the macabre gawking. Instead, I left Samur and returned to Theodora's chambers, where I found her excubitor guardsmen alert and aware of the Empress' ongoing audience with members of Justinian's Court. My status as a brother of their warrior class granted me an audience without delay. The ornate doors cracked open to allow me entry to the warmth and light within.

Inside I found the Empress strangely absent her more formal gowns and jewels in favor of a more delicate shift. No longer bound by the conservative headdress expected of many patrician women, Theodora's long black hair draped across her shoulders and down her back, its ends tangled and frayed from another overlong day. Even her face had been cleared of the powders that provided a mirage of vitality and color, revealing sagging eyes and pale skin. For someone who took great pains on her appearance, Theodora never seemed as haunting as she did in those intimate moments, with perhaps only a half dozen men other than the Emperor having seen her in such a state.

Theodora did not balk at my entry, waving for me to enter and join a discussion between herself, Liberius, and the curious presence of Father Petrus. Devoid of any other servant or advisor, Liberius beckoned for me to draw a bench along their small circle, patting me on the arm before continuing.

"Lord Basilius has taken ill, but I speak with his voice," he proclaimed. "We old men need our sleep, after all."

Theodora clicked her tongue. "Nothing serious, I hope?"

"Only God knows," Father Petrus replied, "although Basilius has rarely been himself these past months. He complains of frequent pains, but one can never know the cause of these things."

Theodora offered sympathetic words to his plight, praying for many years of health and service to the Empire. She then explained Justinian's desire for the riots to come to an end, with the Emperor's thoughts already turned to Constantinople's future. With so much of the city burned or destroyed, massive building projects would be required to restore sanitation, safety, and recreation to the people, giving the Imperial family a rare opportunity to reshape the Empire's capital to their designs.

As details of cavernous churches, new roads, and improved infrastructure swam through my head, so, too, did images of Symeon's wretched body, his face fixed with the terror of the death that had stolen his final moments. Such thoughts would have held me transfixed for the remainder of the night had the Empress not turned to me with words of sudden congratulations.

"A servant informed me of your success, Lord Varus," Theodora said. "As always, I thank God for your safety. But what of the child?"

"Child?" I replied, only to kick myself inwardly.

Theodora chuckled. "The child you were seen carrying into the Palace. I do hope that you haven't been unfaithful to your wife, who is a dear friend of mine!"

"Of course not. I mean, of course I have been faithful, Highness," I stammered. "The boy…"

I considered offering the truth. Theodora had never given me pause to doubt her loyalty, and as Empress, she had gone to considerable pains to accommodate my failures—deliberate or accidental. With Justinian's exchange with Belisarius added to Xerxes' private suspicions of Hermogenes' sudden death, I balked in the face of the woman who held my oath, and therefore my life and soul, in her delicate grasp.

"The boy is a foundling," I explained. "Wandering in the Hippodrome, likely with no parents. It was a distraction, but I could not bring myself to leave the boy to destitution."

Theodora smiled. "An admirable and holy response. Will Mariya mind the added burden?"

"Mariya loves children, and we have more than enough gold and servants to accommodate the lad." I presumed this was so, at least. As I saw the pained look on the Empress' face, I wished I could take back my words.

"Children are a blessing," Theodora said weakly. "Perhaps your Zenobia will join the Court ladies when she is a few years older? I would like that very much."

"Of course, Highness," I answered. "If I may be excused for the evening, Highness, I must go explain to my wife our new situation."

Theodora lifted her eyebrows. "So soon? But you've just arrived. Liberius and I were going to discuss possible reforms to help the people once the riots have ended."

I bowed my head in deference. "My humblest apologies, but I also am quite overtaxed—the retreat from the Hippodrome was… something that I never wish to experience again. Perhaps we may speak tomorrow?"

Theodora nodded stiffly. "Of course, Lord Varus. But stay vigilant. No matter how this evening ends, the world will never be as it was."

How correct Theodora was. For as the disastrous Nika Riots fell to an ignominious conclusion, Justinian and Theodora were free to begin a new era. A new Empire. And a new war.

THE SHADOWS OF
WHAT REMAIN

They say that the Nika Riots ended with a massacre. Such a small a term can hardly contain the carnage it took to restore order in Constantinople.

The true number of dead will never be known, cannot be known. Many months later, over a skin of wine, Baduarius and Ascum described the chaos of that place, where the remaining strength of the Greens fought with nails and fire as much as any soldier's weapon against the steady progress of Belisarius' lines. Enraged by the thick walls of floating corpses that ringed the once-fabled Hippodrome's expanse, Belisarius' men fought with an uncharacteristic hatred, wishing to put an end to the great sin of civil war.

Writing a formal history of the uprising, Procopius reported thirty thousand slain at the last stand of the Hippodrome. Nearly all were Hypatius' men that, though they resisted fiercely, lacked the discipline of the shield wall or the thick armor provided by the Emperor's smiths. With thousands of reinforcements from Mundus and Baduarius, Hypatius' men had little hope for more than a clean death. Some were afforded that privilege; many were not.

As dawn broke over the Hippodrome and exposed the slick horror within, Hypatius was found alone hiding within a pile of rubble.

Other senators had already been rounded up for execution, with each man facing the hangman's noose regardless of how helplessly they bleated for mercy or pissed down their once-expensive robes. Rich or poor, they danced all the same, and Belisarius looked dutifully on as each death was confirmed. Hypatius was saved for last, slobber coating his chin as he cried for Justinian's forgiveness and shaking as a common flaxen noose was secured around his portly neck. Though only rumors followed Hypatius' death notes, it is said that Uliaris yanked on his feet as he began to dance on the gallows, thus breaking the man's neck and putting a swift, merciful stop to what would have been agonizing minutes of strangulation.

To ferry the thousands of corpses that were piled up on the Hippodrome's sands beyond Constantinople's walls for their intended cremation, Justinian ordered those Greens who had been arrested during Belisarius and Mundus' initial campaign to load and haul wagons in and out of the city. The rows of older corpses had putrefied under days of cool sunlight, and flies mauled at the prisoners, many of whom retched and fainted.

The Emperor pardoned those who deposited a set quota of bodies to the outer burn pits, leaving guards to bully those who balked at such backbreaking labor. Though the Hippodrome was cleared of its filth within a week, the scent of deterioration clung to the very essence of the building for months to come. And according to those who still hold to the old pagan beliefs, the spirits of the slain are still trapped within the Hippodrome's expanse, their cries audible on dark winter nights.

Though the number of the lowborn dead remains uncertain, Justinian's tax collectors managed to take an accurate account of vacant properties in and around Constantinople even before the final bodies were ferried from the Hippodrome. Those with no adult relatives had their estates liquidated into the Imperial coffers, while those who hoped to inherit from deceased relatives of questionable loyalty to the Emperor were assigned a weighty tax to ensure against future indiscretions. Some vacant properties were pooled together for future building projects, and many were resold to a number of well-to-do farmers and merchants from the surrounding countryside.

Most profitable were the extensive estates and properties of the seditious senators, whose families were given only a single empty grain sack to fill with possessions before being turned to the streets. Led by Nepotian, the surviving senators who were not directly tied to Hypatius' rebellion offered weighty gifts to the Emperor, the total of which covered the year's payment of gold to secure our Eternal Peace with Shahanshah Khosrow and the Persian Empire.

Ironically, the ensuing wave of gold and silver from these sales allowed Justinian to alleviate the crush of taxes upon the Empire's populace, although the Emperor still hoarded grain, salted mutton, and a number of other perishable foodstuffs that armed detachments of Thracians guarded as they were delivered into the city. Even then, however, the reduction of Constantinople's population temporarily provided an ample supply of food for all, although poorer families, beggars, and outcasts still scraped by on what could be donated or stolen from the more fortunate.

A victorious Justinian commanded peace and order back into the city, including the recruitment of thousands of new city guards to replace entire cohorts that died or deserted during the riots. These recruits were no better trained than their predecessors, and in some ways a great deal worse, yet for a brief time, their loyalty was unquestioned, and corruption minimal. With calm ruling in Constantinople's streets, Justinian turned his attention to a bevy of ideas for the city's reconstruction, allowing his old cadre of ministers under Paulus and Tribonian to creep back to their former positions of authority.

The frenetic turnings of the Court's schemes spared the foederati, who were granted an extended reprieve for their constant duty in guarding the Palace during the riots. Fulcaris led many of my men to the few taverns not ransacked during Hypatius' occupation, and while I distributed ample silver to satiate the men's enjoyment, I spent my repose in the company of my family, embracing the delicious laxity that comes from multiple days of no prior plans and few obligations.

Though shocked at Tiberius' parentage, Mariya showered attention on the curious, frightened boy who found himself in the company of strangers. Sure enough, after a bath and fresh clothes, Tiberius toddled happily to play. Although Joannina and Zenobia were still a half year away from enjoying Tiberius' company, the Palace held other small children eager for a new playmate.

Once the children were passed into the care of a servant, however, Mariya's comforting demeanor gave way to exasperation.

"You can't just take in children without speaking with me, Varus!" Mariya cried. "What am I going to do with this poor boy?"

Howling enemies in the shield wall did not frighten me half as much as an angry Mariya. I had neither defense nor weapons, searching in vain for any words that would assuage her concerns and gain her favor. "I had no choice, Mariya. Hypatius made me take the boy in return for freeing Perenus."

At this, Mariya paled and raised a finger to her lips. "Never say that name in this house ever again. Do you understand the danger you've created for all of us?"

Indeed, I did now. I wondered that I could have so naively assumed this would be simple to manage. "We won't use his formal name, so nobody in Justinian's Court will recognize him," I said. "If they care, that is."

Mariya considered. "And you told Theodora he was a mere foundling?"

I nodded. "An orphan of no note. The only proof otherwise is the ring Hyp— Tiberius' father gave to me."

I produced Anastasius' ring from my belt for Mariya to examine. "Chunky gold, in the Greek style," she said, pursing her lips. "Arabs would have more elegant lines." She pushed it back into my hands. "You cannot keep this ring in the house."

"It will stay with me at all times," I affirmed. "But if we don't care for Tiberius, he'll be dead within months. If an assassin doesn't take him, then life on the streets would—"

"I know!" Mariya snapped. "Jamila can prepare a place for him with Joannina and Zenobia."

Squeezing her hand, I smiled. "Thank you, Mariya. You've told me that you love caring for poorer children, and I just assumed that Tiberius wouldn't be a burden."

Mariya sighed, her shoulders slumping. "I'm happy to help Tiberius. I am. Potentially others, too. I have thought about doing more—for the orphans, and those poor wounded veterans skulking the city's gutters." She paused, her frustration turning into a smile as she considered the thought, only to harden her expression. "But that doesn't mean that I don't want a say in our household, Varus. Especially when it will be *me* caring for the boy when you're off in some godforsaken war." She sighed. "You are a kind man, and I love you, but you have no idea what is required of me to manage the daily affairs of our household."

I raised my hands in surrender, my defenses routed. "I apologize, Mariya. Truly. I will not make this mistake again."

"As for young Tiberius... he must not know about his father until he comes of age," Mariya went on. "There are many in Court who would not hesitate to throttle a child in his bed—or poison those who watch him."

I agreed with her every word. After that conversation, Mariya never once spoke of Tiberius' father, nor used his true name of Constantine. But neither did she show any resentment to the boy. She even managed to break through his shyness with all manner of games and jibes. From then on, Tiberius was our adopted son in all but formality.

In the immediate aftermath of Belisarius' reconquest of the Hippodrome, I was afforded a measure of leisure. Even Theodora's demands for my time were limited. I visited the Empress for daily reports and occasionally joined a somber Belisarius in his own councils, yet otherwise my only duty was to ensure the recuperation of those wounded in the riots. Many injuries were relatively minor—a broken wrist or nastier sprains of limbs—but a few required more frequent attention by the Emperor's doctors and healers.

One such charge was Perenus, who relished his time in the Palace. Seemingly healed after a week of bedrest and rich food, he still moaned and complained of mysterious soreness across his body. As Rosamund eyed each professed ache with careful examination, he secretly winked to me as he insisted on remaining in the Palace for a few more days of recuperation. Knowing what he had experienced in the Hippodrome, I did not deny him the luxury of having nothing to do, which had been earned many times over.

In our meeting, Perenus admitted that his memory of the crash with Magnetius was a mess of broken images and a general sensation of pain and uncertainty. As the mob took control of the stadium, several Greens pulled Perenus' body from the wreckage. He had been miraculously spared crippling injury as he was thrown clear.

Magnetius was not so lucky, however. Street urchins and other unsavory characters of Constantinople's underbelly collected bits of teeth, bone, and an occasional golden ornament that had adorned the champion of the Blues, the price of which fetched a hefty sum from souvenir collectors and secret pagans who put stock in the magical properties of dismembered body parts. Perenus showed little emotion as he detailed Magnetius' end, although he grew remorseful as he informed me of the death of Patroklus, who was slain by the mob as he tried to pry Perenus' body away from the Green leaders. Perenus' lip quivered. He drank a small toast of wine in memory of the surly trainer of charioteers.

After an appropriate interlude, I raised a related topic that had itched at my curiosity since his rescue. The hanged sentries outside the stadium had been hastily removed after its recapture, leaving me no opportunity to inspect the bloodied figure that stood apart from the rest. A body that had been sliced and tortured while still alive, its suffering unique against a sea of decaying men and women who were summarily hanged for crimes against Hypatius' revolution, yet without any real sense of malice or vengeance.

"Do you remember Symeon, the Thracian spearman at my trial?"

"Hardly," Perenus replied, wincing as he stretched bruised muscles. "I do know that Hermogenes threw him out of the army. Why?"

"I saw his body in the Hippodrome," I explained. "If he'd have still been in the army..."

"Then he'd be jeopardizing his entire banda," Perenus said. "The man was a coward and a weakling. It isn't your fault that the man got caught up in the riots. Symeon's death is upsetting, but it happens."

"I assume you're right," I replied. "By the way, did you know that Hermogenes was found hanged in his room?"

Perenus jerked in surprise. "What?"

"He's dead," I said. "It was declared a suicide. Hermogenes had been shamed by Theodora earlier that evening."

"I don't believe it." Perenus gaped. "Hermogenes was too stubborn to kill himself. He'd consider it a weakness."

I shrugged, harboring suspicions yet beholden to Theodora to keep silent. "That's all I know, but the matter appears closed."

With Perenus hinting at a desire for sleep, I departed his company, venturing back to hallways bustling with activity. My desires were not to seek out another meeting of the Emperor's ministers, nor did I yearn to meet with Belisarius, who had taken to melancholy and aloofness in the days after the Hippodrome's liberation. Instead I stepped into the quarters reserved for Xerxes, still convalescent from the dozen wounds taken in our escape from the Greens.

I had regularly checked in on Xerxes during his recovery, only to find Rosamund insisting that he required the regular and dreamless sleep of her elixirs and was not to be disturbed. It was not until this day, a full week after the end of the riots, that I was granted an audience with the weak, conscious Zhayedan prince.

Thinner but otherwise clean and healthy, Xerxes sat propped on a cot. His head cocked toward the door as I entered, a light bob acknowledging my presence that revealed bruises just now yellowing in their slow healing. I grabbed a dented wooden stool along the far wall and dragged it noisily across the carpeted floor, sitting but a few paces from his alert and unmoving form.

"That Gepid witch," Xerxes croaked. "She knows what she's doing."

"Oh?" I asked.

"She's a skilled healer," he explained. "Better than many of my father's, and as careful as many of the magi. If you wanted to kill me, you could have just left me with the quacks that ply their trade to the city's noble families."

Xerxes flashed a smirk, but lacked the passionate scorn he often reserved for much of Roman culture. Though his mouth curled and nose wrinkled, his eyes remained sad and drooping, as though a measure of fight had been stripped from his soul.

"I do not wish you dead," I answered. "If I did, I could have easily allowed Hermogenes to quietly poison you and take Azarethes' considerable offer of gold."

Xerxes snorted. "True," he said in the clipped Greek of the royal Persian schoolroom. "Neither loved by friends nor enemies, yet unable to be killed by either. My life is a cruel joke."

"Xerxes," I said, interrupting his wallowing. "I need to know— why did you sacrifice yourself that evening when we escaped the Hippodrome? You owed no loyalty to any of the rest of us."

"Ah," he said. "You initially thought I'd leave Perenus to the wolves or turn on you and the boy? Fitting for the butcher of Armenian women and children?"

"Truthfully, yes. And I still don't understand it."

Xerxes' gaze fixed on my own, his features hard and momentarily frozen with cold fury. Then he turned, grimacing, and reached for the simple clay cup full of a foul-smelling liquid of Rosamund's design. As he sat in silence, I considered rising to depart, but then he sighed and answered at last.

"I was the youngest Persian general since Cyrus. Did you know?" he asked. "My father was so proud when he handed me his mantle and scepter, even as he pretended that I belonged to another."

He paused to sip once more, sputtering at a taste that must have matched the pungent odor, but taking a full draught that seemed to relax his stiffened muscles and joints.

"I know nothing but how to fight as an Immortal," he went on. "The earliest memory in the fogged corners of my mind is an image of Hakhamanish, berating me for crying for my mother when I should have been hardening my body for the great trials ahead."

"Hakhamanish?" I said quietly.

"The darkness encroaches on Persia's borders, the magus would say," Xerxes said. "We had a reprieve when Attila's hordes faltered in their destruction, but the Dark God would choose another soon enough as a harbinger of destruction. That is what the Zhayedan train ceaselessly for—to defend the Ahura Mazda, and to keep the truth of his flames burning. When my father gave me an army to retake territory that had not been in Persian hands since the time of Alexander, I believed that we'd swipe away the creeping dark that's nested under the noses of the Greeks."

I burned to respond to the charge, yet Xerxes raised himself into a more upright position, his eyes turning to a low iron brazier wrought with flowers native to Thrace. His fist clenched and released as he gathered the strength to speak again, the veins of his forearms pulsing underneath purpled flesh.

"I was wrong," he said. "My father cared nothing for glory or truth. What he wanted was nothing short of total subjugation and a conquest equal to the devastation wrought by the hordes who left your own western cousins lost in the abyss. He called in the Hephthalites and paid them to torch villages and rape women as our army tore into Roman Armenia and Mesopotamia."

"To what end?"

"Your end," Xerxes explained. "Kavadh was a wise ruler, but he had grown tired of the rules and restrictions from the priests and the noble families. Rome was his enemy, and his enemy had never been weaker. The Hephthalites are nothing if not conquerors, slaughtering young babes the same way you or I would skewer an apple or butcher a chicken. And it nearly worked—may the fires cleanse my soul—

the Hephthalites nearly swept the weakened clutches of Rome from Kavadh's desires."

"But they didn't." I frowned. "The Hephthalites failed, despite their devastation."

"Because I ordered them away!" Xerxes cried. "Khingila resisted at first, but I threatened to kill the man myself for slaughtering thousands of innocent villagers who did nothing wrong but to exist on this earth."

My mouth dropped as I fixed on his watering eyes. He laughed at my expression, even as a tear ran onto his thin beard.

"Yes, the man who all of you call a child killer sent away the brutes responsible," he mocked. "And so I gathered my Persians to attack the Romans at Thannuris, trusting in their honor as men, not monsters. My father fumed at the Zhayedan killed in the battle and ordered me wrought into chains for my defiance."

At this, Xerxes rose further, his face finally turned back to mine. He leaned close to me, thick tears streaming from his eyes, and snarled with a hatred that belied his aloofness.

"My father ordered me killed for daring to spare Romans all the horrors the Hephthalites were prepared to unleash upon the world." Xerxes wept angrily. "For following an oath of my conscience, rather than a sworn command of my lord and master. Hakhamanish prevented the executioner from taking my head, yet I spent the remainder of that war behind bars, sitting in filth and wondering whether I had made the wrong decision. I must have, for what kind of son could be so terrible that their father would desire their death?"

Xerxes dropped his head as he cried aloud, his chest rising and falling with angry rasps against his lingering infirmity. For a moment, I was transported back to the grime-scaled pits of Barbalissus, sharing a cell with this Persian warrior who had been blamed for so much chaos and death in Rome's armies and territory. I placed a hand on Xerxes' matted scalp, patting the sweat-strewn hair as he calmed his anger.

"Why didn't you explain your actions to someone? To me?"

"Would you have listened? I am already condemned in Roman eyes—only tolerated to live to supposedly keep the Eternal Peace alive. My half brother, Khosrow, would happily see me dead, and Azarethes will ensure no Persian army will ever allow me to return safely or with honor."

"I was wrong for not giving you the opportunity to explain," I said firmly. "And when you're healed, Belisarius will have need of your services in the wars to come. The men will see your honor as I do now."

Xerxes nodded, shuddering with a final sob. "The wars to come," he said bitterly. "The wars that will never end, until we're all consumed by grief and loss. Why do we fight for tyrants who hunger for the blood of others?"

"We don't," I answered. "I fight to protect my friends, in hopes that one day we will bring back the peace and plenty that our world once had. Even if I'm never thanked for the struggle, the result will be reward enough."

We sat in silence for a time. Xerxes accepted my assistance as I called for freshly baked bread and seasonal winter fruit. As we shared that light fare, Xerxes accepted my offer, pledging himself to the service of the Roman army. He offered a lone smile as I left, thanking me, and I allowed Rosamund to observe her ward and brew more of the pain-relieving elixir that Xerxes guzzled despite its offensive taste.

Though I departed Xerxes' company in good spirits, less fortunate tidings had already converged to break my idyll. Rather than one of Justinian's sycophants, however, these ill omens arose from Liberius, who cornered me as I passed through the Palace's main level.

"Theodora informed me last night," Liberius muttered, careful to keep his voice muffled. "The army is leaving for Africa at the onset of spring, per Justinian's command."

Flinching in shock, I frowned as I met Liberius' serious gaze. "You can't be serious," I said softly. "The capital is in ruins, and it will take months, maybe even years, before commerce returns to normal. A war now would be ruinously expensive."

"You're beginning to sound like Paulus." Liberius chuckled. "Avarice is perhaps the worst of all sins, because it's the only one that we often raise to be a virtue."

"Gold isn't half of the problem," I said. "Invading the Vandals... even before the riots, the risk was enormous. Justinian wants us to invade a country whose people live for nothing but war with an army exhausted by constant battle."

"Indeed," Liberius said. "And in his benevolence, Justinian will provide ten thousand men for the expedition."

"Ten thousand!" I cursed. "Basiliscus had a hundred thousand Roman soldiers when he invaded Africa... and the Vandals still slaughtered them to a man. And that was a hundred years ago. The Vandals have only grown in strength, not weakened."

"I am pleased that you remember at least some of your lessons with me, Varus," Liberius said, "and I do understand the absurdity of the request. I do not think the Emperor expects a total victory against Gelimer—just threaten them into paying tribute, or maybe surrendering the province of Tripolitania as compensation for the Vandals' attacks in Egypt in the previous year."

"It's still madness," I said, wringing my hands. "The Vandals are crazy—they don't think on terms of surrender or diplomacy."

Liberius bowed his head. "You are not required to attend the expedition if you would prefer otherwise. However, I intend to join the army, of which Justinian has given command to Belisarius."

"Of course I will go!" I shot back, my pride wounded. "And Belisarius as commander? It seems that Basilius got his wish after all."

Liberius nodded. "With Hermogenes no longer present to register complaints against his character or capabilities, the Emperor has seen fit to return Belisarius to his former position. A proper reward for loyalty in the riots."

Liberius paused, his face impassive, perhaps parsing how my elation at Belisarius' return to favor mingled with my horror at the prospect of invading a faraway kingdom thirsty for Roman blood. At last, he seemed satisfied, for he added, "Belisarius will need you in Africa, Varus. And so will I, barring one impediment."

"Of course, Lord. Anything."

"Your misgivings with the Empress," Liberius began. "She has noticed. I do not know what has transpired between the two of you, but I urge you to bury it at once. We all share a common dream, and there are too many enemies to begin squabbling amongst ourselves."

Armed with Liberius' information and warning, I took greater care of my actions in the following weeks, taking pains to attend regular private audiences with the Empress and war councils with Belisarius. Though her words showed little concern per Liberius' caution, Theodora did appear pleased with my newfound vigor and conferred to me with otherwise secret details of the Emperor's plans for Constantinople and beyond. Likewise, Belisarius' aloofness eased as the Hippodrome slid further into history, his features eased as he joined me for regular morning prayer with Father Petrus.

Belisarius and I worked feverishly into each evening, preparing drafts of supplies and recalling soldiers from far-flung provinces on the Empire's borders. Lone notes of optimism included the continued health and safety of our cavalry, which had been furiously guarded against Hypatius' raids throughout the uprising. Further, the dozens of ships that were previously commissioned for our expedition to Africa remained intact, with Paulus charged to continue the supply of food and goods that would be needed for a Roman army marching in distant enemy territory.

Mariya grew disconcerted after learning of our all-too-soon departure, worrying at tales of Vandal conquests and the inept performance of Rome's past armies against the Vandal hordes. As if drawing lessons from Rosamund, Mariya begged once more that I resign my post and retire in peace, weeping as her pleas were met with naught but resistance. Her anger lasted for a worrying amount of time, yet at the end of the first month from the riots, Mariya relented, explaining her own desires.

"I'm not telling you this to weight your oath with guilt," Mariya began. "Just to make it clear that I need you to survive this war."

"Mariya…" I said, my chest pounding as I worried at the dozen horrible scenarios that could be the cause of her baleful preamble.

"I'm not entirely sure yet," Mariya replied calmly, "but I believe that I am pregnant. And as much as I want to support you on your journey, I cannot wait helplessly in some far-flung city for news of the latest battle. I need something… more."

My ears grew deaf for a moment at her pronouncement, the confusing feelings of joy and terror bringing bile to the base of my throat. Fighting back a rising urge to vomit, I looked sickly on at Mariya, who giggled at my expression as a single tear ran down her cheeks and traced the thin lines of her jaw.

"What do you need?" I asked. "Will you go to your brother in Arabia?"

"No," Mariya replied bitterly. "If I go back to the Ghassanids, I'll be forced back into a role of quiet subservience, sheltered away from the world while my brother humps servant girls in the palace larder. I was thinking of going to your estate in Pella, and taking the children with me."

Dumbstruck and numb, I nodded. "You think you're pregnant?"

Mariya's chuckle broke into a throaty laugh. "The brave and loyal excubitor, rendered tongue-tied by the inner workings of a woman?"

Blushing, I dropped my gaze to the floor. Mariya moved a hand along my face, her fingers raising my eyes to her own as her fingertips grazed my beard and rested at the corner of my lips. Her laughter ceased as she smiled at me, planting an affectionate kiss before continuing.

"But why Pella?"

"Well, it's yours, for starters." She smiled. "I need to get out of this city and do something with the wealth and ability I've been given in this life. I was thinking of bringing a number of wounded veterans to help till the farm or fletch arrows, or do something to help Theodora's plans for the Empire."

I nodded. "We provide silver for those too injured to march or fight, but it doesn't last long."

"And this would help provide a roof over their heads and food in their bellies," Mariya replied happily. "Not to mention, the fresh air and freedom of the Macedonian countryside will be good for the children. I was thinking of spending some gold to bring some of the children orphaned in the riots with us, to be given an education and time to play without starving in fear in Constantinople's streets."

"A noble goal," I concluded. "I would, of course, rather not be parted from you... but I understand your wishes."

Mariya kissed me again. "All the more reason for you to win quickly and come home to me!" she teased. "Antonina even asked if Joannina could join Zenobia and Tiberius, so Belisarius may be of a similar mind."

My brow furrowed as I considered Antonina's actions. "Antonina means to join the expedition?"

"She claims that she does not want to be far from her husband, and that a war with the Vandals is no place for a daughter of the magister militium," Mariya explained. "However, it seems that Sergius will also be accompanying the army..."

I shook my head. "Those accusations are dangerous, Mariya. And illogical besides. Why would Antonina commit such a crime?"

"The world is not as simple as you make it out to be," Mariya replied. "Logic is nothing next to passion. Why did I defy my father and brother to chase you? Is my decision any less illogical?"

I felt routed but was unwilling to surrender. "Betrothal to Solomon is not the same as marriage to Belisarius. If Belisarius mistreated Antonina, then I might understand, but from what I can tell, he worships her."

"Worship is boring," Mariya countered. I sputtered a reply, yet Mariya smiled. "You are a loyal and kind man, Varus. But I chose you because you offered me friendship and freedom. Antonina is powerful, and she certainly delights in the attention, but Belisarius does not offer Antonina what she desires."

Privately, I felt Mariya had granted Antonina too much credit. "And what is that?"

"To feel valued and included," Mariya answered. "Belisarius may worship Antonina, but he would never seek her advice, nor include her in his troubles."

"You make him seem oafish and cruel."

Again, Mariya placed a hand upon my arm as a gesture of reassurance. "That was not my intent. But what you, or I, or the world entire believes doesn't matter in this situation—only how Antonina feels. And she feels slighted."

It was all too much. Beyond my interests or talents, and lacking in evidence. "But you haven't actually seen Antonina and Sergius together in that way?"

"No," Mariya admitted. "But it doesn't matter."

"Of course it matters! Belisarius would be within his rights to kill her if he knew," I said incredulously. "And I doubt even Theodora would be able to intervene to stop him."

Mariya nodded. "Likely so, and I do hope I am wrong. As for Theodora, I've explained my wishes to the Empress, who begged me to stay in Constantinople for another year."

"But you refused?"

"Theodora was graceful about it," Mariya said. "Poor woman, she must be so lonely, surrounded by enemies and with few friends to trust."

My nose flared as I reasoned with Mariya's words. "Theodora can trust me," I said. "I'm her excubitor, after all."

Mariya smiled sweetly again, lowering her forehead to my own. "Yes, but you're off again to the edge of the world, and we're left behind to deal with the problems that remain. I wish I had the patience to help Theodora, but I just cannot remain in this city without a reprieve, not after what I've seen… and not with another child coming."

Though initially private, Mariya's intended enterprise spread throughout the city, filling taverns and brothels with tales of how the vast wealth of the late Emperor Justin was being opened to the poor and crippled who had survived the horrors of the Nika Riots. Petitioners had even begun to line the Palace's outbuildings, begging an audience with the Ghassanid princess to beg a place in the new venture in Pella.

Mariya was soon joined by the pregnant Auria in her planning, the Mauri woman reluctant to travel with her husband to Africa, despite her father's people being native to the region. Together, the two women enlisted the assistance of clerks and merchants to help prepare for their arrival at Justin's former estate in Pella, ordering the construction of additional sleeping quarters and new buildings for the benefit of children and villagers alike. Theodora offered her blessings on the venture and even ordered Narses to add personal donations to the care of widows and orphans that would venture from Constantinople to the Macedonian province. As she sat in solace during the Palace's chill evenings, it was plain that the Empress' loneliness had begun to crack through her guise.

To house Belisarius' reassembling armies, one of Justinian's first acts of reconstruction included a vast Imperial Barracks, its facilities far larger than even the previous complex. Offering double the standard wages of a laborer, the outline of the barracks rose quickly, and bunkrooms were soon declared fit for habitation while the larger halls and armories continued their construction. Both Mundus' men and my own foederati were relocated there, joined soon thereafter by Baduarius' Cappadocians.

Over the next two months, contingents of Roman spearmen and cavalry converged on Constantinople. Bessas was the first of Belisarius' senior commanders to return, his cataphracts ordered to make camp on the Asian side of the Bosphorus to ease their eventual boarding into the bellies of massive transport ships capable of ferrying such weight across the Mediterranean Sea. Germanus followed soon thereafter, trailed by thousands of raw Thracian and Moesian spearmen, who filled Germanus' losses from Callinicum. Last to return was John, who led the reformed Hunnic foederati to the outer forts of Constantinople before venturing back to the capital for an audience with the Emperor and Belisarius. He beamed as he was rejoined with his oldest childhood friend, the two embracing as their fortunes reunited them as the spearpoint of the Emperor's will.

"It's good to see you back in charge," John said. "This madness I've heard about the city riots…"

"The tales are all true, and worse," Belisarius said balefully. "But let's turn toward brighter thoughts and how we are going to fend off these Vandals!"

"I wouldn't call that a brighter thought," John muttered. "But where Justinian beckons, we have no choice but to obey."

As the last gales of winter licked Constantinople's coastline, Justinian summoned a formal council of war to discuss the impending expedition to Africa. With many of the senior officers separated since the early weeks after Callinicum, the Emperor allowed a brief, informal reunion amongst the men, their general excitement mixed with an undertone of apprehension, not just of the logistical difficulties facing the officers, but also a lingering concern that the army's new recruits would be unreliable in the shield wall, let alone against a charge of screaming Vandals.

As the proceedings came to order, the Emperor's Great Hall was filled to the brim with observers and onlookers. The Palace's marble floors had been polished and cleaned to a burnished shine, removing layers of soot and grime that had been ignored since the Herulians took charge in the Palace's defense. Equally dressed for the purpose, Justinian raised an arm to the massed audience, his ministers standing close behind and his military officers arrayed below the dais at his feet. Though few expressed love for the Emperor, the attending audience roared in approval of this display of strength, forcing the excubitores to use their spear butts to call for silence.

"In just a few weeks' time, Roman men will go to Africa to seek vengeance against the crimes of the usurper Gelimer," Justinian began formally. "They will be led by Belisarius, the victor of Dara and pacifier of the Nika Riots."

Though I would not have predicted that those in attendance would applaud Belisarius' leadership in the final assault on the Hippodrome, many began chanting his name with the same alacrity as would be found at the conclusion of a victorious battle. Justinian's features narrowed for a moment as he processed the crowd's noise before continuing.

"Even though Belisarius will retain full command over the military strategy of this expedition, I name Lord Liberius as my legate, to advise the Roman military command and seek a just and fitting end to this war when the time reveals itself," Justinian bellowed.

While many again readopted chants of Belisarius, Liberius walked to Justinian's dais and bowed to the Emperor, accepting the mantle of authority as the representative and embodiment of the Roman government overseas. Despite the solemn atmosphere amongst the military commanders, I applauded noisily. Liberius winked in happy response.

With the public portion of the meeting concluded, the excubitores drove away spectators, leaving the room emptier and a fair bit cooler from the reduction of body heat. A vast wooden table was hauled toward the center of the room as maps of the Vandal Kingdom were unfurled for all to see, detailing cities and encampments that had once been home to some of the wealthiest regions of the Western Roman Empire. At the map's center was Carthage, the booming port city that had once been home to Hannibal and had later been rebuilt by Julius Caesar himself.

Joined by Theodora, Justinian dropped from the dais and moved to the head of the table, his dark eyes glancing hungrily at the legacy of his forebears. Marcellus nodded as the last members of the public were removed to the city streets, allowing the Emperor's men to speak more candidly. Basilius coughed and wheezed as the meeting began, leaning on Father Petrus as the pair sought water and honeyed wine for his gurgling lungs.

It was John who spoke first. "Highness, we thank you for returning Belisarius to us," he began, "but it is unclear how many men will be sent to Africa, or what you would have your soldiers accomplish in your name."

Justinian closed his eyes for a moment, rubbing at the thin layer of skin beneath them. "Belisarius will have the Thracians under Germanus," Justinian said, beckoning to his cousin, "and the Cappadocians under yourself and Baduarius," he said to John.

Ascum scoffed. "But Emperor Justinian, that's only nine thousand men at best! No force has ever tried to assault Africa with anything less than four times that number."

"I understand," Justinian replied irritably, "and I've dispatched another four bandas from Corinth. That will give you another two hundred Roman spearmen and eight hundred Gothic mercenaries."

Ascum groaned, his discontent echoed by others who decried the use of Gothic mercenaries in a foreign war. Baduarius raised his meaty hands in mock offense, arguing that many a Goth had served in the armies of Justin and Anastasius before him, yet Justinian had no patience for unhappiness or banter, demanding order as he explained our mission.

"The Ostrogoth mercenaries are led by a man named Indulf, who is oathsworn to Amalasuntha," Justinian explained. "As many of you know, Amalasuntha is a sworn friend of Rome and has promised to keep the heretics that plague the Vandals or the Visigoths out of Italy."

"Promises are wind," Germanus replied to Justinian with perhaps an excessive note of familiarity, "and who knows how long that Gothic queen will remain alive. How can we trust hundreds of Ostrogoth mercenaries if she dies?"

Justinian narrowed his eyes, his expression passionless despite the direct challenge. "Amalasuntha is my friend," he declared. "If a course of events were to make that change, the perpetrators would be dealt with severely. Including the Ostrogothic nobility."

"Highness," Belisarius interjected diplomatically, "perhaps if you could unveil your desires, as Tribune John has requested, we may better serve you against the Vandals. God willing, there will be no conflict with the Goths, yet those events can surely wait given the immense challenge already facing us."

The Emperor offered a thin smile, taking Belisarius' opportunity to move away from the unpopular subject of Goths in the Roman army. Tracing the outlines of the African coastline, the Emperor's ravenous gaze fed upon the Roman remnants of Mauretania, Numidia, Libya, and Carthage proper, but forced himself to settle for a more realistic goal.

"I do not expect you to conquer the Vandals outright," Justinian explained. "Make them swear fealty as vassals of Constantinople and pay homage for their attacks on our cities in Cyrenaica."

"The Vandals will never agree to that," Baduarius said next to me, his voice low to avoid confrontation.

"And as a final demand," Justinian said, asserting each word with deliberate force, "Gelimer, his family, and all the Vandal nobility must abandon their heretic Arian faith and embrace the teachings of the Pope and the Patriarch. This is nonnegotiable."

It was that statement that ended any pretense of Justinian's moderation in the Vandal War. The already complex goals of seeking tribute from a people as warlike as the Vandals was laughable but not impossible, yet to forcibly convert the Vandal tribe to a religion that they had scoffed at and plundered for a century was nigh impossible. Not two years prior did Gelimer murder hundreds of Justinian's priests, professing allegiance to that detestable Arianism that claimed that the physical form of Jesus was less than divine. As with Hermogenes, many within the senior officers grumbled, but none spoke against the Emperor who had coolly ordered the deaths of tens of thousands of his own citizens to preserve order in the capital.

"Seeing as you all concur," Justinian continued, "I would ask those of you with information on Vandal strength and customs to speak now, to better plan the expedition's path."

Many sought to speak, but that right was given by a figure standing silently behind the Emperor and Empress. Narses rose at the table, followed closely behind by Procopius, and unfurled a dozen smaller scrolls that had been etched with Latin and Greek. The eunuch was clad in his usual silks, his waist protruding above a thin leather belt whose golden clasp strained from its burden. Nothing of Narses' movements betrayed any sign of softness, his features highlighted by the same threat of violence that had characterized his actions just prior to entering the Hippodrome.

"The Vandals are unlike any of the barbarian tribes who swept across the Western Empire," Narses began. "Where the Goths, the Franks, or the Saxons seek land and wealth for their descendants, the Vandals seek only battle. Their leaders are followed only because of their strength and courage on the battlefield, not out of blind loyalty to any bloodline or heritage."

"So they want us to attack them?" John asked.

"Precisely," Narses responded. "Not only do they want you to attack, they yearn for it. Defeating a Roman army in the field will give legitimacy to Gelimer's rule not just over the Vandals, but over his less-willing subjects in the Mauri."

"The Mauri only follow the Vandal kings out of fear of their wrath," Troglita added, his status as a son-in-law to a Mauri king adding credence to his words. "Given the chance, they will abandon Gelimer and ally with Rome."

Murmurs of skepticism rose from the room as Justinian, Theodora, and Belisarius looked silently on at the advice of their followers. Baduarius roared his own challenge, insisting that the Roman army head straight for Carthage and take the city by glorious storm. Germanus rejected that notion outright, haunted by the memory of similar past attempts to retake Carthage by seaborne assault. Those efforts had always ended in ruinous failure and the deaths of thousands.

"If it helps aid your decision, Gelimer's hold over the Vandals is driven largely by his trust in his family," Narses said. "Two brothers, Tzazon and Ammatas, and a number of nephews and cousins. Well-placed assassinations would weaken Gelimer's control over the countryside."

Normally taciturn in these moments, Belisarius now rose in

solemn anger. "Poison and daggers in one's sleep are no weapons for Romans," he declared. "There will be no more talk of assassination. We overcome our challenges through battle or diplomacy, not cowardice."

Narses blushed, his brow furrowed. "As you wish, General," he said disdainfully. "But know that the Vandals can summon tens of thousands of screaming riders, and the Mauri tens of thousands more. Your idea of courage may change under the African sun."

Arguments broke out again as a number of officers rose in Belisarius' defense, shaking fists at Narses and forcing the man to retire from the table. It was Liberius who kept the peace, however, using his newfound status as Imperial legate to reinforce Belisarius' intent.

"Belisarius has the right of it; we must be seen to be strong," Liberius said. "Most who live in the area are descendants of Romans and will welcome freedom if their safety can be guaranteed. However, that means that we must defeat the Vandals in open battle. A single defeat, and even the more rebellious African families will hesitate to rise against their Vandal overlords."

"Defeat the Vandals in open battle?" Ascum groaned. "What happened to intimidate them or do enough damage to demand tribute?"

"That is our minimum goal," Liberius said. "But if the Vandals force our hand, we must respond. Do nothing foolish, but do not give them a chance to make the army appear weak."

Justinian rose before further squabbles could erupt in the hall. Rather than appear disgruntled or irritated, the Emperor wore a bemused look on his face, a mixture of triumph and curiosity.

"Liberius has the right of it—lure the Vandals into battle, and force them to recognize Roman dominance," Justinian declared. "It's time that these dogs suffer for taking Africa away from our predecessors. To assist Belisarius with this effort, I am expanding his bucellarii, his household retainers, to include Komes Bessas and the cataphract cavalry. The Palace treasury will pay additional stipends to others who wish to join Bessas."

"Sire, the treasury—" Paulus began.

"Can afford this honor," Justinian finished for him.

Belisarius bowed deeply to the Emperor, keeping his head fixed as he waited for Justinian to call him back to ease. "You honor me, Highness," he said. "We will not disappoint you."

"Whip the Vandals into submission, and I'll count the debt as repaid," Justinian said. "You all will be wealthy and loved!"

"Or we'll be dead men," Baduarius muttered to me. "But aye, I've a mind to see Carthage."

And so the war was declared, not with a roar, but with the sound of polite acclimation. For it was a war that few outside the Imperial Palace truly desired or stood to benefit from. Whether from wounded pride from the Nika Riots or a lust for the past glories of Rome, the Emperor was committed to his gamble, and his soldiers would obey. Even against a howling mass that had never known defeat, who two generations prior sacked Rome and brought the civilized world to its knees in a manner not dissimilar to Attila and the Huns. Even, it so turns out, if none of us knew what we were doing or how we would emerge alive from this trial.

TO THE SHORES OF AFRICA

$\mathbf{B}$olstered by an Imperial decree, dozens of clerks and ministers made final preparations for the Army's departure for the Vandal Kingdom. Even with the direct support of the Emperor and the tireless labors of Belisarius, a month was required to fully equip the expedition with its necessary supplies.

Where our previous voyage to Trapezous had been a brief affair marked by safe ports and robust supply lines, an expedition to Africa meant that Belisarius' forces would be all but cut off from the Roman world entirely. Anticipating this, Justinian commissioned a vast array of transport ships to ferry men, horses, and supplies to the distant Vandal shores, a figure that tallied to five hundred transport craft. The Emperor further charged a massive fleet of dromons to protect Belisarius' transports, with each warship bearing fifty oars and fully equipped to fend off even the most determined assaults by enemy craft. Ironically, the naval detachment dwarfed the forces available to Belisarius, with thirty thousand Roman sailors charged with oaring the ships and maintaining their rigging.

In the last days before departure, perishable items were loaded in countless pine crates and barrels. Organized by Paulus, Belisarius' men were provided with twice-baked bread, salt pork and beef, casks of sour wine, and countless other items to complement the heavy loads of nails, rope, spare weapons and armor, and other nonperishables. The loading of the fleet revitalized a hive of activity at Constantinople's harbors, a sight sorely needed to improve the local economy. Belisarius and I both spent considerable sums of our own household fortunes to accrue additional items of protection or comfort for the men, entrusting Thurimuth and Perenus to fairly dole out silver to be spent at the city's markets.

As preparations thundered along the wharf day and night, Belisarius' officers scrutinized the nominal details that could mean the difference between victory and death a thousand miles from friendly territory. Ascum was particularly attentive to the two dozen ballistae, recently crafted to replace his losses at Callinicum. Their beams still smelled of sawdust and sap as he leaned close to inspect each part. He growled at the slaves responsible for carrying each piece of equipment onto the boats, berating one tearful boy who knocked one of the ballista's arms along the ship's gangway.

In the midst of our preparations, Belisarius summoned me to his offices in the Palace. Thinking this little more than another of the hundreds of minor gatherings related to the latest shipment of arrows or reports from Narses' spies in Carthage, I sauntered into the room, greeting Belisarius informally before taking a seat on a worn, sturdy oak bench. However, Belisarius' demeanor immediately denoted that this meeting would be a more sensitive one, with possibly grave implications for the army moving ahead.

"I'm appointing John as second-in-command."

"Of course," I said, neither unsurprised nor unhappy at his choice. "He deserves it, and will perform admirably."

Belisarius smiled. "I appreciate your sentiments, but that isn't why I've asked you here," he began. "I have two favors to ask of you."

I nodded. "If it is within my power, I would be happy to help."

"Don't be so eager. You haven't heard what I'm asking yet." Belisarius chuckled. "First, I would like you to serve as third in the hierarchy. John will retain direct control of the cataphracts and the bucellarii, but you would command the Hun and Heruli foederati, as well as the remaining Cappadocians. If you agree, I will write to the Empress at once, supporting your increase in rank to tribune."

"Lord…" I could barely form the words. "You honor me with this responsibility. But surely Germanus would be more appropriate?"

Belisarius shook his head. "Germanus is a good man, but unimaginative. He is happier with his feet on the ground and his spear in front. I intend to honor him as well with command of the rearguard, but I doubt he will care either way."

"If you are sure."

Belisarius nodded. "Second, I want your brother to command the Huns. He's fearless, which is an admirable quality for a cavalry officer. Sunicas also spoke of his creativity, which is equally admirable—if not more—yet far more difficult to teach."

At that, I frowned. "Only a Hun can directly lead other Huns," I explained. "Sunicas loved my brother and may have promoted him after the Persian war, but now…"

Belisarius smiled. "I've spoken with Aigan and Sinnion, the new leaders of the Hun foederati," he replied. "They will retain command but agree to follow Samur into battle. You should give Samur more credit. It appears that he made quite an impression on the Huns."

"He deserves it, Lord," I answered. "I will tell him your decision."

"Before you do," Belisarius said. "There is one more thing. I've heard rumors of what happened to Samur in Barbalissus. Are they true?"

I hesitated. Sweat pooled under my coarse woolen shirt, heat flooding across my skin despite the cool weather of early spring. I considered demurring or deflecting the question entirely but decided against it.

"While lying in recovery from injuries taken in Callinicum, Samur was attacked and sodomized by a centurion named Marcian, as well as other Thracians under his command," I recounted. "In my rage, I confronted Marcian and killed him. I have no excuse for my behavior, Lord, although Hermogenes was unable to convict me of my crimes."

Belisarius shuddered. "Thank you for your honesty. I knew about your case, but less about Samur. Does he seem recovered from the attack?"

"I believe so," I responded, "and I know that he wants to continue to serve."

"That is good to hear. Tell Samur of my intentions. I will not command him to take the role if he does not desire it, but it would be a fitting use of his talents, and an honor to Sunicas' wishes."

When presented with Belisarius' offer, however, Samur laughed — and refused. Initially, at least. My brother argued that not only would the Huns reject his authority, but also — and more importantly — the recruits there to replace the devastating losses at Callinicum lacked the discipline of the troops Sunicas and Simmas once commanded. I explained his support from Sinnion and Aigan, and to his second point, argued only the need for time.

"They're already accomplished horse archers; they just need Roman discipline," I said.

Samur shrugged, but I could see he had yielded. "All right. I'll do it for you, and for Sunicas," he replied darkly. "But not for the Romans. I've given enough pieces of myself to those people."

As Samur replaced his Herulian ringmail for Hunnic leather and furs, other preparations for departure left me little time to do more than wish Samur well on his new venture. Gold and silver flowed freely into the merchant and smithy quarters of Constantinople, with entire forges burning throughout the pitch of night to form reserve weapons and armor for each element of Belisarius' army. I personally paid for the crafting and painting of an additional ouroboros shield for each of my men as well as thousands of shorter-length arrows that made for easier handling at full gallop. Additional gifts were made to a slowly mending Xerxes, who shyly accepted my coin to have his Immortal armor and sword repaired in a manner fitting of Persian royalty.

Among my other belated preparations was a meeting with young Vitalius. Though I had recommended that the lad remain in

Constantinople to complete his education, Father Petrus urged me to allow Vitalius to accompany me to Africa, especially given his role in the early nights of the riots.

"He has little enough family, though he comes from a famous name," Father Petrus explained to me, "and he has few to look out for his welfare. Vitalius can be useful to you on the expedition, and Liberius and I will further see to his education along the way."

Reluctantly, I agreed, and informed Vitalius of my offer. Through sagging eyes and mottled skin, Vitalius stared back at me, his dour expression breaking into relief as he happily accepted my offer. Though not a servant like Cephalas, Vitalius would care for my weapons and armor as he learned the warrior's trade and, if required, would accompany the foederati into battle. Vitalius assured me that he was an expert rider. I prayed I would never have to discover the truth behind those words.

Despite weary bones, departure day came all too soon. Bored by months of inactivity, many of the younger men flashed teeth in wide excitement of a journey to a foreign land, and even Belisarius joined their mirth as he aided Antonina into her private cabin on board his flagship. Other veterans were less enthusiastic, however, with many of my Herulians purchasing additional wine to fortify themselves against the tossing of the waves. I did not begrudge them those libations, although I warned Fulcaris that the consequences of extreme drunkenness would be felt at length when sailing in the Mediterranean for weeks at a time.

Though Belisarius intended to land several ships at Corinth to join Indulf and the Gothic mercenaries with our assembled armies, only one more stop at Syracuse was expected on the journey, with my men bottled into the hold of the ship for weeks on end.

Rosamund and Cephalas packed and labeled my personal possessions that would accompany the army to our destination. Of all others, Rosamund by far appeared the cheeriest, nearly skipping as she carefully wrapped each of her instruments and powders. Curious, I asked the cause of her happiness, especially for one who spoke so frequently against Roman wars and the freedom of the frontier.

"It's an adventure, isn't it?" she said. "The oldest civilizations in the world, whose gods were old when Rome wasn't even a collection of hovels on some backwater river."

"We aren't headed to Egypt," I said pointedly. "And what's in Numidia or Libya that interests you?"

Rosamund laughed. "If you must know, the Carthaginians used to worship Baal and Tanit before the Christians pulverized their statues and burned their priests. Your own priest may say those gods are dead, but they still linger, just waiting for someone to find them."

As they often did, Rosamund's comments made me shudder. Though many of my men retained pagan faiths that had been scorned under Justinian's leadership, she alone appeared to take a passionate interest in such religious practices, but she was careful to keep them shrouded while in Constantinople. She claimed that her healing powers were only remotely connected to the arcane arts, and in my hour of need of her attentions, I chose to believe her.

With Perenus and Samur each leading their contingents of foederati to their assigned docks, I was afforded final moments of peace with my family. Our rooms were nearly bare, as servants had already begun to pack Mariya's possessions for her move to Pella, which would begin a week after the Army's departure. Mariya half laughed, half sobbed as I propped Zenobia onto her feet, encouraging her to take her first steps while still in my presence. Her chunky legs kicked yet held no weight, and the babe merely gurgled and laughed at my labors.

A realization that soon I would be unable to hold my squirming daughter each morning or slide my beaten and exhausted body next to my bride each night weighed heavily on my spirits, deflating any sense of wonder at the adventures ahead. How long would we be gone? What would I not be able to see? In my melancholy, calculations of months apart rose into vast sums that might as well have been an eternity. Mariya's tears mixed with mine as a knocking at our door indicated the moment of my departure, and we squished Zenobia between us as we shared a final embrace. Mariya kissed the dragon pendant at my neck and unfastened a crimson ribbon from her hair, tying it firmly to my shield-bearing arm. Her perfume wafted from the soft fabrics for weeks after our parting, yet in that moment, I only had a mind for the touch of my wife and daughter.

Upon parting, I joined a small gathering of senior officers huddled on the Palace's main floor. Troglita waved me over as I joined the gathering, which included the detachment of Aksumites who still pledged to follow me into the oncoming war at Mariya's insistence. A dozen wounded veterans had all promised to safeguard their sponsors in Pella, yet Sembrouthes still assigned Wazeba and two other Aksumites to shadow their princess.

Our gathering was brief, as Narses soon signaled our need to move to the awaiting ships. With Antonina already aboard her ship and leaving Joannina in Mariya and Auria's care, Belisarius joined his officers as we marched into Constantinople's streets, his bucellarii hoisting a dozen banners bearing our various sigils. Highest and grandest of all fluttered the Chi-Rho and eagle of Justinian, its purple and gold proclaiming the Emperor's presence through his newly appointed legate, Liberius.

Horns blared, announcing our procession to the docks. Passing several charred buildings and other visible evidence of the too-recent devastation of the riots, the officers held to a somber mood, following servants of Narses as we were guided to our assigned craft. Most unsettling was the lack of onlookers lining the buildings and alleys as the army passed by, their normally curious eyes seeking a glimpse of fabled victors of battles from far away. Instead, the echo of blaring horns mixed with the stamping of hobnailed boots against stone pathways, an otherwise eerie silence following the percussion of our procession.

"Strange to not see well-wishers," John remarked as we crossed into the Forum of Constantine. "Where are all the crowds?"

"They're dead," Mundus replied sourly. "Nothing but bones and ash."

Near the port, however, crowds did form, albeit comprised of Justinian's raw city guard and those senators and attendants who had not been hanged for treason. Several docked ships were lined with onlooking soldiers, and I quickly spotted my black-shielded Herulians split across two separate transport craft. One included the Imperial flagship *Victoria*, which also bore Antonina and a number of Belisarius' bucellarii.

After offering a quick embrace to John and the other officers, Belisarius and I walked down the port's raised piers, the aged wood creaking uneasily underneath our feet. Despite my best attempts to disguise my concerns, Belisarius chuckled behind me, clapping my shoulder in reassurance.

"We've a long way to go yet!" he called cheerily. "A dock is the least of our worries."

Grumbling, I boarded the ship to the greeting of Rosamund and Cephalas. With Perenus, Fulcaris, and Irilar accompanying the other half of the Herulian foederati, the only senior officer available to me was Sindual, who promised to keep the men well-behaved for Antonina's sake. I nodded, but quietly grew disconcerted at the sly wink that the young Herulian offered at the conclusion of his promise. He proceeded to show me to the ship's main deck as Belisarius and I looked down upon Constantinople's harbor.

We did not wait long for further instruction. Horns sounded again, and Narses led a more glamorous procession of the Emperor, Empress, and various members of Court. Though Paulus was conspicuously absent, greater attention was placed upon the ancient figure of the Patriarch, who hobbled on a gnarled cane at the Emperor's side.

The Patriarch and members of Court dressed in their usual fine silks, yet Justinian and Theodora wore a ragtag assortment of loose-fitting sackcloth that formed crude hoods over their faces. Justinian's face was further caked in ashes, his features melancholy as he attempted to appear penitent before his assembled armies and the people of Constantinople.

As the Imperial party approached, a hand tapped my shoulder, and someone pushed between Belisarius and myself. Liberius winked as he joined our vigil, his eyebrows arched in curiosity as the Patriarch stood atop a low platform to address the soldiers. Belisarius knelt in respect for the Patriarch, and I signaled for others on our ship to do the same, listening as the leader of Constantinople's Christians prayed for our safe voyage across the sea and the defense of our arms in the face of the heathen enemy.

After the Patriarch concluded, Justinian ordered the onlooking soldiers to rise. His order obeyed, the Emperor knelt, knees in a shallow pool of grime produced by hundreds or even thousands of feet. Theodora immediately followed her husband's example, bowing her head as he bellowed his oath.

"Lord God, who sent his Son to die so that we loathsome creatures may have another opportunity at salvation, we thank you for guiding us through the darkness of civil strife," the Emperor said loudly, ensuring each word was pronounced with appropriate force and dignity. "I, Justinian, Emperor of the Romans, will repay your trust and providence with my life's work. As our army is being sent on its great journey to liberate God-fearing Christians from pagans and heretics, I will personally see that the Empire is rebuilt in your glory and majesty."

Pausing, Justinian's chest rose and fell as he struggled to keep his voice clear and even. None interrupted as his clutched hands swung into a wide embrace of the heavens, his head lifted to the clouds as he began again.

"I will rebuild and rededicate the Hagia Sophia to be the greatest building ever devised by man," Justinian swore, "so that any who venture into Constantinople, the City of God, will see the power and the light of our faith. Lord God, I swear this oath to you before the peoples of my dominion. Defend my people as they bring war to the Vandals, and shine your favor upon your Roman subjects, who love and cherish your name."

As he finished, Justinian bowed low in supplication, his forehead touching the wet stones of the dock. Once again, Theodora followed his motions, with the rest of the Imperial Court falling to their knees out of respect for their monarch. Only a light breeze and the lapping of waves broke the silence of Justinian's pledge—until men from an adjoining ship began to stomp their feet and pound their fists into the ship's railing, the thudding initially muted but soon bouncing off the walls of the buildings facing the Imperial docks.

Justinian rose to his knees, his features confused and curious about the rising wave of noise. With each passing beat, other ships joined the percussion, the roaring boom capturing even the Herulians and Aksumites of my own ship. Discordant cheers rose from many ships, yet it was not until Cephalas rose in song that the chanting had any direction.

Few expect sweet sounds to rise from the throats of the twisted and the deformed—a prejudice I can scarcely understand, for Cephalas had a voice to earn showers of silver for his songs had Greek aristocrats not been so shamelessly affronted by his looks. He sang a tale of Agamemnon leading the Greek ships to Troy, a ballad that seemed to be well known by the Greek sailors and spearmen from adjoining ships. Unfamiliar with the words or the story, several of my Herulians politely hummed along, yet a thousand Greeks boomed in camaraderie as the Emperor rose to his feet. Justinian flashed a wide grin as he joined in the song, the notes of the swirling mass rising above Constantinople's buildings and filling the city with a fleeting hope that had been long absent in the prior months.

The singing continued as our anchors were raised and the ships pulled out into the Marmara Sea, aligning with the transports and dromons that awaited our initial journey to Corinth. Joining the others, I waved excitedly to the onlooking crowd, finding Theodora's watchful gaze for a moment. As the ship began to move, I searched hurriedly for any sign of Mariya, a rising awareness of our extended separation rising in my gullet like rancid bile. I did not find her until many on deck had filed to the cabins below, her arm waving as she moved toward the pier to close the distance between us. I kept my eyes on her outline as Constantinople faded into the distance, initially unaware of my painfully tight grip on the ship's wooden railing.

It was Liberius who broke my malaise. The older man returned to my side as we fixed upon the waves of the Marmara Sea, the wind driving our sails south and west along the Aegean. We stood together silently as my grief eased into a numb acceptance of my fate, my eyes no longer threatening to betray my manhood. When Liberius did break the silence, however, his words were of casual warning.

"The Emperor insisted that Procopius accompany the expedition to document its victories," Liberius whispered amidst the racket. "I doubt Procopius' intentions are so benign. Tread carefully around him."

"Is he aboard this ship?" I asked, looking around.

Liberius laughed. "Of course not. The fellow followed me onto a transport ship carrying Belisarius' horses that I managed to escape from just before it launched to sea. Procopius is likely enjoying their company as we speak."

The initial journey to Corinth was generally uneventful. As with my normal routine in Constantinople, I rose each morning for prayers with Father Petrus, and spent my days with Belisarius and Liberius to debate our strategy for the invasion of Africa. Unchanged from his original strategy, Belisarius was reluctant to charge headlong into Cap Bon, the landing sites closest to the city of Carthage. Narses' spies had discovered little of the Vandal strength, although they noted their heavy dependence upon cavalry for all attacks. As our planning sessions progressed, Belisarius settled upon a launching point at Caput Vada, over a hundred miles south of Carthage and well distant of any marauding Vandal pirates.

Aboard the ship, my men drank themselves merry, singing songs and recounting glories of their ancestors or their own actions from prior battles. And at the center of the merriment was Rosamund, regaling listeners with tales of the pagan gods and stories of her Gepid homeland, once shared with the Heruli people. She frequently tried to bring me into the gatherings, and occasionally I acquiesced, but I was careful to stay moderate with the wine—for my own dignity, but more for Rosamund's safety. She was one of two women on the ship, and so, despite no signs of anything other than friendship and joy from her compatriots, I took pains to escort Rosamund to her private cabin, which adjoined my own. On quieter evenings, Rosamund occasionally drew me from my cabin, happy to play a game of dice or speak of hoped-for dreams as the rest of the ship slept soundly.

A day prior to our landing in Carthage, several of my men complained of stomach ailments and general weakness. At first I brushed aside these concerns as an unfortunate commonality in any significant gathering of soldiers, yet I grew concerned as Belisarius received word from adjoining ships of similar ailments. Delivered on a message tied to an arrow, Germanus even warned that several of his Thracian recruits had died of bloody flux, their bodies tossed into the opaque waters of the Aegean so as to not to create a miasma for the other men to become infected.

As several ships closed in on Corinth's harbor, Belisarius ordered an inspection of the men's food and water, finding many loaves of bread spotted with green mold. Gritting his teeth, Belisarius cursed under his breath and ordered each ship to conduct similar inspections, and to toss any corrupted foodstuffs into the water.

"How could the food have spoiled so fast?" I asked.

"Paulus must have ordered it baked only once to save on cost," Belisarius said, plainly exasperated. "Even the least-experienced soldier knows to bake bread twice to keep it from spoiling."

"Nothing we can do about it now but inform the Emperor," Liberius said bracingly.

Though Belisarius' inspections staved off further illness amongst the army, the damage had by and large been done. Five hundred men of the expedition perished, all because Paulus tried to save a few coins on equipping and outfitting the ships. Most of the dead were from Germanus and Mundus' Thracians, and their bodies were promptly removed from the ships, with Father Petrus and other adjoining priests offering prayers of salvation for the departed. Belisarius replaced the lost rations with considerable sums of his own fortune, instructing servants to spread coin around to Corinth's bakers to provide the appropriate twice-baked bread for the fleet of ships in their harbor. The task took several days to complete, yet still winds would have made for poor sailing at any rate, and few complained at the opportunity to walk on dry land—even if for half of a day at a time.

It was in this temporary respite that I met Indulf. I have to admit, I found the man both handsome and charismatic, unlike most of the other hairy and bulging Goths that I had encountered in my time with the army. Indulf bore a thick mane that reached his shoulders that framed two piercing eyes that bore differing colors, with one a yellowish green and another blue. He also possessed a rare set of healthy teeth, unlike his countryman Baduarius, which, along with his ornate dress and uncharacteristically proper hygiene, would have made him the darling of many a Roman woman. The only evidence that the man was not some pagan god of old was his average stature, although his broad torso and thick legs spoke to years of strenuous training.

Indulf greeted Belisarius and the other commanders with a warm opening of formal Latin, yet I noticed a stoniness behind the man's eyes. Much later, Rosamund warned that no normal man bore the curse of such mismatched eyes, evidence of being touched by the gods. With his calming words, Indulf appeared neither mad nor malicious, and I brushed her superstitions aside.

With the formalities observed with Indulf's introduction to the army, Belisarius' intentions were shared with all gathered.

"I'm grateful for the reinforcements," Valerian began, "but what is a cohort of Ostrogoths doing fighting in a Roman war?"

Indulf flashed his bright teeth in a show of geniality. "Our queen, Amalasuntha, is close friends with your Justinian and asked us to assist with your war. Besides, we Goths share no love with the Vandals, violent savages that they are."

"But Amalasuntha doesn't rule the Italian Ostrogoths?" John replied skeptically.

Indulf smiled again. "No, but her son is a boy, and his council are not of the Amal blood, of Theodoric or mighty Valamir. Do not worry, Romans, we will not disappoint on your endeavor."

And with a stroke, the ranks depleted from moldy bread and Paulus' avarice were replenished with Gothic mercenaries. Few seemed pleased with the exchange, although Baduarius roared in approval as he embraced his kinsmen. Indulf grimaced as he was drawn into Baduarius' meaty embrace, yet he did not decline to share a flagon of wine as the officers toasted to good fortune and safe seas on the journey ahead. After our provisions were restocked and the additional spearmen and horses loaded onto our transport ships, we set sail for our penultimate destination of Syracuse, the ancient city of Archimedes and a seat of power in Sicily.

Though a nexus of power in the Ostrogothic Kingdom, Narses assured our army's leadership that our fleet would find opportunity for rest and refreshment here before continuing on our final leg to Africa. We discovered in Corinth that, according to Indulf, the landing had been approved by Amalasuntha herself, who would not even begrudge the Romans for the usual taxes and fees to dock along the city's winding harbors. Belisarius disapproved of falling into the debt of a rival monarch, insisting that all costs borne by the army would be swiftly repaid by the Imperial Treasury or his own household.

Bypassing Athens and rounding the Peloponnesus, our fleet diverged from land into truly open water for the first time. Fair weather and swift wind drew heavily on our sails, yet many of my Herulians grew timid and fearful at the sign of the lightest swell. A landlocked people, most Heruli had never seen the open sea, and our previous journeys to Trapezous or from Antioch had never ventured far from sight of land. As a week passed along the open water, many turned to Rosamund to interpret the smallest omen or portent, encouraging her to lead a prayer on the ship's deck in the darkest portion of evening. Many Christians on the boat objected, but Belisarius asserted that the Empire could not forcibly convert members of a foederati that had rendered loyal service in battle. Though less cheerful about it, Father

Petrus agreed, saying that it was through tolerance and love that the Herulians would come to know Jesus Christ, not mandatory prayers. Sindual and the rest of my men ignored all such discussion entirely and prayed to whatever gods would hear their pleas to see them safely off our accursed ship.

When we finally sighted land, Father Petrus uttered cries of religious devotion and thanksgiving. Amidst a low-hanging fog, verdant hills rose in the distance, backed by distant mountains and evidence of long-forgotten settlements from the Western Empire.

"Italy," he said in awe. "I can't believe I'm seeing it again."

"We're close to Rhegium," Liberius said. "We'll be in Syracuse in a day if the wind keeps up."

"So close," Father Petrus said longingly. "If God wills it so."

"He will," Liberius said. "He must."

Though not part of Italy proper, the island of Sicily still bore striking evidence of Roman industry and civilization, even under Gothic rule. As our ships once again hugged the coastline, many bustling ports passed in the distance, their inhabitants stopping to gawk at the procession of hundreds of ships bearing the Imperial Eagle once more. As a child, I remember that Liberius had lectured on the immense wealth in Sicily's fields, the harvests of which could nourish the entire Italian Peninsula if left to incorruptible management and defended from invasion.

Unlike the smaller ports we encountered, however, Syracuse was a massive metropolis whose harbor jutted out into the sea. Capable of supporting dozens of transport ships or dromons at a time, the port city lay along Sicily's eastern coast, split between the outlying Ortygia Island and mainland Sicily proper. Separated by a narrow inlet from the mainland, the Ortygia Island portion of Syracuse held most of the historic acropolis and port, its snaking form jutting into the Ionian Sea and forming a natural harbor for deep-hulled ships of a thousand years of Greek and Roman navies.

At Belisarius' instruction, Indulf's ship was the first to disembark in Syracuse, and the Goth was charged with assuring Roman goodwill upon entrance to the Gothic port. Both Samur and Germanus watched Indulf's movements closely from the adjoining ships, and I spotted the glint of an arrowhead coming from the Hunnic transport, yet Indulf quickly gained the army's entry into the city's ports, assuring all that Narses' promises of safe harbor were valid.

Truthfully, I found little evidence of Gothic settlement on the Ancient Greek city. Syracuse had an Ostrogothic governor and a detachment of a hundred spearmen or so, but otherwise its inhabitants bore closer resemblance to the Greeks or Romans who took residence in Constantinople. Nearly all spoke a dialect of Latin that Belisarius, Liberius, and I were able to easily follow along, though many of the common spearmen or riders within Justinian's forces had considerable difficulty understanding the language of the curious and well-meaning descendants of a wealthy Roman province.

All men were granted the freedom to roam into Syracuse's markets and sample its wares, yet Belisarius insisted upon two unbreakable rules that all under his power were required to follow. First, all ships must be manned by a guard to prevent predictable attempts at theft or espionage amongst the expedition's fleet. Second, theft, rudeness, violence, or general disruption would not be tolerated, under pain of flogging or even death.

Inevitably, a handful of men engaged in a drunken, good-natured brawl at a city tavern. Belisarius exacted swift punishment with multiple bloody lashes along the offenders' backs. After that initial example, all purchases were paid with fair coin, and any grievances were quickly addressed in a civilized manner. While Belisarius permitted more raucous behavior to continue for those on board the ships, the Syracusans came to trust in his protection of their rights and properties, with many of the wealthier merchants presenting gifts to Belisarius and the other officers for their profitable custom.

Of all gifts provided to the officers, however, the most valuable of all was the priceless gift of information. Conferred onto an irate Procopius, the Emperor's secretary burst into an office that had been rented out for Belisarius' private use, panting as he begged forgiveness for interrupting a private meeting of the general's officers.

"Lord Belisarius," Procopius began, sweat pouring down his face and stinging his eyes. "The Vandals..."

As Procopius coughed and heaved, Troglita rose from the gathering and produced a cup of cool water for the secretary, chilled with precious ice chips carved from the heights of a nearby mountain. Procopius slurped happily upon the drink, pausing only to refill.

"What about the Vandals?" Germanus asked.

"The Vandals have dispatched an army to Sardinia, lords," Procopius spat back excitedly, gulping for air. "Their most experienced and best armed fighters, under the leadership of Gelimer's brother Tzazon."

A murmur of confusion swept over many as voices questioned the meaning and importance of Procopius' words. Liberius silenced them all as he stood to face the Emperor's secretary, his face as stern as ever.

"How do you know this?"

"One of the fur merchants in port arrived from Carthage not four days ago," Procopius explained. "I met him a few years ago in Constantinople, when he sold a tanned bear pelt to the Emperor."

As Liberius waved a hand to bring a halt to Procopius' further details, Belisarius drew his legate's attention. "Sardinia?" he asked. "Did the Emperor send agents to foment rebellion?"

"Justinian had mentioned the possibility, but he never confirmed it with me," Liberius replied grimly. "This leaves us in a precarious situation—if this is so, we must set sail for Africa immediately. If not..."

"Then we still sail for Africa," John concluded. "This information changes nothing, except raises the possibility that fewer Vandals are available to face our landing."

As others fought to be heard, Belisarius turned back to the timid figure of Procopius, who more calmly requested the floor. Hair thinning and bony fingers stained with ink, Procopius stood and licked his lips, relishing the chance to shape the army's destiny.

"Lords, what the merchant also confessed to me," he began, his voice more measured as he paused for dramatic effect, "is that the Vandals have no idea that we are coming."

Whatever hesitancy remained died within moments of that revelation. Even Ascum, always cynical and wary of charging into the unknown, voiced urgency at boarding the ships once more, charging headlong into Carthage and reclaiming the jewel of Africa that few dreamed as a plausible prize from this diminutive expedition. Belisarius listened to each of the pleas in turn but ultimately rose to outline his own strategy, charting a path to Caput Vada farther south of the Vandal capital. Despite many protests, Belisarius' strategy was reaffirmed by John and Liberius, who argued that a longer route to Carthage would provide greater opportunities to earn the love of the thousands of Romans still living under the Vandal yoke.

"Treat them well, and they'll abandon the Vandals as soon as we defeat them in battle."

John's reasoning was optimistic, I thought. Others grumbled at the thought of charging headlong into a larger Vandal force, yet none countermanded the general who had plucked victory from the impossible odds of Dara. At any rate, Belisarius' plans set them on a course for a brief war that avoided protracted sieges or years of attrition on the battlefield—either the Vandals would fall under superior Roman tactics or the army would be swept aside in a bloody rout, a footnote to the larger and grander Roman armies that previously faced the howling Vandals and fell to death or slavery.

I admit I have not always been a devout Christian. I pray when I have need of God and often forget to give thanks when my life is full of plenty. And thus it was then, as I begged God for Belisarius to be correct in his stratagems. For as our course was set and we departed Syracuse, I feared that none of us would live to see friendly shores ever again.

LANDING PARTY

With our larders refilled, our ships departed Syracuse soon thereafter. Our accompanying dromons skirted ahead of the fleet as we crossed into Vandal waters, the archers on each ship eager for any sign of surprise or ambush that could have sent thousands of Roman soldiers into the depths of the sea. As our ships moved in a southeasterly direction toward the African coast, we saw no evidence of the enemy.

Another week passed as we evaded outlying African islands in our urge to reach land. Several dromons did stop to inspect the larger island of Melitene, but Belisarius urged the transports to the shores along Caput Vada. Watches aboard the lead ships were doubled, and a prize of a gold solidus was pledged to the man who first spotted the African shoreline, with Belisarius' flagship rushing headlong at the front of the formation. Messages were passed from ship to ship bearing news or stratagems from various other officers, yet little changed as excitement rippled amongst the men.

Of all those who strained for any sign of the Vandal coastline, it was Rosamund who won the solidus. As the rising sun illuminated our backs, she shouted in excitement as an outline of the African coast came into view, its long beaches strewn with occasional rocks and exotic trees that rose along the distant hills. Even in the morning, the heat of the place cooked Belisarius' army, punishing those in boiled leather and polished metal with an angry sun.

As the larger transports closed the still considerable distance to the shores of Caput Vada, Belisarius ordered the foederati and bucellarii to arms. Ordered to leave their personal effects on the ship, each man donned his armor and weapons from the heavy packs distributed to them. Soldiers ready for departure were led in groups of ten to the edges of the flagship, where smaller landing craft were being loaded into position, ready to be lowered to the waters below.

Eschewing my excubitor's armor, Vitalius and Cephalas tugged my custom lamellar and scale armor over my head and tied its leather thongs securely along my sides. While Cephalas fell into something of a routine, Vitalius' eyes grew wide as he rechecked each section of my armor, trembling fingers searching for gaps in my defenses.

"You've done this before, lad," I reassured him. "You know what you're doing. And I want you to stay on the ship for now."

"But, Lord..." Vitalius began.

"Stay on the ship, and help Liberius," I repeated. "There's time enough for you to accompany me into battle."

Vitalius obeyed and moved to complete my armament, only for Rosamund to brush him aside angrily, insisting that *she* hand over my weapons, which I allowed. She began with my dagger and axe, held tight against my belt, then slid Khingila's bow and quiver into a secure hold along my back. Next, she tied my dragon-hilted sword to my left side before handing over my spear and shield, her eyes fierce as she held my gaze.

"You will not die this day," Rosamund said darkly. "I have seen it."

"I'll take that as reassurance," I said with a grin I did not feel.

I could not tell if she saw through my pretense or not. Having seen plenty of battle and bloodshed, Rosamund was no stranger to the fear that grips every man or woman before combat, and I have no shame in admitting being of their number. Godilas always said that a man who fights without fear is a man without sense—and will have a short career in the Emperor's service besides.

"The point of war isn't for you to die for the Emperor," Godilas had barked on the training sands of the Palace, "but for you to make the bastards on the other side die for theirs!"

Rosamund kissed my cheek before lifting my helmet over my head, the rich crimson plume denoting my elevated rank as a senior officer under Belisarius and John. Instinctively, I clutched at the cross and pendant at my neck as Rosamund guided me to my assigned boat at the front of the ship, the Aksumites and several Herulians all inspecting me for any sign of reluctance.

"Can you swim?" Sembrouthes asked.

"A little," I responded. "You?"

"Not at all. If I drown, I'm coming back to haunt you for dragging me to this place."

Within moments, our boat was lowered onto the sea, its deck rolling lightly at the pulsing tides. From the opposite side of the deck, Belisarius called out to me, wishing us a safe landing and promising to meet on the seashore. Uliaris and others of the bucellarii raised Belisarius' wolf banner high alongside the Imperial Chi-Rho and Eagle, their faces grim as they prepared to storm the Vandal beach, wary of attackers that could easily pluck victims from the smaller boats with a well-placed spear or arrow.

A nest of thick flaxen ropes was lowered to that landing craft, allowing each of its intended occupants to climb precariously downward. Before I followed several of my men into that rocking transport I looked along the African shoreline, finding a dozen other craft performing a similar dangerous exercise.

The last to board my boat was Altan, who bore the twin banners of my ouroboros and the Emperor's sigil. Leaping down, Altan yelped as he nearly toppled into the water, but he was grabbed by Sembrouthes before suffering such a fatal fall into the sea's depths.

"Sorry, Lord!" he replied excitedly.

"At least you didn't drop the banners." I chuckled, impressed at his calm.

Stacking spears, bows, and shields, half of the boat drew wooden oars and pushed away from our larger transport ship. Altan attempted to raise the banners but was quickly blown aside by the force of the wind, nearly losing the precious emblems in the process.

"Wait until we land!" I ordered. Altan nodded.

Though our initial efforts at rowing were utter chaos, Sembrouthes began to bark a cadence that eventually organized the men into a steady rhythm of timed strokes. Helped along by the current, our boat drifted to the gradually rising coastline, the white caps of its waves coming into view. About thirty paces to my right, I spotted Perenus and Xerxes, each leading their own boat as they bayed orders to keep their own rowers in line. Beyond those two, I found a third boat captained by Fulcaris, who retched into the water and stained the wooden siding of his boat with his most recent meal.

We did not sing, and we did not cheer. Other than grunts and shouts to keep order, the men remained silent as they stole glances along the African coast, alert to even the slightest hint of movement on the approaching hills. One of the Aksumites hissed as he warned of a creeping figure darting between rocks along the beach, yet others calmed the man as the figure's tail hinted at some sort of a jackal or fox than any Vandal.

Fifty paces from the shore, I ordered those not on oars to raise their shields to protect the heads of those aboard the boat. Several squirmed and moaned as the rising coastal waves jerked all of us violently, but none dared break the protective layer of blackened shields for fear of a sudden attack.

At twenty paces, sea spray lashed onto our benches and formed small puddles at our feet. Many panicked despite our close proximity to shore. As the waters receded to half the height of a man, I grabbed a spear and shield and ordered our protective shell to part, tying my cloak around my shoulders before jumping into the warm African waters below.

With waters rising to waist level, the current threatened to knock me off balance, yet I steadied myself with an arm against the boat and drove my waterlogged boots forward. Others followed my example as we tugged our landing craft the final few paces ashore, with others forming a protective shield wall as we moved to dry sand. The boat's keel cut a path through the fine grains of the beach, and when it was sufficiently beyond the tide, the remainder of my men joined the burgeoning wall. Staring off into the hills, I trained my attentions on spotting any sign of movement, tracking flickers of wind as I prepared for sudden attack.

All that we discovered were miles of vacant seashore. With more landing craft reaching the coastline of Caput Vada, makeshift shield walls edged near higher ground, and that strange, contradictory feeling of elation and dread permeated the environment.

"Where are they?" Perenus yelled to me.

"Maybe Procopius was right," I responded abruptly. "It seems we're alone."

Ordering the men to break into smaller detachments, we crested the nearest hill. Patches of olive trees dotted the horizon, its colors melding from yellows to greens along a generally flat landscape. White stone buildings dotted the distant western horizon, yet we remained alone, an invading army unmolested in its attempt to form a beachhead onto Vandal territory.

Belisarius immediately sent scouts into the countryside. As we were initially without horses, the swiftest runners were chosen from the various detachments of his army, each given a bag of silver coins bearing the likeness of Justinian. All soldiers were instructed to leave all unarmed civilians in peace, with all food and supplies paid with coin and no drunkenness or violence tolerated at any time. Belisarius took pains to stress that our survival in Africa depended upon earning the trust and love of those who claimed Roman ancestry, proving that Roman overlordship would be far more desirable than remaining under Vandal tyranny.

As the sun reached its zenith, Belisarius finally gave the order for the ships to disembark their holds onto the shores of Caput Vada. Given the need to ferry horses and equipment on makeshift barges, our progress was painstakingly slow, taking an entire day and night to satisfactorily complete. Vitalius accompanied Ignis as he fought to keep the stallion calm against the gently rocking waves, while Rosamund and Cephalas ferried heavy loads of the foederati's equipment and my personal effects. His face melted into a sickly green as the heavily laden barge sat low in the waters, relying on Rosamund to bail water with a pathetically small wooden bucket before mercifully reaching the African coastline.

Liberius and Father Petrus arrived on a far less precarious boat, their appearances oddly joyful at the complex and dangerous task ahead. Concerned with the rigors of our upcoming march, I had offered to leave servants available to Father Petrus aboard the *Victoria*, but he adamantly refused to be left behind. He muttered a prayer of thanksgiving as he reached the ancient Roman province, gripping tight to Liberius' robes as he struggled for footing on the soft sand.

While horses and supplies were organized along the beaches, Germanus and John ordered trenches dug and palisade walls cut from transported lumber and local exotic trees. Distributing hundreds of iron-tipped shovels, the Thracian and Cappadocian spearmen made quick work of the square fort, keeping their grumbling to a minimum as they performed the most common duty ever asked of a Roman soldier. Additional latrines and supply pits were dug along the camp's expanse, further disrupting the local terrain and increasing the hazard of an unsuspecting cavalry charge in the night.

As commander of the foederati, Belisarius left me with the responsibility of guarding the camp and strengthening our outriders to warn of any incoming attack. As soon as the first ponies came available, I charged Samur and a force of Huns with supplementing our existing scouting parties, issuing identical orders to treat the local populace well and avoid unnecessary confrontation with suspected enemies. Donning his furs, Samur barked orders in the crude Hunnic tongue, forming groups of ten that ranged far into the African hinterlands.

Overseeing the construction of Belisarius' fort, I was approached by the taciturn figure of Thurimuth. Greeting the decorated centurion, Thurimuth bowed his head in respect as he approached, speaking in deep and near-inaudible tones.

"Lord, about your trial..." Thurimuth began, his features unreadable as his eyes met mine. "I hope there is no ill feeling between us."

"None, centurion," I responded truthfully. "You performed your duty and office with honor, and I've said the same to Germanus and Mundus."

As Thurimuth nodded, I grasped his forearm, and he left as unceremoniously as he arrived, returning to the Thracians as more outlying trenches were cut in a diagonal pattern, facing the interior. Amused, Perenus approached as he offered his report of the foederati's condition, pausing to add an additional thought on Thurimuth's conduct.

"He's a joyless bastard, but a rare good man," Perenus whispered. "After you were arrested, Thurimuth insisted on covering the cost of Samur's care, blaming himself for allowing the attack to happen on his watch."

"But he couldn't have known," I replied. "The only men who could have stopped the attack were Solomon and Symeon, and the latter met his own gruesome end in the Hippodrome."

Perenus nodded. "The Alemanni have a strange sense of honor. Not fun to drink with, maybe, but that man will never disobey an order, no matter how insane it might be."

As our defenses strengthened and the outline of the fort rose into the sky, dozens of tents were erected to facilitate various functions of a larger Roman fort. While ample quarters were made available to Belisarius, Liberius, and Father Petrus, I also reserved a larger tent for the private use of Antonina and Rosamund as the only two women remaining on the expedition. Antonina complained noisily at having to share such rough accommodations, yet after a few hours, she seemed to have struck up an unlikely friendship with Rosamund. The unconventional camaraderie left me oddly jealous.

"You made Antonina seem like Medusa," Rosamund teased, sharing a meal with me on our first evening in Africa.

"And I was wrong?" I asked.

Rosamund shrugged. "She's an overprivileged Roman, all right, but she's smart and seems to dislike all the same haughty old Roman men that I do."

Foolish as it was, I felt betrayed. "You don't know Antonina like I do. She was a brat as a child, and age has not softened her into someone kinder or more modest."

"You were children!" Rosamund guffawed, swiping the air dismissively. "And modesty is for your priests. In my tribe, virtue is for the loudest, and the bravest. Besides, Antonina told me stories of *you* as a child, too."

I could tell she meant only to lessen the tension, but I still felt this fact as an affront. "You two speak of me?"

"Not gossip, nothing *harmful*," Rosamund shot back. "Mostly we tell stories of our families, our lives—and yes, of our early experiences with you. You *are* the only thing we have in common, after all."

First Mariya, now Rosamund—all seemed to fall under Antonina's spell. Samur would nearly suffocate from laughter at the thought, for as a tormentor, Antonina had been second only to Solomon and his gang. My concerns were vague, perhaps unfounded, but unable to be dismissed. Rosamund was my sworn servant, who held secrets that I had never told Perenus or Samur—or, God, even Mariya. I badly wished to forbid her further contact with Antonina but found I could not justify such a measure, even to myself.

"I trust that your conversations are discreet?" I asked, keeping my voice level. "And you aren't revealing anything that would harm me?"

"Oh, Varus!" Rosamund sighed. "You worry far too much about

things that do not matter in this life, and far too little about things that do."

I never grew comfortable with Rosamund's friendship with Antonina. Most off-putting was witnessing Rosamund giggle and gossip like any other young Roman woman in Justinian's Court. Since Moesia, I had only known Rosamund as just another companion amongst my soldiers, and watching the same woman who quaffed cups of sour wine with the Herulians or run about Belisarius' camp in mail armor as she carried on with Antonina was almost too strange to believe. Though I trusted Rosamund would always keep my interests paramount, losing pieces of her attention to another, especially someone I loathed, shook my confidence.

That ill feeling only worsened in the days ahead as our boats were unloaded and Belisarius planned the course of the army toward Carthage. In our meals together, Rosamund chattered about something humorous that Antonina had shared with her, to which I either nodded or ignored altogether. Later in the week, Rosamund requested permission to join Antonina for an evening meal, which I begrudgingly allowed.

"You could try to deny her," Samur said in private conversation. "But Rosamund isn't exactly a person that obeys rules she believes are unjust."

"Nothing to be done," I agreed. "But Antonina... I just don't understand it."

Samur shrugged. "Me neither. That's why I won't let a woman bind me in wedlock."

After days of deliberation, a decision was made to maintain a permanent presence in Caput Vada—at least until a larger city with an established harbor could be seized. Following reports from our scouts, the army would venture to one city or another, leaving behind depots of food and spare weapons, as well as a detachment of forty men under Sergius to maintain a guard. All camp servants would remain at Caput Vada, while Antonina and Rosamund would share a more lavish tent at the camp's center.

"Is this for our current encampment or for the duration of the war?" Sergius asked me, sweat beading the cropped edge of his hair.

"For the foreseeable future," I replied carefully, Mariya's warning circling in my mind.

Sergius huffed. "I didn't join the army to be a nursemaid," he said. "But orders are orders." Though not as immediately striking as Indulf, Sergius had the clean features of an ancient Roman senator, striking a figure of Augustus or Caesar with a cleanshaven jaw and pronounced brow.

Antonina was content with Sergius' command over Caput Vada, but Rosamund was displeased and voiced her worries in whispers to me. "Does Sergius *have* to stay here?"

"Antonina requests that Sergius stay, and Belisarius has agreed," I said. "Why?"

"He devours me with his eyes." Rosamund shuddered. "He speaks honeyed words and pays respect to his superiors, but when his sight falls on something he desires..."

I froze. "Sergius? Did he—"

"No," Rosamund insisted. "But all the same, I would sleep more peacefully with a blade."

I tried to gauge Rosamund's worry. "Then I can't leave you here. I can tell Belisarius that I need you with me."

Rosamund shook her head. "Normally, I would insist on accompanying you, but not this time."

"No?" I asked. Given the opportunity, Rosamund had never denied herself a chance to leave camp and venture with me onto some journey or another. "You just said—"

"I said I don't trust Sergius," she interrupted. "And I won't abandon Antonina here with him. Not until we arrive at a bigger town."

Again, I could not escape the headaches of Antonina. I had no choice but to be forthright. "Rosamund, Mariya claims that Sergius and Rosamund are lovers," I told her. "Although she has no evidence to corroborate that claim," I added.

I expected surprise, or even anger, at her new friend's dishonorable secret. As always, however, Rosamund bucked convention. "I'm no fool and am not surprised. In my tribe, none would even bother with secrecy."

This puzzled me. "Then why worry about Antonina? If the rumor is true, then Sergius is no aggressor here."

"Because it is as you said." Rosamund was unmoved. "There is no evidence to corroborate. I know nothing other than these suspicions of Mariya's you've shared and what little I have seen with my own eyes. I am capable of defending myself, Varus. And we won't be at Caput Vada for more than a week or two. All I ask is a blade."

I could have commanded her to accompany me, although Rosamund would have resented any imposition against her freedom. "Very well. I will leave Cephalas and two guards still weak from flux to watch over you. That is not negotiable."

Rosamund smiled. "Thank you, Varus. I know this is difficult for you, but while I am your servant, I have my own mind as well."

She was right. I had promised her freedom of action and thought when we first met in Moesia, and I could only ever stand by those words. "I expect nothing less," I replied.

The entire situation suffused me with doubt. Perhaps I should have raised Belisarius' attention to the matter—however I might do so tactfully—or ignored Antonina's wishes and dispatched Sergius back to Constantinople. Though I worried for Rosamund, whose concern about Sergius was unusually pronounced, I had little proven cause to act. After all, wagging tongues had riven the Empire's patrician families for hundreds of years, often from ill-founded gossip. I trusted Mariya, yet I wanted to believe this debacle was another example of circumstance and coincidence.

Cephalas accepted my order to remain in Caput Vada and did not pry as I requested he keep Rosamund safe in the encampment. By morning, anxieties of Sergius melted into the background in the face of a broader concern—now that Belisarius' army had arrived in Africa, in which direction would it go?

ON THE ROAD TO
CARTHAGE

The first detachments of Hunnic scouts returned well before dawn. Men under Sinnion ventured far into the interior, encountering a barren landscape yet no recent signs of life. Others led by Aigan galloped south along the beaches, coming across smaller fishing villages whose inhabitants refused to leave the safety of their thatched huts. Yet it was Samur's report that Belisarius' officers most eagerly awaited, with my brother not returning to camp until the sun crested above the eastern seas.

Samur dismounted inside Belisarius' fort, his horse slathered in a viscous layer of sweat and blood, and he momentarily wavered on unsteady legs before finding his balance. He winced, stretching and teasing at a knotted muscle in his thigh. After his men were afforded refreshment, Samur detailed his journey north along the road leading to Carthage.

"We went as far as Thapsus," he recounted. "Plenty of people, but no Vandals. The locals refused to meet with us at first but were persuaded after we passed around Justinian's silver."

"What was their mood? Did they understand we came from the Empire?" Belisarius asked.

Samur nodded. "They were shocked to see the Imperial banners. They didn't even know there was a war on. One of the city officials agreed to meet with me privately, but I assured him of Belisarius' pledge that no civilians would be harassed by Roman soldiers. It's clear they didn't trust Huns, however."

"You only saw locals? No Vandals or Mauri?" John asked.

Samur shook his head. "I can't speak for the Mauri, but Thapsus' representatives made it clear that the Vandals left their city in force a couple of months ago."

Beaming, Procopius moved his quill furiously and with zest, undoubtedly pleased that his report of the Vandal assault on Sardinia appeared valid. John dug into a heavy stack of documents and withdrew a sweeping map of the African coastline, its cities and villages detailed from the time of Roman occupation a century prior. Together with Bessas, John began to position figures denoting Belisarius' current position at Caput Vada, as well as suspected Vandal remnants farther north.

"The Vandals would have left a sizeable garrison in Carthage," Bessas said, "and smaller forces in Hippo Regius and Caesarea, where they exact tribute from local Romans and the nomadic Mauri tribes."

Pieces shifted on the map, with Vandal shadow armies occupying the northern coast of Numidia and Mauretania. After removing the figures near Thapsus and Hadrumetum, the road from Caput Vada to Carthage was shockingly clear of Vandal armies, with only token forces of Romans or Mauri blocking Belisarius from the Vandal capital.

"What of the local garrisons?" Baduarius asked. "Would they fight us if we moved close by?"

"No," Valerian and Liberius replied simultaneously. Neither elaborated until Liberius, clearly curious, bobbed his head to allow the younger officer a chance to speak, his eyes twinkling against the multiple open flames of Belisarius' tent.

"My grandfather was a young centurion in Numidia," Valerian explained. "When the Vandals came, Rome abandoned the province to its fate, leaving its few soldiers to fend for themselves. Those with enough coin bribed their way onto a boat for the east, while those that couldn't…"

Valerian gestured resignedly to the map, his thick fingers knocking over figurines symbolizing local guardsmen in Thapsus and Hadrumetum. Sweeping the fallen soldiers aside, the path to Carthage was entirely clear, with only faded markers for notable cities and villages that had been stripped of their Vandal guards to bolster Tzazon's attack on Sardinia.

"No Roman will fight for the Vandals if they don't have to," he said. "My guess, all the city dwellers will throw open their gates and welcome the Emperor's banners in with a party."

"That sounds like a good plan!" Baduarius' roared proclamation drew irritated glances from John and Germanus.

Valerian continued. "The Mauri, however, are less predictable."

"They avoid the coastal cities outside of Mauretania," Troglita chimed in. "Auria told me stories of how the Vandals would raid Mauri villages, taking girls as comfort slaves and boys as soldiers for their wars. The Mauri hate the Vandals, but they're too afraid of them to do anything about it."

"But why?" Germanus asked. "We've all heard the stories, but what about the Vandals keeps the Romans and Mauri docile? They easily outnumber Gelimer's men."

Liberius chuckled sadly. "In two hundred years, the only decisive defeat that any Vandal king has suffered was at the hands of Attila. Even then, the Vandal lords were still strong enough to escape rather than be absorbed into the Hunnic hordes. Their descendants fought and burned their way across Gaul, Hispania, and all the way to Carthage, enslaving thousands and forcing others into meek surrender. When the Empire tried to stop their carnage, the Vandals beat back an invasion of a hundred thousand Roman soldiers and boarded their own ships to put Rome to the sack. The Vandals are unlike any other barbarian tribe we've yet encountered—they care for nothing but the joy of battle. They let the African Romans and

Mauri collect taxes and administer a semblance of government, but the Vandals themselves do nothing but prepare for war. I can't think of a worse enemy to have."

While several in attendance knew the facts Liberius recited, the reinforcement of our enemy's prowess was nevertheless sobering, if not unsettling. Even with the more experienced Vandal units in Sardinia, Gelimer had thousands of Vandal warriors still available within Africa's north coast. This is assuming that neither the Mauri nor the Romans would take up arms to defend their masters, which was a gamble that many were unwilling to take.

Ascum grunted as he sized up the challenges facing Belisarius' army. "So, should we go north and risk attacking Gelimer's remaining forces, or go south and seize the entire province of Tripolitania bloodlessly? All the Emperor wanted was some measure of victory against these people, and acquiring a plump new region with two wealthy cities seems like fair reward."

Liberius shrugged. "That would be more than a proper renumeration for the Emperor," the legate concluded. "But the Emperor will not be jeopardizing his safety or comfort—that unhappy responsibility falls on you men. It must be your decision what choice we take."

Unused to the freedom to select their futures, each of the men offered their opinion of what was possible, or at least preferred. John served as the lone voice advocating for a more aggressive line of attack, with even Baduarius arguing for less costly methods of seizing the more southerly province of Tripolitania. My instinct was to add my weight to Ascum, Baduarius, and the dozen others who sought a near-bloodless end to the conflict, my concerns less about the reputation of the Vandals and more about the many months such a campaign would demand.

Yet I could not follow through with my nagging wish to be reunited with my family in Pella. Recalling Justin's long-ago oath, my eyes fixed upon Belisarius' map, the marker of Carthage melding with the late Emperor's pledge.

"We must rebuild our Empire. We must take Carthage, we must take Ravenna, we must take Rome!"

Sighing, I joined John. Baduarius rolled his eyes playfully. "We may never again get this opportunity," I said. "Carthage was once a jewel of the Empire and a fountain of culture. The Vandals nearly destroyed this ancient city—I say we take it back."

"Varus the Poet!" Mundus laughed. "Who would have known?"

I crossed my arms, blushing, as others took up Mundus' epithet for me. The phrase "fountain of culture," was repeated by many, and I burned at my own foolishness until Belisarius ended the mirth.

He smiled at me. "Varus, do you remember my reasons for attacking the Avars in such a violent fashion?"

I nodded. "If not completely broken, the Avars would simply come back to attack Cherson as soon as our army departed."

"Correct," he replied. "I wish it were not so, but I fear we are in a similar predicament here. If we take Tripolis, or Leptis Magna, or anything that the Vandals lay claim to, they will not recognize their defeat."

"But why is that *our* problem?" Ascum blurted out. "All the Emperor wants is something to show his ability to produce victory. Look what happened when we sacrificed ourselves at Dara. Or at Callinicum."

With that, Ascum removed his gloves and drew back the thick woolen sleeve that masked his scarred and deformed arm. Bringing the gnarled hand into a crude fist, he raised the arm so all could see the cost of Callinicum, when the army was forced into another avoidable conflict. Though Ascum's words trended perilously close to sedition against the previous Imperial legate, Liberius did nothing to stifle the discussion, only rubbing his aged eyes as the man made his point.

"You are right, Ascum," Belisarius began. "It is not our responsibility to deal with the aftermath of this war, only to bring justice to the Vandals for their attacks on Roman Egypt. But even if we keep our aims limited, we place innocent Romans and Mauri at grave risk of reprisals once we leave. I gave my oath to God and the Emperor that I would defend our people, and I cannot in good conscience leave them exposed to brutality and slaughter."

Defeated, Ascum hung his head in surrender. "I'll follow you wherever you want to go," he promised. "I just wish it didn't always have to be the more difficult path."

"I know it, and I am honored by the loyalty from each of you." Belisarius chuckled. "But my mind is made up—I intend to march north and knock Gelimer from his throne. It's time Carthage was Roman once more."

Uliaris and others within the bucellarii rapped their hands on nearby wooden tables and posts, a thundering chant quickly adopted by even those officers who requested a more peaceful end to our current conflict. Ascum shrugged and joined the din, a declaration to all the gods who ever walked along the shores of Africa that Rome would drive forward or fall in the attempt.

Our strategy determined, Belisarius gave the men one additional day to readjust from their long sea voyage before venturing north to Thapsus and Hadrumetum. Many groaned as the day turned to an extended training bout, with most units being led in drill and weapons practice. Yet John and I secretly rejoiced at the chance to observe the disparate elements of Belisarius' forces, many of whom were still unbloodied recruits who had yet to stand in a shield wall.

Most of all, I was curious about the abilities of our Gothic mercenaries. Pairing my Herulians with Indulf's Gothic bandas, I observed how the Goths parried and jabbed with spears and swords, adjusting their feet as they transitioned from attack to defense. Most of my veterans outmatched their sparring partners, with Fulcaris and Sindual both descending into more aggressive bouts that threatened to turn bloody. However, it was Indulf who offered the greatest surprise as he bested Perenus, sending the foederati officer tumbling to the dirt after an exchange of blows.

As Perenus spat dust and swore vengeance, I summoned Xerxes close.

"Test Indulf's skill," I requested. "Don't humiliate the man, but don't let up either. Let's see who he really is."

Xerxes nodded, eager to tangle with a mysterious foe. Grabbing a blunted spatha, the Immortal challenged the Gothic tribune, who nodded gracefully as he turned to face his newfound enemy. Though custom would dictate a fair initiation, Indulf rushed toward Xerxes, leaving him no time to mount a defense.

Xerxes ducked and dodged between Indulf's blows. Indulf's sword cut and stabbed viciously, though not without a measure of poise, as he drove Xerxes backward, keeping the Zhayedan from mounting a more vigorous defense. Yet it was not Indulf's sword that caused the greatest havoc, but the dust that kicked his boots, which nearly blinded Xerxes as he struggled to keep trained on his enemy's blade.

After a time, Xerxes ducked under Indulf's sword, rolling away before popping upright a safe distance from the Goth. Lancing forward like a scorpion, Xerxes battered at Indulf's defenses until he could do little more than parry and retreat. Xerxes struck hard before twirling around Indulf's shield arm, the tip of his sword jabbing into the exposed armpit.

I nodded. "Well done by all," I replied, relieved as the men separated and ended the bout with a handshake. Indulf straightened pieces of dark hair that had become matted to his forehead and complimented his Persian foe on his exceptional ability.

Later that evening, Xerxes offered a more candid assessment of the Goths.

"They fight well in teams, but less so as individuals. Now, Indulf has somewhat above-average technique, nothing extraordinary," Xerxes confided to me, "but he's one of the trickier opponents I've faced. Very fluid, and very creative. Few would think quickly enough to strike in such an unorthodox manner."

Training halted before the heat of the day threatened to overtax the men, offering an extended period of rest before the morrow's march. Using additional food purchased from Syracuse, Belisarius ordered extra rations be distributed amongst the men, although no wine was permitted with the meal. Satiated but humming with anticipation, many chatted around low cookfires into the night, with many of the less-experienced men showing false bravado in their eagerness to engage the Vandals. I found Altan and Vitalius around one such fire, discussing camp rumors about Vandal tendencies in battle.

"Lord, what was it like to stand against the Avars? At Dara?" Vitalius asked innocently.

I sighed. "Battle is a test of wills as much as a contest of skill with shields and weapons. If you trust the men next to you and believe in your commander, the enemy's strength becomes less important."

"Is that why you follow Belisarius?" Altan asked. "I've heard Sindual tell stories of Dara and Callinicum... It's hard to believe that such things really happened."

"They did," I responded. "I follow Belisarius because there are few men alive more dedicated to the mission and to his men than the general is. Avars, Hephthalites, Vandals... it doesn't matter."

Surprised by the sudden chill in the coastal night, I warmed my hands over their open fire. Others from various sections of the army soon joined our circle, asking their own questions of Belisarius' stand at Dara or my own experience in the household of Emperor Justin. Acknowledging each man, I answered their questions in turn, resisting an urge to sneak away for sleep. Eventually, though, I did insist that the men return to their tents, noting the long march that would soon begin.

Soon after dawn, the camp at Caput Vada was almost entirely evacuated. Camp attendants packed supplies and weapons, while pack horses dragged carts along the old Roman road that snaked along the African coastline. As the army left the fort's raised gateway, a team of sailors took command of the area, ensuring that Belisarius would have a route of escape to the sea should catastrophe strike. Their task complete, many of the armed dromons sailed north to Carthage, seeking to destroy any ships that might ferry Tzazon and his thousands of Vandal warriors from Sardinia back to the Vandal homeland.

Leaving behind the camp servants, most clerks, and a small detachment of men still weak from the sea voyage, Belisarius' army departed Caput Vada in columns bristling with twelve abreast. I offered farewells to Rosamund—who once again declined my offer to venture north—and watched as Belisarius embraced Antonina. Both appeared happy enough, I thought. Rumors of Sergius and the general's wife were nothing but gossip.

Our journey was planned to avoid the worst of the midday heat, although careful precautions were taken to keep the men and horses lightly attired as they walked along the coastal African road. Built hundreds of years prior at the close of Rome's wars with the ancient Phoenicians of Carthage, the smooth cobbles that cut a path between rocks, sand, and thick grasses had retained their form and usefulness despite nearly a century of Vandal neglect.

Following the coastline, we curled slightly to the northeast, encountering famously rich and fertile soil that had made Africa such a valuable province to the old Western emperors. Sea air helped assuage the worst of the baking heat, yet Belisarius and Liberius still ordered the column to halt at regular intervals, tasking mounted scouts with seeking out wells and springs that had dotted the outdated maps of the region.

As leader of the foederati, that duty fell to me. Each scouting party contained no fewer than six men, with orders to remain vigilant for any sign of possible ambushes or enemy activity. As before, the scouts also bore pouches of silver coins, their contents entrusted to those with established records of honesty and loyalty to Belisarius or myself. Fulcaris led one group of Herulians and Samur another for the Huns, their orders to sweep outward and report back within regular half-day intervals. Though I was reluctant to make similar use of the Goths, Indulf insisted on demonstrating his value, and as these men fell under my command, I allowed Indulf to lead his own scouting party farther into the African interior.

"When I joined the army, I never thought I'd be *giving away* treasure," Fulcaris grumbled as he returned from his duty, a half-empty bag of silver coins the evidence of his interaction with locals.

"Be thankful you're giving it away, and it isn't being taken from your corpse."

Fulcaris noted that the army's northern progress placed it closer to a number of villages, most of which were built in an older Roman fashion. Few Mauri willingly agreed to meet with the roving band of Herulians, yet more curious Romans happily took Belisarius' coins, offering praise to Justinian in hopes that their bondage to the Vandals would soon be ended.

"They absolutely detested Gelimer," Fulcaris added. "Apparently he allowed the Vandal nobles the right to sleep with a bride on the night of her wedding to any Roman or Mauri subject. Those who refuse have their tongues slit in half as a reminder of speaking against their rightful overlords."

Such fanciful tales often followed many barbarian tribes who invaded Roman territory, and I initially scoffed. The Huns had once been said to eat the flesh of babes for strength before battle, and even the Heruli had been accused of sacrifice to their pagan gods long ago, although all of my men swore against the validity of the rumors. Yet as the army marched passed Thapsus, dozens of mutilated Romans stood along the roads and gawked as our soldiers passed. Many were missing noses or ears, angry scars forming where a blade had been taken to the soft flesh. Others were absent hands or feet. We even found several with the split tongues as rumored by Fulcaris.

One older woman wept as Belisarius rode by, reaching for his horse and planting a kiss on his boots. Uliaris and Bessas both dismounted and quickly threatened to skewer the perceived attacker, but Belisarius dropped from Xanthos and kissed the older woman on both cheeks. The woman wept again, showing a mouth bereft of teeth, the result of a Vandal assault on her village decades prior. Belisarius handed her a heavy bag of silver coins and ordered a spare mount be gifted to the gray-haired wretch, who bowed in gratitude and promised to speak highly of the Emperor's warriors.

"She's just as likely to spend the coin on a boat out of Africa," Bessas said.

"Possible, but I doubt it," Belisarius said. "Besides, we need to earn the love of these people if we want to leave here alive. They may be Roman, but past emperors abandoned them to this terrible fate, and most are not likely to forget that slight without considerable effort."

As men of the army waded through swelling crowds from Thapsus, Belisarius distributed gift after financially ruinous gift to these hundreds of threadbare peasants. So many grasping hands reached out to touch his cloak or boots that Uliaris and the bucellarii had difficulty keeping the swarming mass at bay. Belisarius had only smiles and laughter for his professed countrymen. Several shouted praises to the Emperor for their deliverance. Then a stubborn call rang out as dozens of voices cheered the general directly, bringing a look of momentary fear onto Belisarius' face.

Elders from Thapsus confirmed Samur and Procopius' previous reports of Tzazon's departure, denuding the coastline of the Vandals' most experienced men. Doctors were made available for our soldiers who suffered from flux or blistered feet, while donations of food and water were pressed to John and other officers with hopes of a decisive defeat of Gelimer. But Belisarius would take no gift without proper repayment, leaving the residents of Thapsus far wealthier from his brief visit.

By the time the army reached Hadrumetum, ten days after our departure from Caput Vada, curiosity and excitement had grown into a fevered frenzy as hundreds of Romans awaited Belisarius' arrival. Much larger than Thapsus, the half-ruined city of Hadrumetum threw open its gates as it allowed Belisarius and his bucellarii through the gates and into the forum, welcomed by a sea of cheers. Many had even produced ancient banners of the Western Empire, the faded and torn cloth billowing even decades after its defeat. A Vandal banner bearing their symbol of a bent cross was tossed from the magistrate's offices, allowed to clatter to the ground as Belisarius unfurled the eagle and

Chi-Rho of Justinian. John warned of spies and Vandal sympathizers that would be watching every move, to which Belisarius shrugged.

"We aren't staying long, and they're a mounted people," Belisarius reasoned. "There's no way they haven't seen ten thousand Romans marching toward Carthage by now."

It was here that small embassies of Mauri confronted our officers, with Belisarius summoning Troglita as an ambassador of Justinian's goodwill to the Mauri people. One of the men present was a distant cousin of Auria and flashed his teeth in a giddy grin as he embraced the more reserved and decorated figure of Troglita.

"The Mauri want to be left in peace," the man said, "but we have long ties with Rome. Most of the Mauri nobility are half Roman themselves. We respect Vandal rule, but we do not desire it."

Though ditches were dug and temporary walls erected on an outer fort to house the army, we only stayed near Hadrumetum for a single night. However, Belisarius did concede to city leaders' requests for a formal garrison, noting that he could spare a hundred men as a token of the army's intention to remain in Africa. Germanus quickly recommended Solomon. Liberius nodded with a knowing wink.

For his part, Solomon did not complain and most likely relished the opportunity, for it gave him direct control over Belisarius' only major port to easily connect with the Imperial fleet while also removing him from the threat of battle. I cared little for Solomon's perceived honors, relieved at not having to worry about a knife in the back in any upcoming battle. The only person unhappy with the predicament was Samur, who scowled as Solomon made a show of garrisoning his banda in Hadrumetum's decaying barracks.

Restocked and energized by the display of the Romans and Mauri, we moved swiftly north from Hadrumetum toward Carthage. Other, smaller villages and towns sent delegations to profess their love and loyalty along the way, with each allowed to return home with coins bearing the image of the Emperor and Empress. Turning inland, our scouts were greeted by a similar display of excitement at the village of Thuburbo, although its residents were wary of accepting the

Emperor's banner and warned of Vandal forces nearby.

The march continued at a determined pace, conquering over half of the hundred-mile distance that separated Caput Vada from the outskirts of Carthage. Samur and I voiced amazement at the ease of our journey, finding no resistance or even any evidence of war along the way. Many boasted that the Vandals had already surrendered, fearing Belisarius' prowess and insisting there would be no battle after all.

Until our first group of scouts vanished.

Though the disappearance of six Huns was unsettling, it was not unexpected within a campaign the size that Belisarius intended to wage. The scouting party could have been delayed by a split hoof or an opportunity to spy upon enemy resources, requiring additional time outside of expected practices. More concerning was the likelihood that the Huns deserted, made all the more likely by grumbling from the newer recruits at being transported far from their homeland to such a distant and foreign land. Sinnion noted some fears amongst his men that the Huns would be left for dead should a sacrifice be needed to save the army from a Vandal onslaught, citing the recent examples of Sunicas and Simmas along the shores of the Euphrates. Regardless of whether this was desertion or delay, I noted the scouts' absence but did not fear the worst.

That fear came soon after. First, the disappearance of two more Gothic parties, and then the delay of a third, led by Samur himself. In a show of surprising fury, Indulf demanded to send a broader expedition to seek out his missing men, spitting in anger when I refused to cleave hundreds of mounted soldiers under my command away from the rolling procession of Belisarius' column. At a minimum, these men were needed to guard the rumbling train of carts that bore stacks of weapons, armor, and food, while the larger body of Huns and Herulians were given flanking duty to protect against sudden strikes from the African interior. Blue veins pulsing along his neck, Indulf immediately calmed his actions, bowing to my demands and returning to the hundreds of Goths under his orders.

Yet Indulf had been right to worry. His fears of Vandal attacks on our scouts were echoed by Bessas and John.

"Don't send any wide-ranging parties," Bessas said, "and set tighter circuits. If that strategy worked against the Avars, it'll work against the Vandals."

"Tauris was tiny in comparison to the African continent, though," John countered. "We'll be blind to any incoming attacks if we restrict the movement of our scouts."

Against John's concerns, I sided with Bessas. Many amongst the Herulian and Hunnic foederati had expressed an unwillingness to volunteer for further scouting duty, their former bravado against the Vandals quickly melting into a fear that these barbarians moved faster, fought harder, and showed not the slightest hint of mercy to perceived enemies. Aigan warned that certain detachments of Huns may outright refuse the scouting order, while Fulcaris and Perenus requested a more conservative approach to protect their own men.

Recognizing our rising challenges, Belisarius slowed the pace of the army, accommodating the quicker return of less-adventurous scouting parties as they reported on the local terrain and presence of locals. Through it all, I struggled to keep my thoughts from Samur, a task that grew more difficult as his absence continued for a further two days.

Any worries were dispelled when Samur and a Hunnic companion galloped furiously toward the slow-moving Roman army. Their tunics ripped and furs disheveled with a spray of grass and dried blood, my foederati initially moved to attack the interlopers, believing them likely Vandals. Then Samur was able to identify himself to Sindual and was allowed to reach Belisarius and myself.

"They're here," Samur panted. "The Vandals. They know we're coming."

Servants fetched fresh robes and refreshment as Samur gave his report, his eyelids heavy and speech stunted as he told of his extended foray to the north. Aware of my brother's fatigue, Belisarius asked only for key details, listening patiently as Samur offered his tale.

"We made our way toward Carthage and had reached its outermost farmlands when we were attacked," Samur went on. "I've never seen anything like it. It's like they came from nowhere."

"This is their country, and they know it better than we could hope to," Belisarius said, attempting to assuage my grieving brother. "But be specific, what did you see? How were they armed? How many were there?"

Samur closed his eyes. "Maybe twenty. Wearing mail and leather, all mounted. Huge axes, some with lances. And they were all tall— taller than our men—and they spoke a kind of Latin that I barely understood."

"Vulgar Latin," Liberius said. "Definitely the Vandals."

Samur nodded. "They didn't handle our bows well, and we feathered at least two or three of them. But they just charged in, butchering my men. Mundzuc and I were able to fight our way free, but the others were killed. But that wasn't even the strangest part."

"Strangest part?" John asked. "What do you mean?"

Samur bowed his head. "They laughed. I first thought some were choking from my arrows, but others joined in. They laughed hysterically as they swung their blades and as they executed my men."

Slowly, eyes turned to Belisarius, Samur's tale as unsettling as it was informative of the threat facing the army.

"Double our sentries," Belisarius ordered, "and keep Samur's story secret. We don't need fear sweeping through our camp."

"One more thing, Lord," I interjected, turning back to Samur. "How close to Carthage did you get?"

"From here, maybe a day's march. Signposts made it clear that Carthage would be another day's ride after that," he said, referring to distance markers that lined most major Roman roads and indicated distance to regional capitals.

"What did the signs say?" I asked.

"Ad Decimum," Samur replied in Latin.

"Ten-mile marker," I translated into Greek. Many of the other officers nodded in recognition.

A mundane name, all things considered. An unremarkable place. How ironic it is that it proved so decisive in our lives.

AD DECIMUM

Belisarius ordered the army to continue for a half day longer, his order to halt coming only after the vanguard under John encountered a new marker along the road. Belisarius asked for Liberius and me to follow, and we galloped toward the front of the army's column.

Over a hill and beyond the sight of the core of the army stood a post, its reinforced wooden beams jutting twice the height of a man. Atop that post was a corpse of a spearman, empty sockets glaring accusingly at his Roman onlookers as a series of ropes held its body and limbs safely in place. His thick beard and moustache were caked in blood and filth, although their plaits indicated the man's Gothic heritage. Flies buzzed as I walked closer, inspecting a curled scroll that had been hung around the corpse's neck, its message scribbled in a crude Latin hand.

Welcome to Africa.

Moving closer, I inspected his neck and torso for any sign of a killing stroke. Reaching out with my left hand, I checked to see if any other scrolls or messages had been stored in the folds of the man's robes, finding little other than hidden coins sewn into the fabric. I turned back to face the other officers, shaking my head as I found few details other than the macabre welcome.

And then the corpse screamed.

I drew my sword and jerked back from the figure, more from instinct than anything else. His voice was hoarse and rasping as he babbled in the foreign Gothic tongue. The body thrashed weakly as I moved closer, muttering a prayer to the saints that made me shiver in fear.

"Bring Indulf immediately!" Belisarius ordered John, who galloped hard back to the column.

Indulf appeared soon thereafter, dismounting near the body as he snarled in rage. Speaking to the man, Indulf's tone was as insistent as it was furious, and he drew a dagger as he awaited a response from his former tribesman. Instead, the hanging man lifted his head weakly, calling out in crude and slurred Latin.

"Romans," the man blathered in his thick Gothic accent. "Kill me! Kill me!"

Indulf roared, his dagger piercing the suffering man's chest and shattering his heart. The man gave one piteous moan before he once again fell silent, a trail of blood flowing from the source of the wound.

"His name was Wulfila, from Tarentum," Indulf explained.

Belisarius nodded. "I will have a pyre made and prayers said for Wulfila."

Indulf shrugged. "Why bother? He is dead and will not hear you. Dig a shallow grave so the rest of the men will not see, and let's move on."

Belisarius narrowed his eyes but did not countermand the Gothic tribune in his command over the Ostrogothic spearmen. John fetched three shovels as he joined Indulf and me in excavating a shallow grave, its depth falling only to knee height before we lowered the still-warm corpse to its place of rest. While I mouthed a prayer for Wulfila's salvation, Indulf returned to his men, leaving John and me alone at the head of the army.

Ordering the army to halt and fortify its position, Belisarius immediately drew his officers together once more, particularly requesting the presence of Samur. Many whispered in confusion at the sudden halt to the army's progress, with Belisarius dispelling their concerns after recounting John's recent discovery.

"We have to assume that Gelimer's forces are nearby," Belisarius explained. "And given the terrain, they could sweep against us from a number of angles, and we'd be blind to their intentions. Samur, what did you see near the ten-mile marker?"

Samur shrugged. "It was relatively flat, with some rolling hills that would be easy terrain for most horses. A wide lake to the north forces any travelers to take a circuitous route to reach Carthage, while the west is an equally large array of salt pans."

"Salt pans?" Baduarius said, his brow furrowed in confusion.

"Extremely dry and flat land, almost like a desert," Liberius explained. "Africa and Mauretania have large areas of them. Easy to walk upon, but entirely lacking in water or vegetation."

Grabbing a large sheet of parchment and quill from Procopius, John traced Samur's understanding of the road ahead with hurried strokes. A thin line marking the stone path snaked around Carthage's lake, while a few small hills were noted to the north and west of the roadway.

"It's a trap," John muttered, his eyes wide as he sketched further details onto the scroll. "Gelimer could attack us from any side, and there's nothing we could do about it."

"No natural defenses?" Germanus asked.

"Other than the lake? None," Samur confirmed. "We could see mountains much farther north, but they are well beyond the Roman road."

"Like I said, a trap," John said. "The Vandals don't even care to disguise their motives, because we have no choice but to continue on."

Ascum grunted. "We could turn around, return to Hadrumetum."

"We would still be open to attack, and the Vandals would sweep behind and besiege any of our forces who are able to return to safety," John continued. "We must continue to Carthage now, before Tzazon returns from Sardinia and Gelimer's numbers become overwhelming."

Belisarius closed his eyes, breathing slowly. "Troglita has the right of it," he said. "And John is also correct. But that doesn't mean that we need to proceed meekly into the Vandals' strategy."

Leaning over John's hand-sketched map, Belisarius began to place pieces representing the various detachments of his army. Less certain of Vandal positions, Belisarius positioned several likely ambush points around Ad Decimum, his fingers tracing the few options his forces would have in the event of a collapse in the Roman lines. Belisarius shook his head in frustration as he considered alternate scenarios, his corps of officers watching silently on as our strategy was determined.

Of all possible ideas, Belisarius' suggestion defied centuries of Roman military doctrine. Even Liberius' eyebrows rose at his commands, yet he did not dispute the strategy.

"Our infantry, archers, and ballistae will encamp here," Belisarius began, taking John's quill as he traced a neat square that denoted the relative position of our trenches and walls. "Germanus will have command and will serve as rearguard."

"Belisarius..." Germanus began, "you mean to leave our cavalry unprotected and alone?"

He nodded. "Precisely," he said. "If Narses' reports and our scouting of the Vandals is correct, they'll prefer to fight as an entirely mounted force. They presume to retain superior agility and range of motion and would seek to surround our slower infantry."

"But, General, our cavalry is less than half of our forces," Baduarius added. "You would attack Gelimer with reduced numbers when he already outnumbers us?"

"Yes," Belisarius replied. "If our horse archers and cataphracts can tear off pieces of the Vandal attack piecemeal, we can grind them down one at a time. Their numbers would be pointless."

Belisarius' fingers pushed Vandal figurines atop Ad Decimum, with Roman cavalry moving to meet each force in turn. Samur stole a glance at me as he noted the heavy use of foederati, his features holding the same look of reluctance and concern he shared before our battle with the Avars years prior. No officer dared to speak against

Belisarius' strategy, leaving it to Liberius to ask the question which, if true, would have doomed us all.

"How do you know that the Vandals will attack in separate units and not join together in a single massive assault?"

Belisarius smiled weakly. "Because it's what I'd do. If I depended upon speed and flexibility, I'd break off my men and outflank my less-mobile enemy."

"And if you're wrong?" Liberius prodded further.

"That's why the infantry will dig defenses here, providing our cavalry with a safe means of retreat," Belisarius explained. "But God willing, it will not come to that."

"Jesus," Mundus said sharply. "I hope your instincts are correct."

As the meeting concluded, Samur pulled me aside. Though substantially recovered from Barbalissus, Samur nevertheless appeared older, his face weathered and creased from his time in the saddle.

"Varus, if Belisarius is wrong, we're all going to be butchered out there," Samur whispered. "If we get cut off or overrun, that's it. There's no reserve force to come to our rescue… no cataphracts to break Tzul or Khingila."

"I know."

"Then why go along with it?" Samur wondered. "This stopped being our fight the moment Justinian decided to send his army a thousand miles away as a test of manhood. We aren't defending anyone here."

It was a near-constant argument that I shared with Rosamund. "There are thousands upon thousands of Romans who live in terror under the Vandals. This is our chance to liberate them, just as Justin dreamed."

"Bugger Justin!" Samur cried. "And who cares about the Carthaginian Romans? They'll happily let you and me die for them in a fight, but they'll call us barbarian and spit derision as we pass in peace."

Samur's fury against Justin caught me unawares. "I made an oath to Justin, Samur, and that means something. It has to."

"Justin's dead, Varus." Samur groaned. "And his maniac nephew is willing to slaughter tens of thousands of his own people, most of whom only wanted to feed their starving children or find a warm home to sleep in."

"I've made other oaths," I countered weakly. "To Belisarius, who risks his life the same as we do, and to Theodora."

Samur paused, running a hand through his hair, which had been oiled in mutton grease to protect against the coastal winds. "If Belisarius was smart, he'd think as I do. His Emperor imprisoned him for that antiquated oaf Hermogenes, after preventing the Persians from swarming over our eastern provinces. If Belisarius wants to stay, then he's as big a fool as any other."

"Belisarius is a great man," I said, anger mixing with my discomfort at Samur's conversation.

Samur did not protest the point. "Yes, on that I will agree with you, but it doesn't change our predicament. As for Theodora, she's as cunning as any of Justinian's ministers, and a great deal more vicious. I think she slew Hermogenes and made it appear a suicide."

"That's a terrible accusation!" I shot back, inwardly disguising my own suspicions of Theodora's intentions. "I saw Hermogenes' body, and there's no way Theodora could have lifted him to the ceiling. She was just as surprised as I was at the man's death."

"Then she had help." Samur shrugged. "It's beside the point. Yes, I'm appreciative of Justin and Liberius, and I miss Godilas dearly, and I honor Belisarius as our commander. But if we keep blindly following orders of this Emperor, it's going to cost us everything."

It was a grim warning, adding to the stack of worries that robbed me of peaceful sleep. Yet Samur said nothing more of our conversation and performed his duties in the Hunnic foederati admirably, revealing no signs of discontent to any other in Belisarius' command. Nor did I question Samur's loyalty, for though his grievances were weighty, he would never abandon me. Of that, and few other things in life, I was certain.

That evening, I wrote letters to the Empress and to Mariya, informing them of my situation, offering what sentimental details I could muster in the darkness of my tent. Each scroll was closed with crimson wax, the melted substance stamped with the ouroboros that adorned my shields and banners. Handing both to Vitalius, I ordered the youth to ride hard for Hadrumetum and send any missives on to Constantinople via the first ship out of port. Vitalius resisted at first, desiring to follow me into battle, yet I patted the boy on his head as I insisted upon the order.

"You will have your chance soon enough," I said. "For now, I need you to obey my order."

Clouds shrouded the sun the following morning, keeping the land cool yet free of rain in a lone positive omen that Belisarius' strategy had been well-founded. Thracian and Cappadocian spearmen worked throughout the night to bolster their defenses with a maze of trenches and palisade walls, leaving a narrow strip of land for Belisarius' cavalry to pour forth to Ad Decimum.

Armor and weapons were distributed and banners unfurled as the morning sun snuck above the horizon. I shared formal acknowledgments with John and Belisarius before embracing Samur and preparing my foederati for the conflict ahead.

"Who knows, maybe there won't even be a fight today," I offered.

"Unlikely," Samur replied grimly. "It's up to the gods now."

Donning his flowing white plume, Belisarius saluted the army. The infantry called out praises and goodwill as their brethren formed to depart, with Baduarius bellowing for our men to discipline Gelimer and be done with this war.

"Kick him square in the balls, lads!" Baduarius barked. "That's between the legs, for those of you less knowledgeable of the subject!"

With Belisarius at the head of the reduced force, we filed through the entrance of Germanus' fort and proceeded farther along the stone road to Carthage. The bulk of Belisarius' forces were led by Bessas, with the armored cataphracts and other bucellarii trotting in front of Valerian's more lightly armored lancers. John was given leadership over our vanguard while Samur, Indulf, and I guarded the army's flank facing the interior. A small reserve of lightly armored horsemen under Valerian made up the rear of our formation, although I doubted their role would be little more than to help secure our escape back to the fort if Belisarius' maneuvers proved faulty.

A calm wind made our banners billow and sway, accompanied by the pleasant crashing of waves along a nearby beach. If our men had not been beset by crippling fear and worry, the march would have been a pleasant one, but all were fixed upon the horizon for any sign of Vandal movements. Outriders were stationed at established distances around the army's progress, yet Belisarius explicitly ordered them not to stray far from eyeshot, insisting on the need to reform at the sound of a horn blast.

Moving away from the seashore, we encountered the southern edge of Carthage's vast interior lake. This, too, appeared idyllic; ripples swept across the lake, and dense clouds allowed for easy visibility. Yet even those luxuries were soon disrupted by sightings of the ten-mile marker.

Ordering the formation to halt, Belisarius signaled for me to meet him along the Roman vanguard. Bringing Samur and Perenus along with me, we found him already speaking with John, their orders decided.

"My forward scouts spotted Ad Decimum in a narrow defile beyond the hill ahead of us," John explained. "We're tracking movement, but no sign of the enemy yet."

"John will send a probing attack to the marker," Belisarius ordered. "Varus, be ready to move hard to the salt pans. I'm also ordering Valerian to protect our rear, but I may need your foederati to respond if any sizeable Vandal detachment hits Valerian in force."

We saluted him and returned to the foederati, stopping short of our men to keep a clear view of John's initial attack. Soon enough, forty armored cataphracts split off of John's force, an immense purple banner projecting Justinian's will in this distant land. The force moved swiftly over the hill and into the defile of Ad Decimum, moving just beyond visibility of the rest of the army.

At first, nothing extraordinary happened. We waited, and even hoped that all of our planning had been useless, and that no Vandals awaited us in such an inopportune place. I dared not speak my hopes as my eyes strained on the hill ahead, seeking out any sign of struggle.

Suddenly, dust clouds swarmed ahead. Any noise was muffled by a rock-strewn hill and the lingering crash of waves along the seashore, yet the unmistakable clink of iron could be heard echoing along the countryside. John sat motionless as he, too, waited for any sign of what the Fates had construed for him, shifting constantly in the saddle as he straightened his helmet and plume.

And then we received our answer. At first it was no more than a riderless horse, its armored scales soaked in a thick layer of blood that sprayed with each step of its massive hooves as it found its way back to our army. This was followed soon by two other horses, one of which limped and screamed in pain. Still, John sat motionless as he interpreted the signs before him, his fists tightening around his horse's reins.

When the first wounded survivors began trailing over the hill, John roared an order to form up. Only a dozen of the cataphracts sent in the initial attack returned, many bearing broken arms or gaping wounds that caused at least one rider to fall from the saddle and crash to the ground. The man was urged to his feet, yet he stumbled drunkenly as he moved to safety.

John's horn sounded its high-pitched noted of advance, sending nearly five hundred of Belisarius' veteran cataphracts bounding through Ad Decimum's pass. As John crested the hill, he lowered his lance against an unseen enemy, sending a cry of defiance streaming through his men as they, too, disappeared.

"Time to go!" I yelled, leading Perenus and Samur back to our respective positions.

Samur separated from Perenus and me as he galloped toward the Hunnic foederati, frequently turning his head in anticipation of further orders. This signal came as Belisarius blew his silver-tipped horn and dipped the ouroboros in the direction of the salt pans, as clear an order as could be given under the circumstances.

"Unsling your bows!" I yelled to the Herulians, an order that was similarly passed to the nearby Huns. "We're moving southwest to the salt pans. Remember your training, listen to your officers, and stay in formation!"

Wild cheering rose from my foederati, the gnawing trepidation of waiting for battle finally concluded. Holstering my spear and shield, I drew Khingila's bow before thrusting a fist into the air. Belisarius' horse archers thundered into motion. Nearly all followed my example, with Sembrouthes and his remaining Aksumites rejecting archery in favor of the melee that inevitably ensues in combat situations. To my surprise, Xerxes drew his own bow, grinning as he caught me gaping.

"We Immortals have been doing this a lot longer than you!" he teased, his body loose and calm despite the rising crescendo of battle.

Noting the urgency in Belisarius' horn, we moved at a near full gallop toward the salt pans. A low hill rose into our view as we neared our objective, and I signaled to Perenus and Fulcaris my intended target.

"Take that hill and we'll have control over the flats!" I yelled.

Both men nodded in recognition.

I pushed Ignis hard, remaining a half length in front of my men as we neared our new target. Nearby Samur and the Huns split off as they moved away to the flats, allowing his nimbler and lightly armored Huns the freedom to maneuver on flat terrain. My confidence soared as the foederati swallowed additional ground on both fronts, cresting the hill as more horns from John and Belisarius boomed with the more distant sounds of farther battle.

Until we reached the hilltop, where we found at least two thousand Vandals less than a hundred paces from our position. Doubtlessly hoping to achieve a similar objective, the Vandal leader bellowed as he lowered his lance, urging his men to charge into their Roman enemy.

"Draw and loose!" I cried urgently, signaling for the foederati to turn and veer away from the impending Vandal assault.

It was only as this first volley sprung into the skies that I managed to get a view of the Vandal warriors. Dressed in an array of mail and furs, the Vandals utilized select pieces of Roman armor alongside those of their nomadic heritage. None carried bows and few wielded throwing spears, whose range would have been laughable against Hunnic or Herulian composite bows, with most bearing heavy lances, swords, axes, and maces in no particular standardization. The wealthier Vandals—fewer than one in one hundred, just about—were encased in lamellar plate that seemed a lighter relative to those bore by Justinian's excubitores. Our arrows sliced through mail, leather, and fur with bloodcurdling ease, dropping a handful of Vandal riders to the stinging dust of the salt pans.

Most bounded toward our position, including several with arrows jutting from chests, arms, or legs. They shouted and howled as they closed in on my Herulians. I urged my men away. Perenus and Fulcaris continued the cadence of drawing and loosing arrows in a pitiless cloud of iron and wood, yet even the horrendous casualties taken from fifty paces distant did not dissuade the Vandals from their murderous charge.

As I began to order the front ranks of the foederati to dismount and form the shield wall, Samur's Huns pelted the Vandals with their own barrage of bow fire, far deadlier and more accurate than even my Herulians had been. Other Vandals to the extreme right of the hill tangled with Indulf's Gothic riders, the Vandals' howls mixing with a booming drum. Several Vandals turned to attack these new nuisances, allowing my men precious time to regroup.

"Varus!" Xerxes screamed to get my attention. "The Vandals have no archers! Form a forward wall and let the rest of your men pick them off!"

Realizing Xerxes' strategy, I quickly barked the order. "Foederati!" I yelled, "First banda form the wall, the rest keep up the arrow fire. Fulcaris has command of the archers!"

My men swiftly obeyed, sliding from their mounts and driving their horses behind friendly lines. Within ten heartbeats, three ranks of fifty spearmen clapped their blackened shields together, the twin banners of my ouroboros and the Emperor's sigil dominating the hilltop. The Vandal leader grinned hungrily as he saw our change in strategy, roaring for his men to complete their charge.

"Brace!" I yelled. "Keep the wall tight!"

Sembrouthes and Xerxes fell in on either side of my shield, their spears sharpened to a vicious point as we formed our defense against the Vandal charge. Even as the rows of screaming Vandals bore down on our position, I fully expected their charge to turn before making significant impact upon my men. Few warriors or their horses would willingly plunge into a well-formed and disciplined shield wall, and my men had been honed for that very purpose. The stream of arrows sailing overhead as gifts from Fulcaris' mounted warriors further added to the hazards facing any Vandal who tested my ranks, their accuracy almost guaranteed at this limited range.

Yet they kept coming.

Even with multiple arrows sprouting from several of the Vandals, they charged headlong toward our position. Fulcaris ordered his mounted archers to aim for the Vandals' horses, which did succeed in throwing several riders from the saddle, yet hundreds pushed ever onward. Their leader wheeled against a center-right section of my lines led by Irilar, his broad wedge aiming for the centurion's red-plumed helmet.

"They're going to crack right through us!" one of the younger Herulians cried out.

"Hold!" Perenus yelled, a call echoed by several of the other officers. "Keep this line straight, or I'll beat you myself!"

Without so much as a momentary pause, the Vandals crashed into our lines. The Herulian wall wavered as Vandal riders connected with each section of the wall, slamming axes and maces onto their enemies' helmets. One rider drove the iron tip of his lance clean through Xerxes' shield. The Immortal thrust his spear into the Vandal's lesser-armored throat and sent its iron tip impaled upon a mop of matted hair on the other side. Xerxes cursed as he withdrew the spear, his shield listing from the additional weight of the broken lance as he called to be replaced along the wall.

As the Vandals did not attack in a single cohesive line, my shield was not struck until Xerxes had departed. My attacker was an older man whose yellow hair was streaked with gray, his arms bulging as he lowered his lance at my helmet. Raising my shield abruptly, the lance's edge broke clean against my shield's wooden boards, although the force of the blow drove me back a full pace before I was able to counter with my spear. Sembrouthes added his own lunge, with our spears filleting the man in his stomach and ribs. The Vandal snarled as blood pooled from the corners of his mouth and drew an axe as I struggled to free my spear, then the Vandal jerked as an arrow buried itself deep in the man's nose.

Stealing a glance back, I found Fulcaris grinning at his victory, yet his attentions were immediately drawn toward the right of my lines. Unable to concern myself with Fulcaris' strategy, I freed my spear from the man's guts and prepared for the next attacker, my shield arm numb from the force of the charge.

Several other Vandal riders slammed into our section of the Herulian lines, jabbing lances and swinging maces with desperate and murderous purpose. One mace, its edge studded with bent nails, slammed hard onto the upper rim of my shield, tearing free sections of wooden paneling and leaving it vulnerable to attack. One of the mace wielder's companions followed by throwing a short spear that would have cut through my shoulder had it not been for the spearman positioned to my right. I found Sindual taking up the role, and the centurion ordered the rear ranks to throw their own spears in return, joining a thin barrage of Herulian arrows firing into the Vandal mass. My own attacker was thrown from the saddle by Sembrouthes and disemboweled by another Aksumite, blunting the Vandal charge in our section as a replacement shield was passed to me.

Men adjacent to me began to cheer at their success, yet those chants soon turned to sweeping horror as Irilar's ranks began to buckle and break. Unable to move to meet the challenge, I watched as Fulcaris dismounted, leading twenty men to reinforce the wall and shore up its gaps. A rearmed Xerxes attempted to join the effort, yet every thrust and slash was parried, even as the Vandal leader led more horsemen into the gap in my lines.

I looked to Samur for help, but the twin bandas of Aigan and Sinnion were locked in their own stalemate as they launched withering arrow fire onto a resilient Vandal enemy. Though few Huns had been wounded in the engagement, Samur appeared wary to venture too close to the Vandal ranks and expose his lightly armored men to close combat, although he did motion for his officers to attempt to flank the Vandals' position.

From my rear, Perenus yelled for my attention, just loud enough for me to hear. "Varus, Irilar is dead, and the lines are going to buckle. We need to readjust now!"

I nodded, barking my own orders in return as I brushed blood from my eyes. "Grab a horse and find reinforcements immediately!" I yelled. "Stop for nothing!"

Perenus slipped back to the rear of my lines to obey the order. Not waiting for Perenus' response, I ordered the wall to advance, jamming my spear into the thigh of another Vandal rider who spat as he slammed a mace into the side of my helmet. My vision dimmed and grew dark as I faded from consciousness, still hearing the chaos of battle and feeling hands tugging at my armor yet unable to move my arms or legs. A voice blared my name, and for a moment I was returned to Constantinople, listening to Mariya rock our daughter to sleep.

That image faded as rough hands shook me back to Ad Decimum. My head throbbed as I struggled to sharpen my vision, my senses slowly flooding back.

"Varus! Can you hear me?" Sindual yelled.

"Yes," I croaked. "Where are the lines? How long was I not in my body?"

Sindual shook his head in confusion. "You were struck on the head not long ago, Lord. Our right is curling backward, and the Vandals are threatening to turn our flank. Perenus asks for your orders."

Resisting the urge to tug my helmet free, I gained an awareness that I had been carried behind our shield wall. Horsemen trotted down the lines as they fired their continuous stream of arrows, while our center and left held firm against the lighter attacks of those Vandals too slow to reach the vulnerable crack in the Herulian shield wall.

"Hit the bastards back," I replied nonsensically, my mind still a dense fog of confusion.

"Commander?" Sindual asked, his brows wrinkled in confusion.

"You heard me, centurion," I answered. "Stand me up, and let's go charge these savages."

Sindual made to resist, yet he merely complied with my order as he helped me to my feet. I staggered but remained standing, leaning on Sindual's shoulder as I regained my balance.

"Herulians!" I yelled, wanting to act quickly before they saw the extent of their leader's infirmity. "Our right needs help! Move forward, and send these Vandals to hell!"

A cheer rose from the left flank as they complied. Centurions and dekarchoi alike commanded the center left to swing round, pressing against those Vandals who pushed and scratched against the rearmost ranks of the Herulian right. His yellow robes swishing in the wind, Sembrouthes led that charge, screaming in his native tongue as he threw his spear.

Surprised at the sudden motion, the pressure on my right appeared to ease as many of the Vandals moved to push back at the angry Roman counterattack. Vandal swords and axes chipped against our blackened shields as wounded men screamed in pain and hatred, leaving dozens of twitching bodies and disemboweled horses to pile along the ground. A thick mud brewed as gore and guts from the dying watered the dry African soil, trampling its fine grasses and leaving only a vile-smelling horror in its wake.

Yet as my maneuver began to drive many Vandals away from the fight, I realized the error of my strategy. Regrouping Vandal riders pointed to a gap in my center, their progress slowed only by those arrows that my rearward riders were able to launch against their incoming death. As I ordered the lines to reform, a massive crash sounded to my extreme right, and I heard my doom calling as a thousand horsemen thundered into my lines.

By the grace of God alone, those forces belonged to Indulf and not another Vandal commander. Our enemies were caught off guard as the Goths charged in, with Perenus directing them to outflank and surround a huge swatch of the burly African warriors. As quickly as the fight began, it finished. A detachment of two or three hundred Vandals not encircled by fresh Roman riders galloped hard to the safety of the west, only to be ridden down by Samur's Huns. Dozens of arrows pinioned the slower and defeated Vandal riders. No Vandals asked for quarter, and Samur gave no order for restraint, screaming for the slaughter of his enemies to a man.

A cry of disbelief and utter euphoria rippled through my foederati. "By the Gods, we did it!" Altan cried out. "We beat the Vandals!"

Cheers and boasts swelled as others noted with amazement the few casualties the combined foederati sustained against the vicious Vandal attack. Yet I had no patience for mirth as I half staggered toward my right flank, soon finding Fulcaris weeping over the body of his dead cousin.

Though no man truly wishes to die in the press of blood and iron in the shield wall, a small mercy granted to Irilar was that he was killed quickly, and with little suffering. His chest was speared with a Vandal lance that seemingly shattered the centurion's heart upon impact, rendering death within mere moments if not instantaneously. Fulcaris wept as he lay atop Irilar's blood-spattered corpse, his eyes staring lifelessly to the sun as his blood mixed with that of a hundred others.

Kneeling next to Fulcaris, I wrapped my arm around the grieving man's shoulders. Fulcaris sat upright before leaning into me, his wails dying amidst rising cheers of victory amongst my men.

"His term of service was complete in half a year's time," Fulcaris mumbled. "He was much older than me, and always spoke of retirement and children. Now he will have none of those things."

I clutched Fulcaris closer as I nodded. A dozen others kneeled in respect for one of the original officers of the Herulian foederati, their show of respect drawing fresh bouts of tears from Fulcaris' swollen eyes. We would have sat there for a considerable time had the cheers of my left flank not suddenly stopped, replaced with cries of concern.

Rising to my feet, I found Xerxes and Perenus, their faces equally confused at the sudden shift in mood. A man helped me atop Ignis, and I clutched hard at the reins, trotting toward my left flank. Instinctively, I patted the white Avar wolf pelt hanging from Ignis' saddle, a sign of reassurance that I had led men into more desperate fights and emerged living to tell the tale.

"This is nothing like Tauris," I attempted to convince myself, almost like a prayer. "Or Dara."

It was ridiculously naïve. And as I peered upon twenty thousand howling Vandal warriors galloping over the nearby hill, at least twice Belisarius' full strength, I knew I was wrong. This confrontation was nothing less than a battle of extermination—either of the Vandal Kingdom or of Belisarius' diminutive army, and Gelimer had no intention of submitting. At the center of the Vandal host stood a crowned and bearded monarch, flanked by looming standards of the bent cross.

"Gelimer," I muttered.

"You mean we only fought off a scouting party?" Perenus asked, incredulous.

"Worse," I replied. "We were lured here to be slaughtered. Tell the men to mount up immediately."

"You mean abandon the hill?"

"We have no choice," Xerxes answered for me. "It's retreat or die."

Perenus clenched his fists, his neck reddening as he breathed heavily. Yet he nodded in recognition of our newfound situation and galloped back to the men to inform them of our latest need.

"So many," Xerxes remarked, almost in awe.

"Who knows how many more there are," I replied. "We don't know how many John encountered, or whether his forces are still fighting fit. Our only hope is to reach the army as soon as possible."

Despite the order, Fulcaris resisted abandoning Irilar's corpse. He blubbered in protest as he begged to be left behind, so I slapped the man hard along his exposed cheek.

"Irilar wouldn't want you to die here too!" I growled, shaking Fulcaris to his senses. "You have a responsibility to your men, and to me. I promise that we will find Irilar later and pay him all respects to see him to the afterlife."

Almost childlike, Fulcaris rubbed his face as he threatened to cry again. Yet he grimaced as he mounted his horse, stealing one final glance at the small number of Roman dead as we retreated toward Belisarius' forces. Both Samur and Indulf did the same, urging their mounts north to escape the swelling trap that the Vandal king had wrought. We galloped hard to the east for several hundred paces, climbing one of the low coastal hills that rolled for miles along the African and Libyan seashore.

Until, cresting the hilltop and expecting to find Belisarius' army, we found another detachment of Vandals crashing into Valerian's lighter-armored rearguard.

"They're hitting us on all sides!" Perenus yelled, his eyes searching for other signs of attack.

With the larger Vandal army moving slowly behind us, I scanned Valerian's struggle with his own Vandal detachment. Though the younger Italian officer stood firm, his forces lacked the experience or heavy scaled armor to repel a determined enemy assault. The Roman lines prevented an outright breakthrough, threatening to buckle as pressure from a more numerous and resolute Vandal attack mounted at each of Valerian's flanks.

My head pulsed in pain, and I desired nothing more than to lay in the grass, yet I clenched my fists to keep my mind fixed on the battle.

"Signal Samur and Indulf," I ordered. "We're going to save Valerian and hit the Vandals on each side."

"But what of Gelimer?" Xerxes asked.

I shook my head. "We need to move quickly, and we need to trust that Bessas and Belisarius will deflect any attack at our rear. If Valerian falls, the entire army will be surrounded."

As my orders were relayed, I looked along the narrow valley leading to the crevasse at the Ad Decimum marker. A few cohorts of cataphracts could be seen in the distance, yet my vision was blurred and unable to decipher whose sigil flapped on the faraway Roman banners. Bile rose in my chest as a creeping fear of defeat gnawed at my gut, with Belisarius not present to rescue the army from an overwhelming rout. Plucking my horn from Ignis' saddlebag, I blew three panicked notes in procession, repeating the signal for urgent rescue several times before kicking Ignis to another gallop.

Both Samur and Indulf reacted to the sudden change of strategy with admirable agility, rushing their mounted warriors toward the several thousand Vandals who swarmed along Valerian's lines. As we drew closer, I made out a massive Vandal warrior at the center of the fighting, raising his head in laughter as he slammed an axe down upon a helpless Roman soldier. Though my view was blocked, the axe seemingly cut clean through the Roman's leg and severed his horse into two separate pieces, its screams cut short as a pool of blood fountained into the air.

"Perenus, Fulcaris!" I yelled, the two officers looking for further instruction as I pointed to the Vandal giant. "That's Gunderic, the Vandal general! Kill him, and the rest will flee!"

Our strategy clearer, my Herulians formed into two separate columns as dictated by their months of training. Samur's Huns swept farther east while Indulf's Goths hurried along the coastline, forming a thin arc of leather and iron against the Vandal formation. As we galloped closer, Belisarius' horn sounded far to the east, bringing a roar of triumph from my men just as Valerian's lines finally began to break.

Yet Gunderic seemingly recognized the tightening noose around his own detachment. With incredible discipline, the once-snarling and blood-drunk Vandals swirled away from their retreating foe, leaving a low mound of bodies of friend and enemy alike. Gunderic's head turned across the horizon as he measured up the Romans facing him, and he roared an order in the savage tongue of his warrior people.

At first, it was difficult to determine Gunderic's route of attack. Samur ordered a flight of arrows at the massed cavalry, yet given the extreme distance, few arrows reached their targets, and all had been sapped of their lethality as they fell against Vandal shields and armor. Moving away from the Huns, Gunderic motioned toward the Herulian lines. The Vandals charged into a dead sprint against my position.

However, the move was a feint. Just outside of Herulian bowshot, Gunderic maneuvered his men west, lowering lances as they barreled into Indulf's Goths. Unprepared, Indulf's men were cleaved apart, sending many scurrying away in panic. Pockets of Goths retained their discipline as they grappled with Gunderic's Vandals, yet even urgent instructions from Indulf were unable to maintain consistent order across the Gothic lines. Seemingly euphoric in his maniacal laughter, Gunderic swung his massive axe once more as he charged headlong into a Gothic dekarchos, throwing horse and rider several paces back and into the swirling dust as Gunderic thundered away.

As quickly as the Vandal attack began, Gunderic signaled for his men to gallop to the south. Avoiding Herulian and Hunnic horse archers alike, Gunderic whooped and jeered as he led his men back toward Gelimer, leaving a small yet embarrassing trail of Gothic dead in his wake.

I signaled for the combined foederati to move farther north and east as we rushed away from Gunderic's soldiers, who mysteriously halted atop the hill that had been my previous battle site. A small detachment of Vandals rushed into the Ad Decimum defile, sending the small detachments of Bessas' cataphracts rushing back to the east, yet Gelimer made no motion to press his advantage upon my disorganized and bloodied foederati.

Belisarius' horns blared once more as the bulk of his army

swarmed west. He raised a hand in greeting as my Herulians approached, finding the Roman cataphracts and bucellarii bloodied yet whole. Uliaris grinned as my men approached. The Frank waved his francisca in a macabre welcome as others gazed ominously at the Vandal army in the distance. Samur's Huns arrived soon thereafter, trailed by Indulf's Goths, whose officers had to reknit broken units into a cohesive mass.

"General," I began, struggling to breathe as my vision slipped in and out. "We defeated a separate engagement of Vandals atop that hill but were nearly ambushed by a larger force likely led by Gelimer himself."

Belisarius nodded. "A thousand of Gelimer's men attempted to cut off the army from the road to Hadrumetum, but Bessas ruined their efforts. We took several prisoners, and it seems that Gelimer was far more clever than Liberius or I gave him credit for."

"Lord?" I asked. "How so?"

"Gelimer's army was broken into separate units intended to ambush our approach to Ad Decimum in a simultaneous action," Belisarius explained hurriedly. "The separate detachment you defeated belonged to Gibamund, Gelimer's nephew."

"Gibamund," I muttered, the foreign name slurring against my tongue. "He's dead now."

"Good," Belisarius said. "I haven't seen John, though. Have you?"

I shook my head. "Nothing from beyond the canyon ahead since the start of battle."

Belisarius' eyes twitched in an evanescent moment of weakness and worry, replaced soon thereafter by coolness. "It seems that John's forces engaged those of Ammatas, leading the garrison from Carthage."

"Gelimer's brother?" I asked.

"The younger one," Belisarius confirmed, his eyes moving toward the distant horizon of billowing Vandal banners. "What can you tell me of Gelimer's main army?"

Recounting my brief observations of the massive Vandal force, I confirmed previous reports of an entirely mounted army. "No archers or infantry," I added, "but they aren't afraid to use their cavalry with insane charges."

Belisarius grunted in acknowledgment. "They need our lines to break," he reasoned. "But they've lost the element of surprise. Why is Gelimer not advancing on my position?"

"No idea," I admitted. "It doesn't make sense."

"Indeed," Belisarius agreed, his attention momentarily turned to the encroaching figure of Indulf. The Goth threw a fist wildly as he raged in frustration, swearing vengeance against Gunderic, Gelimer, and any other Vandals he came across in Africa.

"Motherless bastards!" Indulf shouted, a spray of blood smeared across his cheeks. "I'll pull their entrails out with fishhooks while they watch!"

Belisarius observed him with distaste. "Tribune, I need you to calm yourself," he commanded, his voice low so that few could hear. "Our day isn't yet done."

"Fine," Indulf spat angrily, "but that giant is mine when this is over."

Dismissing Indulf, Belisarius issued commands for his cavalry to retake the field. The detachment of Vandals who scouted Ad Decimum's narrow defile galloped hard back to the main Vandal army, its lines swelling along the horizon. Yet even though they obviously outnumbered Belisarius' remaining forces by a considerable margin, Gelimer hesitated. Against a pulsing headache, I fixed my mind on the figure of the Vandal king, the man in a heated discussion with Gunderic as the huge commander flailed his arms about pugnaciously. Belisarius silently judged his enemy, mouthing a brief prayer before trotting ten paces out to face his men.

"Gelimer had his chance to take hundreds of casualties, but for whatever reason did not seize it," Belisarius reasoned loudly to his forward ranks. "Their trap failed! One good push, and we'll sweep the Vandals clean away!"

Belisarius drew his blade once more, its steel edge not fully cleaned from the blood of its previous victim. Thrusting its tip against the muted sun, he began to trot along his lines, their spears and lances raised as they chanted their commander's name.

"For God and the Emperor!" Belisarius yelled, driving Xanthos into a full gallop.

Hundreds of Belisarius' elite cavalry roared their response, their chants pulsing along the countryside and overtaking the din from the Vandal lines. Still Gelimer remained indecisive as Belisarius returned to the center of his lines, issuing his final orders to Bessas and myself.

"Form wedges," he instructed. "Foederati toward the African interior, cataphracts facing the Vandal center, all other cavalry following closely behind in reserve."

With neither the time nor request for debate, Belisarius' officers saluted in acknowledgment before returning to their appointed section on the lines. His horn blared the signal for a full advance, bringing a booming thunder of hooves to push toward the Vandal lines. Outnumbered and on enemy soil, Belisarius placed his strength into a single throw of the dice, all before the noonday sun reached its maximum.

Though many along the Vandals began to form into more organized lines, confusion appeared to dominate Gelimer's forces. Liberius had once lectured that of the barbarians who invaded the Western Empire, the Vandals adopted the least of Rome's customs or traditions, preferring to abide by the historical customs that drove them across Europe and into Carthage to begin with. Rather than relying upon an intricate system of junior officers, as all Roman armies had since the earliest beginnings of our city, Liberius noted that the Vandals followed a smaller number of warlords, reducing opportunities for disloyalty yet making their forces far more reliant upon the rapid decision-making of their leaders. Gunderic's deep roar drove his riders into neat lines, yet Gelimer's other warlords looked to their king for instruction, finding little to be had.

"Bows!" I yelled as we reached two hundred paces distant.

My commands taken up by a dozen other voices, Belisarius'

wedges moved at a slower trot, saving a final burst for the last stretch of low hill that would bring man and beast crashing into the Vandal lines. Though the entire sequence could not have taken more than a hundred heartbeats, it felt like an eternity as we rumbled ahead, the Vandal banners coming into view as we selected our targets.

At a hundred and fifty paces, I judged the winds favorable to Herulian and Hunnic attack. Plucking an arrow from Ignis' quiver, my gaze fell upon Gelimer as I judged the wind and distance to my target, seeking to end this war in a single strike.

"Draw!" I yelled as we moved another thirty faces.

To the north, Belisarius gave the command for Bessas' cataphracts to charge, an order that was immediately obeyed. Belisarius' and Bessas' wedge moved swiftly against the center right of the Vandal lines, their spears and lances lowered toward their enemies as they reached the final thirty paces before impact. My foederati remained at a slow trot, I timed our volley to the last possible moment, my intent fixed upon the Vandal king.

"Loose!" I roared.

Hundreds of Herulians and Huns showered the Vandals with a narrow arc of our arrows.

As before, many Vandals were struck by our flurry, and several fell dead to the ground, yet most wounded snarled as they hefted their weapons for combat. My own arrow missed its mark, sailing just over Gelimer's head and landing in the shoulder of a more ornately armored Vandal just behind the king. Other Vandals filled the void and drew Gelimer back to safety, seeking to form a more consistent defense against our arrows.

Yet the efforts were futile. The few holes the foederati were able to carve into the frontmost Vandal ranks were all that our cataphracts required, their wedge hammering into a gap and splitting Gelimer's forces into two panicked mobs. After releasing several more volleys, I gave an order for Samur to continue his posture, signaling for the Herulians and Goths to prepare their own charge. Indulf accepted that command hungrily, a Gothic drum booming as their reorganized forces prepared to slam into Gelimer's disorderly lines.

Holstering my bow, I drew my spear. "Form a wedge!" I ordered. "Let's go!"

Of all the officers who repeated my orders, Fulcaris' voice rang above the rest with a thick twinge of hatred. My Herulians formed two smaller wedges behind Perenus and myself, with the Aksumites and Xerxes falling into my own formation. Though tiny in comparison to the massive attack of Bessas and Belisarius, the swirling chaos of the Vandal front left them shockingly vulnerable to attack.

I repeated the order to advance, guiding Ignis into one final assault. My Herulians burst into their own provincial cheers as they urged one another into the assault, followed closely by Indulf and the Goths. Within moments, we neared the crest of the hill, and I selected one younger Vandal whose battle joy had been tainted with the stink of fear. Lowering my spear, I saw only a dead man still riding, my spearpoint aimed firmly at the man's torso.

We collided with a sickening crash. Catching my victim high in his chest, my spear tore through his boiled leather like soft cheese, driving cleanly through the other side of the man's body before shattering from the force of the blow. Drawing my sword, I veered Ignis into my next opponent, my sides reinforced as Xerxes and Sembrouthes completed their own onslaught.

Many Vandals howled and cheered, yet many others looked warily and fearfully to their commanders for sorely needed orders and organization. Though I lost sight of Belisarius, my own wedge cut cleanly through the Vandal first line and well into the second, continuing to push as the more numerous Vandal lines were driven back from the ferocity of our assault.

Yet our progress was stunted as Gunderic plowed his way to the front of the Vandal lines, pushing his more timid countrymen aside as he drew an immense sword that would have required a man of normal size two hands to wield.

"Varus, you bastard!" Gunderic boomed in frustration. "Starting the fight without me!"

He swung the blade effortlessly, leaving me little time to do anything other than duck as the steel whirred a hand length above my face. Gunderic laughed as he positioned his horse diagonal to my own, the mount of an equally large size to accommodate such a heavy rider.

"Come on, you're supposed to be a fighter!" Gunderic's words were a merry taunt. "Here I come!"

The Vandal commander jabbed the sword forward, my instincts allowing me to raise my shield to absorb the blow. The tip of the blade embedded itself into the shield's panels as Gunderic was thrown off of his rhythm, struggling to tug the blade free from its impediment. Seizing the opportunity, I swung my own sword, aiming for Gunderic's great melon of a head.

Only for the warrior to grab my wrist, pinning me close and preventing another strike. Absent a shield, Gunderic optioned for a more aggressive attack. He nearly choked with joy as he met my gaze.

"There it is, the fighting spirit!" he roared. "And such a pretty blade, too!"

I gritted my teeth as his meaty fingers twisted the bones of my wrist, almost entirely unimpeded by the scaled vambraces that protected my forearms. Jerking away at the thought that Gunderic would snap my arm cleanly in two, fear rose as the massive Vandal freed his sword from the ruins of my shield.

He was disrupted by a vicious strike from Sembrouthes. Gunderic jerked away from the Aksumite's spear, its edge carving a rent into Gunderic's horse's haunch. The horse whinnied angrily as it jerked Gunderic backward. The Vandal moaned in irritation. As Gunderic struggled to keep balance, I pulled my sword arm free, swinging down once more onto Gunderic's head.

The Vandal raised his sword in defense, leaving my blade to scrape angrily against the side of Gunderic's helmet. Sparks jumped as my sword cut superficially into the iron, causing the helm to fly off and leave Gunderic's head bare. Grinning, the Vandal swung at me once more, leaving me to throw all of my strength into a counterblow.

The wake of the two blades nearly threw me off Ignis' saddle, the sound ringing well above the noise of battle. We exchanged several more blows as Gunderic tried to use his great strength to knock me to the ground, nearly succeeding on multiple attempts.

"Come on, Varus! I'm disappointed!"

Gunderic's thick straw-like hair was matted into short spikes that swayed as he moved his head. Hoping to cut at the exposed flesh of his face, I jabbed, my blade parried by deft slashes backed with unmatchable strength. Sembrouthes attempted to throw Gunderic off balance once more with another spear thrust, yet the Vandal hooted with laughter as he easily dodged the blow. It was to the sound of that laughter that my foederati's advance stalled, and I became stuck in a crucible of men and horses atop the hill of Ad Decimum.

As our fortunes waned, Belisarius suffered no such trouble. Gunderic raised his head in curiosity as he found the opposite Vandal flank crumbling, its survivors put to flight as Bessas' wedge broke clean through the Vandal lines.

"Come on!" Gunderic wailed. "Just when it was getting good!"

"Surrender, Lord Gunderic!" I yelled, my men roaring in triumph behind me as Indulf's Goths redirected themselves toward widening gaps in Gelimer's army.

"Lord, he calls me!" Gunderic said as he swung another blow. "Our time today has come to an end!"

Gunderic swung a wide arc with his blade as he backed his horse away from the fight, the blow designed more to separate himself from his enemies than to carve limbs or heads from their intended joints. Spying the Vandal banners in the distance, Gunderic joined his king in retreat, leaving hundreds of dead and dying Vandal warriors on the battlefield.

"Coward!" I yelled angrily, seeking to taunt the man into a rash action.

Before melding into the crowd, Gunderic turned back to face me. Raising a blood-soaked glove to his chest, Gunderic mimed a broken heart, frowning sadly at me before his horse began a gallop.

Any remaining semblance of organization collapsed, as those Vandals too slow to retreat were reduced to tiny pockets of resistance. Samur's Huns thundered at the outskirts of the battle as they shot arrow after arrow at the routed Vandals, prying a small number of victims but otherwise unable to impede Gelimer's retreat west. As midday broke, the battle at Ad Decimum drew to a close, leaving Belisarius alone the master of the road to Carthage.

THE GATES OF CARTHAGE

Our victory at Ad Decimum was so swift and so complete that even Belisarius did not recognize the incredible turn of fortune. With few men raising cries of victory, Belisarius immediately dispatched a thousand riders under Bessas to ascertain John's whereabouts and mount a rescue if necessary. Valerian ordered riders to scout the countryside around Carthage, seeking any hint of further ambush from Gelimer, though they found nothing but stragglers and a Vandal army in full flight westward.

Few Vandal captives had not acquired serious wounds. The few dozen arrested by Belisarius were dragged back to the battlefield as he considered their fate, while small bands took it upon themselves to ferry Roman wounded away from the blood and shit that stained the fields, while offering a mercy stroke to those Vandals who lay twitching, yet alive. Altan explained later that many of the mortally wounded Vandals offered notes of gratitude as daggers and swords were lowered over their hearts, clutching at weapons but offering no resistance as the killing blow ended their suffering.

With our task complete, I ordered two dozen Herulians to accompany Fulcaris to retrieve our dead in the fight against

Gibamund. Irilar and six others were carried back—a miracle given the ferocity of the Vandal attack—with my men carefully cradling each of the bodies as if they were fragile babes. Weeping once more, Fulcaris offered a rich cloak and a half dozen intricate golden chains from Gibamund's body, yet I insisted that Fulcaris keep the bounty for himself. Other plunder was divided into equal portions between the Herulians, Huns, and Goths, the thousands of Vandal dead leaving behind enough wealth from a century of domination over the Romans and Mauri of Africa to make each of my men far wealthier than they could have hoped for.

Still wary, Belisarius sent riders to summon the remainder of his army that took no part at Ad Decimum. Others circled the Roman formation as tallies of wounded and dead were accounted for, leaving Belisarius busy as he set up a makeshift command post along the road. Amidst this uneasy relief, I heard distant shouts of anger and pain. I raised my horn to my lips in warning of another attack. Yet, as I found the noise emanating from a formation of Goths, I resisted summoning Belisarius, dropping the horn back into Ignis' saddle and trotting toward the source of anguish. Sembrouthes and Xerxes followed close behind, their features equally concerned at the sounds of fresh violence.

We found Indulf smashing a studded mace into the bodies of disarmed Vandal captives. A half dozen Ostrogoths joined in on the brutalization of perhaps twice their number, while the overwhelming majority of Indulf's men looked away from the torture, their faces green with sickness and disgust.

"Lord Indulf!" I screamed in rage. "What have these men done to deserve such treatment?"

"They are Vandals, the enemy," he replied. "They killed a few dozen of my men and tortured several others like Wulfila, who you saw on the signpost. I am repaying their hospitality with my own."

"At least we gave you Gothic shits a chance to fight back, coward!" one of the Vandals spat in crude Latin, his eye socket cracked and oozing blood. "Even those we captured skulking about our lands."

Indulf raised his mace for another blow. He would have continued in that manner for hours had I not drawn my own blade, leveling it at his exposed throat.

"Withdraw your weapon, Lord Indulf," I said slowly, "and allow the prisoners to be placed in General Belisarius' care."

"Fool," Indulf replied. "You would kill me, your ally? My men would roast you on a spit for your treachery."

"They can try," I replied, hearing Xerxes and Sembrouthes draw their weapons in turn. "But you'll be dead long before me if you keep making threats. I am giving you a chance to forget this unhappy episode, but I'll need you to drop the mace and allow the Vandal prisoners to go free."

Indulf turned his gaze upon me, pausing for several heartbeats. He spat angrily onto the ground as he complied, muttering orders in the Gothic tongue that brought his men to stand down.

"Lord Varus, the tender-hearted one," Indulf said. "Do you think these dogs would offer the same treatment if given the chance?"

"I would hope so," I replied optimistically. "But I pray that fate may never befall anyone, neither you nor myself."

Pointing at several of the younger Ostrogoths, Indulf growled orders. The men raised those Vandals still living and carried their bodies over to the rest of Belisarius' Vandal captives. Turning away from Indulf's rage, I sheathed my sword, careful lest the men see my hand shaking as I drew my cloak over my body.

"You shouldn't have angered him," Sembrouthes whispered to me. "Who knows if he'll retaliate against you later."

"He won't," I lied, unconfident in my professed answer. "And besides, I have you to guard me."

Sembrouthes sighed. "You never make my task any easier."

Trotting back to Belisarius, the growing ease of the army was suddenly disrupted as a horn blew from up the road to Carthage. Belisarius ordered his men back into lines, a precaution that was soon deemed unnecessary as Roman banners emerged from Ad Decimum's narrow defile. Led by Bessas and John, they blew their horns again in triumph, with many of John's men decorated in thick robes and heavy gold.

Abandoning decorum, Belisarius mounted his horse and galloped hard to his boyhood companion. Following close behind, I found Belisarius laughing as John exclaimed his successes, his body covered in cloaks that would have been more befitting of Justinian himself.

"My enemy was Ammatas, brother of Gelimer," John said. "The fool took Carthage's entire garrison and galloped ahead with only a hundred men to prepare an ambush. He killed most of my initial scouts but was overrun before the rest of his forces could come to his defense."

"And the rest of Ammatas' men?" Belisarius asked, finally relaxing his shoulders and head.

"Dead or captive," John declared. "If the captives can be believed, Carthage is virtually undefended. Gelimer's scouts found Ammatas' body, and it seems like the Vandal king fell into a deep shock."

Belisarius bowed his head. "That would make more sense than willingly abandoning the momentum of battle after taking Ad Decimum's hill," he declared. "Varus' men took down Gelimer's nephew as well."

Other reports from Vandal captives validated John's account and Belisarius' theories. Several near Gelimer noted the king's intense grief as he encountered the mangled body of Gibamund, and inconsolable shock after being informed of Ammatas' death. Rather than seek vengeance, Gelimer ordered many of his men to begin building pyres for the slain Vandal lords, a fool's task given the difficulty of procuring lumber in the midst of battle.

Though savage in battle, the Vandals proved surprisingly docile and cooperative in captivity, with all attempts of escape ceasing after Belisarius provided their first meal under Roman captivity. Water was made available for washing as well as drinking, with many scouring away layers of blood and grime as they cleaned themselves of battle. In my surprise, I found most of the Vandals to be relatively pale in their features, their skin artificially darkened by the African sun. Though not nearly as pale as the near-translucent Gepids, the Vandals seemed more a people of the far north, where the sun remained weak year-round and ice prevented the land from yielding crops for sustenance. Yet here, thousands of Gelimer's people remained, resigned to their fate as prisoners of Justinian.

"In Vandal culture, when a man is defeated in battle, all his followers and wealth are by rights the property of the victor," one man named Guntarith explained later. "General Belisarius defeated many Vandal lords and by right is our master as a result."

By late afternoon, the remainder of Belisarius' army arrived in Ad Decimum. Voices of incredulity and jubilation rose from the men as they gaped at the extent of Belisarius' improbable victory, yet strict orders were delivered to avoid goading or insulting our Vandal captives. Both Germanus and Mundus congratulated our officers on their skill, and even Ascum acknowledged the providence that the Fates had bestowed upon Belisarius, embracing him for plucking the army again from certain defeat. Baduarius alone appeared unhappy at the result, unable to test his skills against a Vandal in battle and worrying that the war would be over before he would have any further chances to do so.

It was Liberius alone who looked upon the road ahead. "If what John says is true, then the most important city on this continent is undefended by any Vandal garrison and abandoned by Gelimer."

Bessas nodded. "No Vandals went north, only west. They likely went to Hippo Regius, the only other wealthy city under Vandal control."

Liberius smiled warmly. "Well, then, what are we waiting for?"

Even with no impediment facing the army, ten miles that late in the day was a daunting task for any army—let alone one that had just experienced the rigors of battle. After teams were assigned to attend to Rome's dead and wounded, Belisarius admitted to the wisdom of Liberius' strategy and the need to close in on Carthage as soon as possible. When asked about assigning a rearguard to protect the critical crossroads of Ad Decimum as well as to see to a formal and respectful treatment of the Vandal dead, including Ammatas and Gibamund, it was Thurimuth who volunteered for the task.

Hearing Thurimuth's words, I enthusiastically supported his request. Belisarius left him with five hundred warriors to oversee the task. As Thurimuth bowed in acknowledgment of the order, Belisarius also conferred Thurimuth's promotion to komes, arguing that a leader of so many men could not remain a mere centurion.

Other promotions were conferred onto Samur and Perenus. Aided by John, Belisarius called both men to his tent.

"Samur the Herulian and Perenus of Lazica," Belisarius said, gesturing to both amidst fifty assembled officers. "You have acquitted yourselves with honor and distinction. With the Emperor's blessing through his legate, the honorable Liberius, you are both raised to the rank of komes as well."

Perenus beamed, shifting from side to side, while Samur simply grinned at me. As with Thurimuth, Belisarius offered an explanation of what the promotion entailed.

"Perenus, you will command the Herulian foederati and obey Varus in all things. You shall name a second-in-command to aid you in this task."

"Fulcaris is my choice, General."

"Granted," Belisarius said. "Although he may wish to remain at Ad Decimum to stand vigil over his brother?"

Fulcaris refused. "With your permission, Lord, I would have Irilar carried in a wagon to Carthage. There, I intend to honor him with a pyre."

"May Irilar know peace in the afterlife," Belisarius replied, turning his attentions to my brother. "Samur, you have guided the Huns under Sinnion and Aigan in a manner that would have made Sunicas proud. You shall continue these duties formally and better enable your brother to fulfill the army's needs."

"That's a tall task, if you know my brother." Samur winked, earning a laugh from Belisarius.

Despite his japes, Samur basked in the praise of Belisarius, of

Liberius, and dozens of others. His cheeks reddened at the mention of Sunicas—rendering Samur bashful under the weight of so much praise. I was the last to offer my congratulations, grasping him by both shoulders.

"Who would have thought two palace slaves would have made it this far?" I asked.

"Certainly not me."

We embraced. After so many seasons of turmoil—of Tauris and Callinicum, and of the horrors of Barbalissus, it was a rare moment of peace. And even though it was fleeting, it was as sweet as any I can recall.

Riders were dispatched to Thapsus, Hadrumetum, and Caput Vada—the lattermost responding with small boats that ferried Antonina, Rosamund, and Sergius' men to our position near Ad Decimum. Rosamund's skills were in fast demand—she gaped annoyingly at my bruised head, unwilling to be dissuaded by my insistence that it was a minor wound.

"Injuries along the skull are tricky," Rosamund explained. "I watched my grandfather treat terrible injuries with cracked bone, and the victim recovered swiftly and without complication. Others are minor, almost imperceptible, but cause death. You must inform me if you feel off, even if only for a brief time."

"Of course." I shrugged. "But there are others who would benefit more from your help now."

I should have listened and allowed Rosamund to more closely inspect my wound. I felt as if my legs possessed no strength, and the world around me swam like a river. Instead, I sent Rosamund first to the foederati, and later to John's cataphracts, knowing well that despite the battle's brevity, there were a range of hurts that would fester without her trained eye. Though Cephalas and a pair of Herulian guards trailed Rosamund through our camp, I joined her as she cared for several of my Heruli, watching as they gazed upon her with reverence. As with Samur in Antioch, she prayed as she mixed powders, applied poultices, or set bones straight. Nearly all accepted her care with hearty praise, although one man of John's cavalry spat in derision as Rosamund inspected a hobbled foot.

"Get away from me, witch!" the cataphract yelled.

Rosamund was unperturbed by the accusation, having borne the same criticism many times in service to the Empire. "The bones of your foot are splintered. If I don't correct them, you will limp for the rest of your days."

"I'll take my chances," the cataphract argued. "Thou shalt not suffer a witch to live!"

I hustled between Rosamund and the warrior, recognizing that ancient biblical passage. "Rosamund is a healer, not a witch. And if you're so keen on dying, perhaps I'll be the one to aid you!"

"Better than to accept favors from a sorceress," the warrior spat. "You're fortunate that Belisarius allows you to reside in our camp."

My fingers wrapped into a fist, yet Rosamund tugged on my arm. "Varus, he's in pain. If he needs help later, all he needs to do is ask."

"Perhaps," I spat, my face coming within a hand's length of my enemy.

"Witch lover," the cataphract mumbled. "You should be ashamed of yourself, Varus!"

Most others accepted Rosamund's aid with gratitude or even shared in her prayers. As my vision blurred and my stomach roiled, the cataphract's curses melded in my mind with those of Hermogenes.

Witch lover!

Scion of sin!

I slept badly that evening, waking to vomit in the middle of the night, yet refused to warn Rosamund of my need. Instead, I returned to Belisarius' side the following morning, leaving Rosamund and her swelling band of followers to trail about Belisarius' camp.

A more prudent strategy would have been to consolidate our victory and scout Gelimer's forces to anticipate their next maneuver. Still, drunk on another impossible victory against an ancient and hated foe, morale and excitement were far too high to contain. Instead, Belisarius and John ordered the army's vast column forward within ten days of the battle, our progress winding around Carthage's vast inland lake.

Though Liberius and Father Petrus joined Belisarius and John at the head of the column, I opted to remain with my men, surrounded by Samur, Rosamund, Perenus, Cephalas, Sembrouthes, and Xerxes, all of whom consoled a grieving Fulcaris. In all my years, I had never felt more invincible than at that moment, even as my head swelled and pounded from my previous injury and my muscles screamed for the distant relief of sleep.

Evidence of such incredible momentum was the singing. Without instruction, spontaneous song rose across the ranks, a Greek tune that praised Alexander's exploits as he took his army far into Persia. Xerxes rolled his eyes at the tune but appreciated the compliment of Immortal valor, the song describing Alexander's battles with the Zhayedan as deciding the fate of the world. Even Rosamund asked Cephalas to teach her the lyrics as thousands of Romans sang in horrible pitch and worse intonation. Her normally frail and wispy voice formed a soft harmony amidst a sea of cracking tones, resembling more a herd of bleating sheep than a chorus of men.

Rumors flooded through the ranks that the Romans had only sustained two hundred casualties against thousands of Vandals slain or captured, adding depth to the singing as our noise filled the African twilight. Even the Visigoths and the Suevi in far-off Hispania must have heard our racket, though none cared as months of tension in the face of an unbeatable enemy was released from a single morning of combat.

The outline of Carthage came into view as the sun dipped below the horizon, its orange rays illuminating the city as a signal for all our desires. Our song was interrupted only in the moments when Belisarius ordered a camp raised along the city's outskirts, noting the limits and dimensions of the defenses and tents that would house the army for at least one evening. Valerian inquired why the army would not continue on to Carthage itself, an urgency echoed by many amongst the army's leadership.

"Because we don't know if any traps await us," Belisarius reasoned, "and spending one evening outside of Carthage will provide a fuller understanding of the area."

Many protested halfheartedly, but none disobeyed the victor of both Ad Decimum and Dara. Instead, under a half mile from Carthage's walls, Justinian's army encamped outside of the jewel of Africa, a city so lost to Constantinople that it had befallen more myths and legends than any attainable goal. Finding Liberius, I stood alone with the legate as we gazed at that timeless city, and I smiled as I imagined Justin watching from the afterlife as his dreams finally bore the sweetest of fruit. Liberius said nothing as we gazed onward, ignoring the grunts and laughter of the rising camp behind us as the lights of the city illuminated the darkness along the African coastline.

Until, curiously, the gates of Carthage swung open. Though the legate remained oddly still, I jerked in alarm, intending to run into the camp to raise the alarm of an impending attack. Liberius grabbed my arm, raising his other hand as he again pointed to Carthage.

"Look," Liberius said in awe. "Listen."

It was dull at first, almost indecipherable. As Liberius grinned, I strained my ears toward the noise rising from the vast city, hearing only a thrum in the distance as I shook my head in confusion.

And then, as vast and ancient eagles and Chi-Rho of the Western Roman Empire rose into the sky, I heard it. The same song that our army had belted for hours echoed from the walls of Carthage, its gates open and welcoming of their long-lost brethren. The song grew clearer as more along Carthage's walls joined the effort, their bodies tiny figures from the half mile of distance that separated us. More Roman banners raised along the many towers of the walls as those of the Vandals were cut down, falling into the dirt and grass without a note of pomp or ceremony.

Belisarius was soon alerted, and he stood and gaped with the rest of us at the sign of Carthage's welcome for the Roman army. Even Father Petrus begged him to continue onward to meet the people, yet a beaming Belisarius still declined.

"Tomorrow will come soon enough," Belisarius replied soberly. "For now, we wait and watch, and make sure of our safety."

While some, like Perenus, snored noisily in their tents, I doubt that many traded the experience of the Carthaginian welcome for the allure of sleep. Some even joked of sneaking off toward the African capital, though none seriously considered robbing Belisarius of the honor of stepping foot into Carthage and returning its people to the bosom of Constantinople.

The only notable distraction from our reverie was the funeral pyre of Irilar, with hundreds of Herulians and Huns gathered several hundred yards from Belisarius' camp. Dozens of men were assigned to gather branches and logs to form a raised pedestal for the deceased, which, when completed, rose nearly the height of a man as it held Irilar's body up the cloud-strewn sky.

Amidst the backdrop of Carthage's continued singing, Rosamund carried a flaming torch from the Roman camp toward the massed kindling. Even Ascum, who had great reason to fear the dangers of fire, joined in the gathering, his status as the highest-ranking pagan in Belisarius' army well known by most. As hundreds of the pagan foederati circled around Irilar's pyre, Rosamund began to speak.

"We, standing in this ancient land that existed before our first breaths and that will remain long after we take our lasts, honor Irilar, who was taken from us."

Rosamund glided astride the pyre, gracefully climbing its branches as she stood over Irilar's prone form. Fulcaris wept again as his cousin was memorialized, with Rosamund commending his soul to a blissful afterlife and away from the pain of sickness and death.

"Do not weep or fear, for Irilar feels no more pain!" Rosamund shouted. "Instead, his memory brings us all closer to the gods, in reminder that they are mighty, and we are as insignificant as grains of sand on a beach."

Rosamund looked down upon Irilar's face, closing her eyes as she muttered words of prayer. Then she turned back to the enraptured crowd, completing her eulogy.

"Irilar was a brave soldier and a loyal friend," Rosamund concluded. "He will not be forgotten, and we shall not look upon another like him again."

As Rosamund had been a fixture of Belisarius' army and had saved the lives of many in attendance, none begrudged her reciting the warrior's words of parting. Indeed, dozens called out in response, their emotions fueled by Rosamund's theatrics. The Gepid woman carefully crept down from the pyre and allowed her torch to fall into its stacked branches, the flame slowly catching around Irilar's leather boots.

Rosamund embraced Fulcaris as the fire snaked around the body, its blaze rising as it consumed the vast fuel of dried timber that had been prepared for the moment. Fulcaris clutched hard at Rosamund as the fires rose, blanketing Irilar's form in an impenetrable array of white-hot flame.

Either from the intense heat of the bonfire or from the utter limits of exhaustion, my vision began to blur as the pagans observed the cremation of their fallen comrade. With my temples throbbing, I backed away from the circle, moving twenty paces toward Belisarius' camp and to the cooler air of the African night. As I turned back for one final glimpse of the flames, Rosamund's unsmiling face turned to meet my own, her expression featureless as she locked onto my gaze. Such a thing would have been unremarkable in most circumstances, though as I fixed upon her stare, I recoiled in horror, clutching the cross at my neck.

For I saw the same burning red eyes as the creature in my dream.

In my experiences across the Empire, I have found one universal truth behind human behavior—men and women fear what they do not understand. A thousand explanations could have reasoned away my experience that evening, and others would have happily disregarded these visions as a trick of light or an overstimulated mind. All of which may be true of my experience with Rosamund, and likely are. No amount of rationalization could sweep those angry crimson eyes from my memory, and I left the pillar of fire for the safety of my private tent in Belisarius' camp. An Aksumite sentry looked upon me with concern yet did not follow as I requested privacy, closing the tent flap and ignoring further questions.

Alone, I unfastened my helmet and tugged hurriedly at the iron and leather armor that covered my body. The pounding in my head intensified as I stumbled into the darkness, freeing myself of the greaves, vambraces, boots, and gloves that had accompanied me into the battle at Ad Decimum.

Delirious, I prayed to God as images of the men who had fallen at my hand filled the room, begging forgiveness of the numerous sins that had marked my life. I prayed that I had not damned my soul by granting fertile opportunity for paganism to spread in Belisarius' army, and that my sins would not be paid upon Zenobia or my unborn child. Through it all, God remained silent, leaving me to be tormented by visages of Marcian and Hakhamanish, their eyes twinkling the same burning red as they mocked my fear.

As my chest tightened and limbs grew numb, a muffled noise sounded from the tent's entrance. Suddenly aware of my lack of arms or armor, I felt blindly for my cache of weapons, plucking my axe and raising it against the unseen intruder. The tent flap opened as Rosamund slinked into the darkened space, her long white hair getting tangled in the woolen tent cloth before she painfully tugged it free.

"Varus?" Rosamund whispered, her voice tinged with fear.

Clutching my axe, I backed away from the creature, my head throbbing to the point of near blindness. "Stay back!"

Rosamund raised her hands as she had many times before. "Varus, everything is okay, everyone is safe," she cooed. "Put down the axe and let me look at you. You've been behaving strangely all evening."

I began to shake my head, yet the pulsing paralyzed me with pain. Groaning, I slowly sank to the floor as Rosamund ducked her head from under the tent flap, shouting orders for a servant to fetch her box of powders and herbs. Returning inside with a candle, Rosamund gasped as the flickering light unveiled the extent of my injury, giving her the courage to approach my crumpled form.

"Stay back…" I muttered weakly, my free hand reaching once more for the cross at my neck, the axe clattering harmlessly to the ground.

In the height of confusion, my fingers missed the cross and clasped onto Rosamund's thin arm, causing her to take my head into her lap. As servants returned with the medicines and a pitcher of cool water, Rosamund cleaned the burning flesh along my hairline, her touch an agony as I attempted to jerk free. Not to be denied, Rosamund pulled a jar from her box, upending the liquid onto my lips. I sputtered most of the foreign-smelling material, its scent smelling heavily of earth and bark, though some inevitably found its way into my throat. Rosamund stroked my hair as she bade me to sleep, an order that I reluctantly obeyed. The last thing I remember of that evening was a faint murmur of the magus' laughter, the darkness consuming my vision as I finally surrendered to my fate.

I awoke early the following morning, my body transferred to its cot and wrapped in fresh clothing. Thick bandages were tied around my head like a padded if overtight helmet, the flesh underneath expressing a burning itch. Sitting up, I tugged at the bandages, only to be chastised by a voice in the tent's corner.

"Don't do that," Samur warned. "It took Rosamund most of the night to clean that wound. The last thing you need is for the skin to rot with infection."

Moaning from stiff limbs, my eyes slowly came to Samur's outline. Illuminated by a small collection of tapers along the tent's edge, Samur's haggard face was framed by dark circles under his eyes and the same clothing and furs as the prior day. He showed no sign of fatigue or irritation as he watched my movements, jumping to his feet as I moved to sit up at the edge of the bed.

"You took a nasty blow. It made Rosamund weep to look at it," Samur said. "If you'd have gotten treatment earlier, it wouldn't have been a problem."

"M'fine," I grunted. "What time is it?"

"Midmorning, or thereabouts," Samur replied. "Liberius and the old priest came to see you around dawn and left after Rosamund assured your recovery."

"And the army?"

"Still camped outside Carthage, by Belisarius' order," Samur answered. "Belisarius also asked for you, although Rosamund asked that I send him away."

I shook my head, loosing another bout of pounding head pain. "Help me up. I'll go see him now."

Samur refused at first, asking me to rest and leave the army to the toil of others. When I stubbornly refused, he helped me don my cloak and belt, dressing me in the semblance of a Roman soldier despite the lack of armor. I did strap my sword to my belt, however, the weighty scabbard offering a sense of reassurance and completeness as Samur helped me from the tent and into the fresh air beyond.

Belisarius was not difficult to find despite the ongoing hive of activity in the camp. He smiled as I approached, Samur following closely behind, keeping an arm next to my body.

"I'm glad to see you up!" Belisarius exclaimed. "Rosamund had said that you require several days to recover."

"Recovery can wait," I answered sarcastically. "You wanted to see me, Lord?"

Belisarius sighed as he shook his head. "You need to take better care of yourself, Varus, as we discussed after Dara. Take care of your wounds, or you'll be of no use to anyone."

I bobbed my head in acknowledgment, saying nothing. Belisarius chuckled and drew close to inspect my bandaged head, nodding at Rosamund's craftsmanship.

"But since I can't convince you to follow sound medical advice, I thought you'd like to join me at Carthage."

"Of course, Lord," I replied, "but why have you waited so long?"

Belisarius grin turned into a hearty chuckle. "How ungrateful you must think me if you'd assume I'd leave my third-in-command behind while I took all the glory of conquest for myself! I waited for you, of course."

I attempted to bow again, yet my head swirled and I lost my orientation. Samur's hands grasped immediately at my wavering arms, steadying me once more as Belisarius grabbed a chair for me to rest upon.

Belisarius shook his head once more. "I could command you to return to your rest for as long as Rosamund recommends."

"You may never see me again at that rate." I smiled weakly. "Rosamund would definitely abuse that power. I am fine, Lord, just dizzy is all."

"Very well," Belisarius replied. "Our delegation leaves at midday, if you are able to ride your horse."

Despite my unspoken fears of staying balanced atop Ignis, I found that task relatively simple as long as the pace was kept to a slow trot. Rosamund huffed and pouted when she saw my preparations for the final journey to Constantinople, begging and cursing me to heed her guidance for once in my life. Grinning, I offered instead for Rosamund to join me atop her own mount, to which she made a show of considerable reluctance and frustration at the request. Rosamund yipped in joy as she donned her own mail and blackened robes and joined Samur and me near the front of the camp, awaiting Belisarius' signal to complete our final journey to Carthage.

Still wary of a potential ambush, Belisarius left half of the army in camp under the command of Germanus. Rather than be perturbed at being left behind, Germanus instead showed signs of relief, not caring for such displays of pomp.

"Better you than me," Germanus said to John and me as Belisarius' request was distributed. "It'll give me time to catch up on my reports to Justinian. That man sends more mail than is polite, even if he is my cousin."

With Belisarius leading the army, we followed the double-wide Roman road to the city, finding evidence of John's victory over Ammatas as we progressed closer to the open gates. Booming horns and sweeping displays of song rang down upon Belisarius' soldiers, the Imperial flags waving vigorously along Carthage's ramparts. My foederati chatted excitedly amongst themselves as praise was heaped upon their heroics, the sound of joy and love a far departure from the scorn held by many in Constantinople for the foreign-born.

Even Fulcaris smiled sadly as a troop of Carthaginian children slipped out of the city gates and ran onto each side of the army's column, distributing flowers as signs of welcome. One auburn-headed girl of no greater than eight years handed one such yellow flower to Fulcaris, thanking him in a Latin dialect unfamiliar to Herulian ears. Fulcaris nodded in thanks as he pressed the gift to his face, offering a silver coin in trade.

Ten paces from the city gates, Belisarius ordered a halt to the column. Offering a formal salute, the swell of excitement momentarily reduced its volume as Belisarius addressed those city leaders who remained after the Vandal departure, their faces confused yet joyful as the Emperor's emissary formally joined Carthage back to the Empire.

"Children of Rome, your long bondage is over!" Belisarius boomed in his formal and flowery Latin. Those along the city walls erupted into further cheers, which he politely allowed to swell and diminish before continuing.

"We, soldiers of the Emperor Justinian, have shed blood for your liberation, which is long overdue," Belisarius said. "But our work is not complete. As we continue our conflict against your Vandal oppressors, know that any grievance will be given my utmost attention, and all food and goods acquired for the army's use will be repaid above their market value. In the presence of the Emperor's legate, the honorable Minister Liberius, I, General Flavius Belisarius, magister militum of the Armies of the East, swear these oaths to you with God as my witness."

And so, to the euphoria of thousands whose parents and grandparents knew nothing but slavery and fear, we entered Carthage. The wounds along my scalp burned and pounded amidst the din, though nothing could ruin that moment of jubilation. As

I crossed the threshold into Carthage, I gave thanks to God and whispered the names of those who dared to hope that such dreams could come true yet were no longer here to take succor in the blazing light of the Empire. For Irilar, Alaric and Opilio, Sunicas and Simmas, Barzanes, Dagisthaeus, Isaacius, and most of all the Emperor Justin, whose dream remained alive in the tears of joy shed by Father Petrus, Liberius, and me most of all.

THE RETURN OF TZAZON

Fate afforded us a woefully brief respite to celebrate along Carthage's forums. Overlooking the city's famed and ancient docks, Belisarius brought the army's senior leadership toward a raised dais, welcoming Liberius, John, and myself to embrace hundreds of Carthaginians who thronged close to their beloved general. Many began shouting his name in a cheer that was quickly echoed by those within the army, a call of victory that had been absent in the stunningly brief victory at Ad Decimum.

Thanks largely to the ruminations of Procopius, one of the more famous details of Belisarius' entry into Carthage was his subsequent march to the city's vast palace. Overlooking the sea, that palace dated from Carthage's reconstruction under Julius Caesar himself, engineered and decorated for lightness and openness in contrast to the shadowy and secretive Imperial Palace in Constantinople.

Accompanied only by his more senior officers, Belisarius was led by a delegation of the city's leaders to the golden throne that sat on an elevated platform in the Palace's Great Hall, still fixed with the trappings of the Vandal kings. Though Belisarius protested mightily at approaching that throne, the leaders of Carthage insisted upon its symbolic value, begging him to formally claim the reintegration of Carthage in the Emperor's name.

To avoid undue rudeness Belisarius acquiesced, throwing aside Vandal decorations and sweeping aside his crimson cloak before taking his seat. A thousand voices roared at the gesture, with servants even ferrying in a meal that had been intended for Gelimer's consumption after his return from Ad Decimum. Belisarius politely consumed the bread and wine and made sounds of pleasure at the adoration of the Carthaginians, though I could easily tell that he felt uncomfortable with such displays of grandeur in the Emperor's absence.

With so many local officials and commoners wishing an audience with the general's men, we four split our time in different sections of Carthage for the next two days. Accompanied by my household and foederati officers, I was feasted and toasted at a dozen separate celebrations near Carthage's vast port and dockyard, with sailors and merchants alike offering gifts to my men and praise for General Belisarius. In the midst of such polite and occasionally raucous ceremony, I was able to clear space for our transport ships and dromons to safely dock at port, with many of those vessels arriving in the city within the coming weeks.

While Germanus and Thurimuth kept tight rings of scouts to assess signs of movement from the Vandal strongholds in the west, Belisarius slowly put Carthage back into a semblance of order. Though civil authority legally fell upon Liberius, the Emperor's legate contented himself with scouring Carthage's library and resolving the more serious disputes regarding the organization of the new African province.

Belisarius' retinue was left to resolve hundreds of petty disputes regarding the division of Vandal property that had been taken by force a century prior. I can only assume that many such petitions had little merit and were largely driven by greed and opportunity, yet Belisarius gave each petitioner ample time and respect to make their case. He ended each day well after sunset, with even the hundreds of candles and dozens of braziers used to light the palace's rooms burning low before he returned to Antonina and the opportunity for sleep.

Several days passed before Belisarius reassembled his war council in one of the more confined halls within Carthage's palace. Wary of Vandal spies, Belisarius insisted on absolute privacy, the only servants allowed to carry food or fetch parchment being those beyond reproach and well known to the general and legate personally. Leaving Thurimuth temporarily in charge of the Thracian camp, even Germanus was able to attend the summons, his arms sagging from dozens of scouting reports of the Carthaginian hinterlands.

The meeting began innocuously enough, the morale of the men soaring to incredible heights. Many japed about the relative ease of Ad Decimum, boasting that the Vandals were not at all as ferocious as the stories had hinted at. Liberius merely shook his head, not interrupting the bravado, as many deemed the Vandal War all but over.

"I can't believe the battle ended that quickly," John uttered. "No sieges, no long campaign... just one battle."

"And it very nearly cost us everything," Belisarius said. "If Gelimer had been a bit more organized, it might be him toasting over a fire, counting the Emperor's coins and deciding whether to enslave or kill our men."

"But it didn't," Germanus added. "Within a matter of hours, they ran from the field."

"With an intact army," I replied cautiously. "My men killed hundreds when we took the hill at Ad Decimum, but Gelimer has more than enough trained warriors to match us. And next time, he won't be so reckless."

Bessas frowned as he sought to counter my proclamation, insisting that the Vandals lacked any semblance of professional archers or even armored cavalry. Others pointed to weaknesses in Gelimer's capabilities, making the Vandals appear predictable and limited in their ability to project force. Belisarius rose to my defense, his features drawn in concern at the lack of seriousness given to his enemy.

"I saw plenty of fighting at Ad Decimum," Belisarius began. "And the Vandals are talented fighters. Fearless and half mad, but skilled in their art. Though we hold Carthage, we are still the invader here, and Gelimer will not make similar mistakes with his next strike."

"More reason to execute the Vandal prisoners," Indulf muttered, sipping at a goblet of honeyed water. "Less food from our stores, and more reason to sleep safely."

Belisarius closed his eyes as he took several deep breaths. "I thank you for the sacrifices of you and your men, Lord Indulf," he said. "But we will not execute any prisoners. The Emperor intends to rule these people, not eradicate them."

"As you say," Indulf replied deferentially. "But they would easily rise up if given the chance and slit the throats of you and your family as you sleep."

Clenching his teeth for a heartbeat, Belisarius nodded. "This fear is understandable. Which is why we need to seek battle with Gelimer again soon, and before winter closes the campaign season."

Baduarius pounded on the table in approval. "Finally!" he bellowed. "This time, don't leave me with the shit shovelers, though."

With that, Belisarius unveiled his broader strategy to force Gelimer into battle. Scouts had tracked the Vandal army split between Hippo Regius and Bulla Regia, which Liberius had cautioned was a traditional Vandal strongpoint.

"Gelimer will have an easier time recruiting soldiers in Numidia than he did near Carthage," Liberius said. "Fewer Romans and more Vandals and Mauri, who will all be soon receiving ample coin from Gelimer's purse."

Armed patrols under Valerian would harass Vandal supply lines in the region yet also avoid pitched battle where at all possible and seek to retain the love and respect of the local civilian population as far as possible. With Valerian's protection, emissaries would soon discreetly meet with the Mauri tribes of the interior, seeking to draw them in alliance with Justinian and reject the overlordship of the Vandal nobles.

By sea, Belisarius divided his naval forces into two separate cohorts. A smaller force would sail southeast for Tripolis and Leptis

Magna, occupying the cities and requesting further assistance from garrisons in neighboring Roman Cyrenaica. Second, the larger section of dromons would be dispatched to block the return of Tzazon from Sardinia, effectively preventing thousands of Gelimer's elite forces from joining a final battle against Gelimer's African forces. In such duties, a smaller detachment of dromons would sail for Lilybaeum, the Vandal outpost in Sicily and further bulwark against Tzazon's attempts to sail around the Roman blockage of Sardinia.

Amidst the approval of the officers, Procopius recorded each detail with zeal, readying coded messages to send back to the Emperor in Constantinople on the first ship leaving port. I made a note to write additional letters to the Empress and Mariya, as my previous letters from Hadrumetum had become far outdated, and I did not trust Procopius to relay the whole truth to the Imperial capital.

It was an excellent strategy. So excellent that few found reasons to doubt their general, who put the orders into place that very same day. As far as war strategies go, it fell apart almost as soon as the dispatch riders exited Carthage's gates and ports.

For Tzazon had already set sail from Sardinia, and Gelimer had reinforced Mauri loyalty by taking hostages from dozens of their leading families. This alone was concerning, and sure enough, within a week of Ad Decimum, the specter of doubt and treachery crept across the Roman army.

All rumors, until substantiated by evidence of one's senses, should be treated as the warrantless gossip that they are. These rumors emerged from the throats of hateful men and women who sought to destroy with words just as any army would kill and conquer with the sword. The worst rumors could wreak far more devastation than Attila's Huns ever could. For Belisarius, that rumor was the wavering allegiance of the Huns, who were tempted by offers of gold and freedom by the Vandal king.

And, as with most persistent rumors, concern of the Huns was founded by kernels of truth. Few of our remaining Hunnic foederati had hailed from the time of Sunicas and Simmas, whose

THE GATES OF CARTHAGE

THE GATES OF CARTHAGE

total devotion to Belisarius had instilled an unshakable loyalty from each of the Hunnic riders. Though still pagan and committed to destruction and plunder, these men had risen to be Belisarius' elite, who drew the army from its moments of utter peril and toward improbable victory. The more recent recruits were as vicious and capable as their predecessors, yet few had spent much time with the general, nor did Sinnion or Aigan command blind respect with their mere presence.

Most of all, many of those recent entrants to the Hunnic foederati feared being sacrificed in battle. Or worse—to be abandoned at some remote edge of the world as bodyguards, wasting away on an African desert instead of riding along the endless plains of the steppe. Many had turned to Samur to voice their concerns, and my brother did all he could to assuage their fears, though the grumbling rose as the Huns yearned to return to greener and cooler climates.

These concerns soon reached Belisarius' ears. He assured me of his trust in Samur and overall disregard for gossip, but I could tell that these nagging concerns had infected his mind with worry. Belisarius eventually requested a private meeting with Samur to discuss such matters, at the end of which my brother stormed away from the Carthaginian Palace pulsing in anger. When pressed, Samur merely grunted and shook his head, returning to his men to relay the latest round of orders.

Other veins of misfortune arrived at Carthage within a month of the city's liberation. Led by Tzazon, the Vandal general's fleet escaped from Sardinia amidst heavy fog without suffering noticeable casualties, leaving the Emperor's dromons searching fruitlessly for their escaped enemy. Likewise, an emissary to the Mauri was nearly captured and slain, with Troglita galloping for a day and night until reaching the safety of a Roman outpost. Valerian's scouts confirmed this turn of fate, taking several casualties as various Mauri tribes unleashed their bows against the Emperor's sigil.

By the harvest season, Gelimer's strategy had become plain. Vandal detachments probed the African coastline for signs of

– 453 –

weakness in Belisarius' defenses, sacking villages and destroying mills and bridges that served as the lifeblood of the more provincial African towns. Through it all, Belisarius' Huns were ordered to remain within Carthage as others in the army formed a protective ring along loyal Roman towns of the coastline—a fact that Samur was bitterly aware of in the coming weeks. Roman patrols were dispatched to each instance of Vandal destruction, and even I led several sorties of Herulian foederati, yet only one smaller detachment of Vandals was ever caught.

Finding a dozen Vandals in the midst of rape and plunder of a settlement just thirty miles from Carthage, we killed seven of the raiders outright, while I ordered the remaining five fitted with nooses and hanged from a nearby tree. One of the younger Vandal riders, of perhaps no more than fifteen years, cried for reprieve so fiercely that he nearly persuaded me to spare his life, yet the livid anger of the village's women forced me to harden my heart against a rapist and murderer. As the other Vandals scolded the youth to stop pissing his pants, I ordered two of my Herulians to hang the boy first, showing a modicum of mercy, as his pain would pass sooner. After pronouncing sentences of heinous crimes against the Emperor's subjects, the five Vandals soon left this world, while refugees were escorted back to the safety of Carthage.

Carthage itself was not an easy and tranquil exercise of Belisarius' governing ability. With hundreds of Roman refugees arriving each week, the city's population swelled, raising the cost of grain and other staples to painful heights. Petitioners begged for relief that, when given, was still less than would be desired, leaving few pleased with the Roman army's largesse. Belisarius requested additional support from Constantinople, as well as Rome's cities in Greece and Egypt, though any assistance from governors would not likely arrive until months later.

Thankfully, the strict disciplinary requirements enforced on the army were generally respected. No alcohol or theft or otherwise improper or disrespectful behaviors were tolerated, with Belisarius' officers stressing the need to retain the love of the local people against our shared Vandal adversaries. However, I was forced to address one incident that violated the general's peace, with the offenders falling within my own Herulian foederati.

Despite Belisarius' wishes, it was nearly impossible to prevent soldiers from seeking out wine. This task became doubly arduous when soldiers were garrisoned near a major city, with Carthage receiving several transport ships each week whose cargo holds were filled with barrels and casks of wine from Gaul, Hispania, Italy, and Greece. Seizing an opportunity to raise significant coin, one Carthaginian merchant ferried dozens of wineskins to the quarters of a Herulian detachment, finding two of my men willing to discreetly purchase libations and charging hefty premiums for the luxury of trading in prohibited goods. That alone would likely not have raised the suspicions of the city guards, yet what happened after removed any possibility of a discreet transaction.

The merchant, seeking to line his pockets with weighty sums of the army's silver, threatened to reveal the two men's crime to Belisarius personally, demanding additional payment for his continued silence on the matter. Unused to such sinister treatment, my men immediately beat the merchant and his bodyguards for their insolence, stripping the man naked and releasing him near a less populated corner of the city. Foolishly, the merchant still pressed the issue further, making good on his threat and informing Belisarius of the Herulians' disobedience. After a brief investigation, the wine merchant was found equally culpable of the crime and was levied a heavy financial punishment for his actions, leaving him all the poorer for his efforts.

Belisarius could not be seen to forgive this direct defiance of his orders, regardless of how temptation was forced upon his men. He commanded me to devise a swift and harsh punishment, yet he thankfully insisted that no whipping or other punishment would be required.

Such unhappy duties are an unfortunate requirement of any

military leader. I was not unsympathetic to the pleas of the offenders, whose actions would be permitted within any normal campaign or war. Sindual, their centurion, begged for a reprieve, or at least to share in the burden of punishment as their immediate officer. Belisarius' struggle against Gelimer could not afford the loss of respect or trust from the Carthaginian people, and for that we had to be seen issuing stern justice. Thankfully, an idea from Xerxes allowed me to spare the two of any permanent humiliation or harm, while still providing Belisarius with enough justification that punishment had been meted out.

"In the Zhayedan, any infraction is deemed the fault of the unit, rather than the individual."

Perenus gaped in mock horror. "If Archelaus adopted that form of discipline, Varus and I wouldn't have lived a fortnight."

"A day," I concurred. "But the Persians truly teach in this manner?"

Xerxes nodded. "Our teachers made it clear that the battlefield is a place for cohesive armies, not individuals, and therefore our duty to one another was to collectively shoulder burdens and successes alike."

It made little sense, yet Xerxes' confidence was difficult to ignore. "You're saying I should have the entire unit flogged or hanged for defiance? That seems harsh…"

"You're not listening." Xerxes rolled his eyes. "Use this opportunity to teach as much as rectify. Sindual will honor you for your mercy and will not allow his men to act outside of Belisarius' permission."

Perenus, brushing the horsehair plume of his freshly conferred komes' helmet, shrugged. "If Belisarius didn't specify how to impose discipline, I don't see the harm in following Xerxes' plan."

I surrendered. "You are their komes, and I trust you with the foederati. Work on an appropriate punishment between yourselves, and I will support you."

Leaving the two to their schemes, I did not have long to wait for an answer. Their result might be viewed as comical—if one did not flinch at the hardships Sindual's forty men would bear in their repentance. I agreed, ordering a scribe to dictate the punishment, and signed. Sindual and the two offenders were told few details—only to assemble in Carthage's forum at dawn in full gear. Neither they nor Perenus were disappointed.

"Listen, you ingrates," Perenus growled theatrically, his features framed by dancing flames of nearby braziers, "your command has decided, in their magnanimity, to spare your lives for defying the general."

"Gratitude, Perenus." Sindual bowed. Turning to me, he quickly added, "And to you, Lord Varus."

"However, your actions placed yourselves and all others in the army in grave peril," Perenus lectured angrily. "We are at war, and two of you would rather drink and whore against the general's express fucking wishes!"

Again, the two men bowed and begged forgiveness as Sindual and his men looked on, unmoved. Perenus paced several steps as he allowed the two men to blubber in a mixture of relief and embarrassment, asking for an opportunity to regain Belisarius' trust.

"It isn't your fault!" Perenus yelled, drawing confused looks. "No, it is the fault of your unit, who did not properly guide you. And that will be rectified shortly."

Perenus instructed Sindual that his men would run to the fields of Ad Decimum and back to the Carthaginian Palace within the span of a single day. Sindual nodded as he accepted responsibility, offering gruff and hearty apologies for his failings as centurion. Others seemed less pleased, yet none spoke against any perceived unfairness of the order. To ensure his message was properly received, Perenus ordered that the two offenders take the entire journey from horseback while their comrades continued on foot. I nearly laughed, though I approved of Perenus' logic, ensuring that neither of the two Herulians would ever think of defying an order ever again.

"And I expect not one hair on these men to be harmed!" Perenus warned. "The foederati is one body and one mind. Use this experience as a lesson and return from your trials forgiven of your crimes."

Led by Sindual, each of the Herulians saluted before grabbing their packs and forming into lines outside the walls of the palace. With Perenus, Xerxes, and myself as observers, Sindual began their strenuous run, their rear brought up by the two mounted offenders.

The skies had turned a deep orange as their column returned later that afternoon, their bodies caked in layers of sweat, froth, and dust. To prove their achievement, Sindual handed a broken arrowhead to Perenus upon their return, panting and shivering as he completed his task. Nodding, Perenus offered his reprieve and secretly excused the century from further drill or training on the following day. Though the measures may have seemed cruel, I can happily note that the two offenders were not privately beaten or punished for subjecting their comrades to such strenuous activity, instead performing all duties in an exemplary fashion from that moment on.

As different sections of the Roman army prepared for the next clash with Gelimer, Samur's Huns were offered only the titular duties of ferrying messages to Hadrumetum and Thapsus. No Huns participated in the massive construction efforts to reinforce Constantinople's gates and walls, with Ascum leading efforts to install several of his ballistae along several of the looming towers and fighting platforms. Nor did they join Valerian or Bessas on any of the increasingly hazardous scouting parties, even when the missions turned from simple reconnaissance into more hurried raids to disrupt the Vandal supply lines. Even Indulf and the Goths were given greater responsibility than the Hunnic triumvirate of Samur, Sinnion, and Aigan, whose only distraction on most days was training and drills. Samur did not show any displeasure to his men, yet he voiced considerable frustration to me, questioning why the Huns had been brought to the shores of Africa in the first place.

A welcome distraction of our worries arrived in the form of messages dispatched from Constantinople. While Belisarius received over a dozen, two heftier scrolls were intended for me, with Vitalius retrieving the words excitedly from Procopius' offices.

The first was from the Empress. Uncharacteristically written in her own hand instead of that of Narses, the Empress offered her heartfelt congratulations at the army's considerable fortune, although she cautioned me from overstretching our luck. The Empress went on to describe Justinian's early efforts to rebuild the Hagia Sophia, including reference of sketches from my old weapons master Godilas as an inspiration for an impossibly large dome that capped the most ambitious construction project since the Colosseum of old.

Theodora offered a litany of more minute details. Notes of embassies from both the Visigoths and Ostrogoths, as well as concerns of growing strength of the dozens of Hunnic tribes beyond Roman Tauris. Sadly, Theodora also noted the worsening sickness of Basilius, instructing me that the information should only be shared with the legate, as it would unduly worry Antonina at a moment where Belisarius' wife had no ability to return to care for her father. The Empress also noted additional gold paid to Khosrow to maintain the Eternal Peace as well as curious questions regarding the Zhayedan prince who served under my command. I smiled as I began to note a response, insisting Xerxes' honor was beyond reproach and that any slanders that permeated Constantinople's forums were the construction of more ignorant or jealous minds.

As her letter drew to its conclusion, Theodora warned of the continuing influence of Paulus. After our departure for Caput Vada, the Empress described Justinian's measures to reform his government, including a reduction in prestige of Tribonian and Cassiodorus alike. Surprisingly, Paulus was not reprimanded for any of his failings, although his work in managing the Imperial Treasury had been temporarily simplified by an influx of coin from the thousands of dead heaped into piles and burned outside the capital's massive walls. Paulus' strength would be concerning enough, although Theodora's final warning brought up more immediate concerns for my time in Carthage.

We still do not know the reason for our former enemy's demise, Theodora wrote, speaking by implication of Hermogenes. *Though we have no reason to fear, be vigilant, for I presume that his attacker must be one trained for death and war, and likely resides within Belisarius' forces on our great African expedition.*

These ominous words were swept away by the second letter, its vellum sealed with my own ouroboros and written from Mariya in Pella. Both Zenobia and Joannina seemed to enjoy the vast expanse of my estates at Pella, which had dramatically increased in population as the Ghassanid princess spent considerable gold to house, feed, and care for hundreds of wounded veterans and orphans from Constantinople's riots. Mills were repaired and crops planted, tilled, and harvested, providing further revenue to cover the cost of raising more housing and offering healthy stipends for educators and doctors to care for Mariya's wards. Mariya noted that Tiberius had been sullen and withdrawn at first, but seemed to brighten at the freedom and safety of Macedonia, suppressing the hellish horrors of the Hippodrome into an unpleasant memory.

Nearing the harvest season, Auria had given birth to a healthy son. Both mother and child recovered quickly, with Auria naming her son after Troglita's late father. Mariya happily described little Evanthes as a clear image of his father, already possessing a heavyset nose and a sharp chin. Troglita wept silently when I showed him Mariya's words, later hosting a private feast to thank God for his wife and son.

Mariya's own pregnancy was more ominous, although she appeared to dismiss any hardship. I skimmed her note, my chest thundering as I searched for any hint of worry in Mariya's honeyed words. Upon my first pass, Mariya expressed no imminent danger, yet as I read in more detail, worry swelled in my gut.

While her first pregnancy with Zenobia had been a challenge, Mariya described considerable fatigue throughout the day and nauseous illness at other times. Bouts of pain had given her pause to seek out a doctor, who concluded that little else could be done other than to recommend against overstimulating her days. I considered dispatching Rosamund to Pella on the first ship from Carthage, yet Mariya would likely only send her back with fury at depriving my men of the army's finest healer. Likewise, by the time Rosamund arrived in Pella, Mariya's pregnancy might be well over. I scratched a response to Mariya and prayed for her safety in such a trying time, pressing the scroll to my lips before sealing it with wax and sending Vitalius back down to Carthage's docks.

Memories of triumph had long faded into endless challenge and worry as the harvest season came to an end. However, at a time when the fighting season would normally be exchanged for a season of shelter from the tumult of winter, Gelimer began his reconquest. And rather than an arrogant or overcomplex strategy like what had plagued the Vandal forces at Ad Decimum, Gelimer handed control of the reconquest to his brother Tzazon, veteran of a hundred battles for the Vandal nation.

As the Vandal army massed outside Hippo Regius, Vandal scouts formed a near impenetrable perimeter that thwarted nearly all of Valerian's scouting missions, leaving several to never be heard from again. Those who did return to Carthage told of an entire people on the move, with Gelimer stripping soldiers from all of his Numidian and Mauretanian cities and placing swords into the hands of all Vandal men and boys. Thousands of Mauri flocked to augment Gelimer and Tzazon's swelling forces, fighting on foot rather than with the Vandals atop a horse. Gelimer's army swept against Carthage with alarming sped, with only a week's march separating the Vandal king from his former throne in the Carthaginian palace.

It was at the height of Roman fear of the incoming Vandal horde that Belisarius finally summoned a war council. Forces from the southern coastline were recalled to Carthage, leaving behind only token forces of wounded or civilians to represent the Emperor's interests in Hadrumetum, Thapsus, and Caput Vada. One of those allowed to remain at his post was Solomon, who, arguing that his leadership in Hadrumetum was instrumental in keeping order to the Roman coastline, was given a reprieve from the upcoming battle. However, Solomon was deprived of most of his banda, as Belisarius politely noted that those spearmen were required elsewhere. Solomon obliged the order by transferring temporary leadership to a centurion named Gratian, who had kept Solomon's confidence for years and succeeded Marcian as the komes' second-in-command.

Once in the meeting, he assured that any and all opinions would be fully considered, for no Roman army had faced such dire and unprecedented circumstances since Aetius himself. That meeting did not begin fortuitously. Stotzas, a half Roman who served as a magistrate of Carthage under the Vandal kings, urged Belisarius to surrender the city and evacuate to the eastern regions of Libya.

"When Gelimer comes, he will spare none who sided with the Romans," Stotzas warned. "Tzazon will outnumber you, and he has more battlefield experience than any Roman living. Best to take what spoils can be had and reinforce Tripolis or Leptis Magna."

Others urged for similar strategies. Ascum added his voice to Stotzas', noting the indefensibility of the region.

"The walls have been strengthened, but it would take a year at minimum to repair decades of crumbling stones and decaying gates," Ascum recounted. "Even with ballistae at every guard tower and a thousand archers along the walls, I can't guarantee we'd be able to hold off a massed attack."

Germanus concluded with Ascum's assessment. "My men won't run, but many have no battle experience and have no knowledge of siege craft."

Both Mundus and Troglita bowed to their general's decision, with Mundus advocating for the outright repositioning of those forces to more easily defensible positions at Hadrumetum or Leptis. Troglita, however, did ask that a final attempt be made to join with the Mauri, or even that we seek the support of the Visigoths or Suevi in Hispania for help.

"No chance of that," Valerian concluded abruptly. "The Mauri have fired upon any of my riders who approach them, even those bearing no armor or weapons."

"And even if the Visigoths agreed to support our endeavor, they'd want half of the African provinces as payment," John reasoned. "We'd have fought this whole war for Theudis, who'd love nothing more than to use Vandal soldiers to attack Roman Egypt in two or three years' time."

Baduarius grunted his disapproval. "I haven't raised my sword in anger since we've landed in this heat-buggered place," he complained. "I don't like fighting uselessly as much as anyone else, but Belisarius beat this army in the span of a morning, and without his spearmen! Why would we run when they come back?"

"Because you have too few men," Stotzas replied immediately. "You can't even properly garrison the cities that you have, and even if you defeat Gelimer in the field, you wouldn't have enough men left to control all of the African provinces. Even if you somehow defeat Gelimer and Tzazon's army—and that is a questionable if—you would still lose the war."

Anger rose like bile within the closed confines of the council chambers. Baduarius accused Stotzas of cowardice, hinting that the half Roman's rumored Vandal blood tugged at his loyalties to Belisarius and the Emperor. Samur rose in support of Baduarius' claim, complaining that the disrespect shown to his Hunnic foederati should have been placed upon the Romans of Carthage for their lack of support in our struggles. Stotzas snarled as the Thracian officers defended their position, their thoughts joined by Bessas, who feared that heavy losses of cataphracts would deprive Belisarius' forces of any advantage beyond the next battle. Perenus and I remained silent as more officers joined in the disagreement, with even Thurimuth suggesting that a more organized retreat was preferable to a prolonged siege within a city of few resources a thousand miles distant from Constantinople.

Amidst the cacophony, however, it was Liberius who silenced debate. The much older legate's words were initially lost in the scrum, yet they soon became discernable as the warring parties drew back in silence. Belisarius' eyes remained fixed on Liberius as Baduarius and Stotzas finally ceased their confrontation, ceding the floor to the legate.

"I wonder," Liberius began, pausing for an extended time as his gaze scanned a map resting along the table before him. "What have we learned of Gelimer thus far?"

"Little," Indulf answered gruffly. "He is distrustful of others."

"Ah, but that teaches us quite a bit," Liberius countered. "If Gelimer distrusts many, who does he take counsel from?"

"His relatives," John replied. "Two of which are now dead, thanks to our intervention at Ad Decimum."

Liberius bobbed his head as he winked at John. "Gibamund and Ammatas. I wonder, does he have any others that he trusts?"

Stotzas rolled his eyes at the exercise. "As we've said repeatedly, Lord, Tzazon is the officer to be concerned with. Gibamund was hardly a man at eighteen years, and Ammatas had the tiniest portion of Tzazon's experience or ability to command."

Liberius smiled. "Yes, forgive me, old fool that I am, with little knowledge of war," he said. "But how did we previously deprive Gelimer of his trusted relatives?"

"We killed them." I grinned knowingly, realizing Liberius' intentions. "Vandal commanders led from the front lines—and died in their attacks."

"Ah, but of course!" Liberius' eyebrows arched. "And what happened when these two unfortunate men were sent to the hell that was prepared for them?"

"Gelimer retreated," Belisarius added in a note of finality. "Even as he held advantage on the battlefield, he paused in certain moments, and fled at the end."

Stotzas sought to interject at the insanity of a military strategy dependent upon the death of a single man, yet Belisarius was soon convinced of Liberius' wisdom. None spoke as Belisarius rendered his judgment that he would stand and fight against Gelimer, using the agility and flexibility of his own forces against the more ponderous Vandal hordes. Even Ascum pounded on the table before him as all backed Belisarius' intentions, with only John holding the courage to ask a nagging question.

"But what if Gelimer doesn't retreat?" John asked just prior to the meeting's closure.

Liberius bowed. "No great venture is without considerable risk," Liberius concluded. "You must decide whether the prospects before you are worth the risk of losing all you hold dear. For as my friend Father Petrus would say, God does not provide the same opportunity twice."

"No indeed," Belisarius concluded. "John, ready the army. Wherever we meet Gelimer and Tzazon, we will decide this war."

THE BATTLE OF
TRICAMARUM

Gelimer's progress slowed as he moved from Numidia toward Carthage, though the effects of the Vandal advance were clearly visible from a string of hundreds of refugees who thronged into Carthage's protective walls. Already overburdened housing swelled to unhygienic levels as Belisarius' men sought to accommodate many who arrived with few possessions and little coin. A recent shipment of grain from Alexandria alleviated the direst concerns of hunger along the city's streets, yet Gelimer's dominance of the rich farmland along the African coastline threatened to incur long-term challenges to the sustainability of Justinian's hold over the region.

Amidst preparations for war, civilians residing within Carthage continued to petition Belisarius for assistance or guidance on any number of mundane topics—a task that Liberius had previously shunned but now engaged with considerable zeal. One topic that garnered Belisarius' personal attention was the protection of any attendants to his army who had no place on the battlefield; those men insisted upon armed protection once Belisarius' forces left Carthage's gates to challenge Gelimer.

Procopius in particular complained of a need for the Emperor's secretary to be assured protection in the event of a Vandal attack, a claim that was laughable in the absence of similar claims by Liberius or Father Petrus. However, Procopius' arguments found weight with Belisarius after Antonina voiced a request to bolster her own security. On a more memorable meeting, Antonina stumbled upon me as I waited in Belisarius' offices for him to return from an inspection of fresh arrows from a Carthaginian fletcher.

"What are *you* doing here?" Antonina said.

"Serving your husband faithfully," I retorted. "What are *you* doing?"

Antonina's face flickered first with shock, and then by a flushed anger. Was there truth to the rumors of her tryst with Sergius? Both Mariya and Rosamund insisted upon it. Though I considered myself seasoned from my years in the palace at detecting scandal, I still did not believe in Antonina's disgrace. She was many things, my former classmate, but an idiot was not among them. Adultery was a heinous crime in the Empire, and doubly so for those women who dared to shame husbands favored by the Imperial Court. Besides, what reason did Antonina have to bring disgrace onto herself? Or to Belisarius? That question yielded nothing but headaches and sapped my will to pursue the issue further. Instead, I opted for belief in Antonina's innocence.

"My business is not your concern," Antonina replied, lifting her chin as if an unpleasant smell emanated from my body.

We waited at opposite sides of Belisarius' office—me near a table piled with maps and Antonina sitting stiffly upon an uncushioned bench that Belisarius favored. After a minute, I realized that the door to Belisarius' office had closed, and I rushed to prop it open. Though I was willing to grant Antonina reprieve from my own suspicions, I was not fool enough to be caught alone, in a closed room, with another man's wife.

Antonina scowled as I paced back to my table, her eyes fixed upon her husband's empty chair. The room was altogether too silent— attempts to quell fidgeting feet only made me more uncomfortable, aware that Antonina silently judged every action I took. The room itself seemed to bake despite its proximity to the sea, and a coat of sweat matted the back of my neck. Through it all, Antonina sat, occasionally straightening a silk dress that could have paid the wages of ten spearmen for a year, stealing glances upon her nails when she suspected that I was not watching her movements.

I had to stymie a sigh of relief when Belisarius arrived. He nodded to me, though he beamed at Antonina. "My love, I hope all is well? I would have come to find you, if you required."

"You're always busy," Antonina complained. "And slaves aren't assertive enough to bring you to me. I require a boon, if you are able."

Belisarius grinned. "Anything."

"You left a centurion named Sergius in charge of my safety when you ventured into Mesopotamia," Antonina explained, "a task he performed adequately. If you could spare the centurion with a hundred men, I would sleep much easier."

Sergius. Again with that man. Again, I suppressed thoughts of impropriety—after all, Sergius and his men had provided dutiful guard over Antonina's household for more than a year. She was a woman who trusted few, and who was I to question her choice of bodyguard?

Belisarius' smile vanished. "My love, I don't have a hundred men to spare, although you will be perfectly safe behind Carthage's walls."

"This city crawls with vermin and worse," Antonina said. "Many who would attack me to hurt you."

"Never!" Belisarius cried. "Besides, I've made arrangements for a ship to ferry you safely to Alexandria should the battle not go as I would wish."

Antonina groaned. "You don't understand how difficult things are when you leave! Give me Sergius and ten men. Such a small number would not be missed."

Belisarius frowned, yet upon further pleas from his wife, he relented. "As you wish. I will write the order as soon as I finish with Varus here."

"Perhaps I could volunteer those too wounded to fight in battle

THE GATES OF CARTHAGE

but still capable of serving as a guardsman?" I offered, wondering whether I could pry Sergius from Antonina's grasp.

"That would not do, not at all," Antonina declared, narrowing her eyes upon me as she continued. "What would men say if the Strategos of the Roman Armies cannot offer more than cripples and broken men to protect his wife? No, Sergius performed his duties admirably, and I would feel more comfortable with him remaining behind."

Outmaneuvered, I made no further attempt to impede Antonina's requests, although did note Belisarius' details regarding the safe evacuation of many within his expedition should Gelimer prevail. The plans included the safe passage of my own household, although I doubted that Rosamund would willingly leave the city without full knowledge of the fates of Samur, Perenus, and myself. Despite the grim possibility, Belisarius' face brightened as he found a way to fulfill Antonina's wishes, an aura that remained with him as he plunged into an extended day of planning and oversight of the army's various detachments.

As the first hints of winter swept through the streets of Carthage, Belisarius' army formed within Carthage's looming forum and prepared for departure. Though this more southerly region possessed a greater warmth and temperance than the Empire's European provinces, bitter winds still required many to don thicker trousers and heavier cloaks for the journey ahead, while our thousands of horses were protected by thick blankets at each stage of the march ahead. Sizeable detachments of scouting forces were sent ahead to shadow Gelimer's advance to prevent any ambush or surprise, as had been the case at Ad Decimum, a task that was denied Samur's Huns in favor of Valerian's lighter horsemen.

There was little celebration or excitement as the army exited Carthage's gates. Father Petrus offered prayers as Liberius and I mounted our horses, retiring to his more comfortable quarters in the nearly vacant palace. Soon thereafter, I offered my farewells to Rosamund and Cephalas, yet both insisted upon following the army's march to battle. Though I was able to convince Cephalas to remain in

Carthage and discreetly note the actions of Sergius, Rosamund flatly refused to be left behind. I made arguments to insist upon her safety, but Rosamund merely ignored my arguments and found a spare horse to transport her belongings before vaulting onto its back.

"If you won't listen to me, then I'm not listening to you," Rosamund replied stubbornly. "So I'm going."

Vitalius was equally as stubborn as Rosamund, although I had even less reason to restrict him from the army's march. Assigned a horse and weapons, Vitalius would not be asked to perform the duties of an enlisted foederati, but he was expected to assist with any needs that I may have regardless of the danger to his person. Still glum due to his exile from Ad Decimum, Vitalius followed just a few paces behind me for fear that I would leave him behind once more, bobbing and smiling anytime one of my officers assigned him even the simplest of tasks.

Our departure from Carthage echoed the hum of fear that filled Carthage's shops and houses at the thought of the return of the Vandals—especially to those spearmen who had been absent at the prior battle. Idle songs filled the first day's march west, following signals of Belisarius' scouts regarding Gelimer's sweep across the coastline. Sleep was a difficult achievement on our first night away from the comforts of the city, and I did not begrudge those men who secreted a wineskin to ease worried souls as they crawled into tents for protection from the elements.

As the skies melded into shades of violet that signaled the daylight soon to come, Vitalius shook me urgently awake. Rushing out of my tent and toward Belisarius', I found others in varying states of undress and fatigue, their features equally perplexed and concerned as we sprinted to attend to Belisarius. Notably, Baduarius ran into the center of camp with his sword drawn and yelling for sign of the enemy, otherwise completely denuded of any clothing. His body was covered in a thick layer of hair that disguised layers of stout muscles underneath, marked occasionally by puckered scars and healed wounds from dozens of fights throughout his life. Taken aback by the sight, I yelled for Baduarius to clothe himself, arguing that Gelimer had not successfully infiltrated our camp. Confused, Baduarius looked upon me with understanding, running clumsily back to his tent in search of trousers that had been discarded in his haste.

Already awake and attired with armor and weapons, Belisarius and John busily positioned markers of Gelimer's forces along another hand-drawn map of the region. Each of the officers was acknowledged as we entered the enclosure, a half dozen fires illuminating our figures as many huddled around the flames for warmth.

"Reports from an hour ago," John began. "Gelimer is a bit more than a half day's ride from our position and marching hard in our direction."

"Through the night?" I asked skeptically.

"Not all, but some of it," John replied. "Tzazon's outriders have been chasing our scouts away, but we've had enough sightings of the main Vandal army to understand their movements."

"What of their strength?" Mundus rasped, clearing his throat of phlegm. "Do they know our movements?"

"Fifteen thousand Vandals, or thereabouts," Belisarius replied calmly. "Perhaps another five to ten thousand Mauri and other mercenaries. We should assume Gelimer knows of our approach, unfortunately."

Baduarius whistled. "Against ten thousand Romans?"

"Eight," Belisarius corrected, "subtracting the dead and wounded from Ad Decimum, garrisons for the coastline, and a larger contingent of those too ill to march or fight."

Baduarius shook his head with a chuckle. "When you're knee deep in shit, the only choice is to pull your way out."

"Or to wash oneself clean of filth in the first place," Troglita replied with a Latin tone befitting an Italian of more noble birth.

Belisarius expressed no patience for the usual banter of his war councils. As Liberius entered the tent, the general called the meeting to order, the sounds of a camp coming to life whirring on all sides of Belisarius' quarters. Uliaris tied the door flap shut and returned to his side, patiently listening for the fateful orders to come.

"This is our best opportunity," Belisarius began, his voice low and uncharacteristically stern. "Gelimer's men will be tired, sore, and hungry. Ours are relatively rested from only a single march. Even better, they know if they lose this battle, Gelimer will show little mercy to any survivors."

"Charming," Ascum grunted, drawing an irritated look from Belisarius before he continued.

"But John is also correct: We need a crushing victory, and to keep our strength intact," Belisarius said. "We need to hit them fast and hard, and with an absolute determination to break Gelimer by destroying his brother."

As he spoke, Belisarius' finger traced a thin westward road from his own forces on the outskirts of Carthage, toward Gelimer's less orderly mass approaching from Hippo Regius. His hand came to a stop on a small town near the center of the two armies. He pounded his hand on the table with determination.

"And we'll crush Gelimer here," Belisarius said, reinforcing his intended destination a short ride away. "At Tricamarum. No lengthy maneuvers, no drawn-out battles. The Vandals are fierce but unruly and disorganized, and they will fall if we drive a spear through the heart of their lines."

He soon reflected on how the various segments of the army would be arrayed at Tricamarum with his strategy. Aided by John, Belisarius sketched instructions for the cataphracts under Bessas. They were to form along the center-front lines, flanked by the Herulian and Gothic foederati. Staggered behind the cataphracts would be the Roman spearmen, those under Germanus on the right and Baduarius on the left, who would sweep toward the edges of the Roman lines to hit any opposing Vandals or Mauri. Along with a reserve of Valerian's lighter cavalry were Ascum's archers and Samur's Huns, their purpose being to seize opportunities and exploit any gaps produced by attacks in the foremost ranks. Arguing that speed and agility were a fundamental requirement of victory, no ballistae would be put into service, with most left behind to guard the walls of Carthage.

"Terrible land for ballistae anyways," Ascum offered. "Too many hills, and the Vandals would be able to run from our bolts."

Seeing no questions, Belisarius explained that orders had already been given to break camp and move for Tricamarum at once. By John's calculations, the endeavor would be achieved by midday, giving the army more than enough time to engage and defeat Gelimer's and Tzazon's forces, regardless of their superior numbers.

Before the council concluded, Belisarius added one more surprise to a morning already filled with worry, hope, and the lingering stench of dread.

"Many of you know that I have relied upon John for all of our battle plans," Belisarius said, offering a smile to diminish the tense mood. "Tauris, Dara, Ad Decimum… John's instincts have guided us toward unprecedented success against the Empire's enemies. While I will remain in the rearguard to offer overall commands, I am naming John the operational commander for our assault against Gelimer. Uliaris and the elite of my bucellarii will guard John as he navigates the battle."

Momentary confusion gave way to a battery of hooting and cheering as John's peers gave their approval. Initially stunned, John lowered his head to the floor as he buried his face in his hands, a traditional symbol of deference to Greek leader.

"You honor me," John stammered, his voice uneven and weighty. "I promise you, I will win this battle!"

"Damned right!" Uliaris barked. "Or we're all good and fucked!"

In hindsight, I doubt that little had actually changed in the aftermath of Belisarius' decision. Belisarius and John had worked so closely for so many years that there was little John would do that Belisarius could not anticipate. With a mere flick of his quill, Belisarius had restored morale amongst his officers by recognizing their own successes and demonstrating confidence that he was not the only Roman to bring Gelimer to his knees.

At dawn, our camp broke. Many still marched bereft of weapons or armor, although the equipment was already prepared for distribution at a moment's notice. The army's banners were unfurled, and they flapped against a stiff southerly breeze, with Justinian's own sigil flying high above those of his commanders. As orders flowed through the army, Belisarius' columns marched in near silence, their position guarded by a ring of outriders who indicated any threats or opportunities at the army's front or sides. Little enough was passed to John as we marched, enjoying an otherwise uneventful morning with brisk yet tolerable weather along one of Rome's oldest roads.

Until we crested a rolling knoll a few miles from the town of Tricamarum and found the Vandals' frontmost ranks atop a higher elevation on a far hill. Though the elevations of the mounds conferred little strategic advantage over the surrounding region, Tzazon's men still possessed the high ground of the area, forcing any attacking Roman forces to fight uphill against a more numerous foe. Vandal horns blared to announce our arrival, with a deep howl rising from thousands of throats as a note of welcome. The Vandals were organized in deep lines that were flanked on either side of dismounted Mauri, showing no ballistae and few archers as they formed into a defensive position atop their hill.

We wasted little time preparing for the fight ahead. Armor, swords, lances, and bows were all distributed in a flurry of furious activity, while Vitalius and Rosamund prepared me for the challenge ahead. While Rosamund tolerated the youth to an extent, she sent Vitalius away as she completed her ritual, strapping my sword and dagger to my belt before handing over my shield and spear. I mounted Ignis, and Rosamund grabbed for my arm and removed my leather glove, planting a kiss on the torn skin of my knuckles.

"Come back alive," she whispered in Herulian. "That's all that matters."

Belisarius gave his final operational orders as the Roman column spread into more organized lines along our intended position. Samur and I exchanged an embrace before parting, my brother's bitter frustration temporarily shelved as he worried for my safety along the

Roman flank. With Vitalius bearing the ouroboros banner, I galloped away from Rosamund and toward the Herulian foederati, nodding to Perenus and Fulcaris as they issued orders for our men to form into lines.

Brisk orders were given for the Romans to close the distance separating the two armies, pausing with a mere two hundred paces between the armies' foremost lines. Gelimer was easily visible along the battlements with his ornate armor and huge guardsmen, with Gunderic standing two heads higher than most. Farther down the line was a similarly well-armored figure, his forces far better armed and armored than much of the Vandal masses we spied at Ad Decimum.

"Tzazon." Sembrouthes spoke nonchalantly, yet his brow furrowed as he scanned the Vandal lines.

"They're well disciplined," Xerxes added. "None of the bravado or recklessness that fosters disorganization in the ranks."

I nodded. "All Tzazon needs to do is hold that hill, and he knows it," I replied. "I'll give a hundred gold coins to the man that puts an arrow into Tzazon's heart."

"A hundred?" Fulcaris laughed, cantering beside me. "I would have done it for ten."

"Aye, that's because you're cheap and unskilled," Perenus shot back. "A hundred for me, now that's a fair deal."

With the day still in the clutches of late morning, John galloped before the arrayed Roman ranks, snatching an Imperial banner from one of the bucellarii and galloping hard down the ranks of cataphracts. A low hum sounded as he raised the Chi-Rho high into the air, the noise rising into a cheer of defiance against the Vandal hordes who would send Roman Carthage back into slavery and ruin. My own foederati added their voices to the din. John beamed as, for a few precious heartbeats, he sat alone before the Roman formation. As the Roman cheering diminished, a stillness flowed through the plains of Tricamarum, with John stretching both arms wide to take in the cool breeze pleasantly mixed with the clouded African sun.

That reverie was broken by howling from the Vandal lines, with

John trotting back to his cataphracts and returning the Imperial banner to its previous owner. At his signal, a horn blared in five staggered notes, the sign for the battle to begin.

As with many of our pitched battles, it started with jeers and applause. Not far from my position, the Cappadocian ranks parted as Baduarius jogged forward, the Goth encased in a thick wall of iron and reinforced leather as he moved to answer John's call. Baduarius thrust his spear into the air as he yelled for the army's support, cajoling those he deemed as being insufficiently excited for the demonstration of arms to come.

With the Roman army at his back, Baduarius walked fifty paces into the grasslands that separated Romans and Vandals alike. The great Goth planted his spear into the ground with one swift motion before unsheathing his sword and dancing in a curious and outlandish manner, bringing his blood to rise in anticipation of the fight. After taking several practice strokes, Baduarius leveled the blade toward Gelimer, bellowing for the Vandal king to come and face him like any true warrior would.

Gelimer remained still. Several of the Vandals stirred as Baduarius skipped ahead, hurling insults in crude Latin as he called Gelimer's mother a whore mounted by a dozen Mauri goats. Both Tzazon and Gelimer growled for the Vandals to avoid confronting the menace before them. Confused, Baduarius switched tactics, yelling that the Vandals were led by cowards who allowed others to fight and die in their stead.

"Gibamund died squealing as he ran from the battlefield," Baduarius said, "while Ammatas, that timid child, pissed his pants like a little girl as Roman cavalry bore down on him. He didn't even try to defend himself, just raised his hands and pled for mercy."

Roars of anger rose once again across the Vandal lines. Tzazon struggled to control them. Yelling for order, Tzazon's officers galloped down the lines, chastising those who would disobey the Vandal battle plan and reinstating calm into their vanguard.

Amidst it all, Baduarius shrugged, plucking his spear in the ground and hurling it skyward. Its point hurtled into the sky before thrusting itself into the turf at Gelimer's feet. The Vandal king's horse reared in surprise, and Baduarius raised his arms in triumph, laughing as he turned back to John and rejoined the ranks of the army.

"We win the first attack!" Baduarius said.

John wasted little time in seizing upon the reduced morale in the Vandal ranks. Roman horns blared once more as Bessas' cavalry formed into a massive wedge, the armored cavalry congealing into a thick mass of flesh and armor that sought to tear into the Vandal lines. I stole a glance upon the Roman rear as I found Belisarius riding beside Liberius, nodding at John's command as he moved for a better view along the flanks.

After another sounding of John's horn, Bessas' massed cataphracts thundered ahead, their horses churning grass into a sandy mud as they wheeled toward the Vandal center. Their advance began slowly at first, soon gathering momentum as they edged uphill against the Vandal lines, their lances lowered against defined targets amongst the Vandal horsemen.

The wedge's aim shifted at the last possible moment for the mass of experienced riders surrounding Tzazon. The initial collision boomed along the plains as several Vandals were tossed aside, their limbs flailing helplessly as the incredible mass of cataphracts bowled into their lines. Yet Tzazon anticipated the move, swinging his riders to press hard against the walls of the wedge and blunting its force as it dug farther into the Vandal mass. As quickly as the charge began, its progress ceased, with a brief melee soon ended as John blared his horn for Bessas' men to return. Nearly all were successful in this order, although a half dozen cataphracts remained trapped behind Tzazon's men, helplessly cut down and butchered in sight of the Roman army.

"This won't be easy."

"No," Xerxes replied. "It won't."

As the cataphracts returned, John ordered the two flanks of Roman spearmen forward, their targets assigned as the Mauri lines protecting Gelimer's sides. Ascum's archers were commanded to march to the

Roman front, their arrows flying into the Vandal center. While these barrages were a clear impediment to the Vandals reinforcing their Mauri allies, it did little to thin out their ranks, with Gelimer ordering small detachments of Vandal riders to launch javelins against the slower and less agile archers. Led by the rasping cadence of Ascum, the Romans traded casualties with the Vandals as Baduarius and Germanus marched forward, their shield wall strengthening as it approached that of the Mauri just twenty paces distant.

It was at that moment that John called the Herulians and Goths to the fight. While Indulf kicked his lancers closer to the fighting, I signaled for Perenus and Fulcaris to ready our own bowmen, pointing to Baduarius' shield wall along the Vandal flank.

"Hit them hard, but do not dismount!" I yelled. "Give Baduarius cover!"

Initially motionless, my Herulian foederati kicked into a full gallop within two paces. Drawing my bow, I spotted young Vitalius trailing close behind, his arms gripped tight around my banner as he shouted his own battle cry.

"Nock and draw!" I yelled at a hundred paces, watching the Cappadocian wall collide against the firm resistance of the Mauri.

"Arrows high! Don't hit our own men!" Perenus warned, our horses slowing and turning left as we neared the enemy.

"Loose!" I barked, and hundreds of arrows sailed into flight.

They sailed above Baduarius' ranks and sank into the unsuspecting heads of the Mauri reserves. That first volley dropped dozens of spearmen and gave me hope that the flank might break, until the Mauri leaders adjusted their defenses and ordered a protective layer of shields to guard against the second and third volleys. Thwarted, I obeyed John's call to withdraw, watching as Baduarius' advance lost its vigor and was soon required to return to its previous position. On the far side of the battlefield, the Thracians fared little better, with Indulf's Goths taking terrible casualties as they attempted a charge against a steady wall of spears and javelins. Indulf slammed into the Mauri lines and impaled one officer with his lance, but otherwise the

Goths did little to alter the balance in the Thracians' favor.

Ascum's archers were also ordered to return, allowing Bessas' cataphracts to reform for a second wedge against the Vandal lines. This time, however, my Herulians were ordered to precede the attack with mounted fire. My officers kicked our horses toward the center of the battlefield and targeted those who broke from the safety of the Vandal lines. Dodging a number of clumsy Vandal darts, I attempted to target Gelimer, Gunderic, or Tzazon, yet found little success as their shields absorbed the worst of our volleys.

As Bessas began the charge once more, John's horns blared the Thracian and Cappadocian spearmen into another attack along the Vandal flanks, with lighter cavalry under Valerian adding strength to Indulf's Goths as they skirted along the Mauri lines. Through it all, my men loosed volley after volley at set targets. And while we were occasionally successful at plucking a careless or foolish warrior, it did little to soften the Vandals against Bessas' attack. Gunderic's laughter boomed across the Vandal lines as they howled and jeered at our failure, seemingly ignoring fatigue or pain at each attack.

Before or since, I have never seen a battle with so much activity occur simultaneously. Dozens of senior officers heeded a flood of orders from John's messengers or horn blasts, the constant violence seeking to throw Gelimer and Tzazon off balance, and struggling to respond to such discipline and coordination. While the Vandals were forced to remain still and did take losses, Tzazon's leadership ensured the Vandal lines held firm, preventing a Roman breakthrough or Vandal rout.

Bessas' second wedge had more success than the first, driving apart the Vandal lines and nearly cutting their massive army into two crude halves. Shards of broken lances and cracked spears showered around plumed helmets, leaving at least one man blinded by a piece of unlucky shrapnel. While initial Roman cheers rang atop the hill, Tzazon sounded his own horn. His own armored riders cut hard into the cataphract wedge and threatened to encircle Bessas' men. Sensing the danger, Bessas quickly withdrew, again leaving behind a half dozen riders who were unable to flee to safety.

Bloodied and showing signs of fatigue, Belisarius' fabled cataphracts returned to the lines, with many horses and riders nursing wounds or wincing at pain acquired from the crush of men and beasts at close quarters. At the army's rear, Belisarius sent a courier galloping to John, who then rushed to the front ranks of the army himself, leaving Liberius behind with twelve bucellarii as a guard and escort.

As both flanks of Roman infantry continued to clash against their implacable Mauri adversaries, a courier soon reached my position along the Roman flank. Urging me to attend John at the Roman center, I beckoned to my own senior officers and galloped to my commander, leaving Fulcaris and Sindual in temporary command of the stationary Herulian foederati.

Galloping as fast as his mount would carry him, Samur arrived at John's position at nearly the same time I did. Fresh and unused in the battle, Samur's fists clenched and nostrils flared as he glared at John and Belisarius, dismounting before pushing toward their position.

"You're wasting my men, and for what?" Samur scolded the commanders. "If you're so fearful of Hun treachery, then let me leave here and not squander any more time."

John raised a hand in surrender. "You're right, Samur. And I need you now."

Belisarius glanced to Bessas as the cataphract commander arrived, panting as he removed his helmet. A thick cut lined Bessas' forehead from the force of a previous impact, and he grasped at his ribs while remaining in his mount.

"Bessas, can you give me one more?" Belisarius asked.

Bessas nodded. "It won't work, though," he concluded. "They know our strategy, and if they surround my men, we'll be cut to pieces."

"Not this time," John replied, turning to Samur and me. "Samur will approach from the right, and Varus the left. Tzazon will either have to defend against bowshot or the cataphract charge, but not both."

Belisarius shook his head. "Not enough force or surprise," he added. "Varus, can any of your men wield a lance?"

Confused, I shrugged. "If necessary, Lord. But few have the armor for a frontal attack on horseback."

John's eyes widened. "I just need a dozen or so," John explained. "Most of your men will hold their fire until the last possible moment, releasing a volley before the front ranks collide with the Vandal lines."

"We'll need to hit multiple places to keep Tzazon from preparing his men," Bessas said between pants. "That's the biggest worry, although it would sap the strength of the cataphracts."

"Take Valerian and Indulf as reserves for the charge," John explained. "Form three separate wedges—one at Gelimer, one near Tzazon, and another near the juncture between the Mauri and the Vandals on our left. Varus, your attack will be near Tzazon, while Samur's Huns will fire atop the charging force."

"It's suicidal," Samur said. "If it doesn't work..."

"It *will* work," John answered. "Cut through the Vandals, kill Tzazon, and send their army into disarray. This is our last chance to win this battle before taking too many casualties."

Others looked to Belisarius, though he bowed to John's wisdom. "This is our fate. All the ingenuity of Rome against the might of the Vandal horde."

"And we thought Varus was the only poet," Perenus chuckled.

At John's orders, lances were delivered to the Herulians while each section of the army worked its way into place. Heftier than a common spear, these iron-tipped lances were intended to provide a rider with additional heft to batter shields and puncture mail or scale armor. Though normally reserved for our cataphracts, I had required all of my new recruits to drill with the more unwieldy weapons. I never suspected that they would be utilized for a headlong assault. For that task, I selected a dozen of my most heavily armored foederati, preferring those few who had encased their horses in layers of hardened leather and iron scales over the majority who favored speed and agility as horse archers.

In the end, the duty fell upon Perenus, Xerxes, the Aksumites, and a half dozen other Herulian riders who agreed to volunteer for the task. Each was handed the heavy lances before our formation quickly moved alongside those of Bessas. Fulcaris and Sindual retained command of the Herulian bowmen, their task to shower a murderous volley at the last possible moment before the clash of armies.

"And don't miss, either!" I joked. "If one of your arrows hits me, I'll turn around and ride you down myself."

All this frenetic activity occurred within moments, a note of desperation in John's voice as he set his complex attack into order. Even Belisarius joined one of the other wedges, his presence intended to convince Gelimer that the focus of the Roman attack lay elsewhere along the Vandal front. My men appeared tiny next to the heavily armored cataphracts, with several chattering in Heruli with apprehension at the insane charge that John had committed us to.

The two halves of Belisarius' spearmen continued to occupy the enemy's attention, with Gelimer even sending detachments of his own Vandal guardsmen to assist the reeling Mauri against Baduarius' onslaught. On the right, the Thracians encountered stiffer resistance, requiring John to deploy Samur's Huns earlier than had been desired as Mundus' lines began to fall back from a sudden Mauri advance. Sensing the tide of battle beginning to shift in Gelimer's favor, John issued his final instructions.

"One more push, men!" John yelled. "One more push, then our place in history is assured! Gallop hard, choose your targets, and above all else, do not stop pushing until you've cut the Vandals in half!"

At John's signal, dozens of lesser officers barked orders to their men. The Romans advanced in a grinding start. Dozens of banners dipped as the vast bulk of John's army streamed uphill, spurring Tzazon to respond by arranging his own forces in a formation intended to swallow the incoming wedge. Though initially calm,

Tzazon devolved into furious shouting as our three wedges separated and diverged toward their intended targets. Eyeing the larger mass of riders forming around Belisarius and the Vandal king, Tzazon dispatched hundreds of more heavily armored Vandals to protect Gelimer, thinning his own lines against a less-imposing formation of cataphracts and Heruli.

Initially moving at a slow walk, our formations grew more cohesive as we advanced, our pace rising to a trot. John's horn blew to prepare Samur's Huns for the impending attack, while John himself screamed his final orders of encouragement at the wedge's center. Uliaris and the bucellarii pounded lances against their shields in recognition of the order, with the Roman army rising into a final roar of hatred, fear, and death.

As our pace heightened once more, we slowly closed the two hundred paces separating the rival walls. Jeers and shouts emanated near Gelimer while Tzazon remained taciturn, his preparations completed for John's attack. Gripping my lance, I turned my head back to the archers behind me.

"Prepare your bows!" I yelled. "Do not fire your volley until I command."

Our trot accelerated into a canter as Ignis' hooves pounded at the sea of frothing mud underneath. Bessas shouted his own orders as the cataphracts prepared their lances, tightening their formation into a denser wedge. At just over a hundred paces out, I directed my foederati to follow their example, using the cataphracts to protect our right flank, hoping that our own lancers would not become separated inside a murderous Vandal encirclement. Horns blared as the two other wedges charged down the line, signaling for ours to do so as well.

"Hold!" I bellowed, kicking Ignis into a gallop.

John's wedge spilled towards the enemy, quickly closing the distance to the Vandal front. Our horses began to climb the gentle slope of the hill, our footing increasingly treacherous as its grasses and soil were tossed about to reveal harder clay underneath.

"Hold!" I yelled again, preventing any behind me from launching their arrows.

At fifty paces, a dozen Vandals launched smaller spears and javelins at our wedge, with most connecting against the reinforced shields of the cataphracts. However, one did sneak past the guard of one of Bessas' horsemen, its iron tip piercing through the more flexible neck guard and boring into the man's neck. Initially the rider appeared unhurt, yet as blood emptied beneath his helmet, the rider tipped from the saddle, disappearing within a sea of other horsemen, who immediately closed the gap in the wedge.

"Hold!!" I urged again, desperate, our riders now close enough to discern the movements and features of each of the Vandals before us.

At Bessas' order, hundreds of lances lowered at twenty paces out. Mere heartbeats separated us from impact as the Vandal cavalry structured their shields to repel the Roman assault, opening a narrow gap in their protection. John blared his horn once more, and I finally gave the order to attack.

"Loose!" I screamed, sending a hail of arrows sailing overhead.

In that narrow moment before our crash into Tzazon's Vandals, I saw dozens of arrows connect with the exposed necks, chests, and faces of our enemy. Screams of pain and rage rose as the Vandals were sapped of their cohesion, unable to defend against the foederati's onslaught in order to protect against the incoming charge. Roaring in victory, I zeroed in on a thickly bearded Vandal not far from Tzazon, aiming my lance at the man's exposed chest.

I didn't see the spear leveled directly at Ignis' chest until it was far too late. Its heavy point jammed between the iron scales of his armor. The wooden shaft snapped from the sheer force of the charge. Ignis screamed as we barreled into the Vandal lines, and my world went black.

All I remember was flying through the air. On the ground, my mind entered a deep fog as, vaguely aware of my surroundings, I made sense of my predicament and prayed to God that my body had not been mangled beyond repair. My feet wriggled, and despite searing pain, my hands responded to instructions, and for a moment I was relieved to find myself alive and reasonably whole.

And then, as if awoken by a revelation, I realized that I had been projected several ranks into the Vandal lines. The thunderclaps of hooves pounded in my ears as I raised my arms to protect my head, feeling the disturbed wind of nearby movement yet not trampled into further misery. Though I cannot be sure, it only took a few heartbeats for my foederati to react.

"Fall on your commander!" Xerxes roared.

"Push them back!" Sembrouthes added. "Spears and lances!"

Still making sense of my surroundings, I moved upright, tugging my cloak free from a weight that threatened to pin me to the ground. Though I was successful, I found my glove slick with blood, shrouding me in confusion as I pieced my memories together.

I had little time. Cutting into the stalled wedge, one Vandal howled as he slashed down at my helmet, shaving its plume and grazing the metal that protected my skull. The man dismounted and lifted his sword for the killing thrust, leaving me just a heartbeat to free my dagger and jam it hard into the Vandal attacker's throat. Hot gore flooded over my arms and face as his body twitched and slumped onto my own, pinning me into an awkward sitting position as my back fell against another dying body.

The Vandal lines pushed hard as they drove away my men, thwarting desperate attacks by Xerxes and Sembrouthes to free me of my bondage. Restrained and too weak to pry myself from the viscous morass of bodies, mud, and gore, I pushed bodies from my legs in vain, unable to defend myself as Tzazon rushed forward.

Richly armored, the Vandal general snarled as he met my gaze, drawing his sword for an imminent attack. Unable to free my own sword, I snatched at a loose blade along the ground, raising it in defense as Tzazon swung hard at my chest. The Vandal commander knocked aside my pathetic attempt at a parry and drove my borrowed weapon back into the mud, preparing his own blade for a fatal thrust as he lunged.

Only to be blown back by a sudden charge from one of my foederati. A wooden pole splintered into thousands of shards as the ouroboros banner slammed into Tzazon's exposed body. Triumphant, Vitalius dismounted and swung the broken wooden beam once more. Tzazon screamed for the Vandals to attack.

Drawing a simple Roman spatha, Vitalius parried an attacker and slashed viciously at the Vandal's exposed face, severing the soft tissues of his nose and lips into a macabre cleft in the man's face. Using Vitalius' opportunity, Sembrouthes cut a path to me, throwing aside the corpses at my legs and allowing me an opportunity to steal a look at the horror that engulfed the army.

"Ignis..." I groaned, finding my horse lying still, a spear jutting from his heart, its shaft splintered and cracked. It was only then that I realized that I had been lying against Ignis' body, sensing his final twitches as his lifeblood pooled into the chaos of Tricamarum.

As Sembrouthes lifted my body, he placed me atop a vacant saddle, ordering the Aksumites to protect their charge.

"Can you ride?" Sembrouthes yelled, smacking my arm to get my attention.

Yet my mind was on Vitalius. The lad slashed against another attacker and shouted in glorious triumph as the foederati formed around him, laughing at his success and ability to save his commander from certain death.

Until his body jerked, his face melting from boundless joy to a mixture of surprise and discomfort, a javelin jutting out just under the bone that connects the shoulder to the chest plate. Flecks of blood dripping from his beard, Tzazon roared, his arm extended from the mortal throw. Spitting defiance, Perenus lashed against Vandal.

"Vitalius!" I moaned hoarsely. "Get Vitalius."

"I will do it!" Xerxes yelled back, freeing his horse from an attacker. "Get Varus out of here!"

Screaming, I raged at the helplessness of my situation, unable to resist Sembrouthes as he remounted his own horse and galloped through a gap in the foederati lines that allowed me to escape. Several offered words of support or revenge to me as they fired their arrows into the Vandal masses, yet they, too, began to back away from the reforming and surging enemy. Sembrouthes' fist was gripped tightly around my reins and guided my borrowed mount back to the Roman front.

My neck stiff and pained, I turned to view the battlefield behind me, finding each of the three wedges faltering. While Samur's Huns inflicted ruinous casualties upon the Vandal right, John's horn blew, signaling the cataphracts to retreat and reform, ending the last Roman assault at Tricamarum.

We had failed.

The Roman infantry fought on, but the stalemate with the Mauri prevented any attempt to outflank and surround Gelimer's forces. Shouts of triumph rose from the Vandal lines, and I caught a glimpse of Gelimer galloping the length of the Vandal front as he surveyed the strength remaining to his men. Gunderic gestured lewdly toward his Roman adversary and signaled for an assault, though Gelimer resisted the pleas, moving to Tzazon's position to coordinate their counterattack against John.

Though each of John's wedges had absorbed few serious casualties, the young Armenian general hurriedly surveyed his forces, seeking damage reports from each of the commanders as he reorganized the exhausted cataphracts for a fourth assault against the Vandal center. Sembrouthes helped me dismount, lowering me gently to the grass despite my insistence that I would be fine on my own. It was in that pandemonium, with shouts of triumph and death rising along the Vandal lines, that I spied the figure of Xerxes, who trotted urgently as he ferried the limp form of Vitalius draped across his lap.

As Xerxes cantered beside me, the distant shouts of Perenus screamed toward the Roman lines.

"He's dead!" Perenus yelled excitedly. "Tzazon's fallen! What are you doing?"

Jerking in the saddle, John searched for outline of Gelimer, the Vandal king cradling the ornate armor of his fallen brother. Many near the dead general grew visibly fearful, with Gunderic yelling at Gelimer for orders to attack the hated Romans. Yet, as Godilas had often told in his lessons of my youth, the loss of fortune can bring even the most disciplined army into panic and flight, and Gelimer's heady emotions left him in little state to navigate the intricacies of the Roman attack. Both Belisarius and John reformed their assault as, overcoming wounds and pushing beyond the limits of exhaustion, the Roman cavalry galloped atop the hill of Tricamarum once more. Lacking the steadying influence of Tzazon, Gelimer ran from the field, leaving his headless army to swirl into one of the most terrible routs that Rome had ever taken part in.

As the conclusion of the battle unfolded, Xerxes lowered the still-breathing body of Vitalius onto the grass beside me. I immediately ordered one of the foederati to retrieve Rosamund for another emergency, taking Vitalius' limp hand into my own as I scanned the extent of his injuries. Rosamund sprinted to my location and did the same, yet even as she did, she whispered in Heruli that nothing could be done. I begged her to try, but she simply shook her head.

"It would only bring pain," she whispered. "Bordering on torture."

A low rumble emanated from Vitalius' throat.

I kneeled close. "What is it, Vitalius? Anything you want, I will bring."

"Did I do the right thing, Lord?" Vitalius murmured, his lips quivering as his body shivered from loss of blood.

"You saved my life," I answered, "you saved us all. You were magnificent, Vitalius."

Vitalius smiled weakly before wincing, tears flowing down his sallow cheeks as he moaned. He shuddered, his fingers offering little force as he turned to speak his final words.

"I don't want to die, Lord," Vitalius said, his voice little more than a throaty gurgle. "I'm afraid."

I nodded, fighting tears that welled in my eyes. As Vitalius' teeth clenched from another spasm, I leaned close to his ear.

"God will protect you, Vitalius," I replied confidently. "Go and find our brothers and sisters, and save a place for me for when I come to join you."

Leaning back, Vitalius gripped my hand once more and shuddered, his spasms weak and fleeting. A single tear fell as his eyes locked upon mine, their light diminishing as Vitalius' soul left his body on the stained grounds of Tricamarum. I sat with his body as it cooled, ignoring the hallowed chant of "Roma Victrix!" as the battle drew to its conclusion.

THE COST OF VICTORY

Procopius later wrote that the Battle of Tricamarum was a brisk and simple affair, with the Romans suffering few casualties or hardships as they swept aside Gelimer's final great attempt to restore his throne. I have never cared for scribes, finding that those who tell the stories of others reap much of the glory and pay little of the cost required to capture the minds of millions.

Leaderless, thousands of Vandals surrendered as John swept across Tricamarum's hill, although Gelimer did manage to escape with several hundred of his closest retainers. None of the Mauri joined Gelimer's flight, however, with the Mauri leaders tossing aside the Vandal banners as they raised signs of truce for Germanus and Baduarius. Not long after midday, the last pockets of fighting came to an abrupt end, with many officers dispatched to organize their newfound prisoners as others returned to the Roman camp.

Atop a swifter horse, Perenus was among the first to return to the original Roman lines, leaving Fulcaris to organize the Herulians as he searched for me amidst the confusion. Finding our small group huddled around Vitalius' cooling body, Perenus dismounted, removing his helmet for the relief of cool air across his sweat-streaked forehead.

"It seems that I owe you a hundred gold coins," I said.

Perenus shook his head, sighing as he made out Vitalius' prone form. "I struck him down, but it was Vitalius that scored the fatal blow," he explained. "Tzazon had the tip of a sharpened stake in his gullet when I found him."

I chuckled darkly, nodding. "Watch over his body," I ordered Perenus and Xerxes. "He deserves a hero's funeral. I'm going to go make sense of Belisarius' instructions."

Shadowed by Aksumites still wary of my health, I struggled atop the unfamiliar horse, suddenly mourning the loss of a friend that had carried me through Armenia, Mesopotamia, Syria, and through the gauntlet of Ad Decimum. Making a note to retrieve Ignis from the mound of bodies that lined the battlefield, I pushed my thoughts toward the challenge of reconstituting the army in the aftermath of battle, and the remaining need to capture Gelimer to end further conflict.

I found John and Belisarius ecstatic at the totality of their victory. John's hands shook as he addressed the general and the legate, struggling to contain his excitement as he informed his superiors of the following actions needed to end the war. It was Liberius who acknowledged me first, interrupting the meeting with his own concerns. A look of relief flashed across Liberius' face that was soon erased in favor of his usual austere gaze, and he addressed me informally before the other officers.

"Varus, it is good to see you recovered so quickly from the assault," Liberius began calmly. "I heard that it was your ward Vitalius who struck the fatal blow against Tzazon but not what became of him."

"He perished defending me," I explained. "He slew two Vandals outright and impaled Tzazon with my banner."

Liberius' face dropped, and John and Belisarius offered their gratitude and condolences for the younger man. Nodding, Liberius sighed as he pieced together the events that brought victory to the Roman army.

"A great loss. He was the last of an ancient Italian family, whose grandfather had been a dear friend to Petrus," Liberius said. "His sacrifice will not be forgotten."

"No indeed," Belisarius responded firmly. "I will personally see that the Emperor is informed of to whom we owe so much."

We shared details of the army's status, interrupted occasionally by shouts of anger along the horizon as Vandal prisoners were deprived of their weapons and organized into gangs for pacification and control. John told of the relatively light numbers of Roman wounded or dead in the attack, thanks largely to the brevity of the battle and despite the savage fighting along the front. As John reflected further on the few hundred Vandals who escaped with Gelimer, a detachment under Germanus escorted a group of Vandal officers before the army's leaders. Still armed, one younger Vandal dismounted and slowly approached Belisarius, dropping to his knees and sliding his blade from his scabbard.

"Lord Belisarius, we recognize you as lord and master of all the Vandals living and still to come," the man began, offering the naked blade with one hand on its hilt and another near its point. "As our leaders have either died or disgraced themselves, I, Wisimar of the Hasdingi Vandals, place my life and the lives of our men into your judgment."

Stepping forward, Belisarius did not hesitate and grasped the sword from Wisimar. The Vandal warrior bowed his head as Belisarius raised the blade to face the sun, finding it stained with drying blood. Belisarius kept the blade aloft for several heartbeats, then thrust its point to defy the sun, casting a long shadow along his face. Behind him, a thousand Roman voices roared, yet Belisarius did not lend his voice to their chants. Instead, he closed his eyes, mouthing a silent prayer.

Belisarius was never a man for excess. So many teachers emphasized the Roman virtue of stoicism, and while I have never encountered any who perfectly possessed such passionless balance, Belisarius came closest to the ideals of Marcus Aurelius. He was the last living reminder of old traditions, the last of the Romans. After

Tricamarum, Belisarius celebrated in his own preferred manner.

Belisarius did not allow the moment to linger. Soon, he lowered the sword, offering the hilt back to Wisimar.

"I am neither your lord nor master," Belisarius said. "That privilege belongs to Emperor Justinian, who will reorganize this province in accordance with his wishes."

Wisimar shook his head, his eyes fixed upon the disturbed soil. "Great Lord Belisarius, in Vandal culture, a man who does not fight is not entitled to the spoils of victory," Wisimar replied deferentially. "The Vandals see you as the rightful victor. We do not know of this Emperor Justinian."

I flinched at the insult—one that Justinian would invariably hear of through Narses' spies. Belisarius glowered at Wisimar, unwilling to accept the mantle of conquest in Justinian's place.

"You will soon enough," Belisarius mumbled. "For now, keep your men docile, and await further instructions. No harm will come to any who do not raise trouble, and ample food and medicine will be distributed to all."

Wisimar bowed, remaining still until dismissed by Belisarius and returned to the Vandal captives with Germanus. After a safe distance separated the commanders from Wisimar, John's head bobbed excitedly, his face breaking into a wide grin.

"We did it!" he exclaimed, keeping his voice hushed as his face brightened and teeth flashed.

"Nearly," Belisarius replied. "While Gelimer lives, the Emperor's enemies will still have reason to rise against us."

"Consider it done," John declared. "With your permission, I will track him down and have him back to camp immediately."

Belisarius chuckled. "You have no need to ask permission anymore," he answered, "but take several banda with you. We still don't know how many men Gelimer escaped with. I assume he will ride for Hippo Regius while he still can."

John clasped Belisarius' arm before calling for Uliaris and the bucellarii. Assigned fresh mounts and packs of food and waterskins,

John's forces cheered as they galloped off to the west, trailing Gelimer's whereabouts. One band of Cappadocians saluted John as he dashed by, praising his unabashed successes as they looted corpses for plunder and dispatched dozens of the gravely wounded who lay helpless in a pool of blood and dung for miles around.

Not expecting John to return quickly, Belisarius installed his own orders over the army once more, insisting that all prisoners be treated kindly and mercifully. All Mauri were immediately freed and allowed to depart with their weapons and gold, their only requirement to swear allegiance to the Emperor before departing for their camps at the edge of the Great African Desert. Fearing the miasma of disease, a massive camp was carved along an adjoining hillside a fair distance from any corpses, with tents readied and a celebratory feast cooked for the thousands of Romans who could now claim ownership of the conquest of Africa.

An evening of rest was ordered for each section of the army, with Liberius administering to various tasks of organizing the Vandal captives and informing Carthage of our unmatched success at Tricamarum. Enlisting the support of several of the foederati, we retrieved Ignis' corpse and dragged it on a sled closer to the Roman camp. Sindual and Altan shot curious looks at me for taking so much trouble for a beast, yet I did not rush farewells to my friend, wrapping my arms around his limp and cooling neck and burying my face into his damp mane. I allowed only Rosamund to help me wash and prepare Ignis' body, unfastening his saddle and gently removing the white wolf pelt to leave the once-tireless Nisean stallion naked to the world. Using logs stacked around the body, we burned Ignis in silence, offering prayers of gratitude for his faithful service.

Nearly the entire Herulian and Hunnic foederati assisted with Vitalius' own pyre. Though I would have preferred to carry the boy's corpse back to Carthage for a proper burial, such duties placed the men at considerable risk, and the body would have decayed too quickly to be preserved in the African sun. With Vitalius in the center, a dozen bodies were neatly arrayed, their figures resting upon piles of wood and kindling as prayers from pagans and Christians alike raised them to the heavens.

As the words concluded, I grabbed one of my banners and carried it to Vitalius' pyre, wrapping his body in the black ouroboros cloth with careful hands. As he had still been small, the banner's cloth easily cloaked his legs and torso, leaving only his thin arms and his head poking out into the air. My fingers traced Vitalius' neck as I teased a small cross from underneath his shirt, allowing the coarse silver to rest atop the banner as a final profession of the lad's faith. Clutching at my own bronze cross, I muttered a prayer for Vitalius' soul, my eyes closed as dozens of torches were lit along the periphery. Fulcaris brought forth a torch with an outstretched arm and inserted the rising flame into the pyre, watching the flames rise to consume one who had died far too young.

At Rosamund's insistence, I received a thorough examination of my head and body. Rosamund poked and frowned at thick bruises that had formed from my fall, but eventually concluded that no serious damage had been added to the nest of wounds that had slowly come to paint my flesh. Salves were applied to improve healing, and other medicines were prescribed to ensure dreamless sleep, a gift that I readily obliged as the foederati received Belisarius' orders to rest for the evening.

Given our procrastination, the following morning was far busier. Hundreds of Vandal and Mauri bodies had to be gathered and burned, while several dozen Roman dead had to be attended to in more respectful manners. Belisarius allowed a hundred Vandal captives to serve the needs of Tzazon, his body abandoned by Gelimer in the final moments of the preceding day's battle. In a show of respect, Belisarius even allowed several of those Vandals to take part in mock duels as Tzazon's body burned, his soul sent to the afterlife amidst the sound of a clash of arms as opposed to wailing or tears.

Of a relatively minor note was one body amongst Mundus' Thracians. In most circumstances, these casualties would have been mourned but otherwise unworthy of investigation, though Mundus and Troglita both insisted upon further deliberation. Finding both officers back on the torn battlefield, I was directed to the bloated corpse of Gratian, his features almost peaceful as his tendons stiffened underneath bloodless and waxy skin.

Except for the arrow jutting from his chest, its tip piercing the layers of mail that protected his heart. The shaft was stubby and thin, with shaved goose feathers glued to its terminus to improve the bowman's accuracy.

"I didn't see any archers in the Vandal lines," Mundus reasoned, "and I've only seen Huns use arrows like this."

Mundus' assessment caused me to shiver. "This is a Hunnic arrow, crafted for quick firing atop the saddle. The Herulians use longer shafts."

"Such accidents are unfortunate, especially when the shield walls are wrapped together, but they do happen," Troglita replied. "And it's likely impossible to know how this occurred. However, Solomon will wish to know how his proxy was killed."

"Friendly fire," I answered. The others fell to the same conclusion.

Though my answer was an honest one, a neglected thought troubled my mind as I returned to the Roman encampment, leaving the Thracians to remove the arrow and offer Gratian a proper funeral. If a Hun arrow had accidentally killed a Thracian, why did it strike the man toward the front of his body?

Asked later in private conversation, Samur had no explanation for the strange event.

"Perhaps he turned around and was just unlucky?" Samur reasoned aloud. "It would have been easy for any of my foederati to mistake Gratian for an enemy, given that he was facing our forces near the shield wall."

If we discussed a typical archer within the Roman army, Samur's answer might have been satisfactory. Accidents were a fact of war. Yet the Huns were a different breed of warrior and unlikely to have made so grievous an error. Especially against a plumed Roman officer facing the Huns rather than struggling in the melee of a shield wall.

And especially not a Roman officer holding patronage from Solomon. "Would any of the Hun foederati want to impress you or gain favor by taking Gratian's life?"

Samur snorted. "The Huns aren't courtiers and don't seek to curry favor with anyone. No, Gratian was just an unlucky fool. As you and I both know, ill luck happens."

It was a reasonable answer, but not one that placed me at ease. "You're certain?"

Scowling, Samur looked upon me with irritation. "On my oath as a Roman soldier, I am certain."

Though I still did not understand Gratian's death, Samur's oath satisfied my suspicions. And, as Gratian burned, so, too, did my fleeting concern for that mystery. Belisarius wrote a missive to Hadrumetum to explain the unhappy event, assuring Solomon that his officer had been given all respects and that any family back in the Empire would be handsomely compensated for Gratian's service to the Emperor. He allowed me to include my own letters to Constantinople, adding further words to parchment as I updated Mariya and Theodora of the events of Tricamarum and my status in its aftermath.

Another two days passed uneventfully. Indulf attempted to take several dozen Vandals as slaves for his men, a request that was flatly denied by Belisarius. He placated Gothic honor with a choice selection of seized Vandal weapons and a heavy bag of gold. Indulf bowed and voiced his appreciation for Belisarius' wisdom. To avoid further confrontation, Liberius led a thousand Romans back to Carthage, with those Vandals hale enough to march trailing close behind under armed guard. On the following day, Belisarius dispatched another column of several hundred of the wounded and sick, pairing them with plentiful assistance and multiple mounts to see them safely back to the coastal cities and improved chances at rest and recuperation.

Under Rosamund's incessant care, my own injuries quickly faded, although sensitive bruises remained to prompt me of our great charge against the Vandal lines. Rosamund tutted and lectured for hours at my infirmities, rolling her eyes at my stubbornness and wondering how long I would live if not for her following closely behind. As the fourth day after Tricamarum dawned, I felt as limber and strong as ever, rejoining my men around the cookfires and lightly training with swords and spears for any future fights to come.

By that fourth day, Belisarius' messengers had reached many of Gelimer's former strongholds, with most capitulating upon hearing news of Gelimer's escape from another rout on the battlefield. Upon seeing evidence of Tzazon's torn standards, the leaders of Bulla Regia replied with the symbolic keys to the city gates, swearing allegiance to Belisarius the Conqueror. A dozen smaller towns and villages echoed this example, although it was not until receiving a similar surrender from Hippo Regius that Belisarius began to take worried notice. For Gelimer had avoided the former city along the Numidian coastline, its leaders surrendering the immense Vandal treasure hoard to forty Romans under Thurimuth. Two full bandas were dispatched to secure that fortune, rumored to contain immense rooms of gold, silver, and gems that had been looted from the Vandal sack of Rome eighty years prior.

In our private planning sessions, we rejoiced again as divine providence yielded enough gold to reimburse the Emperor ten times over for the expense of the expedition, ensuring that all who sacrificed for this headstrong expedition would be treated to a substantial reward. Even Belisarius managed a brief smile as the other officers drooled at the imagined sums of Gelimer's treasury, the accumulated wealth of a hundred years of Vandal pillage and plunder.

Belisarius admitted to me in the months that followed that he would have returned that mountain of gold and never have set foot in Africa if the expedition's costs had been clearer from the onset. Enough wealth to pay a dozen armies was simply not worth what Belisarius had to pay.

For as the sun set on that fourth day after Tricamarum, John's expedition returned with the grimmest tidings imaginable.

Given the diminutive size of John's returning party, I initially suspected that John's forces had taken heavy casualties against Gelimer's outriders, leaving most dead or wounded as the remainder escaped back to Belisarius' camp. The initial party hurried to Belisarius' tent, screaming for healers as a long line of riders snaked along the low hills of the western roads. As Rosamund and I sprinted toward Belisarius' tent, my jaw swung open, a chill sweeping along my spine as my legs became rooted to the Numidian soil.

"Get out!" Belisarius barked at Uliaris, who fell to the ground.

"I'm sorry, Lord!" Uliaris wept, his hands outstretched as he buried his disheveled moustache into the dirt.

Belisarius roared as he jumped back toward his cot, unsheathing a sword that rested against a low beam and raising it high over his head. I rushed to meet the commotion, placing one hand on Belisarius' sword arm and wrapping another around his body, struggling to restrain his unprecedented fury and grief.

"Let go of me, Varus!" Belisarius screamed.

"No, Lord! This is not the way. Just put the blade down and we can talk."

Unable to unbind himself from my clutches, Belisarius roared again as tears flooded his face. He began to argue with me once more until his curses were interrupted by the faintest of voices just paces away, its body strewn across a low wooden table that had borne so many of Belisarius' brilliant war plans.

"It wasn't Uliaris' fault, my friend," John whispered, his speech slurred and uneven as blood pooled at the corners of his mouth. "It was mine."

Rosamund sprinted out of Belisarius' tent, ordering camp attendants to fetch her supplies and as many bandages and jars of clean water that could be found. As Belisarius relaxed, I released him from my grip, the sword falling from his hand and clattering uselessly onto the floor. Uliaris wailed apologies and requested that the general take his life as repayment, so I ordered the Frankish bucellarii to depart to my own quarters and into the company of Xerxes and Perenus until further notice.

Much later, the tale of John's injury and Belisarius' rage grew clearer as more cataphracts thundered back to camp, privately speaking with me regarding what had transpired. From what I could gather, John had led his forces on an extended chase to the south and west, trailing Gelimer and pausing for only the briefest of breaks as men reached the limits of their endurance. Gelimer frequently diverted his path or lay ambushes to dissuade John from further attacks, slowing the Romans' progress despite the limited distance that Gelimer was able to travel away from Tricamarum.

On the third day, however, John's riders finally caught up to those of Gelimer. Both forces were hardly capable of standing as their commanders initiated their skirmish, yet neither could retreat or regroup out of the desperation of their situation. As John's forces nearly overcame what limited resistance Gelimer could still muster, John himself became lost in the fighting, surrounded by a haze of sand and dust that stung exposed eyes and rendered poor the judgment of dozens who had been long deprived of food or water. Believing John an attacking Vandal, Uliaris launched his francisca at the supposed attacker, the axe mistakenly burying within John's guts instead. The attack on Gelimer was immediately ceased, and Uliaris mounted the freshest horse available, galloping hard for Tricamarum or the nearest sign of civilization to heal John of his injury.

As he lay bleeding in Belisarius' tent, John held no animosity for his attacker, taking all blame upon himself. Instead, his limited force was trained on Belisarius, his haggard voice forcing him to lean close to his boyhood friend.

"We really did it," John choked once more. "I never stopped believing it was possible, not since we were children."

Belisarius wept bitterly, swallowing hard as he nodded to John. "We did it together," he replied. "I couldn't have done this without you."

John took a haggard breath as his eyes widened, his own tears matching Belisarius'. A hand reached toward Belisarius' collar as the blood-soaked Armenian lifted himself from the table, ignoring

Rosamund's protests as he stared into the general's eyes.

"Promise me," John croaked. "Promise me that you'll see this to the end. See our dream fulfilled."

Belisarius shook his head. "The war is over," he replied angrily. "We should never have come here."

"Only the dead have seen the end of war," John said, the quote stirring memories of his identical warning in Cherson after the war with Persia was declared. "You know that Justinian isn't finished."

Gritting his teeth, Belisarius grasped John's arms to offer a measure of support as his friend weakened from blood loss. "I can't do it without you," Belisarius replied, fat tears falling to his beard.

"You must," John answered, his words as firm as they had ever been. "I just wish I could have been there to see Rome with you."

Belisarius embraced John, his arm wrapped around John's head as he cried aloud. Placing a gentle hand along Belisarius' back, Rosamund insisted that she be given room to work her art upon John's body, already preparing salves that would help staunch the open wound along John's abdomen. It seemed ludicrous that such a minor wound could cause so much damage, a thin arc in the shape of a francisca that could have been easily reknit within a few moments. Yet Rosamund worried more about the dozens of veins severed on John's insides, the blood mixing with bile and toxic humors that poisoned the Armenian tribune and left him unable to rise or sit. After he planted a kiss on John's forehead, he nodded to Rosamund, signaling me to follow to an unknown destination.

Stabilized by Rosamund's labors, John lived through that evening and into the following morning. Belisarius and I sat in silence throughout that time, not even deigning to eat or drink as he peered into the shrinking flames of a nearby brazier. Oddly, Belisarius insisted that I consume my own meal, going so far as to order servants to fetch bread and hardened cheese. He showed little surprise when Rosamund glided into our tent and gave him a somber nod, her clothing layered in all manner of bodily humors as testament to John's inevitable fate. Nodding, Belisarius rose from the fire and disappeared back into his own tent, his screams muffled by the heavy cloth lining the tent's frame.

Ignoring all inquests, he remained aloof from the world for an entire day and night, refusing to answer requests that John's body be taken for cleaning and preparation for its consignment to the fire. Lacking guidance, many of Belisarius' attendants and officers turned to me for orders or advice, although I did little more than continue his instructions to gain control over remaining Vandal holdouts. I did request a detachment of Indulf's Goths to seek out Gelimer's position and attempt to force his peaceful surrender, a task that Indulf welcomed with relish. Aside from that, I ordered camp servants to continue to prepare Belisarius' meals, finding one tray emptied of its contents later that evening.

"We should send for Antonina," Rosamund said in the privacy of my tent. "If Belisarius won't seek comfort with his men, he will with his wife."

Rosamund's suggestion was well intentioned but impractical. "By the time we send a messenger to Carthage, and Antonina rides out, Belisarius will have guided the army back to the coast."

"Antonina deserves to know," Rosamund said. "Perhaps I can dictate a letter to her? The messenger would arrive before Belisarius would."

"As you please," I concluded. "Although, knowing Antonina, she won't want to be inconvenienced by someone else's needs."

"You misjudge her," Rosamund countered but offered no further fight.

John's death was devastating, and not only to Belisarius. John was beloved throughout the ranks—a man who possessed an ingenuity for organization that allowed a motley array of Romans to prevail against far superior foes. He was no Belisarius, lacking his commander's ease at walking through the ranks, committing each man's deeds to memory. His loss left a void in our command. And for one unlucky servant, it destroyed his soul.

The following day, members of Belisarius' bucellarii alerted me to angry shouts emanating from their leader's tent, despite entertaining no company, his pitiful voice backed by sounds of crashing metal and cracking wood. None dared to approach John's killer. Hardening against fears of a sudden attack, I called out to Uliaris before throwing his tent flap open, finding a noose wrapped around his neck, his dirt-crusted feet balancing against a rough wooden stool. In one swift motion, I drew my sword from its sheath and severed the rope secured to the topmost tent beam. Uliaris crashed to the ground in a squall of curses and self-pity. Rolling on the ground, he vomited noisily as his body slammed against several emptied wineskins, his cries a nearly incomprehensible mixture of Frankish and Latin.

Lifting Uliaris by the collar of his wine-sodden shirt, I snarled into his face. "You think that killing yourself will make up for any sins?"

Uliaris wept inconsolably, his head lolling from one shoulder to the other. "I killed John," he muttered. "I was given everything, and I had one job. Belisarius would be right to behead me."

Slapping Uliaris painfully with my leather gloves, I sat the man on the stool that had held his filthy feet. "And drunk!" I yelled. "Those beams wouldn't even hold your weight! You'd just fall in a big useless heap, the tent all around you."

The scolding made Uliaris bawl all the harder, falling back to the ground in a stinking heap. "Just let me die," he begged. "I can't live with the shame."

I shook my head. "Even John said it wasn't your fault. I'm not letting you sleep alone until you're sober."

Uliaris' feeble protests did nothing to stop Altan or Sindual from hauling him to his feet and toward the neat formation of tents that sheltered the foederati. I was told later that Uliaris slept in a daze for half of a day, puking painfully between fits of sobs and self-pity. Uliaris soon calmed in the presence of other soldiers, including several bucellarii who validated John's recount of his final skirmish.

Greeted by storm-wracked skies, Belisarius emerged from his tent the next morning, his face gaunt and features disheveled as members of his elite bucellarii jumped to attention. Finding me sitting patiently nearby, Belisarius strode slowly to my position. I rose and offered a formal salute.

"Build a pyre," Belisarius said hoarsely. "As big as you can make it."

Outfitted in full war dress and placed into neat formations, the entire Roman army assembled for John's funeral that evening. Rosamund painstakingly cleaned John's wounds and washed grime from his face and hands, helping Belisarius fasten John's intricate armor around his body. Copying my example with Vitalius, Belisarius wrapped the armored soldier in the Emperor's banners, the vast Chi-Rho positioned directly over the outline of his torso and legs. A shield and spear were placed at John's side, although Belisarius kept the spatha that John carried into all their battles together, refusing to be parted with that last memento of their shared triumphs, dreams, and defeats.

True to Belisarius' orders, John's pyre was the height of a soldier, the wooden pillar placed at the tallest point of Tricamarum's hill so all could pay respects to their fallen leader. Adorned in his finest armor and the plumed helmet of a magister militum, Belisarius strode to the base of the pyre, facing the neat rows of thousands of Roman soldiers.

"His name was John, hailing from the distant mountains of Armenia," Belisarius said, his voice even and firm as it carried across the valley below. "By virtue of his success, he was a general of the Roman Empire, who sacrificed his life in service of the Roman people."

Belisarius paused several heartbeats, his chest heaving as he gathered the words to carry on. A single torch was placed into his grasp as he straightened, his eyes fixed far into the distance and unseeing of any soldiers in his employ.

"And he was my friend, whom I loved," Belisarius went on. "He will not be forgotten, and we shall not look upon another like him again."

As Belisarius lowered the torch onto John's pyre, the pillar of flames that followed quickly consumed the body, leaving behind a massive arc that trailed above the height of a dozen men stacked one atop the other. We all stood in silence for several heartbeats as the flames grew, their heat glowing along Belisarius' armor. He ignored any discomfort as he remained fixed upon John, slowly raising his arm in salute as the man's body was devoured in the conflagration.

Then, amidst the silence, a single voice roared from a column of Thracian spearmen. From my position, it was initially difficult to decipher, yet soon I made out the chant of Baduarius, his deep tenor rising above the crackling fire in his own send-off for John's memory.

"Roma Victrix! John! John!" Baduarius yelled, his voice initially alone in the disruption of the somber atmosphere.

Other Thracians soon took up the call, their voices rising in harmonious unison. A thousand spears stamped into the earth while others bashed swords against their shields, the percussion deafening yet not outstripped by calls of John's name. The chanting continued for some time, as none tired and few desired to be outdone in their praise by others in the army, as great a victory chant as ever had been shared by any force of Romans who walked the earth. Though Belisarius did not join in the music, I did see him offer the briefest of smiles as he stood alone on the ramparts.

In the morning, the fire's remnants still glowed, though its heat had consumed any trace of a man whose mind had given birth to the strategies that brought the Empire glory against countless enemies.

Another day passed before Belisarius summoned me to discuss our strategy to conclude the war. Alone, we sat together as Belisarius poured two cups of cool water into simple clay cups, handing one to me as he explained his intentions.

"I'm taking the bulk of the army back to Carthage," Belisarius began. "I can't stay here any longer, and we still have hundreds of miles to pacify and reintegrate into the Empire. Not to mention, I must notify the Emperor of our position and needs and seek further guidance."

"What do we do about Gelimer?"

Belisarius gave a grim nod. "I need you to take the entire foederati and seek Gelimer out in whatever mountain fastness that he's clung to," Belisarius declared, his tone dark and bitter as he issued the order. "By whatever means necessary, end this war. I will send you any supplies or reinforcements as they become necessary, but do not fail me in this."

Rising, I saluted. Belisarius handed me several of John's hand-sketched maps of the surrounding region, including markings from recent scouting reports of Gelimer's last-known position in the interior Numidian mountains near Bulla Regia. Believing myself dismissed, I rose from the chair and moved to execute his orders, stopping only as Belisarius added one final note.

"And take Uliaris with you," Belisarius said in a note of finality. "See this done, and we can all go home."

THE DUEL

We departed camp the following morning, well before Belisarius led the majority of the army back to Carthage. Having had plenty of time to rest and refit in the aftermath of battle, the Herulians and Huns gathered supplies for an extended foray to the west, following John's instructions as we traced Gelimer's footsteps. Of those who ventured with our war band, only Rosamund lacked the formal weapons and training of a soldier, yet she politely refused to return with Belisarius to the safety of Carthage. Instead, Rosamund rode alongside my officers as we moved deeper into Numidia, sending messengers to find Indulf and request his assistance in our search for Gelimer's whereabouts.

Uliaris rode with my Herulians, and while thankfully sober, he was constantly morose along our journey. Lacking the will or strength to perform even simple tasks, he refused to bathe or eat, and it wasn't until Perenus dumped a bucket of freezing water over his dirt-crusted clothing that Uliaris rose with indigent anger. Nevertheless, I gave him time to grieve in his own way, visiting at regular intervals while providing as much privacy as could be had within an army on the march. However, I made sure that at least one of my men had a close eye on his activities, fearful that his clearer and more determined mind may succeed where more drunken efforts at constructing a hangman's noose had failed miserably.

Within two days, our scouts succeeded in their task, ferrying messages from Indulf that confirmed the Goth's intentions to link up with the foederati's larger force. Further, Indulf's own reports suggested that Gelimer had not departed, with his banners spotted along the foothills of Mount Papua. Samur and I analyzed John's map as we added markings of Indulf's sightings, placing Mount Papua roughly halfway between the isolated fortress of Bulla Regia and the rich coastal trading post of Hippo Regius.

"It makes sense," Samur reasoned. "Bulla Regia is linked to roads and easy to besiege. But a mountain? Belisarius lacks the supply lines to effectively blockade each slope or hidden trail."

Even Samur was surprised by the veracity of his words. Nearing Gelimer's supposed location, we finally encountered Indulf's forces, confirming his previous report and providing an improved understanding of the surrounding region.

"Gelimer is definitely somewhere near the top of Mount Papua," Indulf began. "Eight hundred souls, maybe a thousand? At least half are wounded or infirm, or are women."

"I wouldn't underestimate the Vandal women," Perenus said, drawing Rosamund's interest. "They seem vicious enough."

"As you wish," Indulf replied. "But Gelimer's greater ally is the terrain itself. Only one trail is known to us that is amenable to horses, and a dozen Vandal soldiers could hold off hundreds of our foederati without suffering serious losses. We could rise along the hills by foot, but many will snap ankles or simply get lost in the forest, and all would make enough noise to warn Gelimer well in advance of our coming."

"So what do you suggest?" Sembrouthes asked. "Both options seem equally unproductive."

Indulf smirked. "Burn them out," he answered. "Light fires at multiple points and watch Gelimer roast for his hubris."

As monstrous a suggestion as it was, Indulf's idea was tantalizing in that it would bring a swift end to the debacle, which threatened to spill over into the frosts and snows of winter. Absent the warmth of the African coastline, the interior Numidian mountains had already grown frigid as winter set in early in the region, leaving me thankful for the heavy cloaks and blankets that Belisarius had forced our men to carry.

Yet I declined.

"We need to have verifiable proof of Gelimer's death or surrender," I answered. "Even if the fire killed him, a dozen imposters could sprout up later, claiming to have escaped by magic. We need Gelimer's head or voice to bring the war to a close."

Routed, Indulf shrugged. "You are correct, of course," he replied. "But it will be difficult going, I fear."

Using our superior numbers to our advantage, I stationed the three sections of foederati into separate camps around the mountain. Thankfully narrow, we were never more than a few hours' ride from reaching one another, allowing for an ease of coordination in the event of a sudden Vandal sally. However, no such attack came, with only a few glimpses of Vandal banners along the mountain's trails to signify the presence of a great barbarian king.

Indulf and Fulcaris spent the next two days probing the entrances to Mount Papua, seeking out any hidden paths or fortuitous leads that would offer an easier trek toward the mountain's summit. Though we gained greater knowledge of the thick forests and brush along Papua's base, we found little to exploit, with two Goths disappearing in the process of their search. All that was ever recovered from their final position was a half-eaten apple and a blunted dagger, leaving Indulf in a fury at the loss of more Goths.

Indulf's rage made him insist upon a full assault, a request that I had little opportunity or strategy to decline with no alternate strategies having revealed themselves. Each section of the foederati offered up a hundred men to march to the summit, instructed to clear away any resistance, yet retreat if Vandal forces threatened to overwhelm our positions. Fulcaris, Sinnion, and Indulf all led their separate efforts, each departing at an appointed hour in hopes that Gelimer's broken, discouraged, and hungry forces would fall at the sight of an ever-determined Roman foe.

By nightfall, the attacking forces had all withdrawn in utter failure. Rising along a steeper slope, Indulf's Goths frequently halted near crevasses or exceedingly dense tree coverage, forcing them to maneuver toward more favorable ground as they rose in elevation. All they accomplished was to become lost, forcing Indulf to retreat back to the relative safety of the mountain's base in a cloud of frustration and embarrassment.

Fulcaris had better luck, finding an easier route of ascension that allowed the Herulians to reach an approximate middle point along the mountain. However, as Indulf had previously warned, the considerable noise that rose from crushed leaves and snapping branches offered ample warning to Gelimer's forces, bringing a Vandal shield wall bearing down upon their Herulian attackers. Forced to fight an uncomfortable angle uphill, Fulcaris took a half dozen losses before sounding a horn to retreat, unwilling to force the issue at the risk of dozens of his foederati.

Sinnion had the worst of it. Following the cleared path to Mount Papua's summit, Sinnion quickly ascended to the upper reaches of Gelimer's fastness, disappearing from view as dense plant life blocked most light or visibility to the Hunnic forces. Guided by torches, Sinnion reached the outline of a crude palisade gate, then found himself surrounded by armed Vandals in the dim glow of the mountain. Though Sinnion was able to lead the Huns to freedom, two dozen of his men were left behind along the trail, although he later swore that his men cut down an equal number of Gelimer's Vandals.

In the week that followed, we attempted several further forays, all of which bore only the fruit of exhaustion and frustration. Though each officer was far more careful to avoid unnecessary casualties, another half dozen of the foederati either disappeared or were cut down along the mountain's expanse, leaving us little improved in prying Gelimer from his hold. Against my hopes, our siege fell into a monotonous rhythm, the hopes of a quick victory melting away as more comfortable lodgings and stronger defensive fortifications were raised to protect my foederati in their mission.

The worst would soon befall our forces, for the first snows arrived on the mountain with a vengeance. Thick flakes accumulated first above a man's feet and soon thereafter near his boot line, making it all the more difficult to traipse about the mountain's thick vegetation. Gusting winds blew piles of snow about in various directions, masking footprints and making it deceptively easy to find oneself lost in a pristine expanse of thick woods—a death sentence regardless of whether Vandals found the unfortunate scouts first. By the end of that miserable day, I made up my mind in frustrated determination, eager to end this struggle and bring Belisarius news of Gelimer's final defeat.

"Don't be a fool!" Rosamund screamed, throwing an empty iron pot at my head.

Ducking to avoid the missile, I responded calmly, gesturing to the mountaintop. "It's the only way," I replied. "We could remain here for weeks or even months. Who knows how well supplied Gelimer is up there?"

Sembrouthes was not convinced. "Rosamund speaks reason," the Aksumite replied, shivering against the cold. "There's no guarantee it would work."

"None," I admitted. "But it's the only option I have."

Later that day, I gathered leaders of each arm of the foederati, explaining my intended strategy and issuing orders if fate should leave me another corpse amongst the brush.

"I'm raising a flag of truce and going to speak with Gelimer face-to-face," I explained. "If he will surrender, I'll let him return to Carthage in honor and comfort, his people safe and free."

"And if Gelimer refuses?" Samur questioned skeptically. "Why not send another in your place? I would take this burden from you."

I shook my head. "I need each of you to lead your men if I should fall," I explained. "And Gelimer would have reason to believe the words of an oathsworn to the Empress, and to Belisarius. It must be me."

Rosamund scoffed, furious at my decision. "Then I'm going too. I lead no foederati."

"Me as well," Xerxes replied immediately after.

"And me," Sembrouthes offered in a note of finality. "But I still think it is a fool's errand. If Gelimer wants to keep his crown, all he has to do is wait for weather or hunger or disease to sap our strength."

"Then let's hope his people are hungrier, dirtier, and more miserable than we are," I replied.

Reluctant to remain behind, Samur, Perenus, and Fulcaris each offered their embrace and words of luck before our tiny band marched up the fixed path of Mount Papua. Tying a white flag atop a spear and carrying our shields in reverse, we four marched ever higher, leaving behind the tempting warmth and safety of the foederati in favor of the damp and frigid darkness of the mountain.

It required a surprising length of time to ascend that hill, the weight of our armor and gear punishing our bodies with each step through the murky darkness. Rosamund alone appeared unaffected by the cumbersome burden, her feet sliding lightly atop the path as she moved like a wraith up its expanse. Few words were exchanged, as we remained on alert at all times, our progress halted on several occasions as whisperings of the forest took on the tones of men at our sides.

Together with their weapons and equipment, Xerxes and Sembrouthes bore torches at either side of our formation. Our boots crunched and squelched along the ground as we initially attempted a measure of stealth but soon surrendered into a brisker pace, any attempt at not emitting considerable noise hopeless as we stumbled upward. Though light from the sun bored through the thick overgrowth of the path, shadows danced from our torches, producing enough light to see a dozen paces before our eyes, yet not well enough to warn of stones or torn branches that threatened to maim or trip.

Xerxes cursed mightily as he stubbed his toe on a mercifully smooth stone, its mass hidden by a thick coat of leaves that had fallen to the earth in the weeks prior.

After hours of searching, we arrived at our first verified signs of life along Mount Papua. Or what had once been life. Eyeing a number of Hunnic corpses, I raised my truce-strewn spear high into the air, hoping that no hidden Vandals would project javelins into my exposed chest. Though blanketed by snow and preserved by cold, the Huns had begun to decay, their eyes liquifying and mouths agape as the few remaining insects of the area feasted on their bodies. Regardless of their likely status as pagans, I muttered a prayer over their corpses, asking forgiveness for leading these men into as unforgiving and unfamiliar a place as the slopes of Mount Papua. Rosamund copied my efforts, crouching close to the bodies as she searched for clues of their demise.

"There's nothing we can do for them now," Sembrouthes said. "If we mean to grab Gelimer's notice, now is the time."

Taking a deep breath, I nodded and committed the four of us to a potentially suicidal strategy that Belisarius certainly would not have approved of, regardless of the desperation of our situation. Hefting my truce-mounted spear and raising my reversed shield as high as my arm would allow, I stepped ahead of my group, awaiting a hidden strike that would pierce my armor and send me tumbling to the ground.

"We come in peace!" I yelled, repeating the statement in Greek and in Latin several times in hopes that some amongst Gelimer's survivors would speak these more elegant tongues. "I am Varus, tribune of the Roman foederati, excubitor to Emperor Justinian and oathsworn to the Empress Theodora. I come under a banner of truce to entreat with Gelimer, king of the Vandals."

My shouts mounted no response. Violent winds blew along the trees as snow flurries slid between the entwined trees, leaving my call answered only by the noises of winter.

After a time, I repeated my entreaty. The same eerie silence was all that responded, leaving me to continue my attempt for a third and final time.

Discouraged, I made to retreat, until cracking noises from the darker portion of the woods brought me to freeze in icy fear. Their clothing torn and bodies filthy, dozens of Vandals formed a half circle around our expedition. Xerxes and Sembrouthes lowered their spears in a meaningless defense.

"I was beginning to wonder if you Romans were daft." Gunderic chuckled. "But now I see you are merely insane. Why else would you fly the coward's flag?"

Emerging from the darkness, Gunderic's bulging frame was caked in dirt and patched with a number of healing cuts and scratches. Despite these conditions, Gunderic appeared reasonably well nourished, defying reports of our scouts that most of the Vandal force had been reduced to roasting vermin or gathering acorns for soup.

"A message for Gelimer," I replied formally, "from General Belisarius. The war is over, the question is what terms Gelimer would like to discuss for his surrender."

Gunderic's eye twitched as he scanned my body. A fist ground against the pommel of his sword, and Gunderic grunted. The grunts became the foundation for booming laughter, a sound that was raised by each of the massive Vandal's men.

"Yes, I remember you, Lord Varus of the Herulians," Gunderic said between snorts. "A Heruli who fights for Romans. Why do you hate yourself so much?"

First Rosamund, then Xerxes, and now a Vandal giant who wanted little else than to see me carved in half. Ignoring the barbs, I attempted to remain in line with my intended goal. "The Emperor is prepared to allow Gelimer to live in peace and wealth if he surrenders his crown now, without further bloodshed," I explained. "I insist that you take me to see him."

Gunderic laughed playfully again. "Aye, but what if we want bloodshed?"

Despite myself, I smiled in response. "If that is your wish, the Emperor is prepared to provide that as well, although you would not appreciate the results."

Gunderic hooted in appreciation for my riposte. "There's the sense of humor! Now I can trust you aren't one of those Roman cunts with a tree branch lodged in his arse, always walking about with a glum face."

I sighed. "Lord Gunderic, you have three choices," I began. "You can kill us, you can allow us safe passage back to the valley, or you can bring me to your king. I prefer the third option, but any are preferable to idle chat."

"That's unfortunate," Gunderic replied. The Vandal warlord considered his options, making a show of weighing choices with his meaty hands as he shrugged with indifference. "I'll take you to Gelimer—if you answer one question."

"As you wish," I responded, "if it is my right to answer, I will."

"Why do you ride with Huns?" Gunderic asked, genuinely curious. "These are a people that nearly annihilated my ancestors and came within an arse hair of putting your Empire under their heel. If they weren't hopelessly divided into their dozens of tribes, they still might have the power to do so."

I chuckled, having wondered the same several times previously. "The Huns are excellent warriors, and loyal," I explained. "And besides, the Emperor prefers Huns and Vandals killing one another to his own citizens dying on the battlefield."

"As would I!" Gunderic beamed happily. "Very well, I will take you to Gelimer if you wish. But be warned, you may not be allowed to leave alive."

"I have faith," I responded weakly.

Gunderic's armed band filed through the path from their hiding posts, unveiling dozens of men that had been artfully disguised within the natural concealment of the forest's trees and brush. Climbing uphill through a steadily steepening path, we soon came upon a freshly hewn palisade wall, its lone tower housing a guardsman whose face was concealed behind thick scarves over his nose and mouth.

"Heilar, open the gate!" Gunderic yelled. "I'm freezing my arse out here, and the king has guests."

Acknowledging Gunderic, the sentry nodded to invisible figures below, who soon unbarred and opened the wooden portal into Gelimer's camp. Gunderic stomped ahead and signaled for us to follow. Rosamund gaped.

By the looks of the numerous soot-caked huts strewn along the mountain, hundreds had followed Gelimer's desperate retreat. Though many bore arms like Gunderic, others were old, wounded, or infirm, yet their menacing glares left me little doubt that they would fight with mattocks and clubs if Gelimer commanded men and women alike to fight to the death. Though resilient, many bore signs of wasting and constant discomfort, leaving a spark of hope that the Vandal king would surrender his final fortress in favor of a more luxurious existence.

Though I had observed Gelimer on the battlefield, I was unprepared for the king's features and demeanor as Gunderic led our party into a slightly cleaner and more intricate hut along a narrow stream. Far from an unwashed or uncouth savage, Gelimer bathed often, plucking lice and knots from his straw-yellow hair and beard with a comb shaped from deer antler. Further, Gelimer appeared every bit the warrior that any of his men had been, defying my expectations of a sniveling coward or a weakling with thoughts of survival over honor. Even Gelimer's manners would not have been out of place in Justinian's Court as he waved his guests aside and ordered a meeting in the expansive clearing at the center of the settlement, although Gelimer's crude Latin would have been mocked by children due to its coarse accent and simple diction.

"We've slain your scouts, so why should I allow you to live?" Gelimer asked suddenly, watching impatiently as a wooden chair and stool were made available for the king's use.

"We are no scouts. We are emissaries from General Belisarius and

Emperor Justinian," I offered. "The Emperor offers you peace and prosperity in return for your obedience and abdication."

Gelimer laughed, a cruel mocking tone as his nostrils flared. "The Emperor? I see an Aksumite, a Persian, a Gepid, and a plainsrider all standing before me, but no Romans. Not even those cockless Greek boys your Emperor likes to bandy about on his business, paying gold to keep stronger men contented and at bay."

"Regardless of our origins, we are all Roman," I replied defiantly. "And our message remains unchanged, if you have ears to hear it."

Though many kept clear of Gelimer's throne and bodyguards, dozens of faces peered into the clearing, watching curiously and hopefully upon the four strange figures who brought an opportunity to end this savage conflict. Gelimer considered my words before countering with his own, his voice low and menacing as his deep-green eyes peered unblinking at each of my party.

"You come to entreat with the king of all the Vandals and demand the end of our kingdom, which would be egregious enough," Gelimer boomed. "But you do so without proper tribute."

I rolled my eyes. "It is not the Emperor's position to pay tribute to the vanquished," I began, "but what is it that you require?"

Gelimer smiled mockingly at that question. "As long as any gathering of Vandals has breath, we are not vanquished," he began. "A simple gift of bread, wine, and a lyre would go far to ease the rigors of this place, but I fear it is not enough to satisfy our ancient customs."

My gut tightened as I anticipated Gelimer's demand, yet I went through the ritual of banter as the Empire's representative. "And what would that entail?"

"In the days of my ancestor Geiseric, who protected his people from Attila and conquered Africa, no foreigner could make a demand of the king without a sacrifice of blood," Gelimer explained mischievously. "We have been negligent, thanks to the laxness of my predecessor, but perhaps it is an appropriate time to bring these customs back in style."

I shook my head. "Christians do not participate in human sacrifice, and I will not be subject to those requirements."

Gelimer laughed. "You mistake me, Tribune Varus. Not human sacrifice, but a trial by single combat."

Dozens of Gelimer's spearmen clapped and howled, while Sembrouthes hissed. In hurried Greek, he translated to Xerxes and Rosamund, who huffed.

Gelimer was not finished. "However, I will not have it said that Gelimer was unreasonable to the unwarriorlike Romans," he declared. "If you would rather avoid such trials, I will allow you to leave my camp unharmed. Your companions, however, will remain here as my slaves, a fair payment for the insults you have lain at the feet of the Vandal king."

"Not a chance in hell," I snarled.

"I'll slay any you would throw against us!" Xerxes called from behind me, his words translated into Gelimer's ear by a nearby attendant.

Gelimer shook his head. "As the leader of your party, it will be Varus or none at all!" Gelimer roared, raising a hand and leveling a pointed finger at my body. "Choose, and let it be done."

"I accept your challenge," I said. "Your time in Africa has come to an end."

The swelling crowd stirred in a mixture of curiosity and approval, although shouts of joy or excitement were reserved for Gelimer's remaining warriors. Smiling at my decision, Gelimer agreed to my terms.

"Vanquish my champion, and you will have your audience," the Vandal king declared. "However, I wouldn't place many coins upon your chances."

"Whoever it is, send them out," I barked, bile rising in my throat. I knew who my enemy would be.

"A true fighter. Very good!" Gelimer responded, clapping his hands. "A worthy sacrifice, deserving of only one man to butcher."

Rubbing his hands together, Gelimer looked to the hundred

warriors stationed at his side, their ranks increasing with each moment as word spread throughout the encampment of the looming duel. His mouth spreading in a wide grin, Gelimer glanced upon his champion, charging him with the defense of Vandal honor.

"Gunderic, there are intruders present!" Gelimer yelled. "Slaughter them for me."

Though tired and hungry, even the less warlike Vandals in Gelimer's mountain village cheered their champion. Grubby children fought for viewing space as a wide circle formed along the camp's center clearing, a human barricade that marked the dueling arena. Thankfully, my comrades were not mistreated at this point, allowed to retain their belongings and directed toward an edge of the expanse.

Protected by interlocking layers of segmented bronze and iron, Gunderic's armor must have weighed double the standard scale chestpiece and leg armor of a cataphract lancer. Its design reminded me of the more ancient armors of Rome's legionaries whose visage had been etched in stone motifs along the Hippodrome's walls, the layered metal providing an equal measure of flexibility as well as balanced protection from any attacking sword or arrow. A wealthy encasement, Gunderic required the assistance of two other Vandals as he girded himself for combat.

Preparing his thick bronze and iron armor, Gunderic yelled out to me, his beard dancing as he threw out a throaty laugh.

"You called me a coward at Ad Decimum," Gunderic said. "It made me quite upset!"

"You ran; I didn't!" I retorted.

Gunderic's men laughed at the war of words.

While we waited for my opponent to prepare, Xerxes jogged to my side, urging in whispered Persian for me to clear my mind against the enemy.

"How am I supposed to take him down? He's basically a walking tree!"

Xerxes sighed. "Big shiteater like that, all you can do is tire him out," Xerxes murmured. "Jab and turn, and avoid getting tangled with him at all costs. One punch from those fists, and you're as good as dead. But he has to tire eventually."

"Eventually," I groaned.

"My advice: go for the legs," Xerxes responded, knocking away my souring mood. "You're unlikely to win this fight with a single overpowering blow, but rather with a hundred tiny cuts."

Clapping his hands, Gelimer ordered onlookers to back away from the flat dirt and grass of the dueling grounds. Rechecking the knotted straps on my helmet and armor, Xerxes nodded as he offered his final words of encouragement.

"You can do this!" Xerxes yelled at me, clapping me hard on my shoulders. "Send this bastard back to whatever underworld belched him forth."

Shooting a final glance back to Rosamund, I tore the flag of truce from my spear and hefted my shield upright. As Gunderic and I approached within ten paces of one another, Gelimer fell into a separate conversation with one of his warriors, relishing the entertainment to come.

"You shouldn't have come here," Gunderic said in stilted Greek, his thickly protected head towering well above my own.

I grunted. "Even if you kill me, more Romans will come and swarm this place. You'll never leave this place of your own accord."

My defiance was met by joyful laughter. "Aye, but that's life!" Gunderic smiled cheerily. "And don't be so cynical, my friend, it might be you that defeats me!"

"Then why not surrender peacefully?" I asked. "Belisarius has promised your safety and wealth if Gelimer surrenders now. The Emperor would happily honor that pact if it meant Africa rejoins the Empire."

Gunderic nodded sadly. "Yes, I could do that," he responded slowly. "But my king, the ungrateful cock that he is, wants me to cut your head off. Men may tell many stories of me, but I've never disobeyed an order."

"Pointless." I glowered. "Wasteful."

Gunderic smiled sadly as he nodded. "But would you do any different if our fates were reversed?"

Closing my eyes, I considered the larger man's unexpected reflection. "No," I responded forcefully, "I wouldn't."

Flexing his fingers around his own shield and spear, Gunderic nodded. "Our choices are rarely our own to make," he said. "I've lived a happy life that my ancestors would respect. Perhaps in the next, you and I will be kinsmen instead of enemies."

"Perhaps," I answered, smiling weakly despite myself. "We shall see."

"Gunderic!" Gelimer shouted, his distraction concluded as a slave carried a heavy burden to the king. "As we are invoking the laws of the undefeated Geiseric, it is only right that you wield his blade to butcher another Roman dog."

Grabbing the cumbersome scabbard in both hands, Gelimer handed the sword to another warrior, who trotted toward Gunderic to hand over the weapon with a look of reverence. Though its hilt and blade lacked the intricate designs of many more famous Roman blades, its construction appeared sturdy and looked to be made of iron of the highest quality despite its considerable age. Sizing its weight, Gunderic temporarily unsheathed the blade, its edge stretching nearly the height of a full-grown man. Though its ponderous weight would have quickly exhausted a seasoned warrior using two hands, Gunderic used one to swing the massive blade about, shrugging at the simplicity of Gelimer's orders. Unbuckling his own blade, Gunderic returned his new sword to its scabbard and tied both behind his back before reequipping his spear and shield.

Gelimer rose to speak of the terms of the duel and of the customs of the Vandals, who prized conquest above all other things in this world. Yet I had no ears for bloodlust. My thoughts turned to my friends and my family, and I whispered a prayer to God to keep them safe. Wishing that Father Petrus were present to ease my worries, I begged forgiveness for my sins, praying that God would hear my words in this far-flung and desolate place. Most of all, I thought of

Zenobia, Mariya, and my unborn child, praying for their safety and protection as Gelimer concluded his gaudy pronouncements.

"Let only the strongest survive!" Gelimer yelled. "Begin!"

Within a heartbeat, Gunderic rushed against me, shifting his balance on either foot as he sought to mask his intended strike by forcing me to adjust my guard with each step. In my youth, Godilas had lectured that such beasts of men should be feared for their strength though were generally slow of foot and easy to outwit with a sober mind. As I was overlarge in comparison to most in the army, there were few who possessed greater strength or height, with Godilas' teachings generally unveiling the truth of how to defeat these foes. Archelaus had been one such monster who defied conventions, his speed and skill unrivaled even by Xerxes, yet I have no doubt that his movements were stunted by wine and poor weather. Neither advantage was made available to me here as Gunderic leveled his spear toward my body with swiftness that seemed impossible for his immense size, leaving me little other choice than to defend.

Muscles pulsing along his neck, Gunderic grunted as he thrust forward, driving the iron point of his spear clean through the wooden panels of my shield. While I was temporarily thankful that the weapon struck empty space rather than the flesh of my arm, I yelped as Gunderic yanked the spear back, nearly throwing me from my feet. In desperation, I thrust at Gelimer's exposed torso with my own spear, its progress halted as Gunderic wrapped a gloved hand near the top of my spear shaft. My spearhead cut a deep rent into Gunderic's armor, yet its impossibly thick layers left the Vandal warlord unharmed as he tugged my weapon from my grasp.

Separating, I quickly untied the straps of my shield, allowing that blessed layer of protection to fall to the ground due to the heavy spear hanging from its edge. Chortling at my display, Gunderic tossed my seized spear aside before disposing of his own bulwark, throwing it lightly toward a nearby Vandal warrior who shouted bawdy encouragement to Gelimer's champion.

"I never liked spears," Gunderic yelled to me jokingly. "Poking things is for lovemaking, not for fighting!"

Rising in frustration at the perceived invincibility of the man, I yelled back whatever insults I could muster. "Neither did Tzazon or Ammatas, which cost them their lives!" I replied clumsily in Latin.

Gunderic's brows rose, yet someone other than my intended victim rose from his chair, his once happy face purpling. "Gunderic, slay this dog!" the Vandal king screamed. "Enough joking around!"

Gunderic shrugged, unsheathing the greatsword at his back and taking two practice swings to reacquaint himself with its weight and balance. I followed Gunderic's example and drew my own sword, its bluish tinge catching narrow rays of light along the arena as its runes flickered in my defense. Rosamund's voice sounded urgently behind me in words that were too muffled to comprehend. I tightened my thoughts before jerking violently ahead.

In a dead sprint, I charged Gunderic, surprising the warlord, who likely had not encountered many enemies willing to assault him directly. Gunderic parried a combination of cuts and slashed as I fought to keep the larger man from mounting his own offensive, depriving him of any measure of brute strength behind his riposte. Through it all, I could find no fault or imperfection in Gunderic's footwork or technique, our blades dancing in a crash of metal that brought hundreds of Vandals to cheer in delight.

Gunderic quickly bored of the exchange. Jumping back, Gunderic's blade swung in a backhanded arc, forcing me to duck to avoid the blow. The blade whistled as violent waves of disturbed air crashing along my face, leaving me but a moment to resume my offensive. Gunderic, however, had no intention of allowing me to deprive him of any momentum.

While his sword was completing its upward trajectory, Gunderic lashed with a hobnailed boot, its heavy tip cracking into my gut and sending me tumbling back into the grass. Struggling for air, I fought against swelling panic to continue rolling backward, creating sorely needed space from Gunderic as I struggled to rise from my feet.

Gunderic roared as I gasped for breath. My vision blurred from the sharp pain of the blow.

Charging, Gunderic raised his blade for another attack, using the sword's considerable length to his advantage as he swung from three paces away. With one arm clutching at my wounded stomach, I dove, tripping from a lack of coordination and forcing my body into a roll as I maneuvered underneath Gunderic's attack. My arms flailed out as my plume caught along the grass for a heartbeat, forcing me to scramble upright in a mixture of pain and desperation.

"Well, goddamn." Gunderic snorted.

Though it is tempting to credit skill for an unanticipated victory, however minor it may be, Gunderic's wound was nothing more than pure accident. While I thankfully retained a grip along my dragon-hilted sword in my frantic escape, its edge scythed along the weaker joints along the armor of Gunderic's knees, cutting a deep gash along the side of his leg.

As he staggered, I watched Gunderic lower an empty hand to his leg, his gloves contacting a thin sheet of blood that bubbled underneath several layers of iron and leather. People in the crowd gasped at the inopportune sight of first blood, yet Gunderic rose and shrugged off any concerns.

"A nasty trick."

"No trick," I choked out. "Surrender now while you still can."

Gunderic hooted, amused as he gathered his blade and resumed his attack. Blurred stabs and slashes whirred about my body as quickly as before, yet the warlord was noticeably cautious when planting his injured left leg. Though showing no sign of pain or discomfort, Gunderic's hesitation afforded me sorely needed time to anticipate and dodge the Vandal's attacks, reducing my need to parry and allowing me to regather strength despite my sore stomach.

In our exchange of blows, I avoided an outright contest of strength where possible. I did not fear my blade snapping under Gunderic's unmatchable strength—before or since, I have never seen a stronger blade than the runed sword of Emperor Justin—though

I worried about overtaxing muscles and tendons as I countered Gunderic's slashes. On one occasion when our blades did cross, a ripple of lightning shot across my arm, rendering the nerves numb as I struggled to keep a strong guard against further attacks.

However, Gunderic was no fool, and he understood how to use the lengthy greatsword to its ultimate advantages in single combat. Placing more weight upon his uninjured leg, Gunderic advanced aggressively, jabbing to force me to shuffle in retreat and beyond the effective range of my own blade. Nearing the starting location of our bout, Gunderic jabbed and slashed to force me into a less-mobile defensive stance, and then executed an attack to end the bout in his favor.

None other than Gunderic could have maneuvered so broad a blade that swiftly or effortlessly. In one fluid motion, Gunderic ended his slash by lifting the point of the blade to the heavens and cutting in a broad arc into my unguarded hip. In desperation, I used two hands to guard the sweeping blade, unable to dodge or deflect the blow in any other way. Numb fingers gave testament to my ability to soften the blade's damage, yet its edge connected firmly against the thick iron layers that protected my hip. I hissed as Gunderic's sword sawed against leather and skin, jerking away before fatal damage could be inflicted from the wound. The Vandal crowd cheered while Rosamund shouted for the bout to end regardless of the cost.

"Stupid," I muttered. I had fallen for the same attack by Archelaus years before.

"Tiring of the fight?" Gunderic asked. "Tell me now, and I'll spare your life. I always need more servants to fetch my food and clean my dung."

Grinning bloody teeth, I faced Gunderic with all the pretense I could muster. "You think this bothers me?" I asked savagely, ignoring a trickle of blood that flowed down my leg. "I've taken dozens of wounds across the world... this is nothing more than an angry kiss."

Raising his hands in mock praise, Gunderic's eyebrows rose as he paused his attack. "Why fight for these Romans?" he asked. "Come fight with the Vandals, and live free. No emperors or ungrateful aristocrats with their fine silks and honeyed wine, just your iron will against the world."

"You follow the orders of a king that would readily abandon you on the battlefield," I shot back. "How is that any different?"

"Aye, but only because I choose to follow him," Gunderic replied. "The freedom of choice, that is the difference between you and I."

Gelimer roared with indignation at the delay in our combat. "Gunderic, the Roman rat is stalling. Finish this fight now and be done with him!"

On cue, Gunderic charged once more, the slightest of limps forming on his left leg. Not that I was in much better shape, for as I twisted to avoid the blow, the pain nearly prevented me from mounting a defense to preserve my life. I dodged Gunderic's assault where possible and parried where I could not, the swing of our battle continuing as both combatants leaked crimson blood onto Mount Papua's soil.

Until Gunderic's limp caused him to stumble, leaving him to stagger as he lost his balance. Summoning all my reserves, I shot forward, chopping hard at the Vandal warlord's sword arm, aiming just above his gloved and mailed hand and connecting forcefully against the thick steel of his blade. Ill aimed, the force of my attack brought Gunderic to drop his blade and leave his hands empty of any weapon. Whirling around, I angled the point of my sword into his unguarded torso and slashed with the most savage backhand I could muster.

Only for Gunderic to slam a huge fist into my forearm. I dropped my blade. With his other hand, Gunderic grabbed my throat and lifted me into the air, his fingers tightening as my legs dangled helplessly off the ground, my body screaming for oxygen. My near-useless sword arm battered futilely at Gunderic's hand, doing little to lessen the terrible force the Vandal giant inflicted upon my airway.

Desperate to avoid swelling panic, I dropped my free hand to my belt and withdrew the dagger still tied to my belt. Slashing wildly, I cut a superficial wound in Gunderic's arm. He scowled as he loosened his grip just enough for me to steal a breath. Any attempts at a further attack were thwarted as Gunderic wrapped his other hand around my wrist, wringing the dagger from my grip and watching it fall peaceably to the ground.

Gritting his teeth, Gunderic laughed cruelly as he held me aloft, my vision beginning to blur and peripheries melding together as my mouth gaped open, tongue wagging for a desperate taste of fresh air.

"I've been looking for a warrior strong enough to give me a glorious death," Gunderic muttered as he tightened his grip. "Unfortunately, you are not him."

At the precipice of death, a strange temptation to surrender remaining resistance and embrace an end to the pain flooded my mind. Pieces of my body grew foreign and distant, and I remained aware only of my head and body, my limbs seeming to float beyond my universe. With all the power remaining to me, I committed to one final attack, my thoughts burning with an image of Mariya and Zenobia as every fiber of my soul yearned to do pain to my attacker.

Swinging my head slightly back, I jerked my forehead toward Gunderic, its range of motion diminutive as Gunderic's grip about my throat sapped any real force from the blow. My plume and its iron fastenings collided into Gunderic's face, rubbing against his exposed eyes. His grip loosened again, and I gulped a single breath before using my enhanced momentum to swing my helmeted head back again, diving forward once more at my singular opportunity.

This time, my helmet collided sickeningly with Gunderic's face, a snapping noise echoing across the field as blood fountained from Gunderic's ruined nose. Dropping me to the ground, Gunderic staggered, his hands assessing his damaged nose as he moaned, dazed.

Still weak and befuddled, I gasped as I charged at Gunderic, lowering my shoulder and launching from my feet. Gunderic choked as the force of my blow crushed the air from his lungs, driving the giant from his feet and causing him to fall to the ground with a thundering crash of metal and flesh. I landed painfully atop my enemy, slowly sitting upright as I raised an arm to slam into Gunderic's gore-soaked face.

An unanticipated blow from Gunderic's fist connected against my shoulder, knocking me several paces beyond Gunderic's body. Though my arm was thankfully unbroken, it had come unlocked from its socket, and I hurriedly gritted my teeth as I snapped it into its correct position, yelling as the wave of pain quickly subsided and I regained use of the limb. Panting and limping, Gunderic rose to his feet and charged at me, seeking to use the sheer weight of his body to smother his wounded opponent.

With no other options, I rolled to the side, my hand brushing against a snapped half of a spear that Gunderic had begun the battle with. Wrapping my fingers around one end, I waited for Gunderic to charge a few more paces, then swung the wooden pole hard.

Blinded by blood, Gunderic did not see the attack until the last possible moment. Thinking the spear intended for his face, Gunderic raised his arms in a crude guard, leaving his stomach unprotected as I slammed the long edge of my spear shaft against Gunderic's guts. Gunderic was wordless as he doubled over, mouth gaping as he struggled to suck air through a battered body. I launched forward in my final opportunity to end the fight before my bleeding hip sapped me of the strength to continue.

With only a heartbeat to attack, I punched Gunderic hard in the gut before hauling his massive body onto my shoulders, draping his bulk on either side of my body like some crude overlarge cloak. Unable to hold the stance for more than a moment, I succumbed to my injury, slamming Gunderic's body to the earth with as much violence as I could muster.

Gunderic's limbs flailed lifelessly as he connected with the rough soil. Grabbing at the broken spear, I slammed its lengthy side into his gut one more time, bringing a croak of pained resistance but no more. Walking several paces away, I plucked my sword from the ground and returned to Gunderic's shattered body amidst a sea of shocked wails and roars of anger.

Shouting, I raised my sword into the air, looking down at Gunderic's face before sending him to whatever afterlife he prayed to. I paused as my eyes locked on his, finding his bruised and blood-soaked face full of tears as he choked out his final words.

"Do it," Gunderic blubbered, a thin glob of blood choking his breath. "Please."

Weariness overtook my limbs as I breathed sweet air, never before so thankful for so simple a luxury. Gunderic begged once more, his words slurred from pain as both his arms remained outstretched and of little use to the once-invincible giant.

My sword suspended in midair, I turned my gaze back to Gelimer. "The fight is over," I said. "As victor, I demand my right to petition you and see the war between Emperor Justinian and the Vandals ended."

A look of bemused shock on his face, Gelimer sat back on his throne, considering his answer. Then he shook his head, his eyes cruel as he levied his reply.

"Your opponent remains alive," Gelimer declared. "Kill him, and we can talk. Prove your resolve as a rightful conqueror of my kingdom."

Exasperated, I returned my gaze back to Gunderic. He inhaled hoarsely as he moaned with each movement, trying in vain to roll over, yet finding himself still unable to move from his injuries. Closing his eyes, Gunderic bowed his head in anticipation of my attack, offering no resistance as Gelimer ordered Gunderic's death.

"No," I said angrily. "I refuse."

"Then by Vandal law, you forfeit your rights of conquest here."

I shook my head. "This is all pointless!" I yelled. "Vandal law is over, and one more death doesn't change the fact that Belisarius will descend upon you with ten thousand Roman spearmen if that's what it takes to end this war. And if it comes to that, none of you will remain alive when the smoke clears from the destruction of Mount Papua."

Unblinking, Gelimer stared on. "If the Vandals are so weak that an army of Romans can conquer our entire nation, then we have no right to remain alive," the Vandal king answered with a note of finality. "I will allow your party to leave here unmolested. Let none say that King Gelimer was unjust to the laws of combat."

"Just end this," Gunderic replied. "With one stroke, I go to paradise, and my people will live on."

I shook my head, gathering my dagger and motioning to my party. "A good man's life is no fair trade for a rotten king," I whispered to Gunderic as I moved away.

The Vandal warlord chuckled painfully, spitting blood as two of Gelimer's slaves sprinted over to assist their fallen champion. "You're beginning to understand!" Gunderic rasped, his laughter rising as I moved to the encampment's gate.

Utterly unsuccessful, we descended Mount Papua, our steps aided by the downhill progression toward the mountain's base. Rosamund worried at the troublesome cut along my hip and begged to stop to treat the wound, though I insisted that we proceed onto the Herulian camp, fearful of being exposed to heavier snow and frost or a vengeful Vandal outrider eager to ignore Gelimer's command in the name of vengeance and hatred. However, it did not take long to reach level ground once more, and we found a detachment of Herulians waiting a safe distance away to aid our return to our assigned tents.

THE GHOSTS OF
MOUNT PAPUA

Another three weeks passed as I remained indecisive of our further course of action. A single courier was dispatched to Belisarius to tell of our location and continuing battle with Gelimer, yet no reinforcements were requested due to the poor conditions of the local environment as well as the depleted strength of the Vandals facing us. Nor did I order any assaults up the mountain, although sizeable bands of scouting forces were sent to keep watch over any possible Vandal sally and breakout. As Uliaris had taken little part in the previous raids, I assigned him the responsibility of organizing and conducting much of the scouting effort, tracking any sign of Vandal attack. None came, however, and we were left alone along the barren Numidian interior in what we discovered later was one of the bitterest winters that region had ever seen.

Ignoring concerns of impropriety, Rosamund slept on a cot located at the far edge of my tent, requiring frequent examinations of my hip, ribs, arms, and neck, her brow furrowed with concern at any hint of the threat of illness. Ever awkward of rumors or gossip, my tent entrance remained open throughout all hours of day or night, giving messengers from the Hun and Gothic camps easy access with updates or questions from Samur or Indulf. Rosamund did not appear to mind, seemingly joyful and carefree as she set about organizing my affairs and coordinating camp needs with the other Herulian officers to survive a winter more comfortably and hygienically near Mount Papua.

Belisarius did send a depot of supplies as winter's chill grew more severe, forcing men to remain huddled behind thick cloaks and heavy blankets even while on sentry duty. On the most frigid evening, any bare flesh that touched a spearhead or sword blade would be quickly stuck to the metal, leaving a painful mark where the torn skin had once rested and the man suffering all the more from exposure to snow and cold.

Each of the three camps continued patrols regardless of hardship, but none complained at the long hours spent around a roaring campfire, roasting donated meats whose rich drippings mixed within the coarse beards of the Goths and Heruli or the wispier hair of Samur's Huns. Many from each camp sought Rosamund's guidance, either in terms of interpreting omens or healing minor injuries, and she grew happier when swaddled in heavy woolen blankets in our oversized shared tent, her long white hair wrapped with a scarf as she gazed at the blowing snow in the outside world.

Our routine continued in this manner until excited shouts rose along the edge of our camp. Altan galloped hard until he reached my tent. I rose from my cot, my body still covered in a thin layer of bandages as I neared the end of my healing period.

"Yes?" I asked, scanning his excited features.

"The Vandals, Lord," Altan replied. "They're asking to meet you."

"How many?"

"Twelve in the party," Altan answered. "Shall we fight?"

"No," I answered. "Bring them to me, but keep a close guard."

Amidst a rising cacophony of noise throughout the Herulian camp, the dozen Vandals walked through our palisade walls and were directed to the great firepit in its center. Emerging from my tent, I threw a cloak over the exposed flesh of my torso and walked to greet our visitors, pretending to not feel the chill as I reached my destination. Rosamund followed closely behind, her eyes falling upon our Vandal guests, whose eyes darted amongst my men, seeking an ambush that would slaughter Gelimer's survivors.

They had little to fear. With torn and filthy clothing, the Vandals waited near the fire, their heads bowed as they awaited a chance to state their business. Many had wasted into a horrifying skin of bones and organs, and I ordered hot meals and fresh water be delivered to all as I made my approach. Bearing the scars of a former warrior, one of the Vandals sank to his knees, weeping for joy as he thanked me for my largesse.

"It is good to see you healed, Varus," Gunderic said, his face still a mess of yellowing bruises despite his broken nose set right.

"And you, Gunderic," I replied honestly. "I feared that you would be crippled for life."

"So did I," he admitted, "but fate has other intentions in mind."

"And what might those be?"

Gunderic sighed, his head bowed in surprisingly joyless deference. "You mentioned that Belisarius would accept our surrender, leaving our honor intact and our families with a measure of wealth?"

I nodded. "I speak with the voices of the general and the Emperor."

Gunderic smiled weakly. "My king agrees to your terms, if they still stand," the Vandal warlord replied. "Peaceful surrender while Gelimer abdicates his crown for Emperor Justinian, on guarantees that he and his people will not be reduced to slavery to the Mauri or poverty to the Empire."

"That is acceptable to us," I answered. "But what has changed since our duel?"

Gunderic closed his eyes. "It is easy to laugh death in the face when it comes suddenly or gloriously," he answered darkly. "It is something else entirely when it comes in the guise of disease or starvation, or simply freezing to death. We've butchered most of our horses for meat but have little else to survive until the spring. Recognizing Belisarius as our conqueror is favorable to any such terrible end."

We spoke of details and logistics for a while longer, allowing Gunderic and his men time to warm along the fire and gain a measure of nourishment from our bountiful rations. Perenus sent mounted messengers to the other camps to inform them of our decision to return to Carthage, while Fulcaris prepared to break the Herulian camp and ready several packs of supplies for the starving and exhausted Vandal survivors. After our conversation, however, Gunderic offered one final gift in gratitude for my mercy.

At first, Sembrouthes and Xerxes both jumped as Gunderic unslung the Vandal greatsword from underneath his vast cloak. Their spears lowered as Gunderic handed the vast blade to me hilt first, allowing me to grab its lengthy pommel. Though I had little control with a single hand, I found it easy enough to wield with two, taking several practice cuts above the camp's fire before returning the blade to its scabbard.

"This rightfully belongs to you now," Gunderic explained. "You may not understand now, but its value is considerable to my people. It allows us to remember a time when we were mighty, and our enemies were few."

Gunderic and I embraced before he returned to Gelimer's camp, the giant still bearing the Vandal banners proudly as he led his procession away. Each of the twelve were provided with ponies to aid their journey, a gift of friendship gratefully accepted. It took only two more days for the Vandal camp to clear itself of its survivors, with Gelimer departing with the final honor guard of Vandal banners and spearmen as my massed foederati prepared to depart on the following day.

Gunderic warned me not to, yet I felt an indescribable pull to return to the summit of Mount Papua for one final inspection of the vacated Vandal fortress. Commandeering spare ponies, I trotted up the mountain's main path, followed closely behind by Rosamund, her pale skin glittering in the frost as her breath clouded in a sea of crystals as we ascended the hill. Requiring little time due to our mounted and uncontested procession, we soon arrived at Mount Papua's gates, bearing torches to light our path through the more heavily wooded sections of the darkened trail.

Though less than a month had separated our previous arrival to the summit, it bore little resemblance to the onetime fastness of Gelimer. Piles of waste had accumulated in frozen pyramids of filth, while dozens of earthen mounds lined the edges of the summit's clearing.

"Bodies," Rosamund murmured. "We shouldn't be here, Varus."

"I need to check for holdouts." My reply was dishonest; I was still unsure of my call to this place.

A dozen smaller huts bore evidence of muck, suffering, and pain. Splotches of blood lined several walls, while a rancid stink haunted the air as we walked further to the encampment's interior. On the floor of one hut, I found the frayed remnants of a grass doll, a plaything for a child forced to bear the consequences of Justinian and Gelimer's war. I was tempted to place the doll in a pouch at my belt, yet visions of my own family warned me to leave it where it lay. Rosamund had often told that such objects held pieces of souls of their past owners, pieces that bore witness to years of joys and terrible suffering alike. I have no doubt that the doll, its limbs formed from the half-dried strands of grass that grew on the mountain's expanse, had seen far more misery than would be desired for any future owner.

Walking on, the silence of the place brought me to melancholy. I clutched at the decorations on my neck as well as Theodora's ring in my pouch and wondered at my own family's safety. Had my second child been born? Was Mariya safe and hale? Did Theodora have the strength to force the Empire into a semblance of order from the chaos of depravity and war? Though my soul itched for a positive answer, horrible scenes of pain and suffering filled my imagination as I considered their fates.

The stench of the camp grew unbearable as we neared Gelimer's quarters, its covering more intricate and far larger than the arrangement of crude wooden huts arrayed throughout the clearing. Thick musk brought me to gag, yet I forced myself forward, eager to complete my vague sense of duty and return to the Herulian camp.

"Varus… there isn't anyone here," Rosamund said, her voice low and urgent. "This place whispers of evil and is no home for us."

"If there's nobody here, then we have no reason to be fearful." I insisted.

Ascending the steps to Gelimer's quarters, I was greeted by the buzzing of flies and the scent of burnt offal as I neared the door. Undaunted, I pushed on the rough wooden boards, finding they resisted my efforts.

"It's blocked from the inside," Rosamund said warily.

"All the more reason to investigate."

Lifting my hobnailed boot, I kicked hard against the door. The wooden hinge on the other side splintered under the force of my blow. Light from the outdoors flooded the room's interior, the source of the crippling stench unveiled to the world. Rosamund muttered a prayer to her pagan gods as I retched, failing to reclose the broken door once more.

At least a hundred withered corpses had been stacked in a heap inside the vaulted ceiling. Many bore frostbitten noses and limbs, while others showed evidence of disease and rot from untreated wounds. Nearly all told of starvation, their ribs and hips jutting through sallow skin in a manner that resembled skeletons instead of living bodies.

Though the stacked corpses had been unsettling enough, the separate pile of children offered visions of the blackest depths of hell that all the priests of Constantinople warned about. Many appeared lifelike, their deaths having only come within a few days at most, yet their sunken eyes and distended bellies gave evidence of suffering prior to their demise. Atop the pyramid, one Vandal girl of approximately eight summers had been carefully stacked above the rest, her clothing flattened and cleaned to instill a manner of respect in the afterlife. Her cheeks sunken, one of the girl's fingers had been gnawed to the bone, its tip pointed accusingly toward the entrance to this corpse hall.

I vomited. By that point, I had seen countless bodies with all manner of injuries, yet that immersive and terrible vision was what brought me to the breaking point. Justin had once warned that all men reach that crux at one moment or another, though it was not until the very end of the Vandal War that I understood the utter exhaustion and disgust of myself and everyone else who contributed to these ends.

"Burn it," I said, ignoring Rosamund's protestations of needing the torches to head back down the slopes of the mountain.

I did not bother to check if any survivors remained along the hill's walls or outposts. By that point, I did not care, for anyone willing to remain was welcome to the haunted ramparts of the Gelimer's last stand. Brittle and dry, the wood of Gelimer's quarters was consumed by the blaze of our torches, yet I did not stay to watch that great pyre of forgotten souls. Turning away, I remounted my horse and led Rosamund back to the massing foederati and the more sensible world.

Slowed by sick and injured Vandal survivors, our pace back to Carthage was unfavorable. None perished as we followed stone-dressed roads and were greeted at various intervals by Belisarius' scouts, their packs ready with additional food and fresh mounts for our return. Each night we made camp and each dawn we trudged along, my men excited and proud for their success. As they behaved themselves, I did not begrudge the celebrations.

But I did not join them. For every time I closed my eyes, I saw the pile of desiccated corpses topped by the Vandal girl. Only a few years older than Zenobia, and guilty of nothing.

Rosamund and I never spoke of our visions atop Mount Papua. Neither did Gelimer explain the sufferings of his people, nor did he seek to interact with my officers or his own people as he rode back to his onetime capital. The Vandal king remained silent even as he entered Carthage's gates, its walls refortified and strengthened to discourage any further attack by those who would deprive the Emperor of that great city along the African coast.

Gelimer's capitulation was all arranged well in advance. While most of the foederati were escorted to various barracks throughout the city by Cephalas, our senior officers led the Vandal king to the Carthaginian Palace, and were soon joined by Belisarius' war council. Many winked or voiced congratulations as I passed, and I made a pretense of sharing in their camaraderie, yet all I yearned for was a measure of peace and the ability to go home to a family that I had not seen for most of a year.

I embraced Liberius and Father Petrus as I entered the room, leaving Gelimer and Gunderic behind under armed guard. Belisarius, too, offered his heartfelt thanks and congratulations, noting with swelling pleasure that Mariya had given birth to a son who she had named Alexander, with both mother and child safe and well. Both Belisarius and Antonina offered their enthusiastic embrace as they delivered the news.

"A son..." I babbled. "Alexander and Zenobia."

"More friends for Joannina!" Belisarius smiled.

Antonina nodded, grasping for Belisarius' hand. For any other couple, something so innocuous would not be worthy of attention, yet I never knew Antonina to seek Belisarius' touch. Belisarius' smile faded, returning to a grief-weary gaze. "We shall discuss later."

"My love, perhaps you can delay your work for a day?" Antonina suggested. "After all, we'll be stuck in Carthage for many months. One day of rest won't change that."

"Would that I could, my dear," Belisarius replied. "But the Vandals aren't likely to accept disrespect with grace. I'd see this war ended."

Antonina frowned, biting her lip. "Of course."

Silently, I agreed with Antonina—Belisarius desperately needed a reprieve. There was no convincing him otherwise, especially when John's victory and sacrifice had led to this result. At his order, the palace hall's doorway was swept open, with a richly adorned and crowned Gelimer striding inside. Gunderic and a dozen unarmed Vandals followed closely behind, two of their banners bearing the bent cross filling much of the hall's open space. Stopping before the raised dais that held Belisarius and Liberius, Gelimer dropped to his knees.

"I am Gelimer, last king of the Vandals," he declared proudly. "And on behalf of all Vandals living and still to come, I recognize the authority of Belisarius and Justinian as our rightful overlords."

"Justinian," Liberius corrected. "You recognize the Emperor."

Gelimer nodded. "All I ask is that you treat my people as any subject, with honor and opportunity," he begged. "We bow to your will."

With that, Gelimer removed his golden crown, its jewels and fixtures digging impressions into the wild mane of his hair. Taking the crown in both hands, Gelimer threw it at Belisarius' feet, the former king falling to the ground in worship of his conqueror. Gunderic and his men immediately followed Gelimer's example, allowing the Vandal banners to fall with a symbolic clatter. Belisarius allowed silence to rule Carthage's hall, his features haunted and gaunt as he gazed at the origin of so much pain and anguish for him and thousands of other Romans in the century prior. His eyes dark, a tear crept down Belisarius' face, yet he did not quiver or weep as he gazed upon his vanquished foe, a people whom all had said were invincible.

Then, several heartbeats later, Belisarius rose from the Emperor's throne. Walking to the edge of the dais, he straightened his back, his eyes staring beyond the bowed figures of those Vandals who remained unmoving before him.

"On behalf of Emperor Justinian, I accept your surrender and pardon you of any crimes against the Empire," Belisarius boomed, an audience of a hundred officers gazing at their accomplishment. "Go now, and await further orders for what will be required of you."

And so the Vandal War came to an end to the sound of applause and celebration. Justinian would rejoice at his blessings, and others would mark a rebirth of the Empire's fortunes after two centuries of decline and decay. For Belisarius, the cost was altogether too much to bear.

Fortune never lingered in our favor for long. For as Belisarius accepted Gelimer's vacated crown, dark omens had slipped from distant shores, hastily written scrolls containing desperate pleas for aid that had been sealed for sea voyage to Carthage's vast harbor. The Vandal War had come to a decisive close, but the Great War had finally begun, and it promised to be unlike anything the Empire had yet experienced.

We were not prepared for what came next.

AUTHOR'S NOTE

As with *The Last Dying Light* and *Immortal*, *The Gates of Carthage* is a work of fiction. While I attempted to stay true to the period, its core actors, and its customs, a certain measure of creative license is required, both to fill in the considerable blanks of historical record, as well as to weave a story. Timelines are altered and characters are invented to fulfill this goal.

The end of Belisarius' and Varus' war with Persia, known today as the Iberian War, concluded after repeated failures by Persia to invade, conquer, and hold Roman provinces in Mesopotamia and Armenia. Shahanshah Kavadh's primary aim—the subjugation of Persian Armenia (known as Iberia, which had defected as a client state to the Romans) was suppressed and returned to Persian rule. However, Belisarius' victory at Dara shocked the Persians and returned the war to a relative stalemate. Under Azarethes, the Battle of Callinicum was viewed by the Romans as a defeat, yet the losses that Belisarius inflicted upon the Persian army were extensive and debilitating. Some debate Callinicum's true outcome, but for me, Belisarius accomplished a difficult goal: keeping the Persians from sweeping through Mesopotamia and Syria and cutting the Roman Empire in half.

The Iberian War experienced a few other battles. Not long after Callinicum, however, the vaunted Kavadh died. His successor, Khosrow, was not secure in his throne and urgently needed to conclude the Iberian War that had cost his empire dearly in lives and in resources. The result, negotiated between Hermogenes and Khosrow's representatives, was the Perpetual Peace. In it, hostilities immediately ceased, borders would be somewhat demilitarized, and territory was allocated *status quo ante bellum* (same holdings and borders as pre-war).

While Constantinople agreed to pay Khosrow 110 centenaria, or roughly 11,000 pounds of gold, any refugees from Persian Armenia were permitted to flee to Roman territory. Relative to the potential permanent loss of the Eastern Roman Empire's Mesopotamian and Armenian provinces, this outcome should be viewed as a success, as it stabilized the Roman-Persian border for a time.

Belisarius received little gratitude for his accomplishments. Regardless of his astounding victory at Dara or the tremendous sacrifice of Callinicum, Belisarius was treated icily by Justinian's Court and was eventually charged with incompetence in leadership and responsible for defeats in the east. Though accounts differ, it is likely that jealousies of Belisarius' tremendous victory at Dara rankled the Imperial Court and swayed their judgment of the young general. He was eventually cleared of wrongdoing, but Belisarius' treatment by Justinian after the Iberian War would characterize their relationship for decades.

Chariot racing had long been a beloved sport across the Roman Empire, particularly after Constantine outlawed gladiatorial matches in AD 325, and the last *ludi* (gladiatorial schools) were thoroughly shuttered between 399 and 404 by Honorius. By Justinian's reign, chariot racing had come to dominate social and business life — virtually all residents within Constantinople professed affinity to one of four color-coded factions known as the Blues, Greens, Reds, and Whites. Attendees often wore colors of their favored faction, and even styled their hair to match those of beloved drivers. The Blues and Greens were overwhelmingly popular, with the Blues typically favored by the wealthy elite and the Greens for much of the general populace.

The Hippodrome, or the vast racing track that housed Constantinople's Games, could comfortably seat fifty thousand patrons, numbers that swelled on a particularly tense racing day. An extended oval, observers lined the track, while the center was demarcated by a *spina*, a center stone median. The Hippodrome's spina contained many fabulous monuments, such as the Imperial Quadriga (the Horses of St. Mark, which were plundered in the Fourth Crusade and now reside in Venice), the Obelisk of Thutmose III (originally erected around 1490 BC, brought by Theodosius the Great from Egypt), the Serpent Column (celebrating the victory of Greece over Persia in the fifth century BC), and others. Several monuments remain in Sultanahmet Square (modern Istanbul, Turkey), and visitors to Istanbul can walk upon marked pavement that denoted the links and bends of the racing track. Alas, the Imperial Palace and most other buildings of Justinian's day no longer remain in Istanbul, including most of the area around the Hippodrome. An exception includes the Hagia Sophia. The construction of that marvelous building shall be discussed in a later book.

The Blue and Green factions were increasingly prone to violence by the sixth century. Well beyond modern hooliganism in international football, street violence became a predictable sight after notable races, including arson, theft, and all manner of violence and murder. One of these riots included the arson and razing of an older version of the Hagia Sophia. During his brief reign as Emperor, Justin I attempted to instill greater order and security over the Hippodrome but did not live long enough to see his reforms fulfilled. Justinian continued and even expanded the games, including the reconstruction of a lavish *kathisma*, or the Emperor's private viewing box, which was connected to the Imperial Palace.

If chariot racing was so dangerous and bolstered the authority of street gangs, why did the Imperial government permit the races to continue? Mainly, it was the Imperial government's easiest opportunity to interface with the masses and mollify most concerns before they became uncontrollable. The Emperor or his ministers would regularly hear petitions before and during a race, often framed as a request from the "Blues" or the "Greens." Shrewd ministers could diagnose potential causes of conflict before they erupted. Unfortunately for Justinian, neither he nor his ministers were able or willing to identify the serious threat of revolt in AD 532, known today as the Nika Riots.

Justinian was a supporter of the Blues and was noted for his dismissiveness of the Greens to the point of granting financial, social, and political favors to Blue adherents. This blatant favoritism, contrary to the semi-representative role that the groups were intended to play in petitioning the Imperial Court, was enough to antagonize gangs and groups of honest petitioners alike. Resentment festered upon the imposition of sweeping reforms by Justinian's ministers.

Two individuals stand out in history as the cause of many complaints: John the Cappadocian (in this series, Paulus, to distinguish him from Belisarius' second-in-command) and Tribonian. John the Cappadocian enacted crippling taxes upon an already overburdened populace, including severe punishments for debtors, while Tribonian's legal reforms had disenfranchised many in Imperial civil service. Likewise, corruption was rampant in Justinian's government, with Tribonian's reforms viewed as threatening to centuries-old practices of extracting a living by the Empire's civil service. By AD 532, there was considerable resentment against Justinian and the wealthy of Constantinople.

While the path to the Nika Riots was a complex series of events kindled over several years, the immediate trigger was a murder during a chariot race. Several perpetrators were caught and executed for this crime, but two—a Blue and a Green—escaped to a nearby church. The Blue and Green gangs demanded that the men be allowed to go free, while Justinian, surprised and threatened by the swelling mob, commuted their sentences to imprisonment. Shortly thereafter, when Justinian opened the Hippodrome for games, he was met by a raucous crowd spitting insults at his government. Eventually, after several races, the chants morphed into "Nika! Nika!" or Koine Greek for "Victory!" Chaos ensued as many attacked Justinian's entourage, who retreated into the Imperial Palace.

What happened next was critical not only for Justinian's legacy, but for Theodora, Belisarius, and many others. Hearing of defections of Constantinople's Senate to the rioters, who proclaimed Anastasius' nephew Hypatius the new emperor, Justinian and his remaining followers consigned themselves to defeat and readied themselves for a sea voyage with ample wealth to live out the remainder of their days in exile. However, Theodora alone refused to leave, emboldening and shaming Justinian into remaining and fighting for his crown.

Many sayings have been attributed to Theodora in this moment, such as "purple makes a fine shroud," referring to a rare and expensive dyed garment that signified royal status. Ultimately, Justinian elected to remain in Constantinople and empowered three men with the responsibility of reclaiming the city. First, Narses spread dissent amongst those Blues who sided with the Greens. Second, Belisarius shored up the Imperial army within the city, repelling attacks from the Imperial palace. Last, Mundus arrived with detachments of men from nearby Thrace.

Justinian permitted no mercy to the defeated mob. After clearing the city of rioters, Belisarius and Mundus besieged the Hippodrome, slew its inhabitants, and hanged Hypatius. Contemporaries note that tens of thousands were killed, with modern estimates ranging from thirty to sixty thousand individuals. In that stroke of brutality, Justinian had removed most of his political rivals, and he then worked with Theodora to strengthen their throne for the task of reconstruction and war.

Eventually, Justinian turned his interests to Carthage and the Vandals. Once a wealthy and grain-rich province, Carthage and its hinterlands were conquered by the Vandals in the mid-fifth century. Horrified, the East and West Roman Empires jointly mounted a ruinously expensive and equally unsuccessful counterattack, which was responded to in kind by a Vandal invasion of Italy. The term "vandalism" is associated with the Vandals' brutal sacking and plundering of Rome in AD 455.

Though they returned to Carthage, the Vandals maintained a reputation for ferocity as well as an unwillingness to cooperate with Constantinople. When one Vandal king attempted reproachment with Justinian, he was soon toppled and slain by a Vandal warlord named Gelimer, who ignored Justinian's threats of war. After securing the neutrality of the Ostrogoths under Amalasuntha, Justinian dispatched an army to Africa. Whether that expedition was intended to seize Carthage or carve off easier targets like Tripolis continues to be debated.

Fresh from his demonstration of loyalty in the Nika Riots, Belisarius was rewarded with leadership over the campaign. Many others in this book accompanied him—his wife Antonina, the secretary Procopius, the loyal and capable John the Armenian, and Pharas the Herulian (the Varus of this book). Belisarius' army was pitifully small, including some ten thousand infantry of questionable training and skill, as well as several thousand cavalry and foederati that held Belisarius' trust. Scholars today debate the size of the Vandal army, yet the fact that the Imperial army was outmatched and under-supported is difficult to argue. Along with roughly some thirty to forty thousand Vandal warriors, the Vandal chiefs had reduced many of the local Mauri to a tributary status, although the Mauri were reluctant participants in the coming war with the Romans.

Belisarius' voyage began with tragedy. Within weeks of leaving Constantinople, five hundred of his warriors died from flux due to moldy bread, brought on by poor preparation, baked once rather than twice, which is a method used to prevent the easy onset of mold and other toxins. Procopius argued this was the fault of John the Cappadocian (our Paulus), who saved on the costs of bread-baking and thought little of the risk to Belisarius' men.

However, the voyage sailed on, including hundreds of transports and ninety-two dromons, which were the famed warships of the Eastern Empire that relied upon projectiles and boarding enemy ships rather than carving through enemy hulls with bronze-capped rams. They eventually landed in Syracuse, where Procopius learned of the lack of Vandal preparation or foreknowledge of Belisarius' advance. Immediately, Belisarius ordered the expedition to venture for Caput Vada, which is along the coast in modern Tunisia and roughly 240 kilometers from Carthage.

The war contrasted against the drawn-out affair with Persia in that it was brief (two battles over less than a year) and relatively light in Roman casualties. At Ad Decimum, Belisarius repelled a clever but ill-timed assault by Gelimer, leaving the road to Carthage open. Belisarius proceeded cautiously, and though the Carthaginians threw open their gates and sang songs of welcome, Belisarius hesitated for an evening, making sure that no Vandals waited in ambush. None came, and Belisarius soon found himself master of the wealthy and fabled city of Hannibal.

Gelimer recovered, infused by the hardened veterans of his brother Tzazon. Regrouping to the west, Gelimer and Tzazon, who had recently returned from suppressing a revolt in Sardinia, charged toward Carthage and met Belisarius' army near Tricamarum. In this battle, Belisarius gave John overall command, remaining in an advisory role. Together, they succeeded, although John was mortally wounded by friendly fire in the subsequent rout of Gelimer's army. The chase was called off as John suffered from his wounds, begging Belisarius to forgive the warrior—Uliaris, both in history and in this novel—who had caused his death. John, who had been widely respected by the army, was mourned, particularly by Belisarius, who had been a childhood friend.

Inconsolable, Belisarius entrusted Pharas with hunting down Gelimer and his few remaining retainers. Pharas was initially successful, isolating Gelimer atop the mountain fortress of Mount Papua, yet he struggled mightily to force Gelimer into submission. Cut off from food, Gelimer's followers resisted Pharas for a winter, suffering starvation. Pharas made several pleas to Gelimer to end the war as well as the suffering of his people. One of these exchanges was noted by Procopius and translated by Edward Gibbon. It remains one of the few direct quotes we possess today that was spoken by Pharas.

"Like yourself, I am an illiterate Barbarian, but I speak the language of plain sense and an honest heart. Why will you persist in hopeless obstinacy? Why will you ruin yourself, your family, and nation? The love of freedom and abhorrence of slavery? Alas! my dearest Gelimer, are you not already the worst of slaves, the slave of the vile nation of the Moors? Would it not be preferable to sustain at Constantinople a life of poverty and servitude, rather than to reign the undoubted monarch of the mountain of Papua? Do you think it a disgrace to be the subject of Justinian? Belisarius is his subject, and we ourselves, whose birth is not inferior to your own, are not ashamed of our obedience to the Roman emperor. That generous prince will grant you a rich inheritance of lands, a place in the Senate, and the dignity of Patrician. Such are his gracious intentions, and you may depend with full assurance on the word of Belisarius. So long as heaven has condemned us to suffer, patience is a virtue; but, if we reject the proffered deliverance, it degenerates into blind and stupid despair."

Gelimer joined Pharas and surrendered to Belisarius, ending both the Vandal War as well as the Vandal Kingdom. Survivors of the once-vaunted Vandal army were formed into foederati, known as Justinian's Vandals. Over time, the Vandals slowly disappear from history, with only a few warlords remaining to cause trouble in the years ahead.

The Gates of Carthage was a pleasure to write but required the diligent support of many to bring to fruition. Blair Thornburgh of The Author Studio provided the developmental and line edits. I'm grateful for her technical abilities as much as her knowledge and diligence to realism for the time period! Crystal Watanabe of Pikko's House provided the copyediting, proofreading, and formatting, and crafted beautiful interiors. The supremely talented Dusan Markovic illustrated the book's cover. Likewise, Cyowari provided the book's three maps. I am grateful to them, as well as my beta readers, for working so hard to make this book better.

If you enjoyed *The Gates of Carthage*, please consider leaving a review on Amazon and Goodreads. I am so thankful for your time in this—ratings and reviews are what allow the series to continue! Ultimately, Belisarius' and Varus' story is not even half over, and Justinian's ambitions range far beyond the African coastline. And despite the terrible sacrifices of Varus and Belisarius, there are far more battles ahead than behind. What comes next includes the continued pacification of the former Vandal holdings and the lingering threat of war from the Visigoths and Ostrogoths alike.

Printed in Great Britain
by Amazon

37343998R00320